D0981928

THE FAR FIELD

THE FAR FIELD

A Novel of Ceylon

Edie Meidav

HOUGHTON MIFFLIN COMPANY

BOSTON • NEW YORK

2001

Copyright © 2001 by Edie Meidav
All rights reserved

For information about permission to reproduce selections
from this book, write to Permissions, Houghton Mifflin Company,
215 Park Avenue South, New York, New York 10003.

Visit our Web site: www.houghtonmifflinbooks.com.

Library of Congress Cataloging-in-Publication Data
Meidav, Edie, date.
The far field : a novel of Ceylon / Edie Meidav.
p.   cm.
ISBN 0-618-01366-0
1. Sri Lanka — Fiction. 2. Americans —
Sri Lanka — Fiction. I. Title.
PS3563.E3447 F37 2001
813'.6 — dc21   00-053879

Printed in the United States of America

Book design by Robert Overholtzer

DOC 10 9 8 7 6 5 4 3 2 1

Earlier versions of portions of this book were originally published
in *The Kenyon Review* and in *Terra Nova* (MIT Press).

The author is grateful for permission to quote from the following works. All efforts
were made to obtain permission for all excerpts used; omissions will be corrected in
subsequent editions. Untitled poem, by Rainer Maria Rilke, from *The Selected Poetry
of Rainer Maria Rilke*, edited and translated by Stephen Mitchell. Copyright © 1982
by Stephen Mitchell. Reprinted by permission of Random House Inc. Excerpt from
Letters of Wallace Stevens, edited by Holly Stevens. Reprinted by permission of
Alfred A Knopf, a division of Random House Inc. Excerpts from *The Smaller Buddhist Catechism*, compiled by C. W. Leadbeater (1983), translated from the Sinhala
by C. Jinarajadasa, and from *The Buddhist Catechism*, by H. S. Olcott (1986), re-
printed by permission of The Theosophical Publishing House, Adyar, Chennai,
India. Excerpts from *The Mahavamsa*, translated by Wilhelm Geiger and Mabel
Haynes Bode (1993) and from *The Sinhalese-English Dictionary*, by the Reverend
B. Clough (1892/1982), reprinted by permission of Asian Educational Services,
India. Excerpts from *The Mahaparinibbana Sutta*, translated from the Pali by Sister
Vajira and Francis Story (revised edition, 1988), and *The Dhammapada*, translated
by Acharya Buddharakkhita (1985), reprinted by permission of Buddhist Publica-
tion Society, Sri Lanka. Excerpt from *The Village Folk Tales of Ceylon*, Volume I, by
H. Parker (1982), reprinted by permission of Tisara Prakasakaye Ltd., Sri Lanka.
Excerpts that open Chapter 46, on Italy and England, and in Chapter 127, on
Rome, are paraphrased from an article by Jim Thornton from *Men's Journal*, August
1998. Reprinted by permission of Men's Journal Company, L.P. 1998. All rights
reserved. Excerpt from *The Story of Ceylon*, by E.F.C. Ludowyk (1985), reprinted by
permission of Navrang Booksellers and Publishers, India.

To those disappeared since 1980:
one percent of the actual Lanka

You who never arrived
in my arms, Beloved, who were lost
from the start,
I don't even know what songs
would please you. I have given up trying
to recognize you in the surging wave of the next
moment. All the immense
images in me — the far-off, deeply felt landscape,
cities, towers, and bridges, and un-
suspected turns in the path,
and those powerful lands that were once
pulsing with the life of the gods —
all rise within me to mean
you, who forever elude me.

You, Beloved, who are all
the gardens I have ever gazed at,
longing. An open window
in a country house — and you almost
stepped out, pensive, to meet me. Streets that I chanced
    upon, —
you had just walked down them and vanished.
And sometimes, the mirrors
were still dizzy with your presence and, startled, gave
    back
my too-sudden image. Who knows? perhaps the same
bird echoed through both of us
yesterday, separate, in the evening . . .

—RAINER MARIA RILKE

In Ceylon, life is almost wholly a thesis;
there is no end of sea and no end of mountains.

— WALLACE STEVENS

PROLOGUE

GOD GOT this much right.

For weeks the water and air shared the same lustrous darkness, clouds making up a mackerel sky. Only rounding the Cape did the wind tear off the haze for a spell. The ship's captain called the weather bad. Unseasonable. But no one could say Henry was blind to possibility. This voyage, his little assault on history, might turbine him into a wrathful chamber he'd be lucky to exit. Because the beauty of land had disappeared.

In its place came vibration: new golds flecked the surrounding gray, sea brine turned sweet as plum and night made the overtime engines wheeze some godawful hunger.

Truth was, Henry had never been victim to such unrelenting weather. It consumed him and he didn't want to admit it. He resorted to deck promenades amid the scudding gusts, private constitutionals against the sky to make his will affect something in the world. It was 1936 and he'd listened with his American nod when the sailors had predicted the cold of these last straits. Nothing unusual to it. This vortex of winds, a particular patch of swells. But the cold for Henry was overkill. He tried to think it sublime even as it entered his waistcoat like a drunken beggar, insistent, tickling his bones. The cold wouldn't let him forget that no one he loved was about to joke or just shiver next to him.

Despite Henry's age, the return of solitude always startled him. The only spawn of a rector, some forty-odd years earlier, Henry had shot out from the womb of an invalid mother, sequestered in a blue and white gabled house filled with drafts and surrounded by rhododendron forests, a home toppling over on upstate New York's silty land. The attending doctor later said the infant had practically self-propelled — Henry's arms hadn't stopped their willful swimming until hours after the birth.

His mother had this boy then, along with her cigarette-stained glamour and a tired mouth twisting all the lullabies: Mary had a little lump; baa baa black sheep have you any jewels? She loved him; he believed that; the scent of her talc and cigarettes stayed a close memory; her only fault being she ended up dying sooner than most, thus abandoning him to a father passionate only for the congregation, for the congregation and God.

His father's choice of unending sameness, of arched rectory walls and nodding parishioners over better potentials — hills and rivers and stone bridges — had made Gould senior appear as remote to Henry as, say, the idea of Corsica or orangutans. Any change or progress would have made the father less mysterious. Had Gould senior chosen to *flee* his routine — say, had Gould gone to live like a baboon in a Rhinebeck cave — *that* Henry could have understood. Instead, the father's routine stunned the boy into rebellion. One which made not a few of the housekeepers, in unwitnessed moments, chide Henry for being an impatient boy.

Every tolerant Sunday, Henry swept between pews — all of it dust the dying-off laity had not disturbed. He attended his father's sermons in which Gould senior said things like *life gives you a premise and you carry it out no matter what*. Henry never felt more remote than during hours crouched against the grille with the other choir singers. With them he watched his father's lantern jaw open and shut as though directly wired by God. With them he sang, upset mostly by how black flies tended to fly into his open mouth.

He managed to act like one of the boys, either awkward or oily, the only choices seemingly available to boys of a certain age. Henry was neither. He was offshore. In himself a little world was growing. He could talk about it to no one. He could barely breathe to the end of a breath. What more or less kept him company was his Bible. He wanted this stage called childhood to hurry up and be done with.

In the privacy of his own room, he would talk to a mini-friend roughly the size of his palm, a boy resembling the Matthew he'd known in first grade. He'd never spoken to the actual Matthew, a towheaded boy with a striking laugh like F-sharp, who had moved to White Plains to live with his grandmother, only to leave the year after. From across the classroom Henry had loved the boy: golden Matthew. He later acquired this habit of dragging tiny invented Matthew out from under his bed. A habit of holding Matthew in a steeplebox he could create with his hands. In the steeplebox he could whisper to Matthew the day's events and ideas.

There were intermittently people who came in and out of the house: housekeepers, for example. If an adult entered the room, Henry would quickly stow Matthew away under something. Couches were best. Chairs were too exposed. He had never been afraid of shadows or closets or the dark himself, so neither was Matthew.

He and Matthew started to classify the housekeepers his father hired. At first Henry had charmed and befriended each in her turn, developing what he deemed his ability to know innermost secrets immediately, before anyone ever said a word. Then he gave up being charming after one housekeeper too many arrived only to depart a year or so later with a piece of his love.

The Pegeens, Bridgets, Morags, Ophelias — he tried to memorize them as a single freckled, ginger-haired bulk, and in this way each one's power to hurt him was lessened. They could be laughing colleens with a rascal's air. Or brackish tipplers with bosoms migrating waistward past disappointed rib-cages. Women who let him run wild in the hills behind the house. The worst were those stern and silent as his father, specifically religious women who made china and dust their only companions. Women tending toward banishing things like parsley, salt, and pet dogs, christening them vexations for a young boy's spirit. One of this last sort had been a Scottish nanny who combed his hair with punitive strength, as had been done to her in the orphanage, whose only indulgence for him was butter, big dabs of it on the bran toast his father considered most ethically correct.

In later years, trying to tease out his pa's severity, Henry Gould would aim for compassion and think: his father before him — and before him, and all the way back to the Revolution, long before the *Mayflower*; the Anglicans having chartered their own boat to Jamestown and its quagmire — came from a line of stern men who hardly used incense in their services. Men whose main delights might have been the Psalms and the mystery of the Eucharist, sole prophylactics against dying from a lack of joy.

3

1

HE SHOULD HAVE GUESSED the augury of Ceylon. The day before had stormed mildly on and off but the air had calmed toward midnight. Henry strolled the decks as tall and loud as he wanted without worrying about shipmen gossiping in his wake. Three weeks on board in abysmal weather and he'd gotten no reprieve from these hissing characters with their names like Tiny and Junior and their purple-nosed conviction that Henry must be a missionary. The nights had been cold, the moon a swollen disc, the scuttlebutt insidious.

On board he wouldn't have minded making some pleasant new acquaintance. A philologist or dreamer, a man of business, an anthropometrist. Anything. He and the cattle had been the only passengers. And whether above hold or below, the sea dogs never stopped playing their salty games. Crowing out petty successes, their voices bobbing out into the night.

Everyone else knew how to bide time, make it pass. This might be a skill to employ with the Ceylonese, Henry has told himself. He always feels time slipping away, an effigy burning beyond. Patience raised to a higher power — stamina — might be useful in what he has begun to think of as *his* village. The masthead light's dim but he wished he had pen and paper to write the reminder: *Biding time can be a virtue.*

Descending spiral stairs to the billiards room, where he'd never been, his boot caught an annoying loose rivet.

'Horseshoes,' he cursed.

A sculler hidden somewhere behind a mound of life preservers laughed at him.

'I'm funny, right?' said Henry into the dark.

'Naw, mon. They think you're funny 'cause they don't know you. You're a regular walking tragedy. No one's recognized you yet —' floated back to him along with a rank cloud of smoke.

Just past the windlass and inside the billiards den, the coxswain and skipper were playing checkers, the rest commentary. 'Could've kinged that one, what I'm telling you,' a Tiny or Junior snorted.

4

The checker players were sweating like last-round gladiators and Henry Fyre Gould slid into a squat corner table. The air sank heavy on his lungs with iron's blood scent, his mildewed kerchief being not much better.

'No drink for the cloth man?' a voice asked from behind. Almost all of the seafarers possessed this rolling accent. Too many years on water. 'The man of the cloth, I mean.'

The captain rested into a seat across the child's table. What was it about his eyes? Shrouded by drooping flesh, whether from public martyrdom or private corruption in steerage, they couldn't be any more feeble. He could be in his early seventies but stayed spry on the ladders. Overall, he presented a tricky read for Henry.

'Probably should be taking all offers.' Henry smiled.

Somewhere underneath his rake's whiskers the captain smiled back. The gaslamp striped over him, making his eyes two bullet holes. 'Colonel Henry, right?'

'Call me Henry.'

'Colonel Henry,' exaggerating. 'It's rich. I like it.'

The two had exchanged no more than ten words the entire voyage.

And this had been the case though Henry did not consider himself a superstitious man. During his years as a fraud inspector, his employees had prized his sober gaze. So he liked to think. Nevertheless. On this voyage, and Henry had known it to be irrational, he'd felt speaking too much to the man in the chart room, the one controlling the ship's destiny, *that* would screw with his own fate.

Rounding near Good Hope, a swamp drift of vapors had made the African cliffs vein into a mirage of faces. The world around the ship had turned into a revolving stage, one clocking in each morning. Of all this and more, the captain had been master and sure steerer, always luffing their vessel back into the wind.

Henry reproached himself. He wanted to have raised his glass for these few weeks with this salty man. There could've been a manly rapport. A certain respect over stew. Instead Henry had chosen constant nausea, or so it seemed, having eaten tinned fish and dried limes alone in his quarters, tasting the lead of his own fork and feeling he made up a pretty lonely little town.

Thing was, up close the captain turned out not to be so old after all. He could be a peer of Henry's. Perhaps it was only the fluidity of his parentage, his varied origins, which aged his face. 'Forgive me, I have an interest in genealogy —'

'— you're wanting to know if I'm from India or Australia.' The captain mimicked voices low and high: 'Dover? Don't tell me, the Antilles? Maybe Cork. Cadiz. Hokkaido. Montego Bay?'

'Smart man.'

'Your first time here we don't know your likes, Colonel. I'm onto grappa myself.'

Henry shrugged.

'Brandy for floating peasants —' The captain signaled for two snifters, sighing. 'Me I'm saying. I'm the peasant. My genealogy is seamen going all the way back one generation. Not you. I know about you Yankees.'

'What about us?'

'Save yourselves with plans. Figure you must be out to fortune-hunt in Ceylon.'

'There's fortune?'

'Don't look greedy, man. It's not polite.' He slid the snifter over. 'I'm teasing.'

'Of course.' Henry tasted the grappa: earthy crushed vines and stems. 'Strong drink.'

'Ain't heard of the northern gems, man? Ceylon's a hope chest. Wouldn't believe the mines. Diamonds big as eggs. Then you'd go kaput. The instant you hit middle age better off leaving certain speculations to young fools.'

'Absolutely.'

'You're off to be a god, then.' At Henry's glance, the captain explained. 'Between Fiji and Togo there's an island, Wantoks, made one of the British princes a god. Because of the king, you see.'

Henry did not but gave a good nod anyway.

'In fact, judging strict from your beard, we're thinking you're off to a mission.'

'Only of my own making —' Henry choked out an impostor's laugh.

'So then?'

He sipped again. 'Maybe you should call me an anti-missionary,' he told the captain.

For this, the whiskers rearranged themselves into something approaching a grin. 'God's sake, man. You're vanilla.'

The captain refilled the glasses and Henry took this as generous. He was in a good state now and thought it might hold. Still, the drink curdled his throat and made the table beneath his fingers heave into several varieties of breast.

6

'Ship's a slaver tonight,' the captain apologized. 'No wind. Though we're crossing the swells.'

'Not that bad,' said Henry, the table torquing into a mesa, a moor, a belly, a penis. The two men fell silent and to their drink with greater dedication. Until the captain tapped Henry's shoulder.

'I'm no believer, see.'

'Fine.'

'You're no cuttle. Guess if you go anti a few missionaries for me my life's well-lived, Colonel.'

'Right.'

'You ain't having me on the block for supper due to not believing?'

Henry grinned more at the table's throb.

'I'm saying there's belief and belief, see.' The captain hunched to speak confidentially. 'You may know already. On a ship especially. Our superstitions, see?'

He pulled a long black silk thread out from under his collar to wave the pendant at Henry: a tiny brown and dried baby's hand with nails perfect yellow half-moons. A whiff of formaldehyde stung the American's nose. For a second Henry thought the hand a deformed appendage from the captain's own body.

'It's real, touch it! Brings smooth winds. What else do we have except our beliefs, Colonel? Small or not. Ain't afraid to tell you. At the start of any voyage you'll find me lighting candles with the rest in front of this darling. Don't tell me, Reverend.'

'I gave up being a —'

'It's swindling kismet. I know. I'm foolish. But see, Rev, in point of fact, thing's as predictable as fishing. Zero nil, okay, maybe, but it's brought me more calm seas than any doytch compass. This casts out for the big catch.'

Henry shuddered. The faces in the billiards room were made of rough edges. All a little too near and angry. He rose to leave. 'Maybe you're a lucky man.' He listened to the absurdity of his words too late.

The captain gripped his wrist to keep him. 'Lucky, not lucky. Just some savvyfair about the world and what works. Luck don't exist. If you don't find out nowhere, Colonel, you'll find out in Ceylon. Whatever it is you're forecasting to do in that godforsaken place.'

2

AT NOON the next day, rows of shipmen burst down the ladders from the chart room and up from the quarters. Marking his lunch-time constitutional on deck, Henry found himself pummeled by sailors from the container holds and the engines. Why would they be so eager, rushing to one end of the vessel? The wind distorted their shouts — *Ty-nee!*

And in response — *Joo-nee-yoor!*

Henry took his time navigating the crowd that had just navigated him. Today no mass parted easily for anything. Because Henry stood a lighthouse taller, once he found footing, he could see over the mill-ing crew.

In the forecastle clearing, two men had stripped to the waist and now huffed, shaking themselves ready to wrestle. One had a goofy grin and noodle arms whipping up and down in preparation for the match — the other being a sullen soul, a compact spitting fireplug of a man, his back's tattoo a cutlass.

Above them, a swabbie mounted a steel cargo riser. To make him-self heard over the readiness to see blood, he intoned through a cone: 'Before we begin,' cracking at each word, 'we'll recite the mar-iner's oath. Special for wrestlers.'

An oath? The crowd hushed into solemnity. The two fighters re-peated each line responsively:

> O guardsmen, o friends,
> > O red and gold water —
> A time has come —
> > For us to praise honor.
> There cannot be surface —
> > Without any depths,
> Nor can there be wand'rings —
> > Without any wrecks.

Henry could understand this need for a recitation. His own main fear in childhood had been that were he to mistakenly voice certain words or sounds, someone across the world unknown to him could

8

die. If he said *murder* or *how you are today?* a budding violence could erupt.

Was his own son prone to such ideas? Daniel lost in the hinterlands, somewhere without his mother, tying flies or spinning tops. In Ceylon, Henry would write Daniel. Tell the boy he mattered more than Henry had ever mattered to Henry senior.

'Now!' the fight-hungry crowd was shouting. 'Now, now, now —'

— it was the swabbie's whistle that launched the match. At first, the crowd tugged in, obscuring Henry's sightlines. Someone kept nudging him. When the bodies parted slightly, Tiny the featherweight could be seen sparring with agility, the man's arms swiping back with a violent perfection.

'Uppercut!' Junior tended to brake the backsweep, to duck and block, showing mostly the warier art of self-defense. 'Ju-NIOR!' one faction yelled hard by Henry's eardrum. 'Go for the jaw! JUNIOR!'

A nudge again. 'Rev, excuse, borrow paper off you?' a short pistareen on the other side asked, only to start up again. 'Excuse, Rev, paper?'

Inside Henry's waistcoat pocket was a card. Even as the sailor jabbered on, Henry's fingers traced its nubby outlines, the expensive woven stock. The sailor amplified: 'To keep notes, ha? Bets, you know? Gambling?'

That was funny. Gambling on deck when voyaging was already a gamble. Needing a record sheet for gambling when the chief risk Henry had ever known involved his concealed card.

It had been handed him by James — who dubbed himself *Jay-meez* — yet another of Madame's friends. Just moments before the ship's send-off from New York, James had come offering this particular record sheet.

There Henry had parked himself at the gangway, admiring the *Colossus*, the vessel having turned out to be a turbine on her maiden voyage, a ship replete with yawning hatchways, gold anchors painted on her belly and the forecastle done up with red and yellow banners as if the queen of some minor archipelago were expected. As now, the sailors had poured down the ladders of the seaworthy ark, its virgin itinerary New York around the Cape, direct to Ceylon, then on to India and beyond. Henry's companions on the voyage were to be his own satchel and trunk, the crew, a farmload of unhappy Raj-bound cattle and a shipment of Cape Breton scotch.

Twenty-one days on board — Henry had never been at sea so long. Stunned by risk he'd sized up the ship, keeping one foot firm on New York soil and the other on the gangway. In an ecru tunic and skirt, James had shown up only to immediately dispense with chatter. Ceremonial, hair sleek and groomed, rippled with a single forehead curl, this man had business to conduct. Henry had liked the avid calculus in James' eyes, Henry's first Ceylonese acquaintance being a man who acted more rigorous and alive toward the world than one could generally hope to be.

James came, he announced immediately, with a written message from their mutual Russian friend. In the last month, allegedly, Madame had disbanded her anything-goes salon. She'd found lifeblood with a sikh who'd seduced her into taking a ten-year vow of silence. Her name had 'reverted' to something like Guru Singh Kalpa. She would not write to Henry in Ceylon, according to James. Yet before taking her vows, Madame had made an offering.

With passion James had delivered a creamy envelope. Inside, the handwriting was so familiar — the high lofty purple Ts, the wassailing dots and imperative slant:

> A reminder: We should never let the pettiness of others become the ambition of our souls. Yours, Elena

Determined to get in a closing word, and a circular, tail-biting one it was. Henry had stared at the card and laughed: she was doing it to him again. Trying to insert a snake of doubt, to poison his grand venture. What did she mean, with all that transparent clarity? He was to avoid *the pettiness of others*. Where, in Ceylon? Undeniably, pettiness and ambition were to be kept separate. It was practically a tautology, something explaining itself, the tail-biting snake of kundalini.

'She also gave you this —' James proffered a bookmark. A lovely rarity of a thing. A pressed lavender flower behind a waxen seal —

'And these' — a large packet marked *Lavender Seeds*. 'You'll be a free man in Ceylon,' James was saying, words stinging Henry.

'True enough. Sometimes I wish I were less free,' Henry had said.

He was being given gifts when he was just a bunch of raffish extra manflesh, voyaging on. A man at loose ends, now familyless, still hungry for the world. And this when Madame had shown unbeatable sophistication by becoming a modern-day monk. Madame, that false guru: all those years and she had led him wrong.

James had bowed a purposeful amount, a muted commotion, enough to indicate courtesy, not obeisance. He had already done a heap of things for Henry. Unfortunately, this last month, some of James' favors had entailed using Madame's web of acquaintances. Nevertheless, in this way he'd apparently rented an immense house for Henry in a perfectly traditional village. Now he would inscribe its name for Henry right there on Madame's card.

'Ask anyone,' said James, using the gangway railing to write. 'They'll direct you. Ceylon will be an atoll compared to what you're used to. Small, of course, but with an uncountable number of climates. People say it's the world's most majestic island.' Henry would have to find his own transport from Colombo. 'You'll stumble upon Rajottama easily. An old village.' He savored it. 'The temple there. Magnificent! And the Sacred Tree. You have also the ancient Kamaraga canal. It cuts between the two mountains.'

'What about the people? local industries? Are they —'

As if a smile could answer all questions, James smiled. 'Don't you think you're better off, as you say, if you're left to your own devices?'

And with that said, James had shimmied off, leaving Henry to imagine a paradise and cradle for his future — a tabula rasa surrounded by palm trees and quick-sighted natives ready for direction. Evidently the elegant James didn't worry what his wake had stirred up. He displayed a talent for vanishing into the dockyard crowd's loud oblivion, one intent on its own destinations and ideas.

'Stakes good today. You're the kind don't like fights much?' the short gambler was asking Henry.

'Depends.' From Henry's perspective, the featherweight and his sly dance had just sewn up the results. The noodle would outsmart the plug. Why should anyone stick around to see blood? 'Wouldn't bet on this match if I were you.'

'Where you from anyway? Got no friends in Ceylon? or New York?' the sailor went right on.

'Sure,' Henry said opaquely and then remembered Madame's salon-goers, all of the sheep. 'Actually. No friends. Not really anywhere.'

Jammed too snugly against the gambler, the other sailors, Henry desperately needed air. He pulled Madame's card out of his pocket and passed it to his tipster. 'You want to write? This is what I have. Now, please, you'll excuse me —' sidling away from the dogfight.

The crowd shoved forward and rebounded, resisting all attempts to flee. This in itself was auspicious. Because Henry again changed his mind. 'Sorry —' and without explanation seized his lucky card back from the gambler. Her very last contact with him and he needed to hang on to it.

'Don't want to see how this ends?' the sailor asked, unshocked. He had begun working the inside of his nose with his thumb. 'I'm no bookie but the end, that's when you get the real ante.'

Wasn't it over already? Tiny lay surrounded by his splinter group near the life preservers, his mouth a bloody geyser, those expert arms now crossed over his chest. Jumping up and down, Junior made a hollow victory salute, a maniac who'd just conquered some world of his own creation and expected others to care.

With it over, who *did* care? — everyone too involved in ceding purses back and forth, fighting over respective currencies and prowess in appraising odds. The brief game had concluded and beyond the barbaric practice itself, Tiny's blood distressed Henry. Should Henry have intervened? Tiny had lost, Junior had won, blood had been spilled, money had exchanged hands.

And Henry had just watched. With the card intact, deep next to his thigh, he swam through the bodies and their celebration. Desperate to cross to the ship's peaceful side.

Once Henry reached the benches, to fool his nausea he bent over the rail and studied the spit of their wake. And saw too the splay of clouds pillared above, pure mother-of-pearl, clouds grabbing the light like a hand taking in alms. He shivered, alone. As though erased upward, the sky cleared. Not a bad sign at all, this clearing. And now the captain gave out from the observation deck a knuckle-duster, a shout taken up by foretopman down to the sous-chef down to where the wind swallowed all sound. *Sighted!* And the crew got so caught up screaming their single word — SIGHTED! — that it became an earsplitting mumbo jumbo. A regular live round — how long could they go on like that? Minutes. Henry held tight, scared he might vomit in public.

'What is?' asked Henry, disoriented, stomach boiling. Best he could do was grip the rail. The light had changed, big deal — let those sailors shout all they wanted.

When finally he turned from the rail, it was with the slowness of a man nearing death. 'What is it?' he managed.

The captain curved down toward Henry, oddly delicate in saying, 'Colonel, it's right in front of you.'

Henry whipsawed back and saw.

The whole spindrift dome of the sky had lifted, along with his spirits: a miracle, creation revealed, a perfect ocean gem pushing up. Land. It had hoved into view and Henry had missed its first arrival. Something like Ceylon was already yawing toward them.

3

WHERE THE LANDSCAPE of America is all foreground, your attention slammed to the front of things, whether it be a storefront or a mountain's base, and that of Europe is all background, some winding country road leading off amid obsessively stone-walled hills, Ceylon is both, simultaneously, Henry decided, focusing on the sea wall and breakwater leading into the serviceably pretty Dutch town.

He took it in: the soapy spume dashing against a promontory bordering a long sandy breakaway. At the quay, a wooden fishing jetty had been guffed out with flags; behind them, long, stalwart official buildings looked blankly out as though only recently pressed into service. To the south a fort towered over a customs-house and lighthouse. Just beyond, breathing darkly, cramped coaling sheds lined up. And the reefs — ugly and exquisite, stringing a blind man's braid out through the harbor's surf.

Through field glasses useless until now, Henry could make out in detail how this picturesque isle would make the past a good premise. A group of raw-backed boys pulled in a hefty fishnet, laughing with enough charm to shelter Henry. Beyond the small defined beach, after a main road, he found the impudent palm trees he had imagined, if somewhat slimmer. They flocked up a slope, tentpoles for a canopy of a green so brilliant he thought too close your eyes would hurt. This landscape accosted him. As a rejoinder, he listed climes he knew, to locate Ceylon's combination of them: kingly California villas, the dustiness of old Spanish towns, Florida's palm-lined promenades, the syrupy river air of St. Louis summers, the quarrelsome density of New Hampshire forests, the ornate metalwork along Louisiana delta houses, the craggy lost coasts of Cape Cod, Cornwall's tumbling scale — and this list-making comforted him.

Foreign as this first glimpse of Ceylon was, he believed he discerned a bold routine, a welcoming, domestic body thriving inside. Floury dwellings pocked the verdure in a pleasing fashion; smoke wafted from red-tiled roofs. And above everything were distant peaks, competing for height, the nearest wearing a perfect judge's-wig of cumulus clouds.

What he recalled was Zion's foundation stone, a precious corner stone, how he that believeth shall not make haste. There would be no fumbling for keys in this new place; the very soil itself would exhale patience and renewal. Ceylon had been no mistake.

You would have thought from the captain's physiognomy he would move unhurriedly. Instead he was a heavy marine fly, flitting from position to position, inhabiting each. He had landed next to Henry. 'The air,' he said, before lighting his pipe. 'Take a whiff. Ceylon air's great.'

'Why's that?'

'You're a joker, Colonel. Name it, they got it in Ceylon. Unexplored headwaters. Any spice you want.'

Was it then cinnamon that Henry smelled? His stomach calmed at the thought. Or camphor and sandalwood? the captain's pipe? the aftertaste of potted chicken?

'Maybe just a warm breeze,' said Henry, to nothing. The captain had flittered off again, more concerned with weighing anchor than with classifying air.

But classification could be put to good use here, *here* where body and instinct could equally share the rewards of the correct life. Henry would be dedicating his next step to the Ceylonese, however long it took. To them he would turn over his blotter sheet of a life with its terrors and kinder moments, his fractioned memories and the specters that trailed him.

The closest peak loomed above and because of the captain's gift, Henry could almost name it. That morning, with a gravedigger's respect, the captain had given Henry a logbook: a ledger kept by a former government agent, Wooves, in the last years of the previous century. According to the captain's innuendoes, Wooves had dutifully notated his years on the island before he went foaming mad.

In what Henry saw as a fortuitous coincidence — the captain hadn't known — the house Henry would be renting out is the one Wooves inhabited. At least that's what James' inscription on the envelope said — *Wooves' Residence, Rutaeva, Kandy District . . .*

And Henry would probably not have to pay anything to any agent of Wooves. In New York, James had promised him that it could be worked out later, surely. Especially as the house had stood empty for so long. James' good friend in London had a friend whose uncle's acquaintance had coordinated the place for Henry. The American was not to worry; even if the Ceylonese had the telegraph and roads, the power of the provincial colonials was much less than it once was. No one would be needing the house. James said that anyway, nowadays, most colonials administered from the capital, not from the outstations.

Henry had only to arrive.

'An Englishman,' the captain said of agent Wooves. 'House should be pleasant enough. Guy was a decent old codger, I thought. Until he went and jumped ship before we hit New York. My virgin voyage — '88. Just shy of twenty and had to sit in on a tribunal about it. The strange thing was his jumping. The man always went on about his expat years. Expat this, expat that. Missing his table at the Algae-quin. His round table in New York where he was meant to swill his gin.'

Henry couldn't think of a nippy response. The government agent had committed suicide after his years in Ceylon. A colorless expat blocked by life. People always showcased themselves so dramatically. This was largely due to the inability to find meaning and service in one's own trajectory. He was about to tell the captain this but the captain needed no response to keep the conversation flowing.

'Me,' the captain was saying, 'I keep the book like a souvenir. They wanted it back in Ceylon to keep continuity for the next guy mugwumped there. Now I'm done with it. You'll see, it's a nail-biter until the man goes — well, you'll figure it out. Never thought I'd have a passenger who could exploit it. You're the one, Colonel,' and handed it over with no little ceremony, waiting for Henry to poke through it.

First thing Henry had opened to were Wooves' descriptions of topography, something about the mountain he thought neighbored them, the second highest in Ceylon. Wooves in his governed script had called it a hoary streak, beyond town, tree, hill and road:

Adam's Peak: God placed the first man here with the command to name the beasts. It is said Adam revisited the peak after being expelled from Eden and that Noah's Ark came to rest on the mount

the civil servant had written in the center of the page; while in the margins he had scribbled spidery additions:

December butterflies migrate to Adam's Peak Local mythology has it that the apostle beloved by India, skeptical Saint Thomas, set foot in Ceylon on Adam's Peak. Wrathful Lord Shiva also alleged here. Yet commemorated most is the footprint of Buddha, Buddha the unspeakable . . .

I

WRONG SPEAKING

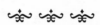

And when he had eaten his meal at evening time near the lake, the Conqueror, in the ninth month of his Buddhahood, at the full moon, himself set forth for the isle of Lanka, to win Lanka for the faith. For Lanka was known to the Conqueror as a place where his doctrine should thereafter shine in glory, and he knew that from Lanka, filled with demons, the demons must first be driven forth.

— *The Mahavamsa, or The Great Chronicle of Ceylon*

Q. What are the sins of the mind?
A. They are:

      i. Covetousness
     ii. Malice
   iii. Wrong belief

4

THEY DOCK in what Henry understands is Ceylon's capital, Colombo.

In that first surveillance, Henry must have missed the procession. By the time he checks again, hems of orange are billowing down the paths. A whole phalanx of orange and brown spreads toward him in royal promenade. Who would have organized this for him? but it was the case and he had to be grateful.

A thousand monks have turned out to meet Henry, and he may be estimating low: the saffron robes convene and swell into a greeting. The orange thickening on shore, awaiting him, these monks and their bald brown pates, taking spiritual soundings with their fans on the dock, all under the sky's loving azure expanse.

Someone must have alerted these devotees to his arrival. Will he be understood here? His heart leaps to his throat. He is modest, yes, will back away from the honor. He thought the organizer might have been James, if more likely that it was Madame, she the only one with motivation enough to summon these handsome holy men. Could this be a last gift from her? These anointed ones, how they hold their straw fans close as breastplates.

What can he call them — these exotics? — such holy figures born into a religion not his father's and not his own? The ones he has come, in a sense, to help. And yet he's certain they summon him.

Henry mirrors the holy men's bows as best he can. Here, no doubt, success awaits him. Of course, he tells himself, he has earned this. He'd lived a life of integrity. About time he's recognized, after all; he has come to help rid these people of their colonial whitewashing. These sepia, saturnine faces are his first blessings on the isle of Ceylon.

Let this crew of Tinys and Juniors make all the quips they want as they help winch Henry down the ladder. Who needs such white crabs?

Below, a longshoreman awaits him in a catamaran. The water is bottle green and through it Henry can detect the jagged edge of the coral reef below, marvelously swift glitterfish rushing alongside. All he has with him is his satchel and this suits him. Light-handed, light-*headed*, he can wait for the trunk later. The seaman starts his oar-plying, feathering through the ambrosial water, hardly fast enough. Henry can't wait to step onto land and be embraced by the dignitaries.

He glances back just once to see the captain with his mouth fallen open.

What kind of story will the captain spin for his next passenger about his American anti-missionary? Henry cannot stop thinking — and for the moment doesn't *try* to stop — how this must be the best reception anyone short of royalty has ever received.

On land, the throng clamors for him: 'Holy man,' they cry. 'Saddhu, saddhu!'

What makes these faces so splendid? That there's nothing but kindness in them? Such good spirit will make his work all the easier. It is not just the monks, gathering, more of them surging down the hill toward him, awaiting in a serene and aureate moment, beatitude apparent. It is how the lane of fishing boats and the road beyond are garlanded with banners. And how the young boy on the pier pulls a cloth that could have been stitched from the very snows of Kilimanjaro, it is that white, all to make a carpet for the visitor. 'I'm sorry, maybe pull just a bit faster?' Henry asks the old mariner.

The man just grimaces back, his oars gutting and shucking the clean water, getting the sweeps out. 'You're here, Colonel,' he eventually gasps, sagging forward.

'Thank you,' Henry says, no coin ready for a tip. The crowd raises a cheer. He leaps out onto the white-carpeted berth, leaving the boat rocking.

A dignified monk parades forward, removes his spectacles. Kneels — the better to cup his hands together from the sanctity of Henry's feet. 'Welcome,' says the monk, sounding as though he rolls marbles around in the back of his tongue. James' accent had been smooth and Britishized, Henry now realized.

'Please,' Henry says to the monk, embarrassed. 'Stand. I don't need anyone bowing to me.'

'Of course.' The monk jumps to his feet and instead makes a nuanced bow. 'You're wise as your work.'

'Have your little love scene,' the longshoreman yells to Henry. 'Your bag's here. I'm heading back.'

A young Ceylonese heaves up the satchel and begins marching through the spectators toward a waiting bullock carriage. Everything here is so mysterious — how the gulls nose-dive and cry around the crowd as if the sublimity of flight hurts them. Telling it like it is, Henry has never heard birds so full-voiced. 'Shall we?' the monk asks, leading Henry with a statesman's certainty.

This monk almost certainly knows everything about Henry Fyre Gould so perhaps it's best to proceed as if no introductions are needed. 'Colombo's *beautiful*. Air's so clean and sweet. Don't tell me — cinnamon? or is that jasmine? pod of cardamom?'

'Sir, all due respect, this is no Colombo.' Behind the monk shines an empire, the day a scorcher despite the wind, palm fronds and red bottlebrush swaying a welcome. Young barefoot girls on the burnt almond road tilt their heads and loll their tongues with a curiosity à la coquette.

'Right,' Henry says to the monk, dabbing his forehead. Wishing he could take off his waistcoat. 'Here you have a kind of heaven.'

'Sir's accent in English proves difficult for us only. Would it be prudent for us to continue in Sinhalese?'

These are not gulls, Henry comprehends, gulls making pained cries — they are crows, speckled black and gray. How sharp their caws are, arrowing toward the dock's end where a hoard of silver flesh shimmers. They perch on what Henry makes out as a pile of fish heads and bones, motionless scurf clogged together. A crush of silent robed men tightens around Henry and the monk. Henry hears something he had missed before.

'Pardon?' he asks. 'I'm sorry. Not Colombo?'

'Sir has arrived in Galle. Not the capital.'

'What serendipity,' Henry laughs, still drunk with pleasure. He wants to ask one of the monks whether someone might be sent for a glass of fresh water. Or gallons of it. His palate is dry as road dust. 'Then we're closer to Wooves' house?' He knows he might be babbling. But thinks he'll be forgiven.

And Henry will also have to forgive Madame everything — she'd perhaps used James to ensure that no matter the harbor of Henry's docking, he'd receive a hero's welcome. Maybe she was on the island? That would be hoping for too much. He misses her suddenly, weird thing that she is, a keen gallop that makes him catch his breath.

'I'm sorry. I'm no expert in Ceylonese. Of course, I'm eager,' says

Henry. The truth is that ahead he spies some bleached official building, a marvelous erection of a thing. With its stonework, mortared edifice and solid colonial steps leading up to the main door, it beckons like part of a valid legacy, makes Henry's nose itch with the yearning to enter. He knows this kind of building, the single fraction of the landscape he *can* label: inside would be ammoniated corridors and wooden chairs, the muted light from tall windows falling on ink-stained blond paneling. He needs just a moment to regain his land legs. He would be happy for half an hour just to sit in a corridor while dusky customs clerks ran by him, clerks who could perhaps be asked for a bottle of fresh water.

'Would Sanskrit suit Sir more —?'

'Please. Say *you*,' continuing to promenade with the genteel man. He sees, closer, what garish trinkets the girls use to ornament their hair. This heat has gotten its gummy hold on Henry and says it won't release him now. Inside his stained shirt, new rills of sweat are ruling him.

'We don't —' The monk straightens himself. Takes a moment to adjust his spectacles. 'Oh! Is it possible Sir is not Wilhelm —?'

In the moment Henry understands his situation, the monk has understood it far better. They have come to the necropolis of dead fish and the wind whippets the stink his way.

The monk continues unperturbed, as though syntax could right the wrong and conjure up the intended. 'Sir is not the distinguished German translator of the Pali Canon? Mister Wilhelm? the exegesis that has illumined . . .'

'Stop,' Henry implores. 'I'm no Wilhelm.' His guts boil and seize. He stares longingly up at the customs house. There is to be no welcome for him. Only this hillock of dreggy fish, these greedy crows, these letdown faces, the jaundiced papers sick-listing by in a wind hot as a simoom. He may as well be in the desert.

Would drowning on the way to land have been any worse?

The monk has the decency to accompany his white fake on a reverse gangplank. To send a shout up to the *Colossus* for another rowboat, a mournful cry that trolls along the mirage, the sallow earnest sea of monks. Henry returns then, past the ricket of fishing boats with their gaudy masts. His stomach gurgles like a sad drainpipe. By the time they reach dock's end, its posts smothered by bracken, the captain himself awaits, leaning on the rowboat's daggerboard.

'Would've tried to stop you,' the captain hee-haws. He chews a eucalyptus leaf and is cheerful down to his breath. At the oars, he pulls and heaves his Yankee freight back to the *Colossus*. 'I was too damn happy.'

'Why?' Henry asks, sullen. 'Should've told me.' He keeps his eyes on the water teeming with unnamable, manic fish. 'Not fair.'

'You don't know these people. They only accept their own. And for once they *recognized* one of my passengers. Hospitable, right?'

Henry can't answer. His throat pinches too tightly. Alongside the boat a discarded label with a watery pink soldier on it floats by.

'Come on, it was better than being a prince. It was like escorting a king. Admit it' — the captain punches his arm with feeling —'you were king for a moment. Most people never get that even once in their lives. You were lucky.'

'Show me when that's true,' says Henry, grabbing his satchel before clambering up the ship's ladder, back to where he belongs.

5

IT WILL TAKE only a few mortified hours to get to the correct capital — Colombo — but each moment until then stretches like winter's worst blizzard. Seeking succor, Henry enters crew quarters below deck, clutching the guard rail. A tubby sailor brushes by in the gloom, a cabin door whining and slamming behind him. Henry inches toward the door, budging it ajar, entering when no one answers his whispered *hello?* — and the room's wideness slumps over him but for the door's split of light.

He manages to fling himself down on the sailor's bunk, finding a relief in such a hasty exchange of identities. What nights had soiled this scratchy, wool-covered bed? The room stinks of ash and animals and something worse. On the preposterously low ceiling and tight walls posters are peeling off, glue undone by the damp. Leering at him are ghostlike pictures of women with beestung lips, whose enormous pale breasts float out of a rosy-petaled haze. Half the rooms in half the boats on water must be rooms like this. All might. In the bad light he can't discern too much about which genus of women sailors prefer; and were he to open the door to let in more light he would be discovered. It is cozier to stay crammed into this dollhouse, the door inert for the moment.

His head pops with random thoughts and contempt for his own harmlessness. The correct mooring is Colombo. He should write to his son. Colombo. The wormy white of the wall women's breasts. Lady B.

Lady B. There he sticks. A woman with no breasts who had brought him down.

Another woman altogether, a body utterly self-possessed and self-abandoning. The woman he had come clean about to his wife Clara. The woman she blamed for everything. The woman who — after his flood of candor — made his wife refuse to take him back.

Lady B. and her wormy-white neck. Whose existence had made Clara tell him he'd better trolley off and save heathens elsewhere: Aryan beggars, Asian elite, Carpathian drunks. Whatever his new ministry was, she had no time for it. Lady B. the one code he could not dismiss from Clara's mind, the woman who'd made him take up quarters on this ship. Lady B. who'd made Mrs. Gould and son flee New York for her father and his resigned midwestern rectory. It is Lady B. flooding his gutters. She and her narrow cameo head and the choice she suggested.

She'd really been no one to him, he'd told himself repeatedly. Wasn't he just participating in a *milieu?* hadn't he always been an intellectual vagabond, an explorer? And those late-night New York salon discussions had not infrequently concerned this idea of free love.

Only months before Henry's defection, Madame had stooped forward, crushing her voluminous purple velvet dress, eyes aglow, her most possessed, inspired look. Madame, the proudest celibate Henry had ever met, addressed the motley salon members. They craned their necks around the salon's stuffed Gibraltar ape to hear her. This inconvenience to them was zilch.

They'd dangle from the rafters if she required it. Just to be near her, dressed as she always was in blues, greens, purples. Ocean colors. They died to be near her and the energy Madame channeled, thinking the whole spectacle would heal them of bedsores and hemorrhoids. Of neurasthenia and ingrown toenails. Of female troubles and forgetfulness. Of illnesses that sounded better in Swedish. These spiritualists were ready to be cured of all afflictions, new or old. Even monogamy.

'Don't you see?' the impetuous Russian had cried that night. 'We are talking about metamor-*pho*-sis. If we demand fundamental equality and universal brotherhood, we in the Society must strip away bourgeois declarations. Forget monogamy! Examine fidelity!'

One knowledgeable salon guest had been wiping her brow and breathing heavily all night. She had to outclass the dead souls who had, she claimed, imperialized her body. Now she mustered up verve, enough to raise her hand. 'Exactly! You're talking about karmic entrapment. My husband and I were together for six lives. Every life he was taken away from me. Maimed, strangled. Didn't matter. Burned at the stake. Then a few weeks ago, I had a lucid dream of his death. I knew I'd scorched away that karma.' She sighed to unfetter herself of another dead soul. 'Now I don't need to hold on to him. I'm not losing sleep anymore. Nothing bad will happen to him. Now we're no longer karmically entrapped.'

A man with long mustaches of a fools'-gold yellow bowed his approval. 'That's a case of dharma burning away the karma.'

Madame exploded in a joyful shout. 'Wonderful! Meta-mor-PHO-sis!' She regained herself. 'Fidelity is our last god! We think chastity an unimpeachable value?' The company laughed knowingly. 'We must consent to our incarnation. Free ourselves from this Western idea of bodylessness as the ultimate goal! There's your dharma!'

She paused. No one understood but her words put them into spiritual estrus, ready for anything.

'You see why monogamy's wrong?' — a Socratic twinkle lighting her up. 'I ask you. Gentlemen. Ladies!' In Madame's unsettling gaze (one eye placid, the other popfish-opened) she included the newly stuffed ape. 'Weren't we,' Madame continued, 'given these singular bodies as vessels for universal spirit?'

The room held its breath before Henry heard someone refer to Madame's unbeltable girth: 'In some cases, more than singular bodies.'

'Call avoirdupois a manifestation from the Masters,' she sighed with some weariness, exhaling clouds from her perennial hookah. 'You need bigness to channel and contain the highest truths.'

Henry missed Madame and her avoirdupois. If she were the jewel at the center of their Lamasery, the whole room, having been done to her taste, proved a dazzling setting for all their communal convulsions. A gilded hollow Shiva danced forever before the whittled fancies of Chinese and Japanese cabinets. From the walls hung a maja's tainted, embroidered fans; on the window ledge rested a sultan's pipes; and in the corner rolled Persian rugs, mildewed, awaited the opening of future Society branches.

Once Henry had loved how her séances left nothing untouched and arrogantly hodgepodged everything. *Her* Buddhism would never stay Buddhism. Instead it would spatter into some crazy Vajrayana-Theravada-Hindu-Jainist-Episcopal-Zoroastrian-Eastern-Orthodox-Sufi-Hopi-American-Kabbalistic stew. She believed herself inspired and directed by the Masters whose physical apparitions, as she sketched them, resembled no one so much as Christ in his various sweaty Renaissance aspects.

Henry had arrayed the salon's divans and couches to promote conversation undeterred by the mechanical bronze bird who (if wound properly) sang 'La Marseillaise' every sixty-one minutes. Over every surface Madame had scattered albums, scrapbooks, lacquered cigarette boxes, papers and ashpots. Presiding over them all, mere curiosity-seekers and true friends alike, strangers and intimates, keeping them ready for some moment's revelation, the Russian woman sat, observant at one moment, a loud cigar-chomper the next.

Around the drawing room people from all strata of New York society felt compelled to stare at shape-shifting Madame. How she shuttled between personae more quickly than you could say *avatar*. Even the Gibraltar ape, freshly stuffed on Fifth Avenue, in his white dickey, spectacles, and the manuscript of *The Eye That I Am: Osiris* clenched in permanent rigor mortis, seemed to hang on Madame's words. Above the mantelpiece, frozen in a death-defying cry, jutted a stuffed leopard, whose glare threatened to take in those whose jokes at Madame's expense were less than kind.

During one of Madame's outbursts, a curiosity-seeker she had attracted, Lady B., visiting from London for months already, had glanced over her lorgnette with enough sauciness to let Henry know he could approach her at a break. Though he had seen Lady B. at a farmhouse séance the previous spring, they had never spoken.

Now he lit her cigarette, saying *Permettez-moi, Madame*, realizing with self-disdain that with these exact words he had made the acquaintance of his Madame.

Am I such an impoverished creature, he thought — as the lady leaned forward with a shade too much coyness, with a shaking of broad curls she must have considered fetching — that I'm doomed to repeat yesterday's phrases, even if they've brought me such past success?

It was the last day of the year. He admitted to the then-popular ailment of depression. Seeing Lady B.'s considered curls hanging from her narrow cameo face, he wondered whether some diversion could be had.

She was, as they said, well-preserved. Around her, he thought, clung the slight shame of a recent divorce, a knowledge of empty piers. She also had that knowing gleam in her eyes, the suggestion he found so alluring in older women.

What was she asking him? 'Then you have these evenings often, Henry?'

He couldn't answer immediately. Madame had just 'manifested' a letter in her Irish maid's hands. The girl lilted aloud the instructions — from a Master's handwriting — for the entire assembled party to retire to the Brooklyn Promenade. There they were to view the fireworks display close to midnight.

Henry arranged to enter a carriage with Lady B. He knew a whole encyclopedia of things. The most important was knowing a kindred spirit when he found one.

'Really,' said the lady, her curls at work. 'I found her comments to be so enlightening.'

'Which would those be?' asked Henry, aware of the warm privacy surrounding them. They were all to meet at the harbor, Madame and the meaningless others having raced over the cobblestones ahead of the pair.

'What she said about free love. The imperative in the Body's birthright. You haven't been listening!'

'Of course,' said Henry, inspired to take hold of those angora-clad hands. 'It's just — I'm distracted.'

That was how the evening had begun.

It ended with Henry dispatching loiterers. He retired with Lady B. to his chambers, the ones that had scandalized salongoers until Madame had clarified that between her and Henri, on the physical plane, there was nothing, nothing!

What he told Lady B. was that the up-shooting light was the only proper one in which to examine a piece of his patrimony: David

27

Roberts' lithographs on Holy Land travel with the turbaned natives forever on their hazy plateaus. He checked on Madame in her downstairs apartments; his mystical Russian snored away.

'Madame's unlit hookah is hanging on for its life out of her mouth,' he explained to the lady. Like a schoolboy on leave, he imitated Madame's fat lips.

Lady B. just busied herself (an aristocratic hand adjusting her pearls) by professing interest in lithos of Bedouins ogling the Old City. How *dedicated* she was to gorgeous landscapes, *stricken* as they were by such sapphire rivulets. Moreover, she found prints in general to be *enchanting*, and the *perception* of spiritual seekers in particular . . .

By the time Henry and the spiritual lady had entered a not wholly soulless entanglement involving a pearl necklace and items of clothing in unstrapped, flung, enchanted state —

— Madame had materialized out of Henry's own closet, puffing on that hookah, saying: *But Henri, I come here for peace and you turn me into a commonplace voyeuse! a spy!*

Shame struck both Henry and Lady B. hard. They had already said too much and too little. Intoxicated things. Like you know I thought of you since the first time I saw you in that farmhouse and you could be one of the world's wonders and now I will always have you in me and I always thought being a wife was bad business but tonight I could be yours and I can't stand my hands separated from your body.

After his Madame had sauntered out, whistling her spoils, Lady B.'s narrow head tucked ostrich-like behind her pale arm (whose graces Henry had been citing only a moment earlier). And, a trifle stuck, the lady gulped, ostensibly doomed to repeating: 'This will be the *last* New York sees of me for a while!'

The last, perhaps, of her — but on the humiliated day that followed, gazing out over the window's boxed morning glories, free love convinced Henry to make the declaration. Thirteen years into being married and, squalid as it was to own up, maybe he wasn't ready to be hampered in the world. Clara had been an intelligent plucky partner, and still she'd be the first to admit they were not well-matched. Even Henry's association with Madame alarmed her a tad. That morning, down to the very bridge of her nose, Clara looked like the habit, long-believed, that all these years had kept him mediocre.

Having made a decision without having really made it, just know-ing he was about to do something momentous, something requir-ing heroic resolve, something deep within himself all these many months, he trod into the weighted atmosphere of his own living room.

His sex and temples throbbed an off-rhythm. He was about to do something —

Big. Something big. What he'd been developing in a sneaky compartment within himself, after months of disagreeing with Madame's helter-skelter direction of the Society. What Daddy had been developing while lecturing from the Central Park stairs — he made his announcement to Clara and to little Daniel who was play-ing in a corner with a caboose — was something Daddy needed to tell them both, he found himself saying.

He was leaving to take a long trip. No return date estimated. Here the wind began to whistle out of Henry. He had to continue. His thighs chafed and he wanted to run away from what he had begun. He was too guilty about Lady B. to have thought this one through precisely. His mouth followed through with its own momentum.

What he figured, he went on, was that the two of them (meaning wife and son) would be better off returning to Clara's father's parish in St. Louis. It would be good to see where things led (meaning for himself and his wife), because legalities could always be taken care of later. He was sorry to have to tell them (meaning his wife) this way but sometimes it was necessary to just get things over with. Because no one instructs any of us on how to live, that was the problem (at this point his mouth shocked him more than it could have shocked them; he listened to it in horror). He knew in his bones he was doing the right thing. Every choice has a consequence, doesn't it —

'Don't tell us. We know. It's the blood of your mongrel mother acting up,' interrupted Clara, nonsensically.

'No laughing,' he instructed his wife. A second later: 'Don't laugh, I say —' Her laugh was horrible and unquenchable. Nothing could stop it but itself. When it turned into a cry, one that accused him of having taken 'an executive decision' without her, he offered what he thought might be a consolation, saying it was only what was best for everyone.

He could not get her to agree that a separation was best. She possessed larger ideas about their togetherness, she said. *Her* to-getherness was Unconditional — at this she concurrently laughed and cried. Like a demon, he thought.

Yet wasn't it natural that he believe her? That, hearing about her Unconditional, he would decide to come clean about Lady B.? Did honesty have no part in the Unconditional? But when he told her, it only made their separation imminent. After he described Lady B., Clara would brook no part of him, especially not his wavering. Once he changed his mind about the journey, once he decided that he might instead like to stay and keep the marriage intact, it had become *her* turn to refuse him.

And what about their son? Was she forgetting Daniel? he'd asked.

'No. Maybe *you* forgot?' she retorted. Adding a false doubt: 'If he is our son.' Obviously, Clara would not take him back. With nothing greater than horseshoe nails he had ruined a family.

At the time Daniel had been all of eight.

He had reddish curls like his mother and a tendency to dream. He named pets after spices like pepper and paprika. And he refused to watch his father during that first mostly public speech of sundering.

'What do *you* think?' Henry asked the boy after the initial volley had more or less finished.

The boy glowered at his father with something between hate and horror. He had never seen his father make his mother both laugh and rush out of the room to do what sounded like cry. He tried to escape from the man now kneeling before him holding his hands.

'You're going to be gone,' said the boy. 'Who cares what I think?'

'What, though?'

'Don't know,' Henry's son answered, wriggling away. 'Don't think anything. Let me go.'

A bloody sense of his own meanness solidified in the back of Henry's throat. At the time he'd thought what was said could be taken back. When the words had already flown out and away from him.

And in the end it was his tongue or hands or some other part of him at fault. He could not turn anything back, certainly not the end of his marriage, and no one could blame Lady B. The disintegration must have been in the tedious works; Lady B. was just the wrench. Henry knew he'd been a coward. He determined to make it up to Clara somehow, with a show of bravery or — if this was all that was allowed — making things easy on her pocket.

The making-things-easier part would come later. Once he got settled and became successful. For now he'd give her a heap of money to stash away, tithings from the *salonistes*, with more to come. At the outset he would have to preserve some of his savings, migrate on the rims of things for a while, invest with Charlie Merrill and hope for the best.

Last he heard, just before he set sail, Clara had deposited Daniel with her mother in St. Louis and gone off on an Episcopal mission to Freetown. Little Daniel had stayed, doing (what Henry imagined) whatever it is that small boys in St. Louis tend to do. Catching lightning bugs, making up frantic songs, acting out wars.

The irony being, of course, that despite Henry's forty-odd years of walking about the world, Lady B. constituted only the second woman he had ever embraced. She was as much to blame as a trigger is for a murder — she had merely suggested the havoc of pleasure. Days after his interlude with the lady he imagined women dancing with him, arms pulling him down. Had a city ever corroded from lust? There did not seem to be anything *absolutely* wrong with that realm. If godliness was distant from nothing, couldn't unexpected boons come from everywhere? For example: who could say it wasn't better for Daniel to be raised by his grandparents? Better to grow up with grandparents than stick around a resentful mother and absentee father in New York, wasn't it?

One never knows Life and its intentions, reasoned Henry. Silence roars at our backs. Everything we venture tends toward the hypothetical. If man is forced to inhabit what the Buddhists called this fathom-long mortal shell, should he not enjoy, if not necessarily free love, at least the stimulation of his senses?

An emphatic shout sounds down the corridor —
'COLOMBO! El capital! Calling Henry Gold-dust!'
He wakes marooned by the fear that the voices have been combing through all his forbidden memories. No. They rib him. A joke. Gold dust. Again he hears the gulls with their devouring cries. He unkinks his legs, gathers the wrinkled satchel and leaves the ladies with their ghostly breasts.

6

COLOMBO — THE CORRECT MOORING. Yet on the gangway, Henry hesitates; fears provisionally pocketed, sea legs (not nerves) trembling. He scans a crowd that looks mostly stunned into an August torpor. On land, two comely, well-dressed Ceylonese children wave with such ecstasy that it is probably not at him.

No, not at him — he will repeat no mistakes, he gives no sign back. He is as determined to forget the Galle episode as a man weak from thirst or hunger or embarrassment can be. He has few expectations.

He has read his card with Wooves' disappointed address on it more than twenty times already, sweat making the writing into a herringbone of sorts. Now his task is to read the name of his destination to some bronchial train conductor or alcoholic carriage driver or god knows what type of person. There are a hundred blueprints for arrival. And which were superior to any other?

Expect nothing, he tells himself. No virginal flesh bursting over laced bodices. No cream-suited dignitaries — women thrust against him offering garlands and honeyed pastries — no round-bottomed babies to dandle — no golden carpets unrolling into bright futures. Nothing he might have fancied, especially at the height of their New York salon's celebrity, say, at the time of the public cremation, when he had thought himself more than a co-leader of sheep.

'Be acceptance itself,' he murmurs. Around him mariners jostle importantly, tying salt-encrusted ropes on the grommets, preparing for land, certain of their social adjustments.

Almost anything would improve stepping off into a harbor where apart from the seamen the air drones hot and solitary. Where the only thing Henry hears moving with purpose is the sharp tongue of a Portuguese, seated on his horse, the better to command his bareback boys.

He descends the gangway slowly, shuffling through the swelter. All he can think of is how to make it to a sliver of cooler shade, next to the port building. To that bench. He is seeing those tiny silver rippings of the world around him. Is he about to have a fit? He cannot. A fit must be sidestepped. All those weeks on board he was spared. No fits now. Would they please just bring out his trunk soon?

Henry mops his face with his stinking handkerchief. Ceylon is heat. This heat and a rickety bench and a slow trunk.

In front of him, the beautiful Ceylonese girl and boy he'd seen from the ramp dance around their father, who'd just descended from the *Colossus* — a rough-featured shiphand Henry had not noticed much. The man must have stayed below deck much of the time. If this mariner had been a pauper on board, buttressing the ship's totem, in homecoming he becomes king. The girl in her clean-collared blouse ferrets in the father's pockets and the boy is lost in some chatter. The father — he must be the father, he shares the boy's long curving eyes — scoops his son up onto his hip and walks on, his girl holding the other hand.

Henry's heart does a wiggle and suck. Why should this man's son have so much *life* given him unthinkingly when Henry had missed out on most of the ordinary pleasures? why should Henry have been burdened with a father so hemmed in by rectitude, he never would've openly carried and kissed a son, any son? On a legal pad Henry had once made a list of things he'd missed out on, and then immediately burned it, annoyed with such self-involvement. Still, he recalls what he had written, long before he had met Madame. His main regret, trivial in sound, deep in root: he had only observed Clara, his *wife*, putting on lipstick; had never seen his own mother have a go at it, with her breed of aristocratic pretension. Pink, orange, red, it wouldn't have mattered the color, just the handsome wrist-flick, that's what he craved, the attention she would give her reflection. Rounded brown hair, pearl-drop earrings, a scent of talc, bent cigarettes in a crystal ashtray. And a mirror surrounded by golden laurels, the mirror he could not fully remember her in. All these years he had carried around more than a few ribs aching for her.

Self-pity! he scolds himself. Baa baa black sheep yourself.

Some urge to ask these swarthy citizens what time everything is supposed to happen comes over him — to step up and ask whether they might include him in their full life. Their happiness. Whether his son too might be brought over on the next humming tur-

33

bine ship. Little hydrant-plug Daniel could descend in some glory. Blue eyes fastening him in their judgmental but ultimately forgiving light. A boy with a gleeful intelligence, palpable even in his most surly moments, Henry's sparkling redness, his Daniel.

He withdraws Wooves' morocco logbook and crosses out the name of the retired agent on the frontispiece.

Village Book belonging to Henry Fyre Gould

he writes. He tries to ignore Wooves' curbed writing smack in the middle of the book:

June 8, 1886

For too long I had been content with my own province and found myself wishing to roam farther. On the outer lip of the Kandy District there is said to exist a marvelous field, practically an estate, which I have long wished to visit. Locals say it represents the very best in native effort, both human and natural. Meanwhile, all have given contradictory instructions on how to reach it. One will say it lies due west, toward the final range of mountains. Another tells me it can be found should one follow the ridge-crest trail beyond the lake before descending. Yet each time this previous month that I have set out to find the estate, something else has insisted on intervening. Urgent affairs and the like. Perhaps the illustrious field does not exist as such and remains another enterprising example of the colorful indigenous stories they like to tell as if to please me. Allegedly they have made of this far field something quite special — a turf dappled with vines, rimmed with peekaboo hedges and rare aromatic flowers. They call its vegetation nutritive, its mood sublime, its inspiration supreme; it is never too distant from their conversations. Such is its fame that a visiting

rajah once reposed under the shade of its mangoes,
later calling the place a lapsed paradise. At its border
it is planted up with coconuts and the whole thing
does quite well though labor is done by women who
come from villages several miles away to work with
the mamotty.

Planted up. Henry envies the dead man. Had Wooves survived the passage home and made it to his curtained corner at the Algonquin, he would've known so much more about Ceylon than Henry does right now in this roasting port.

I'll understand these people as instantly as he did, Henry tells himself. Quicker. He sits up, flips to the book's end section. Begins his own notation:

Arrival, August 10, 1936

He performs a reconnaissance of his environs, his pen aloft for a second before effecting an A-1 landing:

A lithe & noble race. What is the Latin for: Intelligent obedience prospers? What renders the first-time visitor to Ceylon speechless is the profundity of life here: with cool head & tranquil judgment, the Ceylonese

such as he can see them, herded about are mostly sailors, decorous if palsied dockmen, harbor drunks, stray souls, only a few *local* families because mostly there are chlorinated English civil servants in creased khakis skimming about the lot in military jeeps. An Italian merchant ship is leaving bound for Ethiopia, that's what Henry has overheard, and while the young sailors leaning over the railing look more *dulce* than *decorum*, practically virginal, British soldiers patrol the quay as tightly as if they'd been told they could single-handedly forestall another Great War. One platoon executes a smart about-face and unfazed by the heat begins a relay system Henry Ford would have admired: loading systematically from one truck onto another well-girded, skull-faced boxes marked FRAGILE. UNITED KINGDOM. EXPLOSIVES.

seem to know that gorging oneself with the pleasures of acquisition & accumulation (of material and experience) turns one into the grossest of men. Content instead with Fate, they take pleasure in the abiding of their families.

Around them, yes, circumnavigate English soldiers. All the while, the Ceylonese beware & wait for a higher, more metaphysical gateway. A lustrous people of infinite courage & variety, as unstable as water, they too, like water, might perhaps prevail.

The next bench over someone's rustling; no one he'd noticed when he'd sat.

A long-legged local boy in Western spectacles. What Henry can't take his gaze away from is the imperative frostiness of the shirt against that hot dark skin. The spotless boy scans a faded newspaper, his nose pushing close enough to risk perforating the print. His lips appear to rehearse speech, pursing, unpursing, light and shade at play in his cheeks' triangular hollows.

An off-beat character sits nearby,

narrates Henry. He's always prided himself on being an excellent judge of character, knowing who someone would become three years down the line in any relationship, and this boy — what is it, he must be absorbed or in hiding, some soot of intrigue on him. He's tapping his spit-polished shoes on the sandy ground as if his paper were sheet music. All Henry can see is the headline: LEAGUE OF NATIONS' MANDATE QUESTIONED.

Forget cinnamon, the air smells as if a scumload of rats had died last month in this very spot. It wouldn't be the boy, now barbing at Henry's attention —

'Just now you disembarked?' He swivels toward Henry like a mechanical pivot. The accent is a Britisher-than-thou, radio-perfect, saddled-with-responsibility English; the attitude is courtesy raised to its highest power.

'Shouldn't I have?'

'Yes, for me as well, this prior week has proven *interminable*,' the boy already commiserates. No one needs Henry's response to continue speaking. 'I was to meet someone. Now they're telling me he may have jumped ship at Portsmouth. Whether to give up hope entirely, I'm unsure.'

'Sorry, can't help,' Henry shrugs, feeling American down to his posture. Anyway, what does this fellow want from him? Money? Food and shelter? Most likely some slippage of identity. A visa, a passport, isn't that what they usually want, these port types? Even if the fellow is legit, a wobbly proposition, Henry has no extra energy to help anyone else. All he wants is his trunk.

Through the glimmer some lumpy bureaucratic progress is being made. Inch by inch. It seems procedure is vital. He overhears an English customs official take over for the Portuguese steward and explain in glossy, fluted accents to a Tiny or Junior how before the cattle can be counted and tagged on *dock* they jolly well ought to be counted and so forth aboard the ship. After which any personal luggage can be released.

The cattle before his trunk? Henry'll get up and protest. Given sufficient cause or self-interest, he can muckrake as well as anyone. Muckraking has unbonded most bonds, vaulted him long ago out of his ministry and into journalism. Yet it must be this rat-stinking mugginess that has stripped Henry of volition. Somewhere inside the ship cattle get counted; he's reduced to waiting. Just to touch the new place he forces himself to write:

> My heaven might have been a well-stuffed armchair, a steady
> lamp, & the complete Roman histories; yet for forty-some
> years I have been well-fed & well-slaked with eau de vie.
> Now the crystal happiness of Ceylon & its radiant, finely
> tuned people is mine, mine to help achieve a zenith of

The tolerant official has returned to the safety of his customs office. Smart man. Henry wonders whether in this sear one's brains could start to sizzle. Tiny or Junior slips an indiscreet roll of bills to the Portuguese steward; the steward then raises a slow hand at one of his men; the peon creaks open the ship's belly. The bulls, horns roped together, untagged, ramped, are already shoving forward on awkward legs, grunting heartfelt complaints. And the boy next to him has just said something.

'What? Best thing is talk to the captain,' Henry says, fanning himself with the destination note.

'I'd speak — why not? — but in disembarking the captain takes his time.' The boy whittles vowels with full lips. Each sentence jolts him with self-love. 'That hold doesn't look too pleasant, does it?' He practically vibrates.

'Not after the cattle, I wouldn't think.' Henry considers. After the bullocks' exit the ship has a disemboweled air. Caught inside somewhere are those beestung women with their appended buoys. 'Portsmouth you said?' The heat makes showing civility difficult but

Henry tries, though the boy's anxiety makes him a suspect character. 'Far as I know, we didn't go by way of Portsmouth. Who told you about your man?'

'A sailor who introduced himself as Tiny?' From the way the boy emphasizes *sailor*, odds-on you were meant to think badly of the profession.

'Bizarre.'

'I don't joke. That was his name. A sailor named Tiny. They take quite long in disembarking. Heading to Cochi, do you know? or would there be another mooring before that?'

'Sorry,' said Henry, without meaning it. What does this boy want? Condolences? an introduction? 'Wish I could help.'

And the boy is so damned possessed. It would be a bad idea to get drawn into the scam of such an invasive stranger. No rubbish will undo Henry now. He pats his pocket to feel his wallet still there. A comforting wad, though dollars don't work well here, he's been told.

The exchange rate is slippery and the world is teetering for a thousand and one reasons. Or else for one reason, eternally the same reason.

Henry could say it was because five years earlier the Japanese war had never fully ended. Or that people stayed shocked by the bad winter of 1931 when banks closed, lines formed, and the cold never lifted. Henry could cite the ten ways Hitler had been kept busy ignoring the Treaty of Versailles. He knew who argued that entire lands had been invaded to help out the French. He too had fingered newspapers, had contemplated the British in straits tight enough to leave the accords behind and perform the lonely act — signing away to Berlin something like a third of the Royal Navy. Nor had it entirely escaped his notice how Franco had just led a revolt in Morocco and then invaded Spain. A former journalist named Mussolini had just conquered Ethiopia for Italy and — so far as Henry had understood — now both he and Hitler were out to help Franco, or something close to that. Was everything falling apart more rapidly than it usually did?

And Henry had come to Ceylon, when doubtless he might have gone to Spain and sung 'The Red River Valley' and joined the Lincoln Brigade. The sailors had asked him this — why would an American do-gooder head to Ceylon and not Spain? Henry had asked back: Couldn't Ceylon be a different good fight? Then the sailors had insisted he must be a missionary, if a somewhat zany one.

Henry had already been involved in war. Sort of. To close the discussion he said he wanted his own fight, not someone else's. This made them call Henry not a missionary but a mercenary. Made them describe colonial tariffs and how they kept rising, along with the new black market in Ceylonese tea and Indian rubber.

Definitely, the world had just gotten more slippery. Yet he would prefer not to look at it this way. Dollars continue to calm Henry. Especially when what he wants right now is simple passage. Dollars might speed his passage to a nice British house with all the conveniences and a heartwood bed or at least one that didn't dodder like his cabin bunk.

It's not that he's such a bad traveler. He has just passed the longest three weeks of his life, all without bathing, having resorted on board to Louis the Fourteenth perfume deceits to keep himself civilized.

One might say that one is made for land;

he writes. And adds

an island will do.

A broken advertisement over the customs house reads SHRIVER'S POTTED GOODS — YOU CAN NEVER GET ENOU. In a fit of graphomania Henry writes this too and notes the shiny boy staring at him like a gangster. Or is it as though some decision is being made? His first rude native. Henry can't be the only white man this fellow's ever seen. He is on the brink of asking the boy this. *So am I your first white native?* The staring is rude but there's no other bench. No other shade.

Is it too much to ask for privacy? Henry doesn't ask. He's waiting for his trunk. And watches how he himself is being inventoried, again and then again.

This boy keeps up a cloak-and-dagger routine which goes as follows: he performs his surreptitious check of Henry; Henry notices; the boy joggles that handsome head back into his paper. Possibly had read the same article several times over. They are both solitary here. Some compassion for the lot of port rats and other lonely men washes over Henry. And if he plays it candid with this type, calls the ruse, he'll release them both from their labors.

'Listen,' says Henry. 'Maybe we did dock in Portsmouth. Had a lot of queasy nights when I wasn't aware of much beyond my night bucket.'

The boy evidently doesn't want to imagine a night bucket. He pulls back into himself like a prim telescope and inexplicably embarrasses Henry. Constant little shames, will they compose Henry's life here? If the monks and this boy are authentic reps, Henry will have to get used to more politicking, not to this constant unsettling.

The boy studies his paper and, it seems, comes to some necessary decision. He's reemerged from primness and is all angles standing over him, scanning the message and smelling of a talc which Henry doesn't find unwelcome. This is a boy apt to consider scent a life-or-death matter.

'Whoever wrote that should've written *Rajottama*,' the boy says now, close and hidden all at once. His voice mostly a lament. 'Only locals get to call it Rutaeva.'

What does he really want? He comes across less as a scammer and more as the kind of pedant Henry had fled at Harvard. 'Rajottama means universal king. Rutaeva means slippage. An outsider should never call it Slippage. You understand.'

'I'm not exactly intending to be an outsider for long,' says Henry.

The boy smiles back. He is a kind of blood-horse, a steeplechaser, and his responses are quick. Perhaps Henry's had been a good answer. 'That so?'

'Why should I come somewhere to stay an outsider?'

'Righto.'

'Certain men want to get right in. They learn the language. The culture. That's my kind, I suppose —'

The boy hangs off his words. 'Your kind, exactly.'

'I find it a virtue to be joined with people, you see.' Henry means what he says yet hearing his tone thinks, being a former fraud inspector, he might have inspected their sincerity.

'Wonderful!' the boy explodes. 'Joined?' He reacts with more spastic enthusiasm than Henry would've imagined he could summon. He sits down, stands up, and sits down again. This time closer to Henry. Caressing and thrashing, either a con artist or an odd duck: 'You'd like to be joined?'

'One must always investigate, at the outset —'

'Not many foreigners would want that, you can understand. Joined! You disown a certain status.'

'Status?'

'The foreigner's status. Pardon me. I'm Jehan Nelligodam. Nelligo*da*.'

'Nice to meet you, Jenaga —'

'Call me Jehan.'

'John is fine,' Henry assures him, grateful.

'Speaking bluntly, Rajottama is a small village.'

'Yes?' Henry floats up, a little.

'Right in the center of our beautiful country. Easy to understand.' The boy again inventories him, scanning the Yankee. 'So for what are you searching?'

'I was told' — lying a tad, desiring an equivalent mastery —'there are different ways of approaching Wooves' home?'

The boy removes his glasses. '*Now* you say so! the Main House? Wooves'? You must be the colonel himself.'

'Henry Fyre . . .'

'You never overheard me speaking with the ship's first mate?' the boy accuses. He's in Henry's face, all angles again.

Should we be having this conversation? Henry thinks, put off by the angry charm as much as by his own passivity. The old fraud inspector in him wonders how to classify this boy and into which character system.

'Hardly,' he says. 'I barely had time to —'

The boy thumps his newspaper. He's a circus gymnast taking a bow. A magician who just produced the whole lady. 'You have extremely good friends, Colonel!'

'Henry. Please.'

'Henree. They've taken care of everything, you know. Trust me.'

As John begins to elaborate the tasks for which some mysterious friends have hired him — tutor, guide, gardener, cook, butler — Henry takes him in, remembering the first and most common mistake: relying on instinct. And Henry cannot get lazy, especially in a foreign country where instinct could be upset. Easily. No, one must always reconcile signs systematically.

Here the signs are blatant: the boy's twitching foot must be contrasted to his youthful but steady gaze. According to the manual Henry himself had written after careful empirical study, the two traits — Twitch + Cerebral Steadiness — would suggest the boy to be Archetype C: an essentially honest person placed under extreme pressure to prove himself. 'No need to be nervous,' Henry interrupts, as a test of the boy.

As Cs are prone to do at interruptions, John stops short, and, predictably, finds it hard to return to his initial stream. 'I — you — what —'

'You show terrific initiative,' Henry says, using a compliment, promptly followed by a Challenge + Interrogation. 'Still, to work in concert, you can understand, I must know who hired you.'

Displaying another C-trait, the boy reverts to Tactics of Physical Displacement. He stows his paper under the bench as if packing fine linen, also revealing, to Henry's eye, a desire to take good care of all that falls under his jurisdiction. 'My apologies. I'm under oath.'

Would this be a freakish native taboo? to never cite the name of one's employer? Perhaps only truer Buddhists stay clean of such superstitions. Fairly sure now who had sent John to him, Henry tries a positive assertion. 'Then it must have been Madame.'

'Madame?' The boy's smile is ambiguous, again fitting a C-type, not at all approaching the poker face of a crook. Henry studies the boy's hands, twisting now. Yes; it must have been Madame who had gotten her claws into this boy. The boy, then, is conceivably innocent. The question remains, however, why would Madame want to send Henry an envoy? Should Henry consider the boy a gift? Or a new means for Madame to maintain control of her Henri?

All Henry needs from the boy is just a spot more information.

'We are going to work together,' Henry says patiently, 'if I understand what you are proposing —'

'Yes' — the boy sits down —'should you like —' A textbook C_1, the boy doesn't seem to know what to do with his hands. They operate as though someone else instructs them, fluttering about madly. What further proof would Henry need that the boy is one of Madame's gullible adherents? 'Of course, this must be disorienting,' the boy rushes in. 'You wonder how can we start working together without your having a full —'

'— a full understanding,' completing the boy's thought. If the boy permits this without complimenting Henry, the boy could be nothing but a C_1.

'Exactly!' Admittedly, John's agreement jars the interpretation. 'Without someone's full background,' John almost verging into Archetype B territory, 'yes, please imagine for a second, Henree,' and a C would not usually be so free with someone's first name so readily, 'what might have happened if' — and here the boy's eyes roll about, temporarily forsaking all impression of steadiness —'if, forgive me for being incorrect in any way, say, Joseph or Mary had refused the

Magi's gifts. Just because the Magi did not present a full dossier, say, on which road they had taken to Bethlehem. You see the point?'

'That's clever,' Henry concedes. He is suddenly tired, having arrived at a mixed conclusion. The boy is a C with workable wings in B. Because Archetype B stays essentially an honest person, albeit with a small tendency, when strained, to deceive. For the right system, however, Bs could be creative thinkers and partners — one should never sneeze at the idea of having a B along for the ride in any endeavor. Even Darwin was a B. Anyway, were Henry to add up the numeric values of all John's C-traits, Henry is sure they would outdistance the B-traits. And the boy was also a C_1, meaning he was an enthusiastic type. After all the sub-eights and -nines Henry has had to suffer in his one life, those lugubrious lugabouts, Henry needs some sub-one partners.

Having completely satisfied himself with his testing, a secret rush of poetry starts up in Henry's blood. He lets himself relax into the knowledge: bounteous lucky soil awaits him here in Ceylon. All signs line up enough. Henry needs no baby-hand pendant. This may be the life he was meant to live all along. All disgraces might be redeemed here, those he doesn't want to recall.

He can get going without a C.V. And here's a boy, a C with useful B-traits, who could be what he has long lacked: an ally. A potent, knowledgeable ally in the project. But caution is advisable, he reminds himself: he *might* have this boy, this C-and-B.

If Henry still believed in the Brotherhood, Madame's ethereal Masters, the holy eternal beings who appeared before her during hours of séances in their New York salon, he could say they have guided him here.

But it's exactly that kind of foolish superstition which he has renounced. No more Masters. Let Madame stay there entangled with her hokey mesmerism, her tea leaves and treatises. Henry wants no part of it. He will try one last time to find the truth: 'Won't you tell me who hired you, John?'

'Single condition of my employment. Silence about who hired me,' studying his fingers.

'No problem,' says Henry, turned amiable.

'But I'll be your great guide. I know how to lead you there. Trust me. Without a doubt, the house has been abandoned.'

'We'll have no trouble then, right?'

The pronoun slips out. *We. We'll have no trouble.* It's true the boy is a real find. Indispensable. But Henry should hang fire. The basis of any decision is information. 'Did our New York society contact you?'

'Not your society, I'm sorry, Henree.'

'I thought Wooves' house was to be rented.'

'From the last old family left in Rajottama. That would be the Pilimas.'

'The Palimas.'

'The Pi-li-mas.' John practically slobbers over the name. 'Wooves went mad building a house on the Pilimas' land. An Englishman. Believe the coincidence?'

Henry fails to see any.

'It's plausible he might have looked like you. Poor fellow never stopped adding wings on. Had to be shipped back, I believe. The house must've reverted to the Pilimas. So you will not be renting. You must be *staying* there. Pilimas would be too high and mighty to ask for rent. But it will be important to get in on their graces.'

'Why would they rent it out?'

'Sorry, not sure about that.'

'You're young to know so much.' Another test. If the boy answers with modest self-praise, Henry will take him on.

'There's no one with whom I don't know how to speak. Truly. I know all the stories on the island. I almost know this house of yours. It's big enough to be your Holy See. They say no room's less than thirty cubits —' and the boy laughs, a disconcertingly high bray. Seeing Henry's appraisal he taps his protruding front teeth: 'My cow-catchers, isn't it? as though on the front of a train, you know?'

'Cow-catchers. Right,' says Henry, wondering — did the boy see him as some kind of American cow to be steered? Type Cs could not avoid insulting people unintentionally.

John — who strikes Henry as more of a Johnny — is the first to see the sailor pulling a trunk through the groaning cattle. How does Johnny know to identify it? But he leaps to accost the man — to use a tip? — to make the sailor surrender the scarred box. With a strength remarkable for such a wiry boy, Johnny drags the trunk roadward. And over his shoulder, he shines his teeth back at Henry, luring him. 'Come,' he's shouting, 'sorry, must charter a vehicle, we're already starting late.'

'But that's not my trunk,' Henry shouts back.

44

It *is* marked COMESTIBLES; the boy's already racing back to the tar. A roared argument ensues, the outcome being two juniors sent to scour the hold.

Made helpless momentarily, in true C fashion, Johnny gapes back at Henry. Finally the deckhands return breathless: there is, apparently, no trunk. From above, the captain waggles his head at them, irked or amused.

'Mebbe the Reverend's things was taken off when we docked in Montevideo,' says the first mate.

'We didn't dock there,' one of the younger hands protests.

'Well, somewhere —' simpers the other. He changes to a businesslike tone. 'Go on, check the ship yourself.'

Henry does, forced to retreat back up the gangway, along the poop deck and below, peeking into room after room. Around him, sailors whoop it up, pushing through, happy to be anchored, playing beast-and-master with halyard, Henry muttering *pardon, pardon* through clenched teeth. He knows the thing is lost, inevitably, the trunk with his many books and fine sturdy clothes ordered for travel. Still he engages in the ritual, leaving his name and new address with the first mate, who promises, should it be found, it will be delivered.

Perhaps it is superior to enter Ceylon with only his ship clothes and books, Henry tells himself. Less to carry. And by the time he disembarks, Johnny has already hired a cart, an equipage attached to two bulls. The boy is enterprising.

7

TRUE, THIS HUNGER to arrive, to arrive at a *new* land — it had started with Madame.

When, back in New York, he'd had enough of seeing the vacant-moon faces of all of Madame's admirers, the itch had begun. He had started to despise Madame's salon-goers, who just took it in so unthinkingly, as though their own mothers had never taught them to discriminate between breast and pabulum. They liked to hear and then regurgitate a drivel so highly sweetened it could explain away all of life's missteps.

The sheep!

With genuine sheep one trusted they might find their way through a previously unencountered hole in a fence. They'd be able to clamber up a craggy escarpment. These *salonistes*, however — each clung so tightly to a bizarre individual faith.

When Henry quizzed them, the sheep could never say why they had signed over most of their minds to Madame. 'Was it the war?' Henry had asked more than once. 'The lindy? the crash? the loss of valuable assets?' They had balked, would glisten but say nothing. Or else they turned even more sheepish. In their habits and eyes they had banished death.

And one day, as though out of the blue, Henry recognized his own sheeplike reflection in them: *his* whiskers and muttonchop beliefs. He too ran up and down the hills of bellwether Madame.

Immediately he shaved off the whiskers and reexamined her. In Madame's ruminations were culled all the world's 'wisdom traditions.' This last part meant the esoteric was wise and the exoteric usually a version of man's foolish lust to extend himself into the world. Even Plato was too knowable, ultimately, like arithmetic. Though paradoxically in conversation the sheep might use the old Western ideas to prove the precision of their oozing Eastern esoteric.

One night a hunter's moon casting a rare glow had given him the botheration to ask her the thing, without preamble, right where they stood, huddled close on a Fifth Avenue terrace overlooking Central Park. She was smoking her favorite cheroot. Inside was a luxe apartment: the honeyed clink of a dinner party, held by one of Madame's countless admirers to commemorate the success of *The Eye That I Am: Osiris*, her first book. From the sound of it, the party was going smoothly enough, voices in symphonic lucubration, enjoying one another's cadences.

'Elena, please, don't take offense,' Henry had begun.

She had beamed palely through the smoke. He construed this as invitation to continue.

'Why's it *you* never ask questions?' He had moved closer to her. His was no idle demand. But her expression pulled around some amused central pursestring. He wasn't being taken seriously; she *would* be in an insolent party mood.

He defied her. He asked her why spirits and Masters should channel through her and her alone. Why would *she* be elected to know this one's past life and that one's future? Didn't she think we're in a kind of tunnel? That we know nothing of any world beyond? That we assign all these causes just to imagine for a second that we're in control?

She had puffed the cigar. Had then turned on him her full soak of a smile, with its rows of rotted European teeth. 'Typical.'

'What's typical?'

'The child in the womb would say nothing exists beyond darkness and pumping blood. You're saying we muddle our way through just the best we can?' This was derision; he understood it immediately, even without her doing a bad sham of his Yankee accent.

A cascade of laughter sounded from inside, one that grew on itself, finding its mark in those unlucky enough not to have some part of that tight world, its amber light, their unstated agreement with one another. That was what they wanted, those sheep — to stay well-grouted inside with their hobbies; a succulent bleat of a community, eyes widened or crinkled in esoteric discernment. They had no interest in the topography of shadows behind a bar, if it couldn't be linked to something bigger, their *beyond* which imprisoned them.

They turned the metaphysical into a bawdy story relevant only to them. Paid little mind, for example, to what made small children everywhere like to run up and down a few stairs, unless the idea could be pulped into a parable about repetition and morphic resonance, about the akashic record and the universal mind.

Sheep! they wanted to roam beyond what is known, beyond what could be known, toward the traditional and away from it. To wander in vacuous idea castles constructed entirely so they could escape the isolations, pietisms and tyrannies of their own fathers' stories. Their mothers' beliefs. Their pedigrees' whole nooselike set of associations back to Adam. Sheep! they wanted to mush and mash and so pioneer beyond. To be part of a land where they too could be first and necessary and beyond all popular entertainments.

'If there's another side to *this* life,' Henry had persevered with Madame. She had one bloated foot in this world, the other off on the lonesome moon. Just once he wanted her to grant that perhaps someone more pragmatic could know more than she did.

He hated the sound of himself treading so flatly, so literally in argument. Just once he needed to know whether she could see the other side of her certainty, its penumbra. 'You don't think it's our mundane anxiety which makes us think we can define the next life — a story to keep the cavemen sedated?'

In answer, his know-it-all had squinted up — toward the spirits of the air. 'You've never been with anyone at their moment of death, have you,' singsonging a non sequitur. And then remembered. 'Sorry, Henri,' making the apology all gravel. 'Your mother, forgive me. I forget —' She *would* bring up another's losses.

Still, he wouldn't weaken. He faced Elena, her eyes which at night burned bluer. He needed her to blaze through the soppage of their five-some years working as one. To prove he hadn't been wasting his time. He'd allow for no dismissal. 'Please, Elena, it's not as sure as death and taxes, is it? Don't we simply give people fairytales so they'll understand their *lives* better? A séance, be honest, isn't that just *your* way to make people know that nothing's a cinched bet?'

She could shut him up by saying yes. Instead she insisted on gazing out like a sphinx. He may have been gaining ground. 'All your spiritual fireworks are just an efficient way to make people grasp less. To make them kinder. To give them better priorities, perhaps. So they live their lives better. You don't *really* believe we can be certain of everything.' She shook her head ambiguously. 'Because wouldn't it be hubris to think we could? Define it all, I mean. What would be the interest in living then, if we knew all the other spheres? Isn't serendipity part of why we live?'

Now her mouth itself became a rebuke. She practically winked at him. He had failed to push through that sponginess. 'Honi soit qui mal y pense,' she'd said, pseudo-sad. This evil-to-him-who-evil-thinks meant nothing. She stayed trapped by her own ideas. Without them she would be nothing, adrift in the universe, that particular severity.

Such a woman! When cornered she would prattle. From her he'd learned how to make this same deflection of an answer. The high-flown pretense at genius meant she could always stay inside that jellified persona.

He used to believe that the two of them, cosmic twins, brought revelation to the masses. At the biggest event he and Madame had arranged, the public cremation of one of their most avidly rich supporters — four thousand attending in a hall with lung-like organ pipes stretching upward, situated not far from city hall — he'd thought he and Madame had been perfectly simpatico. Perfectly.

In the middle of the *Stabat Mater*, played by Andean flutes, he'd never believed anything more deeply: We get the sheep to abandon their last bourgeois sanctities! We get them to reject all Victorian vestiges! Here a body is being burned — the materialistic, dandified shell!

Sounds sharpened, light increased. Here they helped their followers enter the century's third decade. Freed of deep-pocket showdowns, of grabbing monkey minds. While the Hindus had chanted wishes and blessings over the dead nab's smoke, Henry's mood had been ardent, soaring above.

Now his blinders were off: all they'd done was confirm for the sheep the most worldly desires, for security or novelty. All he and Madame had done was serve up fairytales. Or tasks with fast, placating rewards. The result was inside: the party with its mellifluous spirit, the oyster crackers and self-congratulation, faces lit by crystal chandeliers and flattery.

Outside on the terrace, under that moon's flattened fist, Henry had studied his Madame and given up. How could he have not seen?

8

WHEN, AT THE NEW YORK harbor's gangway, James had told Henry he'd be a free man, the Ceylonese did not know about the son and wife whom Henry had chosen to leave behind in New York. The limbs of his body he had practically amputated, with Daniel off to Clara's parents in the Midwest and Clara herself off to Freetown. No kin to Henry joined him in his new gamble and his gut felt riddled.

Yet, to take the other side — Henry had reasoned just after the farewell — what if he had instead lacked all ambition? How would Henry Fyre Gould be contributing to humanity? He'd be wearing out a seat in some accounting job in Arlington or Butte, Lexington or Kansas City. It wouldn't matter. He might have stayed a journalist. Or a fraud inspector. And to all that he had shouted no: he had refused to do what others expected. He'd kept his future apart from the dictates of Commerce and Institutional Affiliation and Tradition. It was just that no middle ground had yet been invented for him.

At least — as the *Colossus* began to chuff away — he tried for something original. Hadn't he checked behind every nail-headed door? Looked into every nook, every museum and church corner of the great cities and plains? And Madame's last written words to him, there in July as he boarded the *Colossus*, confirmed that he had made the right choice.

To say he shouldn't let *the pettiness of others be the ambition of our souls?* She only wanted to keep him tied to her. Not to hear he could occupy his destiny. Not to hear he could rival her in matters of the spirit. Not to know he would live life fully and that one day he would be memorized and loved and answered fully by his own son's eyes: a blue like no other blue. A blue that would fill with respect for a father capable of the best brand of independence.

9

JOHNNY'S A GRACIOUS HOST: he has given Henry something to nibble, a small coconut-and-nut confection, like a confiserie libanaise Madame used to serve the salon, leftover from wartime bootleg. He's also discussing routes with the new driver, named Ganesh, captain of the bullock cart, this phaeton with its roof of dried banyan rounding a skeleton over the carriage.

The driver winks and throws a tarp over the top ribs. Johnny translates: 'He told me the red-barked foreigner would burn otherwise.'

Seated on his straw mat, his new aide huddled next to him, red-barked foreigner or not, Henry becomes as tranquil as a hot child cooled. He doesn't need his trunk. Or any Madame, any spoken English, any familiar landscape. On a road paved Westminster gray, the snouts of the plodding bulls begin pulling, step by resolute step, taking their time pushing through Colombo's chaos, one rivaling Times Square's. In the back, grabbing the rail, the men clatter against each other like pins; for once, Henry is happy to be inconsequential, a passenger of fate.

They have a ways to go, a ways before they even reach the Kandy road which will lead up to the village. This is just the capital's congestion, Johnny says, tour-guiding, Colombo with its laissez-faire roads and crowds.

Henry will have to acquaint himself with this set-up. With streets clotted by roof-and-bullock teams and these devil-may-care drivers. Entirely blithe Ceylonese families stack in the buffalo wagons, one child atop the other, all in loud cloths. And then a few disgruntled British administrators ride alone in trishaws, a man running before them, legs corded, feet bare, the colonials wincing, holding the rail as if for their lives, their private go-carts jerking away from the free-wheeling gurneys that carry sticks or rotund silver fuel cans.

On the roadside, Ceylonese men swarm unperturbed by any of the road's madness. Usually in long ivory Western shirts; and, below, exaggerating their reediness, a colorfully patterned cloth-skirt, blue brown white, the sarong (Johnny calls it a dhoti) tied with prominent knots. The native mustaches, the gestures — Henry cannot quite take it all in. His entire past is collapsing into dust behind him. Mostly he cannot imagine how Ceylonese have time in the middle of a weekday to throng, arms braided behind their backs. What do they discuss with such solemnity, such pursed lips and passion? He will know all this and more. He will unlock everything.

Everything, even the thoughts of women hoisting coy baskets of vegetables atop head or hip, their bodices a revealing white or the colors of tropical birds. Midriffs stark over a skirt similar to the men's. Whether hillock or plain, stout or emaciated, old or young, each woman gawks at Henry with some undisguised laughter.

'They think it's odd for an American to be bouncing around in the back of a cart?' he asks his guide.

'Not more than any of this, no?' Johnny says, gesturing to the cows heedlessly owning the road. 'This all must be quite strange for you —' and Henry flashes appreciation back. The country is so foreign, it hurts his eyes, made up from buzzing squads of things never before seen. Alizarins, roses, coppers. Hairy vegetables.

There *are* a few nice touches: the first being these natty roadside stalls without any sellers. On small tables are laid Lincoln-green coconuts and bananas, round fruit with a peel that could come direct from elephant hide, stationed on trays under the thinnest of thatch roofs. Just a coinbox in attendance.

'All based on the honor system, Henree.'

'Honor,' applauding, 'wonderful! And entrepreneurs to boot!'

As though a principle of order, every now and again a brown motor car makes a dead-straight line by them — carrying khaki-suited

British officers, faces blurred, beige a ruling principle. Through the window of one such car Henry makes out what at first he takes to be packing materials, until he realizes these are instead the mouths of guns.

A different model of car zigs by, a sporty number filled with young men and women in Western dress. Elbows and legs askew, they are from a lighter palette than Henry has seen. If their chauffeur isn't drunk, wearing a giddy beryl cap, he acts like he is, traversing the road back and forth before tooting off to a roadside stall where the seller already hands over a drinking-straw and a coconut.

'Burghers,' Johnny explains, lip slightly curled. 'Climate hits them harder. They especially need to drink thambili juice to refresh themselves.'

'Burgers?'

'English speakers. The ones left behind by the Dutch and Portuguese.'

'Look wealthy,' more to himself.

'Burghers get the promotions — they come out of the womb understanding the European system.' At Henry's sharp glance the boy adds, 'In my coming-up days, my best friends were Burghers. They mixed well. Nice people, Burghers.'

Whether Burgher or not, people begin to thin out once they start ascending a mountain Henry must have seen at a different vantage from the ship, because now its planes are softened. As the city trickles out, he enjoys the ride more — the palms' chlorophyllic sheen, the outpourings of banana plants. Such profusion to this green, unimpeachable, a jungle green to keep you at a distance, a beneficence that seems a glance from God.

He and Johnny have fallen into a silence unusual for new acquaintances; he can't help it; his head feels like a cap unscrewed, such bizarre streams flow before him.

Truth is, none of his remembered landscapes come close to this island's intimacy. The urgent ivory of the palm tree trunks. An occasional monkey with its wizened face slanted in desire, scampering behind plantain leaves more like the ears of a green elephant. Another monkey comrade shaking the red hibiscus buds. All caught in a green that encroaches on everything.

What would it mean to come from this Ceylonese landscape? Because (Henry will write this when they stop) this green doesn't need them. Nothing could measure it. Jade, celadon, whatever; it is huge and forgiving and omnivorous, a monster to inspire and absolve you right before it swallows you. Instead Henry tries to take it in like one of the cows who leave grazing only to meander across the road. The guileless fields, filled with pert wildflowers like buttercups, faces at attention, suspended in a moment of no time. How within the palm-tree forests, purplish shadows stretch, deep as the leaves are naked and expansive. How light lifts off mountains' indigo rim.

He especially likes the gentle elephants who bathe in streams, their backs gray humped islands. And the fleshy water buffalo: a ball of fat lying on the mulberry-stained road as you encounter them head-on, who at the cart's approach cannot heave themselves off ground or hill without a strenuous tectonics. An epicenter vibrates above their arse and then rolls forward, a glissando toward the head until they jerk up to all fours, flesh hanging off bones like thick canvas. Beasts apparently free to roam hill and unfenced road. No cattle grids exist here, apparently, no gestures at containment or any visible proprietary markers are needed. No fringed sheep dyed blue or given cattle tags. This is a true Buddhism, thinks Henry, one in which all beasts, down to dogs and their lifeless tails, can wander on endless hunts for nourishment.

These dwellers can see beyond the one-to-one correspondence of names. Beyond what the Chinese had dubbed *Ceilan* and the Arabs called Serendib and what the Dutch later changed to *Ceylon*, the outsiders' name for the island that finally stuck. Johnny says that for the Tamils and Sinhalese, since before even the Great Chronicle, the name had been curtailed from the Tamil for island, *illangai*, concluding as *Lankaave*.

'Lanka —'

'Ceylon might be easier for you to say.'

Serendib, Ceylon, Lankaave, *whatever*: now they are hurtling along lush canyons which tuck villages and paradise's own waterfalls into their bowls. Everywhere there is exuberance, the enumerations of green. They are losing the coast's brine, the air becoming a saner cold. They pass the young wet shoulders of roadside bathing women who giggle at Henry, and his good humor has returned, armies of it —

— mostly because of the women's chubby children, foamed into soap demons, who from their wells salute or cry out gibberish at the cart's trek. This may be the most sociable country he has ever seen.

One woman, fully dressed, carries a basket of tendriled leaves —
leaves! the whimsicality! — on her head as she wades through a
field, mud splashing up her waist. Up her snug bleached blouse, too,
and when she looks back at the road, she also smiles significantly;
Henry finds her another jubilation, a regular hosanna of existence.
He would love to muck about with the women, the children. No,
he'd love to *be* them.

They have to pause only where railroad ties and tracks cross the
road. The train lurches past with its cars reading *Ceylon Tea* in royal
blue script.

'Who works the tea?' Henry asks, impressed.

'Tamils the British brought from India just recently. A divide-and-
conquer project that works. Hill Tamils, we call them. You see them
painted on the side of tea cartons? no? Pretty women with long
noses? They aren't like us along the coast. Like the coastal Tamils,
I mean. Those who've been here since before history. Anyway,'
Johnny adds irrelevantly, changing the subject, 'tea country is beautiful, you know. Much farther in than Rajottama.' Just the idea of tea
country gladdens Henry. Here there will be industry because there is
abundance already.

'There is also a passenger train,' Johnny is saying. Later this train
will be one of the things Henry loves most about Ceylon, its view an
epic of mountains and valleys. Now he rebukes his guide gently:
'Could we not have taken the train instead? Perhaps —'

At this the boy laughs, inappropriately, a chainsaw of a laugh that
begins high and ends low and starts all over again, a regular arpeg-
gio. 'We couldn't have taken the train, oh no —'

Henry didn't see what was so amusing.

'It's not done, ah no —'

'You're saying my being foreign and —'

'Don't worry.' The boy wipes tears from his eyes, puts a hand on
the air above Henry's shoulder. 'You'll see.' He realigns himself and
carries on, as it were, a solo conversation, resuming its proper tones.
'Of course it's quite natural you'd want to try the railroad, being that
the English launched this Kandy–Colombo line in, ah, last century,
'67, a good year, one of their better legacies to us.'

'Foreigners don't ride the train?'

The boy turns on him: 'Of course they do, but the two of us, no, it
would hardly do, no, let's say, it wouldn't be an honor for a first-time

guest. A *public* train? Of course we could get off now, if you insist, try to intercept one of the cars —' And Henry protests, the boy's hospitality had been perfect, he liked very much what the boy had rigged up with the cart.

And the idea dawns: he might eventually create a full-size cart, smaller than a lorry, something to break down this private and public distinction. He could practically live in the cart, use it as a base from town to town. No doubt there would be lecture tours, presentations of the success he'd wreak in this natural waiting wonderland. A land one could help explode into a cultural magnet, a city of jasper and chrysolyte —

— and in the planning of this cart, his spirits return full force. In the distance beyond the valley, beyond the paddy pleated into squares, he spies a prehistoric massif which Johnny calls Bible Rock.

Despite herself, how well his eminent Madame has switch-conducted his future, leading him to Ceylon, this awesome spectacle. She'd steered him in. Had introduced him to the princely James just so Henry could claim this beauty as his own. She had fought with Henry and he had fought with her. As she had said during that last small conference with the New York press, she'd *relinquished* him as her student. This meant Henry was now free to institute his model society, one combining West and East.

He coughs and burps, all at once, and mashed-up bits of coconut fly out everywhere: onto the banyan, the tarp, Johnny's glasses, his own coat.

Johnny pats his back. 'You all right?'

'Choked,' Henry splutters and splutters, 'a bit.' Embarrassed again.

'Sorry, hard to digest those things,' says Johnny. 'I should've known. For some people.' He appears more perplexed than his voice's sympathy suggests. 'You have some on your chin. Sure you're all right?'

Henry mops his face with his awful handkerchief. 'I'm fine, thanks.'

'Really, it happens to me as well. You know, if I eat too many. I should've mentioned. They're rather rich —'

'You did fine. You were just being a good guide.'

'Foreigners have to be careful here. Certain things are indigestible. From what I've understood.'

'Thanks. Don't worry. Just nothing.'

'My fault really,' and wipes the coconut snow off his spectacles before replacing them.

Henry grabs the boy's hand. 'Please. No problema. I'm like those cows over there. I have ninety stomachs. Sometimes a few work better than others. Today one didn't. Or it's my windpipe closing up. No, John — you can't go and make yourself responsible for some stranger's hiccups.'

The boy grins. 'Right. You're a good one.' He turns the grab into something else, seeming to relish the chance. 'A handshake. We don't observe that particular custom here like they do in the West.' They're still shaking hands. 'Your hand is swollen?' the boy asks.

'A medical condition. Why don't people shake hands?' Some mildness toward this boy is settling into him.

'They say here *honde minisu* and *adu minisu*. Good and bad people.'

'Caste? don't tell me you have such ideas —'

'Oh no. I don't mind. What caste you might be, for example? I can't even begin to deduce *that*. Our distinctions have more meaning in the backward places. More in the country than the cities.'

The two hands — one sandstone soft, the other swollen and sweaty — hold each other until Henry releases the grip gently. He needs to gather himself again and remember: he is Henry Fyre Gould finally ready for this strip of illumination, Henry finally in Ceylon.

11

THE CANAL

Q. What are the duties of a servant toward his master?
A. i. To rise before him in the morning
    ii. To retire later to rest
    iii. To take only what the master gives
    iv. To work well
    v. To praise him as a good master

10

IN THE VILLAGE of Rutaeva, a dream burrowed into Sonali.

Later considerations reveal how this dream might have foretold most of everything.

But later didn't matter. Even if the dream had come true immediately, Sonali's older sister, Kumari, would never have conceded clairvoyance to Soni. An akka would not admit such talent to a nangi. That was just the way of the world — little sisters weren't supposed to know too much.

Because anyway it was Kumari as akka who fancied herself to have a spot of the herb doctor's magic. A handful of the powers. Just enough to fix a merchant who had shorted her a half-gram of oil. And enough genius to teach a lesson to boys who brought her coconuts with most of the fruit rotted meat — which meant the nuts had been gleaned off the ground and not harvested from above as the boys swore!

How such boys would promise anything for a half-rupee! These manners! Especially sinful when she and her nangi, Soni, barely charged the students anything to learn the dance and its basic tay-kita-taya-tam. Pow lokuy, it was a big sin how they treated her.

Meanwhile, Kumari kept her enchantment skills veiled. The world of akkas has more potency than the empire where nangis flaunt their braggart comedies and charm. So not many would guess Kumari used a sprinkle of black magic to fix folk, whether boys or merchants or anyone else. With the proper chant or offering of flowers and twiddling of rice to the right god, she could give this one unexplainable black eyes and that one stomachache. Easily she could remedy the balance of anyone who shortchanged what was already, all would agree, a shortfallen position in life. And shortfallen not because she or her younger sister or her nephew had committed sin in a previous life. They had not! Their karma couldn't be *that* bad.

Still she couldn't explain having been born into the drummer caste. But that didn't mean she didn't try. Maybe someone else's karma had long ago polluted her own. That happens sometimes. Her illustrious father, a famous drummer, might have taken more pains to prevent his daughters from being treated, frankly, like low-castes.

Because while the Gunadasas are indisputably beira caste, some call it low, many centuries ago history — or rather, the king — had blessed them. With chants and dance, the drummer family had restored to the reigning king the ability to enter the garden of womanly pleasures. For this achievement, the Gunadasas had gained three extra names from the king; plus, ten generations ago, a fine reputation.

Still, sometimes ten generations was too long where honor was concerned. Kumari was not well-off. For that matter, neither was Soni, but round-eyed Soni stayed plump with her *personal* good fortune. She had a beautiful son and a happy sinecure cooking for the local herb doctor. It was just a speck possible that Soni had some greater connection than Kumari did to their surrounding planetary deities.

How unfair! It was as though in their respective births some deity had decided to slight the elder sister! And had given Kumari a lesser portion to make sure enough would remain for the younger and whoever else might follow. When Soni — not a brother to continue the line of drummers, *that* Kumari could have handled! — was the last to be born, the deity may have handed this youngest all the rest of the coconut. A much larger portion than was fair. And everyone knows no milk spills upward.

From the first day of life Soni had received way too much: the best coconuts, the cornucopia, the new year's bird, the good harvest. Thus it was natural Kumari would resent Soni's peepings about future events. Because, in the end, Soni's best audience was Kumari, and who really cared about Soni's dreams beyond their family? Certainly not Sonali's son, with his mischievous ways, quivering on the verge of manhood with his gift for the dance but feeling his wildness, call it his mahasonas, every which way.

And what Soni had dreamt of was, as she said it, something quite simple: There is a new man come who is bad for the village — but maybe, just maybe, Kumi, maybe this one, this time, maybe he won't be so bad for us. This she had recited during an evening meal during the time when drought had been killing off everyone's hopes for a good rice harvest.

In the next room, the yellow dance hall, Soni's son had also been murdering, slowly, one by one, his crickets. Though his mother couldn't see him, his aunt could. Was she supposed to jump up and intervene in his karma? Was it Kumari's place to make sure everyone *else* got good karma all the time? Let her nephew accrue the merit or sin due him. She did nothing.

Now Sonali finished reciting her dream, with the same hushing she always had. Tones that often made Kumari wonder whether Sonali expected her listeners to bow down in praise before her, shrieking *Soni, you miracle, has anyone ever seen such visions?* Soni *was* accomplished. Yet why should Kumari be the one to tell her so?

Instead Kumari continued to mix and fold her rice with its single curry.

'Well?' her younger sister pressed, an impetuous moment later. 'Could this mean something Kumi?'

'Whatever you think it does,' said Kumari.

'What does THAT mean?'

Kumari deliberated on her food. 'Would it hurt for you to salt our curries more?' she said finally, enough to make Soni huff out in one of her fits.

But could Soni's dream be about the herb doctor? This is what Kumari would wonder later. No. Appuhamy was not a new man come to the village. The doctor had been in Rutaeva forever. What had Soni said? Something about *a new man coming to the village who will not be so bad for the Gunadasa sisters.*

What did it mean? Kumari let her bun spill down in her room with its single mat, the room where no matter how many times she poured coconut oil on her head and brushed her hair long and thick, no admirer would arrive. She was past the age when, without magic helping things along, a new man would come her way. And any day her husband *could* come home, it still being unclear why he'd left long ago for the plantations' promises. Especially when he and she had lacked the time to make children. Similarly murky hopes could attend his comeback. Her husband, old by now — he could hardly be called a new man. And so he might return.

There is a new man come who's maybe not so bad for us. Little sister had dreamed of eggs and blood and a man emerging from the sea — but more important, this new man would be good for the Gunadasa dance school and the sisters. So for once let something be a golden crow falling into Kumari's hands, ready to bless her again. She would let something come from the outside. Because magic requires greater effort and decisions. And Kumari had often questioned whether all her supernatural knowledge kept her from life.

For once she would cast no fortunes. For once she need know nothing. She would just wait for joy, attend to surprise.

11

THEY HAVE BEEN junketing up the mountain for a good enough time that occasionally a fog of disorientation descends in Henry, a certain scrabbling to keep the tentposts of his existence firm in their place. Confused, he studies the tall guide who sits proudly erect, facing backward, a ship's deranged figurehead.

All of Henry's years burrowing in others' moldering papers, photographs and daguerreotypes, whether as fraud inspector or journalist, and he had never found such an astounding character as this one — Napoleonic in his stance, Washington crossing the Delaware, Sherman heading toward Atlanta. A bit crazed. So maybe crazed would help in conducting these Ceylonese to the latent higher truth of their heritage.

'Happy dreaming?' Johnny asks, as though having read Henry's mind. Henry wouldn't consider clairvoyance past his guide who, nonetheless, had a flair for getting them lost on more than one occasion. At which point Johnny would hurriedly consult Henry's scrap of paper, annoyed, bridling at himself, Henry, the cart, Ganesh, anyone who had collaborated in this generalized wrongness to things.

Only a few times does Johnny lose track of the road, failing to direct Ganesh well. Only a few times, Henry tells himself, and it could happen to any guide.

'Nothing lost,' Henry comforts the boy.

Johnny hisses through his cow-catchers. 'Shouldn't be happening! The Kandy road is one of the easiest. Pardon, I know this country, I've traveled *every*where.'

Even when the boy's nervous — or is it especially when he's nervous? — there's something superb about him. He could be an Indian Valentino, his mouth is that full. Henry imagines him as a bust in the

National Gallery, something small girls touch when no one's watching, a head shaped of blades, made from a rock darker than sandstone. Obsidian wouldn't do the trick. It would have to be metamorphic stone, thrust up by volcanoes.

The first town they go through is Kandy, not at all metamorphic, its lake so still the clouds are etched into its surface: the shameless curves of a young girl's cheek. A child's town, Henry wants to write, this is a child's *country*. So many things here seem to belong to children. The people's exultation as he passes, for one. He writes nothing and instead admires a sizable bulb, no, a palace that could have been sculpted from birthday ice cream.

A temple, not a palace, overlooking the town, its boundary fence made up of stuffed elephant heads, trunks extended in a final roar. 'The Temple of the Tooth,' Johnny narrates. He has a certain talent for flowing easily into tour-guide mode. 'Here the palace is the ancient seat of religious kingship. On the left —'

'So why aren't religion and kingship a contradiction?' Henry interrupts, forgetting England. A hanging sign bangs against a tree, back and forth in the wind. Another publicity piece for the potted ham: it reads SHRIVER'S DOES IT BEST and shows a small pink soldier with blazing pants leaping out of the can while still managing to salute.

'In Ceylon there's not much separation between kingship and religion. You'll understand later. Here the monks hide the Buddha's tooth. It's true. They can be rotten.'

'Rotten?' He was getting distracted from his appreciation of the juvenile aesthetic.

'Yes, rotten, why not? Some monks are awful. Not all. Some just care about their own self-restraint. Their own salvation. Some care nothing for the common man. They won't let a low-caste gain merit by giving puja — food donations — to the Buddha. Poor people end up thinking their karma for this life is ruined if they can't donate to the Buddha. And the main temple keeps a mint of looted gold hiding the Buddha's tooth! Some monks, all they love is their relics, or saffron robes. Their *own* nirvana — no one else's.'

Henry dismisses this. Johnny had already said that in his home village he'd worked for some kind of Catholic priest.

'Henree, I'm not considering you a stranger. I'm hiding nothing from you. Trust me.'

No doubt the boy bears a partisan grudge against Buddhist monks. Of *course* they wouldn't be on the boy's home team; Henry would hardly expect his guide to transcend everything all at once.

An emaciated man in a turban runs to halt their cart at a cross-roads. They wait a few minutes before what must be a rehearsal for a parade passes, a rehearsal unlike any other Henry has seen. Some thirty naked-chested boys pass, one by one, stunted mahouts with slinky arms, each boy leading his own elephant by a grubby tatter of ropes. Some of the boys are sullen, making it look as though they are being mastered, that they are the beasts of burden. Other boys more vigorously ignore the animals, calling to one another with a criminal glee. A few ride the sad-eyed beasts bareback, legs sticks above the massive flanks. Only one beast in the middle is decked out — carrying a gigantic wax replica of a lotus flower in its trunk, wearing a gold-trimmed white blanket with boards, overhung, advertising lodging. A royally painted howdah rides him — inside, two mahouts chatter happily. 'The annual temple parade,' Johnny says, breaking Henry's spell. 'It just ended. The Esala Perahera. Goes on for ten days, eleven,' he says. 'Maybe you'll see it next year. The people go mad.'

'What's the parade for?'

'The temple's glory, really. All the castes dance. They eat fire, walk on stilts. But the elephants and the monks, you'll see, *they* walk the white carpet.'

Who needs white carpets? Henry has no interest in dwelling on the idea of white carpets. Not after Galle. A quick breeze has started up, making the nearby branches crackle. 'Where we heading now?'

'We're close. Thought we could detour. This we call the great city, Maha Nuwara. In English, as you may have inferred, we say *Kandy*.' Their cart totters around the lake, its surface now all distended ripples, flaring silver triangles overlaid upon silver triangles. 'Several centuries earlier' — Johnny heightens his radio announcer's tone and pushes what he calls his specs higher — 'a Buddhist king thought he was entitled to a harem.'

'Why not? A king —'

'He ordered this lake to be built. As a moat. To keep his concubines on an island. Separate from the people. But the Sinhalese refused to help the king in this enterprise.'

'You're not a bad storyteller,' Henry tells the boy. Would they be arriving before nightfall? The dark deepens under the lakeside trees. 'Think we should head out toward Rutae —'

'Rajottama? We'll be there in ten minutes. Ganesh! *Api daen Rajottamate yaneva, naeaede?* Anyway, what did the king do?'

Henry shrugs.

'He chopped off the heads of those workers who resisted him. Then he staked their skulls underwater. All around the harem island.' Johnny brays. 'We call it the skull flower.'

'That's disgusting. Gruesome.'

'Well.' This story apparently excites Johnny. 'That's not quite the end of it. No doubt he kept their skulls quite low. So he wouldn't scrape them with his oars. Can't you see it? The king's rowboat. The women, waiting. The skulls.'

Henry shudders. Barbarism. And in Eden.

Across the lake from the Tooth Temple, a line of saffron-robed monks carrying straw fans heartens Henry. After all, *this* is the Ceylon — backwater monks pacing in meditation — that he'd imagined back in New York.

These monks appear more somber than the Galle monks, Henry believes. Until the cart comes closer — they are young monks. Guffawing. Probably at that exact moment they are relieving themselves into the bushes, covering themselves with the wings of their robes. After a moment's adjustment, the initiates resume their ascent.

'Where are they going?' Henry asks. He draws his stiff legs up to his chest, embarrassed for them.

'That would be the Iri monastery,' Johnny says, seeming to point toward the monastery with his lip's curl. 'It carries the highest pedigree. For the highest caste. By the time these monks are fourteen, they've memorized most of the Buddhist canon. You know, the *suttas*. The Triple Baskets. Call it the Bible . . .'

'No need to translate too much,' says Henry, 'I'd prefer you overestimate me. I've read about the books. Some. But I'm up for all good challenges you want to throw my way.'

'Righto.' The boy is calm, practically conjugating phrases. 'As you Yanks say, you call the pots, isn't it?'

'Shots. To call the shots.'

'Righto.'

Ultimately their cart follows a road out of town past secretive houses in the day's last glare. When doors open, Henry glimpses Moorish patios, flapping laundry, children stunned into a moment of contemplation, mothers who pull veils over their heads to spin away from passersby. The road leads toward what Johnny has started to call *the home village*. And Henry wonders: *home* for how long? He had initially planned to stay in Ceylon, in that first rush of enthusiasm, for a full decade. To really *see things through this time*. He'd be fifty-five when he got out. Something like that. But perhaps he'd been a bit possessed. All plans taste wonderful at the outset. It never did one any good to overestimate, say, an endurance for the exotic.

He pats his wallet, fondles its reassuring wad with something like ardor. Still there. And he's gotten here for free. Meanwhile, no one had ever said that to be altruistic one had to perform some minor self-disembowelment. Two fully focused years — or even just one — might be enough for Henry to begin worthwhile ventures here in Rajowhatever.

As they rattle down the hill, a group of blue-suited British rifle-bearers marches up. At a command, the ensigns stand at ease. Only their eyes, used to gauging silence, follow Henry's trap. 'There's enough of them,' says Henry, jigging away from the low branches that want to scuff his face; 'they make you feel you should salute.'

'Oh, not to worry — Kandy is deficient in the military activity you'll see elsewhere. The English have a surplus of revenue from Ceylon, so they built up security to an insane degree. *In*ternal security.' The boy evidently cannot help reminiscing; there had been the time when the English established martial law in this region, during the riots between the Sinhalese and Muslims. 'Ages ago — 1915. The English mistook the whole mess as anti-king. Then they shot dead anyone they found. These days they're tamer,' he smiles.

'Not where we're going, right?'

'In the time of the Kandyan Rebellion, there was an encampment in Rajottama. My assumption is it's defunct like most of them,' says Johnny and sneezes closure.

The day has already begun to flame and then fade by the time they turn onto a warped main street, or an idea of a street, one that thwarts the very idea of directness. All Henry sees are impassive houses and boarded-up markets. He must scale down his expectations. A model garden is a good thing, a self-sufficient economy better, a revived Buddhist culture the best. He can work this all out in his one village.

Just one village could muddle the British. One seedlet. There are no set programs for these things. Rajotown didn't need to be some sprawling megalopolis. He isn't out to make the next New York. He could begin slowly and leave something *solid*. This could be the theological utopia, the storehouse for pure Buddhism. People would call it, what —

— Henryville? No. Something with a more local feel to it. Hanra? That sounded better, more like a utopia. Even Rajotown would be a mouthful for people.

He reminds himself: keep a steady gaze on the goal. Show how a *valid* society can be built out of small, *considered* steps. He'll keep a daily log, help inspire others. Smallness is the very thing to foil empire. Not omnivorous but local. Maybe one year could be enough. One year. He'll eat coconut, develop physical prowess, learn the language, start things off, find good people — he's done well so far — and delegate, delegate, delegate.

They reach the top of a hill and are slow descending into its valley. Below, Henry can see a low canal and the buildings of the unused coffee plantation, its roofs a dried-blood rust.

'Rajottama's tight but sufficient. If the village were a body' — Johnny purses his lips — 'the bridge over the canal would be its leg, say, the left one. They're having a kind of drought now —'

'Didn't tell me you were a poet,' Henry says, half-delirious with thirst, hunger, an ache for sleep.

The boy seems pleased and continues. 'Thank you. The marketplace would be the left hip. The Sacred Tree temple, with its big tree and its smaller tree, we'll call that the two sides of your waist. The Pilimas and their orphanage, that's your head' — tapping his own — 'and the house in which you'll start the project presumably falls just below. Somewhere on the right side of the clavicle. The right armpit,' Johnny titters, a schoolboy who immediately straightens himself.

Though Henry is dazed, it's the Pilimas' history which most entrances him. These new landlords, Johnny had told him, descend directly from Rajottama's notorious rebels against the British.

The Pilimas came from those who, in 1817, having helped the British capture the Kandyan kingdom, then crossed over to become rebels. Entire families stood their ground — all while the British were forced to send for additional contingents from Bengal and Madras, new English hands to help raze Kandyan houses and gardens, to torch the villages. Brave Pilima rebels had nevertheless prevented the Kandyan crown from being stolen, even managing to protect the Tooth. And they again held their ground in 1848, when the rebellion started among the peasants against new and unfair taxation. Unlike other clans, the Pilimas have stayed together. They still stake claim on land their ancestors had protected against the colonizers.

Because of the Pilima family, the British gave up their desires for everything Henry had just seen in town. The British had surrendered it all: the Temple of the Tooth, the monastery, the manmade lake with its skulls. They had fled the Great City's kingdom, had given up conquering the country's interior. What could be more perfect?

It's something Henry has wanted since he was a child left alone to his own devices: entering an urgent and vast set of connections. All this is better than an adult's version of a toy telescope or a model galleon. This is something big. This dynasty of Ceylonese Pilpimapamapas or whatever are big enough. Because it's not that Henry's coming to any arbitrary plot. No. The story makes poetry sing in him again. This was — *is* — a family of natives with foresight enough to envision destiny. People writ in history who left fear behind and kept their country's heart safe from invaders.

And there is something else that can help him: perversely, if there is a drought — a mild one — it will help his cause. Because from his gentleman-farmer days in New York, Henry knows a little about everything: about irrigation, about German hydroponics. All this possibility mushrooming up everywhere pleases him as much as a new find will please a collector.

They are descending what Johnny calls the hill's crippled right leg. Veering down toward the Kamaraga canal, their cart barely handles the turns. Below, on rock islands in the lifeless waterway, men are bathing. Men who look like nothing less than majestic rulers bared of shirts and chest hair. Until Johnny corrects him, Henry takes them all to be members of the Pilima clan.

'They say that before Vijaya came from India, thousands of years ago, the only inhabitants of the island were demons,' Johnny laughs. '*Yakshas*. They also say the forefather of the Sinhalese was the grandson of a lion —'

The Sinhalese, a lion's descendants? Blind to the cart's arrival, by the canal, villagers leonine or not are busy calling to one another. On the sloped banks women slap dirt out of clothes, all to a heartbeat's sunken rhythm.

Tiny red and white petals of frangipani begin to litter the road: the temple flower, Johnny explains, areliya, here since Vijaya. To their left, up many white stairs, banners festoon a temple's alabaster bulb. Before the temple, a giant plaster Buddha sits facing the canal. The left hand of the Buddha lies calm in that righteous lap but Henry can't figure out whether the right hand is facing forward in a mudra of warning or welcome. And yet the Buddha's entire face is obscured, swaddled by a saffron cloth.

On a terraced pathway next to the Buddha, two people seem to float. Of everyone, these two draw Henry's attention the most. Not because one is a robed monk with a stevedore's build who gazes below, monitoring the canal. Or because a level beneath him, a thin man with gaunt shoulders murmurs to a drum whose tension he is adjusting.

It's that in their composure, the temple their backdrop, there is timelessness: the first tableau Henry has found to be truly peaceful. As though for centuries everything had anticipated Henry; and still awaited him, as a hand from the future might, reaching out to bring him forward. The stairs rising to the Buddha, to the monk and the drummer — when Henry has done almost nothing to get here. And now this incandescent mammary of a temple — what other sight could make Henry's sap start to run again? What wind could chisel such vividness? His whole prior life has been a sleepwalking: he has been walking about with a white stick. Now behind his eyelids he can see: some effulgent mystery reveals itself — opportunity a golden comet — myriad flecks of light.

He blinks. Only now he realizes how much his youthful thinking panhandled from everywhere. What has he ever truly experienced himself? Not only will he live near this monk. He will come to know — without anyone else's mediation! — what philosophy might lie behind that saffron robe.

To the rear of the monk and drummer extend the liberal, profuse branches of a tree on a dais. Levels are everywhere: his past life, his future, a belief everywhere in ascent and descent. This much Henry knows from Madame and her teachings: hierarchies always backbone the world's mystical traditions. She had preached to him how it is especially the body — with its brain commanding the heart and limbs — that shows the nature of hierarchy: 'All is not your egalitarian Americanist reality, Henri!' Only now do her words form logic: one cannot just turn up at the tree. Step by step one moves toward enlightenment. In the last daybeams, the temple's ivory-white makes the promise to him for which he would have bet heartbeats, rather, *years*, off the end of his own life. Just to know this tinge of this familiarly foreign, this so foreignly familiar!

This monk is the first to make him wonder. Perhaps Henry had been in a previous life *here*, in *Ceylon*. He had dismissed reincarnation as claptrap, the kind of hogwash salon-goers lived on. But is it not likely that his father and mother, the entire *absence* of his childhood, all the slippery footholds on various grades, were for *this*, such actualization? Why *would* nothing ever have worked out before?

All the blessed signposts had brought him here. Madame, James, his flops. That when he had started the farming utopia in White Plains, everyone had been all thumbs with the rakes. That during his journalism days, he could only get enthused about stories related to the spirit and his editor had eventually thought him too purple.

In utter rhapsody he turns to Johnny and bows his head — *thank you thank you, how can I thank you* — practically blubbering. Jewels of tears, the first Henry has cried publicly in years, spill from his eyes. This is how the moment must express itself: he may have just come home.

Johnny seethes at his foreign charge, breaking Henry's spell. 'Nod! up there in the temple! They'll think you're slighting them otherwise!'

But only their driver Ganesh grimaces back. Henry is too late. Their cart has hurtled on too quickly. Henry couldn't move out of his momentum swiftly enough to translate the boy's command, clear though it had been, into action.

Madame had long ago told her American colleague that to make his plans work, he must give up planning. Here that won't be feasible. Because Henry will not violate. He *must* start with a plan, if a gentle one. First he must understand the situation at the get-go, methodically, in order to do right by these kind faces. In this way, and only in this way, will he most efficaciously be able to awaken their self-reliance, one surely snoozing but ready for action. The Ceylonese. He knows he already sees them more freely than Wooves did. He is sure of it. He will be their clarion call. He will wake them. He loves them.

12

IT REALLY IS SOMETHING, this house: a pearly castle of a thing, capped with flanking towers and pinnacles, set in a bower of trees. When they swerve left, up a hill, and immediately left again up a steep peagravel drive, Henry admires from afar the sumptuous gabled cloister that will be his. An iridescent aerie with blue shingles, brattices, not all that dissimilar from his childhood home. He is plumb-center, where he always wanted to be, where his fortune will finally hew to the straight mercury.

But the house, splendid from a distance, turns out to be, as they climb, different. Truth is, it's something of a monstrosity — deviant flying yeasty abutments, turrets and wings and belfries bulging out of a basically trapezoidal idea, with the roof a hip-and-valley, a sawtooth, a pavilion. An architect with a penchant for the cancerous and the baroque had gained an upper hand in the design. And this despite a few nice touches: the mansard arch and corbelling over the wooden door. It is white, true, like other houses Henry had seen, but evident water damage, brown braids of it as though from ivy vine tracery, mar the facing. Even the step up to the house looks to have rotted through its core, down to the molding planks spread out below. Meanwhile, there is the hanging rope with, at its end, a tarnished silver crescent — a doorknob not used for years. Closer inspection would depress any first-time guest, not just Henry.

Yet over the handkerchief of lawn, on a rampart wild with crabgrass and Queen Anne's lace, an enormous tree hangs with golden roseate fruit, pendulous. 'Your mangoes will be coming from there, Henree,' Johnny is saying —

— and down the stairs beyond the front yard is a white cottage set among more fruit trees, a habitation which Henry already earmarks for Johnny. That will be the boy's little boîte.

'Perhaps it will make more sense once we're inside,' he says assuringly, half to Johnny and half to himself.

They linger behind the wagon, undecided how best to leave things with the driver. 'Won't be needing a carriage then, Henree?' Johnny has chosen, apparently, to disregard Henry's remark about things making sense. 'Because this driver's good — and help is hard to come by in Ceylon . . .'

'Not sure. Feel uncomfortable *hiring* help . . .'

Ganesh wags his head like a slow water bobber marking the depths of future employment potential. Johnny hurries over for a brief consult with the driver and returns. 'We can get ahold of him later, should you need. For now, I just paid him off.'

Henry protests.

'Don't worry, Henree, we'll sort everything out later.'

Johnny has thousands of varieties of confidence in him, Henry notes with some pleasure. Just now the boy kinged it a bit, behaving like landed gentry — or is this a taste of the Ceylonese hospitality which James had hinted at so enticingly? They walk to the edge of their lawn to watch in silence the sunset, gingery streaks tuning above the mountain. 'This shows us the famous welcome,' says Henry.

And then he hears the rustle.

He turns abruptly but no speed is necessary because what he sees is not stirring.

She is still, in this first deceptive sight of her, when later she will be movement itself. When she will be someone who darts, plucks, slams. She stands in the doorway, one hand shading her eyes. Struck still, as though bright noon has arrived and not a travel-mussed man. As though deciding whether to let down any special bridges for him.

13

Our officers, those under the command of myself, D. T. Wooves, and my superior, brought in women from the village and exerted such force over them that more than anything in all my years of service, it pains me to recount the expedience with which they lay plunder to the most valued holdings of a woman's

*life. I say woman ill-advisedly, for it was girls they
sought, girls from the village in question, so-called
Rajottamah, and particularly those beauties of
the illustrious Pilimah family, known for their long
Egyptian — or Nilotic? — noses of a kind long
forgotten by history but revered in our art. Their eyes
are the shape of pomegranate seeds, their waists
slim like reeds.*

Henry compliments the boy on his fine reading voice. 'You got something going there Johnny! Reverberant! a kind of rumble in the bass! If you didn't want to be a nate —'

'You can say it. A native guide —'

'— no, you're better than any war announcer! No one told me I'd get treated to such renditions! It's wonderful, don't stop.'

*The men of the Pilimahs were angered by our
Government's recent inauguration of taxes on dog-
owners, gun-owners, any merchant with the most
trifling roadside stall or boutique, and on peasants
who only used jungle paths but were being taxed for
stone-paved roads. Thus, the Pilimahs had been
rather vehement in organizing guerrilla attacks
upon our remote garrisons in areas of jungle
where our mother country had not seen fit yet
to create suitable roads by which provisions could
be maintained. Though we were admittedly
vulnerable, these Pilimahs for the most part had
succeeded merely in disrupting our communications
with the seat in Colombo. All the same, the wrath
our men targeted on their village, particularly on
the one family —*

'See, this is why your plans, Henree, are going to succeed here. Once you disclose their scope to me. Which — I'm just saying —

73

you haven't done yet. We have time. You understand, the people of Rajottama —'

'Rajott-ama.'

'Good. They desire change. After the coffee blight and the failed plantation. You couldn't have picked a better place for your village. Change. It's even in the coconut trees around here. *Pol.* Try saying it. *It's in the pol trees.*'

The entire night, the frogs outside in an optimistic gidder, Johnny and Henry had dizzied themselves, in the old library, on shot after shot of Wooves' port, served up in beveled glasses.

Henry's gesture, never mind his vision, is as misty and grand as his plans. He waves the boy to continue but instead knocks over his own glass, barely missing the kerosene lamp. Before the glass hits the straw mat, Johnny manages to catch it.

'Oh you're sober!' Henry accuses the boy, who shakes his head. The boy wipes his hands on his handkerchief but can't stop laughing. 'Then you're adroit!'

'They didn't say you came to Ceylon to tame us droits?'

'They?'

'The pol trees. No, I'm more clumsy than you think. Hardly adroit.'

'Don't you ever take those glasses off?'

'Why?' The boy is touchingly vulnerable setting his specs down.

'Nice to see the man behind the mountain. You have yourself a good jaw.'

Johnny juts it at him. 'Does it augur success?'

'Tonight maybe.'

Henry couldn't be more pleased with the wide good feeling flowing between him and the boy, here in this room with its balmy light. After all, his local guide *can* make something of a joke. He might end up being decent company. Especially for an American isolated in the tropics. But a moment of decent company might require a formula: tank the boy up to the chin, let him read aloud. He seems to enjoy that enough.

'C'mon, boyo, don't hold back,' says Henry. 'Put your specs back on if you want. Your readership's all ears.'

No sooner had my colleagues taken one female specimen upon whom they exerted themselves in the

most barbarous manner than they found themselves
like bersaglieri hungry for another. No native meat
could be found young or rare enough to satisfy these
transmogrified bloodthirsty dogs, my erstwhile
colleagues and companions. Since the beginning of
the century, the military had been strengthened,
perhaps too much so, for needs which never surpassed
internal security, and thus had grown restless.

None of the above activities were, of course, in
keeping with the universal character of what Sir
Ralph Soredig had foreseen for our Civil Service, or the
Queen's army, which generally sought to show
forbearance, and which ordinarily conciliated the
sentiments of the natives by adopting a line of
conduct at once firm, but moderate and considerate.

After a few moments of bewilderment —

'How about that?' Johnny hoots. 'Wooves just stood there assessing the pillage.'
'Cowardly, wasn't he?'
Johnny wrinkles his brow. 'How do you mean?' He doesn't wait for an answer but goes on:

— being hardly able to control my men, I removed
myself to a fairer prospect upon a knoll, one which
provided safe vantage upon the area where the
mainstays of the large Pilimah family had organized
firebrands to protect one village front from the
onslaught of the best and brightest our public schools
could offer (as Ceylon in those years was considered
quite a choice assignment).

'Maybe not such a bad man,' Henry observes. 'He knew it was wrong as it was happening.'

'And it took him a while to gather his wits? You're not being a little innocent, Henree? Think. An army man who watches rape without lifting a finger?'

'Conceded. Maybe. Go on.'

In partial explanation for the chthonic frenzy of my colleagues, no doubt one stands to get touched by years of trying and thankless service, carrying the burden in malarial jungles in the name of our respected Queen. Though a wild and entirely unfounded rumor made the rebellion what it was, the people believing the Tooth Relic (by which the natives set such lofty store) to have fallen into our hands, such accidents have caused lesser wars. What finally stemmed the revolt was the same as its cause: our alleged possession of what the people believed to be the Buddha's tooth, a remnant after his cremation. This faulty supposition proved crucial enough to shatter the morale of even the Pilimahs.

'What a race!' Henry muses. 'Losing morale over some dentures.'

'No, Henree,' the boy says. He hits his head in mock impatience. 'Not a race. A *family*. I told you about them. It's true most of them aren't truly related, but they keep the name. Pushpa and Lester, the others —'

The boy swells on about the Pilimas. He knows how many died of water sickness during this year's drought, ever since the southwestern monsoon gave up the ghost three months early, in May. Here it is August and, yes, Pilimas as well as villagers have suffered. He knows which Pilimas control the meager canal and which oversee the irrigation for the peasants' paddy. And how there is no younger generation. How the only true Pilima left is a woman named Manik who's never in Rajottama.

But by what means did the boy come to know so much?

'See, I study these decrepit clans.' — Why *does* the boy have this acute gift for telepathy? 'Anyway, most Sinhalese would know. You can't know too much about people like the Pilimas.'

Ultimately, the main Pilimah rebel had his beheaded skull presented to Scotland's esteemed Phrenological Society, while another Pilimah was exiled to the isle of Mauritius. Today the family remains a thin filament upon Ceylon.

Rather soon after this Rajottaman fiasco, I found pretext enough to quit the Service and return to our green and pleasant land. Only years later, having returned to Ceylon, a spirit of scurrilous self-examination having beset me, did I begin to set down these, my humble memoirs and exegeses. Though not a literary man, I am hard-pressed to admit that all too easily can I conjure before my vision one of those Pilimah girls, her famously beautiful eyes stationed upon me in a plea which, however muted, required no translation. I must confess that, after the Pilimah fiasco, the mere sight of my first name, knowing what it can spell backwards, will occasionally haunt me.

Dennis Thomas Wooves, 1887

'He waited, what, into his sixties? before he left Ceylon?' asks Henry.

'Seventies, I'd say. Who knows? You have time then, isn't it?' — and the boy's disconcerting bray sobers everyone up more than dropping the glass did. With great care, the boy again removes his specs, sets them atop the civil servant's logbook. A spider spools out from the pages and onto the coffee table, and from there onto the wicker pretext for a carpet before scuttling beneath the surface. 'I'd like to be that spider,' Johnny says. 'Don't you think he's a truer artist than all of us? Goes where he likes.'

'You'd no doubt spin better.'

'And have gourmet meals. Play hide and seek whenever I wanted.'

'Hide and seek,' Henry echoes without hearing. He's wondering where the maid is. Some four days ago he'd arrived with Johnny to be greeted by the house with its mildew and spiders, its port wine and books. And the native maid who — by virtue of what? — had, upon arrival, become theirs as well.

14

THEY HAD FINISHED paying off the driver, their cart had rattled away, the sun had begun its last bleed down, and Henry stayed startled to have found her there. You drive up to a castle of a house and find a woman and cannot tell how long she has been pretending to be a doorjamb. Anyone would be startled by this woman looking tired out by too much of something.

As with the monk Henry felt her to be an argument for reincarnation. As though he already knew her. Though she spooked him. And kept her eyes shaded, needlessly. And held a dwarf broom the likes of which he'd never seen. A strong-boned girl, either a territorial neighbor or a refugee: where had she come from?

'Probably one of these coastal types who drift up north. Usually just want a house to clean,' Johnny drawled. 'Want me to take care of it?' but in this Henry could hear how the ten-hour-plus journey had spent both of them. Even Johnny's tongue had tired.

'Sorry, don't mind?' still overdoing the courtesy with Johnny.

Henry's aide mustered a brisk consult with the girl. 'You see, Henree, what I thought.' He strode back as though having just tamed a brutish dog, fingers aiming an invisible double-shooter. 'She came up here when something went funny with her marriage. Nowhere else to go.' His hands continued to shoot. That was the bizarre part: the boy with his shooting hands.

Studying her, Henry had liked the glimpse he'd gotten of her eyes: furtive and strong. She'd be an intelligent one, Henry thought, perhaps a beauty — but she'd ducked back into the house so hastily he couldn't tell. Around those eyes, he had the impression of something sublime, the grandeur he had dreamed the people of Ceylon might possess. Dazzling, shaded, cosseting. Later that first night in his Village Book he wrote in code of her:

Strong. Broad yet delicate. Silk.

On the lawn he'd immediately instructed Johnny: he didn't want to banish her. He wanted to keep her on. 'After all,' rationalizing, 'don't we need somebody to take care of the house?'

'Take care?' Johnny had cocked his head. 'You want help?'

'From here it looks like a hell of a cavern, doesn't it? Why not this one? Should we go find her?'

'You want a *domestic?*' This prospect evidently made Johnny less than happy.

'People don't work with household help here? That's what I heard.'

Johnny cocooned back into some ghostliness. 'A domestic. Fine.'

'Sure?'

'I say it's fine!' practically shouting, but maybe the mountain ascent had plugged everyone's ears.

Once the men had entered, once they'd gotten their travel-tired feet up on settees, once the lamps in all rooms were lit, giving off a faint hiss and stink, she certainly whisked about in a familiar enough manner. Henry lay at the calm eye of a domestic tornado, being brought blankets and cups of beautifully clear water, which Johnny made her take back and boil for the foreigner. She acted as though every whim of theirs took its place in a long tradition, this being the second time that day that Henry had the feeling, eerie, of centuries waiting for him to reappear.

'Why *not* her?' Henry had repeated to Johnny, who with his selective hearing never answered.

Henry could imagine selective hearing to be a useful trait. It enabled one to be a little less earnest all the time. Or a little more. If you only heard what you wanted, your own objectives stayed hub-central. He thought he might share this insight with Johnny later. Perhaps on another night of shots.

But from the moment of their arrival she certainly seemed perfect to Henry. The most perfect thing he'd seen since landing on the island. Surpassing the green, transcending the monk and drummer. Better even than Johnny, which with his jealous intuition the boy may have understood. And she was no dummy. She acted as though she recognized the need to make herself look useful to the boy.

She stayed silent but moved with authority around the house's quirky nooks; removed dustcovers over furniture; opened the front room's draperies; closed doors to wings which Henry later found led nowhere. And also immediately stowed Henry's satchel in one of these nowheres.

He and Johnny toured the house like seigneurs: the stately front library with its french windows, bottles and foxed books. The mustard chaise longue, bordered by heavy ocher curtains. The bedroom next to it — two-doored as if for quick escape — its moth-eaten curtains. An old silvery skeleton key fitting into the mahogany cabinet that Johnny called an almirah, after the Portuguese almeira.

'The Portuguese gave us parangi,' says Johnny, 'which means both *Portuguese* and *disease*. No one knows how to cure parangi. As bad as rinderpest for humans — a terrible skin disease. You feel you'll die from boils.'

'Tell me that later,' Henry says vaguely. 'But I appreciate your ideas, thank you.'

He likes flitting through the house, its vast theater. The old colonial style people had described in America proves true enough. Quaint wings and their eccentricity — cut-off corners, the long corridors — didn't this add to the charm? Perhaps Wooves' home is not such a monstrosity. Because how can a monstrosity be comfortable? It will be, he decides, a good house.

Off the kitchen with its well-used cutting board, its clay water vessel, its ceiling-high shelves, you walk out into a patio, a bailey, where a recessed campfire smolders. Inside is a smaller pantry, protected from the outside only by wind-stripped lattice. Scabbed pots and pans hang over the lead sink bowl. Beyond, a thatched roof bulges over another pit and kindling: husk brooms, plaited palm, objects Henry would find it hard to begin naming.

He had wanted to give the girl a private welcome gift, but Johnny had to be asked to get her to go find his bag. Other than the shirt and trousers he wore, this portmanteau is the only tangible remnant of Henry's other life. She'd stored the thing in an outlandish trapezoid of a closet at the head of a blind corridor.

He followed her back. With his bowie, Henry cut the ropes he'd tied around the bag. Inside, atop his few mildewed clothes and books lay the gift — the lavender flower preserved in its wax bookmark.

Could he say that this gift's appearance — at first chance — is a sign? Maybe he's meant to give up something? To release Madame, his Russian co-conspirator, his shaman and muse?

The girl had stood by him. After his struggle with the bowie, the ropes, his brooding over the satchel's rank contents, she seemed ready to dart off. He'd picked up the bookmark and handed it to her.

'Please. Let this be yours,' he'd said, feeling grand.

She'd bowed her head instantly and flashed her white teeth once at him. Twice. He couldn't help thinking that a girl like her could bite him in half: the road must have burned out his usual wits.

Leaning against a bent wall, Johnny had watched the gift-giving. 'Terrific,' he mugged, surprising Henry. 'Now you've given her that, that *trinket*, she'll be yours for life.'

Was this a pleasantry? Henry smiled his embarrassment. Because he couldn't parse the boy's jokes: they hit just left of what Henry would call good humor.

15

THAT FIRST NIGHT, she'd cooked for them. A simple meal from the exotic breadfruit hung like body parts on the tree out back. She'd served like a woman long used to serving, on what must have been Wooves' chipped china, with its blue trees, bridges, temples.

As she'd prepared the meal, swift on her feet, Johnny had tried to keep her near. The boy querulous, as if her presence alone frustrated him. As if she were something he'd forgotten about. Her voice low in answering. Her glance never long at either of them.

Henry understood. If he'd had a daughter in her situation, he'd want her to behave the same. Not deferential, not flirtatious: pragmatic obedience seemed to be her choice.

He'd christened her the mystery girl. Johnny's queries had gleaned only a strand of her background. Before they'd arrived she'd been in the house two weeks, possibly three. Johnny couldn't tell whether she lied or had a villager's feeling for time. She'd assured Johnny she would pose no problem. She'd been sleeping outside, under the half-shelter of the patio's straw roof. She asked for nothing but to stay on.

They had trusted her enough to eat her food that first night. She didn't seem like someone you wouldn't trust. As far as Henry could tell. And he was proven right, mostly.

Without any doctoring, later she ate the same food as they had — but apart, toward midnight, sitting at the kitchen door facing the patio. The two men had been glazed into late-night inertia at the kitchen table. They didn't want to leave each other, or the girl; they weren't ready to wander from the kitchen to find their new beds, with Johnny to go to his separate cottage just down the hill. Because wasn't their stasis delicious, a grasping of their first day together?

Until both men finally left, her back had remained hunched toward them as she ate, as though to disguise an act of shame or delight.

'It's our way,' Johnny had said austerely. Dismissing her as normal.

Later, unable to sleep, he'd watched her. Through the dust-smeared kitchen window he saw moonlight shed into the patio and her curled into a child atop a thin palm-leaf pad. Only a plum cloth wrapped around her chest, he saw this, a plum cloth around her chest and waist and hips. Arms and legs smooth as dowels and castors. One more cloth over her, but much later in the night, when he peered again from the window, she'd kicked it off. Henry had resisted the urge to cover her. Tried instead to guess her age.

She could be seventeen or thirty-three. How can he know with these people, their skin so smooth? Brown so morally superior. And she was his own personal gift, better than a library of bookmarks from Madame.

The last time he peeked, before he went off to find what Johnny had called the master bedroom, he was pleased to note that sticking out from beneath her pillow — a burlap sack of coconut shells — was the lavender bookmark.

As she washes dishes by the patio well, she hums thrilling tones low in her throat. When dogs skulk for scraps, she shoos them away with a sputtering cry from between her coconut-white teeth.

People use their teeth in a much more active manner here than in America, he writes. In the accounting of her which he begins to keep, he marks a large positive + in the left column — most likely she will be trainable.

With what he thinks is his usual good cheer, Henry starts his instruction to her slowly. He asks that she scrape the mud off his boots. She understands his prancing gestures and loud English. He shows her how to steam his shirts, how to fold back his bed's holey top sheet. They soon move on to greater chores.

He is hardly done demonstrating before she complies and always with that prompt duck of her head. Her hair she keeps up or in a braid. Her nape is forever bare, delicate, inviting.

16

WOULD LIFE have taken a different turn had his father not died when he did?

You aren't supposed to think in that unproductive way but Henry can't help it. The month before graduating from the seminary, May 1913 — aged twenty-two — Henry had been forced to witness his vital father, so monumental, fallen in repose: the head of a grand literalist. The son had the ludic urge to pray to that head as to an idol, so complete was it before the son: a vine without any vine-dresser.

At the bedside of his last parent, Henry was compelled to hear the rattle and hiss of a final breath, see eyes focus on a private distance, a hand clutch at nothing, feel the flight from life. Is the world that bad? His father's last moments so resembled his mother's, some nineteen years earlier, that what most upset Henry was how democratically death levels all.

One thing that shouldn't be egalitarian is death. Once again he could not place where the soul might have been in the room. The truth was, the second after his mother had died he could have stopped believing in the afterlife, but it took his father's death to drive doubt in more profoundly.

With his father's death there was nothing. No change in the room's temperature. No light. No profound thoughts or electric communion. Suddenly in the world there was no one to fear or love on the sly. No one whose root was deeper than his.

Just a lightness spooky only in its mundanity: the nurse asleep downstairs; the kitchen drain tapping. He and his father's body, alone in a room with nothing.

'I'll do the thinking for both of us now, Father,' he had said aloud, needing to make a joke or something to cut the silence because anything was better than such spiraling absence. *None of us*, he decided, forcing each word out in his head, *dies uniquely* — and that became a private epitaph, different from the inanity which ended up gracing his father's headstone. Henry repeated it to himself during the funeral until the words became nonsense, pliéd before him like ravens. *None of us dies uniquely.* This was all he had to hold on to; his closest relations lived in the Yukon territory and hadn't been heard from for years; long ago he had alienated his seminary friends with his relentless questions about their life choices.

In the days after his father's death, he forced himself to think of many similar sayings, but this was his favorite. None of us dies uniquely.

He had never known his father, had only hated the strict literalism of his sin-and-burn account of morality. And yet without that great lanternlike presence, Henry's position in the cosmos shifted. In the year of mourning that marked his twenty-third year, Henry stood at the dark pulpit unordained, lucky to find a position so quickly only because the war had caused attrition in the ranks. Few chaplains were to be had, with so many gone on to ships in torpedo-infested waters, or holding dignified posts on the Continent.

Fresh out of the seminary and the draftable, unordained boy stayed at home, in his father's house, attempting to inspire his father's flock, one that had so loved the grave father they forgave the unripe son his emphases: how Henry junior lingered on Peter and Isaiah and drove home his points with Ecclesiastes or Revelation.

It was all a little too ghostly. He had not been ordained and could never forget his immaturity. His father stayed a graft within him; the same horsetail gestures and fiery rhetoric impregnated him, a volatile spirit that would corrode all traces of Henry junior.

This he could not stand. One had to break away eventually. So when in February a loyal parishioner had suggested Henry be appointed colonel, albeit on the domestic front, Henry was happy. *Colonel* Henry would give up his ministry, reenter the secular world. He'd commandeer a fraud inspection unit outside D.C. and in this way the bereaved young man would be spared a life leading difficult parishioners — as well as the slights of the Great War's shells and bazookas.

The only part of the deal that played the odds was that Henry would have to volunteer first, rather than wait to be drafted. This was no hurdle; young Henry had patriotic inklings; and fraud inspection would mean he finally earned his own keep in the world. This business would, too, dodge fate: the clangor of guns and ships would belong to another.

Henry took the lesser risk. Almost — because what did he know about fraud inspection? Barely. He knew how to spell fraud. He knew more about deer-hunting. He knew he had been gifted solely because of his father once again. Not because of his own work. Not because for nine months, without official imprimatur, he had led a lackluster congregation just a half-mile from his birthplace.

In leaving his father's flock — leaving the entire calling of the rectory — what he hadn't counted on was how his thirty fraud inspection recruits would be at once so bumbling and demoralized. Hardly the innovative recruits he had imagined, boys laboring against the bit, nosing out truth. If anything, he had expected them to be overly hearty and idealistic. Instead, what he got were boys who would have been drafted but for their high-placed relatives or strabismus, their club foot, their claustrophobia.

For the most part, they turned out to be paltry kind souls bent into their own punitive literalisms, Henry's personal cross. And he had to be their bearer. They would go to their death, or the end of a fraud inspection case, following the letter of the law, missing vagaries with their hole-in-the-pocket thinking. Henry felt as though he were forced to live with his father all over again, Gould senior's God-fearing face replicated multiple times over in these young men's secular version of sin-and-burn.

Henry should not have taken this so personally, but he could not help himself. He saw their literal-mindedness as his own failure right from square one. Henry's Thirty approached assignments as they did their lives, shoelaces, perhaps even their future wives. They might tie things up square and firm and never know if the insides of an attaché putrefied or a fiend blew on their shoulder.

Which meant that to boost their morale — and his own as well — Henry had needed to drop in on site offices. He lectured his team on laws of consumer demand and supply, human psychology, modes of thinking, hoodwinking strategies, ideas, dreams, fantasies; anything to give these wet souls enough of a jolt so they would think *laterally*.

Like a criminal. Like a fraud perpetrator.

These were ensigns who were the product of the Empire State Building and Gibson Girl mothers. Something in their training or what Madame would later call incarnation history must have blocked them from thinking in subterranean tunnels.

Lateral thinking! Henry had to preach the new gospel twenty times a day to the literalists. Lateralism! Trouble was, he found himself managing on too microscopic a level, which made his department's efficiency in fraud Identification, Detailment, Education, Apprehension and Surveillance rate (IDEAS) plummet. And Henry would falsify no internal reports. The problem remained his and by gum if he wouldn't conquer it honestly. Start-ups were hard, the general who had dubbed him colonel had told him that much at the outset. In a start-up, you had to be a one-man band.

Two years into the jog of it all, Henry tightened everything, upped standards, devised a new training, instituted daily calisthenics for himself and the unit, created a handbook, a straight line of command. In his spare time in the barracks, he had been reading up on lie detector protocol, private investigations, and courtroom procedure, all to devise the absolutely best way to know when John Q. Public was being diddled.

He listened closely to popular lyrics, polled new colognes among his friends, studied ration tickets' numbering systems, analyzed deviations in the faces of acquaintances. He was being a skeptical inquirer, keeping his ear to the ground, his finger in the wind. He wrote pamphlets on the Archetype A, B and C system he'd invented. No one could have faulted him. No other newly minted colonel, in charge of a department as saggy as fraud inspection, could have done better — and for his troubles, somewhere in the middle of 1917, having worked with his young trainees long enough, he started to see some return.

Their ability to launch bolt-from-the-blue attacks had skyrocketed. They trapped and caught fraudulent purveyors of home remedies, panaceas, pilliwinks, ladies' under-support garments, ball bearings, mailing services, educational materials and bootleg whiskey. Washington's mayor pinned a white badge on Henry in a ceremony which no one related to him by blood attended. Henry was, according to the mayor, helping the war effort, but Henry knew he could not be doing quite as much for the country as it had done for him.

The process of investigation had proven invigorating. He liked following the first whiff of a clue. Approaching; figuring out the right questions; what depths could be sounded, what systems should be used; what tracks needed to be erased, what staying undercover until the right moment meant.

When he was truly in the grip of a case, about to home in on a suspect, light would hurt his eyes, such was his excitement. He had believed this excitement could be contagious, would inspire his thirty. And he had been right: toward the close of the war he had many Henrys, many, all sitting with his same hands-on-the-knees, forward-leaning mannerisms.

After the war Henry resolved *not* to continue on in the same line, not to advance as an inspector of fraud — he would never damn the restlessness that had brought him so far. But yes, he would continue in the broader field of investigation. He had enjoyed investigating too much to let it drop. It was too satisfying to see how he'd transformed his thirty in what he'd thought the most important respect: the boys not only asked questions, finally, they asked the right ones. Had his father not died when he did, Henry would never have been to them, as one of the thirty said in a public farewell, 'as a wind over the reeds.'

17

BUT HE CHIDES HIMSELF! Busy remembering his past so clearly when he should be learning the clarity of Ceylon! First three days in the house and he walks that huge grimy interior remembering earlier selves and careers, pretending to plan. Three days of this, his first three days, and he starts to self-remonstrate: *Indulgent beast!*

Then again, those who cannot remember the past are condemned to repeat it, the philosopher said as much, didn't he? With these new people on board, with Johnny and the girl, he'll prepare for the next stage of his undertaking. It will certainly take method to create blueprints for the model village, to bring it out of its colonial and feudal torpor. Nothing will clobber him. Without supervisor and guidelines —

— and this is the way he prefers things. Overseeing his new maid will be the first priority in the logical step-by-step progression toward the goal.

Begin at home, he tells himself. Move out from there.

18

AS THE TWO MEN continue the fourth morning, hungover in the library, her bare feet slap through the corridors to the patio kitchen where she begins to make a real ruckus with her pots and pans.

'She *is* noisy,' admits Johnny. Maybe it's the port. Or is it that without his spectacles, his eyes float in his face? 'The English camp would have better followers. At least those girls would be quicker around the house.'

'You're wrong. This girl's no follower. But she's quick enough for the two of us,' Henry protests. 'Especially if all we've really done so far is drink port.' Or mosey around remembering the past. He leans back into an extraordinary chair. Made from discarded ship wood or a seasoned packing crate, it bears a lintel of sorts at the top, a horizontal shingle, a roof.

Henry fingers it: 'What do you make of this top piece?'

'Part of a casket?'

'Only a few pieces of wood separate a throne from a casket?'

Johnny stretches, half-cat, half-horse. 'I could grow to like this style of life.'

'And I'm proving what a lazy creature I am.'

'We've been talking ideas. Anyway, Henree, you've been here only a few days. Should give yourself time to settle in. Start to know the names of flowers. Auriculas. Pinks. Croton. Would help you, right?'

'That's what you're here for.'

'Righto.'

'But for example, I don't know about this English camp.'

For the first time Johnny stammers. 'Sorry. I mean, I told you. It's defunct. It's nothing.' When he sees he's failed to satisfy Henry, he adds: 'There are many encampments around the country. But as we discussed, there *used* to be a British camp just above the Sacred Tree temple.'

'Oh?' Henry wants nothing to do with anyone's military.

'Well, remember I told you how the Pilimas practically died out? That's about the time the government decided that with no Pilimas in Rajottama, nothing left to quell, all the soldiers moved out. It's defunct. I wouldn't be here if — nothing to worry about, really.'

'Who says I'm worrying about the British?'

Without any special warrant Johnny's voice rises. 'Telling you, Henree, English or whomever.' He puts his glasses back on. 'I mean simply they're gone.' He resumes in a calmer tone. 'Far as I know. This hypothetical camp or whatever's no threat to anything. I mean of course better maids must exist *somewhere*. Hypothetically. Why not some hypothetical camp somewhere? Hypothetical, Henree. Camp's hypothetical.'

'What's the problem, Johnny? I'm offending you?'

Henry's new aide, whether C or B, is a sulky creature. He shakes his head and turns away.

'Johnny, think I should christen you too. How about Mystery Boy?'

This elicits nothing. Henry touches the boy's sandstone hand. 'Please. Already you've been a wonderful boon.'

'Thank you,' muttered by the turned-away head.

'Please, Johnny. Consider it a dead subject. I don't care about any British whatchamahaveyou. Hypothetical or not.'

'So why'd you be offending me?'

'Sorry!' says Henry. 'Weren't we having a nice morning? Our port. The spider. The tea we're about to have.'

'See, the camp here in Rajottama, as far as I know, it long since disbanded.'

'Well, fine. Typical enough,' says Henry. He'll try once more to smooth the conversation before he surrenders. 'They divide, conquer, disband.'

'That is correct. *They*,' says Johnny. Henry's tactic, whatever it is, appears to have worked. 'They. Too soon for you to know so much!' Johnny laughs his alien bray. 'People like you and me, Henree, we learn quickly. No one told me you'd be a regular scholar.'

Henry's head begins to pound. *Who would've told . . .* He manages to say: 'What else do we learn in American schools but —'

Instead of getting to enjoy the returned good humor, his moment with his aide, the morning in Ceylon, everything, the tiny men in Henry's head start their work upon his skull. Skilled men. Terrible men. Since childhood, Henry has been plagued with their handiwork. With headaches that are a precise grammar of hammer and nails inside his forehead.

The routine is so familiar, he can only succumb. Henry is breathing fast, watching the library, the french doors, the garden and Johnny's eager face stretch into a skein which then rips into silver rags.

'Shhh —' Henry holds a warning finger up to Johnny.

The silver pulls a hot new blind of pain across. Gall and wormwood. Hardening into the vise that becomes the vortex.

He is beckoned across —

— across and then down.

As a child, Henry had come to see his body as a machine with its own will. At the onset of the boy's fits, even his father would retire into his study. Between gasps of consciousness, Henry knew terrible solitude. What he never knew was how long the fits lasted. Once he had broken a pocket watch during a fit, and as punishment had never received another. It could've been minutes, hours, centuries of purgatories during a fit; terrible spiders crawled on him; and then he would come to semiconsciousness, hearing his breath and blood. Beyond that, people clamoring their clichés like *the boy's gone mad* or *don't bite your tongue!*

Once, the ache subsided enough, Henry had peered into his father's study. In his hooded black cape, Gould senior sat, head fallen in his hands. The dormer window's unruly light made the grand Episcopal a dark blot. Aloud the rector argued with God in a voice insistent enough to persuade massive congregations.

The injustice, his father had expostulated. *To afflict such a young boy? A motherless boy.* Little Henry had thrilled. This was no abandonment. This was his father interceding with God.

'Let it be only the smaller pain,' begs Henry.

'What?' and Johnny flinches, still a stranger.

As the men with sledgehammers start their work with a gentle, loving tyranny, Henry tries to suppress his legs' desire to pedal, managing to pat his boy's sleek hand. 'Nothing.'

When he wakes, he is in a garden; short grass stubs his neck, a smell like summer lemonade wafts toward him from an exotic spoiled fruit next to his head. Mango? Above him a boy's face twists. 'Call a doctor?'

'How long was it?' This is key. Fine to lie here on this loamy ground and not recognize anything but time shouldn't be forgotten, should it?

'A few minutes,' says the obedient boy. Henry has already forgotten what question this is supposed to answer. He notes the boy's voice is like water rising and falling. 'Have this often?' The boy replaces a hand, his spectacles steamed, askew. 'It wasn't long.'

A fit, the boy is talking of a fit. There has been a fit; the man knows that. He is Henry, that much is clear, but he's trying to figure out who is this dusky steamy boy. This boy and a mystery girl who could be someone's sister or wife or god knows what alternately dragging and carrying Henry to a bed in a room that in the French style overlooks a garden. That is all. This is the blessing and curse of invalidism, everyone so involved with your body and its secrets. The weight of your ankles. The width of your wristbones. Everything races into a blur between specificity and anonymity.

Whoever she is, she does a stellar job removing Henry's heavy boots. He wants to tell her this but words fail him. Her touch is not unwelcome and her hands are active as a mother. She knows what to do, drawing closed the white curtains, while the boy paces the room.

In the dim light Henry remembers who Johnny is. 'You know last night you were speaking of dignity?' Henry commences in the middle because he can't find the head or tail of things, it is all torn into many colors. 'Last night? something about self-sufficiency? the need for it?'

'Oh, I, after all.' Hedging.

'Don't humor me! Say if you don't remember.'

'I remember.' The boy sits by him, his face a noble horse's. Henry reaches out to stroke the boy's mane and then remembers not to. He stifles the hand under the rigid sheet they've laid over him. He must reassure the boy about something but beginning is the hard part.

'What the sick have is will. This humility stuff is baloney. You know I'm not really a sick man. These little whatevers only attack me when I've had too much change all at once —'

'I was hardly thinking you were a sick . . .'

'Change, you see — I'm not some invalid you have to care for. Some oatmeal-chewing oaf.'

'Of course not.'

'I'm a huge believer that life must go on. So what if you do get occasionally bed-ridden? I call them *whatevers* because . . .'

The boy has hands that dance around, Henry sees them like puppets; they don't know where to station themselves, whether to hang by his side or lie cloistered in his lap. Instead a hand behaves like a necklace, a finger flies to the lips and Johnny clears his throat. Everyone else looks speeded up once Henry's forced to be anchored. The maid scoots around the boy, an intimate laying a damp cloth across Henry's head.

'Johnny,' Henry says. 'People like you and me have a lot in common. You were brilliant last night with your questions. I'm more lucid now. You know, as a seminary student I plagued my teachers with similar questions.'

Johnny doesn't move away. 'Like what?'

'The main one for me was always moral value. How are we to judge the moral value of any choice? If everything was created according to God's will.'

'What did your teachers say?' asks the boy, seeming intent on being found worthy.

'You've heard about respecting the mystery?' Henry asks. 'The contradictions. They would say exactly the same thing about the Eucharist.'

'But what no one's ever explained in a satisfactory way to me, Henree, is why bother judging value at all, when God makes the yardstick at the outset. You know — *I am the true Vine, and my Father is the Vinedresser.*'

'Right, go on.' Henry warms to this boy, one practically speaking his own thoughts. If he could, he would sit up but all strength has drained out of him.

'*He's* the one who gives this one grace and that one an afterlife destiny, no matter how many things you recite. So why does man need to decide what's moral or not?'

The discussion's so interesting Henry almost forgets its purpose. The moments after a fit are the worst. If someone stays close he can make it through. And he has two here. Two people. A girl crouching on the floor nearby, her eyes a numinous sibyl's. This is who? A maid?

His maid. 'Ever find out her name?' Henry asks his boy.

'Nani,' Johnny answers too quickly; the finger jumping again to his lip and the girl ready to bolt at her mention.

'Nani — anyway, in all modesty,' Henry continues; bound to his bed, Henry is determined to tell the boy of his past life.

As he talks, Johnny's face drifts away and Henry finds himself again in the grip of his father. Of childhood in which spare walls led to a single catacomb composed of morning song and mystery: the Episcopal apostolic succession. His father tended toward the Latin, unlike any other local rector, and though he didn't use much incense did sing *ex-cel-sis De-o* instead of *exalted God.* And young Henry got caned for being too scared to address God directly, for singing it as *eggshell seas day show.* Later his seminary teachers in their ivied cloister came to believe that such a promising student as Henry failed because of his passion and the way he let it trip up his reasoning. Henry had to subtract Henry out of Henry's understanding of the world — or that's what it sounded like. He never took that necessary leap toward a semblance of objectivity, injecting too much of his limited life experience into his theology.

And the young student had also lacked faith, never having fully surrendered himself to God's ministry. His Swiss and English mentors hinted about humility. Finally they considered Henry too much a Yankee, too headstrong to surrender to the call. The boy labored under fallacies, thinking all remained his doing and not his Maker's.

'How can you be both objective and humble?' Henry spirals off, remembering his worsening restlessness. 'They were right. I am willful. Otherwise, everything would've been easier for me. It's better to find understated graces in life.'

Johnny leaps up. 'Water?'

'I'll just finish, and then you —'

Henry needs his boy by him. It is only politeness that makes him abbreviate. He tells Johnny of the letter he received in 1914. While the Ceylonese were getting worked up about a nativist temperance movement, Henry was facing the war with his fraud recruits, thinking war had arrived in the nick of time, capable of soothing all betrayals. For ten years after the war, he'd been a journalist investigating bank fraud, Tammany Hall–style corruptions. Then, as a compromise with himself, he full-circled back to the life of spirit. He started to investigate fraudulent occultists, covens and philters. Psychomancers and spirit-raisers. White magicians.

He loved to disrobe their fee-faw-fum and thaumaturgics on page one. To tell of the cheat machinery. The ashamed flying carpet shops forced to close down their jugglery and business. This was a blossoming field, apparently, no one else having dared to declare the trendy emperor naked.

In turn, Henry was offered speaking tours, book contracts, the love of rational women, induction into the Skeptical Inquirers' Society. He would have been able to continue his own fumigation scheme until kingdom come had it not been for the day in the farm-house, when he met Madame conducting one of her notorious séances.

He'd wanted to deny it but he knew. Here were no magical lights or wires or false volunteers. Such a mountain of a woman, there could be no arguing. He had never met anyone like her: all the hairs on his body told him she was the real thing. She set his teeth on edge.

It had been a farmhouse designed by Italian socialists, made up of pine logs and gargoyles leering down. It was under these knotted eaves that five seekers first sat together, in a light strangely stippled. Five around the table, five who would later form the nucleus of the first salon.

Oh, and Madame, how she had cracked her jokes, put them all at ease. 'I am not sure what we are doing here today,' she had admitted, once they had been introduced: a Welsh pharmacist, an Indian professor, Lady B., who confessed she was a sometime student of Balinese dance, and Henry (calling himself Jack Farquhar, a seminarian, not wanting to be unmasked as a journalist).

Madame's séances were known among seekers as the crème de la crème: elite and small gatherings in which what was observed could not be spoken of later. Just to attain entrance, months prior the four had been vetted by a blinking man with wispy blond hair who went by the name of Chateau.

It had been all too easy for Henry to second-guess all of Chateau's questions. Yes, he would not go insane hearing messages from the dead; no, he had never been directly involved in the military; of course, he had loved his pets when he was a child; and certainly, he would consider universal vegetarianism and suffrage values for which he would fight if necessary.

'You know,' Madame had said, after the introductions were through. 'I still love the yak-meat I ate as a child. And I hardly expect you to have been Saint Francis. The questions were only for Chateau to outline how you met them. Whether you'd be suitable for today.'

Like all the seekers, Henry was flattered; there had been no cost to come to this; rather, they had been chosen by some shadowy criteria.

'Call it my gift or my mission. I help people know they can speak with the life beyond.' She had gazed importantly around. The light made them into fantastic leopards, zebras, even Lady B. with her cameo's face. 'I like to divine who might most be in need of this knowledge.' Here Madame's nostrils dilated and she began to breathe fast and sharp little breaths. As if she ran up a hill while staying perfectly in place.

Henry surveyed the faces. He himself had never been called *upon* in any of his investigations. Always he had known how to make himself blend in with the backdrop. Now, with his fraud inspector's eye, he speculated on who might get chosen: Lady B., in his first encounter with her, had exactly the grace a woman like Madame would want to unseat.

But this had not been the case. Madame had pointed a stubby finger directly at *him*. 'You the seminarian! Jack not your name is it? You look like an ex-soldier! Never met a seminary-anything named Jack. Who is it for you? Your mother, right?'

Here is where his hairs rose, signaling she might be real. Henry just hung on to his seat. Yet anyone could say 'your mother' and produce this effect. He had to stay objective.

'How do you mean?' he asked, buying time. He wanted to flee but the door to the barn had been locked from the outside by this woman's creepy assistant.

'You blame everything on her since you were' — and her eyes rolled up, the breaths quicker upon one another — 'three or four? Your father avoided talking to you about it, right?'

'All right.' Henry would let her play bones and ivories with him. This upped the ante of what he had come for.

'Reluctant to talk with her?'

'Why not?' He had the idea about himself that he would never turn truant from a job's demands. Broad-shouldered, brave, he'd never desert, he'd take slings as they came.

But by agreeing to this woman's whim, he waived the chance to withdraw subtly from the séance. And gave up any hopes of objectivity. There went his journalist's penetrating eye. And there went the article. As Madame began her uphill breathing, one more chapter in her life-work, he shrank from the table, his hands simultaneously hot and wet and cold. He wanted to fade into the dark but couldn't: they were all watching him as if he himself were a magic lantern.

And she, she was doing nothing but breathing that rapid oscillation. Slowly she started to make the motions of someone sprucing a table, neatening edges, polishing silver. Trimming wicks, laying placemats and plates. She washed down something that might have been an invisible sideboard; wiped it; stood to mop and swab down the barn's matted hay.

Around the table she walked, eyes fixed on the gargoyles grinning down at them. Climbed up some unseen but evidently narrow stairs, ten of them (he counted), just as many as in his childhood house — one for each commandment.

Piece by piece she removed imaginary items of clothing, down to a slip. Very like his mother: as though Madame had become a thinner, younger woman, one with a brazen strength. She polished shoes, plucked at her eyebrows, hiked up stockings, her movements faster and faster. Washed her hands, yanked on a fan-string; lifted a crying baby and soothed it back to sleep. Sprayed perfume in the air to test it, and then turned it on herself.

He was shivering as she glanced out a window and pulled on a dress. Pinned drop earrings on, brushed her hair, stared appraisingly in the mirror and then with one act sliced Henry's heart: leaning forward, skimmed on lipstick, made her mouth into the lopsided halves of a harp.

Lipstick!

She pressed her lips into a thin line, pouted and gazed again critically at herself.

'Stop,' Henry found himself saying, 'fine, sufficient, I don't need to know more, please —'

— his hands on her, he didn't mean to, he pulled at that velvety waist until she gasped, shaking her head, staring at him with his mother's eyes. With wild eyes. Finally with her own astringent, amused stare. 'Please?' he begged, 'can't you stop please?'

After the séance, he had taken a long walk with her to a windy bluff under elms reaching over the Hudson's gray. She had taken a cheroot with her, sucking on it as they walked. To her he revealed his identity (Henry Fyre Gould, man of many projects) and past (projects not fully realized for reasons mainly extrinsic). He did not undignify Madame by asking for a quid pro quo. For her to unveil, for example, how his mother, so long gone, had come to inhabit the Russian's shiplike body.

Because like so many he was simply grateful to her: for having allowed the moment to occur and, also, for having stopped at his request. Every fiber in him told him that despite all her encrusted persona and eccentricity, Madame was the pukka black diamond, the bedrock he'd been searching for; an incomparable Simon Pure; some kind of home truth, the *ipsissima verba*, the natural *real* thing he'd been craving all his years as a journalist.

She did not do her thing selfishly, bilked no one, supported by contributions 'which come when they come.' She stated again without arrogance that she had a gift and it came with a responsibility. 'I would give it up if I could,' she said, 'but this is not how one should treat such an obvious calling.'

They had an immediate rapport: she told him as much; begged him to call her Elena, not Madame. She had felt their kinship not only when he had walked into the barn but even earlier, when Chateau had described him. And she'd known he was using a guise, whether because of a shared past life or her Masters who told her such things, yet she hadn't wanted to disturb him too much.

She'd also said they should start a salon: 'You and I the founders. We complement each other perfectly. I have been waiting for you. We will create a new society, one better than this.'

I have been waiting for you. That was all he heard. He loved those words more than any others. The idea of someone waiting for him.

'With her, you couldn't exactly answer no,' he tells Johnny, who leans forward, mouth half open, the floor creaking under him. 'How do you refuse a volcano?'

'Extraordinary,' Johnny says. 'I wish I could meet a deva like that.'

'She's no deva!' Henry pounds the bed next to him. 'You're not getting it! I haven't told you the rest. Elena's no mystery! She's just an ordinary woman who happens to have a psychological gift. You and I might think we have a thermometer to gauge people. But she has a million times the mercury we do. It's not extrasensory anything. She just clamps on. It's sensitivity. Nothing more.'

'Clamps on? Anyway, you didn't marry her? No one's coming to fetch you from Ceylon?'

Henry chokes. 'Maybe you're not getting the picture. Madame's more someone who mates with herself. A kind of Russian snail. She's sixty and probably has been sixty since she was three.'

'Righto.' The boy seems at a loss. 'Where is she now?'

'Eating truffles in New York. Or intoning mantras in her salon. No, I forgot. She's taken vows of silence with a lama for ten years.

That's the last I heard. She'll change her name from Elena to some-thing like Guru Nam Kalpa.'

'And you're here in a Ceylon bed.'

'Exactly. We had big dreams together.'

The boy stares at him the way many children do at their adults while the adults reminisce about some Before time. Before the bicycle. Before the War . . . Henry's own son Daniel often had the same look: a child recognizing that adults have their curious mental play-things.

'Know what the extraordinary thing is, Johnny?'

The boy stoops to hear him. Henry's voice is giving out.

'I've never been closer.'

'Closer to what?'

'Closer than I am this moment to that first vision I had with Ma-dame on that bluff.'

'You had some kind of society.'

'And now you're going to help us form the real model society. You're going to be the one, Johnny.'

'The one?' The boy's alarmed voice fades. A potent sleep is re-claiming Henry. 'Which one?'

'You'll help us. We're going to release a tradition's power, Johnny. The sacred . . .'

True friendship, he hears her milk-gargling accents, *true friendship Henri should never depend on anything so incidental as geography autog-raphy pyrography eschatography verminography scatology smutography tautology . . .*

When he wakes, briefly, the light already slanted, the maid — Nani — is whispering as though to him, face urgent, looking be-yond. With all the explosions of her language, its puffs, hisses, rain on aluminum — she is trying to tell him something.

'I'm sorry,' he tells her, 'try in English.' Was he dreaming? That he should actually hear her mouthing words in English as though from a great distance? Slow, Herculean, kneehigh-to-a-grasshopper words. At first he can't understand the scale of this English, the words as though she knew only to read them aloud, perfect words like something that happened to another Nani. Slow at first and then a rush of them formed into a story of a girl — a story about sis-ters and a father and a house.

She goes on talking until the hour when quiet crosses interiors so the only sound left is the rubbing of curtains against each other and a distant hammering across the valley. He awakes alone. Had it been a dream after all or had there been (somewhere in the lifting haze of sickness) her voice?

19

On SEPTEMBER 7, 1886, Wooves wrote:

The tiny man who brings my coconuts just told me an outlandish folktale about how the earth and sky came to coëxist. It is here notated, only slightly embellished, in order to record the temperament of the people. This is what the man said:

A long time ago there lived a servant-girl who found herself annoyed by the clouds afloat while she swept her compound (the enclosure around the house). To her, these clouds were no small aggravation but rather a living nightmare.

One morning while this naughty girl was sweeping her compound as part of her daily routine, the clouds flocked thick as young lambs, bumping and sticking on her broom-stick. She found it hard to continue to push and pull the broom in exactly the way she knew to be best.

Further, this was not a girl famous for patience, as you will see. Finally, when no one was about, she gave a smart blow to the firmament with the broom-stick, stamped her foot and shouted for the clouds to leave. 'Clouds, you are upsetting me,' she cried, 'more than you can know. Please be kind and leave me alone. Find someone else to jumble up with your cloudy ways!'

Of course the sky felt deeply ashamed, as these Ceylonese believe both in shame and that a clout by a broom-stick is the worst affront one human can visit on another. Indeed, demons are afraid of being struck by brooms. Fearing future shames and broom-stick whippings, the sky thus flew far away, far out of human reach, in order to avoid having to lose face in such a grievous manner ever again. This story explains why stars no longer are the lamps on our homes, and why the sky hangs so sadly, so far away from all of us.

'Listen, we've got to get you to learn English,' Henry tells the maid. Having recovered during the night from yesterday's little fit, his initial idea this morning had been to make better use of his legs and get about in the fresh air. Yet despite himself, all morning he has stayed in the library, peeking at Wooves' diary until something about the man disgusts him. He called her then, to get her to help him garden.

They are sowing lavender in a plot behind the house. He admires the attention and understanding her hands show the compact dirt, which presents a challenge — hard at first, what one of his childhood nannies would've called a souse's-brains dirt, crumbly and fertile only after a bit of plowing.

And the care she shows the seeds. She has a knack with *things within her own sphere*, a kindness, and he will develop this thought later, this in-her-own-sphericity, doesn't it promise some fruit?

For now, what he has just said about her learning English needs more explanation. Her eyes probe him as though he's a creature hard to understand.

'English, yes? Because I can't always have Johnny right next to me, you know, translating.'

He repeats himself more loudly. To no avail. She only stares at him. He must have hallucinated her story about a family. After all, how *could* she know his language? It certainly wouldn't have been the first time after a fit that he imagined someone whispering to him in a shared, semiprivate dialect. Her sisters and father: they must be just another part of his dreams, something else he has associated with the wrong person.

'So I'm mistaken,' he says aloud. 'It's not the first time. You don't have to look at me that way.' She is rather rude in her staring and he can't help being aware of the pulse beating at the base of her throat right where the lovely bones knit to make a hollow. The purplish thorn scratchings on her hands and dowel arms. 'Okay, I'll explain later,' he says. 'It's just I think we'd get on much better if you could bring yourself to learn English. Eeeeenglish? No comprendes?'

But she has already returned to furrowing the compact soil.

20

BETWEEN THE GARDEN she has come to and the garden she is beginning, neither has borne any real fruit yet. There are things to buy. Gourds and rampe karapincha, to start with, pumpkins and curry leaf. Her peculiar blushing man has taken a liking to curry, that much is clear, he had shown Nani with huge gestures how much he'd liked hers. With him everything had to be big big big all the time. He had pointed to his big pink tongue. And had lifted his shirt to reveal a stomach with weird red-black hair curling on something too hollow for such a big man. 'I like!' he had shouted in his big way. Was she supposed to be impressed by the tongue or the stomach? Maybe by his slurred language? 'I like!'

In that same language she had dared whisper to him something of her life. But this was when he was so crazy-sick, lying there, eyes rolled up in his head. She'd thought it wouldn't matter what she told him. Because talking could help any sick man, everyone knows that. And it had been easy to see he needed someone to speak to him on any subject. She had worked hard to use the language that was his, what she knew from reading with the herb doctor long ago. That she had bothered to make this attempt, was this what had invited him closer?

Because now he so often weighs upon her, whether she's gardening or cleaning or cooking. He clutches and lunges. Shows up in places most men never go. Nani! he calls in his jabbing voice, one both high and low at the same time. Sometimes she will be cooking and he will carry a stool from the library out to the patio. Sit tight-lipped as though admiring the yard. But really she knows it is to assess her chopping and frying.

I am not interested in poisoning anyone, she wants to tell him. From his roost he watches until her hands get clumsy from such watching. She often has to disappear around a corner long enough to get him to take the hint and his stool and disappear.

Sometimes it is more than a relief to leave the house and instead walk along the canal at the hour of the small chewed-up winds and their afternoon rising. It is soothing to see the same mountains as those flanking her coastal village but set down closer and higher, the same sour-faced palms but bunched tighter and thinner. Here the wind is slower and more exact as though it blows through a sieve. Different yet also the same, this comfortable land — it almost returns childhood's first freedoms.

Walking to the market by the bridge, it is a giddy relief *not* to be known. To move among people who ask the usual *Where are you going?* and to whom she answers *Nearby*. But nothing else needs to be said. The more they would come to know her, the more an inexcusable stranger they would find her — and they seem to guess this, and so leave well enough alone. And she does not care about the whispers that follow her. It is after all a relief to move among villagers who resemble long-ago uncles and aunts and other heroes, yet without their knowing more than her name.

In her wake she has also heard them saying the bad things about the foreigner who moved into the Pilima house. They had been expecting a Pilima scholar named James who would help make the Pilimas' history and needs known to the West. Instead a foreigner came and who knows what he wants exactly? They call him vicious knotted names — a cockroach, a karapote — just as they would any pink man, but they say he's a new and worse kind. Worse than the English, because who knows what a Burgher from America wants? While she thumbs overripe mangosteen and golden keselgedi at the market, she never lets any of their whispers distract her.

Because always on her way to the market, she passes through the devale that faces the big temple. The smaller temple for the gods looks with no appetite from its canalside perch up at the large Buddha, at the Sacred Tree and the monk's temple. The devale is its own place and it is also hers. Here she always sets her empty market basket down. Among other women who pray in their desultory afternoon way, she walks easily, near the skin of the devout without having to meet anyone's gaze. The best part is how each woman raises her own dust and chooses her own god, whether one reared up on a red silk stage, behind an inner lace veil and frosty glass, or a god nude on a tapered iron pedestal, ready for pleadings and small winds.

After her few weeks here at this temple she especially loves Saman, his splendid expensive eyes, and stands before him and his elephant's trunk long enough for him to bless her and this new life. When no one looks she touches his long nose once for good luck. And once again so luck will stay. His eyes recognize her more than any villager does, and to him alone she speaks, barely moving her lips. She has worked hard to be anonymous.

Once Saman has heard her benediction and prayer, she leaves in luxury, taking her basket to proceed along the road, past houses with hillside paths wound tight around them.

But it is today (in looking up one of the paths) that she sees the peculiar: the house's trodden boy, Jehangir with his nervous memory and ways, sitting at a card table hidden behind the palms. Not alone either. Like an old friend he is talking agreeably with a tall cockroach. An English roach, it looks like, someone who despite his thin frame must be — from all the bright gold roti on the uniform — a commander. An aged English commander with so many golden pancakes on his blue shoulders. His face also bluish as though recently bled. And, leaning against the table, between Jehangir and the roach — a long, copper-plated gun, bigger than any she has ever seen.

As a child she had witnessed English troops moving down the main road by her house. Then they had been distant unequal men. Squads alerted to her village because of the frequent sea storms. That's how her father had explained them. No one had ever sat with them like Jehangir is doing now. Jehangir? That oddity friendly with a commander, a man whose face grizzles at the edges before dwindling to nothing. To such a face, she would be invisible and so can stop on the road. And observe the shared labors above, how carefully the commander listens as the boy explains something. And see how the commander slides a pen into the boy's quivering hand and waits. Until Jehangir signs one paper, and then another, and then another yet again.

She stands amazed watching this flourish and signing by the boy with his bad memory. If she could spell out the boy to herself, she would. But she can't, he is too hidden, like house things that want to stay sheltered under fancy ragged cloth. She watches him explain and then sign some more, his hands in speech ever more rapid. She leaves without having to see the boy's finger fly up to his mouth as he does in the house whenever he spots her. But she will not forget, though she will try, how while Jehangir had signed the papers his own face had glowed and then tightened some more, just as though he stood in line getting ready to be shot.

21

A YEAR BEFORE he met the foreigner, Jehan was keeping a map of London folded in his white shirt pocket and was ready to set sail for Oxford. He calculated on jumping aboard a ship, retaining passage by the power of his speech, and landing in the famous square's center. He felt sure he would be recognized as different by a scholar who heard the high class of his elocution.

He would be taken in and have apartments on the Thames. After that his dreams wavered. He would study vast fields. Literature. Jurisprudence. Philosophy.

Oxford and London were identical to him. He loved smokestacks. He would take walking tours of the Lake District, follow the path of those rambunctious pilgrims whose book was forbidden by Ceylon's missionary schools, lose himself in the moors and then have tea at four to discuss his scholarship with an envious peerage.

For this he had fled his village.

He would stake life out on the playing field pitted between those who believed in him and those who had been cruel. With his accomplishments, he would make the believers proud and punish the doubters. When the results of his many games would out, his believers would be rewarded with a meaningful if obscure victory.

But the port British had intercepted his journey by hiring him more quickly than any imagined Oxford don could have set him to parsing Latin. Recognizing certain aptitudes, as well as a forged passport, they set him on various trails: detective, escort, spy.

For a year they'd kept him engaged in certain official tasks, some more interesting than others. Jehan had learned how to beat himself at chess, to announce ship movements from a cramped studio, to tap Morse backwards. He shadowed a card shark by the Colombo port, nabbed a deputy government agent gone mad, and notarized a customs official's fatally greedy words. He never considered stowing away again — being caught once had left him feeling soiled enough.

He so excelled at any task given him that for a finale they set him on the American.

'Not a monster,' Jehan was told. 'This Yankee colonel's nothing compared to some of the types you'd find left over from our Great War. Not like anyone you'd find in some of the contained skirmishes we must manage from time to time. But especially with things' — a wave of the hand from which Jehan was to understand prior discussions touching on aggression, territory, Hitler, holdings, the Sudetanland, unpredictable Americans, a current precipice — 'you understand, things as they are, it is in everyone's interest that we track certain incomers, American or German — does it really matter after a war and with so many battles afoot?'

Jehan had asked what then made the colonel so dangerous. 'He's an old intelligence hand. Yankees call their spies *fraud inspectors* — it is not unlikely this colonel is our first American envoy to Ceylon, performing a little reconnaissance.'

Jehan had wanted to know if an American couldn't be coming to Ceylon just for pleasure. He did not want to feel useless in his employ. That would exhaust him too much before his term expired.

'The Yanks have always called Ceylon strategic. They'll want to start up a masked naval intelligence base. You can count on it. And we have to take care of ourselves. Madras sometimes leaves us Colombo hands in the dark. They don't recognize what we're up against.'

The British had been privileged to receive tip-offs, advance notice of the colonel's arrival, direct from his former friends. News reports of the colonel's American success. Rumors about fraud inspection units involved in counterespionage with the Russians, the Austrians. 'And this man has a clever front. He presents himself as a dumb American, apparently. A bit addled at the kick-off, if you see the point.'

Jehan didn't.

'Everywhere the colonel has gone he makes himself look stupid. It's a ruse. He got involved with some spiritual quackery out in New York. Just to set everyone off his trail. He's gone so far as to claim to be a Buddhist.' It was not improbable that this man would find a way to work with the socialists, the Tamil Congress, or Ceylon's local nationalizers, the young insurgent boys. 'He is dangerous, you'll see. He created a public outrage in New York by cremating a few of his own followers. One can imagine. He needs someone equally clever to keep him in check. We think you're the boy for the job.'

Flushing at the praise, not wanting to flush, Jehan had inquired about the appropriate methods to be used.

'One controls Yanks by pretending to help them. Stay positive. Help with his plans. You'll get a stipend for your private use. Then you'll be allocated certain sums to shunt toward him and his ideas. At the end of it, you'll see, all this will go into your dossier. And each man will catch his prize in due time.'

All Jehan would have to do was file reports, every other day, then weekly once a pattern got established, and that would be it, the sum of his duties. 'Shadow him,' they said. 'Humor him. Never lack for ideas. Most important is keep your cover for the initial period' — only twelve months, Jehan thought, *nothing* compared to a season spent in rice paddy or a clerk's cubicles — 'perhaps an extension to follow, and afterward we guarantee whatever you want. A King's College scholarship? Oxford? No less.'

True to what the Brits had promised about the colonist's bonho-mie, the Yankee had taken him on more quickly than any scholar populating Jehan's dreams. Music danced on the surface of Jehan's skin when he'd seen the pinkness seated next to him at the Colombo port.

Conceivably this would be the man to help young Nelligodam slip-knot his clerk's fate. Henry Fyre Gould could be the final ticket to London and Oxford. As they spoke in the port, it became clear as Kandy's own lake to Jehan that no matter the understanding with the British, he'd do well to attach himself to this Yankee colonel.

This would be work with a man who proved to be generous and, in an additional grace note, blind to class. Their implicit bargain transcended the terms of its creation, didn't it? Jehan would give the foreigner access to the abundant life he so obviously craved. The foreigner would give Jehan a certain foothold on the future. And immediately, the foreigner had designated Jehan apprentice idealist, a role Jehan's been preparing for his whole life, one he's happy enough to play.

Meanwhile, every other day or so, unhampered, Jehan toodles off, and, feeling like a fiendish child, sends a telegram on the American spy's activities from the camphor-stuffy regional office in Kandy. The colony clerk knows the Ceylonese boy by now, beginning to print out the address form as soon as Jehan steps through the door. As for Henree, he has not yet questioned his Johnny's import/export business, one which requires such copious telegraphing. Henree is, as the British had promised him, entirely too self-obsessed a Yankee to pay much notice to any clandestine activity under his own roof. At times, caught up in his planning, the man will speak to Jehan as though to an item ready to be ticked off a laundry list: and then — the necessary moment — he'll seem to remember he is addressing a human, he'll apologize, go deeply into handshaking, punching Jehan's shoulder, performing any one of many bizarre gestures.

Actually, the detail Henree fails to notice is legion. Even the way Jehan had, after that first introduction, taken the *m* off his last name, and so passed as a Sinhala with a name like Nelligoda. Not Nelligoda*m*, which would have been the name of the Tamil he (partly) was. Henree would be too squeamish, perhaps, to sense that his rising sun and protégé was considered a sans-culotte. He would not wish to know how the difference among Sinhalese and Tamil and Muslim might be important to some people.

All cards down, Jehan hasn't gathered a single clue about Henree's purported life as a secret agent. Rather, the man looks to be a do-gooder; at worst, a misinformed busybody. Yet the Oxford deal must not be rescinded — were Jehan to tell the Brits his instincts, he might be dismissed from this lush situation. Because why should a Ceylonese be paid to track just an ordinary American? Infinitely better to pull them along. To keep everyone thinking Henree a spy. His mother used to quote from the vedas: *Unity is knowledge, diversity is ignorance.* Jehan will keep everyone unified with their own knowledge about espionage. He will not give up his charge so quickly. Never before has he had such an interesting case.

22

IN THE MARKET, only Zahir the trader, Roshan the young watch-fixer, and the knife-sharpener whose name no one remembers would say openly that the presence of this new American cockroach could be good for the village. They were the only three to claim, individually, that the foreigner's face, as glimpsed through the hedges, was a kind one. Zahir found it confused, and Roshan happened to find it heedless, a bit bloated with vague good will. But these were the three to argue that from what they had observed it was not an *unkind* face.

No one had seen much more than they had, but such opinions could be quickly discounted. Everyone knew Roshan was too friendly for his own good; Zahir was a Muslim trader, too accustomed to consorting with people who weren't Sinhalese; and the knife-sharpener's mind had been lost somewhere during days strolling the road with his whetstone playing its nationalizing anthems.

The foreigner — they called him either the American cockroach or the Yankee Burgher — he became among marketgoers of low and high breeding the season's topic, more interesting than the usual predictions of drought, the smooth-rimmed rice fields that would be ruined this year, or those whose voices hushed as their fathers' new poverty would keep them from marrying.

Only the old-timers remembered the Englishman Wooves, who'd gone pissu, fully mad, in the same house. Before he'd gotten shipped back to whatever place gives birth to such mad cockroaches, Wooves had tried to cut down some branches from the Sacred Tree. As for the younger Rutaevans, they had never seen a foreigner come to live in their midst, pretending to be a Rutaevan himself.

When new reports came out, the roach had been sighted — and more than once — bathing in the back of his house with a dhoti wrapped around his lower half. They'd seen his bare chest like some fantastic pink loaf of bread, broad and covered with awful red and gray and black hair, a walking jungle for flies.

And when *she*, the roach's girl, would come marketing, the women would slow down choosing vegetables for their baskets. The problem was her proud carriage, as though she came trailing feathers and gold. Had this girl once been pretty queen of her native village? That bothered them. As though having once believed herself to be queen, this girl wasn't going to let anyone in her new village forget it. The insolence, it should be slapped off a person! Who needed such bad behavior?

She maybe took rude cues from that roach of hers. She didn't meet their eyes and answered only dimly. *O, naeae, samehare witte* — who wanted such *yes, no, sometimes, maybe?* Was this Nani girl his wife? his concubine? They asked her where was her village and she would snap: *In the south.* Who were her people? *You wouldn't know them.* Clearly she thought herself too good (even if something soft did stay around the eyes). They left her mostly alone.

In the huge house the Pilimas had long left to ghosts, the American roach lived with that outlandish girl and, worse, with a boy whose Sinhala came out in one big torrent, a Sinhala that made your ears wither. Always a Sinhala which prated on about a model village this and a model village that and wouldn't the boy ever stop talking for a second?

The pragmatists who had never needed any model anything and who spent their afternoons under the ambalama's russet shade came to their decisions. The American roach was certainly a mercenary come to plunder what remained of their local wealth after the tobacco and coffee plantations had crashed. The most pessimistic among the pragmatists believed the roach to be a slave trader, ready to suck the life out of the village — for wasn't it only recently that the African slaves had won their lives back in America, and then not even fully?

Among the pessimists, the more pragmatic decided to protect their children from foreign influence by keeping them at home during the day. No point in being foolishly sociable. Was it impossible that the strange boy Jehan had come as well to kidnap their children, to be more slaves for America, or for some mercenary war? Jehan's talk of a village of the future — was this not just a slave trader's pretty talk?

You could tell the boy almost didn't believe his own words. He spoke like someone spying on himself, flabbergasted to find himself burping out speech. He was not Sinhala or Tamil or Muslim or English but some odd combination of all that. Why should anyone trust a hybrid?

Meanwhile, among the pragmatists, the more pessimistic were to be found among the Pilima family, whose own history warned them. Within the Pilimas, it was Lester who especially resolved to master this foreigner's game and prospects. Already, the Pilimas had been duped into thinking that James, an illustrious Buddhist scholar, had been coming to rent Wooves' house. Not only was James known for his piety, but he was a distant cousin besides, coming from good Pilima lineage. Had the Pilimas realized a *cockroach* would come, an American cockroach at that, no Pilima would ever have consented to loan out the place.

But now the Pilimas (and hence the villagers around them) were stuck with this spiky ménage: the cockroach, the boy, the arrogant girl. The Pilimas' discussions revolved around this: that the three in that house should be managed. Perhaps Pushpa, being a woman, should be sent in their midst, to keep an eye on their doings. Of course, she should only do this to the extent that she could stomach such an unpalatable task. The Pilimas' main verdict was that the three strangers must be kept within the Pilimas' jurisdiction and on Pilima grounds. And it was this last decision that would ooze down, almost to the very bottom of the village's castes.

23

I wished merely to view their sports, as a cricket fan might, and told them as much; but to this, they responded only by goggling at me, as was their custom, their eyes widening until they became platen moons. In order to get anywhere at all, I found instead that I must indeed enter a neighboring dwelling and accept their hospitality. They were keen that I imbibe some of their famous thambili, the

*cooling coconut juice. About this alleged property of
the juice, they showed an exaggerated piety, as
though I had been deemed a person prone to chaleur.
Perhaps needless to record, in drinking during such
canicular heat, I was forced to pay little heed to
the china service, composed of earthenware tureens
in which rough pores had absorbed generations upon
generations of village saliva*

Henry's eyes blur upon Wooves' cagey script. Despite a heat which *was* turning a little doggish, he's set on proceeding methodically, in sections, from the beginning of the government agent's notes through to the end. In this way he can stretch out their pleasure. While he often feels himself superior to Wooves, he is also his student; Wooves' notes will be an almanac to mark his own place. He will write from the middle of the same book onward, a response and bettering of what Wooves may have accomplished during his years as a government agent.

August 19?, 1936

He scrawls this under his own last entry. Is it Wednesday? Thursday? An almond-shaped leaf from the ancient mango tree above falls within the book.

What exists here is creation's fifth-day harmony. I will not be
change in itself but a marker. Just as shoes suggest feet, just
as all abandoned tables and chairs in this boatlike house
point ahead to the life that will fill it, I will signal ahead to
the sixth-day splendors — the wonder of these Ceylonese &
their potential — & the fermentations of the seventh.

There are consequences which a more religious man than
myself would say redound after one's life. May it be so for my
good works here?

What is already here — he orders the list he gathered from Johnny:

Arecanut, banana (7 kinds, including apple banana & the two
curatives for both stomach distresses), betel (bulat), breadfruit (del), cocoa, coriander (for fever, called kottumali),
coconut (king and thambili), guava, jakfruit (kos), kitul palm
(for the sugar the peasants like, & also the liquor arakku),

lime, lovi, mangoes, mangosteen, mora, olive, pawpaw
(papaya), pineapple, plantain, pineapple, pomegranate,
rambutan, rose apple, sapodilla, slime apple, tangerine,
wood apple

Too many kinds of apple, for one thing. The women he sees passing on the canal road below are scrawny. They require greater nutritional variety. His pen poises.

This is temptation, the savoring of an idea from childhood's most
perfect games: how, from a blank enough slate, to create a world
which makes sense.

Apple, he writes, and then adds *Washington* before the apple.

apricot, black currant, cherry, fig, gooseberry, grape,
grapefruit, lemon, mangetout peas, melon, orange, peach,
pear, plum, raspberry, strawberry

On stray papers Henry has begun to sketch *modest* clothing which
will withstand tropical temperatures; dwellings that convect heat;
filtration systems able to suppress damp; canal-dredgers adept at siphoning bottom slime up onto a seagoing raft.

He draws what Johnny describes as being typical of the distant
coast: palms swayed by ocean breezes. Palms which hide clapping
girls in folkloric dress. And the images satisfy him. 'Not half bad,'
says Johnny, when pressed.

Henry's imagination is fired. He draws everything Johnny's described. The young boys who hitch themselves up trees where they
run on tightropes between high stalks while carrying syrup buckets.
He sketches a British officer whose attenuated shoulders carry icons
for rubber pots, tea pots, coffee pots.

'You might have become a political cartoonist,' Johnny tells him
one morning in the library. The new pinkish curtains Nani has hung
filter in enough sun to make Johnny almost ruddy. 'Really. You're
good. Why didn't you?'

'Not enough bravery,' Henry laughs. 'You're flattering me, right?'

Johnny claps his hand to his forehead. 'With flattering lips and a
double heart do they speak —'

Henry finishes it. 'The Lord shall cut off all flattering lips and the
tongue that speaketh proud things. You're well-schooled!'

'You're the flatterer.'

'No, Johnny, I just know a lie when I hear one.'

'Why care about sketches? don't you seem to master most every-thing else?'

Henry takes a swipe at Johnny, who drops back quickly. What wouldn't Henry have given to have had this rapport with his own son? Maybe Daniel has not yet arrived at the right age. When Henry feels better he must consider writing his son. Someone must be force-feeding church to the boy right now — whether it be Clara or Clara's father — good as cod liver oil, open up and down the gullet.

Unforced by anyone, Henry could grow to trust this Johnny. There's been a benefit to staying indoors a bit and getting his Cey-lon legs. And the drawings help define the project ahead. They might be cartoonish but then they're also the equivalent of British voodoo dolls. Little dolls of the colonizers whose plantations have blighted this good people's self-sufficiency; dolls of the colonizers he has come to turn around.

In between drawing he has been making lists:

> Ask Johnny to hire good local men to begin model garden.
> Keep log of observations of locals & customs.
> Find field guide to local plants.
> Translate the people's historic chronicle.
> A tutor for me in local language: Sinhalese? the local monk?
> Tour village & surrounding areas with Johnny.
> Note natural resources. Use abandoned coffee plantation
>   for model garden?
> Start enlisting locals in plans.
> Tour, study & pray with Buddhist monk.
> Write to this area's British Government Agent.
>
> Think of the people's:
>
>> 1) Health & Hygiene
>> 2) Education
>> 3) Agriculture
>> 4) Culture & Religion
>> 5) Morality
>> 6) Other

He is proudest of the sweetener he will institute — for himself first, and then for the locals. Being in principle and action against the sugar trade, he asks Johnny what the locals use for their tea.

'Hakuru,' Johnny says, 'brown palm sugar. The *adu minisu*, lower types, are prone to sipping tea and then eating the sugar in chunks.' Such a separation sounds insane. Plates and saucers could be divided, but certain experiences must happen at the same time: tea *and* sugar.

The plan they come up with is that Henry will have Johnny trade for beeswax from beekeepers down south. Nani will rig muslin bags from the kitchen's open-walled ceiling and let the honey drip through to bowls. This would be Henry's protest against the inequities of sugar plantations. With the used-up wax, the people can make candles.

This will be yet another way in which Rajottama can take a principled stand in the world of villages — being a village of the future. What Henry especially likes is the social idea of wax, which bees transform through effort as a group, each bee knowing its contribution.

Perhaps, too, he will ask Nani to prepare one of the house's abutments as a potential room for Daniel. A bed made to fit his son, a little highboy cabinet, and the gifts Henry would periodically install within: to conjure away his fatherly absence. Tonight perhaps he will leave the first gift for Daniel: a man's bearded head carved out of coconut, which he had found on the main lawn, along with a broken toy ship.

24

How FAR HENRY has come from his first break from Elena, the days of his speechifying, lecturing there on an actual soapbox: under a statue overlooking the desolate faces streaming past the park's southwestern tip, at New York's suicidal buckle, a neat walk from the salon. At the crossroads where dodgy shards of New York mixed and lost themselves, ran out into the streets. Where they needed enlightenment most. Salon-goers had too much time and money on their hands. But Henry's democratic crowd had everything. The recently impoverished, the permanently wealthy. The old-timers, the arrivistes, the wax-skinned shopgirls. The black overcoats and moleskin jackets, Harris tweeds, pillbox hats . . .

He spoke to the unsheeplike cores behind these personae and gathered himself a following with regular hours. Wednesdays at six, Fridays at noon. He did not want their muttonlike obedience. He asked questions, socratically encouraged their own, and all along his ostensible pasture was Buddhism, in which he had read widely but not deeply. As he preached a pure wisdom tradition, he knew on the one hand that he was an utter fraud, the kind he himself might have rummaged out and shamed in his old days as an inspector: what could *he* know about Buddhism? But on the other hand, his questions to them endowed any hapless listener with self-awareness; and the *purity* of it all was superior to this mixing and daubing from everywhere and proclaiming such a syncretic smelting the only truth.

And he also knew — from the shy questions and forward letters that often got thrust his way after he ended a discourse — that he managed to touch some of these people. Or he blotted up their dissatisfactions. He was not his father's son for nothing. For a moment he helped them bear life's little burdens, much as his father had done, much as he had been trained to do in his own forsaken ministry.

At the pith of things, he converted his audience to a way of thinking which — if not entirely at odds with the city's bold gothic — was nonetheless a different sea and dimension. A necromancer's work, one which could transport accountants, secretaries, policemen on horseback away from the quotidian. He did not bury them with a new mentality. He exhumed them from the old, let them mull their own wine. And this was all for the good, that Henry's baritone could solve so much, make people *behold*. He savored the change he might be making in their lives.

But it must have been the humid sop of a day Madame came by with her new friend — apparently by sheer chance, though one never knew with Elena — that Henry thought perhaps he'd gone too far in having started an open-air competition to Madame's salon. He had just finished discussing the first of Buddhism's four noble truths — *Life is suffering* — when he observed poking above the heads the ostrich feather. The feather of her peaked mauve hat, a summer oddity she favored in this Year of the Bird, as she alone had dubbed it.

She was with a small passionate man dressed entirely in ecru, whom she introduced afterward as James. 'I applaud your oration,' she declaimed, the usual cloud of violet perfume about her. Her beluga-fed, milk-gargling accents carried French and Russian in equal parts, and, depending on his mood, could either charm or annoy. In his heart, two months ago on that veranda, he had already said goodbye; had decided to put her and her sheep behind. But today, his guilt gnawed at him; he had been caught. All over again he found her perfect and revolting, in much the same way a starving man might regard an over-candied suckling pig.

The three of them had retired away from the throng of female well-wishers that tended to beset Henry after the discourses. 'You know I'd been wondering why you'd made yourself so scarce.' Elena was being arch, something never lost on Henry, who knew her better than any lover, past or present. She still was *his* Elena; not the public Madame. Because of this he knew, too, that she was somehow using him as a pawn to impress James who had traveled directly (she said with importance) from a reunion of Chicago's World Congress of Religions to attend a smaller parallel assembly in New York.

'In Chicago,' she announced. 'James is said to have cut a magnificent figure. He out-Protestanted a Protestant with watertight rhetoric in debate over Theravada Buddhism. You remember Theravada, Henri?'

One step below them, ignoring everything else, a young bony mother in a bag dress but with a face like satin had heaved herself down. With care she unpacked a half-eaten lunch for two smudged boys, both with the same bushy, serried expressions. She sat, a tranquil beauty with her face solar but vacant while her sons attacked the lunch. Watching her, Henry wanted to be the missing father in the quartet, able to make flare what was now just a hint of brightness.

Madame still carried on in her cartilaginous voice. 'The Theravadans emphasize self-restraint over love and good works. During all your incarnations you can't that easily dedicate yourself to others' salvation over your own. Can't as easily attain the bodhisattva ideal. Then there's that wily question of the no-soul. All the merit you collect in one life ends up in a heap. Castaway clothes for others to pick through, you see. Nothing belongs to your own soul in the next reincarnation. Because there is no consistent soul over all your lives. This is the most frequent Ceylonese view of things.'

'Thank you,' Henry had said. He hadn't known all that and would not have vouched for its truth. But he did know Madame was showing off to James by instructing Henry, Henry who in his public talk had only elaborated on a clear-cut Buddhist idea: what *life is change* and hence *life is suffering* could mean in Western terms: the death of fathers, mothers, friends. The loss of what ambition had promised could be your legacy. Or the endless change a city like New York used as seduction. Thus, in so many elaborate ways, Elena was saying that, in matters of spirit, Henry stayed a simpleton.

Ceylon, though, she knew she would catch Henry's attention uttering the word *Ceylon;* the teardrop-shaped island in the Indian Ocean, the name itself a special code between Madame and Henry. Two years earlier, the Masters in séances had transmitted through Madame's Ouija board, long before any schism or speechifying or James, that Henry and Madame should steam to Ceylon. Until Henry had pointed it out, the Masters had misspelled Ceylon in the Chinese fashion as *Ceilan.*

But why Ceylon? The Masters had stumbled over the alphabet on this point, growing tight-lipped, forcing Henry to dig up reasons. Was it the insularity of an island universe? They'd never explained why, but stayed adamant: Henry and Madame should start a branch of the society in Ceylon.

Henry turned to James. 'If it's true no consistent soul survives incarnations, we're lucky to meet you in this one,' which made no sense, but silenced Madame for a few moments.

'I *am* from Ceylon. Thank you, yes. A Theravada Buddhist but we don't have many other kinds in Ceylon. And actually there *are* good works that need to be done within this type of Buddhism, among the monks most of all,' said James.

This was a gentle correction of Madame. The rigorous calculus in James' eyes had been immediately appealing. But at the time Henry stayed unsure whether a more detailed template helped one distinguish life more carefully, as the novelist said was necessary to do, or in fact kept one from being alive to the surprises of the next moment and the next. He had suspended judgment on Madame's friend. But this was suspending judgment on someone who would, as it turned out, tinker so quickly with the balance of Henry's own fate.

James went on to describe his motherland in such rapture that all rigidity evaporated from the corners of his eyes. Henry could see the man in his former incarnations: James as a young Ceylonese boy teetering on the silvery tightropes between coconut palm fronds, above the red jacaranda, spiriting along syrup buckets.

Or balancing as a fisherman on a stilt-pole, above a sea so clear that at noon you'd find a tiny pebble twenty feet below. At dusk, he would be catching bright seerfish, his fellows similarly slicing the water. Years earlier *he* had been one of the toddlers he'd described, running after a coffee or tobacco train, waving . . .

'Yes, it's true, the English have given us trains and schools. Plantations — but also blight. Telephones in the main cities,' James continued, deep in his recitative. Henry felt like an attorney come to take a deposition from a stock witness, such was James' fluency. For all his vigor, the man lacked irony. 'Before them we had the Dutch, who were peaceful and friendly. Just conducting their business. The Dutch gave us Sinhalese aqueducts and lacy rice treats. Not much harm, you could say. And before them, the Portuguese, too, who gave us Christianity' — he harrumphed — 'and pigs, and dogs, but also married our girls. People cannot hate them wholly because our blood has mixed. O but the English are the best, people think. They are the kindest, with their Magna Carta and their enlightened ruling.'

What interested Henry more than anything was the tightness of the man's recital, strung between sarcasm and full-out anger.

'I'm telling you how people feel. Especially in their cities. But see! these English, they stay separate from us. All the better to rob us clean. Next generation coming up will have no clue about our tradition. What to do? Our people will be sipping their bitters and whiskey sours. Meanwhile they won't be able to recite a single line from our great epic about the Sinhalese nation. They'll stutter if you ask them about Buddhism and its struggles. We Buddhists, you see, we've never killed anyone — we never had a Crusades — and yet we are punished! We will have no clue that Ceylon is the land favored to protect and unite Buddhism' — he beat the air with his hands, winding up only because it was clear he could've kept tunneling deep into the colonizers' evil.

'A Sinhalese *nation?*' Henry asked. The breeze had just made the young mother's brown bag skid atop a border hedge.

'And why not? There are others, yes, among us in Ceylon. Tamils who are decent, whether Hindu or Christian. But you get it plainly from me — *we* are a *Sinhalese* people.'

Only months later would Henry learn how James, avid exponent of nation, had neglected to mention how the indigenous Ceylonese had been *one* people, rooted by prereligions. Even if language separated them, centuries of intermarriage made them like peas in a pod, their proudly invented claims of different Dravidian or Indo-Aryan lineages, heights and colors notwithstanding.

Henry was seized by the thought as if it were his own: 'You think the people could be turned around?'

'Ah, primitive techniques! We're laggards, far behind India's liberation struggle! *Because* we have no sense of ourselves as a single unit. As a nation. Colonialism gave too much — and claimed too little blood! Our accounting is biased! Only recently, now that some leftists have helped peasants with their malaria, now we have a feeling we could revolt against the English —'

'But suppose the revolution were cultural, not practical,' Henry began. He was having a hard time following the man, but thought it worthwhile. 'Say you began with everything you mentioned. The dance, the religious practices. A resurrection of Buddhism —'

James had been gazing upon Henry a long time. For the first time in the conversation, Henry was conscious of the orangey whiteness of his own skin, stretched tight as a drumskin, tingling.

That last month in New York, Henry had set about learning about Ceylon and the American in him had stirred: he was, after all, a body who lusted for origins. For the romance inherent in wheelbarrows, self-propulsion, calisthenics and the quest for truth. In Ceylon he could uplift the people away from the easy delights of railway lines and Catholic or Anglican schools. He could spirit them back to their roots; at least to their original questions.

25

THE TWELFTH MORNING in his room a hot yoke of dread weights down Henry's back.

Already the twelfth?

August 22? 1936 —

— and how is he supposed to begin the model society? He has to get out there. *In the field.* Should he learn the language first? Or risk offending the people and rely on Johnny to translate? He is too late for everything.

Slumped, he doesn't hear her enter. Without glancing at him, she's as much a phenomenon as wind or light. She stacks sheets and towels inside his armoire with a fanaticism he's coming to prize. Quick and neat hands. A braid arrowing down between her protuberant shoulderwings. And her spine's knobs becoming that small of her back, a strong tawny crescent between the short pale bodice and her dark skirt.

'Come here,' he says. Without meaning to, exactly, he pulls the threadbare gold tassel of the bedside servant bell so it clangs.

She turns from the closet, her face an inquiry. 'Mas-ter?' she says, so haltingly that both the word and its delivery half-kill him inside. He suspects she speaks more than this, but with him she uses only two English words. The other word being *Par-don.*

'I want you to knock before you come in,' he says. He doesn't know why he chooses to say this. He is no longer an invalid. He is storing up energy for the grand venture. He pantomimes his words over the fading bell.

'*O, o,*' she says, their *yes, yes* that sounds so much like dread or alarm. She steps back.

'That's fine,' he continues. 'You're fine.' He relaxes into the role. 'Listen, I don't mind about today. You didn't know. Next time.'

Her eyes are still behind the lids' tremble. Their outermost rims are a blue Johnny had derided as coastal, while brown rings around the large pupils. 'Your eyes,' he tells her. 'They're like a well that's stirred. Like sky *and* earth.' He can't help watching the pulse in her neck. 'What do you know about the village here?' he asks, for want of anything else to ask.

She shakes her head, uncomprehending. He mimes village life as he's imagined it from the little he saw on the journey up the mountain. Cooking, meeting. Praying. For once her hands are empty of laundry and she says nothing.

Finally, exasperated, he mimes cutting his throat, to mean *forget it,* and she recoils. 'That's not what I meant,' he says. Now it's clear how much Johnny will have to be his eyes and ears while he recovers from his travels and his little fit. She'll be good for other things; he'll figure out for what.

'That's all, then,' he says, dismissing her.

At noon, without being asked, she crushes a tiny bit of lavender from the new plants into warmed coconut oil and makes an ointment.

'*Indeganne,*' she tells him. Does she mean him to sit?

In her kitchen, on the stool, he sits and investigates as a small boy might. Hung dried chilies. Thick woven garlic ropes. He has given Johnny a packet of money to change and dispense within the household and she has supplied the house well. There is also the question of how much he likes her hair, with its whorl at the top of her head, a fine thing: had he ever seen a Western woman with that whorl?

With these people it's tough to know their age, their ideas, their pasts. Thus he cannot know what his maid thinks as she starts in with her skillful hands, laving and oiling his feet. Perhaps she wishes to give *him* a gift?

He knows he is capable of communing with a woman, he just has never found the one. The one whose back he'd wish to rub at night, hands never satiated. That perfect equilibrium. He won't trouble himself now; he will just concentrate on his feet. It is as though this maid wants to turn the tips of his limbs into precious carvings. Anyone — even a happily married man — would consider this heaven.

26

WOOVES KNEW what kind of heavenly retreat to build. It could survive another flood, the cavernous thing with its add-ons and wings. The house that imposes its own rhythms, making the three of them move painlessly within its tempo. Though it does appear that the maid and Johnny avoid speaking to each other.

'She might have people in the Rajottama area,' answers Johnny, when, in the waning light of the front room, the thirteenth day of their retreat, his boss turns on him and asks what in God's name keeps Johnny and Nani from being more friendly to each other?

That she has people in the Rajottama area? why should that keep the boy from being more civil? Henry can't see the connection and says as much.

'She might have people who come from the other side of the canal, Henree. The Monkeyhead side.'

'Oh,' is all Henry can respond.

Why should he or Johnny or anyone care where she comes from? or whether she's low-caste, as Johnny implies. 'You think,' he tells the boy crossly, 'about this whole caste business a little too much.'

'Righto. But maybe one day you'll see why it matters here,' retorts Johnny. At this first disagreement, Henry feels closer to such an ungilded ally. 'You might by the way consider seeing the village for yourself,' adds the boy.

'Those first days, weren't you telling me to take my time?' Some crisis of faith grips him, only momentarily. 'That's important, do you understand? I'm *trying* to move slowly here. I came for something simple and uncluttered. To live the correct way —'

Johnny laughs, and Henry thinks he lives partly for these moments, when Johnny lets him in fully: 'You aren't already living it?'

The house, decides Henry, is to thank for having so quickly transformed its three inhabitants into intimates. And it is the house, sensitive to their slightest movement, that is to blame for his slowness. It makes him feel existence alone is an accomplishment. Or else he could accuse the country's accent. Cumbrous curries, the overrich sunsets announcing themselves hours ahead of time.

To no one, especially not to Johnny, will he admit how much he enjoys the cadence of these first two weeks. Something is melting off him. He generally rises late to find one of his few pant-and-shirt sets neatly cleaned and pressed, sun-sweet and hanging over his room's mahogany and wicker chair. On the third day of his stay, with fluent gestures, she'd asked him not to lock his door with the big silver key. This was so his clothes could be ready by morning. Sometime in the night — while he sleeps — she must enter to bring the clothes. The lack of privacy is captivating. That she should come in on him sleeping shows a tenderness far better than any childhood housekeeper ever showed.

By midday, his pants and shirts flap on the line strung behind the kitchen patio, sometimes next to her own skirts. In a modest concession, she dries his undergarments somewhere unknown to him. And where does she dry hers? He improvises a hamper from a tall lacquered straw structure Wooves must have used for golf clubs or cricket bats: each morning, his clothes of the previous day have vanished from it.

Later on, from his window, he can peep around the moth-eaten curtains and survey. First he searches through the trim of leaves down to the canal, usually to spot her soaping and rinsing. She gets wet, she perseveres; she wrings and slaps dirt out of his pants with great force on a rock too small for her purposes.

But before she washes his clothes, while he is still propped up in bed, taking notes — while he is still in what must have been Wooves' Chinese sleeping robe, made out of fine madder silk, with its pattern of fat pigtailed boys chasing kites from trees — she always brings ginger tea on the dragon tray and leaves just as quickly.

This is when Henry by and large finds life hewing to the good. Especially when he glimpses smoke exhaling from the chimney atop Johnny's cottage, the boy in his own parallel, sipping tea. In the repose of these morning hours, Henry likes to browse through an agricultural manual with missing pages, one which (he guesses) may have been authored by Wooves and a cohort.

Midmornings, Henry leaps out of bed, naked, ready to perform his usual arm-whirls, jumping jacks and push-ups. His own father had frowned upon such athleticism as vain but Henry thinks it a body's praise of God, his little panegyric. Once awake, he heads out to bathe the native way. This is what she had taught him:

You wear a sheet around the waist. Then pour kettleful after kettleful of cold water from the well onto your back and front and legs. He knows all this religiously but can't help balking and dancing away, the water splashing on the patio around him. Never does anyone show any shame about such half-nudity. Henry takes his cue from the bathing women he'd seen on the ascent up from Colombo. No one had blinked, their bodies bared, and this was a practice of which he approved.

He is not just half-nude, he is heartily half-nude, beaming his broad, hairy-chested self at both of them. If they wouldn't be shy, he wouldn't be either; perhaps he will help inspire both Nani and Johnny to higher plateaus of health, who knows?

Usually Nani is working in the outside kitchen, first squatting over the iron tongue of her coconut scraper so it protrudes out from between her legs, next putting on a big pot of rice. Chopping red peppers and onions and garlic with a lapidary care. She tends the fire, made from coconut refuse and mango wood, the smoke itself a salve to his spirits.

By the time he's done bathing, she has placed two halves of papaya with lime on the table inside, in the immense main room by the front door. Up until this point in the morning, it has just been Henry and Nani, though sometimes Johnny will unnerve him by coming early to discuss the day's plans while Henry still washes. Once he and Johnny are installed in front of their papaya, picking it over — the orange flesh springing and melting against his tongue — Johnny will inform him about what had been learned the previous evening as the boy roved through the marketplace. The gossip. Who set up a new vegetable stall; whose daughter wants to marry; how the terrible drought bruises the rice fields; how uneasily people await the rains. I have my ways of finding out the truth, the boy always says, before going off exploring, leaving Henry free to dabble in his projects.

Henry finds a discarded roll of mosquito netting and manages to sew an elaborate hat plus cover-all plus gloves, all one piece, out of the net. Who needs tentlike structures when one can just wear the net on one's body? He'll have to write to Washington's patent office about this. In his Village Book he sketches dresses and unusual houses, lists lecture topics. Somewhere during this, she leaves to shop at the market.

When Johnny doesn't come home for lunch it is because he has some of his private import/export business to do in town, something that makes him need to telegraph. After such work he always seems all the more eager to help Henry. On one such trip, he sends off Henry's lonely or pride-stripped telegram to Madame:

DESPITE ALL OUR ARGUMENTS WHAT WOULD IT TAKE FOR ME TO CONVINCE YOU TO COME HERE? THERE'S ROOM FOR ALL YOUR ENDEAVORS AND IDEAS MAGICAL OR NOT. YOURS IN APOLOGY HENRY.

27

AFTER EACH DAY of tending and cleaning, of wiping honey spills and preparing tea, Nani pulls a curtain and shuts the door behind her.

She enters what's actually a kitchen closet with an obscure slit to allow in air. If she has been remiss in her attentions, the altar smells sour and her Buddha acts preoccupied. Often, once she enters her secret altar, her Buddha takes his time settling into calm white plaster acceptance of her devotions. He never seems angry, only aloof. One who needs to be brought around. His lips press in a contemplation so inner she has to remind him of herself.

While she waits, there are tasks she can do. She can finger the shirred silk of yesterday's cream areliya petals. Place the petals in a lotus shape around a slim votive. She had found a treasure, a bag of cattlefat candles discarded in a market ditch. With no one else claiming them, she had taken them back to her altar. Now she pushes, horizontally, a canal reed through the fat. So she can light it with one of the man's fancy matches. Greatly extravagant, she lights the reed at both ends. And taps twice the lavender she'd hung with rough coir over her altar.

A special lavender, it doubly ensures her luck will hold. Her peculiar man does not know that those few times she has rubbed his monstrous, ill-smelling feet with muslin and lavender coconut oil, she links him with her altar prayers. At her age, no longer marriageable but before the end of childbearing, she deserves good fortune.

Her little precautions and prayers don't hurt her chances.

Bronze Vishnu is there to help her. On his garuda bird, he holds a wheel and conch shell with his upper hands, his third hand down to reassure her and his mouth open in laughter or shout. He teeters on a crumbling brick just below the Buddha's altar and so helps continue her stay in this Big House of Kindness.

And there are others she has chosen, the small statuettes she'd traded lavender seeds for at a secluded market stall: Saman the elephant with his right hand up, holding the purple manel flower, Skanda the peacock, Vibishena the devil god. The gods shelter her, some more than others, depending on the day and their moods.

The main thing is she refuses to make any more room for cruelty. This is why she won't show the pink stork her altar. She must keep this corner of the Big House her own. Only she sits on the cushion, stolen from one of the house's lost nooks. Only she lights the incense. Only her eyes take in her deities and protector, her Buddha. Her peculiar man will never guess who she is as she sits here. In the next room, with his thick fingers, he flips through books, commenting to himself.

28

EIGHTEEN HAS LONG BEEN the mystic's number. Eighteen whose digits when you add them equal nine. Eighteen the days he has been there when the rains start without warning.

August 29, 1936 —

The night before with hasps rattling on the window frame, Henry had seen birds like little magnetized chips rolling and blending low across the valley underneath hard winds. Once the morning light lifts, Henry lingers in bed watching ambitious rills on his window weave into larger runnels down to the garden. Wondering if weather here is always so violent.

In the roof's heavy drumroll he discerns his own name's rhythm, as though being called — Hen, Henry — but Wooves' haven safeguards him: the weather finally a sign and justification for not having got out and about. In the kitchen he drinks his tea slowly, leaning casual on the counter so as to better oversee Nani, who is in some odd exultation, grabbing brooms and kindling from the patio, light and direction in her face.

Rain

he writes later in his book. Then writes it again. He has nothing more to add and just paces the house. When by early afternoon a slight pause comes, a sigh, it is only for the clouds to roll in heavier, at first fringed like an exotic bird's tail and then overwhelming everything into darkness. The house clatters. Just as thunder booms closer, he and Nani are of one mind about running out, getting soaked, out to construct from mosquito-net and wire a temporary asylum for their young, flattened lavender plants. He is scooping up a windfall of green mangoes when lightning strikes the canal, making him drop half his fruit. She laughs and for once with him, he thinks.

From inside the library, toweling off, he watches the canal white-washed as though several oceans writhe within. The road has become a bog; the lawn the house sits on threatens to slide downhill. And still the sky will not relent.

The last of the day's light has been muzzled when Johnny returns home before tea, out of breath and in some particular froth himself. He had been out visiting, taking advantage of villagers being caught at home during the tumult.

'I like doing reconnaissance for you, Henree,' he says, warming himself in the library, 'I mean I really like it.' His hair slicked behind his ears makes his head into a chrysalis of sorts.

'Why's that?'

'How long have you been here, Henree?'

'Say two weeks.'

'Eighteen days. How much has been accomplished so far?'

'I. We. We've been in the planning stages.'

'Well.' The boy builds up a momentous silence until Henry prods him to continue. The boy starts in about the Yala, the southwestern monsoon — how it had ended early in May, and ever since there'd been a bad drought, crops collapsing . . .

'We know all that,' waving him on.

Apparently the people are now saying the Maha, the northeastern monsoon, has never come so early. And they believe Henry himself had brought the rains. His aide claps him on the shoulder, in a bad imitation.

'That's absurd!' Henry grips the table. That an American brought the rains? Was this to be his introduction to the village? Such superstitious thinking?

Johnny tells him that now the forecast stands in their favor; that the people can't wait to meet Henry; that the Rajottamans especially like the model garden idea. And the subscriber service. The orphanage. 'And your main Pilima man —'

'You went to the Pilimas without me?'

'Lester Pilima was visiting someone else. You know he's a kind of informal Maha Mudaliyar, collects taxes from the locals for the British. A big honor. Anyway, he's suggesting we use one of the abandoned buildings on the old coffee plantation. Roof's rusty but it'll work.'

Henry can't hide his happiness. He pinches Johnny's arm.

The boy winces. 'Why?'

'You done good. Real good.'

'Come on.'

'No. Tell me I could find anyone better.'

'You can't, daresay.' Johnny swipes back at Henry. The boy's embarrassed.

'See? Your immodesty suits you. What I'm saying is you're someone with the good fortune of being perfectly suited to your job.'

'Thank you.'

'Should recognize that. Not many people achieve that in life.'

She enters then — she and her vivid dark eyes and her cantilevered fore and aft. With a ballerina's poise she brings the tea. Johnny slaps his legs.

'I'll go dry off a bit and tell you more after — Henree?'

Henry is studying her. 'Fine,' he tells the boy. Spooky how she's so balanced. Is the perfection of her form and being a sign?

He asks her how is it she knows exactly when tea is needed? She shakes her head and bestows a half-grin. Everyone is bestowing today, everyone celebratory and more alive. Or at least she's bucking up. 'I mean it's like the house instructs all of us, isn't it?'

She bustles off, forgetting the tray. This is something his wife would never have done. Clara in her sensible bones would never have been so flustered by him that she would have forgotten, say, a ring by a sink, her knitting at a charity auction, the ironing of her dresses, her roll calls of soup kitchens, women in benevolent societies, people to contact.

If all of Clara's actions had been well-meant, it was still true that after you groped through all the layers of sensibility, you didn't know where to find the person. Somewhere there might have been a volcano raging inside: but she would express as much passion for a white elephant sale and benefit auction as she did for making sure Daniel did his homework. As she did for Henry's embrace. As she did for polishing silver. She was every bit her father's daughter, proceeding evenly to each of life's tasks with a charnel's measured fatigue.

Only when Henry came under her critical eye, only then would Clara show a fizz of greater life. She had demonstrated this at their leavetaking. A censure almost sexual, strangling, this hot invective had practically pulled him home. But she had made her decision, and carping alone couldn't be enough.

Therein lay the crucial balance. Not *enough*. For all her daily warmth, Clara could have been a meritorious clock —

— and yet Henry was aware he barely knew her. Had she come

with some type of guidebook explaining how one *could* know her, it would've improved everything. But she had remained impenetrable. Sometimes he thought more than marrying the rector's daughter, he had married his courtship of her: her kid gloves and lipstick, the way her full body gave under his, resisted, yielded some more.

His seminary questions heating him, he'd thought the two of them united in a shared passion for the Word of God. Had hoped their union would explore this Word. But this had not been the case; he'd only grown more alienated from his body's relentless search for merging. Never learned much more about her than he did their first night. Her body to him had been rolling sierra and saddle and ridge, a country responding decently enough to his imaginings of Woman or taboo, and yet all the while he had no clue as to what Clara thought of their enigmatic, messy grappling — but all that was past, thank God. Inside is the house, his boy, the tea and the girl. Outside is the rain and a busy canal, the wet mountains, a people's eagerness. And the temple, to which he will soon make the visit for which he's been waiting a lifetime. Meanwhile, he tries to recall the dream he'd had, like something spoken during his sickness, enclosed by the valley's hammering. Had she after all told him something which he might (if given half a chance again) half-understand?

29

WHEN SHE WAS only ten and a half, all bird and fluff, and her father had been dead one hour she'd asked her eldest sister, 'Why?'

This eldest one squinted her eyes at her youngest responsibility. 'He had a pain in his heart,' she explained.

In the afternoon as Nani crouched in the yard, which even the chickens had deserted, she heard from his old workshed the keening of the sister just above her.

The dust inside the ramshackle shed reassured her that the world's colors had not changed entirely. Deka the second had flung herself atop his worktable near the vise. She half-rose and grabbed her younger sister's shoulders, reverberating dry heaves through Nani's chest.

She does the crying for me, Nani thought, relieved, smelling rosewood. Her sister sobbed long streams of things into Nani's shoulder. Was Deka giving up?

'I,' stammered Deka, 'I, I, I, I . . .'

When Deka recovered, Nani understood her as saying either *Now we have no future* or perhaps *Now it is bitter.*

'Why?' she asked, her favorite question. Only later in life would she begin to ask *how*, a more practical word.

Why would a future disappear just like that?

Then she wondered something which seemed borrowed from the mind of one less involved: Which of them was most fragile? who might crack?

Early in the evening when the mosquitoes were just alighting on their bare arms and knees, they sat around the table. The only movement in the room came from Nani's aching hand. She could not shovel the food into her mouth fast enough. The others sat and stared at her and the single pot brought over by a neighbor.

'We don't exactly have milk rice,' Eka commented. It was as though she had said *it might rain* or *that cat's gone and killed another hen*, so little of Eka's usual fire remained.

Nani realized she was the only one eating. But even if the others just sat and watched (why would they just sit and watch?) while she dipped into the pot on the table that connected them she still could not stop. A heated hunger would eat away her stomach's inside lining if she slowed. The rice in all its mustiness was hardly a celebration. She tasted only the dictates of the beast that had taken over her belly.

'Leave her alone,' Deka said too late. 'She must have worms. Or she doesn't understand.'

'She should understand.' Eka trapped Nani's eating hand in her own. 'Listen Miss Wild One . . .'

For the first time Nani stopped chewing.

'You should be mourning.'

'For father?'

'No, foolish. For your own life.'

Eka squeezed her hand hard enough so that Nani had to switch hands to continue eating. The middle twins had been able to preserve their silence up until then but had to gasp.

'See how unclean she is,' Suji said.

'She doesn't know that without a dowry even the lowliest beggar won't have her,' added Hatara.

'Is it any different for us, nangi?' Deka asked Hatara. 'As though it weren't hard enough that. . . !'

Paying her sisters no mind Nani continued eating with her left hand. If she stopped to listen, her hunger would surely eat her up. Anyway, her father had told her marriage was a hira gedere, a prisonhouse . . .

Eka's hand hesitated before flying up and landing with hard decision on Nani's cheek. This was not the first blow visited upon another sister. But it was serious and silenced even Nani's hand scraping the plate. The impress showed, purple fingers on Nani's face.

For the first time the tinny buzz of the mosquitoes could be heard, coming closer all the time.

'Now,' wailed Deka. 'Now look. Now they're eating us.'

For her part, Nani had always entertained a different picture of her prospects. From a young age she had been gifted with a rare and brilliant optimism that brought strangers to her. It also deflected the hereditary morose shames of her family and brought showers of resentment. Perhaps the family's troubles were unique and acute, summoned by an ancestral god. But this same family was also clever. Easily, the sisters could always find some fount of melancholy, of grim lip-biting servitude to some greater god who would carry them forward into their futureless future.

This grimness came not in the least from their father, admittedly a private man with small features growing in toward one another on his face. Still, as he often enough said, before nuzzling his daughters: 'I am one with a nose for jokes.' Her father!

'What difficulties,' Eka told Nani. 'The first time he heads for the coast is the last time because he fell in love with our low-country mother. For her, for one who would die so early, he left such a large drummer family.'

'And gave up everything,' Deka complained. 'He lived in the wet area where we would have had temple lands left to us.'

'But father is good,' Eka overruled her younger sister. 'His troubles would have pulled down a lesser man.'

Her father! Despite all the problems of his impulsive heart which had jumped into coastal love, the slightest provocation could make Nani's father's face widen into a hospitable smile, invariably including her in the moment's humor.

Her father: her heart's own firefly.

And she the only one in the family who shared his humor. Around them a special enclave grew in which they huddled together against the bitter practicality of the sisters who described the world outside.

'Little Gem has no idea,' her sisters were fond of saying about Nani.

'Just wait until she grows up.'

One of them was always yanking a comb through the unruly tangle of her hair.

'Gem gets her craziness from her hair,' Eka explained to the others.

But Nani insisted on getting ideas from the books the herb doctor had taught her to read. This difference from the sisters proved no more exasperating than any of her other attachments. Nani insisted upon noticing the earth's yeasty smell after the rains, the design of leaves and leeches lumped on the front coir mat. The haste of the thin strong river below their house as it hurried to empty itself in the ocean.

From the same vantage her sisters liked to see the potential for spoiled fishing seasons and a lack of employment in the village the coming season. Their sorrows were sustenance, casting the family's gloom long across the face of unseeing history, lending them the substance of tragedy.

'You wait,' they told Nani. 'You'll see soon enough.'

But Nani's optimism, while willing to persevere, could not fully resist the gravity of her sisters' ideas. She had to become the kind of stubbornness which required blinders. Because of this, sometimes she gave an impression of doltishness. Not because she was blind to the world's crevices. She was all too aware of darkness. Still, her patron god of stubbornness demanded that she hold out against her family's dark ideas.

After her father died, her favorite sister was Deka, the second, with her thin-lidded eyes making her appear perpetually startled. She never hid her sympathy and cared for Nani because no one else did. When no other rivals mar the landscape, martyrdom grows more pleasurable.

Before the sun of Nani's universe had been jostled, how different it had been. Though she had maddened them, not one ever used her given name; they called her Little Gem so much she came to believe her own mother to be different from theirs. Her father said Gem had been chipped from a giant glimmering mountain. And Little Gem thrived on the sisters' love. One sister would leave for her a special curry made from the coconut's thick first milk. Another washed her slippers so that not a grain of dust would dirty the youngest one's feet the next morning.

At night the sisters lay entwined across one another in a single large bed, their hair long and brushed over the pillows. They created a mother out of one another, nestled close in the slight seasonal cold off the coast.

III

THE COUNCIL

Q. What is the fourth of the Ten Shackles?
A. Those passions born from the senses, which one must
   renounce, known under the name of Kamaraga.

Q. What happens if you cannot rid yourself of desire?
A. You will be born and reborn, endlessly.

30

YEARS OF MEDITATION, burnishing of lamps, and maintenance of decorum: every bit of the holy man screams this to his new student. The monk's neck shines, thick as a tower, his voice booming even more thickly against the temple's off-white walls. His eyes are heavy-lidded, the shoulder uncovered by the orange robe a full silo. And Henry believes his monk's face to be that of an even-tempered god, one hiding timeless knowledge.

Thirty days into Henry's stay and finally Ceylon's rains had ceased for the time being. A half-rainbow hung over the canal, a terrible and wonderful thing, reproaching Henry for all time ever spent inside. He left the compound, finally, following Johnny and turning right, greeted by a scatter of birds rising from the road's gutted mud.

He found it to be a road comfortable in its antiquity, dividing canal and mountain. Above the road, dwellings — kept hidden this last month by Wooves' frame trees — clump on the embankment, more ramshackle than retrospection would have it. From Henry's first ride in, burned on his retinas was the memory of a gracious, unconcealed village — a paradise possessing evenly spaced homes, each with its own yard and palm trees. He turned, remembering.

Because where is that logic in how they live? These people dwell practically on top of one another! Not what he had remembered. Or imagined. Around their hives were huge undeveloped tracts, plains and mountains surrounding them; across the canal, few houses were visible. Do the Ceylonese require proximity, or do they cling stubbornly to ancestral plots? Are they tribal, or just one big family? Had they been shoved into stingy areas? He decided it was the work of the colonizers.

'How's Ceylon different from India?' he asked the boy. Before coming to Ceylon, Henry had thought the two countries pretty much one subcontinent, culturally as well as geographically.

'You know.' The boy was glancing around, somewhat fretful.

'I don't. Tell me.'

'Many parts of Ceylon look like southern India's Kerala, they say. Same palms and coconuts. Same weather along the coast. During any rumbling of war, our rubber is as good as the Indians — it commands a king's price. But Ceylon is a favorite colony. We're easy to work with. Some people say it's because of Buddhism versus Hinduism. The no-Self versus the Self, you know, not so big a difference as Westerners like to think, believe me. We're easy to work with only because we compare the British to the Dutch or Portuguese. The Brits come out like daisies. So we keep our English masters happy. Our roustabouts stay low. And the poems call Ceylon the world's first and last paradise. Beautiful, isn't it?' he fanned his arm out.

The roofs peeked through the flame trees in pretty enough fashion. Henry was trying to decide whether the houses had an intrinsic order. Meanwhile, some tripwire must have alerted someone to alert someone else who sprang out toward Henry. A shirtless, smooth-barreled man, all hail-fellow-well-met and affable. But he had been drinking, evidently; another man ran to take his arm to keep him standing. Still, both men managed to salute Henry — chests out, wrists tensed.

Henry hesitated, unsure whether he was being mocked or honored. He nodded and kept walking, the salute being a greeting he had not anticipated, especially on his first time out. The second man skipped forward to keep up with them, speaking happily about what Johnny translated as 'the rain, Henree, the crops.' Henry glanced back just once to see the first man already retreated to his lair amid the trees, hugging close the waists of two laughing young girls with looped-back hair, girls who might have been his daughters.

At the next cluster of houses, Johnny told Henry to note someone on the canal bank below: a small, ageless woman in a flesh-colored petticoat and skirt. She alternately studied and poked the banks of the canal — as if scolding the water level — with the point of a white umbrella. 'That is Pushpa, Henree, a Pilima.'

'You'll think it's crazy — before you said it, I guessed she was a Pilima.'

'You knew?'

'The dignity?'

Johnny didn't answer. And, concentrated on her work, the Pilima did not look up, poking, tamping a bush down, even as they continued on, their voices lowered.

'Shall we speak to her now, Henree? It would be a good idea to —'

'Later.' Some timidity had entered him. Leave her to her canal work. He was not yet ready to summon a Pilima. There would be time for that.

At the next hive, a mother called to another, who came bracing babies on her hips. More straggled behind, carrying dishrags and baskets. Soon a mobile crowd had gathered around Henry and Johnny, moving forward with them, a cloud of people lolloping about, crows screaming in giant circles above. An acornlike pod pinged off the back of Henry's neck and he saw up in the palms a small monkey smirking at him. While Henry searched for the pod in the surface dirt, the people fell silent. All Henry wanted to do was paste a specimen into his Village Book. This wasn't hawthorn, maple, pine. Once he found the thing, he shrugged at the people, a smile raking over his face.

The air had started to press on him, the road raised an unforgiving morning mist, his shirtfront sodden against his chest. Henry had walked just over a half-mile from Wooves' house but already he saw how his new aide-de-camp worked: Johnny choreographed more than he spoke. By the time he was done with a welcoming bow at each gaggle of people, he had already begun to expel phrases. Each time, Henry was beside himself watching the performance. There was something in the willed, metallic perfection of Johnny's explosive consonants that invoked bullets speeding through a well-greased rifle shaft.

Henry registered the villagers — the men with their long Western vests and big gappy grins, the women with their outrageously exposed bellies and giggles — the villagers who were, all the while, registering him. By their fixed stares, he could tell the boy especially astounded them. Johnny proudly reported one woman's invitation to tea as if it were a merit badge. 'When I'm alone they don't show me that kind of hospitality,' he said. 'My coastal accent perhaps. But you see how kind our people can be?'

They passed a man with shorn hair who made a shocking sound Henry mistook at first as being sexual: *ssst!* harshly hissed, what passes between doorways in a red-light district. But the man was calling to a friend, who dragged a wagon from out between the hives. Fortunately, it was a hiss to proffer help, not solicit the wrong kind of attention.

The richness of this situation, here in the hinterlands, was over-stimulating Henry: the radical crimson of bottlebrush hung heavily next to the road. The bananas become obscene, cresting their stumpy trees. A group of small boys folded around him, singing *I could eat Shriver's the leevlong day*, boys in oversize white formal shirts and military surplus. Some clung to the tail of his coat, looking expectantly into his face as though he should join in. Didn't these bright young faces have a better way to employ their collective intelligence?

'Now then,' said Henry, raising a gentle hand. He did not know which he wished for more: knowing how to talk to these children or knowing how to get them to scram. First he had to understand the topography. First he wanted to see, for example, the other side of the canal. They wouldn't let him. He kept walking forward, the urchins flanking him down the wrinkled road, their comportment hardly in line with a Buddhist education. Were the waifs just poor or lawless or both? Their grasping condition, no doubt, reflected the presence of the colonizers — it was, in fact, what he had come to remedy. They raced, the little rogues, joyful along what Johnny called 'the village's trunk — toward the temple at its waist.'

It was only at the temple, the road wrung narrow by canal and hills, that Henry's followers dispersed, as if awed by the hooded Buddha. Johnny would wait for him. Henry must walk up alone to ask for language lessons with the monk. 'He'll treat you better if I don't come,' said Johnny, making no sense. 'This is an English-speaking monk. I've heard after four years here he still doesn't mix with too many locals.'

'You're not exactly local.' A good answer, it seemed.

The boy's face gleamed encouragement. 'Go on, then.'

At the stairs' base, Henry removed his boots and left them among a heap of discarded hide sandals. He would not be the first to ascend to this temple. Populations had preceded him. Was it the orange cloth over the Buddha's face that testified to remote origins? Johnny'd said this temple had existed in Rajottama since before the time of any Judas, Christ, Moses.

Henry finally hiked up, the plaster cool on his feet, telling himself all the while to stay simple with this monk. He must surrender pretense, be clothed only by his authentic ignorance.

'See you back home?' called Johnny from below.

Home?

The air was clear and Henry waved back. Everything might as

well have just fallen away. The sun had emerged and as though it were another first day of school, another defloration, he would always remember this moment.

Maybe he would become a monk and live out his life in Ceylon. Could a Westerner become a Sinhalese monk? It was hard to control the tricky, ecstatic sense that he was entering a new empyrean. Because his ascent made him feel once again how Madame (even if across the oceans with her lama and her vow of silence) would always be linked to him.

He would never have expected that a high-placed monk, the highest monk of the region, would say such a quick *yes* to a foreigner. Never would he have thought a Buddhist monk would be surrounded by half-empty cans of Shriver's Potted Ham, forks planted in them like triumphal flags. And never would he have thought a monk would be reading a week-old *Tribune*, the headlines startling Henry as though a line from someone else's dream:

RUSSIAN REINFORCEMENTS TO SPANISH REPUBLICANS — WAR OF 'BROTHERS AGAINST BROTHERS'

'Odd,' Henry cannot help but say to the whole scene, including the old woman sweeping around them. The introductions are quick and cursory, as if he and the monk already know each other. And then Henry on the threshold, eyes adjusted to the semidark, finds himself blurting, 'You wouldn't consider being my teacher, would you? Teach me the language and perhaps' — the monk staring at him, deadpan as his statue — 'Buddhism?'

Just like that the answer came: '*Yes.*' A singing *yes*. Not no but yes. A total yes. Henry felt the hatch to the universe opening: a hand descended to hoist him up. Never mind the rains. With such benediction, it will all work out.

The first lesson, the next day, September 11 — he marks it in his book — it takes hours. There's much to accomplish. This head monk's name is Pandit and he possesses an uncanny gift for patience. The endeavor itself is his salary.

'Money won't buy you a good teacher,' explains the monk, pushing Henry's money away with a folded dharma book, a heartening gesture. 'We're after something bigger here.'

'Indeed,' says Henry, charmed beyond belief. 'Bigger.'

141

'Buddhism isn't just texts and chants. Monks have to think about their own *pinkam* too,' Pandit explains. '*We* need to accrue merit in this life too.'

'Why?' Henry sets down the stylus. 'You accrue the merit and you'll be born into a better life than the one you already have?'

'No. We want *not* to be born again. But as a monk, we find we distress the people if we talk too much about nirvana.' His eyes bind Henry closer. 'A monk talks about nirvana, the people stay away in droves. Who wants cessation of being? They flock to their worldly pleasures like ants to a poison syrup.'

'So how can I thank you for agreeing to teach me?'

'You know the precepts are all don'ts. Don't kill, don't steal, don't indulge in lust, don't lie, don't drink. Teaching ends up being one of the few positive acts left us, Colonel.'

So saying, Pandit leans down to study his student's efforts. They have spent the past hours with Henry pushing his stylus hard against the palm leaf's horizontal grain.

'Really, we don't usually teach a student how to use the stylus on the first day,' explains Pandit. After all these hours, the monk's sonorous faux-English accents have begun to hypnotize Henry. 'It takes years for boys to learn how to draw the letters correctly. In the sand!'

All day Henry has been admiring the letters' beauty. Elaborate circlets like an animal's tail curled in on itself. He has copied letters, laboriously, with his clumsy right hand, the proper and holy hand used for writing. But the protesting grain of the palm leaf starts to seem a terrible literalism. Far more literal than their discussions. In one day the monk and his pupil have covered much more than just circles and dots, or the wonderful, well-omened similarity of certain Sinhalese words to English ones.

'Can I tell you, Pandit,' Henry tells him without waiting, 'in this village knowledge can be shared to everyone's benefit. A certain propinquity' — how to explain intimacy?

'What are you saying, Colonel?'

'This is a village that can excel. Here the people's culture can be revived. In such a beautiful natural setting — who could ask for more?'

'Indeed.' The monk studies his pupil. 'But do not think we are your America.'

'Of course, I wouldn't.'

'Here the people or the religion must be behind one in order to do anything. It seems you have the people, perhaps? The rain —'

'I have you, don't I?'

And the monk's pause after this is not long. But when his answer comes, the tone is sure, the mouth a determined line. 'Indeed, Colonel. You *are* a popular man — with us as well.'

So in its broader outlines is the agreement struck.

The monk shows himself as good-natured, Henry believes, but also as *a discriminating customer, no one's gull:* a holy and insightful man, yes, and hence more able to size up the right kind of newcomer as being *a man out for everyone's good.*

A few minutes later, once they step out to the rosiness, the last paraphrase of the afternoon, to the bench overlooking the canal road, certain agreements are spoken.

Henry should (in addition to the other Plans) begin a General Store. There is a site available just overlooking the canal, where the bridge is: what the monk also calls part of the body, Rajottama's 'left leg' meeting the beginning of the market, 'at the hip.'

Who decided this anatomy? The monk doesn't know, but he will help arrange the lease of land from the temple. Everything can start up immediately. With his savings Henry can begin the store and keep it stocked with the correct goods.

He and the monk also share certain ideas on nutrition.

'Come back in,' invites the monk. 'We'll have an early dinner.'

Together they enjoy a tin of Shriver's ham — that marbled pâté — over rice, brought to them by the older woman scuffling about.

'We like certain plebeian delicacies,' explained Pandit. 'This Shriver's. We're not to eat meat but if it's manufactured, distanced from the killing, we find it to be appropriate. You people must enjoy Shriver's in America, don't you?'

'Not really.' Henry had noticed this Britishism that the monk and Johnny share, this tagline like a caress at the end of a sentence, this *don't you, isn't it, wouldn't you.* On the road this morning, two Sinhalese women within earshot had saluted each other in their missionary-school English, one with a joke: *You've gotten old, haven't you?* The last two words had drawn out some wealth of shared values, consensus, humor. On *this* island, rather than underlining some tyranny of polite-society dictates, the tag came from a higher concord. *Isn't it that you and I are in the same cause, wouldn't you think?* He blurted out: 'How do you say in Sinhalese *isn't it so?* or *don't you think —*'

'*Naeaede* — you heard people say that, we imagine.'

'Naydeh. I like the kindness of it.'

The monk stares at him. 'At any rate — Shriver's? We do favor it. It has what we call the taste of the horizon.'

The older woman — Pandit calls her Rosalin-akka — stays on while they eat, coiled in a corner with hands folded, idle but alert, a common stance, Henry wants to write. Afterward, as entertainment, at the monk's request, she bounds up like a music-box dancer and begins to sing a dramatic ode.

'This song,' the monk explaining, face almost ashamed, 'a favorite of ours from childhood.'

'About enlightenment?'

'Not monastic. A love song. Our Sinhala Buddhism has more to do with self-control and practice. Less with love. That's the criticism, at any rate. Later we'll discuss the bodhisattvas.'

'The melody's beautiful, Pandit. The words — ?'

The monk halts Rosalin-akka so he doesn't miss any. 'About Gascoyne. A Frenchman, a dignitary sentenced to be hung by a Kandyan king, eighteenth century or so. He'd been a swain of the queen, you see. The queen watches Gascoyne marched down the execution walk. He'll die for his misdeeds.'

The monk takes a visceral delight in the recitation, but redrapes his robes as precisely as if he'd just expounded on a Buddhist sutta. He has Rosalin-akka resume *gascoyne sakisanda ikmen gamening*, her voice startling and clear and that of a much younger woman, one who might always have such pride in her posture. She becomes the queen staring out her window, singing the song with eyes so wet you'd think she too had lost a swain.

When she stops, Henry applauds, touched by her transformation. But why does applause break the spell? She is already bolting off behind a curtain — while her song has relaxed the monk. He lights an oil lamp and lets his holy ideas spill out, a regular trove of them. The first concerns Henry's lectures. If the villagers attend them, and if their children attend the new school Henry's planning (so students stay in school past age eight) they will be rewarded with chits, the monk suggests. The chits will induce them to stay involved. 'We know our people!' the monk says, clapping.

With these small tickets, they'll be able to buy goods at the store. And soon the store will become self-sufficient and actually restore the village's economy.

'People say coffee ruined the village but you see, Colonel, it was ruined to begin with.'

'Sure,' agreeing, thinking of Johnny's reports. 'The people can seem a bit lazy.'

'We've needed someone like you, Colonel. This store, these chits, they'll make you even more a popular man. That and the rain.'

'I know,' rueful to the end.

'You should be glad, Colonel! Summum bonum, as you say, the highest good. The people'll be better off because of you!'

A final coup: one of them suggests they collaborate on a Buddhist catechism. Henry or the monk? It doesn't matter who says it first; it will be written as a meritorious act for the schoolchildren who've been losing their heritage in Kandy's missionary schools.

'The children will encode the words,' the American goes on, 'and the words will undergird their actions.'

'Super idea!' says Pandit.

'This catechism will be my best souvenir and contribution.'

'Certainly!' says Pandit, voice round with approval.

And Henry dreams of mailing the finished catechism to Madame, writing to her: *This is what I did, an anonymous man in Ceylon.* If all this doesn't have him hollering inside for joy, nothing will. The catechism *is* a super idea.

Describing village politics makes Pandit most lively. Kandy's chief monk stationed Pandit here only four years ago. And yet Pandit — 'call us *saddhu,* which means holy man' — has a finely tuned sense of Rajottama. Outside the dusk is lingering; Rosalin has lit more lamps; and Pandit is getting only more enthusiastic. He's especially good in cautioning Henry about those in the village whom he must watch.

'The temple drummer for one, Regi, his family is notorious for haggling! Lower castes have that tendency to argue, Colonel. Because of misdeeds in a previous life. Actually, we're waiting for the drummer's son to marry outside their caste. Then they will be disbarred from serving the temple.'

As though the world conspires to confirm the monk, on the road outside a man harangues his woman. The only words that carry up the stairs to them are *burnt rice, burnt rice.*

Pandit translates with a certain spark. 'Your time here's too precious to waste with, how to put it, mongrels.' He regards Henry. 'What you might not know, Colonel, beg pardon, is that the Buddha never came out explicitly against caste structure.'

Henry wishes his monk could tell him exactly what time holds for him. Once he truly ventures out into the village. Today is Friday, what does Monday hold? a month of Mondays?

'You don't believe in oracles, do you?' Henry asks.

'No part of the Buddha's teaching!' A welcome severity. 'We are against magic talismans. Yet we do have a few sacraments in our Buddhism. Consider our Sacred Tree outside —'

Through the window, Henry can discern the tree's contours. During the monk's tale, the drummers have been lighting small torches leading along the temple path. Illuminated by grander fires, the tree itself stands unreachable on its platform, while in and out of its long branches, its eye-shaped leaves, white moths interlace in a mating dance.

Some two thousand years earlier, allegedly, the emperor Ashok's son and other Brahmins carried the sapling from the famous fifty-cubit bo-tree in Bodh Gaya. This being the very tree under which the ascetic prince Siddhartha had fought Mara, the snake of illusion. Day and night under the tree, on a cushion of kusa grass, the prince had stayed immobile until he was clarified and became the awakened one, the Buddha. And the Buddha's tree had produced the sapling for Rajottama's own.

'Pagan, isn't it?' comments Henry, caught by the lights. 'In the West, we used to think there was a spirit for every tree.'

'Yes, but that ours lives is wonderful. A few years back, it was nearly killed by too much coconut milk spilled during the monthly devotions. Before my time, some man had gone mad. He came at night and tried to chop down its branches. We're lucky, you see, it survived. Now you can understand why we're honored to be posted in Rajottama?' asks the holy man.

Henry's unsure whether the monk refers to his student's situation or his own. He says nothing, which increasingly appears to be the right answer; in this case, it makes the monk compliment Henry on his quick mind.

Henry falters: 'You're beyond anything I could've expected.'

'Rain or no rain, Rajottama can get a bit dull. In a sense, you could say we were waiting for you.'

'Sweeter words were never spoken.'

'We are the out-station. You say hinterlands? After all, how many times can one read the suttas?' He waves with his broad palmleaf fan. 'Always the same truths, correct, the same desire for nirvana?'

'Exactly.' Henry's still struck by the monk's echoing of Madame. *Waiting for you.*

'The same canal, you see?'

Waiting for you. The same canal. Is the monk posing him a Ceylonese koan, what Zen practitioners call the unanswerable question, the question designed to provoke enlightenment?

A knock at the door jolts Henry. Nani peeks in and he jumps from his chair. She has said something with her eyes downcast and Pandit translates. 'Your boy sent her, she says he was concerned. This would be your serving girl?' He stiffens and rises.

'Lesson's over, saddhu?'

Pandit coughs. 'Patience with the subject! with yourself, Colonel Fyre!' Colonel Fyre is Pandit's name of choice for his student. 'In the monasteries we spend years tracing letters in the sand and you've guzzled them down. In one day! Tomorrow we'll start with action. With verbs!'

He makes a gesture as though to press his palms at Henry, not fully doing so, before gathering his fan and rushing by Nani without a word.

'Don't worry,' Henry says to Nani, who doesn't understand.

Henry decides what's lacking. In his wake, he upsets one of the monk's wicker chairs. He hurries along one of the temple's still-dark pathways. At the gate just before the Tree the woman Rosalin-akka cowers behind her monk.

'Forgot something?' Even in the flickering light it's easy enough to see Pandit trying to put a good face on Henry's clumsiness.

'You know,' panting. 'I have a proposal.'

On the canal road, the husband continues to hector his young wife. When she runs, he pursues. She turns long enough, pretending to an embrace, so she can instead grab some talisman he wears around his neck. When she scurries away laughing, the husband curses his luck and drops his evidence: the burnt pot.

The monk views his student from under heavy lids, with a slow bemusement. 'Colonel?'

'It's about my maid.'

Here the monk gazes more steadily at Henry: the shine off his head is deflective. 'Your maid.'

She stands on the lowest stair, her back toward them, gazing down the road. Henry continues. 'She needs to learn the language.'

'Don't inconvenience yourself, Colonel. We heard her! She speaks fine,' Pandit answers. He fights with the gate's latch.

'I mean she should learn to speak English, saddhu. You can lift there.'

'Colonel! You're doubting. Don't think your Sinhalese will proceed fast enough?'

'Sorry.' Crows hoot *sorry* back at him, stationed somewhere in the road's banyans. During the day banyans are pale and peeling membranes stretched over clots of roots. At dusk they've become tortured silhouettes. 'Sorry, didn't you just tell me I had to be more patient with the alphabet?'

'Can't you get your low-country boy with the Moorish name to teach her?'

Henry doesn't understand. 'With the Moorish name?'

The monk muses, almost to himself. 'You call him Johnny. If we are charitable, we could think *John* comes from the name *Channa*. Channa being the prince Siddhartha's Sinhalese charioteer at the hour when the future Buddha saw the four signs —'

'It might be Channa. You know I'm not any good with —'

'But from his slate-like skin color, one might think *Jehan*. Short for *Jehangir* which we believe *is* his actual name. Perhaps a Tamil or even a Muslim moniker! Can't say with any certainty —'

'Johnny's going to be pretty busy translating for me in the beginning —' His throat has gone dry. 'I thought the Sinhalese and Tamil were one people.'

'Colonel!'

'Weren't you saying they've had many kings and wives in common?'

The monk begins to turn away. Of course the monk's time is valuable, Henry goes on to say, but if the holy man wouldn't mind, no one speaks half so well as him. It would be compassion itself.

The monk smiles, if faintly.

Quickly becoming an effort beyond what Henry intended. Merely language lessons for the maid. What words did she really need? *Less sugar needed for tea. Dinner at six. Inform callers. Looks like rain. Order the goods. Please, thank you, see you soon. I'll be ready then. Ten dollars. Twenty. Are you comfortable?*

'To be honest, I'm not sure why,' Henry begins, only to change strategy. 'Of course, if it's an imposition. If anything prevents you . . .'

'Nothing prevents us. We wish to help you especially! We'd be' — and finally Pandit succeeds in raising the post — 'delighted to teach your maid! We'll do it on the fifteenth and sixteenth this month! That's it, then!'

He locks the gate after he and Rosalin-akka have made it through, into the holding pen for a monk and his cleaning woman and a tree. 'You might not know,' the holy man turns to tell Henry from inside his corral. 'Hearsay only, but we believe your domestic might have some command of English!'

'Still, if it's a question of money, I'm happy to pay, would you consider —'

The monk simpers: 'Remember what we said about accruing merit. Of course we'd be delighted!'

On the road, the disgruntled husband strides into the bright semicircle created by the temple's lamps. He picks up the rice-burning pot. With an arm uncanny and strong, he flings the evidence into the canal. The pot arcs far toward the other shore before thwocking down hard on the water.

Nani shudders. *Gederete yamude?* she says to Henry, annoying him inexplicably.

'Don't understand,' he shouts back. He taps his temples. 'To me — all right? — English. EEEN-GLISH.'

31

THE MONK had not told the colonel his real story. Why should he have spilled his jewels?

More than twenty years earlier, Pandit had been allowed into the upper-caste monastic order. Just before, there had been an eccentric, profound drying-up of rivers and wells, several degrees worse than this year's drought. The subsequent malaria plague had scoured the monasteries clean, and the sangha, the community of monks, risked significant attrition in the ranks. So during two months in the dry season, the head monks had secretly suspended the rules about caste: they had let in streams of unlettered village youth who loved temples and robes, boys wanting the betterment of a monk's existence. And all the eternal assurances: food, clothing, shelter, possibly enlightenment.

At Pandit's upasampada ceremony, his mother had cried as her boy's wavy black hair was shaved off forever. How her vanity had lived in his hair — and how perfect was that first liberator, the barber, how quick the razor, giving Pandit a first taste of the steely freedom that could be had away from the tyranny of normal attachments and caste.

As anyone of his birth would have had to do, the fourteen-year-old initiate changed his last name. Pandit took on the radala name of a high-country farmer caste, Ehelapola, so no one would know the truth: that he originated within the bathgama caste — among those who in ancient times, for example, had borne the palanquin for the king.

Bathgama was not so far down from govi, the farmer rank that monopolized the top; and it was only an inch down from the pannadura, the caste that glorified itself with the name bodhivanse, meaning *they who care for saplings from the Buddha's tree.* Bathgama was, however, a caste only a smidgen above beira, the drummer caste. Hence it would frustrate anyone, having to preside over a temple with two surly drummers always near.

Only Pandit's mother had known the truth of his origin, and the secret had died with her. No one living knew Pandit was anyone but Pandit Ehelapola, a monk of the highest of castes, hardly bathgama at all.

During her short life, Pandit's mother had made it her custom to weave on her toes human hair from the wealthy uphill ladies into sweaters for him, sweaters she had mailed him at the monastery, sweaters he had burned into acrid smoke, since none of these were correct clothing for a future monk, didn't she know that much?

And during his childhood, as was the custom, high-caste uphill men had used Pandit's mother as a pleasing toy. Only two men made themselves known, brothers with dark glum faces and impecunious ponytails; Pandit had long grown accustomed to seeing this pair skulking around his house.

Whenever a suitor was with her in the house, Pandit had to hang a leather loincloth on the breadfruit tree — to signal the other brother not to enter. One of them, his mother hinted, might be his father — a high-caste man! — and would even help pay for his schooling. But Pandit had stayed proud. He ignored both brothers equally, never wanting to claim either as father or uncle.

When the monastery itself had become a father, life improved. From those first early days as a novice — when Pandit had secreted away his mother's mail parcels and only occasionally faltered over his new name — he had come far in life. He was a monk. And in this way Pandit was more similar to the crazed American and even his loathsome aide, Jehangir, than anyone might have guessed. All of them had taken great strides away from their motherlands!

Perhaps that drone of an aide made the biggest pretense, hiding his origins, when it was clear — if he had any Sinhalese blood at all — Jehangir would at best be something of a karawa, son of the west coast's Catholic fishing people. Only someone from the west would say karawa loomed over bathgama, that happening not to be Pandit's own attitude.

About this foreigner's aide: in his being was something stinkily admirable, nothing Pandit wanted to know too well. *Please keep this aide away from me*, he wanted to beg the foreigner, *it is not good for me to consort with low-spirited people* — but he restrained himself from doing so. It could arouse the wrong species of questions.

The week when the rains pretended to let up a bit, that first week of lessons, Pandit was hardly expecting guests when Ranjit came by. Pandit had already dispatched his American home for the day — to do homework on a difficult sutta regarding detachment — and was musing on his alien student when Ranjit, an old-time friend from first days at the monastery, knocked. As a young novice, Ranjit had kept the precepts central, quoting them at every turn. Hadn't there been one time when Ranjit helped keep Pandit from stealing something, hardly more than a swatch of threads kept in the monastery coffers — a tiny, unnoticeable relic of the Buddha's robes? As loyal a friend as they come, recently Ranjit had been promoted to being a big Maha Nayake Thero himself, a righteous presence at Kandy's biggest temple.

Like Pandit, Ranjit dwells in the highest-caste nikaye of the whole order. But with the lion-face of his caste, Ranjit, unlike Pandit, is the genuine article. And he serves the best temple in the noblest city, in, of course, the most golden country sworn to defend what they call *Sinhala* Buddhism.

For all that, Ranjit is a humble man and honest, one whose manners could not be any more graceful. Even had he not followed his grandfather's grandfather, had his own grandfather not been important — the chief liaison between the British and the monks over the proper handling of the Buddha's tooth! — he'd still be comely and agreeable.

When Ranjit arrived, his face still direct as a lion's but with the uncertain walk of one not used to having accumulated some girth, Pandit had been reading.

'But Ranjit!' Pandit interrupted his own thoughts at the sight of his friend.

'I'm not disturbing you?' and Ranjit cut himself off.

Pandit's gesture was a joke, the honoring palms folded upright, knees almost — but not quite — to the floor, head lowering. All of which would be right only if the visitor were superior to Pandit, which Ranjit didn't know he was.

The beauty of their friendship was how supremely equal Ranjit and Pandit could seem. This was testament to Buddhism; or to Ranjit, perhaps the only man Pandit ever had considered to be one iota enlightened. Pandit indicated one of the ivory chairs.

'It's been too long. A month, is it?'

Ranjit settled himself down, but not before giving the furniture a calibrating nod. 'Fine chairs.'

'Left by my predecessor,' Pandit explained.

'You're always luckier than most.'

'Don't envy me, Ranjit, you're the one who swims over oceans.'

'Not to let a friend rejoice in your merit? Or I forget, you'd call it luck —'

'Lucky or not, such things come and go, don't they? The weather's finally cleared, hasn't it?'

'Without hedging, Pandit, there's a favor to ask.'

'No tea? They have you on honesty vows now?'

'Why talk in circles with a friend?'

'Which is why you have so many friends.'

Ranjit would not admit this. 'You know the British are going to stop paying their required support to the Temple of the Tooth . . .'

As Ranjit went on about his decision to mount a political campaign against this, since the temple would wane without secure donations, his lion's face kept its good humor, at odds with his speech's urgency. It would be easy to confuse Ranjit with a living Buddha. Even his earlobes were long. When his eyes rested on you, you could believe you saw the calm that comes after years of meditation.

'I'm speaking one to one with each group in the Kandy area. Asking people to sign this petition — in this way we'll make some *concerted appeal*,' using English to drive the point home, 'to their commanders and their home officers —'

'Have them see the error of their ways?'

Pandit continued in English because the drummer's son had come into his office bearing a broom — thin pretext! — when he was really just a NOSE-ABOUT!, which Pandit barked, making Manu scud away. Pandit could not help his hatred of the boy drummer, who happened to resemble his mother's dark suitors; the hatred weakened him and made him hate the boy all the more.

The monks sat. Through the window, the sun was striking the rusty steel and aluminum extension of the old coffee plantation. What remained of the roof became a ruddled lake cut by clouds. The Yankee, wearing a pustule-shaped hat made entirely of mosquito netting — or so it appeared from their vantage — had not gone home to do his homework on detachment. Instead with that creature of his, Jehangir, he poked around the building, squinting at its breadth.

'Actually, I'm fed up with these British soldiers,' confessed Pandit with a gravity surprising even to himself.

Just before the rains began last month, Pandit had been approached by a young Englishman, a cheeky lieutenant named Christopher, who half-asked to use the encampment — now vacant, unofficial temple land uphill from the Buddha. 'A kind of military training camp, for not too long,' the soldier had said, with that terrible Western confidence, 'a few months from now. We've been looking for something in hill country that wouldn't be too cold. And you must know, this is a prime village for many reasons. There's an American chap here now, isn't there? It wouldn't hurt you to have additional security here, would it?'

Pandit had agreed to what he'd thought was anyway just a formality. Last month in town he had explained it to Ranjit: 'The cheeky man would do as the man would do — as such type of men do!' he had laughed.

What Pandit had kept from his friend was his own gooseflesh.

At the soldier's overture, the right course of action would have been to call in Lester Pilima; perhaps Pushpa; even that toddy-tapper Chollie. It would have been correct to make the soldier with his accent and manners understand the particular kind of history and resistance that would impede his work in Rajottama. At least to have made the soldier wait. But the event was finished so quickly. And there had been something hideous and irreversible in the speed of Pandit's acquiescence. He had just bowed to the man's Britishness.

The soldier had without words understood this shame and, a gentleman, proposed that no one would ever say the monk had agreed to what Christopher was calling the *graceful reoccupancy of the village*. Pandit could keep his hands untainted. The reoccupancy would not be his doing.

Yet all of this had been a bad bargain. What Pandit would get in return for his consent was nothing but a reputation maintained. A violent and too quick deal. Nothing would be gained for the village by these British soldiers taking it over. There would be nothing for the temple. Nothing for himself.

The finalizing words had been tucked politely and solidly into the soldier's superior speech. *Great*, he had drawled. *That's splendid.*

What the monk also kept from Ranjit but mostly from himself was that generally he went about scared of most people; especially of the English. They wouldn't care to disrobe him but he thought they carried the right amount of ill will to do so. Far more than any newly arrived and clawless Yankee, the English knew about skeletons in the closet; about origins and low caste. They'd stand him on his head if they could, would punt him about in a circle. Worse, they'd be the ones to use his caste, he knew it, to mortifying consequences *within* the village and the community of monks, the sangha. He would lose all he had built up in life.

Pandit pulled his robes close and explained to Ranjit that he had no pull with these people, that the English wouldn't come for a few months, and that besides it was always better to go to the top than pick at the grass roots.

Ranjit's face fastened at this, at the roundabout way Pandit had refused to sign his petition. But it was bad enough to have the Yankee mucking about; and his aide; and now the British encampment coming in. Clearly, Pandit's next few months would be taken over by the need to manage everything. For now, Pandit had effectively nipped any roots Ranjit might have had in Rajottama.

'You know, Ranjit,' Pandit said, favors asked and given the best way to banish discord. 'I've been searching for a ship made in a bottle for a long time now. Does your uncle still sell them in his shop?'

Ranjit rose to leave. 'They'd cost beyond our monks' salaries! But when I talk to my uncle I'll tell him you're interested.'

'Please. That would be kindness itself.'

32

HENRY IS HAPPY to find Wooves' book to be so informative. Apparently old Dennis had quit the service soon after the 1848 debacle, hard for Henry to pinpoint when exactly, as the man had stayed on in Ceylon some forty years. In his emeritus entries, Wooves maintained the habit of keeping stringent records of his life, just as the royal employ had mandated:

> *Through my inquiries with my neighbors, I have finally comprehended the caste system here, of which no one speaks unless pressed, as is not the case in India. That this revelation should come so tardily, when I might have found it more than useful during my years of work in the field, is no mean cause for regret. One must remind oneself that even Job was told not to regret any of his trials. Nonetheless, others might say regret is one of those gifts God gives us so as to learn how to avoid its occasion in the future.*

> *My notes, to be gathered later:*

> *RADALA — the (former) kings' ministers, who control water and land rights; the uppermost division of the farmer caste. Below them come the GOVIGAMA — farmers, usually of rice. The largest caste.*

> *<u>Every following caste believes itself to be nearest to the radala and govigama:</u>*

KARAWA — generally fishermen on the western coast. Tend to be Catholic and shopkeepers.
DURAWA — toddy-tappers, generally from the south, called Madinne in the north-central province, or Hali in the north.
SALAAGAMA — the mat weavers in the Kandyan period. Currently cinnamon peelers.
PANNADURA — those who serve the special temples. They call themselves Bodhivanse, while their former name was Villiburakmane.
BATHGAMA — those who carried the palanquin. Now they are mostly farmers.
NAEKATHI — the drummers.
NAWANDANNA — the potmakers.
KUBAL/WAHAMBURA — the sugarmakers (jaggery).
RADA/DOBIE — the washerpeople.
OLLI — the cane basket weavers.
DEMALAGATTARA/VAHAALU — usually slaves to radala people, usually southern.
KINNARA — matmakers.
RODI — the outcaste, the untouchables, the beggars.

Henry reads something like this and his eyes mist: why should such stratification matter? His model village will render such hierarchies useless. What Wooves regretted in life, in his service, had more to do with that English belief in vertical order. Henry wants no part of it. Instead, as the monk said about the ham: a taste for the horizon. Henry will cultivate in everyone such a taste for the horizon.

IV

RIGHT ACTION, OR, IVORY FOR THE TUSKS

Q. What are the sins of the body?
A. They are:

      i. Murder
     ii. Theft
   iii. Evil indulgence of the bodily passions

33

A BLAZING SATURDAY before the usual afternoon deluge, Henry wakes with the sense he has mislaid something and hears someone working just outside, stone on stone. He shrugs on his previous day's shirt, waistcoat, pants, thinking either a group of men Johnny has hired is working outside, or else Nani is caught up in some private plan. But the canal has played its echoes. The building, such as it is, seems to come from something like half a mile down toward the temple.

Plain curiosity makes him walk slowly toward the construction, ease and familiarity pulsating through him. Leather boots and the paths of Ceylon any day in September would cheer a heartsick wretch: always his feet are ravenous for the roots half-crushed within the soil, the ones creating puddles, footrests, plateaus.

Some twenty paces down, Pushpa Pilima is working, the dignified woman he'd seen on his first walk to the temple. Only a few days ago but it could have been years; time works differently here. He doesn't approach, just watches her laying in and mortaring a stone wall. She could be nature's first principle, he wants to write, someone content with her lot, her skirt muddied, her gestures deliberate, fixing a wall risen around what must be a property annex, one more of the Pilimas' haunts. Small blue flowers border their compound, ending just beyond where she works. Perfect self-perpetuating thing, this Pushpa in her early-morning fence-building.

After a few moments, she raises a hand, 'Hello?' she calls, humor flashing somewhere. Her half-smile a half-torment: an inner burn making him a kind of shy he never felt in New York. Later, he thinks, he will have to meet her later. His hand waves back, awkwardly. And he pantomimes to droll effect that he may have forgotten something. With a bad rush of sauve qui peut, he runs back to the house in a half-defeat.

34

KUMARI HAD HER first sight of the foreigner, his broad beige hat with its strange net and the brim a fallen sun slowly pushing up around the road. He was crossing past the ambalama where travelers could rest under the cadjan shade and drink well water but this one, he wasn't much of a one for resting, even on an unusually hot day plunked dead in the middle of the September rains.

Instead she watches him with her nape pricking as he continued to rise around the turns, past the terraced rice. Paddy too inexplicable this year, flooded by the bluffing Maha that had begun long before October, this monsoon like no other, saber-rattling cloudbursts so everlasting from the northeast that people blessed the foreigner. They said he had authored these rains.

But this foreigner's Maha gave her cold feet. It verged on being too much. Yes, the rains had fed the paddy. Still it was ten ill-omened days before October and everyone worried the crops would get flooded once the real season started. Maybe pink men needed more rain than most and had a rash sense of seasons?

True, what he had done with the rains had switched most people's suspicion to a welcome. Not her sister Sonali's but everyone else's. Yet if he continued to bring the rain on with such defiance, the people might get back to wondering about his intentions.

What most people wanted to know about this mossback, apart from his cloud powers, was could he help cure sick children? No one knew him well enough to ask. And no one dared mention this in front of the herb doctor. The most they knew about the pink man they knew from his aide, foppish thing that he was, Jehan a boy who ignored most of hospitality's laws, an overdone humbug! He came over and drank tea without doing the reciprocal thing, which would have meant inviting them back to his fancy cottage. Jehan was such a dandy, he'd even turned away people who dared visit him just as unannounced as he had been at their homes.

Such rudeness was unthinkable. To turn someone away? Kumari couldn't begin to imagine what prunes and prisms had crossed this boy's birth. Poor foreigner, to hire such a precious aide! If the pink man had an herb doctor's powers, wouldn't he have had better judgment than to appoint a bad ally? But maybe pink men possessed *different* powers from Appuhamy's or any other herb doctor Kumari had seen.

It appeared the pinkness was targeting her house. He was alone, anyway, which made him both vulnerable and safe, freed of that rude boy. He could be carrying a gun. Perhaps he was coming to order them out of their ancestral mansion, with his cloud powers and a gun. This wouldn't be the first time a pink man would have the gall to do such a thing. Who knew? He might want to take the house over for his own use.

'Soni!' Kumari shrieked in a cold sweat. From the top stair she sprinted down to the road; directing her shout into the copse hiding the well where her lazy sister might be bathing yet again. 'Hurry!'

And the man had advanced more quickly than you'd guess him to be capable of, legs insect-long, as though stretched by one of the ancient Kandyan kings' torture machines.

Then all at once he was standing before her. He offered his face so nakedly. A rumpled, concerned face. Rude herself, she backed up her stairs to stare down upon it. The brow was furrowed beyond its years, the skin rough like a lemon's, all of it making him appear like anxiety itself.

Yet some light and friendliness played about the eyes, downsloping as they were, like a China trader's. Overall it was a face hard to understand, made of contradictions. Fleshy pads framed the top of the nose but the chin rounded to a decisive ball. As though it picked through workable things to say, the mouth was monkeyish.

The impression Kumari received was of a baby.

A big pink and yellow baby. But her heart should not go out to him, rains or not. Of course none of him was to be trusted. Still, she had never looked down on a pink man, one who gave up his gaze so freely. And though high on her stair and taut with mistrust, she could not help feeling flattered.

He was taking off his silly hat as though he were a low-caste man and bowing his head before her as though *she* were the inspector. His thick hair was a woodpidgeon's, white-streaked, falling suddenly —

— and then he extended his right hand. Ready to touch her? To grab hold of her sarong and breasts. To rape her. These pink men so prone to their lusts. She'd heard of the famous pillage the Pilimas had helped stop.

She had since her young days often dreamed of this exact pillage and the dreams had returned recently. Still Sonali had not shown up. There were few things that could be done with such an uncontrollable sister.

'Ay-bow-wan!' said the man broadly, finally. He seemed pleased and pressed his palms together, bowing in the proper Sinhalese fashion.

'Hello,' she said back. It had been a while since she had used her missionary-school English. Her father had believed it best for his girls to spend schooltime singing hymns like 'Loving Shepherd of Thy Sheep' and 'O What Can My Little Hands Do?' so that their English could help the girls if interest in the great Kandyan dance tradition ever waned. She had missed the point of all the hymns but still had loved the nuns with their severe copper faces, their habits' black and white.

'How are *you* today?' she continued and this seemed to relax him and his palm-tree body further, there in his long jacket not a far cry from the ceremonial cloth and banian of the great leaders.

'You are —' began the man.

'Fine,' she answered, obedient to her nuns.

'I am Henry,' he said. 'Heard a heap about what you two are up to here.'

What *two?* Then she realized slick Soni had come around the back way only to pant behind her like some crazed pup. Finally the only thing to do was forget about his aide's bad reputation and summon him in for tea.

Like his aide, the pinkness did not stay long. He drank in one long embarrassing slurp without having washed his hands first but otherwise acted decently enough.

Soni, meanwhile, barely enunciated two words to the foreigner. After he left, with many bows and wipings of his sweaty face, she turned voluble. 'He's not good, Kumari. Doesn't see us at all.'

'How can you tell if someone sees you?' Kumari liked to rebuke her sister whenever those eyes grew round with self-importance, as they did now. Kumari for her part had liked the man.

Only when they were pinning wet sheets in a wind blustering with promises of more rain, only then did Sonali bother repeating herself. 'Telling you, Kumi, he has big plans.'

'How can they affect us?' she sniffed. Kumari had been right about the weather. Good luck was in store: the wind had shown some loss of nerve and now the last of the sun shone on her laundry.

'The way he went on' — she stretched it out — 'all those model things. His garden. Aiyo, never mind what he said — to come to us, he must be hiding some bigger hunger.'

35

So when the beggarwoman came with her hot recitation, enough time had passed for Kumari to consider that Soni might have had some sense after all. Six weeks or so the foreigner had been among them and his rains had blasted the crops close to that irredeemable point. It was already October — maybe he needed a check put upon him.

The old beggarwoman with second sight and bugaboo fire in her heart had arrived at the dance school just before the afternoon class gathered, and still the woman had insisted the two sisters come meet her in the yard. She sobbed something about the Dark Prince for a long while and then cried out: ' I saw her! with these two old weepers of mine I saw her.'

They finally got the story. The girl and the pink man had been entwined as vines in the window of their Big House.

Kumi knew history. The Pilimas had become great not by dreaming of being pillaged by lanky pink creatures but by *staving off* pinkness. This is why Manik Pilima, that fine radala woman, had such dignity in her carriage. The poets would say no joints showed in her and that was for the good.

The beggarwoman spoke, poor sad paps sneaking out beyond the cloth, doomed to abstain from all bodices, all previous lives and demerits scripted even on her sad breasts. Seeing the lesson of *her* (not at all like Manik Pilima-that-fortress-against-roaches), Kumari was more ready to jump to action. Because who didn't know this beggarwoman had long been gifted with second sight?

The question — shall we alert the girl to her state (the Prince having conquered her) or just take care of it ourselves? — has barely been asked before they consult their herb doctor Appuhamy.

A subdued holy man, he is busy repainting with pungent resin and last year's tempera the crumbled plaster of a peacock arch over his doorway. Along the paddy-curved road toward the dance school, among the white daub houses, only Appuhamy's vivid green arched door distinguishes his home from the others. Unlike other Ceylonese of drummer rank, he would never want to show wealth with Portuguese tiles on his roof. A woven-thatch cadjan roof suits him fine, he says.

People warn him — snails will eat his roof. He smiles away such concern. They attempt to scare him by mentioning falling snakes, snakes that spiral out of the sky itself. He rises to the challenge: Don't I come from a family of snake doctors? Do I not have the only true snake stone in the island, capable of healing all bites?

Though once some of his patients formed a committee to tile his roof, they disbanded when they discovered philanthropy's one truism — generosity requires its recipient's interest.

Now, neither interested nor troubled, Appuhamy wipes his hands on a cloth and squints at the dance school sisters. Women with good hive instinct are starting to gather behind the sisters, there at the sorcerer's doorfront. Don't they know that the noon hour jinxes planning? But he'll let the women talk their talk.

'That girl is involved with the Dark Prince,' akka Kumari tells the herb doctor right off. Soni sways behind in contented solidarity.

'There's no one who doesn't love you in town, Appuhamy,' Soni explains with her sugar-coated tongue. 'Who among us doesn't need your help? But you travel around more ordinary than anyone. No one can buy you. Anyone would entrust her dead body to you.'

'Even shopkeepers slip extra beans or peppers into your basket, Appuhamy,' Kumari interrupts. Her nangi can never stay to the point.

'They're investing in their own salvation,' Soni derides her sister.

Appuhamy shrugs off the two and asks, 'Do we ever know what insurance the gods will notice?'

After his wife had died from miscarriage, Appuhamy had asked Soni to cook for him. What could nourish a man who keeps the gods nourished? they riddle her in the marketplace, awed by Soni's elect task.

She tells them he takes rice and curry, soft foods, like the monks, like the Lord Buddha, what else would their Appuhamy have?

To the marketers, Kumari always needs to interject a tale of her own talents, how once she had him for lunch when Soni had fallen ill, how she had made one of the island's best curries, using good curry leaf in the onions, a lot of sweet coconut milk, using the first and second milks unlike the lazy . . . 'And once Appuhamy had eaten enough of the tastiest I could make he covered his plate like a monk' — which her long scarred hand always demonstrates, cupped as though tiny fish could escape upward through her fingers.

Sonali smiles now at the herb doctor, holds up the pail for him to wipe off his brush. 'Uncle, you must've accrued much merit in your previous lives for your power to help poor women like us. Truth is, you're more our monk than our actual monk.'

Appuhamy shifts his weight.

Kumari has to take control of the situation before he leaves altogether. The herb doctor may have fallen prey to the illness that comes from too much solitude, terrible tanikam dosa. 'This is how it stands,' she starts by saying. 'The Dark Prince has taken over that girl. The one who cares for the cockroach. The Prince is making her get indiscreet with the cockroach.'

She knows her sister hates labeling pink people *cockroach*, thinking it lessens their threat, but cockroach is the name for them.

Now in their brief audience with Appuhamy they must impress upon the sorcerer the danger of the cockroach and his entanglement with the girl. What good Sinhalese woman would let herself get wrapped up with a pink man? That girl Nani must be possessed. Especially because in a certain light, she could be thought lovely and everyone knows lovely girls attract the Dark Prince's eye.

Appuhamy peers at the sisters. 'So you never spoke about the Dark Prince with her?'

Kumari studies her hands. She's exchanged no more than five polite conversations with Nani, conversations which always possess the same sequence and roles.

When Nani and Kumari meet at the Elephantside market, Kumari asks *Where are you going?* By which she means: *Hello.*

Nearby, Nani says, forcing a kind of smile. Meaning: *none of your business.*

'Why're you telling us this?' Sonali had asked the beggarwoman, after she had finished her tale of lust.

Kumari had broken into laughter. 'Because we're the first who should know! That girl, she's always off. Don't tell me you haven't seen her! She washes so far from everyone at the canal! uses the wrong kind of stone!'

Sonali had considered: 'And she wrings her clothes. Doesn't even know how to rub *on* stones.'

'Worse,' the beggarwoman had gone on. She took a gulp from a bag tied by rope to her waist, a gulp to cool the roof of that hot mouth. 'The girl never talks of the Dark Prince and his afflictions. She always keeps to herself.'

'When the Dark Prince afflicted Shila, the girl never came to the exorcism,' Kumari agreed.

'It's true.' Sonali recognized how little she knew Nani. The girl had a disconcerting face. Uptilted eyes. It was unusual for a new-comer not to show up at one of the most important ceremonies in years. Women came from far away to Shila's exorcism, Sonali re-membered.

'You attend that kind of thing, the Prince stays away,' the beggar-woman added helpfully. 'The girl could have at least crossed the canal.'

Sonali remembered watching Appuhamy during the exorcism. How he'd entreated the Prince to leave Shila's body. To make the young girl's breasts stop hurting. For months, the Prince had made Shila, normally a shy and well-mannered girl, run naked in the mar-ket and along the roads. He'd entered her veins, forcing her to plea-sure herself at midnight out in the potter's field. Appuhamy had pleaded long and sincerely with the fiendish Prince. 'Why would anyone miss that kind of ceremony?' was all Sonali said.

'You know the Prince sometimes strikes good women,' the beggarwoman continued, 'real women, those who offer food at the temple every full moon day. But think how he destroys a woman who never shows up!'

The sisters had quailed at Nani's dismal fate.

'Maybe she's not afraid,' Sonali had ventured.

'No' — Kumari would have her say — 'worse. We misunder-stood. Her morals are already lax. From everything we've said, it's clear. The Dark Prince had gotten to her a long time ago.'

Deities cannot be rushed.

Appuhamy knows this but the women, vying to speak, do not. He closes his eyes to find a faint eggshell-blue afternoon light. The light says jumping to conclusions is one thing, acting upon them is an-other.

Moving slowly is his way. Terror of the gods' vengeance stalks

Appuhamy's dreams and confounds daytime tasks. Sweeping, he finds a pile of lizard guano stacked in an inauspicious half-circle and he halts, alarmed. Passing through, he finds his shrine's candles rotated a quarter turn, his altartop flowers mussed, and he trembles. A papaya tree branch forever scrapes his rear window in a demon's heartbeat rhythm.

Moving quickly spells disaster. Appuhamy's lean acid face creases at the number of listeners from the road, assembling to rustle and twitch around the dance sisters. 'That girl Nani's practically a middle-aged woman!' one tells another.

'She isn't sixteen?'

'— and alone in the world.'

'Unless she secretly married the pink roach.'

'Who wouldn't say she's not a sorcerer herself!'

But when Appuhamy speaks, they stop their buzz. The few words he offers, even when he repeats himself, are precious bees. He addresses the women:

'First, why not talk to her yourselves?'

Having said his piece, the sorcerer emits something like a sigh. It may be a belch from the over-chilied sambol which Sonali brought him for breakfast. No one who cooks for him has ever figured this out but Appuhamy is a man who eats sweets and red-hot curry with the same indifference.

He returns to his peacock arch and continues retouching his door with a honeycomb of dots. For a few moments, the women remain suspended in a corset of assumptions. When Kumari backs away, Sonali and the other women follow.

'Let the man furbish his house,' one woman says.

'Poor man,' Kumari sighs. 'Never one to ask for much. Not even for the right paint.'

As they walk the road to the dance school, losing their hangers-on, Sonali has advice for Kumari. Of course the older sister will be the one to carry out the deed.

'The nuisance will be to get Nani alone,' says Sonali. 'Whatever you think of her, Kumi, can't say she's lazy.'

At that tall pale house the foreigner works her until those coastal bones protrude. And every day she's there at the old plantation, helping gather stones for the fence around the new orphanage and school. No local wants this orphanage. It will attract to their little valley all the runty children left by the last wave of missionaries to hit sinful Durbbhiksha, one village over.

'We're lucky not to be Durbbhikshans.' Kumari beckons her sister over to the well, to help lug bucketfuls of water. She will make a vat of rice tonight and invite over her favorite talkers, just to hear their ideas. But Soni never helps. Sniveler and whiner, anywhere she stands that dreaming nangi just picks her toes and pretends to shoo away mosquitoes.

Soni giggles. 'Can you imagine? a village without any herb doctor like Appuhamy.'

'True, our Appuhamy's slow' — another woman has joined them with her own pail — 'but he produces. All Durbbhiksha has is mat-weavers and sparse paddy, not much else.'

Even the inhabitants of Durbbhiksha, far-off highland village, call themselves by the name others gave them: Mouth-village. What karma: all day on porches mucking with straw and gossip.

'Their gossip,' says Sonali, watching her sister's exertions with the pail and water, 'it flows more quickly than muslin from the throat of that carnival gypsy. Remember? The gypsy who came to the edge of Rutaeva?'

'How could anyone not remember?' Kumari rolls her eyes.

The muslin had unraveled from the fiercely painted broad mouth and unimaginable gut of the gypsy, unreeled in bolt upon desirable bolt until even the adults couldn't take the suspense and had cried for the cloth to cease. That gypsy had smiled like a frog after a good meal of flies, showing a disrespect worthy only of railroad beggars. They had to pay him off before he swallowed the whole cloth back to where (you could imagine) it lay corkscrewed in his gut, awaiting the next crowd for a snake dance.

'Think you have enough water there for twenty months?' the neighbor asks her.

To back off, Kumari invites her for rice later before reprising: the mouths of the Durbbhikshans stay slimy with gossip.

The women concur — what a fact of life this is. As factual as their certainty that the Pilimas and the new Sacred Tree Temple monk will never ensure a fair share of canal water to irrigate paddy. As unchanging as the amount of seedlings apportioned to families by the government agent. As certain as the government coffee plantation never starting up again. Never again to employ men it had emasculated out of ancestral lands. And most predictable of all: the Durbbhikshans will never stop talking.

The Durbbhikshans' saying was true: a fish dies because of its open mouth.

Compared with Durbbhiksha, who doesn't feel lucky to live in Rutaeva? Rutaeva — nestled between the great Elephant and Monkeyhead mountains, its large, tank administered by the Sacred Tree Temple. Rutaeva with its noblest of families, the rebels, the Pilimas.

36

KUMARI TAKES IT upon herself to find Nani when the foreigner's away. She knows from the beggarwoman that both the stork and his twisted-tongue assistant are off to tour Durbbhiksha. Doubtless even the foreigner loves the story of a village gone bad.

And he chose a good day for a trip, one bright enough to occasion a laundry festival at the canal. Women are slicing the air, spanking clothes. Underneath them the canal sinks. A dolorous flock of men pretends to fish.

Loafers, thinks Kumari, there are no fish.

She cuts along the canal on a path among paltry trial rubber plants seeded by plantation owners around the time the coffee project was going to fail. But just before the bridge to Elephantside, she finds she can't raise her foot.

What's this? she cries. Her one foot, and now the other, stick deep in an unforgiving mud.

She hunkers down. No one passes on the tiny path. The women down below don't understand Kumari's frantic sea-creature arms. Joyful with laundry and gossip, they wave back.

Fools. If only Appuhamy could tell her what to do. Or does one of Appuhamy's gods signal her? How the beggarwoman's face had filled with prophetic light when she mentioned the Dark Prince for the first time. Still, could the woman have been hired by someone, by that strange boy Jehan? No, there'd be no reason for the boy to have hired the woman, unless he'd needed to separate the pink foreigner from the girl. The beggarwoman had surely come of her own accord; and perhaps the Dark Prince knows already that Kumari wishes to intervene. But Kumari is ready — her mission is as certain as her sex.

First she will ask what Nani knows of the Dark Prince, and at the girl's answer, Kumari will see whether she chokes back a moan. Whether her gut surges in a laborious heave. Whether she must restrain herself from lunging away, or whether her hands wish to stroke all her womanly traits. Her soft neck, her hands. Whether she's a victim of all the usual manifestations.

Kumari will be firm and motherly. She will give the girl a chance to explain her own detection.

The signs. Did Nani recall when the Prince first cuffed her shoulder, smacked it hard enough to signal his cloaked arrival? Had she counted nights spent in wakeful fever? or did her petticoat bind her chest? When had her breasts and female parts hurt so much she'd tried to wrench them off her body? Most importantly, did the girl remember premonitory dreams about the Prince during her time in the hut of menarche? If Nani knew the signs, she was a girl with some sense.

Then Kumari could go ahead and organize the exorcism with Appuhamy. Together they'd free the girl of the demon's baleful influence. Like silk over muslin, Kumari would shine. All would celebrate. And then Kumari would help her sister cook a regular sorcerer's feast — all would praise her punctilio.

But the Dark Prince must have other plans. They include keeping Kumari from rising and crossing over to the girl.

While the noontime sun climbs high over the tank and shimmers waves down upon her, Kumari must remain curved over in thought. The canal banks empty. Across the canal, only the foreign stork and his odd aide shuffle by, no doubt on their way home to a lunch made by Nani. Ashamed at her imprisonment, Kumari pretends to study the rippled sludge below her. She doesn't want to see the face the foreigner would show her with its kind heckling. Blinking, disheveled, she is left to burn.

Perhaps Nani is fine after all, she tells herself. The beggar-woman's prophetic sense may not be wrong but perhaps Kumari's interpretation wavered. Perhaps the girl is actually managing well in that pale peaked house.

And the foreigner did lessen the rains just when all the paddy could have been ruined. He might be all right after all. He had certainly *seemed* humble before her. So if the Dark Prince had inserted himself into the girl, why should Kumari be the one to intervene? That was none of her business.

The Sacred Tree Temple across the canal thrums with the women's low chant, waking Kumari from her spiraling thoughts. Six o'clock and Regi's drumbeat sounds homage to his family's ancestral gods.

I agree then, Kumari tells the Dark Prince, forming a contract. *Who am I to bother you? Do what you want with that girl Nani. With the new man. Let their bodies rope each other. You see more than we do. You'll get no more bother from us.*

But the Dark Prince cannot be so easily persuaded. He frees her only when mosquitoes alight hungry at sundown. Her feet lift easily from what has become an ashy, charred relic of mud. She barks a harsh laughter to herself, reeling back on the road's thin sash back to her home and the dance hall her husband built before disappearing so many years ago, before he chose the decoy of the coffee plantations over Kumari and her nameless, faceless, wished-for babies.

Forget Soni's first dream: Kumi had thought it likely the new pink man meant well for everyone. And he would most likely do right by the sisters — you could read gentleness in his face. It would not be hard to wheedle him into doing things more to their taste, or at least to hers.

37

Nani wants to tell her story to only one other person in Rutaeva: to Manu, the drummer's son.

Since the end of August, before the bad rains started, he alone of all the villagers had helped her. He alone had chosen vegetables for her at the market — for months he had thrown out rotted cabbage, had selected the least moldy ginger. If free from temple duties, all the way up to the Big House, he'd haul her parcels, in bags glued together from personal letters and children's homework.

At first she thought Manu worked the marketplace but then realized that he lay awaiting especially her, there in September's rains, inside a stand of slanted bamboo and his gift of timing. His perfume tickles her. Better than oleander. He may be younger but he's quick in comprehension. Secretly she wonders whether they are not lost cousins. This is not inconceivable. They share the same last name. It appears that all the while she considers him family, he is trying hard to seduce her.

He's not just quick but mesmerizing and as they walk down the canal road between the rains, small children understand even more than Nani and hoot and tease him. They adore him, he is a natural leader and that is how they call him, Chief and Leader, and asking all the time who is the foreign girl that he's courting. He doesn't care, he is her friend. He tells her not to kick him away like some chipped clay vessel. He bids her goodbye respectfully and stands vigilant as she approaches her cloister.

To him she never speaks of life within the house — not of Honree, not of Jehan — but instead of life before Rutaeva. Over time their steps slow so she can tell him more.

He concentrates on her with all the attention his seventeen years have granted him. On dry nights, crickets drone things he might say to her, a throb of longing. She is the first girl he has ever noticed (though plenty love him in the village) and he wishes he could make himself as illustrious and bold as the nameless people in her stories. Make himself as tremendous as her father, the old herb doctor, her sisters, her failed wedding. As big as the boy who consoled her during her time in the menstruation hut.

One October week when the rains are incessant Manu avoids her so she'll miss him — and believes from her sharp inquiry the following week that he's been successful. She had found it hard and this cheers him more than if she had given him something precious like a golden lotus.

Another week he consults with his bachelor uncle the next village over, a mat weaver in Durbbhiksha with a reputation for masterful courtship skills. Manu describes his passion but hides Nani's identity. 'She calls me cousin,' Manu complains.

His wise uncle tells him that though Manu's young, he'd do better if he had a secret from the girl. A big secret.

'One to impress her. And since a secret doesn't exist unless its existence is guessed,' his uncle advises, 'you must now do grand, brave things. You should busy yourself and only later tell her of your involvement. Otherwise she'll find you contemptible. She sounds like the kind of girl who needs great deeds to admire.'

The boy is foolish with love for her, and his uncle in his time had been no mean lothario. So Manu's legs do the thinking for him. The rains are impatient but he begins his plan slowly, walking from barn to barn along deep ponds and in the mud, even when during yet another battering storm the treetops threaten to fall on him. The skies are alive and hold the message and confirmation. He builds on contacts with trading merchants and distant cousins. Slowly he starts to connect an empire of himself, an empire of secrets, something no one would find laughable.

Yet he may have listened too well to his uncle. The plan builds upon itself too quickly and will not let him go. Its original outlines dim. Now promises and obligations cloak him along with words like *national* and *revolt* and *riot*. And this only after seven weeks. Months from now, when December has almost ended, he will hear leaves in the forest chattering one morning and remember with a pang how frequently she used to talk to him. He will have let the secret grow too big. It will grip like a scar upon him. His uncle being a busy trader, Manu will not have sought advice immediately, having believed it necessary to continue building on what he has done so far.

In many villages they will call him Chief and Leader. He will be responsible for organizing nationalizing *actions*. For drumming up *caste-blind sympathy*. Because he cares less, he will become better than anyone else at a job that will try to devour him. He will fall asleep during temple duties, dreaming of Nani's former life. And his father will speculate madly about where his youngest son's mind has gone, saying *you knockabout!* Rushing from the temple, Manu will have no time to wait for her in the bamboo by the market. For countless days he will not even glimpse her.

'All for the good,' his uncle says somewhere during this period, in a rushed meeting. 'You're doing fine. You see, if you love her enough, your reward will come. I'm telling you, Manu, the bigger the secret, the bigger her love. That's the way it is with women.'

And all the while Manu runs from her (to be closer), she will believe him a great piece of her past and (who knows) future.

38

THE ONE THING Jehan cannot say is what makes him raise a finger to his lips every time he sees Nani. Both self-caress and shackle. Does he warn himself or her? Perhaps many Novembers before this one, Novembers piled on Novembers like so many turtle-months humped on others, he may have turned away from some doleful punishment of which she keeps reminding him.

Because she is so damnably familiar. She bothers him, making him stifle or compel a cough. Why should she have this power over him? How she invokes memory, half-visible. If he were to *choose* memory it would be better. But his mouth, why should it be startled by her into wincing, as though in disapproval or ardor! Who cares about what is, after all, only a maid? It may be irrational but he feels it's *her* fault. He might've had it all under control. He didn't plan for her.

About himself, he knows certain things. For one, his eyes seek the corners more than he'd like.

Once, in an improvement manual, he'd read no man should trust another who cannot maintain a direct gaze. His hair is a wholly separate trouble, in constant revolt against his attempts to slick it into submission. And there's the question of his clumsiness, not so different from Henree's: he rises to his feet and finds his will overwhelming his body's mortal capacity. His impatience for the next part of life makes him stumble — always a buffoon with knocking knees brought before the handmaiden and king in their fools' paradise.

39

WHEN THE EARTH has become a dark womb wracked so often by rain and her life has wilted into the Big House, into dragging laundry out or in, depending on the sky's signs, she starts to feel she will explode from silence. Manu has stopped coming to find her. Far too long ago — though it may have only been a matter of days and weeks in the house, time having become just another wave passing through. At first Manu had been her great savior, leaving her without any need to whisper to anybody. Now he left her with lack. As bad as anyone she had ever known. Bad as her own father.

And worse is that after each day of cooking, the other women rude to her along the canal and market, her Buddha's preoccupation drives her mad. The Buddha doesn't notice all she does for him. Unlike the foreigner who always tells her how grateful he is for her services. *Bohom istuty*, says the pink man, when just a gesture with the head would be enough. His *bohom istuty* annoys as much as the Buddha who doesn't listen or acknowledge a thing.

On an endless night when the sky is screaming thankless murder and she would ordinarily move her pallet into the entrance hall for protection, she instead pads into the foreigner's bedroom on quiet feet.

What is it about his face slack upon the pillow? she wonders.

Though Honree's body is huge, his reposing head becomes gigantic. As a child with her father and sisters on their home seashore, she had once seen a bladderwrack washed up on the sands. A sea vegetable with an appended bulb, its thick skin bloated near to bursting.

She knows the pale man, sleeping, has a head which often thinks of her. This same bulbous head often worries in the next second whether he's left new trowels to rust alongside the fence of the big planned model garden. Just as she can hear air escaping his nose in gentle throttles, she almost sees little monsters escaping this head.

How peculiar he is, this knotted man. How much he loves his little flying pet ideas. He strokes them and loves them to death and thinks that from them an entire house will rise. Not a house, but a village; not just a village but entire fabrics of villages; all borne aloft on those monsters' bony wings that would save everyone. She understands that much and more, from his discussions with Jehan.

What would his children look like were she their mother? and she immediately banishes the thought.

Bohom istuty. Never in her young life did she dream that she would be so intimate with such a man. She washes his underclothes, wringing and pounding their soilage out upon canal rocks, letting parts of him bleed into the great water shimmering between mountains.

What he doesn't know is how his fate made a beeline for her.

He came to where she chose to live: on land that might as well have been her family's ancestral plot. She's letting this belief gather time. From old weathered maps which her father kept creased in his workshed's bronze box, she knows.

The map distinguished her family's high-country land in watery greens and blues and a proud script. *Bandu.* And she is Nani Bandu, a girl holding what had been their name for two thousand years, ever since her family had first brought the Sacred Tree sapling over from India with the other Brahmins. On the map, Bandu was circled at a knoll overlooking a canal leading to the Sacred Temple.

She had never told her family name to Manu, thinking it too big a flirtation. The boy would have thought she wanted to marry him — everyone knows first cousins make the best spouses. The truth was that after what she had seen of her sister's marriage, she didn't think she could be a wife.

How does happiness ever find the right life to lead? Her happiness or Buddha had brought her to this crazy house and its throne on the hill. Arriving in Rutaeva after only the second time on a train, she'd hung off the corroded handle near the front to watch hill and paddy clatter past. When the train slowed at a station far from Rutaeva, the wan house against the red croton-studded hills had made her jump off.

Once, fifteen years ago, she'd jumped off another train, on her way home from her failed wedding night. She knew about jumping.

On this first trip to the house she had gone back and forth on a sludgy path, crossing the canal once, twice, finally back across the hardest way on the hanging bridge. As much as she had ever done, she found her way to a home, to what may have been her lands, feet strong up the road through the village and to the house. This was not such a small village, so at first she thought herself lucky — no one's eyes clasped her with foreknowledge.

In the fringed hatbox she had pilfered from her sister, two pale cloths muffled the thud of a single book and her white plaster Buddha. Her burden was light but each step trampled years whose number she'd prefer to forget. Years like snakes refusing to submit with grace. She wouldn't budge again. This time something would be hers and would stay hers.

Was it better to have a house facing sunrise or sunset?

In this place to which she has come, sunsets boast more clouds and are colorful as ripped wreaths. They are what she'd imagined while still a child in her father's house, collecting leeches for the local herb doctor just before the wide open coast filled into night. Since she has arrived here, it has not been easy to rank the unbidden memories that flock like demons and corpses. This place where a foreigner arrived a few days after she did. Where a foreigner needed to make himself feel more at home by giving her tasks.

Clearly he wanted to belong to the house before he belonged to anything else. She did not begrudge him his orders. Especially because as she cleaned, she kept finding interesting things. For instance, other books to remind her of her father's friend, the herb doctor, the one who'd taught her to read in that language which no one she'd ever met had used. All those years and before his death he'd forgotten to teach her how to *speak* it correctly. He'd bequeathed her this half-knowledge of English: squiggles on a book's page, sense without right sound.

'Honree.'

She savors the stork's name between her teeth and draws it out as an experiment: this second time that she speaks while he sleeps, she will be braver, she tests him more. And Honree is a deep sleeper. Night after storming night, she grows more bold while his sleeping self allows her this new forthright spying.

When, during the day, he asks her for *favors* as he calls them, *one more favor please Nani*, her spying has become a luscious secret, a wedge keeping her intact within that huge deserted palace. She pulls up his shirt and examines the strange hair on his chest. And thinks what she does a superb strategy. Her sisters would have called her, as they usually did, possessed by the fiery snake.

She huddles closer to bite on the pink upward earlobe.

Honree does not stir. She blows on his eyelids and that head maintains its equipoise, the throttled breath.

What would he be seeing now? she wonders, blowing upon his eyes.

40

IT IS STILL DARK but she is laying out the morning tea things when the boy saunters in. He is insolent, he adjusts the cup on the saucer, the hakuru sugar in one solid brown mountain in its dish.

She asks the boy (who has come early) whether he wants tea. Today she finds their game rude. This silent agreement between them. There is a distance like years between them. Once she had tried to get him to speak about it. About what had happened since. But he'd played dumb.

It has been easy enough to take his lead and make up habits. They skittle about the house with the fierce importance of two laborers. One day, she thinks, he might bother to teach her to speak English. He would be better than the monk had been. At least they could be friendlier.

The boy comes to sit on the moss-covered bench in the interior courtyard, next to the kitchen. He watches her through the lattice, hunched as though bound with a load of wood to his back. A finger to his full-lipped mouth, always as though to hush her. What a terrible habit! As she strains the aromatic leaves with cheesecloth, he has risen and steps neatly behind, closer than usual, practically gasping.

'Stop,' she says.

'What?' He backs out into the courtyard, trying to make himself appear dignified. This is what she finds intolerable.

'You've been wanting to play it your way. So now we're in a different time. Excuse me —'

'*Young mad-dam,*' he uses the English, *mad-dam*, bobbing close to her. 'I don't understand.'

She puts her pot down on the bench and sizes him up.

'What do you mean, *mad-dam?*'

It is this closeness and false distance at the same time. She makes as if to strike a dog but stops herself midway.

'You should grab hold of yourself,' he says.

'Shh!' hissing, picking up the pot. 'You're proving it.'

He just stares back.

'It was worth nothing,' she says, trying to get past him and into the house.

But he goes on talking. Blocking her passage. *'Pardon, mad-dam?'*

They can't stop what she had started. 'You're not going to talk about it?'

His finger flies to his lips.

'You must have followed me here,' she says. 'Either way — excuse me —'

He slides to block her again. 'You think your maid position here is permanent?'

'Be polite!' she says. 'Let me get by —'

'It's becoming clear, *mad-dam* —'

'— please!'

She gets by and turns back to him with a cat's fire. 'I know about you,' she sputters — her hair fallen and she blows it away — 'you're the one who should take care. I know how you work —'

And she almost smells the other man before she sees him, in his tired robe like an emperor, inside the house, leaning against the basin-stand. His face is milky and inward, not yet assembled for the day. But he must have been watching them, his two helpers, arguing in Sinhala. He is curious. She can recognize the look, *too* curious, squinting directly out of his unassembled face at them, his unassailable face, the smile not unfriendly.

In his bad Sinhala, he is trying to ask them something.

She is as frozen in place as — by her side — Jehangir is. As though they had both been caught in evil and are now forced as punishment to watch a pink man stammer out Sinhala. The man settles on what he knows how to say. 'Kohomode?' from the shadows, *how are you?* 'Kohomode?' And then without waiting for an answer, 'you all right there? Ah, Johnny? mind coming in half an hour? Talk about our day?' she thinks he says, in a hoarse English which sounds, strangely, just as hesitant.

41

JOHNNY WHISTLES entering the front room only a few minutes later, acting amazed to find Henry, dressed for an outing, already taking notes under Wooves' hurricane lamp.

October 10, 1936

Formerly this mind wandered as it liked, where it wished,
according to its pleasure, but now I shall thoroughly master it
with wisdom, as a mahout controls an elephant in rut.

Delight in heedfulness! Guard well your thoughts! Draw
yourself out of this bog of evil, even as an elephant draws
himself out of the mud.

Henry reads aloud from the monk's translation of the Buddha's
Pali scriptures. 'Most of the night I couldn't sleep,' he says. 'But the
important thing is maybe I've never met such a brilliant man as our
holy Pandit.'

Johnny glances at the book. 'Brilliant,' he agrees. He busies himself with opening the french windows. And turns the lamp-wick so it
drowns in kerosene.

It sounds for a moment like his aide had cursed. 'What's that?'

'Brilliant. I said yes, yes, brilliant.' The boy stands by the door.
'Ready?'

Henry strolls, hands clasped behind, imitating those men he's
seen along the misty canal. He doesn't want to break any spell by
asking what just happened in the kitchen; he can find a way to ask
later. Permeated by the sense that he and his aide continue a new
daily ritual, he wants to stroll — keenly, rigorously, Johnny holding
for him the sanctifying gift they've discussed. Two saris as gifts, ac-
colade and inducement for the dance sisters.

For almost a month, Henry has shown his face around Rajottama.
To and from language lessons with the monk, yes, but also seren-
dipitously: in the market, by the water. The wet warm air has kept
him cloaked in a hearty sweat, like the people's good cheer. Luckily,
he finds most villagers unsqueamish if also not falling over themselves with enthusiasm. They do prove more than willing to discuss the future and their needs. Only one local custom is truly off-
putting: that even after the most passionate interview with the
locals, after all the ceremonious bows have been performed, the
ayubowans said, when nothing more can be done, Henry will walk
away — only to glance back and find the same villagers tightened
into clusters laughing, imitating his own Sinhalese and shoulders-
back posture. He does not relish this. The paradox being that his

two months here feel both timeless and limited, hardly enough to know anything at all.

And as though Henry's blind, during every morning's stroll, Johnny apprises Henry of the news, interpreting all he'd learned in the village the day before. Henry welcomes the presumption: sound man with choice spirit, his Johnny, describing the village. Because this is exactly what Henry had imagined in America: a road, pungency, new friendship, stories.

Later he will remember how in quiet accord, they had headed toward the intended site of the orphanage and school. He will wonder later should he not have managed this particular encounter differently?

A big huffer of a man is waiting for them. The day before on the road, Henry had met this man, if briefly, a man who makes him nervous with his close-set eyes and the up-from-under glare of a charging bull. Whenever the man had made one of many points, his shoulders had rolled uncontrollably, his breath stinking of the local liquor. It was the scent of kasippu, according to Johnny, kasippu that kills men young here — a strong bootleg made from what-have-you and whatever-else-besides.

'Remind me, Johnny — how do you say the name?' whispered, but too late.

Too late. On this day the man wields English like a knife: 'Yoohoo!' shouting, rising. 'What's this, Fyre?' Fortunately the man doesn't smell of ethylated spirits — maybe the exchange would be pleasant.

'What's what?' Henry smiles. He must put these people at ease. What would help? He pats his waistcoat pocket and feels only a fountain pen and his Village Book. The man would be insulted with the gift of a pen. But the name comes back: Lester Pilima. A bearlike man. Eyes ready for some hunting sport. All topped by a pathetic toupee.

'You people, Fyre! Gone and used the wrong stones.'

'Sorry, what?' Henry extends his southpaw hand to pat the man's shoulder and stops himself, remembering this could be construed as an insult. He retracts it and presents the right one instead. Which goes ignored.

'These?' Lester kicks a pile of stones. 'Got these from the top of the hill?'

'Oh, I — ' For the last few weeks, Johnny has been overseeing the maid as, in imitation of Pushpa, step by laborious step, she gathered the rocks to build a boundary fence between the road and the orphanage-cum-school.

'Weren't we supposed to be bringing stones up from the canal?' Henry turns to Johnny. To be honest, Henry hadn't put much mind to where the desired stones would come from. He'd just given instructions that a few should be gathered.

'Was the Pilima name on these rocks?' asks Johnny, sotto voce.

This makes Lester's shoulders roll, an earthquake suppressed in his musculature. Aggrieved propriety. He adjusts his hairpiece. 'Yoohoo,' more quietly. 'As Maha Mudaliyar for this village —'

'How can you be mudaliyar?' Johnny interrupts. 'I heard the British never nominated you. They just accept your help in collecting taxes.'

'This boy, Fyre! Those that *belong* here would have more smarts. Next month we're using these stones to build our fence. But this boy is a loose cannon. Makes you seem —'

'Point's well-taken.' Henry grins. 'All of you. Actually, what my trusted aide here is not telling you is we really *wanted* to use Pilima stones.'

'What?'

'The Pilima name. And the stones. Say you were building a start-up venture, any kind of wall in Rajottama, doesn't matter, you'd want a mark, a brand, wouldn't you? You'd also want to use Pilima stones, right? They'd be the best for any project, wouldn't they? Never mind for the people's morale?'

Lester acts confused by this tactic. 'Of course.'

'You understand, we want our project to succeed. If that's the case, wouldn't we need the blessing and participation of the Pilimas? Right down to the name itself? The stones?'

'That *is* how things work here. Except you haven't paid us any formal visit yet, Fyre! Or asked our help or —'

'Sorry — Johnny, what's on the program for —'

'Tomorrow? Righto. Pilima compound.' Johnny eats crow but still plays his part. Henry has to give him credit. The boy holds up admirably. Doesn't try to save his own face or need a blaze of glory, his breed of loyalty an old-fashioned virtue.

'Actually, Lester,' Henry continues, 'you've helped all of us by coming so early.'

'Nothing really. You're coming to the compound though? What kind of hosts would we be if you didn't come? You'll have some tea with us.'

'And we've heard about your compound's beauty,' lies Henry. He's not even sure what a compound is. It sounds militaristic, something to do with berms and foxholes.

Now Lester truly becomes a boy. 'Well! It's nothing yet. We just started the renovations. You should wait and see what we're doing with the door. It'll be a miniature replica of the Temple of the Tooth. Elephant heads, you know' — he imitates them — 'we might even use actual ivory for the tusks. Get it? Ivory for the tusks?'

'Incredible. Since you're here, Lester,' says Henry, on a roll, 'perhaps you could advise us a little? the directionality of the boundary wall here?'

Johnny has to translate this last bit for Lester.

The big man nods. 'Yes, Fyre. Laylines, they go west–east here. You wouldn't want to disturb those. Also your girl carrying the stones — that's not women's work. Should hire men from Rajottama to help. Tell them Lester Pilima said it was all right.'

'Could you consider overseeing the entire school construction? You'd be in charge. We'll have lots of men — volunteers.'

Here Lester's speech slows. 'About how many do you need?'

'We can figure that out, right?'

'Sure,' parleyed back. 'Anyone who knows Lester Pilima knows he can manage well.'

A few minutes later, the man makes an august bow to Henry. He even sends a cursory half of something in Johnny's general direction. But stops on the way out. 'Tell me, Fyre. You people believe in tombstones, don't you?'

Henry stiffens. *You people.* He summons up some statement about commemorative markers.

'Because whether a man's white or brown or purple, what he wants on his grave says everything, no?'

Henry agrees.

'Ever give thought to yours?' Lester holds conclave as a boxer would — standing too close and with such a heavy breath.

Believing it prudent to avoid tangling with any bully, Henry lies again: 'I always thought I'd want chrysanthemums on my grave.'

'No, a message. You people write things, don't you?'

'Oh, something like, not sure, HE DID HIS BEST.'

'He did his best?'

'That's right.'

Johnny stifles a laugh. 'What about you?' An aggressive boy but loyal. 'What would be on yours?'

'We don't use such things in Rajottama,' shot back proudly. Lester tosses his head; the toupee stays solidly fixed. 'We remember who we are without messages. Good day!' lumbering off, the wrestler's back an unceremonious goodbye.

Johnny whistles coolly. 'Turned a mean trick there with Lester.'

'Was a tall order.'

'You're quite the man of the hour.'

'Am not.'

'Enough to flatter him. Enough to bring him around.'

'Heard what he just said about epitaphs?'

'Don't worry so much,' says his aide. 'He was testing you.'

A light slap to the boy's arm. 'You think flattery's the only way I win my spurs.'

'No. All this was my oversight,' the boy says, again showing nobility. 'Tomorrow we'll go there.'

'For now we have everything to gain. He came over to our side.'

'With these people don't speak too soon. Around here these Pilimas command the rag, tag and bobtail.' There are other, greater tasks and the boy ticks them off — for starters, the dance sisters want Henry to watch a rehearsal.

'Wish they'd come to us.' So early in the day and Henry wouldn't mind a chance to talk to his maid. To show her, perhaps, how something is done in the garden or the house. A task of some variety —

'Don't get lazy on us, Henree.'

'Lazy? one thing I'm not.'

'But you want your plan to succeed?'

'Say *our* plans.'

'*Our* plans, then.' Johnny is walking backward and laughing.

'Say it louder.'

'I won't,' waving his employer forward. 'Come, Henree.'

Now they cross not a bridge — Henry's heart having leapt into his throat — but more a series of loose palm and wood snippets suspended over the abyss of the canal. Henry describes the moment to escape fear, unable to watch the confident grip of his aide sliding his hands upon two waist-high ropes. His mind runs dry and he panics. Finally eases himself by trying to repeat Madame's frequent quotation of the Talmudic formula. *All the world is a narrow bridge; the essential point is not to fear.*

All the world is an essential bridge, the narrow point being not to fear, all the world is essential, the bridge — and Henry's booted foot slips on a slat, making him cling one-legged and paralyzed. With the dark canal beckoning him.

Johnny on the other side, holding the saris, urges him to replace his errant foot on the plank, hands like so, then a bit forward on the rope, speaking Henry through the motions of walking to the other side. *The essential point is* —

Once both heavy feet are solid on land, Henry swallows the desire to embrace the boy. Outlandish and beautiful thing that he is. No part of any herd, every inch a prince.

'Guess we'll have to build a better bridge to cross back later,' Johnny offers. 'Or a ferry.' This is intended, clearly, to cover any potential embarrassment.

Henry can't help thinking the boy shows an admirable reserve of sensitivity and perhaps even native affection for his employer. Replacing his spectacles quickly, the boy resumes his didactic tone, surely to help the moment pass.

'You remember we have just arrived at the side of Monkeyhead Mountain. Here the lowest castes live — the drummers and dancers. The toddy-tappers. And out-caste beggars.'

'You talk big.'

Johnny believes it better, he says, better for 'the projects at hand,' that he and Henry live on the side of Elephant mountain, among the farmer caste, in the shadow of the Sacred Tree Temple. Still terra incognita, then, this Monkeyhead road that they follow, flexed above the paddy's cheerful piecework. Cultivated on plains and low hills, engineered with exceptional simplicity, the paddy's layered terraces continue to impress Henry, with their low mud dykes just wide enough to walk on, their sluices keeping the water dribbling down.

As the two climb by, children and women missing teeth rush to the doors of have-not shanties patched with aluminum bits and cinder blocks. Just to offer him that ardor, that cackle and wave. The unwashed treating him as though he were a baron? It's colonialism that had taught this people how to be flunkies; and Henry has come to free such subjects. In his model village there will be no boot-licking.

'Relax!' he calls to them. 'Please!' But they stand taller and straighter as though one more government census daguerreotyper pulls an invisible cord up through their spines. Henry waves to signal they can move. *Go on. Please.*

'Listen! I'm not taking photographs!' Henry shouts. 'No! none! nicht!' But he could be parading through a magic forest where his effect is to turn everyone but the animals into born fawners.

Meanwhile a gang of dogs follows, trying to get in jabs at Henry's groin. This serves to titillate the audience along the road. Only now do they dissolve into something far more cavalier, a free-and-easy laughter. Hoi polloi, gripping their sides, gurgling as if Henry were a comic gala barnstorming the town. Their joking only increases when he stops to pet a few of the strays.

'They have diseases,' warns Johnny. 'Careful.'

'I have an iron stomach.' Henry himself inflates his chest in mockery of someone diffuse on the horizon. His father at the pulpit.

'Can't be whimsical about this. This is exactly the kind of thing,' Johnny almost bleating, 'foreigners in my charge have to be careful. Even with your penchant for — once, I was helping a Danish man, about your age, with his papers, you know — ' and the boy cuts himself off.

'What were you doing for him?'

'Hear the drums?'

They have passed the down-and-outs and continue to hike the path past the trees, unwitnessed during an only temporary purdah. Now as they round up the last hill, a crescendo thunders down from the yellow mansion alone on the hill.

'What's the name of that flower?' asks Henry. 'Dahlia? daffodil?'

Above them in the yard a woman dashes judicially between laundry lines, a harried ambassador of the clean. 'You remember Kumari, Henree?'

The woman's face has both the incredulity of a three-year-old's and the worry of an eighty-year-old's, while her carriage remains a young girl's, powerful on full haunches.

Once Henry produces the saris, for her and her silent sister, Kumari gibes him. 'You stopped the rains. Now gifts!' It may sound like an insult but she probably means no harm. Without pausing she tucks the saris under her arm and is already scurrying back toward the house.

Later Henry will learn nobody admires a gift when it is first given. That would be considered rude. Instead, they hide it away for later appraisal. As though to say *the gift doesn't matter, in this moment our relation matters far more.* This is hard for an American who craves appreciation. Just a citation of thoughtfulness. A suspended moment in which a blue ribbon for a sleek sow is granted. But from the threshold Kumari is already calling to them in her broken English.

'The rehearsal, come,' bringing them up the stairs as she shouts into the empty hall. 'Sonali, *wature geene.*' Go bring water.

Over the door hangs a handsome frieze and Johnny translates: 'Wards off the devil Balagiri — says *difficulties not today, tomorrow.*'

'Tomorrow?' says Henry, purifying the word. But no time to speculate, they are following Kumari into the kitchen where she finally stops and surveys her guests.

'Excuse me. Just a moment,' says Henry, the first to sit. He takes out his Village Book and writes:

> Ceylonese observation: Certain women feel comfortable only
> in their kitchens.

Henry has never noticed this proprietary smile of Johnny's. 'A habit he has,' his aide explains for Kumari. 'A man who writes everything, no? Doesn't leave too much to chance. Or memory.'

Has Kumari understood? 'O, nice. You two are like kinds of bulls, very clear. Sit down yourself.'

Henry can mostly tell who Kumari is because everything about her suggests corners, down to the smallest flick of her hand, while Sonali, her younger sister, has been cut from a softer clay. It must be, however, the dance that has given both sisters the same proud, stately bearing.

For now it is certainly pleasant to sit again in this kitchen with its checked yellow-and-cream oilcloth on the table and light hazing through the window. Even off-duty the women dance. They perform an elaborate do-si-do around the boiling of the water over the fire out back and the choice of which tea and the final steeping of it in the appropriate china pot and how black it should get and where Henry should sit.

They fuss with each other and their fingertips and the tea and all of it is over him. Johnny had taught him the idiom: there are a thousand ways to be happy in Ceylon. Here Henry finds a new fascination and certainly no bad blood. This is what he'd pined for all his previous life.

Yet happiness is so often the most contingent of feelings. Would the dance sisters be this kind to any stranger? or does something in *him* invite their hospitality?

Henry lets himself drift into a dream, listening to the boy's rapid Sinhala. His thoughts pop and dissolve and he is responsible to no one. One of travel's particular pleasures, he wants to write, is that before you grasp the language you can steal moments of privacy. You view others without needing to be viewed yourself. And the sisters *are* beautiful to watch.

But now Sonali, the shorter one, is pointing Johnny to a closed door that lets off from the kitchen. In the silence that falls, Henry and the women hear everything as his aide enters through the door and latches it. Somewhere behind that door the boy relieves himself with a disconcerting fusillade of groans.

This architecture really turns the stomach

Henry notes: a water closet adjoining the kitchen? At least Wooves' W.C. abuts the house's rear and is a tin bucket with a top that Nani can empty daily into the garden or canal. Henry cares not to be on friendly terms with this, with where waste goes, it hardly concerns him. But this C lacks a W before it. Johnny emerges and washes his hands in the same bucket in which several teacups rest.

Henry will lecture Johnny on hygiene; his sulky aide should memorize some medical advice on the handling of germs. Scads of hot water; abrasive soap; soak thirty seconds; rinse five times; dry on a fresh towel. So far, Nani has helped him maintain such simple surgical precautions in Wooves' house.

But to Henry's horror, Sonali scoops up the teacups from the same contaminated bucket and into these Kumari pours the tea.

What can he do? spill out a little, hoping that hot milk will rinse away Johnny's castaway tsetse bacteria, germs that could attack everyone's systems? But these sisters with their jovial faces have survived after drinking tea from cups washed in adulterated water. He will just have to swallow all Johnny's little microbes and bear them, let the beasties run down his tubes and nest in his sides.

Somewhere in the middle of Henry's cogitations on hygiene, a son slinks in. The son who will be rehearsing, long and skinny as his mother Sonali is a bundle. Putu — which Johnny translates unnecessarily (hasn't Henry been studying every day with the monk?) as meaning Son — Putu has already slurped his tea without a greeting and hurried out.

Now in the kitchen it's not just Henry and Johnny but a gaggle of teenagers from the village who charge into the house with great ownership. By the time the troupe has drunk two pots of tea, Putu is a new man. In the center of the large hall built by his grandfather's grandfather, the boy stands utterly transformed.

Around his neck hang prize silver loops big as escutcheons, his wrists and ankles ringed by intricate votary chains. A silver chandelier of a headdress, its canopy recalling the Temple of the Tooth's roof, crowns the boy. He is timid in his new splendor, not unfeminine, swaying and jangling.

'Whoa!' Henry burps, taken aback, microbes restless.

Indulgent, Kumari leads Henry to sit on the low stage. 'Lovely no? Next week my nephew has initiation as dancer. Why we allow him dress for rehearsal!'

For once Henry is stripped of words. Everything else falls away. *This* boy is the richness of the Ceylonese. Such a royal spectacle. A regular trophy for the culture, all magnet and lure, Putu half-squats, legs apart and bent, splayed, palms pressed before him as though in protest, thumbs rotated down, elbows out.

It is Kumari who begins to chant and beat the drum slung over her shoulder. *'Tay kita taya tam!'* Her words over the drum signal his movements. *'Tajika ta tam!'* The boy's hands, slow at first, alternate an expressive dialect. He pushes admirers away and brings them in, legs akimbo. *'Taytita taytita taytita tayatam!'*

Explaining. Dismissing. Cocking his head back and forth, the chandelier crown jingling. The drums rolling louder. Faster. More martial. Yet the boy preserves his equanimity. Head and face stay calm above the kicks and emphatic hands. He holds no brief for idleness.

'A young master,' Sonali breathes. 'Not because my son.'

'What do the words mean?' Henry shouts over the drums but she just shakes her head at him. Maybe her English is not so good. Henry tries to clap, softly, a four-four beat over the drumming but finds it difficult to continue. He has gone thirsty for something inside this dance and sets his mind on understanding it.

'Takaji, ta tam!' Already the dance climaxes. And resolves to a finish: the boy with sweat above his lip, arms framing a torso sighing and heaving under all the metal.

Johnny manages a smile back at Henry. Shakes his head. 'Believe it?'

'Wonderful!' Henry applauds. And they all startle, strangers to him. He stops and repeats himself in Sinhala. '*Honday! hari honday!*'

The sisters find it difficult to pull off Putu's complicated kingly headgear. The boy butts until they get it off and he is shoved back into his mundane youthfulness.

Henry whispers to his aide: 'Fairly ruttish, isn't it? Chaotic. Like the boy was in heat, don't you think? We'll need to find a way to stick a story into the dance. Or something people can relate to in all this — this —' and Henry imitates the boy's arms during the dance pushing, bringing in, pushing away. 'Otherwise it's just about beasts —'

Kumari cries out, 'You new student, Mister Gould!'

'Not quite,' holding tight to the stage.

'Come,' toying with him or is she? She grabs his hand and pulls him onto the floor. 'Try. Like this? *Tay*,' sticking her leg out but his won't move like that, '*kita taya tam*. Try? You are not a tree! *Tay kita taya tam!*'

No. He *can't* move like that. His body is straitjacketed differently from theirs. An insane fear grips him: they will coerce him into dancing. Little children gathered along the wall are hooting *Tay! Kita! Taya! Tam!* Everyone always laughing and imitating him. Unbidden, unknown, loveless. 'Stop please,' pleading. 'Please I can't.'

'All right.' She's laughing too. 'No worry. Maybe later.'

'No.' Johnny steps in. 'No later with Henree. But Putu! what a talent.'

On the way home Henry decides the day has been a triumph. He is partial to these dance school denizens. The very spirit of light, love and beauty. That's how he describes them to Johnny. Bright flags fill his vision. He speaks of his plans to focus the whole new conservatory. Yes, hadn't James even hinted, long ago in New York, that a dance troupe from Rajottama could tour the island?

'Don't know what you're getting so excited about, Henree.' The boy sounds cross, chewing on a pit of some sort.

'You don't see the panorama —' Madame's trill sneaks into his voice. 'We get children from all castes to be involved. This brings attention to the real society we're building. People will see someone like Putu today and be moved.'

'He *is* something.' Johnny shakes his head.

'We wage a hearts and minds campaign. The whole thing will be a model of indigenous cultural wealth. No one —'

'You gave those women how much money today?' Johnny interrupts.

'For their costumes? Why?'

'Curiosity.'

'You want partners, you need to invest. They're going to buy costumes for kids from the entire valley. Starting next week students'll be flocking to them.'

'Our people hold on to money pretty loosely, Henree.'

'Then we'll give more. Don't fret over such trivia.'

'You know only a certain child will come to them.'

'What do you mean?'

Johnny counts off on his fingers. He thinks the dance sisters will only get students from castes that might arguably be considered *beneath* the drummer caste — potter, tapper, washerman, basket-weaver, and matmaker families. 'But, for example, no one will tolerate if the rodis come. The beggars.' Ahead of them a mixed crowd of birds skitters down, cawing, landing on a mound of darkened peels left in the center of the road. These scavenging birds never get enough. Johnny goes on to explain how Rajottama lacks a few of the castes. Evidently, here are only high farmer, low farmer, cinnamon peeler, metal-worker, drummer —

Henry stops. 'Caste caste caste. You're enough to make a man fall out of love.' He slaps his head. 'Would you stop grousing? This high farmer low farmer business. You're worse than Jonah. When you find fault so much, all I hear is I'm the one to keep things afloat! You'd check the sea seven times and never find water!'

'No,' and Johnny kicks sand toward the squab. 'If *you* hadn't learned at least a shred about Jonah, you'd think you were some kind of messiah. You'd build castles in Spain. Don't you need someone to be your peephole into how things work here?'

'Where did all this come from?'

'My implicit job description.'

Henry cups Johnny's cheeks, obliges the boy to face him close and tight. 'Listen. You of all people have got to be my teammate. Can't keep naysaying —'

'Oh.' Johnny ducks out of his grip. 'You're saying you want enthusiasm?'

Henry nods.

'A dance to show my enthusiasm?' Johnny stirs up the dust now in his imitation of Putu. His long limbs jerk into an approximation of grace. Making a blacksmith pounding inside one of the dark sheds stop his work to laugh.

'Johnny! Okay!'

'Satisfied?'

'Should be in the troupe.'

'See? I'm excited, see?' When Johnny pats the American's shoulder, the good feeling between them gushes back, restored. Johnny has the requisite good cheer. He is again, and Henry reminds himself for the hundredth time, a real and unforced ally, perhaps the ally of a lifetime.

42

THIS SECOND TIME that the pink man had come to Kumari's house, she had, at the end of the day, done what she could to drag him onto the dance floor. If Kumari could see just once how the pink man moved to a simple tay kita taya tam, she would know his core. She already more or less liked him. He had arrived with his helper bringing the dance sisters many gifts. It had been years since she'd had a man bring her gifts. And he'd said he wanted to include the Gunadasa dance school as part of his whole plan.

'You're well-respected,' was how the aide translated the pink roach to her. Jehan had what Kumari considered an almost intolerable accent, explaining the foreigner in bad Sinhalese. The sisters could barely understand the boy. Only Kumari, with her missionary-school English better than Soni's, could talk to the man himself.

How tall he was — she had forgotten.

He was slowly growing something like a Muslim's beard but his skin stayed the color of fruit jelly with swirled-in egg white. She felt sorry for him as she would for anything that had fallen too soon off a tree. Such a lost man deserved hospitality.

In their kitchen he appeared sick just drinking tea. He wanted them to be *partners*, he said. He wanted to revive culture in and away from Rutaeva.

'*Culture?*' Kumari had exclaimed, tittering behind her hands.

Sonali had joined her. 'You want *culture?*' She'd forgotten what this English word meant. But she wanted to be a good hostess. 'Ah, let us have music.'

After Putu's performance the American's pink face had appeared a sponge that made everything around him too dark, as if he floated alone through life. 'We've got to run,' he'd said. Poor running beast. 'But what do you say?'

'Of course we'll help you with culture.' She was thinking of the nuns' beaked hats as culture.

'Tell him to bring us some tins of Shriver's ham,' Sonali had whispered at the goodbyes, not ceasing until Kumari stepped on her toe. Her sister couldn't take the long view about the pink roach. He meant well.

Kumari could tell that even if the American were foreign he was not that far from the marrying type. You could never tell with men. Some would look it but would run away soon as they could get nothing more from you. Others would seem the exact opposite of the marrying type. Men shy against the market's edge, men who refused to dance. Then the following week you'd hear about them being grooms at other women's weddings. But face to face with someone, you know who they are. That's why she'd pulled him onto the dance floor. So what if he'd resisted her. He was still not such a terrible man.

43

THE DAY AFTER the visit to the dance school ladies, the dawn breaks all at once, too sudden and intense, with scarcely a breath between night and day. Henry has been up since two and feels his bearings are off. He can't help it; he must shout down the stairs to Johnny's cottage.

'Do us a favor. Get our maid to leave her pots? She should come with us, to see where we'll get our stones from now on.'

The boy jumps from his hut in pressed knickers and a white shirt. He performs a mock salute, probably imitating the villagers again. 'Atten — *tion!*' There is an element of surprise to Johnny recently. The boy's capable of many small insubordinations.

'Come on, John, my tone couldn't have been that bad.'
Apparently it had been. Henry gets no reply.

In the early light along the river, she walks behind.
'Should have been a diplomat, Henree,' Johnny's saying.
'Not what my housekeepers said.'
'Ah.' Johnny studies him through the impermeable air. 'I get it.
It's Lester. You don't want us to impose on Lester. That's why we're
awakened so early to go stone-foraging?'
'Is Lester really the tax man?'
'There's a surprise for you, Henree. It may be too late for us *not* to
use the Pilima stones —'
A small coterie of boys runs after, in between him and Nani. They
cosset his heels, tranquil in their endeavor of chasing Henry, smell-
ing of boyhood and sweat and pleasure. They quote what must be a
radio advertisement and don't stop with one recitation: *I could eat
Shriver's the leevlong day, I could eat Shriver's the leevlong day.* He loses
her and the boy in the crowd of them.

This is hardly the first of the freebooters he has to get used to.
When they arrive at the putative site for the orphanage, a shock
awaits: a perfect, refined fence already encircles the old barn. In con-
cession to the practical, space has been left for a door. The light ris-
ing off the canal reveals how the stones — who could have done
such fussy work? — had been aligned so evenly their red iron veins
are vertical stripes. And the top is level enough to dance on.
Someone *is* watching over him. A fence had grown up overnight.
'You're right about the surprise,' Henry says. 'So?'
To which Johnny only shrugs. 'So.'
The little boys take up their own call and response: *So so so Mees
Hanree Mees Hanree so so so.*
'Come on,' Henry says, both annoyed and pleased. Whom should
he thank or bless? 'Someone did this for us. Nani? You? Not
Lester?'
A spindly older man rises from his bed, the ground behind a stack
of banyan wood. Of the four teeth in his smile, one is gold. His eyes
are unfixed as if a blindfold has just been lifted.
'Today's your birthday, isn't it, Henree?'
'No. June. Who's this —'
'I hired him,' says Johnny. 'Yesterday. You said you wanted this
done in two weeks?'

'Right —'

'I made an executive decision. Joseph must have worked all night.'

'Well, but why?'

'First, it's true that Nani, her working alone on the fence, doesn't help your cause in the village. Lester's right. A woman working like that won't make you any friends. And —' he stops. 'Anyway it's hard on her.' Seated on a woodpile, Nani cringes at their looks. 'Anyway, Henree — this is Joseph.'

'Pleased to meet you.'

Joseph nods as though accepting a wreath of laurels.

'A Tamil, hired from India for the tea. They laid him off a high-country plantation once he got the spooks from the chemicals.'

'*Something* did a number on him. Hello,' says Henry.

'Think he's a mute, Henree.'

'Then where'd you learn about him, Mr. Genius?'

'Some boy brought him to me at the market. A nephew who'd heard a rich foreigner was hiring.' This puzzles Henry but Jehan continues: 'Someone like Joseph, he can be an all-around handy-man. Work the garden. He'll open our gate and watch over the house. That is the custom for these grand houses, you know.'

'Could've gone into sales. I mean it, Johnny. You're good.'

Joseph half-chortles as though he has followed every beat of the conversation. Inexplicably he shows them the burnt palms of his hands where the skin has been pared to a bright rosiness. A bubble of saliva at the corner of that smashed smile.

Henry bows at him, but to no avail. 'Nani, maybe you can go home, then? Looks like we don't need your labor.'

She stares back. She refuses to be connected to him as he is to her. Or she just doesn't understand and makes him try his new Sinhalese. After his days of intensive lessons he should be able to say *something* but the words splutter on the back of his tongue and he forces them forward. '*Gedere yaneva?*' stammering a mistake. Nonetheless she understands. She bites her lip — mocking him? — and turns back toward the house.

Joseph works his mouth — in imitation of Henry or as if air chokes him? — but still says nothing. 'Come with us,' Henry motions the man grandly. 'We'll set you up.'

On the way to the Pilimas' compound, Joseph trails, his face that of a knight whose battle glory has been restored. Henry can't get over that face but Johnny is trying to tell him something about the former orphanage the Pilimas administered. He'd seen it only a few days earlier. 'More a bed for rats. Those low-caste children might have thought themselves lucky to subsist on Pilima land.'

'You're doing wonderfully.'

'Like a scooped-out shell. This terrible brick dungeon! and then a shadowy room which smelled awful. Like mothballs. Or castor oil. Burnt rice. Rotting guts. Someone must've died there.'

What would Nani do to such a place? 'Sounds like my aunts' perfume,' says Henry. He hopes he hadn't been too brusque with her. If her English would progress more quickly, perhaps he could find out what she is thinking all the time, behind that efficient industry of hers: is the efficiency a mask or a plea bargain?

'You have a lot to work with, Henree,' his aide is saying. 'Your children will be an eager bunch.'

Maybe the boy has turned a corner. His social conscience must be developing. Johnny talks of the slum proles and his enthusiasm sounds unforced. He'd found abandoned narrow hospital cots which the orphans had once marked as individual with proud groupings of stones, discarded tools, and (what touches Henry most) dead flower arrangements. Johnny had also learned how the monk used to administer a dharma talk every now and then. And the last Pilima woman, Manik, would occasionally press money into hiring a new matron for the orphans.

'But you're planning something bigger, Henree. No low-caste will ever be a, what do you call it again, a —'

'A born slave. That's true. Don't pump me up, John,' he said with American gravitas. Still he loves it: the boy plies his compliments so sweetly.

'Your vision is greater than anything Rajottama's ever seen. No wonder even Lester was happy to sign on.'

'Now you *are* flattering me!' says Henry, imagining crowds approving his modesty. A ghost of his Madame creeps inside his heart.

They leave their new gardener at the gate to their own house, Joseph venerable, bearing a trace of the sovereign he might have once been, acknowledging them. And they continue on, through the dense trees that protect Lester Pilima's compound. 'Watch the mud,' Johnny warns his employer.

'Actually, isn't it just after sunrise?' Henry wants to hesitate behind a rogue curtain of trees. 'Maybe let's wait.'

'A courtesy to your Pilimas now will feed you well in the future.' The boy's tone is that of a teacher, all agog. 'Trust me.' And as though he didn't make it obvious: 'All this is for you actually. The Pilimas are no favorites of mine either.'

Below a slippery pass, a bare-chested boy opens a back gate for them, one which gives a wanton creak. 'He's one of yours, Henree.'

Henry startles. 'My what?'

'Your orphans-to-be.' The boy's swagger leads the two along the white-limed house. At the front — newly painted a blaring bright blue, unlike any other Rajottaman dwelling — they find a large-beaked man pacing a porch, raising a hand in threat against a serving girl polishing the balustrade. Her chest caves in but she doesn't re-coil, staying busy at her work and moving to a different spot. Once he sees the visitors, the man lowers his hand.

Johnny speaks with him but the man, Samitha, cannot answer. How many mutes can there be on a tiny island? There should be a diploma for each. Samitha is more a commander than Joseph, however, clapping his hands to summon the orphan. He panto-mimes: chairs are to be brought from the house.

'You'll sit?' Henry offers their host, who has something of an un-dertaker's mien about him: the dignity of silence coupled with an improper relishing of secrets.

Johnny reprimands him, whispering that a Pilima would never sit at the same moment as others, even though Samitha only assumed the higher caste that his brother had married into.

'And you?' Henry persists. The serving boy, his job done, cowers at being addressed. He will not sit but regains his swagger toward the back gate. Slumped, he picks his teeth and over his shoulder, glances back to reflect Henry's eyes but not his attempt at a grin. Samitha claps to make the boy return to the house and it is in calm that the men wait until the boy returns with tall earthen mugs of co-conut juice.

'You're being honored, Henree.'

'That is right,' a woman's voice intones in English from within the house's cave. 'Honoring.'

'Oh, come out,' his aide insists. 'Pushpa, you remember her,' he whispers. 'Samitha's wife. A Pilima.' She surfaces into the early light, a huge relief, this gentle fish of a woman with her thick lips, in the same flesh-colored petticoat and skirt as on that early canal morn-ing. She pushes her hair from her forehead with the back of her hand

and streaks ash across it. Henry realizes that no matter how high the Pilima caste, no matter Pushpa's unorthodox dawn of fence-building, no matter how many servants she keeps, like most women she comes from tending fires, from cooking.

'Hello?' in English and targeting her crossed eyes upon him with utter composure. She could lay a spell on someone with those eyes, outstare a fiend. 'So glad to meet you formally at last, Mister. In our homes.'

Johnny understands something and rises. Samitha goes with him on a promenade around the compound's perimeter — two men trolling on a pleasure boat, pointing and signing. Every now and then Johnny says in his overloud way, *mehemay*, it's like that, *mehemay*, it couldn't be any other way.

'You see I know you,' says Pushpa, her eyes unnerving.

Henry has learned the lesson of patience with his monk and waits, the chair's damp beginning an upward seep through his pants. The woman for her part winds up and refuses to sit. Her hands knit an invisible fabric just in front of her navel.

'I know you. You don't mean bad. You just don't know how to talk yet.'

'Is that it? I *am* still studying,' he smiles. Such familiarity stings Henry. He feels like a deer being dressed out slowly, the entrails of his project pulled from inside his skin with her winnowing fingers.

'You must know we were expecting someone else. James' — Jay*meez*, emphasized like a further shame — 'he was supposed to come live in our house. A great scholar, you know. A great Buddhist. Also part of the family.'

'Yes?' going hot and cold and then hot again.

She tells him she doesn't find him that different from the others. From the other colonials.

'Thank you, that is, I'm sorry, I —'

She tells him they, the Pilimas, they hold a different idea. That, yes, the peasants think Henry is good for the village. Because of the rains. 'You've heard them talking this way?'

'Perhaps this isn't a good time for me to visit?'

She tells him she is speaking to him directly. That she means to help. Her voice softens. 'You are going to turn them against you if you don't quiet down for the rest of your stay among us. But if you act just like one of them and participate in activities, you'll accrue good merit. After that they'll take more kindly to anything you say.'

Her hands punctuate that invisible knitting with a sharp force. There is no right of first refusal with her. 'Activities,' Henry echoes.

She delivers when and what she wants. She says she knows from experience. That if he needs this thing of his to fly, the best approach would be if he could forget about it.

'I'm sorry.' This dialogue is costing him strength and momentum. 'I can't just —'

'Mister. Excuse me. This is a slow country.' She tells him she has heard of others like him. That she has known others. That they all learned to get anything done here, they could hold their ideas as intentions in the heart. But they were ruined if, at the first go-round, they went spending their ideas like worthless rocks.

'I'm not really —'

She says that people will listen to him if his ideas have a chance to build. If they come out slowly. That first he should see who is the most respected here; who has the most authority in speaking — and also see who never speaks at all. 'Since you are hardly going to fall into the first category right off. Better to hedge your bets, as you say.' Charmed at her own expression, she sizes up Henry.

'Possibly too late for that approach,' shrugging. 'Hedging bets. I've already built too much. Said too much.'

She says that is ridiculous. That he has done nothing. 'You think we have not heard you types before?'

'Of course not,' he begins. 'It's just I —'

She asks whether he had heard of the English plow problem? All swipe, nick and pinch. That is what she finds his people to be like. What is he thinking? His famous dance and culture school? Does he bother to know, she demands, that all he is doing is rebuilding the Pilima orphanage? Is he so proud of the plan for whatever he called it, the General Store? She'd heard about these plans. And she is telling him candidly that he will do better to err on the side of being too humble.

'Of course —' Henry, herded, tries to interject again. 'I —'

'A few weeks here —'

'Two months.'

Only October, she states, only a few months here and there is no way he could have built anything. 'Do not be foolish. And the right approach never comes too late. You haven't done anything at all.'

'I —'

She tells him she knows about him. About swapping dreams. She too had traveled. When she was young, her uncle had manned a steamer. She'd sailed the seas during her eighth form. Her school years and she'd gone to China and Europe. She asks does he find this surprising or not? She had been a young girl. She had spent time in his part of the world. 'Is it London?'

'America,' says Henry, his voice almost escaping him.

'That's right. You're a Burgher from Europe.' She says she knows his people. How they like get things done right off. Most high-country people would not have the knowledge she has. She had been only thirteen, she reminds him, and she had traveled with her uncle.

'And you came back?'

'What could be better?' She gestures at the abundant jungle pressing beyond her compound. From the table she lifts a pair of tarnished scissors to make a nonsensical snip. 'Believe me, our people are good. They'll just take their time in hearing you. You understand?'

Henry likes the exactitude of her being more than her words. He nods again. 'I'm listening to you.'

That is good for him personally, she says, and better for whatever his plan is. And then she changes the subject: 'Some here say the light at dawn is the prettiest.'

With a ticklish throat bothering him, on impulse Henry asks, 'Perhaps you'd like to be our first teacher at our school?'

She purls: 'You *are* smooth. Why me?'

'You're an educated woman and know the people.'

'Of course I'll consider, Mister —'

'Henry Fyre Gould.'

'Henry Fyre Gould. Be sure you don't travel about giving false praise. That might work with you but not with our people. You'll get a thrashing for falseness. Here you can't annex everything.'

Having finished her homily, she slows her knitting and turns toward the threshold. When the house has almost swallowed her, she offers a final warning — if anyone ever asks him about his success in Ceylon, he is never to say she had given him the best advice.

'How smart you were to ask her,' comments Johnny once the two are alone. Henry is noting how the cornflowers that originate from the Pilimas stop at the invisible border marking the start of Wooves' compound. 'You have some tactics going, Henree.'

'I doubt it.'

Johnny stares at him like a drill-sergeant. He says Henry isn't allowed to doubt or give in when he is always reminding everyone else to have faith. Yes, Pushpa Pilima is a difficult woman, a high-caste snob, but Henry had aced it, says Johnny. Henry is starting a pattern: first with Lester and the stones, then with Pushpa and the school. 'You don't bicker. You just get them to think *your* ideas are *theirs*, Henree,' the boy said, stroking imaginary chin hairs. 'It's brilliant.'

'Maybe we should call the orphanage Embrace Your Enemy.'

Johnny stops, struck. 'Is that an American thing? Embrace your enemy?'

'Never agitate them.'

If Henry gets a Pilima to teach at the school, that's a real coup, according to Johnny. After that all the villagers will rush to send their children. 'Your flotsam and jetsam. Your *rabble*.' He's teasing Henry, probably, because he flashes him an admiration that looks genuine enough.

The rabble school isn't enough. Henry wants his model village to gain an individual fame. He imagines Nani like a good woman from Antwerp presiding over something like a Belgian chocolate shop. The Loire has wine, Andalucía has guitars, Cremona has Stradivarius. America has munitions and strapping machines. If he could only find the right crucible, his cultural revival will pour across the island, spill over continents.

Gaskets, strong hybrid vegetables, hearty chickens?

On their right they pass the temple. A swath of orange cloth still cloaks the massive Buddha's face. Though the high doors remain shut, from near the umbrella of the Sacred Tree, they hear the scratch of Rosalin-akka's broom on dirt.

To their left the more modest bo-tree, its branches ending in eye-shaped leaves, spreads over the canalside rostrum. 'This is the devale, with its lesser tree for the people,' Johnny explains, pointing out the embroidered streamers and tiny oil lamps trimming the platform.

'I *know*,' said impatiently. The evening before, Henry had watched these people: white-clothed villagewomen who gather at six o'clock for their daily practice.

Amid the voluptuous Buddhas and raisin-eyed gods (who sat variously exposed on small altars, lurking behind transparent veils or low to the ground) each woman had followed her own crusade.

He'd hated the scene; it could have been lifted from his former journalist's life exposing poorly run insane asylums: these women wandering, mouths half-open, mumbling at their own doll-like stations, placing rice on a betel leaf here, lighting incense there. The only reminder of sanity was how the women had waited to gossip until the proper period had passed and they were down the road again, seemingly granted immunity from the divine and its requirements, returned back to the quotidian safety zone. This was the part he had understood.

Now, abandoned in early morning, the women's faded streamers and glutted oil lamps charm him. But how such rampant devotion fails. Henry stops to add to his Village Book:

> Like passionate lovers the women thrust their prayers
> forward only to sit spent in meditation, regaining inner
> control, before rising & passing off into the night. The
> women & their fierce white protest against the dark:
> an unignorably tight flock of birds.

His plan would take some doing. Between this moment and the one in which all the women would enter his model plan, there'd need to be a lifetime's worth of touting and hawking.

He slams closed his book and continues on with the boy. 'I mean, you agree Buddhism *should* be a philosophy, don't you?' Henry asks Johnny, as though they had been disputing this very point. 'Not just bent backs. You agree Buddhism is not a religion, don't you?'

'Certainly,' the boy checking him from the corner of his eye.

'I knew a little about this whole Ceylonese idolatry business, but it's still disappointing. Those statues!'

From behind as though preordained comes the podden slap of feet on the ridged dirt road. A bony-shouldered man accosts them with a sleepwalker's confidence. 'The temple drummer,' Johnny whispers again to Henry, a sneer rippling his face. 'Regi, an old —'

'Regi,' trying out the easy name.

'See how he scratches his ears as though to remove a turban in respect to us? To you, rather. Nod! That will let him stop. And that towel over the shoulder? The sign of a real Sinhala peasant. The skirt shows what he is — a real drummer-caste inbreed. Has to use that special knot in the front. His family's been forced to keep the knees uncovered like that forever, since, I don't know, before your history.'

The man catches his breath, his ribs like bellows. He peals to Johnny in a Sinhalese too fast for Henry's new ears to comprehend. All the foreigner understands is *ShriHenry ShriHenry*, a wind through the man's speech, an imploring susurration.

'*Shri* means famous — or exalted. He's calling you Famous Henry,' his aide translates, lip curling. 'Master Henry. He wants us to come to his house. Show you something.'

'Want to?' The moment seduces him. Idolaters will be won over soon enough; his sensational aide is by his side; the village demands him.

'Shall we?' Johnny betrays more allegiance to Henry's impulse than any affection for the drummer.

'We shall, you merchant prince.'

Above them crows fight over a dead rodent caught in the uppermost branches. Because the rainy season stays ruthless upon them, fickle, the day's light can turn so quickly into what it is now, gold as garden-party champagne, a sheen on the crows, something to write about in the Village Book. But it is too late: the low-caste leads down the road, a skinny temple man whose narrow slapping feet reveal more savvy than any other part of his diminutive self. With that slap alone he could lead them and he starts toward the bridge.

This time, in crossing the water, Johnny is ahead of Henry and is kind in guiding him under his breath. *A step, now another.* From Monkeyheadside, the drummer watches their travails. Once they overtake him, before Henry calms his heart, the drummer has already whirred off on a path the American could never repeat alone.

Over grassy knolls fingered by wet luminous wildflowers; through sheaves of rushes where point-snouted lemurs prowl; across riverstones and finally up a steep stone-set-in-mud embankment.

In utter isolation, on a platform cleared away from the slither of Monkeyhead jungle, Regi's home awaits: an expanse of yard — swept dust and raked mud. Stringy trees which cluster together in the center and then waste into a pile of palm refuse, stacked by a small outhouse tethering the periphery. A bigger daub house roofed only at the corners with Portuguese tiles. Under a thatch canopy, a skinny rice sack leaning against clay pots and the wary vestiges of a fire.

At the heart of this empire, the drummer acquires a magisterial grace. His arms can extend no straighter than a set of parentheses (but there's an eloquence in this). He wipes his hands on a rag; his dented chest rises and falls from eagerness. A mongrel mutt yelps and comes to sit at his feet, head tipped at the strangers. In the house's shadows, half-behind the crimson curtain, a woman watches her man talking to the foreigner and his assistant. '*Shri?* Sir Henry? Come, come.'

Henry blushes at Regi's address and coughs.

'The dust,' Henry tells Regi, an isolated lifer in his odd traits, someone who also doesn't understand English. Someone with shoulders that slope in perennial migration toward each other as though limitation itself can become a god.

At Henry's hesitancy, the dog begins to bark. Methodical ever since they arrived at his compound, the drummer waits for his animal to stop. And lights a kerosene lantern from the fire. With a good host's grace of gesture, he now raises what Henry had taken to be a pile of refuse at the yard's center — actually a loosely woven palm-leaf trapdoor. And this is when Regi signals Henry to be the first to descend the earthen stairs beneath the door.

In that damp underground room, sucking up kerosene fumes amid nameless fetor, Henry does not know what in the quivering light he should take in. Johnny gestures at something indistinguishable. Then Henry sees.

On a low cot before them lies the thing. At first Henry takes it to be a large doll with a balloon face, its puffed limbs skewed, its eyes closed under curly mats of hair. A low cot stitched of gunny vegetable sacks supports a body the size of a five-year-old's. The doll sputters; the wide engaging eyes open; Henry realizes he faces a monster baby.

'Sir Henry,' says Regi in his violent and frayed voice.

Would Henry be able to say, later, what in that moment — or in the low-caste man's shoulders and ingrown face — wracks him? He could not. It is hard enough to return the gaze of the doll baby.

Under the peat ceiling shot through with roots, Regi sits next to his child. With great care and an elliptical embrace he stretches her arms to a more natural angle, his lips brushing her cheek. He bends over, replacing the rubber pacifier which had fallen from the mouth — actually a British rifle's discarded stopper-ring.

All the while the drummer strokes the baby's globe face and rolls out a litany. 'Regi thought you were a doctor,' Johnny eventually translates, soft and low as though in church.

'A doctor?' Which from Regi's tone would probably mean a deliverer, a champion, a guardian just short of a god.

'He *thought*. Being a doctor you could cure this son, his firstborn. Now twenty-five years old.'

'Why?' having meant something more somber.

Johnny explains how Regi is drummer caste, a man of few choices. According to the drummers, marrying one's father's sister's daughter is the best achievable pairing, and Regi had done this. 'Even the upper castes consider it good. Purity —'

The drummer reaches up suddenly, saying *SirHenry, SirHenry*. He grabs Henry's hand in his own rough one. And places the foreigner's massive hand upon the child's belly so Henry feels the uncertain throb of the child's miraculous bird heart and the tiny organs trembling against this jest of an extended life.

'He's saying he sold almost all his ancestral land. He spent almost all the money on herb doctors. Even Western doctors. Now he's asking if you could cure his son.'

Henry peers into the father's blue-rimmed and blind-looking eyes, not so dissimilar from Nani's. Reckless and full of mettle, though the father's brim with a love Henry hasn't seen in that spooky girl's gaze. 'Tell him I wish I could cure everything.'

The drummer scratches behind his ears.

'A show of shame,' says his aide. 'Why don't we go?'

'It's —' Henry shuddering badly '— don't you ever have the feeling you're taking up too much space in the world?'

Johnny gets to his feet, telling Henry not to take this one too hard.

'But don't you ever have that feeling?'

'Maybe we should go?' says the boy. 'Or what do you mean?'

'I could so easily *be* him. I could be here with my son asking the foreigner for a cure. It could be me fixing drums all day. It's just an accident the shoe is on one foot and not the other.'

'Sometimes isn't it all right to wear shoes?' Johnny answers, nonsensically.

Henry is nauseous from privilege. Blades of it line his throat. He tells the boy he has the urge to extract himself from his body, he can't explain it —

Johnny coughs and coughs again. Asks shouldn't they go now?

'I mean,' says Henry, 'my conditions are like a husk.' He can see a myriad of little Henrys on a hilltop, risking nothing.

'I'm sorry, Henree, I'd like to — can't quite follow you there.'

Because he needs to, the American again takes the drummer's hands and stares into the man's almost blind-looking eyes. It is possible there might be a heroic truth exchanged in that moment. Henry can't say for sure. The drummer might simply allow himself to be stared into while staying closed as a firewall.

Ceylon eyes? Such striking eyes. No west wind down there.

Johnny stands with an abruptness that thuds his head into the ceiling. Nothing speaks before Johnny translates what only the air must be telling him. 'He says, Henree, we can leave, Henree.'

After they reemerge into the fresh morning, the drummer calls to the half-hidden woman. 'Ruwini!' Her thick hank of hair swings behind her not unlike Nani's (it must be the fashion, Henry thinks) and she hurries to give Henry his gifts: two bulbous gold-flecked green fruit. Henry feels the fruits' weight, tiny breached infants he doesn't know how to carry. He holds Ruwini's bruised gaze until he notices the mineralized waves of scars broken across her puckered belly.

'Pawpaw, Henree. You've been calling it *papaya*. You see,' the boy happy to resume his tour-guide tone, 'most Ceylonese are actually quite hospitable.'

The drummer must have decided this moment to be the apex — he embarks on a final heated plea to Johnny. Watching, Henry feels drowsy or drunk. The man goes on talking even as the visitors clamber down the stone-embedded incline back to the road. And then a toady smile screws up half Regi's face.

Up from a well below the road comes a boy, 'the drummer's *other* son,' whispers Johnny. Though he wears a sarong, refinement makes the son clutch a cloth to his bare chest. A boy you'd never complain about were he yours — broad brows and an expression glowing some tender of intelligence.

Johnny smiles. 'Hello, Manu,' in brisk Sinhalese. 'You've bathed?'

Henry understands this much. *Nanavade?*

The boy eyes Johnny's spit-polished shoes and his white pressed shirt. He cocks his head as though listening to a distant forest call. When Johnny repeats himself, the boy swings his hair so water spirals out. He shrugs and crosses the arena made by the visitors.

'Shall we?' Johnny asks his employer. He pushes his glasses back up his nose, his skin's shine impenetrable. 'You'll see how our people are. There may come a time when you'll think that there's no man alive who doesn't want anything from you.'

'Then what do you want?' — but his boy just swings his head in good imitation of Manu.

Carrying the green-gold fruit, Henry descends the path to the canal bridge. The trip to the drummer's may have cured him of his fear in crossing. He doesn't speak until they reach the side of Elephant Mountain.

'Know anything about all this?' he asks finally.

'They'll be ripe in a few days,' answers Johnny, his bizarre bray of a laugh smothered at the end.

V

THUS HAVE I HEARD

ॐ ॐ ॐ

Q. What are the Ten Shackles which, unless renounced,
keep us being reborn endlessly?
A. Those Ten would be the following:

i.	Illusions promoted by Self and Selfhood	Sakkayaditthi
ii.	Doubt	Vichikichchha
iii.	The belief that absolution arises from oaths and penances which the Buddha would never have accepted	Sillabbata-paramasa
iv.	Those passions born from the senses	Kamaraga
v.	Anger	Vyapada / Patigha
vi.	The desire for life in a world of form	Ruparaga
vii.	The desire for life in a world without form	Aruparaga
viii.	Pride	Mana
ix.	The lack of an ability for concentration in all practices	Uddhachchha
x.	Ignorance	Avijja

44

His head has died atop his neck. Henry bolts up into the night's clammy press and trembles. Slipping Wooves' Chinese robe on, he paces through the still hall to the outer patio. The well-chain protests with a mild squeak but allows him to bring up a bucket of clean water from the Yala. He pours this into his morning teacup which she had left on the counter. The night is so still around him, his exhale almost echoes. This loveless air sweeter than jasmine.

Had Nani left a fire burning? He follows the scent to the outdoor oven where a stubby joss stick smolders through the dust. An unscheduled item which he sifts ash over.

He's glad she's not awake.

He pads so softly that she probably doesn't hear his approach. And there she is, rocking upon a cushion at what can only be a clandestine altar, the closet door ajar behind her. It slakes his thirst to see her. But she has hidden this corpse, this superstition of hers. And just a few weeks ago, she had pretended to be one with him. He'd explained how Buddhism had lost itself. How Buddhism had become a patched pirate of its former glory. And with her listening she had betrayed him — nodding as much as any Western woman would. She had nodded and played agreeable while he'd inveighed against wrongful prayers. Against paganism.

Meanwhile, now her long back is seated before a white Buddha and an appalling algae-scaled bronze god. She bows, unknots a rope hanging from a nail, frees some stalks of dried lavender, rubs the flowers on her cheek, touches them to her forehead, and ties the flowers back up. Such ponderous movements. *Is she a liar like the rest of them?* O the banality of betrayal. She'd kept herself hidden. How can she be part of his house when her behavior is as changeable as a woman's rouge?

If Henry could, he would spy on her longer. But that would be blameworthy and go against everything. All that's left for him to

do is tiptoe away. Her devotions must stay private, his own voluptuous pet.

Ordinarily he would forbid this misbegotten paganism. But life is
so rarely a menu. For the first time, Henry understands why Wooves
in his later years might've held the Algonquin in such high esteem.
At the Algonquin, you could order a whiskey sour and receive it exactly as you'd like, ice cubed in the right glass.

Each of Henry's steps back out to the kitchen is an exercise in
compunction. Secretly, he wouldn't mind joining her. He wouldn't
mind helping her long idolatrous fingers with the rope, the nail, the
lavender, devotions.

45

As the hindus say when speaking of insight, the ears of his heart
finally listened to the voice of his soul. And the idea for the catechism had swelled like a restless newborn.

His pamphlets will unite all the schoolchildren in their knowledge
of Buddhism. As quickly as Henry can during a January when according to everyone the rains should have showed signs of abating
— but didn't, building on one another instead, this monsoon from
an endless sky — he has been working with the monk, compiling
truths, Rosalin-akka kept busy refilling their teacups: ginger, tea,
milk, the taboo pleasure of sugar.

Often Henry arrives at the temple under only the stars' altar, just
after dawn. If Pandit has not yet awakened, Henry will spend the
time in their room, poring over the monk's sutta translations, enjoying the dandyish pulse of the crickets here, insects flirting indeci-
sively between alto and soprano.

Once Pandit comes, they close the doors, banish all truancy, fall
into happy work on the catechism, broken only by courtesies such as
wouldn't you say that and *of course we should never imply that* and *good
job.* The general flurry of papers back and forth is so pleasurable that
repeatedly before Henry knows it father and son outside are beginning the evening drumbeat. At which time the monk must make an
appearance — if only to light incense — among the women and
their pagan tapers before the lesser tree's gods and buddhas.

'Tell me if I'm keeping you from your duties,' says Henry habitually. Sometimes he wants the sanguine monk to be as urgent as he is about the mission.

'We are fine, Colonel,' the monk will respond, serene enough. He goes along, will sit and work out hard theological points with Henry into eternity so long as Henry is there prodding him with questions. And yes, a little less passivity would be welcome but how can Henry complain? Maybe years of meditation take the edge off a man. And the monk has spent entire weeks with the American. All day, with house-trained calm the monk could work — or, equally, watch Henry's progress and be amused. So it seems.

Maybe Henry has to work on shaving off his own edges.

On one occasion the American had departed, forgetting his good pen and Village Book. When he raced back he found the monk snoring in his chair.

'Tell me if I'm tiring you out,' he said to rouse his mentor.

Pandit had awakened with a start. 'You're fine, Colonel! Our duties can wait. You are considerably more interesting than our duties.'

Henry wants to be more than just *interesting* to the monk, more than just a specimen: but this is a greed, one impossible not to recognize. Especially given their work on the catechism:

Q. What are the principal causes which help sin to arise?
A. They are three: greed, anger, and ignorance.

Everyone's interested. As the monk and he work during those long weeks, the drummer and his son file by, casting surreptitious glances into the room. Regi won't acknowledge Henry so long as the monk is with him. But Henry marvels at the drummer's industry: both father and son appear to carry out a great deal of — what *are* they doing exactly? — *activity*, especially when their only real task consists of beating the drums at six every night. They prowl around most of the day, bound by caste laws to the temple, repairing drums, trying out rhythms.

One day he will address this issue of their workload and time commitments. For now, Henry's heart-ears must be flapping, the urgency of the catechism project speaks that strongly to him. This catechism is necessary, he wrote, because:

— The people's pagan devotions arise only from ignorance.
— In a model village, ignorance needs to be eradicated as punctually as evil.

By some grace, he has had only good luck here in Rajottama. But there remains ignorance in the life these blessed villagers live and (Henry has it firmly engrained in his brain from both his father and the suttas) ignorance can produce evil. While these villagers can show wholesome loving souls, Henry knows that anyone choosing a morally correct action *by mistake* can never be a fully moral man. Are they ignorant or lazy?

For example, no one has signed up for his projects, no matter how much he and Johnny had canvassed. Henry's calculations say he needs thirty able-bodied men by the end of January, when the locals say the monsoon should finally have let up.

Only thirty men. Not so many after all. Ten for the school; another ten for the General Store; a final ten for the model garden and the subscriber vegetable service. Thirty volunteers. And he has none. No one has ceded to the newcomer.

In between storms he has roamed the market with Johnny, suggesting to youngish men that they get involved, make the effort, help ensure their children's future by pulling Rajottama out of its poverty et cetera. Johnny has translated all this with noble fidelity.

And the people are listening. No feet tapping or eyes straying. They thank Henry for what he has accomplished with the rains. Because of the deluge and the crops he must be a good man, they say, often with unnerving humility. He has asked for just enough water, but not too much; he must have powers; they certainly would be the last to wish his plans any ill.

Worst is how they will never say no directly. Some scoot away fretful. Others only smile and shake their heads and continue on their business. The shadow that follows him everywhere is the only thing to volunteer. *Miss Hanree, Miss Hanree*, his shadow cries, those scrawnbucket orphans. The urchins scatter only at Johnny's *Ssst!* When Henry's alone, they are there: jumping up and down, interrupting all proceedings, raising hands high in the air as though ready to be called on.

Too bad the orphans can't be his volunteers. How hard it is to relay the message to the villagers. These projects are for *them*. Their delayed enthusiasm ends up siphoning *them* (as well as him). Can't they see that?

46

A FEW EVENINGS LATER, unable to *nikang inneva*, to just exist, and feeling restless in Wooves' library, Henry finds stuck between Gibbon and a field manual a whole different kind of logbook. Fairly well-creased. Entitled *Notations on Amatory Matters Throughout the Ages:*

> Italy 1754 — Italian lothario Casanova boosts his legendary prowess by eating 48 oysters each morning, using a comely female breast as his plate.

That night — is it because there's no rain for once? — neither he nor Johnny can sleep. The boy gets their rapport going further by reading more from the *Notations:*

> England, A.D. 1000 — Burchard I, Bishop of Worms, describes the making of love bread. Naked women frolic in harvested wheat, which is then milled counterclockwise. A male who eats bread from this flour is said to become sexually ensnared by the woman who serves it.

Hardly ensnared by anything, the two of them, levitating free into the night. So what if Henry's spirit got pierced sometimes, it *returned,* that was the gist of things. Maybe it helped keep them both aloft.

Especially after yesterday's affair in the market: Henry had been talking with the friendly marketplace jack-of-all-trades, Roshan, a young fixer with a superb brash face — Roshan who could transform a rusty Mighty Motor engine from Kandy into a propane-powered water-boiler–cum–vegetable-chopper. The marketplace beggar, who with his piebald face and guffaw chooses to dress like a Vedda, thus pretending to be one of the last aboriginal hunters, had charged down the hill costumed in loincloth. At this, the Muslim trader, Zahir, called for help. Apparently the fake Vedda had stolen Zahir's spittoon and escaped. Yet a pall fell over the market. No one would help. Because Zahir was a Muslim, they explained later; because his fruit prices were too high (though no higher than anyone else's). This inertia — such discrimination — it was pure and clear wrong. A terrible sign.

And when Henry later tried to reason with a small group at the market about the model village's need for agricultural volunteers, a Sinhalese man did not listen, just squalled his objections: 'I am rice FARMER,' slapping his chest. 'What I know of model life? PADDY. BULLS. But I KNOW. Poor people when you rich? You find no one work for FREE!'

Henry had tried to make a joke at this, but had also gotten angry, stamped his foot, let himself get a bit carried away. He'd dug into his waistcoat pockets, found a Lincoln-head penny of all things, flashed it high enough that a pretty light hit it hard and bounced back. He had been here since mid-August and now it was January? This *daen* of theirs — which was supposed to mean *now* — hadn't yet worked for him. He needed something to move and now. *Now* in the Yankee sense. 'You want money?' Henry started to shout. 'Here's money *daen!*' thinking the people could use a little scene as motivation.

What would happen if after this constant deferral he fell to the ground foaming and spitting? If mired in sweat he begged for help between drooling gasps? How long would it take for someone to come to his aid with anything? with a doctor or aspirin or laudanum or, never in a million years, Coca-Cola?

When is a doctor coming to help me? he would ask from the ground.

Daen, they would say, as they do to him now, tee-heeing or boo-hooing. *Daen* which really means *next week* or more often than not *never*. *Daen* which is never the now he presumes as his birthright. Never the now that cuts straight through all flab to reality's nitty-gritty. Never the now which means now.

He kept tossing the coin in the air until Johnny managed to pull his arm down, whispering, 'You can't show you're angry here, Henree.' Intuiting more was needed, the boy added: 'Your plan will work only if you never show your frustration.'

Though he and Johnny began their first insomniac night with the *Notations* in the library, the next six nights, rain stilled for the first time in weeks, they prefer to sit outside, where the palm leaves become jagged spokes, dark swords radiating out from the safety of their bench. *She* goes to sleep early, and won't be drawn into any talk after dinner. So Henry rues that the rains hadn't let up earlier. These little bouts of insomnia, shared in the dim outside, save Henry from the chains of nocturnal loneliness.

Finally Johnny gets loosened enough by the port to talk about his family — his mother, and especially about the father who vanished. 'I couldn't bear the perfidy,' says Johnny, a week after they'd seen the marketplace ignore Zahir.

'What does perfidy mean to you?'

'Think I know?' giggles the boy, candor he rarely voices by day. 'I don't.' He looks up at the stars, bountiful tonight. 'That one's Hydra?'

'No, probably Berenice's Hair. Haven't showed you that one yet. Or maybe the Hunting Dogs. See the snout?'

'Henree! last time you said the Charioteer!'

And Henry laughs back, drunkenly. This is amusing: the boy is enough of a gratification to justify all upheaval.

Not knowing what perfidy means and saying it. *I don't know.* And being unsure about the constellations. Creatures of an inferior species would not be able to laugh at themselves so deliciously as Johnny does in these unguarded moments.

Always, on the other side, lies what Jehan has been trying to escape his whole life: the chasm understood by the English and their colonials. A fate worse than a knife stabbed straight through the gut. As a young boy it had been no secret to Jehan that his school's superstitious rows of chairs, memorizations and canings were preparation — all the coconut-oiled heads were getting Morse-coded for a single job.

Clerks. They were to be clerks. The boys were children of desperate mothers. Of fathers stunted in their ambitions. The offspring needed the canings' code and Anglophilia if they were to race forward on that single but coveted track toward the future. In which, if luck prevailed, one could have one's own cubicle.

Jehan knew this much. Any head slicked with precious coconut oil was getting molded into a clerk's cranium. The biggest irony Jehan saw was that the single way for the once-elected clerk to stand out from others was if he conformed, religiously, with all the rules.

Be bright, the code whispered, but not too bright. Erasures should be no neater than anyone else's. Make consistency your deity. Keep your lines and accounts not just straight but as consistent as the rules that had pressed them into being (not a jot more or less). This nation of clerks knew it must keep shirts white and ironed, pants scrubbed and tactically pleated. Then what a kingdom awaited.

A nice girl could be married. If one followed the rules, nicer children would be born who would grow to attend even nicer schools. If they protected their patrimony, these children would soon have acceptable spouses bear the nicest grandchildren, who would one day sight (the clerks could only hope) some more attainable god in their shoes' spit-and-polish.

But never wish to be so unexceptional as to be exceptional. Hope that some superior might peer upon your ledger and exclaim at the inordinate *consistency* of your clerkdom's sir-saying mass. The hope being that the attainment of such machine-like dependability (once noticed and redeemed) would promote its pious to roaming outside the stalls of ledgers. With such power the former accounts-keeper, the ledger-maker, and the line accountant could not only father an appropriate line, but could provide voice to the people from whom he had sprung. Which meant helping his village; and helping a village usually meant his mother's home what with its trustfully swept yards and unclipped shrubbery and its clean sun-scented clothes hiding such longings for her offspring.

But did this sequence ever happen? Jehan often had wondered.

And was it because his father had disappeared — whether while fishing, during a rubber plantation incident, or from sorcery — that Jehan had early on scoffed at both clerkdom and its promises?

'You're listening so carefully, you see,' Johnny shrugs, in answer to who knows what. All their camaraderie and desultory comments are a reward. It is over these shots of port and in the luxury of night that Henry believes the two feel each other's history most keenly. The boy moves Henry, even as he speaks of his childhood with a reporter's false objectivity.

'You get the picture, Henree,' Johnny's voice resumes in the darkness. 'I was the kind of a boy in a room who thought my name practically written on my ceiling's wattle and daub. One of those grandiose boys. You know, whose only toys are ideas about the future —'

'Is that so bad? Maybe we were meant to meet.' Hadn't every lurid sunset of Henry's own childhood been marked with lightning bugs flashing out hope?

'I was ruled by self-pity.'

'Don't know anything about *that*,' swigging a drink now become oddly viscous.

'My stepfather snored one room over. The terrible part was imagining my mother, all those —'

'Dark gropings.'

'Each noise I heard made my real father more awful. Why should he have risked my future life just for some night fishing?' What Jehan is trying to do in telling these stories is simple. To see whether he can bridge the distance between him and the pink man he's supposed to be spying on.

'Couldn't he have died in some plantation trouble? Your area's famous for all those uprisings. The south. The rubber —'

'Sometimes in life Henree you just know certain things?' a volley discharged and then softening. For once — charged with this accepting Yank — Jehan might not have to worry about how well he's blotting his copybook. 'Whenever I saw fishing lanterns on the water at night, I knew. My father didn't die in some rubber marsh. He died at sea and gave up my life.' This freedom between them is so rare, earnestness fills the boy — still, how much the foreigner understands is left for grabs. 'Get it, Henree? Sheer luck how other boats went missing at the same time as my father's. Otherwise like you, everyone would've thought my father had been some kind of insurgent against the colonials. That he'd been silenced. You can imagine how that might've been the end for my mother.'

'And you.'

'We would've been swallowed by gossip. Or punished maybe. Who knows.' Jehan won't breathe to his boss the worse alternative. If his father had left by choice, the gossip could say some evil spirit must reside in the wife and son. And Johnny would never impugn his mother in this way. 'She'd spare no lesson or gift on me, Henree. You can understand. She wanted me to have only the best.'

Even in the dark, Henry thinks, such mother love can never be wiped off the boy's face. How his Johnny must have suffered during his school years. 'I never wanted to save any mementos from that time,' he says, when Henry asks whether he still has his schoolbooks.

From the sound of it, Johnny had been too bright for long rulers. And for teachers grave with discipline. For seniors bent on ragging when all Johnny possessed was height. That explains it. The boy's occasional arrogance. His arched eyebrows and know-it-all tone. 'You found a good front to protect yourself,' is all Henry says and sees the boy surprised to be recognized. 'Your sensitivity probably drove you to exactly the brink your sensitivity couldn't handle.'

Jehan elaborates, inches closer on the bench. 'Say I had one or two classmates willing not to be cruel to me — you know, that childhood way of small kindnesses. I couldn't think they were worthwhile. They pitied me. Then I pitied them back for their altruism.'

'Such a misanthrope?' Henry rises to fix a swallowtail branch made disorderly by the new wind. All during Johnny's sorry history the branch wouldn't stop whacking the mango trunk.

'On my own I thought things could be done better. I raised myself. Or looked for other misanthropes to match me.'

When Johnny tells the story of his childhood (each night a different face gets told) Henry prickles at the boy's vulnerability. 'I'll do right by you,' he finds himself repeating to the boy often, something that generally gets no answer. He says this again tonight. From the mango tree the boy could be a still life, a crustacean poised, glass near his lips, dark thick around him. 'You understand, you're a hard one to help. Because you know too much.'

Tonight praise gets deflected with grace. 'A long bandwidth but it's all low-decibel. I know a little about everything. I'm like a pearl necklace. Not strung very well.'

Henry succeeds in adjusting the branch. Do American elms or beeches behave in such an unruly fashion? By day he'll get the girl to wire-bind it. 'I'm not blind. The problem is you only really listen to me — maybe you're learning from me? — if I talk about self-sufficiency. It's the only topic that makes your ears grow longer.'

'Unfair!' his aide cuts in, jumping up, raining fingers on the back of Henry's neck. Sweet pinpricks. 'I listen to you all the time!'

'You are disconcerting me,' Henry's voice coming out nasal. He turns on the boy and assumes a military posture. 'John, can't you tell me what made you sign on? when you were hired to help me?'

'Nighttime attacks? Unfair! And under the influence of drink? Dirty tactics, Henree. You promised you'd never ask, right? About my hiring,' spluttering, laughing. 'Anyway, should I bring in the other bottle?'

Weaving a little, Jehan takes care reentering the house's cool, caught in musing: can this whiskered man understand a split of his boyhood? *This man who so dares to dream others' lives*, Jehan says aloud. What *does* he know?

Nothing, really, of schemes plotted like constellations on a ceiling, nothing of nights with an ear pressed into the radio. Nothing of the radio's brilliance — *Thank you, and good night from Radio Ceylon, from the heart of the Bay of Bengal!* — which had taught Jehan to speak as though for the first time. The radio which had taught him how to out-priest the priest who had bequeathed it to him.

'So you never told me what caste you were.' The American is practically bubbling over with ideas by the time Johnny returns. He turns up the wick of the lamp so the beveled bottle of crème de menthe looks like a huge diamond. 'You toddy-tapper or what? I got a letter from my friend the insurance poet in Stamford asking me which caste you were. Is that rude to ask? That's all we have left in our cupboard? Isn't crème de menthe a ladies' drink? won't it be too sweet?'

Johnny pays attention to the cargo at hand, smooth at pouring the dark syrup. 'You wouldn't want what the gardener drinks. Arrack's too strong for foreigners.'

'You're probably not toddy-tapper. What then? Farmer? not drummer? metal worker?'

'Maybe I should give you arrack after all.' Johnny makes a move to pour the drink on Henry's swollen hands.

'Johnny!' pigeonlike, parodying himself for the boy's benefit. Mock stentorian. 'It's for — our village!' He beats his chest once then twice then once again. 'Sincerely! We need to know where your sympathies rest. What's your family made of?'

'Coconuts. Do you remember that children's song about the pussycat going to London to visit the queen?'

'So I should think you're made up of coconut meat and oil?'

'The oil's good for hair growth,' pulling Henry's own hair. One avenging second, two, three. 'Makes it less wispy. Fuller.'

'Oil-heads? is that a new caste?'

'My people,' taking a draft of syrup and choking. 'Needs water. We're clerks, Henree. Tell your friend the poet I'm a clerk. Prone to a feeble lack of resolution. All us clerks.'

'What kind is that? Clerrick?' the words separating despite all efforts to fuse them into a single gorgeous sound. 'How long's that been for? shall I call you Clerrick? You know,' Henry sloshes his drink around in its glass, a tiny ocean, and speaks into it with asthmatic sincerity, 'say you had six fingers, I'd still take you.'

Jehan slides next to the benched man. 'What does that mean?

Take me no matter what? what if I were Muslim? or Hindu?' he asks, though it is more than likely certain distinctions mean nothing to Henree.

'I'd take you,' declaiming and stamping his foot, 'Hindoo.' A jolted gecko clacks back.

'What if I were the king's son ready to kidnap you and your ideas and your soul for my court?'

'You're embarrassing me. I'd take you!' He's obliged to stamp again. And in this vaulted night it is easy to laugh together.

As they sip their crème, Jehan eyes the Yankee's form with hungry suspicion. Does this man radiate reliability?

But if my life were at stake I would trust him, the boy finally decides, *more than I would anyone else. More than anyone from Headquarters. This man would do what was right* — he sips again, considering — *what he would believe to be right, in any case.* There is more than flourish between them. There may even be something like love. Or at least affection.

Genteel. Gentlemanly. Gentlemanly affection. He pulls a mango leaf out of his glass and offers it to Henree with a mock bow. *In another few months I could stay on with Henree. Stay of my own free will and then come clean with him. Tell him everything. Really be a partner with him in our projects.* Here he chokes back some disbelief. This Yankee has won Jehan over to some new vista, all on the strength of the man's rampant faith. It's a rare strain of charisma.

47

TELEGRAPHIC DISPATCH FROM KANDY OFFICE TO 'CHILKINS' BY JONATHAN NELLIE AT 16:23, 20 JANUARY 1937:

YANKEE SUBJECT APPEARS TO BE EASILY MANAGED. PROJECTS PROCEEDING OF COURSE UNDER OUR TIGHT GUARDIANSHIP. SITUATION UNDER CONTROL. REQUESTED FUNDS WILL SOON BE SPECIFIED FOR IMMINENT PROJECTS OF LOCAL SCOPE. CONTINUED SUPERVISION BY THE UNDERSIGNED SEEMS ADVISABLE FOR TIME BEING. REGARDS WHOBODY.

48

THE PLACE KNOWN as the plantation in Rajottama is a forgotten dream of a thing. A secular barracks with girded walls and rooms opening on a courtyard amiss with small puddles like a geomantic chart. On one of the loose doors a single rusted nail secures a piece of looking-glass.

If the plantation remained as it was on that very day, and you had found yourself on the interior walkway, you would have discerned on the eastern patio wall a mural's faded outlines. In it, happily tempera'd natives cavort inside sheaves more closely resembling corn than anything you might associate with the coffee bean. There they are in pseudolatin broad hats, the natives, scudding along, raising bright baskets and harvesting in their garners piles of ready-made brown beans which in artistic execution lie not too distant from piles of excrement.

There is something a bit off in the artist's vision, you might have thought, a painter who'd left his work unsigned. Whether the mural was commissioned originally to inspire the coffee bosses or their minions would have been unclear to you.

As for furniture, only a wooden bench and a stack of holey canvas cots had been left behind. Everything still bore the ghostly contours of the chiefs, whatever lot of men they might have been, sincere or arrogant or vain.

But here amid such ruined splendor — rather than in the draped confines of Wooves' house or on temple grounds — Henry had elected to hold the first meeting of the model village. Once again he is inspired by the idea of the phoenix, a concept he believes untranslatable to his Ceylonese villagers. Deep down he knows that if the delegates (he conceives of them as a mini–League of Nations, ambassadors from the canal's different regions and castes) can understand that what started their economic and cultural deprivation began on the plantation, they will, just as quickly, acknowledge the necessity to start something fresh, with Henry's facilitation, right from the seat of their loss.

There is no storm today and for that godalmighty boon he is more than grateful. Because this Maha monsoon pretends to stop and then continues in a constant scrimmage with his patience. Cold rains from the east won't stop blowing and still everyone is thinking this a sign of Henry's particular gumption. Late January and they are asking him about it. 'I'm sorry,' he keeps saying to everyone, wishing they'd take it all as a joke, privately ruing the thing.

Hence the day's fair skies are a timely occurrence — only creepy remnants of life stir *inside* the rooms, with no place on those ghost floors for Henry to commence any meeting. Instead the men form a disjointed ring outside around the map of little lakes, slouched against the hot walls, watching the water evaporate.

For the record, they are:

| Lester X X X X | X Regi |
| X Roshan X | XX Zahir the Muslim |

Henry had suggested that each delegate bring along two 'colleagues'; several X's, unknown men, clustered around the delegates. In the New York salon, Henry would have typified some of these mugs as being either archetypal bourgeois or preening intellectuals. Here in Ceylon, however, Henry knows such men must be up to truer things. Who's he to judge men by their faces? Especially at the moment that he subjects them all to a standing torture.

Yet clouding over everyone's heads are the favors Henry has left undone for each delegate. Their own antipathies toward one another; the mistakes he has already made; that each has made. Even to their host, such clouds are mostly visible.

And none of these men really know how much Henry has sacrificed. He would like to begin the meeting with a tale of some hardship *he* had suffered (he is not just the dispenser of good fortune) but manages to forbear.

Today he arrived like Samson: naked-handed, shorn of the help of Johnny or the monk. And this had been intentional. These delegates should trust him and his tactics. They should discern no desire for evasion. The hope being that a sense of self-sufficiency and surplus value can be stirred up in these men.

Yet and yet: it is only the end of January and after more than four months of intermittent language lessons, speaking and understanding stay a problem. That is, Henry can speak. It's just that outside his household no one fully comprehends all the phonemes he utters.

'*Kohomede?*' he'll have to repeat several times, just for someone to understand *how are you?*

Kohomede? Honday?

Fine. We're all fine. Excellent. After the preliminary greetings (at that, everyone's a natural) Lester has to be pressed: he will perform as translator. But the bear looms over Henry and starts, spitfire, right in the middle of Henry's own sentences.

'We'll be brief,' says Henry at the beginning. 'Thank you for coming. You are the seed of the proposed model village. As such —'

'We are?' Lester preens in English like a real class clown. Then for five chock-a-block minutes translates the foregoing with great importance, while Henry studies the roots of the man's toupee as if reading the codex to an illuminated manuscript.

After he finishes, Henry continues: 'We need to assign paying jobs among the twenty-five-odd families who belong to Rajottama's very heart. Originally, as you probably know, we'd hoped for a show of spirit. For volunteers. Barring that . . .'

'Only twenty-five?' rebuts Lester.

'We will not contrive to draw a geographical boundary line. Because it was dictated by the colonial regime. When this is the kind of imposition our model village argues against. That is why all of us here will rely on families —'

And prompted by some internal stirring Lester growls into another translation. He is interrupted only by Regi, who asks, in a meek Sinhala, whether at the outset he could suggest that he himself, Reginald, temple drummer and servitor, be considered to help man the General Store about which he's heard so much.

'Of course!' Henry sighs; this first show of enthusiasm helps him overcome a growing desire to flee. With a flourish Henry notates the first quasi-volunteer in one of Johnny's blue accounting books:

Regi = General Store

'Shall I continue?' asks Lester, without waiting for an answer. He perorates for another ten or so minutes, a man on a campaign. After which only Roshan the watchmaker raises his hand to say in English that despite any ambivalence anyone might have about the newness of certain plans, the person setting the agenda for the day's meeting should be the foreign mahattea, Mister Gould, since it was he himself who had called them to discuss the model village in the first place.

'Correct!' agrees Lester. 'Let's hear from you. As mudaliyar, I call upon you — Fyre?'

Startled at being called upon, Henry tries to sum up the most important ideas. Number one being who will take on the other jobs? This is done hastily:

1) Lester will oversee the orphanage-cum-school, to be built from the very site where they convene.
2) Someone TBA will oversee the model garden.
3) The delegates will forward to Henry any other suggestions.

Henry departs thinking much verbiage was expended at the cost of later effort. Perhaps he relies too much on consensus. Maybe about now a little authoritarianism would be in order. Even steel filings need a magnet. This doesn't have to be a timocracy, exactly; he can just orient the people's will even while he models it for them.

By February he has become a king of morality, though the rain continues to insult the people's faith in him. As Rajottama lacks a printing press, Henry sends a notice around the village, with the ink barely dry. He's hired the dance sisters in their saris to slosh through mud. To each dweller, the sisters will translate Henry's screed: fountain script on embossed ivory paper:

In the much-regretted ABSENCE of VOLUNTEERS for the Projects on Behalf of Rajottama's Future, its Directors will be hiring men on a permanent part-time basis, to be supervised by Lester Pilima and others TBA.

Meet for Hiring Day at 10 A.M. on February 4, 1937 — On the Site of the Intended School and Orphanage. Wages offered.

49

OFFERING WAGES may be fine and well but February 4 dawns and Johnny on his cottage threshold speaks like a regular laggard. He's still tinkering around his house, he says, 'too many things to do.

Meet you at the site in another half-hour or so?' he offers, retreating back before his boss can do more than gulp.

The boy will come in half an hour? Does he know how Henry must quash a feeling of inauspicious abandonment? It's one thing to choose to go alone; another thing to be left alone. Half an hour? Henry stares into the mean faces of the gladioli growing strong next to the boy's cottage and gathers his senses.

On his cracked pocket watch it is the rational hour of 9:30 as he leaves then, a soloist, walking toward Hiring Day at the abandoned coffee plantation: remembering New York headlines, the way they used to stream before him all day like fiery letters in the sky. Right before he left the States, the front pages kept ranting about the civil war in Spain and how munitions were crossing borders.

But the thing he misses most about the papers in New York is their deceptive smallness: a beam could fall on a Times Square worker at lunchtime and cause him to speak French all of a sudden. And across America the next day, if people chose, they could read about the beam. About the worker's Irish wife, his bright son, the obscure verbs that he conjugated and the dog that ran after the cab taking the worker to the hospital.

He used to love how what happened in New York always got disproportionate documentation. As though the place had been gerrymandered to represent all of America. This, when New York is hardly a microcosm of the States — hardly the capital!

Henry is wondering how to obtain for Rajottama some similar wave through Ceylon; through Southeast Asia and then Asia entire; through the other continents. One by one, modestly, a new vision would open up: seeds of self-reliant communities, free of foreign interference.

Surely what he's trying to accomplish here has more importance than a beam on a worker. Also more relevance. Henry's history of the world outside of the States is a bit shaky — he did come to Ceylon on a fluke — but he is the first to know that there have been colonies all over and in unlikely places. Even in Scotland the Manx could say they had been colonized. Everywhere: colonies. Indigenous wisdom waited to be decolonized and untrapped as far as you could see. Maybe he could write a manual for other Henrys: *Pay wages first; get the volunteering going later and then —*

Trailing onto the road off the plantation is a long queue. Still dreaming, at first Henry has the quaint thought that all the old blights had been conquered. That the defunct colonial coffee farming has arisen again —

he frightens awake realizing instead these men have come for *him*. And what men — people with whom he has not spoken the five months of his stay here. None are men he had canvassed while in the market; none are those he had seen at Roshan's stall.

Instead: sulky ruffians with unruly facial hair. Only a few of the starved children from the main road's shanties. And all with some docility as though what awaits at the top of the line is some blessedly eternal dispensation.

'Our people are good queuers,' Johnny had once told him. 'You have no idea! They will stand in line for hours! Especially for anything from the government.'

'Colonialism,' Henry had said.

'No. Childish hopes.' Johnny had corrected him with something Henry thought no different from colonialism. 'Spirit's been beaten out of them.'

Nothing, but nothing, could justify or gratify the hopes in this queue. Henry studies the people; from behind lowered lids they scrutinize him back. No one makes a move. Their attention cannot be shaken from what must be happening at the start of the line, where perhaps, he prays it's so, some alternative event might be taking place.

He prays it's so. 'Excuse me. *Samawenne*. Going through.' Henry brushes by their stiff bodies. What a nightmare this could turn out to be. Where *is* Johnny? '*Kanegatuy*, con permiso, sorry —'

The men smell of kasippu and craven desire and allow him to squeeze past them and the gates to their old plantation. At the head he is happy to see Nani and Joseph's stone fence around the storage hull; here the line stops, however.

Apparently there's no alternative event.

How numbing. The valley has disgorged body upon body, each expressing some swindled human life. Men with glittery jewels for eyes and loose wrapped rags around arm stumps, men with feet leprous ostrich claws. Men clearly born soldiers and others fit for the wet-nurse. Men who could have been clobbered by anvils and men themselves anvils. Young boys and those short of a limb; the hale elderly and those with ulcerated hulls for bodies. A rare few with vigor and energy in their profiles. But no matter what, all eyes drill into him, all faces line with expectation. For starters, his Sinhala is not up to this.

He should have told Kumari and Sonali to *whom* they were to announce the hiring. A crucial point he has overlooked. There must be over three times thirty here: a hundred unfit men or more. He feels the dizziness that tends to precede a fit and tells himself *not now, you can't, Hank, stay standing.*

'Well,' addressing the crowd in English. 'Hello. Good morning.' Compared to their thundering silence, his voice fizzles. Impassive faces turn on him. 'How should we proceed today?'

In the crowd there are no Lester Pilimas. No Johnnys, Pandits, dance school sisters, or Pushpas. No Nani. No one to help him beyond the impasse he has created. A riot is not out of the question, though these Ceylonese are more peaceful than any American mob would be. He has seen the bloody moments of Tammany Hall employment lines. But here there are no anarchists. No social Darwinists. No danger, he hopes, but what *had* he been hoping for? That by ten in the morning as if by magic thirty able-bodied men would appear ready to work? thirty and no more?

There is no danger. 'How about for today,' mock-folksy, 'let's each write down a name and our qualifications in this —' He pulls the Village Book out of his waistcoat pocket and repeats to find his balance. 'Your name and qualifications.'

A tide of Sinhalese licks through the crowd. Today Henry will exclude no one. Henry beckons the first of the hundred forward. He knows he comes off like some kind of beleaguered milksop but can't switch off his own panic. 'Come, please. Write your name . . .'

Slowly each would-be laborer comes forward. Whether sullen or fearful each shows a formality signing his name, invariably long. Whether disabled or whole, each concentrates on the letters in Sinhalese or, in the rare case, English. This one pushes up his sleeves. That one prays to some unseen deity before entering his curlicue, squiggle, the pothooks and hangers.

Later, Henry'll get Johnny to decipher such cacography, but for now, next to each name, Henry writes in code *(V)F* or *(V)U* to mean *(very) fit* and *(very) unfit.* A way to caption the cuneiform of their physical beings. For his own benefit, more than for the men in line, he keeps up an unremitting patter:

'See, thirty's a prime number for us. Not mathematically, of course. Just means there's a chance your name won't come up. In which case —'

All white shirt and oiled hair, out of breath, Johnny lopes up. 'By gosh what a crowd!'

Henry is so angry he can't speak.

'Look, shall I take over book duties?'

But Henry has gone on strike.

'Had to get a telegram off. I'm sorry about it.' Johnny's words fall like swirls of ticker tape. 'Good show though, don't you think?'

For once Henry will show the boy what it feels like to be unable to rectify a situation — in this case, a silent boss. The thought shames Henry; but his loneliness up until now has stunk more. Finally, after the last man limps up to put his name in, Henry captions him with a big VU, a send-off smile, and then slams shut the vellum book.

He waits a few — but crucial — seconds and then begins his scold: 'Is getting a telegram off more important than what we're doing here?' Each word acid on copper. 'Do you realize it's after noon? You care more about your import-export business than what we're doing here?'

'No.' The boy actually thinks about it. 'That's a lie.'

'Who would be that important you would've needed to send them a telegram?'

'Nobody.'

'But maybe you have a mean streak. You want to hurt me? You're trying to make Henry lonely? Or you think you can just dash off your duties? What is it with you?' He tramps around the boy and comes to a stop. 'Tell me why I'd want to work with someone who does this kind of thing to me.'

Unexpectedly Johnny's face crumples. 'Didn't do it *to* you.'

'Oh for god's sake,' sighs Henry, seeing the boy's spectacles filming over. 'For god's sake.'

The boy's chin rigid back at him. 'Listen, Henree,' bulleted. 'I. Do. What. I. Can. Every. Minute. You've got to see what I'm doing for your projects —'

'— *our* projects,' a little reluctantly voiced.

'Our projects. I am with you. A hundred and seventy-five percent. When I don't even have to be. No one makes me do all I do — you've got to at least give me *that*, Henree —' It's obvious each word convinces the boy more and more of his righteousness.

'I do —' as if they'd just wed on the site of the debacle — 'I think you're with me. You've just spoiled me, is all. I've gotten too used to you. Your help, it's there, we just need it.'

The shade from the plantation building has crept over them. A raw chill travels down Henry's neck. 'Let's get going then? Maybe you'll take the afternoon off?'

Johnny pats his employer's arm. 'No need.' And more than quickly retracts his hand, a five-fingered perfect hand working *with* him, something to be appreciated.

'One day maybe you'll tell me about this business. It gives you enough money to live on?'

'I don't need much,' the boy smiles. 'Isn't there enough coconut here?'

'But you'll tell me?'

'You worry too much, Henree,' and the boy has returned to his other self, 'you're worse than I am. Always thinking your idealism is misplaced.'

'Who says it's misplaced?' It seems the most important thing to do is find a way to be grateful. Henry wants to give up worrying.

'Didn't your Madame once tell you not to trust people too soon?'

'Who says I'm trusting?' He tells himself again that he has this intelligent boy: the kind of ally he had always wanted, the kind people will often die for.

50

ON A FEW NIGHTS Jehan's insomnia goes unanswered by his employer's. He sits alone on the bench, trampling weeds underfoot, practically waiting to dance. He has no radio here: hasn't Henree been better than any radio?

But when Henree is deep in his snoring sleep, nothing can make nighttime pass more swiftly. Sure, Jehan could read; but he knows how reading can both populate your world and intensify your solitude. It takes no stretch of the imagination to understand what Henree means when he complains about being *made* to feel alone.

Whatever Jehan pretends to during the day, night takes his measurements. Leaving the compound and walking alone — that, too, scares him. One dead of night, early February, the monsoon still hasn't decided whether to give up or not. It lingers, ghost and prediction, the air humid and restless. Jehan cannot take it any longer. Night locks him up, that much is unmistakable, fear has become his private warden.

He rises from the bench in unconscious imitation of Henree,

pushing off from the knees, a vertical swimmer. Above the gate stands the gardener Joseph, a flambeau of sorts, Joseph who has taken on the house sickness of not sleeping anymore.

You can tell that Joseph used to be a smart one. As Henree says, that would have been before the hill plantations did their number on him with what must have been close quarters, hard labor, chemicals everywhere. The Wonder-Gro had a way of slowly attacking the nerves. Jehan has heard about it. Any imported Tamil with a shred of independence — which Joseph may have had — would have suffered brutal punishment from the plantation supervisors, until the hour when the workers could gossip and cook their rice in a mud pot over a fire made of spoiled tea leaves and refuse.

Joseph should be about the same age Jehan's father would have been, had he lived. But surely Jehan's father would never have let himself be so abused. From the way the gardener had tried to describe something one day, his head had been pegged from a fight involving planks or a corrugated roof or sharp upward kicks. He had Jehan feel his skull where an iron nail — something worse? — had been jimmied in and could not be taken out.

Now a foolish grin yawns across Joseph's face. Maybe he gets joy from being useful at any hour, in the formal waltz: Joseph waiting, Jehan arriving at the gate, Joseph creaking it open. Passage and closure. In all this ritual lies mysterious reassurance, better than the unpredictable pair in the house. Much better than the isolation of night, a night which grows live around Jehan.

Some carding-wool mist rests low on the road and the trees next to the canal hold themselves unbendable. But he hears a call, the hustle of bodies. Extended among husky palm fibers lies a dead lemur with its entrails fatted worms, its snout split open and gaping, as though to lick the rancid cream scent of the canal and its nightsoil. Away from the temple, for no huge reason, Jehan walks south. Where the road curves and the swamp cleaves around him, he stops to listen.

A crow caws by his ear but he does not jump. It has been good to escape. To see night beyond Henree's compound. And then another noise, a stomp and *whist!* as if the path itself rends cloth.

He turns up a thin road, past hovels which by day boast ever-bathing semi-naked children. He and Henree have never come here together. What need has there been? No one considers it part of the official village of Rajottama. A no-man's-land caught between the administration's laylines for Rajottama and Durbbhiksha, a dense shantytown, it lacks name or government.

The people here live in a universe where the coin is demons and possession. Their religion would laugh at Henree's horrible distress, the covey of clean-clothed Rajottama villagewomen in white who at six in the evening share tapers with their temple Buddhas. Here even the Buddha rests uneasy — just another statuette in the devale, another to be cajoled.

Jehan sniggers, uncomfortable with the diaphonous scene before him: in this area Henree's planned catechism would become first kindling faster than the Yankee could say *I take refuge in the Dhamma*. Villagers would dance around the bonfire . . . I take refuge, murmurs Jehan, the words preventative medicine.

But the words fume away, inconsequential there in the jungle and among the houses. A hostile compromise has been reached: ramshackle dwellings tuft amid what looks to be the stronger order of vinous trees —

— a pain shoots up Jehan's thigh and he slaps his leg. Two leeches have worked their way up inside his trouser leg and suspend from his calf. Little feeding bladders bloating with his blood —

— and he has no cigarette ash. No salt. Unable to see the creatures plumping on him, he does what he should not and wrenches each hard little body off. His childhood Father had taught him never to do that. Tonight he disobeys and disobeys some more until only one leech head lodges just under the surface. Later he will have to sculpt a trough into his skin to extract the creature; yet ridding himself of the feeders had been his only choice. He wants to walk unencumbered. The thin path pulls him through the jungle until he hesitates, barely breathing the charred air, where thin-trunked trees have grown too dense for vines; a clearing is signaled ahead. Brave, he advances through the trees like a larger man careful not to bump into dancers.

The boys stand in the tunneled light moving their hands in wave and frond forms: sea anemones in the heavy atmosphere, these adolescent villagers gesticulating in formation. Across the field, two teams of them approach each other with uncanny synchronization.

Barefoot. Dressed in belted brief pants and collared shirts. Softly applauded — and the glint through the trees reveals the seated female villagers cheering the boys on. Jehan recognizes some of the marketplace girls despite their bell-shaped uniforms, their western skirts.

With utter gravity, the girls are practicing a subtle elbow jab to one side and then to the other. If you chased them, he thinks these people would leave you grasping air. He stands so painfully apart from these specters and their togetherness. Beyond the girls, elders known to Jehan only from cursory greetings attend in silent witness.

From within these, a robust man rises. He slices his hand across his forehead and beats his forearm twice. While the profile is craggy and strangely familiar, slanted moonlight does not render the features distinguishable.

The boys halt as though the sky itself had dropped a directive. As one they crouch low to the earth. Next moment they're jumping high, legs kicked forward, with the colossal mass of girls shifting up thrashing, angry weavers at an invisible loom.

Jehan can barely breathe and his thigh boils. When he pulls up his trousers, he cannot see his calf for all the clustered black bodies, an army of leeches! Nausea burbles up its gall. His lips burn and he turns heedless through the trees, branches snapping, going in the wrong direction. Then through the trees, the tall man's look bores into him: Lester Pilima sees Jehan and is seen back.

Without control the man rolls his shoulders. Now the boy understands how the pseudo-Pilima pseudo-mudaliyar's tolerance has never been a jot more than pseudo. What comes clean are not the leeches but exactly how much the Pilima abhors him. Alarmed by eyes made bald, Jehan backs away from the abutment.

And then runs.

Safely returned to the garden, he hears no terrible boom, which he'd somehow expected all the running way back. His heart beats ready for anything. Catastrophe, brimstone, total collision. But only frogs pulse the heat around him, content creatures. Tonight, he could use a radio. And really use it.

In the kerosene sanctuary of his cottage, Jehan pours salt over his leeched legs. The jokers' bodies spiral off his legs, pinging onto the floor and making a dry crackle, their carcasses balled in a final defense against all incursions. In the morning he will sweep out the leeches, empty out his little graveyard. For now, with one of Nani's tingling herbal ointments, he rubs his legs until they are rawness itself.

Only now does Jehan Nelligodam, late of the coast, a good boy known to some as Jehan Nelligoda (Sinhalese) to others as Johnny (more Yankee) to still others as Jonathan Nellie (more English) and to another as *puta*, as *son*, only then does he throw himself onto his bed, having for the first time forgotten to remove his shirt, a mistake no good aide or Cambridge scholar or even a young clerk would make.

Lost and far from perfection, Jehan Nelligodam — by birth, as far as he knows, a Sinhalese Tamil Muslim Burgher — Jehan Nelligodam has finally become like his boss: lazy and enamored of sleep, that tricky lover.

51

TELEGRAPHIC DISPATCH FROM KANDY OFFICE TO 'CHILKINS' BY JONATHAN NELLIE AT 15:34, 7 FEBRUARY 1937:

AS SUGGESTED IN THREE PREVIOUS UNANSWERED COMMUNICATIONS PRESENT CHARGE COULD PROVE INDISPENSABLE TO CONTROL AND IMPLEMENTATION OF OVERALL COLONIAL PLAN I.E. OVERSIGHT OF PUTATIVE ESPIONAGE. PROMISED FUNDS SHOULD BE REQUISITIONED DIRECTLY AND IMMEDIATELY TO CHARGE'S FOUR MAIN PROJECTS. GENERAL STORE CATECHISM ORPHANAGE AND SCHOOL/CULTURAL CONSERVATORY. REGARDS WHOBODY.

52

BLOW THE TRUMPET in Zion; sanctify a fast; call a solemn assembly. Great passion quickly becomes collective. At lunchtime, during February's most fevered work on the catechism, if the rains don't condemn him indoors, Henry will take his break not by sharing rice and Shriver's potted ham with the monk.

Instead he will rush down to the site of the orphanage to check on Lester Pilima. With respect to Lester, it is hard to remember exactly whether he had *bullied* Henry that day at the plantation or *agreed* to Henry's invitation to foreman the orphanage. Whether bully or not, he is after all (he'll tell you each time) the informal chief of the village, its mudaliyar. Through an exquisite number of shoulder rolls and upward glances and moments of bravado in the initial meeting, the man had virtually set in stone that he would be the school's construction leader.

But Lester looks born to his job. He apparently loves to stand like a low-caste paddy farmer stripped to his waist, tunic wrapped into a turban. His torso is burly and glossy, efficient as a muskrat's and far more than what Henry wants to know about that body. But Lester does seem happy to have men working around him and happiness, no matter whose, each drop of it, doesn't it help the scheme here?

Lester had his men build a banyan scaffolding around the colonial coffee storage hull. This was how things were done, apparently. You innovate within and atop the old — now, however, the whole structure with its scratchy scaffolding bore an unfortunate resemblance to Lester's toupee. 'Why waste a good enough building?' Lester will bristle.

Henry knows it best to be confident in delegation. Trust your men, leaders always say. Destruction of the old, yes, that would have been preferable, the Yankee way generally tending toward total demolition, after which one can always begin again from scratch. Yet now that projects slowly proceed, Henry's legs and spirit should not quake.

'Whatever you think best,' he demurs, as part of his Buddhist practice.

At Henry's site inspections, Lester waves with vigor and import and just as immediately returns to his men. From under that tight brow he stares as though staring will help his charges in their hammer-and-roping. Such a glare must help in collecting taxes. He had probably gotten the tax sinecure with his choler and in most of his dealings manages to prolong the M.O. of the childhood bully, full and intact.

In contrast, the foreman Henry had chosen for the model garden had at the start acted gently. He'd cast a pearly coating over everything by sending his own personal *representatives* on Hiring Day. Not himself.

When Johnny had in the first week of February summoned back the potential employees Henry'd marked as being Fit or Very Fit, Chollie had shown up, *without* his VF minions. And rather than wait for the public meeting just a few hours later at the orphanage, he had paid an unannounced visit to Henry's home.

Nani had knocked on the bedroom door with some alarm. Guests never came like this. Her surprise made Henry stumble out in Wooves' moth-eaten silk robe and his thermals, only to find Chollie there, dignified, already seated in the library's verdigris light, its drapes partially drawn.

When his visitor rose, Henry understood. Chollie leaned on a cane and came to Henry's waist, yet sported a compensatorily long mustache and beard about which Henry would later write *Resembles a hanging marmoset.* This was a man who made no bones about his origins, a man who in a charming English, a guttural, speeded-up lord's, bade Henry to sit down behind his desk.

'I'm the man you'd call to fix things, it's my name Chollie you'll see cut into trees anywhere inside Ceylon's four corners! Don't bother with the last name! You wouldn't know the caste from it! I'll tell you that much. Call me Chollie, Gould, I am from something less common in the high country,' he said, his cane tapping out a syncopation, 'the toddy-tappers. Low but high! You'll see why.' This would perhaps be the last true thing Chollie would say, but Henry's realization of this would come only many months later.

'Why *now?*' Henry blurted, meaning the visit took him aback.

He did not mean to be ungracious. Something in the man commanded both candor and complete obedience. Henry remained behind his desk and its safety, face assuming his default receptive expression, while Chollie was washed with half-dark, being a stunted stopple of a patriarch against the windows and the ambiguous light now stealing across Henry's lawn. 'You hate us, don't you?' Chollie's voice could carve oceans.

'Why say that? In point of fact, I could not be more in love with Ceylon,' this last nonsense drifting low in the room. 'You didn't want to come to Hiring Day?'

'We're trying to help you here, Gould! No use backing us against a wall! You might not have chosen the best man for the job if you'd *seen* me!' He lowered his regal dark eyes, having spoken the truth again: Chollie is VVU.

Still, after months of swimming through the villagers' indirection, Chollie's modest arrogance touched Henry. That first meeting they exchanged only a modicum of chitchat, Henry trying to suss the man out. Some fermented breadlike scent, a certainty, wafted around Chollie and his assured statements. Doubt would be poison to such a man.

Only midway through their little discourse had Henry made the suggestion that made the tapper light up. 'Why not try out as foreman for the model garden? We left it open. If you have experience —'

'Experience? Someone then told you how for four years I've overseen twenty-two acres of palm trees? Practically eighty-eight years. Not to mention the seven years I've guarded three tanks on high ground! Like twenty-one years. Three tanks! All alone I shot and killed sixteen herds of elephants! also leopards! Beasts that came at night to destroy one of our chena fields. Once I saw a pride of leopards kill a lion! But I took care of them. Do you know how delicious leopard meat is? Yours is a very good idea, Gould! A leader should know how to manage, no? And you and I know enough when we see it, enough —'

— the foliage outside the french windows crackled. It was just after dawn but beyond the drapes, Ceylonese children were pressing their noses up against the glass. Even a few adults towered among them, enough to make up a poke-nudge-twinkle mob all over again —

'— enough is right!' rasped Henry. He yanked the drapes closed. Had the gardener let in these clowns? Once before, Joseph had forgotten to close the gate. Then how happily the children had amused themselves. For hours beyond midnight, they'd played catch with coconuts yet to be gathered from the yard, up until the millisecond in which they smashed one of Johnny's windows into a vitrine spiderweb. Then like so many tiddlywinks they scattered.

Such moments when the village spills into Henry's life endear no one to anybody. Henry would have to install a better hasp. And also drill into the gardener the need to keep it closed.

He would soon find that any trucking with Chollie made it impossible to find peace. The dwarf went nowhere without a herd. This may have arisen from Chollie's own instigation but only one person would know this for sure. The man was cagey, that was apparent. 'I keep my back covered, Gould!' he said many times.

In that first meeting with Chollie, Henry had excused himself, had found himself running through the house. Where was she? Seated on her little board in the patio, legs spread forward. On the fixed metal knife between her legs, she was scraping coconut into fine shavings. Her ceaseless tantalizing task. 'Go,' he told her. 'Tell Johnny what's happening. Serve the people coconut juice. Calm them down. Get them to leave our grounds, get Joseph to help. But whatever you do, lock the gate after them.'

At moments like these, she rallied. Strong girl with a thinking head. He could depend on her. Never any protestations. She did not say, for example, that *the people could always storm over the gate should they want*, since Henry's 'grounds' are an only symbolically enclosed paddock. She never said anything ridiculous like *there's not enough coconut left for the midmorning drink*, which she favored and had begun to press on Henry. With her, you'd never find dithering. All godspeed and lightning, she understands commands. Dispatched, she leaves promptly. Much later he would remember these moments, her eyes filling with a gauzy light and yet also taking him in, as if he might be understood.

She and the gardener soon dispersed a crowd made happy with their native treat from the pink man's house. And commandeered all this without having to wake Johnny! This Henry would learn the day after. Much to admire. And she was never vain. Henry often had to press her to learn about her prowess.

In the moment, considering her smoky nature — docility or decisiveness? — he hurried back to the library where Chollie had reseated himself, the man unfazed as ever, hands crossed awkwardly on his lap.

Henry considered him. 'You've got admirers.'

'Not the only one, Gould! *You* know how it is. Some idlers have nothing better to do than gawk and gape.' Smiling out of his unflailing self like a wooden saint. 'But all right! Maybe I do have a few fans. Because there's no escaping dwarfhood.' He must have known mentioning any brand of banishment would make Henry go all soft and runny toward him. He was onto something else. Some difficult contrast. 'You go back to America, Gould, so many pink people, who stares at you? No one. But where could I ever go? To a country of dwarves? Is there such a thing?'

'No —'

'That's right. Nothing for me but my toddy-tappers! You see how it is? With my tappers I stay invisible because of my visibility.'

But Henry cannot remember what invisibility feels like. Especially any time he heads toward the dwarf's model garden. Midway up the hill from the canal his own entourage tends to find him, Henry's orphans who never tire of chanting *Miss Hanree Miss Hanree*.

Some are earnest and try to clasp his swollen hand. Some give him wildflowers with roots stretched like talons through the dirt. Some just tag along. By the time he reaches the garden he's a real Gulliver. How has Chollie ever gotten used to such a cloud?

At first it had been hard to appraise Chollie's leadership style: the man with his reptilian body good at being a pope of repose, lying with a bottle of palm beer under a tree's shade. Only occasionally do any commands burr out, and so huskily that even in English his words overreach Henry's hearing, sounding like cabbala.

Does the beer make the tapper more or less charming? Tappers make this *teleje* drink by spicing holes in the palm trees; sap is said to run through the spices and into their buckets. The idea Henry's heard — from Chollie, of course — is that teleje makes a man stronger than others. Drinking teleje, a man can live for days like a hunter. Because of teleje, tappers are said to have an uncanny link to the earth and the palms' spirit.

These days, whether owing to beer or not, Chollie never smiles at Henry. Instead he forgets charm's whole sway. His main interest is procedure. Salary procedure. He is incurious about Henry's *whatever you think bests*. His own prerogatives, that's what's scaled to a priestly level — almost all else has been defrocked.

He does bother to make assurances to Henry. That for example the garden's under control. O my men! he says. They throw up gobbets of earth! And work double- and triple-time! More than the school workers! And when are they getting paid? A guttural peril to this, as though everything is just a variation on what he'd said that first day: *do you know how delicious leopard meat is?*

Chollie also has a penchant for questions. One of his favorites is the following: what does Henry think of the fact that buffalo stricken by 'the foreign disease' will wander home to their birthplaces, 'no matter how many miles away! They head over roads and through streams! All animals go back to their homeplace, Gould. No?'

Henry stops answering and by the third week of February starts to cut short their meetings. How do men like Chollie and Lester gain their power? How were things given them so easily in life? They were burnished and happy and believed they occupied some proud place in an order of things. Both could rule any room they entered. And *why* exactly Henry had surrendered the garden to Chollie of all people, he can't quite specify. As far as Henry's concerned, Chollie has turned into Lester.

But not a doodad can be changed. From Henry's previous projects he knows going back on your word incurs favor among no one. No horse likes being changed in midstream. You get only rancor for that.

Watching Chollie he speculates on a juggernaut. No matter how carefully prepared the ground, there's *something* in the man, a heaviness brooking no uncertainty. But what if all projects love dictators? No doubt, he reassures himself in Johnny's tones, with someone like Chollie in charge, the garden will end up truly model.

Luckily, in regard to payments, the monk had offered his help. He will oversee administering salaries to the foremen, to Lester and Chollie. This way Henry can stay uninvolved and for this the American's grateful. The whole idea of payment smells sordid; especially when Henry's original hope had been for a completely volunteer effort.

All Henry had asked was that the monk pay the men according to the fair going rate for the out-stations. He'd handed Pandit a wad of bills from his own decreasing bundle.

'You're a trusting man, Colonel,' Pandit had smiled.

'Economics bore me.'

'Also an honest man. That is good.'

'Not so much that. But we have an expression in English.'

'Don't hesitate, Colonel.'

'Well, in terms of money, most people would say I could bullshit the balls off a cast-iron monkey. I'm as good as the next Tom.'

'You are, Colonel.'

'But frankly, I'm not interested. Isn't money ultimately a deception?'

'Yes, and in a world of illusion, what does money become?'

'But *money*, saddhu — how can you buy time or exchange one value for another with money? Isn't it one of our biggest lies?'

The monk sluiced a thinner smile. 'Of course. It is only because of your worthiness that we consent to handle yours.'

The monk's particular breed of irrelevance — a monastery rhetoric? — always manages to balance Henry's mood.

'If we'd had volunteers, I'd have been happier.'

'You're handling all this extremely well, Colonel,' he'd been assured.

So many extremes to handle. If it weren't for Johnny's caretaking, the extremes could knuckle Henry down into their center. For example, there had been concern from Johnny's corner that outfitting the General Store might take forever. And the boy, good for him, takes charge.

In February's second week his aide had suggested they make something like three round trips up and down the mountain to amass all the inventory in one clean go. And the drummer's son will drive them expertly in the carriage which Roshan had just finished equipping.

The first trip down to the capital, Johnny kept warning that even inventory might not be simple. 'Years to establish relations with merchants, Henree. I'm not talking delivery and invoices. I'm talking policy sessions. Long afternoons over tea. Much discussion before any agreement even starts to be voiced.'

'Ridiculous,' retorts Henry. His trip returning *down* the mountain enchants him far more than Johnny's drib-drab pragmatism. Here are all the same waterfalls and quaint villages! the encroaching heat, live as a leopard!

Virtually his trip of last August but in reverse: the same flat palm leaves bend down, irradiated an explosive silver, serfs bowing to a sun king. A tinge of gold, now ash, spangles the trees. Below them tadpoles of light and branches, strewn on alluring jungle paths which he'd love to run on and explore, hungry to crunch things underfoot. And the cliffs with their waterfalls and pools: they're tall, sculpted from a mahogany deeper than any in America.

Then he gets a glimpse of a bather's bare breasts, no mirage but full-tipped, that same rich earth! But wasn't her nipple's berry much darker than mahogany? And if the bather turns away it is only because that is what she does, she *turns* — not because she is afraid of their carriage rattling by.

He has become a constituent element, a component of this landscape.

Even back in America, at city hall, say, when renewing a business license, Henry would feel simpatico with the people who sat patiently on rickety chairs in the corners of rooms. Not with those who shoved forward in their entitlement, speaking impatiently, expecting service. All his life he'd thought himself most aligned with anyone who felt they dwelt most on the margins. He took as adult evidence of this that his few childhood friends, those in the neighborhood who'd consented occasionally to play with him, had been, without exception, children of teachers, preachers, porters and maids.

He may now call himself part of this Ceylon margin — and he may even have accomplished much in this last half-year. Yet too much remains to be done. Henry shores himself up: 'Time is our sole commodity.'

Johnny laughs. He's still in the middle of his monologue about how long everything will take. 'Oh — not sure they'll think that. The merchants. If time's a commodity, you'll find they spend like millionaires —'

'One can change certain systems when one dares model a new way of being!' explains the elder. While speaking, he imagines he outdoes Madame. And in Johnny's young/old face, doesn't he see a mirror of rapture?

By the third trip down the mountain, he thinks time has played its hand too fast against them. He has Johnny hire a city man to help deliver the last bid of goods, a final shipment from America and once again they've whipped time into something like control.

There in the port breezes, they mastermind trunks and packages being thrown down the planks from the *St. Lawrence*. Johnny had endowed a small pay-off to the customs-house man so they can just tick off the order as it tumbles down: there should be Kentucky hominy, cans of condensed milk from Wisconsin, salted turkeys from Vermont. As each box lands on the dock before them, Johnny keeps saying 'fascinating,' especially at the dried oranges from California, the crates covered with paintings of young women in pouting blouses. 'Fascinating.'

'One day,' Henry tells his boy, 'you and I can go to America. Tour, distribute handbooks. This will be after our success. If you are still working with me. Maybe our dance school will be for international communion, in the best sense. It will matter. Everything will be seen, documented.'

Johnny wrinkles the corners of his eyes. 'Sounds good.'

'Doesn't it, though?'

'Actually, *yes*' — the boy acting surprised — 'it does. It sounds fantastic.'

While the hired man loads his cart Henry explains the oranges: 'We don't want anyone to get scurvy in our village.'

'Our villa*ges*,' Johnny says and gets a smile for this.

Under the shade of the same port building that had witnessed Henry's first meeting with Johnny, a man in a pith helmet has fixed himself. Some kind of British civil servant who sights them and raises a hand to greet Johnny. He jogs over, a man made mostly of joints, less of sinew. 'Jonathan!' he calls, once he has rallied back into himself. 'Waiting for a shipment? Of course. Rations and whatnot. You know, we've missed —'

Henry monitors one and then the other.

'Discreet man,' the boy says coolly to the interloper. 'Let me introduce you. Henree Fyre Gould' — wavering a bit — 'allow me to introduce —'

'Chilkins.' The man turns cherry. The way he nods, you'd think the name itself had been a congenital setback.

'Chilkins is —'

'— deputy. Government agent for your region,' finishing for the boy, his tone sharp. 'Deputy GA. New appointment.' This must explain the defensiveness. He changes course: 'Weather all right, isn't it? Perhaps it'll hold this time.'

'Oh,' says Henry. This overbright duet performed by the two men would confuse anyone; Johnny will explain it all later. Henry tries to start up again: 'Did feel we were in for a bad spell but it's lifted. Nice to meet you —'

'Chilkins. Yes. Chilkins.' A repetitive man. 'Deputy GA for the —'

'Greater Central Kandy region,' Johnny rushes in. 'Chilkins here just promoted, it seems. I've been corresponding with Chilkins.'

'Oh, really? That's nice. Johnny's not a bad correspondent, right?'

'Henree, Chilkins is planning,' and here holding the Englishman directly in his gaze, 'to help us.'

'Yes?'

'Nothing quite on the table yet. Chilkin's still firming up the details,' says Johnny with no little insistence. 'But he has access to funds and requisitions. That right? Chilkins probably too modest to say so himself. You'd find him the first to count himself among those' — the boy stutters just a bit — 'among those who can't ignore all we're accomplishing in our model village.'

At this mouthful the civil servant assumes a flabbergasted smile.

'You see, as usual, the boy flatters all of us,' says Henry.

'No, Henree. Not flattery.'

'It's something else,' says the agent, diminished somewhat.

Johnny measures out his words with no small care: 'Actually, Henree, Chilkins is high enough to push the hand of the chief agent. Of Colwether.'

'Colwether? What — concerted movement!' the Brit interrupting as though studying a tennis match. 'Brilliant, Jonathan!'

'You probably came over to tell us that funds for the school, orphanage and General Store' — the boy taps off each project on his fingers — 'have been approved. That right?'

'Something —'

'See, Henree, I've been writing Chilkins. He may still be waiting to see about the garden.'

'Yes,' breathing hard, 'the garden.'

'The boy —' Henry begins but Chilkins finishes, saying, yes, yes, clearly the boy is a wonder, it has been wonderful to have Jonathan on his beat, and with all that H'nry is doing —

'Don't mind my saying so, seems like heat stroke may have got you some,' Henry's first bit of sympathy for an Englishman. 'It levels us all. Want some of our water?'

Chilkins leans against their wagon, squeaking thanks, the weather is just fine, really, anyway, he is meeting someone later at the club for a drink —

'No water?' Henry aims to sustain the rush of kindness over all Chilkins' technicalities. 'So you work under the GA — what's his name, Colwether? I've been wanting to meet you people. How lucky for us to have bumped into each other. So what do you think of Colwether?'

While Chilkins allows that Colwether is a basically good and fair man, Henry butts in with his estimation, unspecified, of how much the British have done in Rajottama. An impression Chilkins wishes to correct, and does, as one should say it is not so much the *British* who've bettered Rajottama but the English *proper*, though the Scots could at times be good negotiators.

The two men are incapable of speaking directly to each other. 'H'nry, is it?'

'How long did you say you've been here? Sorry, Chilkins your first name?'

'That is, my family's name was once Redsleeves but then we were titled and so —'

Henry pities the frail man. Though obviously suffering from sunstroke, he appears forced to keep up a rabbity imperialism. 'Chilkins, sure we can't take you somewhere?'

No, that would be quite impossible, Chilkins saying again how *happy* he is to have run into them, that Henry would be using his brolly, he imagines, there being a concerted movement from the northeast, the big Maha monsoon —

'It just finished,' the boy cuts in. 'Henree here could tell you the difference between the monsoons.'

'I *will* anticipate speaking with you, Jonathan.'

'And when might one be sending those checks?' The boy's smile a real imp of a thing. So Johnny does know how to be forward in the appropriate moments. As an American, Henry would've tried to be a bit more diplomatic than the boy is being.

'Next week, positively,' Chilkins promises.

'Sorry, didn't hear you?'

'The boy is rough,' says Chilkins, 'isn't he, a real operator, when, yes, next week they could receive a check.'

'You can't deny there's money there,' says Johnny, 'for the garden and everything else.' The man sighs, either caught or succumbing. He thinks aloud about discretionary surplus, seed money, something that could be dubbed *development funds*, rattling on without need of intervention. 'A line item'll do. Not such a big sum necessary at first, is it? After all —'

Henry nods. 'Seed money.'

'Legitimate,' Chilkins continuing to talk to himself. 'Development projects. Could be done. Should be acceptable.'

'Good,' says Johnny, taking the agent's hand. 'I'll write you soon. Before that we'll be anticipating —'

'— the cheek.'

'Pardon?'

'Checks!' And Chilkins tries to tweak Johnny but the boy shrinks away. Manu evidently understands Johnny's cue and starts up the cattle. Behind him the second wagon follows.

'H'nry, you're an extraordinary specimen. To put up with that brazen one!' but they are off. Even a few paces away Chilkins starts to talk to himself. They hear him saying 'Seed money. Development funds.'

'Man can be forgetful,' is Johnny's explanation.

'The real wonder's you,' Henry explodes once they're out of earshot. He kisses Johnny's hand (of all things) without having meant to entirely. 'Incredible! Enterprising! You must've read my mind. I was beginning to worry about our money situation. My savings. Almost down to nothing,' warming up just thinking about it, 'and on your own you went and got us an investor!'

Johnny looks volumes. 'In a sense, Henree.'

'The mystery is — don't take this as a backhanded compliment — you sometimes come off colder than a well-digger's ass.'

'Should I thank you?'

'Just then you did something incredible. A bravura performance. They'll be talking about that long as you live.'

'If I survive. Don't know what came over me actually.'

'Your belief!' he crowed. 'It's a goddamned gift! Don't be dark. That's crass in you! You're above that!'

From the front Manu turns around and cuts his eyes at Johnny as though for the first time. 'You *were* good,' in his heavily accented English. 'Very good. And good to get money for village.'

At this Johnny shines, wobbling his head back at Manu. *'Haride?'* he asks, 'that true?'

After they pull onto the main road clotted with colonials — motorists and carriage riders — and with local families stacked in bullock carts for what looks like a morbid joyride, Manu makes an unannounced decision. He pulls over to an anonymous blue shack, completely boarded over. The hired man understands and reins in sharply, making his bulls grunt at their bits.

'Right back,' says Manu, already loping over a discarded plough toward the back. 'Relatives —' and disappears around a corner.

Henry eyes Johnny who shrugs: 'Strong family ties in Ceylon,' without sounding convinced. A scruple and qualm later, the boy asks whether he should go get Manu, but Henry tells him to leave well enough alone, to stay by him; isn't Johnny always counseling patience to everyone else?

They hear men laughing, a chaffing, lovely beautiful obstinacy of a laugh. One man emerges, a wiry fellow in shirtsleeves. In the West, with his unkempt mustache, he'd be considered a radical, the kind to frequent longshoremen halls and to rally communalism. In fact, down to his waist, he is very proper Western but then below the buttoned shirt comes the usual white sarong, the dhoti, which he holds at its corners like a girl might, carrying in its hammock a blazing roll of posters. Behind, Manu holds a can of caulking and a dirty paintbrush.

'This is my' — Manu tries to find the English word — 'my cousin-brother, Nandana. He's giving me gifts for —'

'For his father,' finishes Nandana. He nods to Johnny but shakes Henry's hand with too much vigor. 'Fine to meet you!' warbles Nandana and then just as immediately bids them off with two raised palms. 'Safe journeys! no time to waste!'

Once back on the road, Manu holds a mum court. Henry sees a small lemur along the road and remembers something: he claps his palm to his forehead and cries out, 'We forgot to get the Shriver's ham! For the monk!' to which both Manu and Johnny in tandem telegraph messages Henry would describe only as sour. Their faces say *there is no stopping*. And also: *We are practically already on our way back up the mountain.*

And perhaps? *You should know monks take a vow not to eat meat.*

'Pandit says it's manufactured, the Shriver's, so it's out of the rules!' Henry twits back defensively. But no one seems to understand what he is saying, or so they pretend, and the carriage hurtles on without making any further comment on the monk, the ham or any amoral combination of the two.

53

OPULENCE IS the Saturday in early March when Henry will distribute the catechisms and open the General Store. Thursday night through the trees the wind rustles *success, success,* rising on the second syllable, and this is all for the good. Henry means to place the pamphlets in the free bin outside the store.

After all Manu had turned out to be a friendly sort. Their three trips to Colombo had brought about a final thaw. And after his father made mention of Manu's artistic prowess, Henry persuaded the boy to draw the catechism's cover.

Owing to Manu's artistry, as thanks Henry decided it would be natural to put Regi in charge of running the store, exactly as the drummer had requested during February's first meeting of the model village. 'It won't interfere with Regi's drumming duties at the temple, will it?' Henry had checked with the monk. 'Aren't the hours different?'

Instead of answering, Pandit had studied his own feet, a pair which should have belonged to a much longer man. These people, whenever it pleases them, they know how to ignore Henry. So Henry had veered from the usual decorum and had stuck his face close to Pandit's. 'Saddhu. Regi *offered*. Or is there something unholy about a drummer getting grubby with commerce?' If Pandit won't say what's the matter, Henry's not going to let one sourpuss spoil the whole undertaking.

Trying to maintain the calm mindstream the Buddhists prescribe, Henry himself had played foreman over a final crackerjack team of wage laborers. Four had been paid and thank God one man, Suba, had volunteered. Together they had situated the General Store where the monk had suggested, on a semi-eroded lot near the bridge, at the foot of the general market, just by the canal. This meant they had to pile in compact clay over the rotted soil and pile it high. Also, Henry's ideal had been that people would walk *up* wooden stairs to a porch and from there through a swinging door into the store. This small climb created a lot of extra work but it had been his single attachment, a tip-of-the-hat to the general stores he'd known as a child in White Plains.

For the floor Henry had envisioned some kind of medieval clay-and-stone mosaic. Using regional supplies as much as possible, he had purchased slate from Lester Pilima, direct from the Pilima quarry. While the chips are rough and of uneven quality, indifferent to Henry's plans, the workers — deep-chested, well-oiled — are good at the labor, tin panful after tin panful of chips atop their heads. Unfortunately, Lester had dumped the lot a good five hundred meters up the hill.

So this ends up being the hardest segment of the whole project, the hiking to and fro. Yet how worthwhile: when the floor is done, a sumptuous joy, Henry takes his shoes off and walks up and down. So what if the thing *does* cant up and down like a ship's deck? On his bare feet the stones themselves are as cold and smooth as the best sort of caress.

An enormous accomplishment, this store. The ne plus ultra of all plans prior and progressive. On this foreign isle, Henry is building something big. Though often solitary he is never alone. His urgency to achieve makes him feel forever surrounded by a stadium of cawing or booing sports fans. They run him with their home sympathies and dreams. Nothing is ever too large and no last-minute dash too bold. To balance this, no plan can ever be too deliberate.

And between urgency and the desire for deliberation, a calm mindstream becomes something almost unreachable. Still, he has tried never to raise his voice when giving directions.

Some kindness is due him about now. A kind of reprieve. And yes he'd felt it incumbent upon him to get the store done before more branches start to snap and more skies start to roar because the next monsoon is due to arrive soon. He knew what his catechism said:

Q. How did the Prince attain enlightenment?
A. He meditated through the three watches of the night.

In the first, he acquired omniscience about the past; in the
second, omniscience about the present; and, in the third,
he understood the chain of dependent origination which
reveals the origin of suffering.

The workers had scrabbled to raise the walls and build the roof in the time allotted. The team had been a good one; with all of them he had tried to just shut up and be grateful. Suba, the older Anglophile, his ears rife with radial whiskers, is probably pushing seventy and yet had volunteered along with the paid workers — this alone had made Henry marvel at the team members' strength and merriment. No matter their age. From fifteen on! No matter the lack of meat on their bodies. No matter the makeshift materials. They had been *good*.

'Good,' he clucked constantly. 'Good good good.' This he said when feeling serene. He doesn't like to remember what he says the other times.

Dependent origination can be summed up in this way: none of
our actions are separate from another's, past, present, or future: they depend upon all and occur in a web of causation.

Soon the builders had raised a banyan scaffolding. They managed to wattle-and-daub the walls with enough skill that the sticks are unseen, smooth as a funerary urn. They laid coconut thatch over the roof and weighted it down laterally — rope tied to heavy rocks at each end and running in even parallels crossing the thatch — so the thatch itself bulges up like sausage or a woman's flesh between the rope. All is alive, he had thought, the store becoming more human, heavenly, spectacular.

And a Thursday evening early in March, with the Yala monsoon already threatening from the southwest, Henry saw the last straw, mud and hinge put in, the last bit of inventory stocked. How gloriously the final structure arose out of its lot!

Inside, on the solid mangowood shelves, nothing lonely in any of this, the goods bulge as much as the roof does. Because (and no one would say differently) Henry has spared no effort. Chilkins' checks have not arrived — Johnny still promises they will come, they will come — but to the last moment Henry has been dipping into his shriveling savings to advance inventory.

He had ordered that perfumed hygiene soaps be stocked along with time-saving brooms more effective than the coconut-bristle sweeps the people now use. Had made sure rows overflow with jars of molasses and tins of ham, hominy and condensed cow's milk; with sacks of corn meal that are the finest the American Catalogue could produce and ship.

And in the front he has lined boxes of pure tallow candles. Wooden matches. Bags of ladybugs to patrol against aphids. Worms to burrow within individual compost piles. Many free nutritious recipes written in Sinhalese and English. And marvelous yards of cheap, colorful linen for the women to use as saris, all part of Henry's National Dress program.

In the meantime, the opening of the store will not be grand. It is meant to have taste. Understatement. Saturday, two days after its completion, the store will simply open for business. No villager will turn greedy and charge in. Because no one has been slighted.

The model village doesn't require *money*. It transcends money: these first weeks all the villagers have been given the same amount of chits to use. Soon as possible, the reward of chits will depend upon a family's attendance at the weekly lectures and their children's participation in school. Unfortunately, Henry has been too busy to write any lectures; the school has not yet formalized itself; he must take one step at a time. He won't be able to help them if he himself can't manage time.

Surely the intention behind the store is transparent enough. The people will be freed from household drudgery and dependence on colonial imports: they'll turn toward ends higher than that of brute survival; their potential will fly far beyond their colonial schemes. Any urchin could become a learned Buddhist philosopher, any good student could write treatises, any child could give birth to monastic lineages. The Rajottama School of Thought . . . the Rajottama lineage . . .

The catechism with Manu's Buddha on the cover is just a start. The Buddha smiles a lopsided grin from hundreds of these books at the brown eyes and hands which will soon grasp and memorize his essence.

Buddhist Catechism
Certificate to the First Edition
Rajottama Village, Uva Province
20 February 1937

I hereby certify that I have carefully examined this English Catechism prepared by Colonel H. F. Gould, and that the same is in agreement with the Canon of the Southern Buddhist Church. I recommend the work to teachers in Buddhist schools, and to others who may wish to impart information to beginners about the essential features of our religion.

H. Pandit Ehelapola
High Priest of Rajottama and the Sacred Tree Temple
Principal of the New Rajottama School for All Castes

THE LIFE OF THE BUDDHA

1. Question. Of what religion are you?
   Answer. The Buddhist.

2. Q. What is Buddhism?
   A. It is a body of teachings given out by the great personage known as the Buddha.

3. Q. Is Buddhism the best name for this teaching?
   A. No; that is only a Western term: the best name for it is Buddha Dharma.

4. Q. Would you call a person a Buddhist who had merely
been born of Buddhist parents?
   A. Certainly not. A Buddhist is one who not only professes
   belief in the Buddha as the noblest of Teachers, in the
   Doctrine preached by Him, and in the Brotherhood
   of the Mystical Masters, but practices His precepts in
   daily life.

54

FRIDAY MORNING promises moderation if not more. Henry rises
early. In dawn's light (before anyone disrupts his plan) he will see the
store. Alone. He needs an uninterrupted moment to savor the birth
of this kind of temple.

Whatever charm brought him to this isle, he has broken out of the
prison of his own destiny. Yet he is no dodger, no escapologist. In
this store is a retrieval, the hopes Henry had whispered to his imaginary friend Matthew as a child. With foresight and invention he
might create something that would change people's lives.

Without bathing — he doesn't want to wake Nani — he puts on
the clothes she had laid out for him the night before. She has sprung
him a surprise. Apparently she wants him to go traditional. Instead
of his usual workshirt and khakis, clean underwear, the socks for his
boots, what is laid out over and under his chair are the following
items: a pressed white cloth banian to wear as a tunic, a dhoti (the
men's skirt, what he prefers to call a sarong, actually like a pillow-
case cut off at both ends) and sandals. Yes, the white buttons of
the banian please him immensely: with a child's care, he pops each
in turn. And then the sarong: he still doesn't know how to tie the
sarong-knot but why not take up her gambit? He hazards a guess,
approximates. And from Johnny he knows no self-respecting man
wears undergarments. What freedom, to walk about naked under
cloth! Even the sandals are a liberation!

He would rush to thank her. But if she were to act the startled deer
(would she act the startled deer?) it would ruin the gift of this blessed
morning and its good mood.

Succor is his vision and Rajottama a sleeping giant, the mountains either an old woman's face in profile or a young woman's body curled in, facing him. In the twirl of mist the canal below is a silver littoral, despite the white-gold light from behind the house. The day might stay a clear one. Henry inhales, stretching his arms up. Is he not as vigorous in his pith-and-sap as he'd felt at twenty-one, long before any world became his?

On the road there is only the slappeting of his feet in the new thongs — they take getting used to — and the occasional haHOO-haw of a parrot. Birds here are a dissaffected lot, won't sing just one or two notes, instead carry on complicated melodies for many measures, only to start up again. He can't fully figure out their rationale. By the time he gets to the bridge, where the store rises, a flock resounds like a symphony.

Everything can verge on too much around here. Sound, light, ceremony. Beneath his skin a fever runs. These men must broil, tolerating the stiff cloth of the banian shirt as less of an extravagance, more a sacrament.

The previous day Henry had locked the store door cursorily, with a key hung rather obviously from the padlock outside, and yet is bowled over to find the portal swing open at his touch. Maybe Johnny had checked during the night and forgotten to lock up? But that would be unlike the boy. Either Johnny is an amnesiac's nightmare or savior, he would never forget anything.

'Hallo?' Henry calls into the store's dim nave, a tinted bloom, its shelves and corners swelling with plenty. 'Hallo?' He slips in carefully over the pleasing, worthwhile stone floor.

Then it is that he finds the urchin, one with a brave, tender-bird face whom he had seen on his first walk through Rajottama. A thief? But no, the little boy pretends not to see Henry. Apparently he just wants whatever this store is. He walks along, fingers tracing the goods. Lingering. Henry can understand. This much he knows about psychology.

He crouches down so the boy can't ignore him. 'Like it here?' he asks in Sinhalese. *Mehee kaemiteede?*

The boy raises his head, his profile an armament. He won't admit defeat readily. 'Why not?' he asks in a hesitant English. 'I am Upali.'

'Maybe you'd like to work here, Upali?' persisting in his bad Sinhalese.

This makes the boy's gleam less secretive. 'Yes, Miss Hanree. I can work.' He must be nine or so — or else older and malnourished — but he understands the vision of the store; and this time Henry will make sure to recognize all allies, whatever package they come in.

He considers the boy, how he skips out, content. Certain people know to unkink the contortions of their existence. And this boy *deserves*. Let this be a precedent. The store's workers and users should appear among those capable of appreciation. And Henry hadn't misjudged: this knave Upali will later turn out to be a regular *citizen* of the store, such is his ardor to wrap, stock and sweep among the fancy goods. He will even sleep in the store, 'to stand guard.' This is the attitude that should become contagious.

55

WASN'T MANU's the kind of face that would make any priest worldly? His bones practically threatened to rip up out of the face itself. You could see the skeleton's advantage over the roan skin that said it had seen nothing. And then the eyes with their depths and alleluias and the mockery Jehan always searched for — directed at himself — but never, since their first meetings, had been able to find again. He had liked being mocked by Manu. Being mocked was affirming.

And now the mockery would not be repeated. Why? because their friendship had grown. All their new pretenses veer toward pedagogy, the idea being that Jehan would teach English to Manu. Because Manu wants to practice the little he'd learned before he left the missionary school; and Jehan's accent in Sinhala is also incomprehensible. 'You trill in unusual places, you cut the most necessary words,' he explains to Jehan. 'This is why you should teach me English, no?'

'Or maybe you should teach me Sinhala?'

'But yours is perfect! What do I have to teach you?'

The two find themselves often by the bank, hidden on the slope that slides in one muddy red slop to the canal, the tank shored up by the English so coffee and tobacco plantations could be fed by it. And the foreigner thinks the ancient king alone had created the tank, what he always calls canal or sometimes reservoir. Who'd ever want to apprise him any differently and break up his dreams?

A tree had fallen on a faded tussock by the canal, just before it began to digress into all kinds of swamp farther north near the shanties, and it is on this branchless trunk amid the rambling sedge, brush and debris that they sit. In these late afternoons on the bank, in a respite of dry weather, they begin to find some kind of comfort, which neither really wanted to admit. In the fashion of crib friends, they finish each other's thoughts. And as with new friends, often the other's endings prove surprising.

'I am waiting for —'

'The pink man?' Manu will insert, teasing him. 'What else do you ever wait for? *Oh Henree!* Maybe you too are aiming for detachment?'

'Not the same thing?' Jehan muses, slower-witted but with the same covert roguishness that draws them close like rare and hunted tigers. But Jehan has three years on his friend and is more prone to being overwhelmed with possible affinities than is Manu, who knows better how to have a friendship without needing to name it.

Manu! what a bravery guarded his realm, untested but ready to fight or protect.

And in the umbra of that bravery — did it have something to do with what the boy called his *organizing*, his *sympathies*, his plans for *revolt?* — Jehan felt he could relax in a way he hadn't since leaving his own mother's house.

He was sure this courage might also come from Manu's royal lineage, not that lineage mattered; but the boy's story about the Bandus' ancestry gibed with his gestures' majesty.

Jehan knew that every single caste claims it descends from Brahmins from India. But in Manu's case, Jehan wanted to believe it. Even down to that dismissive suckling noise the boy made at the corner of his mouth — in its rise and fall, Jehan could discern fanfares. Strange how none of this beauty, *none* had anything to do with the father. Jehan would never ask the drummer's son why his father acted like someone from another forest altogether. That didn't mean Jehan wasn't doing what he could to help the family.

Today Jehan did in fact have good news. His friend had guessed correctly.

But Henree had asked that he not convey the news. What he would've told Manu, if he could, was that Henree had been working with the monk to raise Regi's salary (and hence Manu's) so that Manu's deformed brother, the monster baby, could be given medical treatments in the capital. That was the idea, at any rate: to help save and restore the lost life.

This was one of Henree's generosities. The Yankee often put his energy to work wherever his mind alit. Naturally, Jehan had supported this venture. The general trend of things had been that his Yank charge had become unusually tractable. Ever since the store had neared its opening, Henree had been so full of wonder and a readiness to learn that this last month Jehan had started to find espionage more than pleasant. He deemed the job an uncanny gift. This was what he would have hoped for, had he known how to name it, long before the swinging lanterns on the water had started to mean the death of his father.

Every day less and less obscenity remained in his working for a Yankee but he couldn't tell Manu anything, not yet, not about his own spying, nor about what the American wanted to do for Manu's family. And so the boys sat hushed for a bit.

Not long. Manu's fingers in their whittling were quicksilver. How knowing and almost mechanical was his deftness. 'Should I teach you?'

Jehan laughed the offer away. 'In me whittling would be an affectation where in you it is completely natural,' not sure his friend understood what he meant or why. He knew himself to be a clumsier feline than Manu. Even a simple act like coconut-husking meant a dented nut and a wrangled mess of threads in Jehan's hands. Something about the physical world left him ill-equipped.

'You should come to one of our meetings some time,' his friend said without preamble.

'You're organizing?'

The statuary man's long nose and furrowed brow started to emerge under the tutelage of Manu's hands. 'I told you details about my work, no?' and saw he had not.

'You organize something somewhere.'

'I always mean to tell you. You know, Jehan, that story about the leftists? How they helped the villagers with malaria?'

Jehan gave an indiscernible wobble.

Manu continued to pare the legs of his statue with short skims and twists. 'This is an even more underground group.'

Hard for Jehan not to admire his friend and how he didn't lower his voice.

257

'We try to bring *all* the castes into unison. And this has nothing to do with anything the Pilimas may be doing.'

'At night?' said Jehan.

At this understatement the boys exchanged a hot look. Apparently Manu also knew about the Pilimas and their night games. But if Manu knew about the games it seemed no one was allowed to discuss them. Instead they listened nearby as a bird made dirgelike pronouncements about her intentions and then boomeranged low into the canal, only to come up empty-beaked.

'Say what though, Manu? I mean, what will this voice of all castes say?'

Manu's gaze took in his friend without condemnation. 'To get rid of the colonizers.' With quicker strokes Manu rendered boots on his little man. '*Others* try. But we are going to succeed, you know.'

'Of course.'

Jehan hadn't known, exactly. All this had been so many jots and rumors to him. To Henree, yes, he had acted sophisticated about the nationalizing activities. Truth was, his own ambition hid so much from him. Problems which he did not fully wish to understand. Things that would have blocked his sights of Oxford. Phrases he had overheard: bodies floating in rivers in India; a general movement; Ceylonese advocates imprisoned for not paying two rupees to the British as road tax; meetings in Jaffna to form coalitions among the Tamils and Sinhalese and Muslims; the Kandyan Sinhalese asking to administer themselves; the new native congress members asking for at least internal administration under the flag. No, they would never call it freedom, they had said, they were not so foolish as to ask for freedom. This phrase alone had stuck in Jehan's craw. *They were not so foolish as to ask for freedom.*

He lets himself remember only certain moments — how, the first time he went with his mother to the polls, after that 1928 English report gave older women the right to vote, his mother had stood proud in her best silken clothes before the soldiers who guarded the ballot box. Jehan had entered behind the drapes with his mother and observed how carefully she selected representatives on the basis of their family name and caste. For seven years everyone in the village, even the illiterate, had loved this election ritual, the officials, the severity. Some would run after to mind how the wooden ballot box got transported, after all the voting was done, surrounding the soldiers who passed the box from a hall to a carriage to a boat to finally evaporate. For a day many in the village would feel important. And Jehan also let himself remember how this same 1928 report had decided the Ceylonese could manage their own affairs so long as nothing would be detrimental to the interests of empire.

But for years, Jehan had kept most of his other half-knowledge far away; the problems had seemed like so much hatred, wickedness and injustice; old tailors threading needles, exhaling blood, turbid waves, difficulty.

By the canal, Johnny had barely said to Manu of the statue, *It's Henree, isn't it*, before the skies that had been holding themselves in all these days suddenly opened the terrible hatch, heavy globes magnifying into the beginning of the vast Yala monsoon coming down. Would everyone blame this again on Henree? An early Yala. A flood. This time, from the looks of it, there really might be no ceasing.

They ran, struck as if by blows, Manu covering his head with his tiny man, Johnny wearing his new hat. His khaki shirt (a recent gift from Henree) got drenched immediately. Through the mud puddles up the driveway and on the thin path to Jehan's own cottage, they shouted until the cottage, where the door behind them made a satisfying slam.

Inside Manu shivered while Jehan did what he could to get a coal fire started with the few damp pieces left. The coalman had missed last week in what Henree had cried was an abysmal show of laziness. 'Laziness!' the Yankee wouldn't stop shouting. 'Laziness!'

But the cold was not the worst thing in the world. Even with the ratty towel around him Manu was shivering. Jehan would cover him if he could but kept no extra blankets. All he had was his own body. Terrible heat suffused his hands and tingled his lips. He surveyed Manu with such rapacity that the boy finally said *What? what? the fire?* but Jehan glanced at a spot over the drummer's left shoulder for a second to avoid the wet cheekbones and then brought himself to making the fire.

Thunder cracked. Through Jehan's wire-crossed windows, they could see the rain moving in, squadrons of it, horizontal sheets across the canal, powering creation but flattening prostrate the palm leaves.

After a bit what broke the silence was Manu's question: 'Should I maybe teach you whittling now?' That was all he asked; that was what could be exchanged.

And this was how Jehan began the practice; he tried to learn it, a vain attempt to slow his hands. Waiting for Manu on those long afternoons when his duties with and for and against Henree didn't call him away, he engaged in their shared chiseling. At first his miniatures were blocky — houses, churches, carriages which he immediately set upon his windowsill in pride. All testaments to the hours his friend had spent tutoring him. Or hours he had spent thinking of his friend.

Soon he could move on to finer effects. He presented Joseph with a tiny trowel. He made a little drum perfect down to its side-strings which he gave to Manu. In thanks the boy embraced him, like a concave if impulsive nun.

With whittling, the boys' hands when together were kept at work. Jehan especially created hundreds of unnecessary things. Funny how the smaller an object was, the more it could say. The smaller, the better, they'd tell each other, in an endless game to beat each other's miniature.

56

AT THE NEW STORE, open now a few weeks, Pushpa Pilima has come to stock up on the oval soaps imprinted with a ship. She tells the drummer she wants six of those bars nice and wrapped, please. In the outsized sea-green apron Henry has given him, Regi's practically dapper, only tending to lurch over the thing's hem.

Henry's kneeling, arranging the bin of catechisms, ashamed that he enjoys them so much. 'Go ahead, Regi,' in his bad Sinhalese, 'bend the rules a bit.'

But the drummer stands dumb as a sentry in his green webbing. Henry has to explain: the four-soaps-to-a-customer idea can be altered. 'We aren't facing any shortages now,' he continues. 'Anyway, this soap is surplus stock from some London penitentiary.'

He learned this trick from Johnny. Grandstand and filibuster a bit, throw out some extraneous information, and they're satisfied. Then they feel things are *right*. As though the soap's being surplus would affect the village quotas — as though the drummer would understand the idea of a penitentiary!

Pushpa takes matters into her own hands. With sharp tones she translates for the drummer. After his gnarled hands pause, he starts wrapping the soaps.

'These little books of yours,' her English shielding itself, her mood peckish, it seems. 'These catechisms. You've done well, Mister Fyre. Very exceeding well.'

'Why's that?' Henry stands and wipes the dust off his hands. 'You might sweep a little more,' reminding Regi. 'Where's Upali?' He mimes a broom.

'Because it is true I say it.' Pushpa's eyes accuse him.

If her eyes were guns, she might've shot me already. No. He tells himself he's being melodramatic. Pay attention, this woman is friendly enough. In her creamy sari top and bound lungi isn't she just like any other villagewoman? She defers to the same courtesies. Is of the same stuff. She may think the majority of people imbeciles but the truth is *this woman can't hurt you.*

'Given any thought to teaching for us?'

She ignores him. 'No one will say you're not smart. Even these' — she pulls a handful of damp tickets out of her bodice — 'you give these chits to people for coming to your lectures? For working in the model garden? Excellent! For every day a child will attend your school? That we get soap and such with these chits? This is a clever system you've created, Mister Fyre.'

'But?' There's some qualification in her voice. She's not telling him everything.

'I told you I'd speak straight to you.'

'Please.' He notes a few women on their way into the store pausing nervously on the creaky stoop. He beckons for them to enter but apparently they prefer to stay at a distance and giggle behind their hands.

'The chits. You were saying. That was my aide's idea' — Henry's unsure whether he passes blame or shares credit — 'maybe Pandit's idea, as a matter of fact.' He swelters in his listening, dying subtly under the scratchy new tunic.

'Your aide with the Moorish name?'

'Shall we step outside?'

'You know we can't speak freely *there*, Mister Fyre,' says Pushpa. She indicates the women still huddled in gossip, a clump of followers evidently nothing new to her.

Henry leads her to the back office without closing its door behind them. In this room, with its medleyed perfume of fountain ink, san-

261

dalwood incense and glue, he too can feel at ease. Across a wood ta-ble Regi had made are neatly piled blue books, Johnny's records of chits and inventory.

'Who can commend you enough, Mister Fyre,' is what Pushpa's words say. Her bun's so taut the contours of her skull seem to tick. 'You're doing an excellent job.'

This woman's gaze is both too direct and crossed. The two of them are seated across the table from each other. They could sit that way forever. How one must wait with these people. You wait through their reprises and codas long enough and, finally, you're there gasping and they might divulge everything. But push too much and they're closed forever. It was Johnny who'd taught him that patience must be his own patron saint here.

'You're changing how we eat,' she proclaims. 'I've seen it. The people think they need niceties like cheese and ham now. That must have taken a lot of —'

Henry explains the rationale. Too little protein and people be-come slow. Even lazy. Not far from the office, not far from the door, somewhere nearby, Johnny sneezes. Henry goes on — at first he'd thought the people obeyed some Buddhist prohibition against eat-ing meat.

'No, if it moves, we cook it,' she interjects. 'Good meat, well-cooked.'

But what a bunch of contradictions: Henry'd heard them joke about Muslims who couldn't stay far away from the butcher's knife. And how they called the hunters, the Veddas who live beyond the toddy-tappers, *wild men*. Then they would furtively hire butchers to come and slaughter their beef. And call his Hindoo gardener Joseph a *parippu*. A lentil-eater who consumes only vegetables.

The long and the short of it is, whatever their contradictions, these people had hardly been getting enough protein. The monk had understood this immediately. Surely Pushpa could see the bene-fits?

'I'm flattered. You let me in to your plans, Mister Fyre. But you're still ignoring rules. That is wrong. For example, you can't have a low-caste man running your stall.'

He is not sure whether to put more or less of himself into this conversation. Add or subtract Henry. He does a reasonable facsimile of something in between. 'Johnny and Regi both run the store,' he says.

'Worse.' She reaches across to tap his hand. 'Don't bluster. You're going to doom the success of your projects if you don't respect how we do things here —'

'What is it you want? Tell me. Anything.' His patience has reached its end — he doesn't have all day. Not if he's going to be scolded by some older woman. He thought she meant well but some leopards never change their spots.

He gets up to usher her out. 'Still mulling over teaching for us, I hope?'

'You don't listen very well, Mister Fyre,' she says, staying seated. 'That's wrong on your part. And not because I'm a woman or older than you. You might consider whether I could help you.'

'I have. That's why I asked about the teaching.'

'My niece will be starting in your school.' Her face both wily and innocent. 'I wouldn't object to the chance. To oversee what you're doing with education.' He can't hide his annoyance: these Pilimas play shy and then tug hard. Of them, Pushpa especially seems to test whether he stays suitably steel-cabled to her caprice.

'You want me to beg maybe.' He is trying to tease her but it doesn't quite come off. 'Maybe I should get on my knees.'

He is almost ready to kneel on the floor to make some point to her until she usurps him, rising suddenly. 'But yes,' speaking as though to herself, 'I also think it is best for us to stay involved. It's a good idea. And I've considered your offer long enough.' It comes through that she will teach; that Henry might even prevail upon her to teach the catechism. Further, she believes it good for a woman's mind, at an advanced age, to be kept exercised.

'That's really' — finding himself doing a Johnny imitation — 'grand of you. Next week let's discuss everything. On your way out, be sure to take a sample of the new candles.'

> 156. Q. How would a Buddhist describe true merit?
> A. There is no great merit in any merely outward act;
> all depends upon the inward motive that provokes
> the deed.

Johnny is leaning over the catechism bin, pretending to read as Henry and Pushpa reenter the filtered light of the store. He and Pushpa barely give each other the nod particular to people who do not judge themselves equals. She says nothing as she takes a candle and her wrapped soaps before sweeping out of the store.

'Sir! she gave no chits,' Regi protests.

Henry waves his hand. '*Eyaate daene mokakwat*. Give her anything. She's fine for now. Call it a complimentary —'

'A com-plimen-tree!' echoes Regi.

Out on the porch some women cover their mouths and titter as Henry steps out. 'They're laughing at me?'

'Just shy. Bow,' urges his aide, 'deeper. That'll help. It erases some fears, not all.'

Henry tips his head, making the women seize the opportunity to rush by him and into the store.

> 157. Q. Give an example of merit.
>   A. A rich man may expend lakhs of rupees in building
>   temples, in erecting statues of Buddha, in festivals
>   and processions, in feeding priests, in giving alms
>   to the poor, or in planting trees, digging tanks,
>   or constructing rest-houses by the roadside for
>   travelers, and yet have comparatively little merit
>   if it be done for display, or to hear himself praised
>   by men or for any other selfish motives.

'Everything you said to Pushpa was correct,' Johnny announces loudly enough for anyone to hear, if they chose. 'When the people have meat, they eat it and well. The Sinhalese have no idea about the uncleanliness of meat.'

'Do *you?*' Henry starts for the road hurriedly, the boy tagging behind.

'No, rather, don't hold back any of your ideas — I know everything about these people.'

'No doubt.' Again he imitates Johnny: *no doubt.* The boy's tone soothes him as much as a sweet would a colicky child. As does the boy himself, now quoting from the catechism:

> But he who does the least of these good acts with a kind motive, such as love for his fellow-men, gains great merit. A good deed done with a bad motive benefits others, but not the doer.

Nothing makes Henry forget how misbegotten the people's ideas are. Pushpa had wanted to teach — he was not blind to this — more for the *Pilimas* to keep an eye on what he was doing. Not so much from any gargantuan love of teaching. She has not become a new ally. This is a woman who stays as skeptical of him as ever, seeming to relish the anxiety she causes. This last, perhaps, was a Pilima trait.

But for his project, wouldn't two angry monkeys who scratch each other's backs be better than two angry monkeys who stay separate? And he has an unaccountable liking for the cross-eyed woman. She presents herself as rational. Yet he has no doubt that were he to delve beneath her surface even just a bit, he'd find calcified layers. Of wrong information. Of superstition.

As bad as anyone's. *Too much lime burns the blood,* the dancing sisters had confided. *Lime with chilies helps catarrh,* explained the monk once. *Cucumber eaten raw with salt strengthens the kidneys,* Suba said. When children get feverish, they're given a British concoction made of laudanum, alcohol and spices, so the wee things are left mildly addicted and severely dehydrated by the fever's close. And the people always advise that the best thing for thirst on a scorching day is *high tea, wouldn't the foreigner drink a cup more?*

The misbeliefs can topple a person. What becomes crucial are allies and a clear road. Isn't it always the road that binds Henry back to the boy? Once they're on it, the road and its groaning palm trees, Henry asks, 'Am I trying to do too much all at once?'

'You're doing a terrific job, Henree. Don't worry so much. Nothing will happen unless you promote your plans.'

Johnny tells him about the English plow problem. It could help the meat-eating issue. Some years ago, Colwether, the province's current government agent, had convinced the people to use the English plow. With their new plows the people were forced to rent the temple's expensive cattle to prepare their fields. To this day they still rent the cattle. Yet they'd never dreamt of buying and eating the beasts. They hire a butcher to come around every few months and slaughter his bulls right in front of Rajottama. But why not the local cattle?

'It's this kind of misunderstanding you see on the women's scrawny bones,' Henry laughs. Johnny's plan sounds far-fetched as well. 'Sometimes I'm astounded. Might as well feed them on peppermint sticks. To not know about such fundaments as milk? or beef? or ham, turkey, yams —'

'Or corn meal? I know, Henree.' Now the boy returns. 'Be patient. My advice is start with something a little more sensational than cows and cabbage if you want to grab their interest.'

Henry quotes back to the boy:

One who approves of a good deed when done by another shares in the merit, if his sympathy is real, not pretended.

But the boy finishes:

The same rule applies to evil deeds.

'What?' he retorts to his employer's glare. 'That's how it's written, Henree. I'm just quoting your book.'

57

Welsummer: a breed of large poultry with golden plumage. Prolific egg-layers. (After the Dutch village of Welsum, where first bred.)

In his stolen sunrise moments outside, all March, Henry has been studying poultry catalogues. Old thumbed catalogues which (while out of date) inspired a glamorous project. Though the project was doomed, Henry still admires its dream.

Yet another of Madame's ageless friends, a scruffy former Bolshevik whose hair stuck out at obtuse angles from behind his ears, had told him the story. The Bolshevik had described in a conspirator's hoarse voice how he'd wanted to start a poultry cooperative as part of Uganda's new Zionist endeavor. Sadly for Zion he'd boarded the wrong ship. Happy-go-lucky and ready for the world he'd established the same project in Buenos Aires where his incubated Welsummer eggs were hatched for cockfights.

But during dawns on his favorite bench, Henry assures himself that such history wouldn't plague him. Such serendipity. Poultry might be right for the village of the future. Everything could be planned for. This is not a ship on an unknown course. And the local herb doctor had seemed, in a terse discussion, to give the project his blessing. Rajottama would never succumb to cockfights.

The lives of the Ceylonese are too circumscribed by the daily rituals of subsistence to become a gaming folk

Henry predicts to the ever-attentive audience of his Village Book.

The day before, he'd felt lucky to see, unannounced, how in her role as new teacher, Pushpa had drilled the students in his catechism. His catechism! He had peered through a crack in the classroom door. The classroom was still bare but the children's eyes and mouths had opened wide. They had recited without any pain of inflection:

> Q. What plan of discipline did the Buddha adopt to open his
> mind to know the whole truth?
> A. He sat and meditated, concentrating his mind on the
> higher problems of life, and shutting out from his sight
> and hearing all that was likely to interrupt his inward re-
> flections.

No one had seen his spying. Children of all ages and castes speaking English so poorly. He loved them. How awkward they were, perched on their baby benches.

He should get them better benches, perhaps like his own. This front garden's elaborately carved seat is one of the many gifts left him by mad Wooves. From its vantage, the pale early-morning light spilling through the mango trees performs magic tricks in his honor. It makes the canal appear to rise cobralike toward him. Like the days, which also rise and fall in magnificent colors toward and away from him, promising everything: he will find the way to be their pot of gold.

58

TONIGHT SHE WANTS to start with his feet. Because her nighttime man is linked to the daytime man by his feet — awake, in the afternoons, he had stared at her holding his funny feet. He didn't know any better. Tonight she begins at the heels. These feet may have walked miles in their big shoes but they are also cosseted feet, feet that have rarely walked bare. Feet too refined for a man who likes to act as if he has done so much in life. Still, even his feet feel kind, she thinks, they are warm and kind in her hands.

He stirs in his sleep but she believes he will not wake — he never does. Tonight she is taking a bigger risk than usual because the moon is almost ripe and he could just open his eyes and see her. What would she say? That she needed to do a nighttime laundry and was just lifting his feet out of the way? She wants to laugh out loud. She sees her hands like animals burrowing up under the sheets. She already knows the stringiness of the calves but the softness behind the knees surprises her.

His mouth half-opens and he lets out an animal sound, like the end of her name. *Ee?* she whispers back. How can someone sleep so deeply?

She doesn't usually take such risks but tonight is different. Because in front of her Buddha she had found herself crying without reason. Without sound, too, tears just starting on their own. At first she told herself the tears came from too much sandalwood smoke. And then she tried to remember that her days of being cursed by Dragonhead planet are over. There is no good reason for tears. She climbs now onto the bed next to Honree but doesn't breathe onto his face, his eyes — tonight that would risk too much.

Instead she lies atop the sheet, slowly placing her arm on the chest, its rise and fall. And whispers close to it: *I had someone who thought about me. Somebody made sure I didn't go hungry. Pushed rambutans through a hole in the wall. You don't know rambutan. You've never seen a fruit that round. That red . . .*

She listens to his steady breath and it calms her, closes her eyes so it is as though the two of them survive on the same boat, the same wind caressing them. For a moment she feels herself inside his pink skin, the pink a sun on her and winds across the water ferrying them somewhere. He is humid, a balm. She studies the face, a man's face, lets her lips brush the man's neck, once, smells his baby skin. *I know you,* she whispers, *you are not what they say, not a cockroach, you are mine.*

59

Q. What is the aim of the four great efforts?
A. To suppress one's animal desires and grow in goodness.

Q. Try to give me a simile.
A. In the ordinary waking state, one's view of knowledge is
as limited as the sight of a man who walks on a road between high hills. In the higher consciousness of Jñāna
and Samadhi, it is like the sight of the eagle poised in the
upper sky and overlooking a whole country.

One Wednesday toward the end of March he stays barefoot on
the rhapsodic bench until close to noon. He is happy at Nani's busy
enterprise near him. In the morning she had pounded the laundry by
the canal and now hangs it up, prolifically, tenderly, the pins in her
mouth until they clip the line. She sweeps the walk near him and
makes the quotidian a dance. She never meets his eyes.

'You *do* see what we will be able to do here?' he says out of the
blue. Perhaps she understands. 'What a good life for everyone.'
He waves toward the canal. Her neck a harp's curve, her hands
tight around the broomstick, an answer must rest in that lithe
sweeping. 'You amaze me,' he says. 'Really. I'm sure you talk but just
don't.'

He leaves the bench only to go inside and operate the syringe he'd
improvised from a coil wedged into a pricked buffalo-milk stopper,
a gadget that refills his fountain pen. From the window, he sees
Pushpa running up the drive. A second later she is pounding the
door to his library.

Playful, determined to undo whatever her surly urgency is *this*
time, he hurries to the front door to surprise her from behind. Don't
all of them need a little humor in life? He has nothing but benevolence toward Pushpa: she has been teaching for a couple of weeks
but already — his eavesdropping has told him as much — she has
done a fine job.

Seeing him at the door she lets out a bleak little 'Oh!'

In her excitement, she calls him by the wrong name. 'Mister Wolf, come. The children! Gone mad. Can't help it.' Later he realizes she meant to call him Wooves, confusing him with the other foreigner who'd lived in this house. 'Students! Run most way to town.'

'All of them?' A grasp on things — numbers — all are essential. 'All,' she pants.

In the library he pulls on his new thongs. They run, out, down the drive, along the canal road. Past the temple where the monk raises his hand in a curious greeting for which Henry has no time. Up the hill, Pushpa hiking her skirt, strong woman that she is — Henry must struggle to slow his breath, to get that hot glove reaching around his lungs to *quit*. He might as well be in some highland games, it's that hard to keep up with her.

In a spirit of comradely holiday, others begin to run with them. By the time Pushpa pulls Henry off the road and onto a shortcut through a muddy cattlefield, the whole village is after them, so it seems, splashing and muddy, jolly coming from the market with their cadjan baskets of vegetables. Already Henry is beyond exhausted. They are flagging, walking but still insistent, up the main road into Kandy, over a stream and through the hillock's serrated tunnel. Heading into town, they meld into a gigantic rabble, a mob.

'There's one!' Pushpa cries, pointing out a devilish little boy he thinks he has seen before, distinctive because of his rooster's hair tuft. 'Philip!' she calls. 'A boy named after one of our aristocrats. Someone who was a Sinhala from a good Kandyan family,' explaining over her shoulder to Henry. Philip turns about, distraught, and points up the road toward Kandy.

'They didn't wait for me,' he says, in a baby's Sinhalese, unheeding his aristocratic namesake.

Pushpa hoists him up and onto her own ridge of a hip. She gives his wrist a small slap: 'You were bad to go.' But he is happy up on her body.

For the first time Henry admires her without reservation: her mildness with the boy, her crossed eyes, the way she would run like a girl but then shows a woman's acumen.

As though Henry too has misbehaved, as though he couldn't understand otherwise, she commands, 'Come!' with her usual briskness. Today she wouldn't kill him. She's bringing him along. Could any mercury be invented to chart these people?

'They're ahead,' she's saying, 'behind, I don't know. Lost somewhere.'

With Pushpa and Philip, he comes alive. Tagging along and happy. Whatever this all is, it doesn't depend on him. He is less concerned with some minor pedagogical insurrection and mutiny and is just more pleased that he has gotten his boyhood wish. To be close to life and action. To color.

As they pass the rainwashed Muslim homes, the muted roar of a crowd up ahead greets them, the noontime sun blazing so fiercely the day's hues flatten into variations of gray. Once they arrive in Kandy's central square, just in front of the creamy Temple of the Tooth, they succumb to the crowd. Among the bone-white shoulders of the clerks, they could easily lose one another. 'Stay close!' Pushpa snaps and for this he is glad.

A man is booming *revolution, revolution* into his megaphone. In English of all things. Peaceful and exhilarated by the crowd, Henry watches. For once he need not do a thing: life with its own design swivels around him.

'We come here today . . .' and the man's voice echoes, spikes and slides. 'Today, today.' His English could be spoken to the king himself. 'To assert a new fraternity, a camaraderie among men and women. Honest soldiers of the Sinhala nation. When you had malaria, we went into the villages and helped. When you had the water sickness, we taught boiling. But we are more than medics treating the nation's physical body. We are medicine and cure for its head and heart, so long bowed, and you all know what I mean.'

A roar does go up in the crowd, but Henry cannot tell if its cause is natural or cued by the university types flanking the stage. In the wind, red banners from the treetops reading DOWN WITH BRITISH IMPERIALISM and CEYLON MUST LEAVE THE EMPIRE dip and wave over the makeshift stage. Several white-shirted colleagues run to beat the signs higher with the kind of long stick usually reserved for striking down coconuts.

By the lake, bobbies on horses shift uneasily, uniformed in stoic blue, trading sweaty glances. Some twenty of them — are they after all policemen or soldiers? — fringe the crowd. While their surveillance might enslave them, it liberates Henry. He gazes across the eager spread of faces.

From the throng, someone yaps up at the speaker in a tidy English: 'And what are you university leftists doing for the Tamils? the Muslims? the lower castes? Did they teach you that in Oxford? in Peradeniya? You waiting to take over your high-caste uncles' government jobs?'

As though what had been spoken was a salute, the crowd's bellow rises to swallow this salvo. Henry sees the speaker is Nandana, the boyish man whom he'd met in Colombo the day Manu picked up his posters. There by Nandana is, in fact, Manu, at the very rim. But the onstage speaker pays no mind to Nandana, his phrases rolling forward, exigent. 'We are thinking revolution, revolution. Demanding revolution, revolution.'

Henry wonders whether most of those present can understand the speaker's words. He possesses a student intellectual's appeal with his glasses, suit and tie, appearing every bit an Oxford type on holiday who'd ascended to some kind of throne. On the crude stage, he throws his arms around four or five others, all similarly attired, who begin to sing a Sinhala song which Henry can't make out but which many in the crowd begin to hum.

Pushpa looks as transfixed as Henry by the scene but still bothers to translate a few phrases for him:

> Life is like a flowing river,
> No barrier, distinctions . . .

The crowd joins in the song and a weird harmony shimmers on the lake's surface.

The British move in, just slightly, on their horses, not breaking up the crowd or the song or the civil dissent, just presenting the people with the menace of hooves, of stampede — horses are still intimidating here, that much Henry knows. He spies some of his boys and girls, loitering in excitement along the edges, not far from Manu, in the native shirts Henry himself had them dye so laboriously. Were his villagers so easily rented for any cause that they would gather at a second's notice here in the square? Did they notice whether Henry or someone else was speaking to them?

'Come!' he shouts to them.

Pushpa pulls his arm down.

'Yes,' says Henry, 'no, I mean —'

'We go to gather the children ourselves.'

As Henry wrestles through the nest of the crowd, everyone in their turned-up collars smiling, he loses his way for a bit, even among the shorter people, so is surprised when a chamber opens between the bodies and he faces his aide.

'Johnny!' He cuffs the boy on the shoulder as though it has been monsoons since their last meeting. 'Johnny! What do you think?'

The boy's face today is a falcon's, there by Manu and Nandana.

'Yes, Henree.' And too quickly, a wary guide, though there's no need to be ashamed, not before his companion of so many benched nights. 'Shall I return with you?'

'No! we're fine,' says Henry. He wants to cede to the boys, show himself as generous. These two, this Manu and Nandana, they must be new friends of Johnny. Over-energetic smiles are exchanged all around. The blood subsides in Henry until he thinks, inexplicably, he might faint. Is some betrayal afoot? but no, he imagines it. Of course it's healthy for Johnny to get out of Rajottama for a little change. Things are just as they always have been between them. 'See you back on the ranch?'

'Of course, Henree,' with a consoling delicacy.

Henry walks in the early afternoon back with Pushpa on the road to Rajottama, the orphans skipping gleeful, not fearing reprimand, up ahead. It is not so bad that Johnny disappoints him by his silence — it is, after all, just the smallest of breaks with his employer, that Johnny fails to keep Henry informed about *all* his movements.

No, what is worse is that others are trying to resurrect an independent Ceylon. And Henry hadn't known about this exact group. And it is entirely feasible that what he has just witnessed is one of hundreds of groups hatching. Still, Henry can't help but feel a paternal soft spot for this particular breed of young students. They believe in themselves and their singular cause. They lack all sense of life and its complexity, that is clear, life and its obstacles. Yes, the crowd they had attracted was unambiguous, substantial, but wouldn't that go hand-in-hand with their youthful convictions, with their central locale, with their central *age?* While he, Henry alone in Rajottama, he is trying to do something specific. Something specific that will have deeper and more perennial meaning, he tells himself.

'Those kinds of fireworks are good for the young!' he says aloud in English, making Pushpa turn to him. 'What?' she asks.

'Nothing,' smiling back. 'I enjoyed the day.'

It is important to keep his eyes on his work, on his side of the elephant. What did the fable say? You could work on cleaning the leg of an elephant, while someone else worked the head, while another worked the back. And all of you had to hope you were cleaning the same animal, but just because you knew others were working didn't mean you should stop your own work. Eventually, no matter the size of the elephant, everyone would reach the heart, wouldn't they, by their different means.

He slaps himself for feeling lonely, walking back with Pushpa but not with her. He tells himself of course there is one trip on which no one else can really share your load. No matter what you dream of lying in your own bed. Nothing ultimately can be fetched from outside of yourself. You aspire without grasping. You just do your best — you work your side of the elephant. It would not be fair, say, to control Johnny completely. What if he tried to? What if he told the boy he must stay only by Henry's side?

The clouds have moved into Doric columns as they walk. The ground is endless and his mouth twitches without eloquence. The inexplicability of Johnny's falcon face — the demonstration — Manu, Nandana and Johnny on the rim. Once again everything conspires to tell Henry he is clueless, knowing nothing about anyone's intentions.

By the wayside rest years of searching for allies. He has to remember that as much as he might admire — and love, and trust — his boy, *his* Johnny, there is a superior god he can't forget.

60

SELF-RELIANCE. And haven't they too heard of it? 'Please, sir, you asked once how you could be helpful? This is what we need,' Roshan is saying, brashness wrung out of his face.

Henry'd arrived home from the socialists' Kandy event, alone, shocked to find a virtual Pietà on his driveway: Roshan the friendly marketman holding his wife swathed in a huge iridescent cloth, herself cradling a child.

'Help us, sir?' Roshan had asked.

This day had already been too much. From strange dreams to samadhi to politics. The children's mutiny, Pushpa's friendliness, Johnny's hauteur and now Roshan. Henry's first thought, ridiculous though it may have been, was that this plea for help happened to concern his American watch: he *had* asked Roshan to repair its cracked face.

'She's sick,' Roshan went on, 'my wife. Said we should come to you. She was the one made me. We tried kottumali and laudanum and everything else. Nothing worked.'

'I can bring you to a doctor.'

'Our people don't like to ask for help. Because my son, too —'

Henry had not known Roshan had a son, the boy about four, quiet asleep, his face as sloping as his father's.

'Please,' the repair wizard was saying. 'She thinks maybe you can do your you know.' He had trailed off, making the staccato motions of someone scattering dandelions. It had taken Henry a while to understand. He saw Nani standing at the top of the hill near the mango tree. Did she want to explain but couldn't?

'What is it you want me to do?' he asks Roshan, kneeling down, gentle. Henry rocks in the begging position and extends his swollen hand toward the boy's head. Though the child slaps aside the pink thing, Roshan grips it, making the American's hand stroke his own wife's flossy hair. What in god's name does the man want him to do?

Henry must, as is usual here, improvise. And so he makes a small circle in the air above the woman's head —

'That's right, sir,' says Roshan encouragingly. 'Perhaps too sing some of your chants?' Elaborating: 'Songs, you must be knowing what I mean, sir.'

Henry stares up at the eye-shaped hole the trees make above him. There are rain clouds and there are rain clouds. Today they turn determined and serious, rushing in to cover any gaps in the sky. No special dispensations there. Henry gives up. 'A song?' He's been here too long. Long enough not to know which songs he still knows. That is wrong. He recalls one. And starts in a low tone: *My country 'tis of thee* . . .

'That's it, sir,' says Roshan. Closes his eyes devoutly. 'Louder. If you don't mind, sir. Sometimes I've heard that helps —'

> Sweet land of liberty
> Of thee I sing.
> Land where my fathers died —

At this point, the child quits pretending he has been sleeping and sits up *hitapu gamang!* all of a sudden! to hold Henry's look with an intent stare. The mother rises too, her spine sunken but face upward as though to receive a benediction and a gift of light:

> Land of the Pilgrims' pride —

At the bottom of the drive, two women stand lookout: Pushpa, always Pushpa, freshened after their little trip to town. Now accompanied by a fancily dressed woman who must be her famous sister-in-law from the capital, Manik, the last of the Pilimas, the true Pilima. The women carry their vegetable baskets high on their all-purpose hips but notwithstanding, they nod like sovereigns at Henry. Still he will finish the song:

> From every mountainside,
> Let freedom ring.

'That's fine, Mister Wolf,' shouts Pushpa. He tolerates the mistake. Most important, Pushpa's mood is good. For once she is surrendering her ladylike patina. 'Fine! Fine! You are learning about —' and he thinks she says *our kindness* but it is not entirely unlikely that what she says is *surrendering breasts* or *finesse*. She waves with a new brightness. And then moves on, approvingly, until she is beyond the trees. Like any newly minted doctor, of course *he* must stay.

61

THE NEXT MORNING (having woken before Nani) Henry finds a basket of long-stemmed gold-tasseled wildflowers in a wicker basket on the front porch. He is surprised, why not, but the gift wouldn't be from Pushpa and Manik, would it? or something from Johnny?

No; the basket is too ratty.

Inside is a small card in a Sinhala which Henry translates torturously. He gets the basic idea. It seems Roshan's son and wife have made a miraculous recovery from their ailment, the English letters on the card being:

COOLIN GFEVER TH ANKYOU.

But now it also appears that everyone and his mother's cousin's harelipped uncle from two villages over has caught whatever the uncooled fever is, whatever had beset Roshan's family: everyone suddenly needs serious cooling.

By midday, Henry has instructed Joseph to turn away the fevered supplicants that line his drive. They crouch cracking and spitting heaps of sunflower hulls, dogged in their waiting. His hands are cold, it is true, and swollen, but that is from his scleroderma and the associated Raynaud's syndrome. Not from any new powers.

Once again the valley has spewed them forth from unknown crannies. Henry stays quarantined in the house, Johnny bringing excited dispatches from the market. He's back to his usual self, away from the new friends. Yet everything, today, breaks from their usual routine. The boy practically chirps: 'This can only help, Henree! everything will go like fireworks!'

To soothe his anxiety, the famous Yankee healer with the cold hands eats too much fruit and has to spend most of the morning with a spastic colon in and out of the outhouse, Nani amused by his gluttony and its consequences, or so it would seem from her pursed mouth. He has no mind to do anything. The weight of them and their illnesses, invented or real, pushes up the drive toward him, all of them burrowing terrible tunnels through him.

This is hardly what he'd intended. He'd merely always liked Roshan with his wry comments and his polymath talents. And this situation makes him boil — all but his hands. From the canal road he hears a chant which he understands is in his praise:

> Miss Hanree, Hanree!
> *Wessa witerak naemae! Sanipe witerak naemae!*
> Not just the rains!
> Not just health!

By two o'clock, Johnny has gotten fatigued. He spades rice into his mouth in the library, all with more rudeness than Henry has ever seen in the boy. Johnny's friends are breaking him in, perhaps. 'You have to let *some* of the people see you. Otherwise you'll be like a dam that could break.'

'No! They're inside me already,' says Henry from where he lies curled on the chaise. His famous hands are not doing well at cooling his stewing head. 'What I'll do is create daily receiving hours. Or something. But I can't just let everyone come in all at once. Not today.'

'Of course not, Henree.'

When Johnny leaves again, Henry contemplates the idea of sending a real message to the village. Chants and six o'clock offering rituals to the Buddhas at the temple: all this has gone too far. Henry needs a symbol. Something that will speak to the people's private lives. This is when he conceives of the day on which all the altars in the village will achieve a higher, truer end.

The Day of Altars. He christens it himself.

He sends word via Johnny, late in the afternoon, that the monk is invited to come to the house and the monk immediately agrees. Pandit shows himself to be congenial. Right off he states his satisfaction at the jackpot — the supplicants lining the drive.

As soon as tea is served, Henry makes the proposal. While flies contour-map a vertical tornado hole in the center of the room he waits.

Will the monk take on the project?

Pandit swats the flies cheerily. He *will* help with the Day of Altars, which they'll set for a week's time hence. 'Come,' the monk congratulates him. 'It will be one more success for you, Colonel! You're already such a popular man!'

Henry rolls his eyes. 'Even if the popularity doesn't come from me but just as a correlation?'

'Doesn't correlation sometimes work as well as a cause, Colonel?' Pandit brushes a dead fly off his robes. 'You wrote about our Buddhist idea of dependent origination.'

'My popularity's not based on anything real.'

'Of course you do,' the monk sniffs back, not having listened very well, this deafness continuing as a rhetorical trend.

Pandit's alacrity surprises Henry, but no more than it should. What the monk considers seriously on his own way back to the temple, amid the threads of the crowd attracted to the colonel, is whether the bumbling foreigner might be one of those crazy fools who possess supernatural powers. Because the man's hands are unusually cold. Without the aid of any strict regimen of meditation or diet, certain people *can* gain powers in this next instant.

Certain men are allowed to see the light spilling out from behind the cosmic dark. Certain ones can transport their bodies like contraband to the farthest stars. Perhaps the colonel has become one of these men, a man steering a grand vehicle even if with loose hands. He does seem to go about without much heed. He never knows the heart of any moment. And yet all the while he stays strangely protected.

But is the colonel a fool? Association with fools 'is ever painful, like partnership with an enemy,' the Buddha had said, his own light blinding if you remembered it too well.

Perhaps the Yankee had been born into some kind of common-sensical savoir-faire. That much Pandit knows. Common sense is native to America and England. And even if this were not exactly the case, even if the colonel were a fool, it would do no good to cross a man like him. The monkey must have *some* kind of access to the powers beyond all the shields. Why should Pandit fail him on such an inconsequential matter?

The Day of Altars — obviously some restitution the Yankee has created to correct an insult reverberating in his solitary world. And Pandit should never interfere with something of such limited scope.

What he doesn't understand is why the colonel is so upset. Were Pandit the colonel, *he* wouldn't complain about being treated as a great guru or healer. The problem with the Yankee is he always seems to be staring at a mottled screen of the future, what has not yet happened, never knowing how to rest in the bounty of life.

One day Pandit would point his pupil toward the suttas that teach a key wisdom — frantic avoidance of the sensual world binds one all the more to it. He could, perhaps, instruct him in this — utopias necessarily cost a man his own personal salvation. There would be time for teaching the American all that and more. After years as a monk, Pandit has patience, stores of it, a horizonless capacity for nikang inneva. And rests in full anticipation of a calm hour alone in his own study, just before his daily afternoon meditation with Rosalin-akka.

62

MANU'S IDEA was straightforward. A few years earlier, he had been mistaken for a girl often enough. For him to know what the Pilimas were doing, and so to help the boys whom he'd helped to organize, to nationalize, he might attend one of the PILIMAS AGAIN! meetings clothed as a girl.

To do this, he had to enlist the help of Jehan, who obtained from a beggar-caste woman a ponytail woven of human hair.

That afternoon in the cottage, Jehan took a little pride in how he could weave and further plait the wig into a bun atop Manu's head. 'Did this kind of thing for my mum,' was all Jehan said, arranging a tendril here, an artful spit curl there. 'You look better than a theater artist!'

Jehan had also been responsible for procuring a bodice top, which Manu guessed — he hoped — came from Nani's boudoir. He would not be uncouth and ask. What followed — a double-wrapping of Manu's hips in a lungi cloth, a stuffing of the bodice — was something Jehan again proved himself a dream at doing.

Manu, gazing in his cracked reflection in Jehan's mirror, laughed. 'I never could've done this without you.'

'Good,' said Jehan. 'That's what we're here for, isn't it?'

A knock came and Manu ran to hide in his finery, up the two stairs to the boy's bedroom. From behind the almirah he could hear Nani saying, 'The pink man would like you to come discuss plans for the pilgrimage in half an hour,' and luckily she left immediately; no nonsense; she conveyed her message and disappeared.

Coming out, Manu felt titillated by this brush with Nani, as pleased as he'd been afraid of being found out. After all, it was her blouse he wore. And circuitously, it was for her that he was going to a meeting.

The boys resumed their work, plaiting a last strand. 'He wants you, Jehan, doesn't he? Shouldn't you go?'

'Just a bit more,' said Jehan, daubing drops of sandalwood oil in the hollows below his friend's ears.

At dusk the meeting itself was held on the flower-specked field fronting the Pilima compound, one frequently used for impromptu cricket games among boys of the govigama caste. Manu did his best.

He aped a girl's mannerisms. Crossed his hands, lowered his eyes, sat in the back. Did what he could, in short, to go unnoticed. As if by instinct, other girls moved away from him on the bench. No one knew him, the best of all possible cases. And though he thought he saw Nani among them, and ached to walk freely toward her, take claim of her, it turned out not to be Nani. He fidgeted his thumbs, a drumbeat rolling within and unable to come out. When the bench was to be pulled up toward the front by boys he talked to every day, he sat apart from the other girls on flattened straw, smelling the sweat of those nearby.

People were saying, Manu overheard, that maybe it was not be-

cause of the pink stork that the Maha had come. But they stopped
their gossiping soon as Lester strode out in front, a gold sash binding his ceremonial whites. Manu thought the man had become like
Henry: a bird with its balloon of air rising up through the chest, the
heart, and forced to talk!

It was true — Lester had every one of the foreigner's mannerisms,
down to the last talkative detail. When sitting, he could not seem to
keep from leaning forward on his knees. He did not greet anyone
without judicial pomp. This was no longer the Lester who barked
commands as he came to collect taxes supposedly for the British.
This was a Lester who'd learned that ancient claims of honor could
matter less than loutish popularity. Just once, Lester bore down
close to Manu; and the boy shrank back, pretending to sneeze along
his drawn-up legs, succumbing to a regular fit of sneezing.

When Lester started to pontificate, however, he lacked the same
boom and bombast which came so helplessly to the foreigner. The
Pilima had not much to say, it seemed, other than this: 'We are here
today to begin the movement! We call it P.A.!' He gestured for
someone to bring forth a placard. 'And this will be our symbol —'

'— a P and then an A for PILIMAS AGAIN! Pilima-la!'

This was the magic Lester achieved: these motley Rajottamans
with their fingers in the air, drawing circles and loops. Manu saw
that much of the crowd had come from the poorer areas, the shantytown patch along the railroad tracks, and they enjoyed this exercise,
this air-drawing, much more than what followed. Lester's torrent of
speech: 'You have known me as the taxman! I've been your Maha
Mudaliyar for as long as you have memories!'

'Not always such a kind one,' mused a motherly woman near
Manu.

'I have been the face of the British. You feared me! I came for
money for roads when we people, apee minisu, we have always
known and used jungle paths, ones we built with our knowledge. I
made bad mistakes! I was one of them! I came to take! I asked you for
taxes on dogs as pets — when we people, apee minisu, we didn't
keep dogs as pets!'

Those near Manu were getting riled, bodies giving off more
heat, some making tiny interjections to pretend they could·interrupt

Lester Pilima. One woman dabbed her upper lip ritualistically as though before her stood the dark devil Mahasona himself.

'But!' — and here was the apex of Lester's imitation of the pink roach, pounding the placard — 'I am a Pilima by marriage!' — only a few snickered at this — 'and can still speak on behalf of rebels who died so we could be here today!'

Manu knew this was of course an exaggeration. Yet it was a riveting performance, far better than any sorcerers' contest.

'And I say to you!' — here Lester threw off the golden sash — 'I say that after today I WILL COLLECT NO MORE TAXES!'

'But surely they'll appoint someone else to be Mudaliyar,' said a man up front. 'Someone else could be worse!'

'I dare anyone,' and here Lester returned to his normal bearishness, 'to become Maha Mudaliyar to spite me!'

All this Manu later recounted to Jehan by their canal bank. 'But their group is *nothing*. It's not important.'

He did not want Jehan to think less of Manu's own group or even of the leftists they had seen during the Kandy demonstration.

'The truth is I can't keep all these movements straight, Manu. I just know those college boys in town lacked something.'

By this, Manu understood his friend meant the leftists had been too snooty, preaching above the crowd. 'Not what your pink man would call the voice of the common folk, are they?'

Jehan smiled. 'Your movement would be. Probably.'

'Then why *don't* you come to our meetings? You'd be surprised. A person can talk himself into believing something bigger than himself. And then it turns out to be a good thing, Jehan. For your heart, or for — '

'Yes, I agree.' The boy patted Manu's hand. 'Still, some things, don't you think, they're better admired from a distance?'

Manu considered this to be the worst kind of excuse, either lazy or bad thinking, but he let it go. Jehan had to come around whenever it was time for him to do so, not a moment earlier.

63

How these people understand each other. Does it bode ill
for our shared projects that they use the same word for
uncertainty, probability, sufficiency, truth, testicles? Or do I
mishear my monk? Their word for existence is the same as
for waiting. Will that be my history here?

Still waiting to hear from:

American Fruit & Vegetables, Inc.

Seeds for model garden:

1 large Pumpkin variety capable of feeding more families
    than their own slender tubular local variety
1 Cucumber
Spinach (to hybridize with local acidic variety, Gotu Kola,
    with labor-consuming leaves left over from Chinese trade
    routes)

On this dawn he riffles through the book in which he and Johnny
keep their notes.

Behind him the house moans. By some accident of wind and
structure, the edifice emits a racket you could mistake for a woman
in labor.

These last weeks during the slow start to the Yala monsoon,
Johnny and Nani have brought Wooves' vexing shelter into order
and have maintained it without derailing during the whole Roshan/-
Henry-worshiping day, when they had finally managed to disband
the entourage by announcing regular Receiving Hours, offering
fruit bribes, and much smiling all around.

Still Henry could not walk in the marketplace without a wake — a
bit of admiring friction, a few last-ditch pleas. His wake had grown
from the young gossiping boys into a larger one, including scabrous,
pickled folk, people he'd never noticed in Rajottama before, people
who ended up being too darn afraid to come to Wooves' house during the daily Receiving Hours.

This extra drag in his sails he can handle because he has the boy and girl as allies. She especially has shown a decent hand in banishing dust, far better than Henry in his rectory days. Best of all is that without much solicitation, already many weeks ago now, she had begun a certain ritual. Mostly as an afternoon event, she rubs his feet, as often as he can get her to do so.

Rub may not be the right conjuring of what she does. She pummels the tips of his limbs until he is in such pleasure he often has to retire from the kitchen to his room so as not to erupt in some mortifying paroxysm before her wide eyes. All the while she kneads his toes in ways he never could have imagined, he wonders: have I ever been in such ecstasy? Whenever he smells lavender — as he does now — he craves it: the good fortune of it all, her hands on his feet.

But she's slower to vanquish mildew. No one else smells it as much as Henry does. Mildew follows him like the boys of Ceylon. And despite her speed in the garden she's damn slow with cooking. And with niceties like handkerchiefs.

The breaking day promises no rain for once, the sun inching toward the canal. Nani has once again not pressed his handkerchiefs. His whites did go out with her laundry yesterday. If she has finished the task she hasn't yet returned the clean clothes: she's slow as the horizon. Ultimately she may be of a piece with her people, who regardless of new protein are torpor itself.

Henry wants to blow his nose and has nothing to do it with but instead of going to wake her he stays on his bench, atop the highest hill in Rajottama, because the monk is observable now, leaving the temple, heading on the road toward Wooves' house. There's no denying Pandit's admirable restraint. He always looks to be hovering two feet above the road's muck, above the chatter of the shadow-boys he shares with Chollie and the American.

Even when the monk recently complimented Henry on how much had been achieved, Henry felt the monk hovering two feet above him as well. And this despite Pandit chortling something along the lines of *We're glad to have you here, Colonel!* or *You don't know how to judge your progress!* Yet what a resource: this last month Pandit had proven to be a shockingly good source for suggestions, especially strong on the nature of provisions. He'd agreed with Henry that perhaps the women would develop better than scrawny chickens if Henry imported variety into their diet: a hard-working and proud race could be harvested out of such promising soil.

'We're all for your new vegetables,' the monk had said. 'Your arti-
chokes and asphodel.'

'Asparagus.'

'Asparagus. What we're especially proud of is how you use what
you've learned from our lessons.' He had reflected. 'That you're giving these lectures is not insignificant. We're proud of you. How you
can already teach the people their culture.'

The truth is Henry's had to glean knowledge from everywhere.
There is no sleeping on this job. But what a lovely phrase for such
a polished monk to have used: that Henry *teaches the people their
culture.*

Culture? Kumari had said she was all for it. And both dance
school sisters had kindly offered their sizable hall for the lectures.
Problem is, not only do voices reverberate in the hall's lemony confines, silence does as well.

Starting on an every-other-day basis, just to get the thing going,
Henry has already lectured on topics such as dental hygiene or morality and abstinence. While he talks, the people sit on a big carpet.
They fasten their olive-dark eyes upon him as if their spirits have
vacated and left their bodies parked behind. In front of the dance
school's blackboard, Henry spends himself searching for easy
phrases for Johnny to translate to the congregation.

Teeth can rot otherwise. Or: *Fidelity can free a man to fulfill his higher
destiny.*

No matter what he says (or how Johnny translates it) the people stay so unnervingly still. He thinks they pretend to listen. That
they believe Henry to have authored the rains. And the health of
Roshan's family. Occasionally a few of the women bow their heads
and coo. However, as though silence is an article of faith, no one
ever applauds.

In the queue afterward for chits, this is when they show their
animation. Yet not their true faces, the visages of future scholars
and mystagogues, luminaries, leaders, sages. Instead they shove and
chuckle like children waiting to receive gumdrops, all for the chits
they can use at the General Store for cheese and — his small concession — palm wine. He sometimes wishes they would show a little of
the earnestness he'd seen in the clerks' faces at the Kandy nationalists' rally.

All right, Henry admits to himself this morning, his nose itching, the day creeping in slowly, it's a little disappointing. No wonder the monk has chosen to stay distant from the people. They do not reciprocate well. But supposedly many like his talks. 'O, they like,' Kumari had said (after *Morality: Is Elegance Refusal?*). She helped roll up the carpet. 'Tonight they like much.' Even the recalcitrant sister Sonali had enumerated: 'Moral, yes, they are very interesting in moral. They like much.'

Like or not like, each March day has turned his fortunes topsy-turvy. And the mountain has been staring him down. Outside his window each day three bullocks stay stuck against the mountain's impassive surface. Today is no different. Inside that flat, bare mountain of Monkeyhead, he knows, jungle veins swell, transport the viridescent slither that encroaches everywhere. But there is something in the mountain's face, its *flatness*, the stasis of the bulls, that in the wrong mood could seem designed to defeat every ounce of a man's can-do and horizontal thinking. The face of that mountain: you could see in it, if you chose, an ungenerous host waiting for a guest to leave.

On the bench after dawn, the monk walking steadily toward him, Henry studies Johnny's notes on lecture attendance:

The Need for Proper Hygiene — 20 attendees

How Water Conduits Can Save a Civilization: The Romans Onward — 8 attendees

(Chits instituted.)

Moral Purpose — (uncounted)

Why a National Dress? — 51 attendees

The Purity of Buddhism — 74 attendees

How Moral Customs Make a People Proud — 80 attendees

Projected topics:

The Importance of Documenting History: A Split from Myth

What Makes a Nation?

The Benefits of Hydroponics and a Subscriber System of Vegetable Gardening as a Means toward Nutritional Variety

Who needs applause? I am not so bad a synthesizer of ideas, Henry tells himself. *Eighty came last time.* Perhaps it would be better to give lectures only every week, not so often as he has been. He is figuring the percentage of post-chit attendance increase when Johnny passes him by. In a clean but misbuttoned shirt, he pops Henry an all-clear sign.

Johnny had decided the temple grounds should initiate Henry's lustrous venture: the Day of Altars, a Day of Rededication.

But once Henry had specified the site, the monk's protests came in a subtle, new flurry. Could Henry's group not meet at the usual place, at the orphanage and schoolhouse? Had they not considered the abandoned coffee plantation? At the plantation, volunteers could sit on rusted tractor parts to await others. Or why not near the tank at the head of the canal where several roads intersect?

Henry wanted always to respect his teacher. But on this point he grew stubborn. On the Day of Altars the people should go forth from the Sacred Tree Temple, from the very heart of Buddhism in their midst.

Finally, a quick pivot, the monk relented: 'Go on, let the riffraff gather at our temple,' Pandit had joked.

Riffraff was not a word Henry expected from a monk. For the first time Henry tries to fathom what might have been Pandit's family origins: aristocratic, no doubt, a family used to distinctions, the boy sipping coconut water from a filigreed spoon.

From the canal road the monk mounts the drive, his bald pate shining golden. Were he still a Sunday painter, Henry would love to render the monk's skull in oils and glazes. Too much else needs him now. Leave art to the New York salons.

At the gate Pandit passes silent Joseph with his gift of standing stiller than a Ceylonese listening to a self-improvement lecture. 'Your man,' the monk huffs, thinking along Henry's lines, 'a real tree! Like he's sworn to bear witness to dawn.'

'He'd probably enjoy your poetry.'

'Sit,' the round monk commands his student, who'd tried to rise. 'We prefer standing. You're wondering why we came so early? A talk before your Day of Altars. We know you're usually awake at dawn. A little business between friends.'

The monk's Buddha-perfect mouth, the orange robe draped over a regular cannon of an arm — all conspire to rouse Henry. Pandit could ask him to tumble naked in a barrel down the canal road in the name of Buddhism and Henry would probably do it.

Pandit sniffs. There is something to be communicated which is, he puffs, of vital interest to the community. 'Regi's rotten,' jumping right in. 'Didn't we tell you? That boy Upali told us. Turns out Regi's playing favorites with the chits at the store. Can't be trusted.'

Henry doesn't know how to take this so instead of speaking, he strokes his nascent beard, what the monk had earlier called a Muslim trait.

'We *know*, Colonel. For years he has beaten the evening drums for us. To take a little — never enough for his people. His son Manu's worse. Biggest loafer you'll ever find. We told you as much. You know they never attend your lectures?'

'I saw him at Morality.'

'No! he came *after* to pick up his chits. While you were lecturing inside, he was getting intoxicated on the road with his betel-chewing. Spitting on the road.'

'Hard to believe.' Henry regards how Joseph, in a voiding of civic responsibility, kicks a pile of coconut hulls from the garden. The gardener keeps kicking the hulls down the drive until they find their final resting place on the main road as litter. Henry is reminding the monk how it had been Manu who'd drawn the catechism's pictures.

'A rotten seed produces rotten fruit, Colonel! for all you know they're running a business selling chits to others!'

'In the interest of fairness —' begins Henry.

'For your plan to work, Colonel, you can't come in and change everything left and right and immediately!' the monk declares and then drops his eyebrows. He smiles with latinate beneficence. 'Slowly things happen, no? Of course you mean well, Colonel. But you want to be fair — you don't promote what you would call in English a *bounder*. And so quickly. Also customers don't appreciate taking goods from the hands of a low-caste man.'

'That is wrong,' imitating Pushpa.

'That is reality.' The monk paces in front of the bench.

'What to do,' trying out another native locution. 'Please sit.'

'We have another man in mind. Remember Chollie?'

'The dwarf?' but this is reflexive. Chollie's raspy voice, long beard and cane make him distinctive in Rajottama. For all his naps, the dwarf hadn't done a bad job foremanning the garden. He'd at least gotten the job done.

'Small but strong. In his time he was one of the best toddy-tappers,' sighs Pandit. 'You wouldn't believe it. People lined up just to taste the toddy he brought down from the palms. It was that sweet.'

The gardener takes a few swipes at the hedge with a dull machete but soon gives up and returns to his gateside post.

'To be honest, saddhu, maybe I'm blind, but whether we choose Regi the drummer or Chollie the toddy-tapper — to me it's the same as tea with or without milk.'

'A world of difference, Colonel!'

Henry tries to rally. Says that what matters is the larger picture, the native knowledge they can release, ending up tying himself in a rhetorical knot, asking why should it matter who runs the store, or whether the drummer is of lower caste than a toddy-tapper.

'No one can say you're not easy to work with, Colonel.'

Admittedly Henry has a stealthy fondness for the drummer. Perhaps Henry is being unfair: in the village of the future, there should be no favorites.

Strange skinny Regi. Repairing his drum as Henry entered the village and later showing Henry his monster child. The way the drummer strains to please at the store. Henry can never tell the monk that Regi has become as much an amulet as the monk himself. Both the monk and Regi have the significance of dream figures in the Plan. Both mean success.

Madame would've shooed Pandit off with a provocative reply. Henry's own father might have listened with diplomacy, thanked Pandit, and then would have followed his own original plan. Henry chooses neither. Pandit is his ally. Let Pandit decide what's best. With Henry modeling a Buddhistic acceptance in Rajottama, many of its trivial old vendettas might be forgotten.

'I'm more eager to keep you happy,' he answers the monk. 'You know what I mean. Appoint as you please.' Johnny says that if the Pilimas and the monk are on Henry's side, nothing can stop the train. 'Thank you,' Henry finds himself saying. He wobbles his head. '*Bohom istuty*. I appreciate your good counsel. I'm sure you mean well.'

The monk nods in a semblance of relief.

'Sit,' Henry commands again. He has been brushing up on his nativisms and out-nativing the monk is a pleasing test.

The monk finally seats himself but slightly angled away from Henry, fanning himself. 'Dry, isn't it, Colonel?'

'And so early,' adds Henry. The two men stay in something he's learning to appreciate in Asia. The tea-cozy comfort of a silence believed to be companionable.

Henry writes in his book:

> When it comes to the repressed throwing off their respective
> shackles, a strategy of conciliation won't hurt anyone —
> consequently, it will not matter whether it is the Ceylonese
> among the British or the low castes of the village among the
> high. All will come to merge such distinctions & recognize
> their primal quiddity.

From the canal road Johnny raises a hand in surprised greeting.
'Ho!' he calls like a peasant. The sound echoes a maniacal chant
across the canal. 'Ho ho ho ho!'

64

How PUNCTUALLY and eagerly the villagers gather, later that same
morning, for the Day of Altars — and all in the name of destroying
paganism; yes, and helping Henry's model compost bin, too. What a
departure from the thin headphoned men of the wire services, the
mushroom complexions of his fraud trainees, the gravid brows of
the gentlemen farmers and their inept trowels.

A breathtaking sight. But as Johnny and Henry climb toward the
temple grounds, Lester calls out in that sarcastic crescendo of his
missionary English. 'We've lost count, Fyre. You've got people from
at least fifteen households. That must be your magic working?'

It's a pity, thinks Henry, the waste of such an accent. All the
Pilimas speak this highfalutin English and not a one ever sounds
sincere.

But the villagers with their faces fanatical and hands clutching
hammers and mamotties, they are the ones who stir Henry deeply.
For the Day of Altars they've brought their own tools in order to accomplish his mission. Like a giant in the temple yards, Henry stands
among them. If he is a latter-day, smaller John Bunyan — he is modest — it is the people who will together erect something worthwhile
and towering above pagan devotions.

The monk stalls at a remove from the crowd — sniffing, hoisting
his robes up from the mud, nipped by it.

'A bloody hunting party, am I wrong?' Suba says, accosting Henry. Henry can't decide whether he likes this older Anglophile of a man with his habit of touching Henry anywhere he can get a hold. 'Yes, call us maverick soldiers, ready to go beyond duty to serve.'

'True.' Henry ends up pleased at the man's explosion, Suba being just another expression of goodwill. Henry'd agree to almost anything at such a triumphant moment; anything; that at nighttime the globe squeezes into a trumpet or that the Second Coming had already happened. Because what counts is such earnest intention. Henry smiles at Suba. 'You're so right. We're mavericks.'

'Might you heal someone worthy of his gout?' Suba asks, pointing to his knee, but Henry elects to ignore this last query.

People straggle up the road but cannot find entrance to the crowded temple grounds. Henry's synod today is made up of nuzzling families, young men, unsquired women, people to whom he must nod, lacking clues about their names, homes, identities. They call him variously: Mister Henry, Fyre, Miss Gold. He knows he is being addressed by their honorifics: *Hello Mister Henry Fyre mahattea morning!*

He has nothing to do but stand among them. Nothing to do but nod ceremoniously and this he can do easily. Once he tries to share a smile with the monk, but Pandit's face has cooled into its public masks, poised or frigid.

Soon the crowd spills from the temple grounds out into the road and down toward the marketplace, a veritable mob, and one of the dance sisters prompts him. *'Api yamude?'* Shall we go?

Why not? For this unique moment Henry has been ready his whole life. What paradise. His Johnny is just ahead, wearing a khaki hat which had been Henry's gift to the boy. Little Upali, the General Store's server, undercover lover of goods, skips alongside, a perfect emblem for Henry's own perfect heart.

But maybe most important, the powerful Pilima has chosen to partake of the Day of Altars. Lester strides beside Henry and proffers the crowd a gesture half-drawn from the cricket field, half from obeisance, arms raised overhead, hands clasped. This man gives Henry qualms with his game-dog eyes and the tic of rolling his shoulders to punctuate his frequent self-descriptions — nonetheless he's someone good to have along, to help drive this pride of lions.

Behind Lester paces the monk with careful sandals barely scraping the dust, the dwarf Chollie rapping his cane just after in an insistent rhythm; as usual, the two burly bodyguards who rarely leave Chollie sidle along, the dwarf irradiating them with his own extra life. Far in the rear Henry sights the two dance school sisters, true converts, parading with sanctity. Their necks brown scimitars, the new saris glinting from a long way off, making it self-evident what distinctive and good-looking women he has on his team.

As though his head itself is uneven, Johnny's hat won't stay on straight. He joins Henry to whisper how smart Henry has been to arrange this day. 'Still, Henree, it's sad — not all the people are seeing its worth.'

'How do you mean?' If Henry wants, he could get annoyed about Johnny's compulsion to make small alarmist comments.

'Some say you pay the sisters for wearing saris.'

'A fee for wearing certain clothes?' Henry laughs; these ideas! None of this could weigh ballast on a day of such promising winds. And in the flutter of Madrasi golds and reds the women are captivating; their carriage queenly; the draping upon them more giddy than sea-fronds worn by any Miranda.

'Colonel,' the monk hovering, 'your aide fails to translate correctly.'

'Beg pardon?' Johnny's body interpolates itself between the monk and Henry.

'He doesn't understand our Sinhalese and we don't understand his.'

'I'm —' which friend should Henry address? both, neither — 'sorry.'

'Colonel. The people approve of the saris!'

'Heard what I heard.' The boy's gaze black ice at the monk.

'Exactly! *What he heard.* Don't worry, Colonel, your ideas are being received well.'

'Fine,' finishing uncertainly. 'Right, Johnny? We're fine,' he repeats. What he does not say is *Could you all stop squabbling and enjoy the day?* Nowhere did he sign on to be everyone's den mother. But once the monk has moved on, Henry turns on his aide: 'Why should the monk say those kinds of things about you?'

'It's not me you should be suspicious of,' Johnny says. But Henry had not said he was suspicious. 'If you really want to hear stories, I could tell you a thing or two about your monk.' When the boy again gets no answer, he goes on. 'A thing or two. But you don't want to hear.'

'You're right. I don't.'

A shout of good spirits kindles up from the back, a marching song: everyone, without exception, everyone is fine. Henry folds his arms over his chest and reminds himself of the mission. He wants to imbibe the moment. 'You go on ahead.' He stops to range his eyes past the ragtag early-morning brigade. Starvelings and pluto-crats, moneybags and tatty down-and-outs, all on his el dorado. He understands now that the rabble is singing his own particular praise-song:

> Wessa witerak naemae, sanipe witerak naemae

Not only rain, not only health . . . what they think he has accom-plished. They segue into the song Roshan has taught them:

> My country's whiz a gee
> Sweelan of liver tea
> Of Z eye think.

The Ceylonese hike past the emerald rice paddy and the shim-mering canal. All to do Henry's bidding; no one else's. His; and they have gone blessed from the temple; and there are allies among them.

> Lanyard my fodder's dyed
> Lanyard my soul lisps dry —

Carpenter ants take just ninety tries to learn a path and still this Ceylonese landscape shifts around Henry. He can forget where he is all too easily. But, without questioning, Henry had decided to start the Day of Altars on Elephantside, in the wealthier section of Rajottama.

> From any mountebank's sigh,
> Let free-dom ream!

They head away from the region where once Henry had found numerous cones made of palm leaves, the begging bowls of the untouchables. The party of helpers staggers north, up the trunk, away from the left foot where the temple rents its land to those of unnamable caste, away from the bridge and the market at its hip and the abandoned coffee plantation. They pass the upper-caste paddy and the Sacred Tree and Henry's house under the right arm and con-tinue on toward the Pilimas at the head. This much he tries to keep straight. It's not that Henry is blind to the paupers: he'd heard how they use the cones to beg for food and coins. Certainly, the party could return to the paupers' land later, after all the other sites had been sounded and encouraged.

Johnny had told him the untouchables remain, a vestige of the caste decree voiced by an ancient Kandyan king, the one who fell in love with a candala beggarwoman. The paupers live practically atop the railway line. Every day the Colombo express train, a colonial attempt to transport goods and stabilize prices, roars past their grind. Of course, Johnny always tells him, echoing James, 'The train is the legacy that disinherits us. Our British haven't spilled much blood. Which is why so few want to get rid of colonialism. This is what you're working against.'

The train is easier for Henry to understand than the idea of untouchables. Today no real squalor floats among the ranks, no irretrievable shreds and tatters, not so far as he sees; but then he wouldn't know a candala unless one came and begged from him, citing her caste name.

He would like to do some public gesture of embrace of the untouchables; but they have diseases, Johnny had warned, there is talk of contamination.

'Which household we starting at?' asks a skinny man whose wide grin seems happy at its sheer toothlessness. With a man like this, you could build twenty nations. Advanced years have shorn his legs of all but corded sinew and bone, yet a spry boy still lives within him.

Another man laughs and taps Henry's shoulder. 'Ask instead at which home we end, am I wrong?' Suba with his strong chin and unblinking brown eyes gives an impression of steadiness. He points to his leg and whispers conspiratorially, 'Wouldn't mind seeing if your magic works on gout.'

'Nothing stops us from starting at my house, does it!' Lester booms; but it is already done, they are approaching the Pilima compound, as though Lester had invisibly directed them from the start.

Over the last weeks this big man has crossed over from a pretense at hospitality into a constantly belligerent curiosity about Henry's plans. Even on the broadest of roads Lester manages to thrust Henry aside; to jab his arm a little too feelingly.

Don't underestimate Lester, Johnny has often warned him. These high-caste farmers are one clan per village. They never let anyone forget who they are. Even if Lester himself is a self-appointed taxman and chief of the village, even if he comes from some dirt-eating anonymous farmer family and wears a bad toupee, he was smart enough to marry into the Pilimas. In short, history's on his side; one needs to treat him well.

Lester is practically pushing the group to his home, rallying them to be quicker: he insists on being first. Johnny's face clenches unnaturally under his new khaki hat. Whenever his spectacles slip, they get slammed back up with martial speed.

Henry writes as he walks:

> Even Johnny is in awe of the Pilimas' inwardness and pride
> — one of the last stands against England's gentlemanly
> seduction of Ceylon.

Henry does remember the sense of a higher clime in Lester's historic compound. A better breeze, a more loving sun. On that first day he'd barely noticed Lester's domestic, the girl polishing the balustrades. Today she stands on the front porch and the sight of such a crowd seems to sink her chest further. Unmistakable youth keeps her cheeks so full, Henry has to resist the urge to pat reassurance into her.

'*Mehhh — api oyaage deviyo oonae,*' says Lester. Henry understands that much: Look, we *want* your gods. Or we *need* your gods.

Which is it? Want or need? On this Day of Altars the maid leads Lester, Henry and Johnny back through a dark corridor abutting the house. The monk must have stayed outside in front of the porch, no doubt partly to pacify the crowd. What strikes Henry most is Lester's strut, his sheen of well-being, of ownership; clearly the servant girl coddles the man of her house.

Across the boundary wall, Pushpa Pilima steps away from her mute husband's hands and their communication. Back to her usual tricks, she wipes stray hairs from her forehead and, dammit, aims her bright crossed eyes directly at Henry, enough to make him quake a bit.

'Come, Fyre,' snarls Lester, pushing Henry before him. 'You see it isn't mine exactly. But we can take it down.'

'Whose is it?' This is just to buy time. Occasionally he wishes Johnny would interpret English to English.

At her altar the maid hunches, as though wishing she could ebb through a gorge in her chest. Lester strokes the altar's lacy veil and hesitates, grinning at the girl. Is he asking permission for pillage?

Johnny pushes forward. 'May I, Henree?' entreating. 'Today we can't waste too much time,' telling Lester this with an official air. 'Our project's too large.'

Johnny thrusts aside the lacy veil to lift a white ceramic Buddha statue. He hands the Buddha to the maid and she takes it like a torch-bearer.

'Perhaps,' Henry starts, 'we should let her take it down herself?' This is all going too hurriedly. The girl has no idea of what the three men want. Henry wishes she would serve tea or find some other way to stall the moment.

Johnny begins his rapid crazed kind of talking, what Henry wishes he could soothe out of the boy. 'I understand these people, Henree — in a thousand years she would never do it herself — we want your plan to work — sometimes our people are a little backward.' He whispers: 'This girl's *rodi*, from the beggar caste.'

While Johnny's hands are at work, Henry is unsure where to set his gaze. 'If you understood what we are doing, you would be happy,' he tells the maid.

Her lips are trembling — a silent prayer? — while Johnny dismantles, board by precious hand-hewn board, the altar on which she has placed her sacred objects. A small seashell, three contorted red peppers, a dried garland, a birdbone, a bottle top, a miniature pair of scissors and a lightbulb filament.

When Johnny's completely done, she is still squinting but now at Lester. She holds her Buddha aloft. And beats her retreat, a hard one, as though a wind slams her back into the house.

Three orphans have crawled along the house's side wall to see what the pink man is doing with Lester's maid. The boys understand her moment as disgrace and hoot hoarse witticisms at her passing.

From the main door, the beggar-maid guards the departure of her dismantled altar. Her lips move fast and faster as though to summon the altar back to life. Back on the road Henry looks at nothing, nowhere, being not Abraham in Ur nor a Greek desecrating the Maccabees' altar with pig's blood, but not necessarily a man performing an action he will affirm unwaveringly as a placeholder for the greater good.

He strokes the smooth, incense-fragrant planks Johnny piles like a one-man machine into Suba's wheelbarrow. A splinter pierces his thumb and the pain appeases him. When no one's looking — not the helpers, not the monk under the papaya's shade — Henry sucks the finger.

Pushing the wheelbarrow, Johnny guffaws with the orphans. They are fighting over who gets to wear Johnny's new khaki hat and in the melee Johnny appears a leader of midgets. In their leave-taking from Lester's house, Johnny's voice takes on a quite unnecessary stridency. Henry will have to find a suitable moment to mention this to the boy, gentleness always being the best policy.

But he need say nothing. At every house the dismantlement proceeds as evenly as it had at Lester's. People often withdraw at the sight of the crowd. The most cloistered beggars haven't been canvassed about the Day of Altars, the day when the new compost box would be dedicated. Some wave incense before their altars and chant frantically to the god of transitions before Johnny helps them begin the dismantlement and unbinding.

Instead of doing anything himself, Henry stays among the volunteers and tries to rouse good cheer. But all they want is for him to sing the song he sang to Roshan's wife. Caught by their clamor, he finally does reciprocate, with the correct words:

> My country 'tis of thee
> Sweet land of liberty
> Of thee I sing . . .

Not such a bad song, its themes relevant to the supplicants, but they don't understand. They close their eyes so prayerfully as he sings, he worries they really do take it in the wrong context. After he finishes one round, a few women bow to the ground — bowing, he hopes, from gratitude at the vanquishing of the last dregs of non-Buddhist superstition from Rajottama. Today an understanding of the larger picture must be pervading all, among those who, like the little beggar-maid, assist Johnny and comprehend that mud-smeared sticks and stones are not vessels for spirit. These are the pioneers — these understand that their backyard wattle-and-daub or wood altars are undergoing only a symbolic shift: all spirit will remain untouched by any dismantling. As the monk had quoted him a few mornings ago:

> If by renouncing a lesser happiness one may realize a greater
> happiness, let the wise man renounce the lesser, having
> regard for the greater.

Henry had written the Buddha's words in his Village Book and adds today his own commentary on the scene:

How brave. These people will face death with the courage
that comes from truly understanding Buddhism's philosophy,
not its god-worship.

Once he finishes writing, some start an answering chant of their
own, sitting serenely for Johnny and his helpers to be done inside.
They chant in their sacred language and wait: these stalwarts carry
the entire model village on their backs, they are entreating some
kind of good fortune for him, his plan.

But does their praying relay some idolatry? They would seem
more Buddhist if they would sit in a *silent* contemplation.

He has no regrets. None of this, none! mitigates the success of the
Day of Altars: this is a step toward banning British tariffs on Indian
rice. Toward banishing reliance on Brummie fertilizer and English
ploughs. With the model garden in place, the people will slowly free
themselves from dependence. Once again the world will revolve according to their sights and dreams, not to those of the colonizers.

He asks Johnny to lead the last of the helpers across the bridge, up
riverstones and the steep stone-set-in-mud embankment, up to the
house which busies itself keeping away the jungle.

There, the drummer Regi hunkers in his compound's center. He
is oiling his drumhead near the palm-thatch door but drops everything to greet the foreigner's miraculous visitation. 'Sir Henry!'

The drummer's filthy mutt lurks along the periphery before emit-
ting a hyena's wail at these jungle intruders. Lester Pilima blinks at
the low-caste and Henry, unable to hide his grimace.

'Regi-aya,' says Henry. 'Brother. Didn't anyone tell you why
we've come?'

The drummer waits politely. For his dog to relinquish custody
and for Johnny to translate Henry's beginner Sinhalese. He coughs.
'*Naeae ni*, Sir Henry. Not really.'

Something in the drummer's skinny shoulders and ingrown face
inspires Henry.

'You see, Regi-aya,' essaying again. He hates his tongue stumbling
over the language, but likes this locution of *Regi-brother.* 'We're going to need to see your altar.'

Johnny starts forward and explains in his bullet rush of words.

'Good good,' says Regi.

Henry keeps the remaining volunteers — Lester, elderly Suba, the last of the orphans, even Johnny and the monk — from coming along. Alone, Henry follows the low-caste drummer in his pale sarong and thin undershirt, the mongrel dog trailing after. They pick their way behind the house, past the stove, crossing the outhouse toward the stringy trees where the daub altar is set like a crown jewel.

'*Yann'aetule,*' says Regi. The man smiles so much. That effort of jaw and sinew must hurt. *Go inside. See for yourself.*

Henry fights down his liking. He reminds himself that this drummer can slip between two poles. All smiles and eager boy caught in a man's body, Regi can the next moment also appear an oily spinner of some craft. At the end of Henry's first social call, Regi had asked the foreigner to lay hands upon his twenty-five-year-old monster baby. And for money to see real doctors. As though Henry were part of his own father's apostolic succession or, at the very least, the capitalist succession. Capital healer or not, Henry cannot help glancing at the disguised palm-leaf trapdoor. The enigma of that tiny damp room below earth — a murky way of thinking which they're trying now to sort out.

On this second visit, the temple drummer pulls aside a door-length lace curtain. He lets the foreigner stoop into an altar's low closet: here he unveils for Henry his distressing spiritual bounty. Three idols: Lakshman the gilded god of fortune. Skanda the warrior with his many arms and spears, his virtues mainly those of war.

'And don't forget Saraswathie. The special god of our family,' says Regi. 'Beautiful, no? She brings us luck. When we were Brahmins' — Regi speaks with a slow tenderness so Henry can understand — 'we brought the holy sapling from India to the Sacred Tree temple.'

Henry strokes the stringed instrument which Saraswathie holds, not unlike the oud Madame kept in the cosmic twins' New York salon. He laughs, a short bark, remembering how Madame liked to observe a certain ritual during her trances. Her fat lips would press like a trumpeter's upon sharp bursts of air, her nervous eyelids with their short lashes would quiver in that face. And she would break her trance to demand that Henry play the oud. He'd never refused and yet had never mastered the thing. Could Regi's oud be a sign from Madame? — but a chill traces up Henry's neck: he wants to leave all that freakishness behind.

Regi hands a taper to Henry so he can light the incense before the goddess Saraswathie.

'Usually, we don't give this to anyone outside our own family, Sir

Henry,' the drummer says. He is scratching a wooden match on the tile floor. 'Outside our kin. Last year when Manu turned eighteen, I let him begin to light this incense. But you're a very special Sir to us.'

The humor of Regi's mouth is so welcoming it almost makes Henry like the *Sir*.

With the incense lit Henry steps back so Regi can prostrate himself. Why should he stand between this man and his religion? Now Regi beckons to his Sir. With the spotted dog slinking behind, the two return — past outhouse, trapdoor and the outdoor stove where the man's wife crouches amid everlasting nightsticks of smoke.

It is when Henry's back on the road that Regi's son, dressed in temple vestments and a white turban, alights above on the stairs. He casts a gaze, condescending or sympathetic, down on the road group, and Johnny almost trips, jerked by courtesy. '*Manu,*' he says and bites his lip. The inchoate boy smiles back.

Lester cannot stand this exchange, the Pilima with his shoulders rippling that horizontal wave, unable to disguise a great loathing. 'Where's the fellow's altar?' he sniggers. 'Should go back there, no?'

'I think, gentlemen,' says Henry, 'we've probably amassed enough altar material today. Enough to create a fine compost heap.'

'Excuse me, Fyre!' Lester pushes his bulk so close and threatening, a frost could overtake Henry's innards. 'As mudaliyar here, we find it strange you take advice from that loose cannon of yours!'

'Sorry?'

'You're *not* taking Regi's altar, is that it?'

'Maybe we have enough for the first half of the day then,' trailing off, tasting metal — from the incense? 'We can perhaps build the compost box now?' He scrutinizes Johnny, who curls his lip before beginning to translate into a more suave Sinhalese.

Lester's mouth opens as though to tell Henry something of which he thinks better. He opens it again and says only 'Favoritism!'

But as he speaks, his toupee's adhesive, unglued in the day's warmth, irrevocably gives way with an odd suction. The whole matty hairpiece, in a graceful arabesque, spirals to the ground. Lester bends down, pate tacky, only a few hairs marring the surface. Confidence undamaged, he rises, readjusts the thing. Intones, 'Careful, Fyre!'

Lester turns to the last of the volunteers and throws his arms wide. 'You see how things work with our *healer?*' he asks, followed by a stream of mock-plaintive words which Johnny will later translate for Henry. 'First the man pretends to cure just one family among us! Then overlooks this drummer's house! And today I, Lester Pilima, have given up the protection of my own household gods! Given up! for this impostor and his projects!'

All Henry understands in the moment is that Lester is on some kind of trail and had recognized his moment. Suba — who appears incapable of offending anyone — makes like an elf, practically hopping over to the Pilima, trying to nudge him away from his fomenting. 'Let's follow the monk?' asks Suba.

'I, Lester Pilima!' reiterating, his name all of reminder, plea and directive.

'You don't happen to be campaigning for something?' Henry dares to ask. 'Because it sure seems like it.' By now he is used to no one answering him.

As they descend, a pulverized group, Henry promises he will that night, in the privacy of his Village Book, parse his desire to spare Regi his altar.

Let there be no charges of favoritism. Favoritism is a terrible Dutch door, opening the top and excluding the bottom or vice versa. Henry must organize his thinking: no, it cannot be favoritism. Favoritism can occur only in a commodity culture. You don't have to be a Bolshevik to see how Regi offers both everything and nothing. In the universe of Rajottama, this man belongs to the lowest of namable castes. His ash would mix with the wind's like anyone else's, with nothing worse, with nothing better. Regi is just father to a velvet-eyed son who plays the mute until you know him. And father to a monster child who dwells under a palm-leaf trapdoor in a brown warm stink. Also owner of a sullen dog. And member of a family that has served the temple by playing drums for generations. There is more, of course; and also nothing more. Because Henry will make no favorites of anyone. No one, kawurat, mokut naeae.

At four in the afternoon, Johnny tells him no more real work will get done. 'We've done well to muster the early morning hours, Henree.'

He is right. By the afternoon's sixth house — they'd pressed on — most of the original enthusiasts have waltzed off the main path in a vapor of excuses, flagging in their will. After all, the work's demanding. Some complain in a graveside tone at the end of their breath but loud enough for Henry to hear.

True enough, crossed over onto Monkeyheadside, the task begins to require a rude determination. The volunteers must swag dismantled altar pieces across the swinging bridge as though participating in some kind of rifle drill, shedding flak and tracer on a difficult course. Down the canal road they must go again. Then up the hill toward the temple plot where the monk has offered land for the garden and Chollie has overseen its plowing and preparation.

Of course no one would be inexhaustible. Even his thick-lipped warden of truth appears tired: Pandit hovers a little lower than usual. Henry can smell the acridity of the monk's sweat — does Shriver's potted ham taint it? When the sun begins to glaze over around five, Henry's orange-robed sachem fixes himself on a makeshift bench, scanning the garden.

The final volunteers are tossing the last shattered altar bones into the compost heap. But how neatly they've ploughed the plot for the intended snake gourd plants! Henry considers this plot like the mustard seed — a seedlet shooting out such liberal, sprawling branches that far-roving birds lodge permanently under its shadow.

And the expectant poultry pen has a certain charm. Soon there will be feathers and eggs and squawks. For now it awaits the arrival of the Welsummer hens and roosters.

Does Pandit cackle? Can a monk cackle? 'Of course, Colonel, for your compost — you'll have to provide everything.'

'Everything?' relishing his fatigue, 'what do you mean?'

'Indeed, your own worms.'

How can Henry answer this? 'Don't worry,' is what he says. 'It's all planned for. Down to the worms.'

65

TELEGRAPHIC DISPATCH FROM KANDY OFFICE TO 'CHILKINS' BY JONATHAN NELLIE AT 17:14, 29 MARCH 1937:

WE MIGHT BEGIN TO THINK YOU ARE PREOCCUPIED WITH OTHER AFFAIRS. AMERICAN SUBJECT A FORCE TO RECKON WITH. SUCCESSFUL WITH HIS PROJECTS AND CONTINUING

TO RESPOND WELL TO SUPERVISION. CONSIDER THIS A RE-
MINDER RE PROMISED FUNDS FOR ALLOCATION TO SUB-
JECT'S PLAN. AS YOU RECALL THIS IS THE AGREED-UPON
MEANS TO BETTER CONTROL SUBJECT. PLEASE CONSIDER
THIS A PRIORITY REQUEST. REGARDS WHOBODY.

66

MARCH HAD ENDED like a lamb, good signs abound, but Henry rises disgruntled, thinking of Lady B. in the hour when egrets still nest in the mango tree. He's not lonely. Bad dreams are just heaving themselves into him. He resorts to descending the ill-set stone stairs to the cottage. To calling out, 'John! Sorry to wake you! Please do us a favor today and teach our maid how to press handkerchiefs more efficiently?'

Johnny comes to the door rubbing his eyes. 'Can't you show her?'

'It seems she won't take instruction from me. Not anymore.'

Johnny answers with his usual epithet for Nani: 'Silly coastal girl.'

'Not silly. Just — maybe in her village they use their sleeves,' says Henry, turning back up to the study. A few minutes later he will hear Johnny enter the kitchen. At first the boy makes as if talking to the girl in a reasonable enough voice. A promising start. Henry hears the English word *handkerchief*. But she must have whispered something back to provoke the boy. Otherwise why would he raise his voice as he does? Henry hears water slap the ground in the patio. Something tin crashes and rolls around. Now she must be running through the back room and the kitchen in her bare feet. A door slams; the whole house shudders, too sensitive.

'What's going on?' says Henry. But softly. These squabbles between the two of them never cease. He wants to return to his previous night's reading.

Centuries ago the Kandyan kingdom had held a poor Englishman named Knox captive. Half the sleepless night Henry had read Knox's journal, which devotes ample time to the native women:

> And tho I think they be all Whores, yet they abhor the Name
> of Uesous, which is Whore. Neither do they in their anger re-
> proach one another with it, unless they should lay with a Man

303

of an inferior quality to themselves. And the Woman reckons her self as much obliged to the Man for his Company, as he does to her for hers.

In that golden heyday of Buddhism, both man and woman were bound to each other for their sport. Rather than face the new day, Henry would prefer to escape into Knox's world. The man seemed untouched by all he encountered.

'Must've had iron skin,' says Henry aloud with some envy.

Not that the day before had not augured success. It had. Most men would have called it a breakthrough, a day for any month's lion.

In the morning Henry had suffered one of his headaches. Yet afternoon found him recovered: he was happy to have met at the temple both the monk and a surprise guest.

Johnny's friend Chilkins. The rabbity government agent's deputy was paying a courtesy visit at the temple, wearing an elaborately decorated if oversized blue uniform. He nibbled on ham sandwiches with the monk, showing an elaborate protocol for brushing crumbs away from the recess where a chin might ordinarily be situated. Chilkins had arrived only moments ago, according to Pandit, and it was clear to Henry how much the new arrival wanted to be taken as a friendly fellow: Chilkins practically fell over himself rising to greet Henry.

He'd traveled up from Colombo to check up on his acquaintance Jonathan, he said, but mainly to see this famous Rajottama, to tour its famous temple, and of course, of course, to give his very best to H'nry. He told both Henry and the monk he was keen to show he was a man of honor: 'I'm as much someone for H'nry to confide in as anyone else.'

The monk showed no small alarm at this: 'The colonel already has a number of confidants, you could say.' He spoke as if Henry were both absent and absent-minded. As if he needed fatherly instruction. 'The colonel needs to be kept free from distraction.'

Yes, Chilkins went on, he wanted to show he would keep his word not only to Jonathan but also to H'nry. Thus he would confide his own 'personal address' — he kept saying this — to H'nry as well. He supposed the monk would not mind if he 'performed some business right there in the temple.' With a heroic fixing of his pen, Chilkins stated his readiness: he had checks earmarked for the model garden and the store. Another for the school and orphanage. A final check — Pandit made an effort to wink at Henry, since this had perhaps been the monk's suggestion — to help reprint the Buddhist catechism.

'But why would you want to do this?' Henry felt flustered in receiving someone else's generosity, especially someone from the colonial structure which he had come, supposedly, to weaken. He didn't know, moreover, how one should address a deputy.

'H'nry, H'nry — we consider you, in a sense, our own maximum success,' said Chilkins. 'You're volunteer labor, aren't you, a kind of laboratory, one could say. Why shouldn't one help monitor your little experiments here?'

'And support them,' the monk inserted helpfully.

'And support them,' Chilkins echoed.

Pandit had come to his senses, making the intelligent suggestion that the checks be written out to the new entity he had founded, the Sacred Tree Temple Trust. Thus Pandit could help administer the funds and 'leave our Yankee free to dream up his new schemes.'

To Henry's surprise, the weedy deputy had agreed to all this. He'd written an obvious note to himself:

TELL COLWETHER OF AMERICAN PROJECTS:
   AGRICORELIGIOUS
   EDUCATIONAL
   LITERARY

Afterward, the monk and Henry had contemplated the deputy as he made his way down the stairs. At the bottom, in his maladroit way, he'd pulled on his Kent boots made expressly for jungle-walking.

'Goodbye, H'nry. Concerted effort you're making. We'll pray for good weather, shall we? Goodbye, sadd-oo,' Chilkins had called from the road.

'Saddhu,' Pandit had corrected him quietly. 'Not sadd-oo. Saddhu.'

Once Chilkins had vanished around the bend, Pandit revealed his pleasure.

'You've arrived,' he kept saying to Henry. 'Arrived.' He made a gesture Henry considered highly unmonastic: stabbing his finger into his palm. 'In.'

'In?'

The monk gestured for Henry to sit down on the bench. 'Colonel. When you first came to us, you said you wanted Rajottama to be a seed for other villages. We laughed.'

Henry would not deny that.

'When you wanted to banish British imperialism and initiate events like making the Buddha's birthday a universal holiday, we didn't take you seriously.'

'*That* I didn't know.'

'But today we know you're *in*. It's a sign. Something like good merit is behind you. We think you're capable of anything.'

Q. What were the four signs that made the Buddha, when he was a young prince, leave all that men usually love so much and go to the jungle on his way toward his enlightenment?

A. A Deva appeared to him when he was driving in his chariot, on four different occasions, in four different and impressive forms.

Q. What were those forms?

A. Those of a very old man broken down by age; of a sick man; of a decaying corpse; and of a dignified hermit.

Q. Why should these sights, so familiar to everybody, have caused him to go to the jungle?

A. We often see such sights. But astrologers at the Prince's birth had told the King that his son Siddhartha would one day resign his kingdom and become a Buddha.

Not wishing to lose an heir, the King had carefully prevented his son from seeing any sights that might suggest human misery and death. No one was allowed to speak of such things to the Prince. He became a prisoner in his lovely palaces and flower gardens, which were surrounded by high walls. Inside, everything was made as gorgeous as possible, so that the Prince would never wish to go and see the sorrow and distress that are in the world.

67

THIS BRIGHT FIRST of April, Henry stalks out of the compound without a plan. He is unaware that Nani studies his back from the attic window where she's been cleaning.

Without having chosen a path, he heads first to the model garden. In the early heat Chollie's workers are planting what Henry sees as the next indigenous addition to Ceylonese nutrition: the snake gourd crop.

The workers have strong cordoned arms and an unnerving cackle. Their furrows are generous and hold fast. He envies them and had he time enough he too would want to dig deep into the loamy earth and splurt mud on himself, lug buckets of water from the temple's well, gain scars, roughness, girdings of muscle.

But long ago Madame had told him he needed to learn how to delegate. He must fix his sights on the larger goal. The model village will not run without him. Let his delegates work. He must keep his mind clear, his peripheral vision open.

Something about the men's rhythm as they work — more than Chilkins' thin bluish hand signing checks — seeps the renewal of success through his veins. And it is just midmorning.

As he saunters on, the daylight over the Sacred Tree floods him with an uncontainable benevolence. On the sly, a low-caste village-woman is washing clothes from the temple's clean well. '*Master hamuduruwekee hamuwenee?*' she asks him. She quickly hides a General Store soap bar behind her back. 'Did Master meet with the monk?'

Later he will try to think what it was that unbolted his mind. Was it the buttonhook of her smile? or the clothes brazenly stretched across rocks like so many splayed backs? Perhaps it was the satisfaction warming his chest with a sense of purpose. In ways she may not have known, *he had already contributed to this woman.* As much as to anyone in Rajottama. He existed, in a sense, just for her peasant self. Already this faraway place had become his corner.

Whatever the cause, Colonel Henry Fyre Gould, an enlightened man of the world, late of New York, finds himself saying, '*Masterge gedere gihila balanne kamiteede?* Want to go see Master's house?'

Henry has never wanted anyone to use the word *Master*. He'd even asked Nani to quit. Yet he makes an allowance this once: if such a word works as part of a common language, why forbid?

Not that the argot rolls easily into his ear. It does not. *Master* — and the echo lingers but gives him time to examine her. From her trunklike but smooth neck, he thinks she is perhaps no more than sixteen.

She has that amorphous something in her body, that hopeful chaos that has nothing to do with age. Sixteen being the time when he'd been imbibing his share of choral songs, morning prayer and the Episcopal Church's vaunted openness toward other traditions. When he'd been an untouched youth, preparing to follow his father into the ministry.

The difference between Henry at sixteen and this washergirl — under her simple flowered housedress she bears the strong defined flanks of a woman who has known the world. And she has that gaze in her eyes, the one Henry has seen in American women who've lived as fully as any true hosanna.

With care she folds the stretched-out sheets into her laundry basket and hides everything behind a boulder. It's a game of whist between them, her hand a good one apparently from the way she glances at him over her shoulder and lets out a titter: clearly the sound of a pleasured woman. His skin turns sticky as a wineskin, ajuggle inside. Though he tries to walk behind her, or just next to her, this flirtatious girl insists on following Henry along the canal. And today the straight road feels like a maze, tortuous, proleptic, complex and undulating, binding him and his thighs scraping each other.

When they pass Joseph the gatekeeper, Henry looks back, and she is still behind: more and more a collection of globes connected by planes, a continent of hemispheres, more orbicular than ovoid, more flesh than matter, she is already melting in his hands, though there's been no touching yet.

In his bedroom her fingers are hungry as well but they roam the room's possessions. She strokes the gilded hurricane lamp, the fringed pillow, Henry's fountain pen. In the sugarloaf light let in by the drapes, her eyes are knowing — and this is what he will return to later — *her eyes were knowing*, an insuperable fact — she is butter, begging for something.

As it happens, she seems to think he has a gift to offer.

He locks the door and things change. Her eyes flit about like those of an unruly horse caught in a ditch, her Sinhalese grown frantic. She worms and wheezes the syllables: *'Mama nikang dobie kenek, mate karedere keranna epaa.'* He understands her: I am just a washerwoman, please don't bother me.

As though her profession or caste had anything to do with the penumbra she cast in him with her flirt's laugh. Henry knows certain things from his reading: a flirt's laugh is universal. He is about to let the girl leave, though he finds that he is lying on her, or she had placed herself under him, an alley cat, spitting back, fractious as hell, and he realizes with her arms punching him away that there must have been some serious misunderstanding.

He rises but for the second time in his life he has no time to prove anything. Nani enters through the smaller library door — his mistake, yes, having forgotten to lock it — yet she comes in without knocking! Bringing in his laundry, as though she wants to undo him!

His hand: it flies through the space between and smacks Nani's cheek.

Hard.

Much harder than his own shame.

But Nani's hand moves just as fast as his and already smacks back his soft cheek. And all his banians and clean shirts are dropped to the ground. Stunned by the blossoms of folded and steam-pressed clothes spread at his feet, at the fact of the honeyed village girl making a quick exit behind him, he stands a stupid figurehead as Nani's skirt swishes out of the room.

Have I gone crazy? he asks himself. *Should I have become a monk? Maybe a Benedictine rather than a pioneer in Ceylon.*

He licks lips slightly bruised from the day's events; considers; seats himself on his bed; pulls out his Village Book and special pen; lets this pen target paper. Colonel Henry Fyre Gould writes:

April 1

Jakfruit in ripened maturity said to taste like caramel. Large prickly fruit.

Monsoon suspended. We're all thankful here. Yesterday, monk receptive to plan & helpful with deputy government agent.

He peers down at what he has written and rubs his cheek. *Nani would never have glanced up from her washing.* He draws her tall silhouette. *She* would never have said with such brazen invitation: Master go see monk?

He slices that succulent silhouette into finely grained cross-hatchings. His own maid is acquainted with him — she knows too much. She could stare him down with spooky eyes and understand everything.

Her slap still stings. Little silver scraps escape the corner of his vision.

68

HENRY WRITES his dream:

> Toward shore a woman rises out of the ocean. At first she is
> dazzling, her hair like snakes, cloth tight against her skin.
> After days at sea, the sailors love her. But she starts to laugh
> at their love & her laughter quakes the waves, the boat &
> the isle until the sailors are thrown headlong, leagues away.
> She goes on laughing until her laughter veritably drowns
> the island —

69

TELEGRAPHIC DISPATCH FROM KANDY OFFICE TO 'CHILKINS' AND BLIND-COPIED AT SENDER'S REQUEST TO 'HEADQUARTERS' BY JONATHAN NELLIE AT 17:19, 4 APRIL 1937:

NEW TACTIC ADVISED AFTER FIRST MEETING OF CHILKINS AND SUBJECT. SUBJECT APPEARS TEMPERAMENTAL PERHAPS DISPIRITED AT TIMES. IT IS OUR BELIEF THAT SUBJECT IS IMPORTANT BULWARK AGAINST THE SUBVERSIVE NATIONALIST ORGANIZING BEING UNDERTAKEN IN VILLAGE BY ONE

LESTER PILIMA WHO HAS BEEN COLLECTING TAXES AS UNOF-
FICIAL MUDALIYAR AND IS CAMPAIGNING SOON TO RUN FOR
A POSITION IN COLONIAL GOVERNMENT. IT IS THEREFORE
IMPERATIVE FOR HEADQUARTERS TO KEEP SUBJECT IN-
VESTED IN PROJECTS. CONSEQUENTLY A MORE PUBLIC DIS-
PLAY OF SUPPORT FROM COLONIAL ADMINISTRATION
WOULD HELP SUSTAIN OUR UNDERSTANDING OF SITUATION
HERE. CERTAINLY INITIAL CHEQUES WILL BE PUT TO GOOD
USE. BUT THERE IS PROBABLE PROFIT TO COLONIAL STRUC-
TURE ITSELF WERE IT TO COLLABORATE OPENLY WITH SUB-
JECT'S EXPERIMENTAL PROJECTS. BEING EXPLICIT WORKS
BEST WITH SUBJECT. CHILKINS SHOULD ARRANGE TO MEET
WHOBODY AT QUEEN'S HOTEL NOON 8 APRIL FOR EXACT DE-
TAILING OF HOW FURTHER SUPPORT SHOULD BE OFFERED
ALONG WITH AN ENUMERATION OF POTENTIALLY SIZABLE
PROFIT TO THE CROWN COLONY IN A DOUBTLESSLY SIG-
NIFICANT EPOCH. REGARDS WHOBODY.

70

APRIL 6 BURSTS a brindled morning light through the leaves onto
Johnny's polished floor. Every kind of red results, a monochrome Joseph's coat. Henry would like to chart the floor's patterns. Could
there be a universal and finite design for April 6 across the world, a
template for how light falls on all floors?

Because sometimes no one comes to the daily Receiving Hours,
during which he will talk to villagers in Johnny's cottage, Henry
brings with him the *Notations on Amatory Matters* and a book he had
rescued from a rubbish heap in Kandy town, a contemporaneous
history book written by a self-styled Burgher and university man:

> By 1915, a European war had changed the world beyond what
> Ceylon's various realms could have envisioned. Later histori-
> ans would say the war had been fought in the name of small
> nations and their privilege of sovereignty. Of course, such vic-
> tories would affect Anglo-Indian relations, and in the tailspin,
> Ceylon would also find itself questioning that which it had
> long held to be a necessary tenet of existence. While for years

Ceylon had enjoyed an unbroken serenity — disregarding the excitement of 1848 and 1915, as exemplified by the history of one notable Ceylonese family, the Pilimas — a less complacent epoch now heralded its arrival.

Yesterday during Receiving Hours there had been a lot of warm-blooded ballyhoo — mostly from the Pilimas about the annual pilgrimage. According to Lester Pilima, this year Rajottama needs to travel through the jungle.

This matters but Henry is also thinking of Nani — for the last few days, since the rendezvous with the washergirl, he's skirted away from her eyes. Jeremiah at the height of his prophecy wouldn't have had more scorching eyes. But she kept the household running. Lunch with two curries, a ghost's meal on the table. No foot rub, but didn't he find a sprig of lavender atop some folded bed linens? He did; she had placed it there; despite her stare wasn't she trying to tell him not to worry? He'd be forgiven. Good humor would return. She would bring him tea on that elaborate tray again.

Meanwhile, Johnny is explaining the pilgrimage — the villagers must propitiate some guardian god at the god's *main* temple. And must also feed the forest's hermit monks. Henry doesn't understand. Why would hermit monks let some village or another descend on them just to serve rice? It will entail for Rajottama a journey of an entire day each way. It means sleeping in the jungle, in what Henry imagines as a crowd of villagers collected from many localities, each clinging to spindly trees above tired overcargoed horses and plaits of rattling, seething snakes.

'I'm telling you, Johnny,' looking up from his book, 'none of this pilgrimage hullabaloo makes much sense to me. No one's been listening to my lectures.'

His boy's kneeling, busy scumbling a corner of the floor with a sham paintbrush, a stick tied to one of Henry's old shirts. *These people have some inborn necessity to make any red into a hot ruby*, Henry does not write but wants to. 'You know what I'm saying. We've made so much progress toward our —'

'Village of the future,' the boy finishes, intent on his polish.

'Exactly. So why join other villages? Why feed monks in some distant thicket? Doesn't charity begin at home —'

Johnny glances up from his work and flashes scarlet palms. 'Then you might've stayed in America. Shouldn't take this all so personally.'

'But don't they understand what we're talking about here? The philosophy? the catechism? our obstacles?'

Johnny surveys the floor and returns to a missed corner. 'At this point you can't give one convincing reason for the village *not* to go.' In March, Johnny had appeared to grow into his job. Only when he's pressured will he speak in that former, manic rush of words. 'Nothing would keep the peasants from this. Not your philosophy. Not even their own fear of boys organizing the villages against the British. Or —'

Henry has heard nothing of this and it is not unreasonable that he should ask about the boys organizing; whether what Johnny meant to refer to, perhaps, were the Kandy leftists, the mob demonstration in the square with the bobbies on horses and the long sticks and songs of the university boys —

The boy dismisses him. 'There are *those* demonstrations. Then there are other demonstrations that are better organized.' He actually makes a shooing gesture at Henry. 'But really. Things are starting to work well for us here. I have things in control. There's nothing for you to worry about.'

'Why haven't we talked about this more?' Henry gets up to stand over where the boy works. 'Am I missing something? Where are these better demonstrations happening? What is being organized?'

Johnny sighs. 'It's nothing, Henree. It's not worth rocking the boat.' But the man still stands over him. 'We have it good, Henree,' hesitating before the old flood of words surges out, directed floorward: 'Of course. Ceylon's troubles don't compare to India's — we have fewer people disappearing. We don't have the same detention cells.'

'Detention cells?' Henry's pacing the room. 'What are you not telling me? Are you trying to protect me from something?' — and this finally makes the boy look up — 'why didn't we talk about this before?'

'Henree,' laying down his brush. 'Sometimes you worry too much. You're not here to solve every problem. Just look at what you and I are trying to do. That's what matters. Ceylon is peaceful. We don't have young bodies clogging the rivers.'

Outside the sharpener passes on the canal road, calling out his long nasal advertisement. *Today, today. Sharpen knives today.* The sharpener's wheel plays a snatch of anthem before continuing on: *O queen of the hills, the spice has ripened overnight, where are your reapers?*

Henry chews his broad gray-pink thumb, swollen and numb at its base from his syndrome. He is trying hard to listen to the boy's words, not to that painful tone of dismissal. 'You think I'm a child,' he says finally. 'There's something you're keeping from me.'

He buries himself in reading the *Notations:*

> England, 1587 — A cavalry officer who has performed gallantly in the Netherlands, having served under the Earl of Leicester, becomes a favorite of Elizabeth I. As part of the officer's clandestine courtship of the Queen, in the proper season, he makes it a habit to hand to Her Majesty's chambermaid not just black truffles but the related pig snouts, dried and wrapped in a lady's new lace undergarments.

Outside the boy's door, a flurry of feathers falls through the trees and a tuft of fur skids in. No, it is a mongrel dog that rushes around the two men, sniffing the newly polished corners, leading his owner, Regi, in a storm of panting. And on the threshold balancing is the dwarf Chollie, standing as if the entrance itself were a tightrope.

For this Receiving Hour, Chollie has brought along a few more friends than usual, three toddy-tappers, shadows over him, men who scream strength, capable of scrambling up palm trees. Henry hasn't forgotten. On land Chollie's minions seem as aware of danger as they do when carrying syrup buckets on ropes through the trees. They flicker enterprise and ill will, shoving in to flank their leader and occupy the small dry island left on the floor.

What follows is not anything he has asked for. Regi stays rapt on stammering *Sir Henry*, while the dwarf Chollie undams a speech from which Henry finds it hard to pull a single phrase. And the man does this when he is perfectly capable of speaking English.

'Help me, Johnny?' Henry snaps a glance at his aide.

During last week's Receiving Hours, Johnny explains, according to the toddy-tapper, Henry wrote an advance of chits for the drummer. Yet the drummer is malingering, saying so-called religious tasks have kept him from fulfilling his community service. He didn't work his weekly hour at the compost pile — nor had he attended the lecture.

'I'm sorry you missed the meeting, Regi,' Henry inserts. 'Ancient Religious Customs. You would've liked it. We talked about drummers —'

The drummer stares at his benefactor with the visage of a drowning man. Johnny translates more: the chits Henry'd lent the drum-

Manu emerged from the shrine, a crested proposal, leaned against the temple walls with nothing better to do than hum a faux-jolly untruth of a thing, inspecting the monk's imperfect concealments.

'Come, Colonel, we'll discuss your current plans?' There was also a point about grammar we wanted to bring up. Your need to study. When we heard you speak at the Hygiene lecture the other day —'

They entered the monk's book-lined study, books blood red, where Henry took the offer of a single wicker chair. A guest invited into the religion's heart. With a gutsink of certainty, Henry knew even then that there would be no mention of the gods. What had Pandit said long ago? 'We have no magic talismans.'

He that leadeth into captivity shall go into captivity. His monk was staring down on Henry, an attitude which Henry will later remember and in certain forfeited moods, find laughable. Pandit began: 'There are elements you do not yet understand about the conditional. There might be, you see, there could be . . .'

72

THE MAIL CARRIER for Rajottama is a sound family man whose eyes are made of private unreachable contracts. Three times a week he hikes four miles over the treacherous hill path which at its most singular point snakes vertical on greasy stones; and another twelve on the main road in order to connect remote villages with Kandy town.

He returns the same day as he sets forth, loaded with the weight of communication.

Henry has once hazarded this very mountain pass and found his heart boiling in his throat, he was that scared about how in descent the cliffs opened below his feet. He would never repeat that trail, even with his love for devouring as much of Ceylon's variegated landscape as he can by foot.

It turns out the previous mail carrier had died, at seventy, on the same bluff. The current postman confided once to Henry and Johnny that he might not have taken the job, when first suggested to him by one of Colwether's appointees, had the previous postman died from the path itself. 'If from his heart or drinking, that's fine though,' he'd said, face mobile atop a neck skinny as an insect's.

'What's the best part of the job?' Henry had asked, genuinely curious.

'Going and coming. The calm and the challenge.'

'The worst part?'

'Fighting the weather. There's no refuge from that trail, mahattea.'

Johnny had said that being a postman was just as bad as being a fisherman. '*You* ever fished?' Henry asked his boy.

'Sometimes,' Johnny clearly lying; and to cover it over, Henry said his Johnny did tend to show a fisherman's necessarily patient method.

As for the postman, his method requires no punctuality. Sometimes he will arrive not just late but empty-handed, satchel thin and ineffectual as a dull razor, carrying only one or two letters for the Rajottamans. Whether this happens because the postman is forgetful or clumsy, who can tell from those eyes? Of course, this is no way for a family man with a schoolteacher wife and three children to behave. No way to ensure his pension or even a continued civil service job, but Henry is reporting no one's inefficiency to the colonial structure.

And then the man — MySinhalaNameIsTooDifficult Kenneth — is gentle as summer music. He will stop by even if he doesn't have anything to deliver. 'I like the walk and the chats with people.' Henry can understand — rather, he can imagine exchanging his own job for Kenneth's more amiable endeavor.

And every day Henry blisters for mail from Madame. Just one white envelope would still the desire. The woman had willed herself into this obstinate vow of silence, a tundra unto herself, content in the illusion of her enormity. If she would just *come*. He is past the point of thinking he needs no one here.

He needs *her*: a woman with a big mind, an ensign from afar, capable of reconciling the contradictions that stay the hardest for him. Certain inarticulables have started to stick in the craw. He needs to rub ideas against hers, rocks in a tumbler, make his own smooth.

What he really wants, finally, is to convert *her*, have her see the error of her ways. She should know preaching only to a Western audience makes ideas no better than pralines. He wants her to concede, finally, a simple premise, drawn from a world not larger than the sandbox: his idea (coming to Ceylon) had been better than *hers* (finding her Ceylon within).

Only the poetic insurance agent, his rhapsodic acquaintance from the New York salon, remains faithful in writing letters. 'Could your Ceylon be wholly thesis?' the agent scrawls from his Stamford desk. 'And please, if you find a moment, tell us something about the mammoth turtles, those frequenting the southwestern shore.'

When Henry cannot know one of the agent's requests, he invents. 'At the point of midnight, fifty percent of the adult turtles roar like lions,' he writes, 'and are said to roar all the more if someone's expressive art should prove false. For good luck the people garland the creatures with necklaces made from baby turtle skulls.'

But too many of the agent's requests flock, one after another. In a fit of pique one day, Henry drafts back, curtly, that what the man says is true enough. Ceylon is wholly thesis and sketchbook, exactly what the inspired man makes of it. The agent can go figure out the rest in iambic pentameter.

This will be his last communication to anyone, he decides, except for Madame. He cannot bog down his mind with stateside contradictions, such as how one man can be both poet and insurance agent, and never leave Connecticut and yet fantasize constantly about these eccentric lands? All that is untruth and impediment. Henry's task is to take the wings of morning. To be *in* the clear moment of Ceylon.

And Henry will also give up corresponding with a lecherous friend of his, Goodson, whose inquiries about Ceylonese women finally made Henry issue a gag order. In a final letter to the *Mayflower* descendant, Henry's drunk with the fun of renunciation:

> Gg, you damn Balaam, remember the story of the dumb ass.
> Why not for once & for all send away for a catalogue of mail-order Hawaii brides? Yrs, peaceably, H. F. Gould

The only counsel Henry wants is *hers*.

Undaunted by her silence, it being his main witness, he fires missives, recounting stories of Wooves' home, the splurge of garden growth, a vista so fresh it would drain the very blood from her eyes; no other view could ever be like morning mist rising off the Kamaraga canal. He dangles before her the prospect of meditating with a Theravada monk in a transcendent Ceylon, an isle more than wholly thesis.

'Come, friend,' he writes, implores, 'let us heal our breach — at least come argue with me.' He adds: *Tell me what you want, it can be your Taj, your playground.* But their falling-out has been too extreme. She stays stubborn. Or the postman trips in his path and only her letters fly off, kite-wings into the jungle.

The postman and his radiantly false teeth; his bike; that blissful torture of the moment, suspended, when he rummages in the satchel and not a moment too soon takes out something close to — but not exactly — the thing Henry needs.

For example, one day Henry receives a letter from his son:

> Dear Father, I am glad you went saling on a hug boat. Did you row or was it a gondla? One day I will too. I am trying to deside a name for the dog grandpa brought me maybe Shadow. In Sant Louis there are not many pepole like New York and not relly friends. But food is beter than Mothers. School is easyer also. I am alone or with our mutt mostly. Please send a stamp from Ceylon for my colectin. Love your everloving Son Daniel.

Henry has been forgiven, a bit. And yet nothing big has been accomplished so far. Hence nothing is sufficient to write back to the legatee of his loins. Henry has to be gone for a little while longer, risk appearing wild, but one day won't he return? Then he can resume being a father and not a miscreant. Reading the letter temporarily impairs his vision. For now he won't revisit the site of likely remorse. Licking a stamp to his son would send paralyzing guilt through all nerve endings. Can such regret ever be allayed?

Six weeks ago, something better than the usual gifts had come from the satchel; something finally worthy of sending back to Madame or even his son with his dog comforts and lonely voice:

> Hotel Central
> Madras
> March 1, 1937

Dear Mr Henry Fyre Gould,

Recently set free from my duties in New York, I am currently working as a freelance journalist in Madras. Having heard distant reports of your success, I was delighted when I heard directly from one Miss Rose Burns of the Red Cross. Miss Burns had heard news of your successes and told me I should come to report on your village.

Sad to say, other engagements, not to mention small visa quandaries, prevent me from coming to behold your grounds, much as I would like to. Miss Burns had only the kindest words about your efforts.

What follows might strike you as a trifle unconventional.

I thought perhaps you could write a detailed description of your projects. I would be able to incorporate such themes into a larger article. As yours is most assuredly a worthy cause, I am sure the publicity entailed by such an article could only help your purposes. Of course you may indicate those items which you would wish to be off the record.

If you consent to this unusual exercise, please be sure to give me a sense of at least the physical lay-out of the place. You can be in loco journalistico. Please, too, let me know to whom else I might address such a query, in order to garner further background detail.

With only the best wishes,
K. M. Samankumar
Journalist

Henry had drafted a letter in response that very day:

March 5, 1937

Dear K.M.,

It is a wonderful thing indeed to encounter such an insightful voice from somewhere out ~~in the jungle~~ there. I must thank you for your interest in our humble efforts. We are foreseeing boundless change in the months ahead; my task is to submit to you a verbal picture of our affairs and goals, both as they are and as they will become, so it is all more than just ~~air~~ empty plans.

As you may know, we arrived in Rajottama some 7 months ago, ~~ignorant~~ open to its information, only to meet head-on a pre-monsoonal village which, while boasting natural abundance, rich in palm products and rice paddy, found itself in a sorry state of affairs.

~~Suspecting~~ Two salient features distinguish Rajottama: the Kamaraga canal, erected by ancients more worthy of geometric cerebration than we are; and a temple, which helps orient the people's philosophy. Many of the people possess a prominent frontal lobe, indicating an aptitude for things visual and theoretical, I believe; coincidentally, most people are front-agers, residing along the canal. It is this canal and its relation to the marketplace, temple, and dwellings, which might help provide an orienting idea or, dare I say, a frontispiece for your article.

We here in Rajottama are focusing on six primary projects, all essentially situated on what is known as the Elephant side of the canal, after the large mountain with its caudal indentations at the base of which lies our humble village. To wit:

1) The General Store
2) The Model Garden
3) The School/Orphanage
4) The Culture Conservatory, Focusing on Native Dance, Drums, and Apparel
5) The Self-Improvement Lectures
6) The Renewal of World Buddhism in Our Time

We however are not composed of elephant material. As you can imagine from this formidable hexagon, mortality's constraints have meant that we have had to delegate much of the ~~revival~~ stewardship of certain projects over to qualified candidates who keep us apprised of ~~status~~ progress. Thus it is that I cannot detail to you, for example, the name of the ^cheerful^ cook and baker with the perennial flour soiling her face and hands who whispers to me fairly happily each time I visit the orphanage: I just know that she has been hired by one Mrs. Pushpa Pilima, and that this cook keeps the small boys and girls nourished enough that they can exercise their minds alongside schoolmates blessed with intact families.

The accounting point man lets me know, occasionally, whether an order comes from this satisfied cook to the General Store for more rice, spices, vegetables, or protein source.

All this is the most succinct summary of the nominal limitations imposed by our own humility and capacity — perhaps by this date, these two qualities are no longer distinguishable for me, but such conjectures have no room in our current discussion.

On this issue of protein, I happen to take an especial interest. When I arrived, I was struck by the leanness of the women, ~~whose physiognomies more closely resemble~~ and am currently excited by the sense that we will soon be able to reinvigorate this people long stymied by the colonial perception of them as tranquil, or, in the term of worst opprobrium, lazy.

We are implementing a subscriber service for vegetables from our garden (such as the rich snake gourd, pumpkin, etc.) and will soon institute a regular source of protein supplementation so that the village will comprise itself of muscle and sinew, rather than the distended bellies and gauntness of mal-nutrition arising from a barely tamed jungle, one which habit-ually visits scourges of malaria on its denizens at the periphery etc etc.

What we have found, in relation to this idea of hard work, is that our people in Rajottama have proven not to be lazy, not in the slightest whit. Take, for example, the case of the cultural conservatory. On a recent Monday, it was my good fortune to stroll ~~not without, admittedly,~~ on the swinging bridge that crosses the Kamaraga canal, on one of our typically balmy, cordial days, and walk through the rustic picturesque of what is colloquially known as Monkeyside, owing to the pocked mountain of the same name.

Once I arrived at the lemon-colored conservatory, I found the two sisters who are ancestral inheritors of the revered Kandyan dance tradition busy rehearsing for an exhibition of dance (date to be announced), at which your Red Cross lady may be in attendance if all goes according to plan. What I found was that the rhythm of the cousins playing the drums was ~~discorda~~ slightly off, but I was soon able to rectify the sit-uation by clapping and having the children, the dancers, and the drummers clap along in happy concord with me.

Once everyone was back on a regular 4/4 meter, clap-ping together, the dancers and students then showed them-selves relatively able to follow my choral and choreographic suggestions. I wanted the group to start off singing in a tab-leau resembling a Western Pietà, but then quickly to disband into the singular vertical plane of Indian painting, as a means of suggesting the shrugging-off of the malign colonial influ-ences that almost vanquished this people's pride in their culture.

While Ceylonese culture lacks a rich painting tradition, the people are, as I've noted, possessed of prominent frontal lobes, and hence are able to assimilate, and be stimulated by, suggestions which occur in a visual plane. We soon had dancers barreling one atop another, in what might have re-sembled the pyramid of American college's football ritual, had the dancers not been so lithe of limb and graceful in com-portment. All the while the drummers kept up their rhythmic one-two-three-four, as I had suggested, and soon we had all contributed to a product I found most ~~amena~~ aesthetically pleasing, and which will no doubt impress our international visitors. As you can well see, all I did was provide the frame, and the people's native ingenuity showed itself ready for all impetus.

I will write more anon. For now, accept this first missive as a prospectus for what remains to be accomplished, and all that is being accomplished, even as you read this. Perhaps this will help you in your first round of researching toward your article. You may also wish to contact John Nelligoda, my assistant, at the same address; at this point, he may be a far more articulate exponent of our plans than even I am. Further, you may wish to consider corresponding with ~~Pushpa Pilima~~ our monk, Pandit Ehelapola Thero, who can be reached c/o the Sacred Tree Temple, Rajottama. I will, however, attempt to continue this missive as soon as my other duties release me again.

> friendly
> Your servant,
> Henry Fyre Gould
> Rajottama

Henry enjoyed this writing to Samankumar, going on to send several letters to the reporter. He found that organizing a version of his time in Rajottama had been honeysuckle for his spirit, making him feel like some original lucky man.

The day after the monk's disappointing show of pagan devotions, the postman brings a few letters. One is a clipping of the final article: the first international reportage on Henry's efforts. And only Johnny is there to share Henry's pride:

THE INTERNATIONAL HERALD TRIBUNE IS PLEASED
TO PRESENT THE FIRST IN A SERIES
BY K. M. SAMANKUMAR.

OVERTHROWING THE RAJ:
ONE REFORMER'S SPLENDID SUCCESS IN A SEED VILLAGE

One does not know at first that one steps onto consecrated grounds when walking the shaded paths amid the plot of Henry Fyre Gould's model garden, located in Ceylon's high country, his model village of Rajottama.

What one quickly realizes, as Mr Gould will delight in telling even the most casual visitor, is how this humble agricultural plot is the smelting grounds for a grand plan which, like an imposing cannon, comes from but also points toward the very pillars of the colonial structure.

As one treads the paths and notes the young snake gourd vines, the pendulous tomatoes, the pumpkins, and the decidedly nontropical cucumbers which Mr Gould and his fellow Ceylonese volunteers

'Volunteers?' Johnny gulps. 'The fellow's a dreamer all right! Cucumbers? for our natives' tea sandwiches?'

'A detail, Johnny —'

have been able to wrest from an iron-rich soil more accustomed to growing rice, plantains, palms, and the ubiquitous coconut, is that all has been done according to a plan as precise as his furrows are geometrical.

'I just wrote him what our *plans* are, John, that's all' — a bit hurt; the boy needn't carry on so. 'In a few months, we'll have cucumbers. I just told him the basics. It's not *that* big an exaggeration, is it?'

'Ah,' the boy seeming to understand he can't rib Henry too much.

Modest though he may be, Mr Gould, born in the United States but an honorary Ceylonese by devotion after seven months in his adopted country, has proceeded according to a pentagonal plan to help give the colonized peoples of Ceylon a chance for self-determination.

Health, Hygiene, Morality, Cultural Tradition, and Education form his current areas of interest. In respect to the penultimate, he has converted a run-down orphanage into a regional all-caste school with links to a dance and drum conservatory across the canal. This school has produced a cultural troupe which will eventually tour the island.

While in many remote Ceylonese villages, the local temple stores the deeds to ancestral lands surrounding the temple, Gould has tried, with what he calls a vegetable subscriber service, to free the Rajottama villagers' dependence on land dispensations from a temple's chief monk, a system somewhat analogous to the Catholic Church's erstwhile practice of indulgences. Gould's main objective remains this: to liberate the Rajottamans from the government's price-fixing of rice, as well as of vegetables imported from India, a practice which has sent some families into a never-ending spiral of debt to the local Government Agent.

The day that a reporter visited Rajottama was also the day

on which Mr Gould had distributed a Buddhist catechism, the product of many months' work under the tutelage of the dedicated local monk. This is a guide meant to simplify and standardize the knowledge necessary for young children to find pride in their tradition. In marketplace and on terrace, the proud people of Rajottama were busy poring through a copy of the small catechism pamphlet, which had been distributed for free by Mr Gould's able aide Mr Jehan Nelligoda.

Most were busy trying to out-memorize the others, all in a spirit of good fun, as Gould put it. Next month would bring a contest, initiated by Gould, meant to assess these devoted memorizers.

Gould himself was to be found rehearsing the drum and dance troupe which he has organized. One has to cross a perilous narrow rope bridge strung over the main canal near the Sacred Tree Temple and walk several miles up past paddies being reconstructed by hard-working families bought out years before by a blighted coffee plantation plan on the part of the British. Only now do these humble laborers hear the cry of their motherland and are able to restore its manna, the ubiquitous rice.

From across the paddies, one begins to hear the call of the drums. It is a sound pleasant enough, hollow in the bass, full in the treble, capable of calling the most recalcitrant to come join the dance. Inside the echoing yellow dance hall, Mr Gould presides, clapping his hands to choreograph short dances which celebrate themes such as historical and agricultural renewal for a future showcase involving a visit by the local Red Cross.

'You know they canceled,' says the boy — gunning for Henry? 'The Red Cross told us we'd have to bring our people down to Colombo. They can't send anyone up here.'

'Thank you,' waving for the reading to continue.

The choreographers, two sisters who are talented servitors of their family's centuries-old tradition, named only Sonali and Kumari, parade proudly in the saris which Mr Gould has convinced the village evince a necessary national pride. Kumari and Sonali speak with approval of the changes which Mr Gould has effected in their village.

'Before Mr Gould came,' Kumari explained, 'there was no pride or interest in the traditional arts. He has asked us to make what we do standard and accessible. Now it is not just drummers' families who send their children to study with us, but even the farmers' children come.'

In colonial Ceylon where the scarring divisions of caste run as deeply as they do in India, if more of a hidden discussion, farmers remain the highest caste, drummers close to the lowest. There are, however, farmers and farmers: those who are the highest, such as the local Pilima family, often distinguish themselves through charity. These Pilimas have shown characteristic generosity in donating portions of their land to not only the original orphanage-converted-into-a-school which Pushpa Pilima so ably supervises, but also, since the advent of Mr Gould, to the dance and drum conservatory.

As Sonali said, 'We had no goods. We were on the bottom of the pile. At the top were the Pilimas. But when Mr Gould came and transformed the General Store into a place of fine goods, we were able to furnish our homes with the items appropriate to our people's pride. We could have almost as much as the Pilimas now.'

'I hope, Henree, no one thinks he's having a spot of fun — all that exaggeration.'

'Why? because he makes the people sound like bourgeois — ?'

'We don't want to burn bridges, Henree —'

'But isn't it nice to get a *little* attention?'

One watches Mr Gould working with his fellow garden volunteers in turning over the compost pile erected from formerly pagan altars, overseeing the bounteous General Store, or clapping with the drummers to sound a beat more ancient than one's marrow.

One sees a woman from a noble dynasty leading a classroom in a converted orphanage of literate, well-motivated children from ages five to seventeen, and witnesses the well-run household managed by Gould's intrepid aides Jehan Nelligoda and Nani Bandu.

From this evidence alone, one understands that, for one reformer at least, it is possible to begin small and wreak change within a colonial system that surely suffers its last gasps.

It's clear when the boy hates to admit something. Then he shifts; a little smile drags across his face. 'Yes,' drawled, as though accepting the compliment. 'It's brilliant. Don't stare at me like some blushing bride. It is, Henree,' regaining himself. 'How do you do it?'

'A good relation to the writer. Wrote him a few letters, see, gave him words to use . . .'

> Reform, not revolution, emerges as the key concept here.
> To paraphrase the Buddha, though some may think that at the cessation of the Master's word, no more Master exists, in fact the truest of Masters is to be found within a people's pride in their tradition, so ably mirrored in this case by one Henry Fyre Gould.
> Such developments surely herald the surfacing of a people kept too long in the dark. In a time of a war-shaken globe, such burgeoning advancement merits the world's attention, deserving its utmost commendation. For details on how one can contribute to Rajottama, this model village of the future, write to Henry Fyre Gould, c/o the Postmaster General, Kandy Station, Ceylon.

'So we'll get *public* money from this?' asks his boy. 'Incredible.'
'It already came. I didn't know why. A few anonymous bills here and there from different addresses. And in different currencies.'

The maid pads by the man and his aide studying papers in what she has claimed as her inner patio. She unclips the laundry line and proceeds to the kitchen where she begins to bang pots and pans. Is she noisier than usual? Henry shows Johnny the second letter he received:

April 6, 1937

Dear Colonel Henry Fyre,
> On behalf of the Crown Colony Administration for colonial Ceylon, I write to congratulate you on your recent successes. You have attracted international attention and support, controversial but positive nonetheless, for not only the evolution of your worthwhile project here in Ceylon, but for our policies of enlightened reform. As you know, we have always intended to have you as our partner, not our adversary.
> We understand you have only been here for under a year. Yet just today we have seen the recent articles, a veritable watermark of how much you have accomplished for the island's profile. You must be aware that such success exacts a tariff even as it rewards you. The world's eyes are watching you.
> For our part, we are proud that we have been able to contribute in some way, however small, to your progress. We remain with you every step of your endeavor, and appreciate be-

ing kept informed. Your school, your dance troupe and the agricultural reforms you have undertaken are all worthy endeavors. I have made mention of you to Ceylon's Overseeing Government Agent (formerly Governor in Madras) so that he can be aware of your activities.

Hearing of your fine stewardship, we have also allotted a partial sum from our additional annual discretionary fund, freed so long as we remain out of the sticky business of war. You should understand that its use is unrestricted within your village. (Or for the much-anticipated tour of your troupe, for example!) Should time and funding allow, we or our Deputy Agent may also visit on a regular basis.

Given your commendable success in Rajottama, we have also discussed the occasion for hiring you as a special breed of consultant. It is possible we may be interested in creating more of what we understand you call seed villages in other parts of the island, and in this way working together to further everyone's interests.

The plans of a man like you could perhaps benefit some of our more unruly townships. I am only sorry that we have not been formally introduced. Please know that through so many I am aware of your contributions.

> With every wish for success, I remain,
> Yours truly,
> Mr H.A.J. Colwether
> Government Agent for the Uva Province
> In the Honorable Employ of H.R.H. the King

'Henree!' the boy slaps the paper with that fervor of his, making the maid gawk crossly at both of them. 'Isn't it perfect? You do a little thing and the world responds. See what a clear path we have in front of us? When you feel nothing moves fast enough, you have to remember this kind of thing. Now — can't you see it? — nothing can hold us back.'

As always, his aide has a sharp mind. Henry had read only flattery, albeit of a reciprocal nature. The Crown Colony was noticing being noticed. He had just a slight misgiving: 'You don't think it's bad if the model village becomes part of the British administration?'

The boy's face, strangely, falls. 'I thought you should be happy at this! You have to see that things can be of service to you even when they don't march under their proper names.'

'No,' says Henry vaguely, 'of course, they're just names, you're right.' The problem affecting his concentration is the fust of chilies frying in coconut oil. The way she cooks has begun to sicken him, he's sure of it. Her rancid spices have already scalded his throat and stomach to shreds. Not to mention that she is so loud when she cooks . . .

'I'm sorry, Nani,' shouting over the sizzling pots. He hates being a foreigner to everyone but there's no helping it; he can't hide in his own home, can he? 'If it's all right, I'll be having oats again tonight.'

'You know, Henree,' his boy smiles, sincere and gracious, 'we're alike. If I could, every meal I ate would be something as mild as sandwiches at high tea.'

The maid's head appears, a brown bobbin over her pots. She stares a good long moment and then drops back to her work.

73

THROUGHOUT THE YEAR, the Rutaevans act as if the drummer ranks lower than his mongrel mutt, barely domesticated. They bare their teeth at him, stopping short of a smile. Henry has seen it all.

The drummer can never sit when others do and never on the same bench. If he wears a hat, he must shove it back upon his head and doff it when a higher rank approaches. It's just the rules (Rutaevans say) that force him to keep his sarong tied with a special knot so it shows his knees. Just the rules that no one can use a cup or plate he's used. When he drinks water at another's house — even if the other is a friend of sorts — his host must serve it to him in a flimsy earthen mug so it can be smashed into uselessness afterward. One can tell who Regi's assorted half-friends are by their yards and the heights of their shard heaps.

Worse, because of the drummer's caste, never in a thousand kalpas would the monk bless Regi's smallest donation to the Buddha. Yet evidently, because the day for the pilgrimage to the forest monks is fast approaching (and Suba says every pilgrimage needs its drummers and drummers' ceremonies) Regi begins to achieve what Henry notes in his diary as an apotheosis. From the Pilimas on down, people at the market start to nod to Regi. They greet the drummer with a marked courtesy — and Henry has witnessed them pressing miniature gifts into Regi's hands.

Still, what most surprises Henry is not that it is Lester Pilima who organizes the pilgrimage meeting on April 12, some ten days before the planned departure. No; it is rather that the Pilimas had chosen to hold the meeting on the barren weed-threaded field just *below* Regi's house. How can this be? It is as though the Pilimas were trying to offer the highest honor to the drummer, making him a temporary king.

On such an important morning Johnny irritates Henry by mislaying his spectacles. Thus the boy stumbles on the road with its holes filled in by scraps of statuary. He tries to lead Henry toward the lower field and a herd of people gathered upon straw mats, one that turns to stare back. Henry cannot help remarking, 'What a comely group, and assembled so early!'

On this day everyone appears scrubbed, down to the hungry temple helper Rosalin-akka, skitting along the crowd, unmoored without her broom. The two dancing sisters sit queenly, legs tucked to the side, faces shining at Henry as though coconut or great belief creams under the skin. A few pip-size orphans in school uniform whisper near the herb doctor Appuhamy, where bigger business is at hand — Appuhamy is chanting into a child's ear something Henry knows he doesn't want to hear. He just wants to take in the rest. Like the oldest man of the village, all knobs and pommels, chuckling at something Pushpa Pilima has said. Or Pushpa, who continues to careen amid the crowd, wiping hair off her forehead, a faintly hysterical approval fixed on her face.

One man in a gray tunic, unknown to Henry — but then it's just a matter of time before Henry knows everyone — raises his hand. This man seems to be saluting them and calls out something that sounds quite indistinguishable from *coiling undies*.

Coiling undies? Surprised, Henry raises a limp finger back in a half-wave, half-bow, whatever is the right thing to pacify these people. He broadens his smile, shortens his stride and is approaching the gaggle just as a spurt of light detaches itself —

— which is when Regi's dog makes a run for the pink man.

The dog's pique, far more than pique because it is specific, targeted, and potentially fatal, paralyzes the villagers. They fall still mainly because they can't understand for the life of them why a beast should be so angry, so full of desire for the foreigner and the foreigner alone. That a beast should bear some grudge and need to sink its teeth through the thick pants and into that flesh?

They stand like human stonepiles. And watch the bite, how quickly the pink flesh flies unseamed from its ligaments. How tenacious Regi's mutt is, like a laborman teasing out the man's fibers and tendons. How awful when the animal takes a small piece of leg — but still a piece! — and in some mimicry of shame hides behind a well with its pink dripping treasure.

They can't help but notice how pink is an off color, dead as the absence of color, clean and sullied, deader than pure white. And if the moments before the bite are erased by the event's scale, no one forgets the tall man tumbling. As though someone had cut his strings. Falling first to his knees, then on his face — *pow* — practically in the mud.

Pow. A real sin.

So later it's no surprise that no one, not even Pushpa with her high-lady reserve, can keep from remarking how their foreigner screams. His screech cuts into their ears like the sound just before contaminated water spills from the ladle, a roughness in the world you usually don't hear, a voice you'd be tempted to call not a sign of pain but of possession.

At that moment, all they could do was watch. They watched as his aide led away their foreigner, his bleeding pinkish leg rigid as a crutch. They watched as the overwhelmed drummer beat his dog on the flank once, and then twice, and one more time just to balance things. He called the mutt names that would satisfy himself and the village. And did it loudly enough for the villagers to hear: *Cur!* said Regi then *Bastard!* and finally *Ingrate!* Quick as midnight a silence surrounded Regi and by extension everyone else. A few of the gathered shrieked back, laughing, into that silence. Because only exclamation and maybe gossip could satisfy the surprise in their throats.

Lester, he's the one to suggest the villagers suspend the meeting until next week at the same place.

'Here at my field?' mustered the drummer.

Of course it would be at the drummer's field. What did the man think?

Everyone knew, though, what they had seen. Dogs bark at demons. They never bark at gods. Never at men with the least bit of godlike essence in them.

With something like gratitude at such a quick release, the drummer nodded and hoisted his dog to his chest with a father's love. On a day nearing the yearly pilgrimage, the people found it easy in their souls to let the low-caste and his bundle get by, to cut a quick path through their huddled mass.

74

'DON'T TAKE THE LAUGHTER seriously, Henree. No doubt they were alarmed. Can you hike it up just a little?' The boy's ministrations calm Henry. Only a rare person would have such a touch, even while the numbness starts to depart in spikes and barbs.

'If you could go just a bit more lightly, John? Can you ring for —?' His aide tugs the frayed gold tassel: the Englishman's bell. The bright echo bounces off flagstones still damp from Nani's mopping. 'Would the dog have been diseased?'

'We're not that dirty here in the out-station. Of course, on the coast you might expect so because there are beasts who mixed with Portuguese mongrels, but here . . .'

'Mangy, wasn't it?'

'We can't help that, Henree. Dogs are imported. Not really meant to be here. Even in the dry zone, their fur can't take our moisture. Why Regi is the only one to keep a filthy dog as a pet is beyond me —'

'You hate the family.'

'Not the *family*. Sorry, can't hurt that much?'

'Think we could have tea around now?'

The boy ceases his swabbing. 'Like the stuff, eh, Henree?'

Henry would have to be totally deaf not to know the boy props false cheer over his alarm. But the boy should feel reassured. The leg throbs, sure, but so far as Henry's concerned, there's no gangrene or rabies, is there? His hope rests in a tautology: his leg is his by virtue of his long-term claim to it. It would be unimaginable to consider otherwise, to think his leg might go elsewhere.

And he needs no leg medicine. No tea tray with accouterments. What would most soothe Henry would be the sight of her white petticoat and half-open mouth and her listening to the request coming her way. *That* could help salve the pain. He needs her to forgive any past indiscretion. To come to the door displaying that stretched equator of a belly: its exuberant navel popping forward, its smooth cinnamon skin.

She arrives having missed twenty million hints but holding a heavy mug, steaming over. As he slurps the drink down, bitter, she seems to attend his every gurgle. She has forgiven him, after all, hasn't she? She dabs a poultice on him: bandages which reverse Johnny's touch: the hot pins in his leg skulk out until they subside entirely.

'You feel bet-ter soon, Sir,' her slow monk's English says. She had not studied long; still, for once she tries to speak to him.

So the last thing he considers is color and scent, the particular invitation and deflection of cinnamon. Cinnamon — before he goes under into some warm waiting vault. When he awakes, the air is antiseptic, alcoholic, and the two are raising his limb.

'She sewed you up,' Johnny announces as though the pride is all his.

'Luck-y,' she tells him. 'You are luck-y.'

'Yeah,' groaning, all words tasting bad.

His mood slides quickly. How little she understands. He notes for the first time a ledge built high up in his bedroom on which are laid skewers and vises, rusting metal instruments for inexplicable tortures. Optimism flees his pores: he is too far behind everything; none of these people understand. Damn if his plans aren't too young and too new. 'I've come to this village five hundred years too late,' he tells them but they don't catch his meaning. Dreaming of efficiency, he is bitten by a mangy dog.

He can imagine only cynical noblemen joking as they make contracts based on national advantage. It's difficult to see rows of clean, industriously employed orphans resurrecting a heritage wiped away by people with names like Chilkins and Colwether.

If Henry could, he'd move but they've swathed his throbbing leg into an alabaster cast. A sea creature's carapace. With deftness Nani wipes the spittle from the corners of his mouth. If he were defective in intelligence, they'd treat him this way all the time.

Johnny shakes his head. 'Don't turn him into an infant,' he says in his easy-to-understand Sinhalese. 'Our Henree will be fine no doubt.' *Apee Henree honde aeti.*

Our Henree. He wishes a perfect language existed. He'd use it to explain everything to these two aristocrats. They're not arguing for once. He'd explain if he could how Madame's fulgent voice begins to reassure him. Her tone sweeter than sugared Russian liqueur, Madame's cadences, talking to him from the threshold of his mind: *Surely there will be enough time to bring everything back in line,* she says. Henry is sure she approves of these two, Johnny and Nani, behaving as friends, afloat before him with their odd language; having cleansed and swabbed him down, having bandaged his broken skin.

He raises himself enough to see the room has grown crowded. Had he gone under again?

By the wall, the herb doctor Appuhamy chants into a lime. Nearby the dance sisters singsong devotions into their clasped hands. Kumari has a madonna's ironbitten grin — had he never noticed the resemblance before? — as she lays a wreath of woven grass at Henry's feet. Who shirks duty or affection? No one. Had he died already?

Henry's two friendly float-faces are pulling and placing his leg, forking it left and then right and left again. A pillow under, now over, placing and pulling. They do this until the vestibule of sleep claims him into a dream of a village: embroidered hills and pregnant, ripe clouds.

75

Then the Deer said, "Our sister has a longing."
The village headman said, "What can she eat for it?"
The Deer replied, "Our sister can eat the stars in the sky."

He is dreaming, Johnny telling him nighttime stories his own mother had told him — so sick for how long now? He never leaves his bed. He drifts in and out of the World's Fair and his childhood. There are phrases to be muttered from his seminary days *for since the fathers fell asleep, all things continue as they were from the beginning of the creation.*

One morning he sits up all of a sudden, having awoken to the half-dreamed repetition of *brown skin, cinnamon.* Cinnamon? Brown skin? He believes this could augur recovery.

'We may want to train you,' says Henry. Later that day, in what they say is still April, he's alone with her, propped up against pillows. 'To do something you'd like more. Want to teach?'

'Teach?' and here his maid studies the needlepoint loom, her useful bedside activity. 'Sir wants me to teach? I can-not speak yet —'

'No, come on, you speak fine. Beautifully. Didn't the monk say you'd been one of his quickest pupils? Perhaps you could do some independent study now.'

'I am sor-ry, *inde-pendent?*'

'Teach yourself more English from books.'

'Yes, I like to teach. Eas-i-ly I can learn more. Eng-lish Sir wants? I can teach what you call herbs.'

'I'm saying it might be nice for the pupils if someone like you taught English.'

'Sir is sure it is Nani that Sir wants?'

'Oh, Pushpa's doing us a favor. If we're lucky, she'll hold out a few more weeks. But you, you might have a real talent for it. We'll have Johnny get you a book. And then you'll stick with it, yes?'

'Stick? Oh I see, Sir. I stick and study.'

If asked to make a structural engineering diagram, Henry thinks he could probably render some of the forms which create the insolent question mark of her back. He might do justice to the heft of her acorn squash breasts pressed against that white bodice, though the bottom roundness might pose a challenge. Given his draftsmanship, he might be able to sketch her whole strong length.

But he would never be able to do justice to the surprise on his calves of her hands, housed in lavender cloth that early day. Or how she touched his arm once and then again during his convalescence. Nor could he pencil in her uptilted eyes: bemused and spooked. And sometimes reproachful, belying her words' courtesy. Even as she cures him with yet another fruit mash.

Spring, summer, a day in 1937, April?

The belifruit: large hard-shell nutlike spheroid encasing a brown pulpy mass. Ceylonese villagers pound the fruit with palm sugar to be used as an alimentary tonic.

Once he's up that afternoon and walking with a cane, making a slow tap and dig of things around the market, he hears about April's New Year's celebration, in a few days, right before the planned pilgrimage. It is women who especially freight the question: What are you and your people doing for New Year's?

You and your people. *Who are my people?*

'We are such children,' Johnny explains, before heading out to telegraph. 'This country will find any excuse to shut down for days. You'll have to drop in on all the villagers' homes.' Johnny says, too, it's good the pilgrimage comes after New Year's. Even if haphazardly, in not blocking any of this, the American had made the people happy. *I'm doing fine*, Henry repeats to himself as the new year approaches.

Because the holiday seizes control of the people. *I'm doing fine*, he repeats, the next morning, tap-digging about again, the leg more of a dead weight. Without his doing, each hour the village appears to double. At the wellsides the numbers swell — there are more blanket wringers and crouched pot scrubbers, soapy children, worn mothers, amused mothers. More pound their clothes against the rocks with that rhythmic sickling sound. In the kitchens, palm sugar, coconut oil and rice flour are spinning out into trays bearing round raw balls, flowers, and riverside branches — both hard and soft food like that cooked by the Buddha's disciples.

Seeing such devotion, all the culinary labor, he asks himself again, does it not count for something that the women are kind to *what is in their own sphere?* The cooks' hands are kind to sugar and flour. To their children who will always have a sentimental slobber after such treats. Each child will be outfitted with a memory of annual, loving moments. As age visits its indignities, do people later rely on the memory of this epoch of sugary indulgences? When desire, once spiked, is not supplied; if their favorite brothers become drunks and leave offspring virtually orphaned; if wives die in childbirth or husbands on plantations; if the paddy harvest is spoiled; if conscience faces a guilt not to be assuaged by food donations to the monk —

— at such moments, do they remember childhood and this physical mothering? These sweetmeats tell the future that once upon a time, the world took note of a child's most foolish desires and tried to speak them back.

Would it have been better had he stayed to serve like a good rector to his father's congregation? If he'd deferred his ideas of himself;

stayed instead to play catch with Daniel in humid New York evenings, to ferret out the idea behind some recent invention? Had he stayed to sidle into a cozy house whose wainscoting he would've built himself, a house warmed by his work in the church, would he have been superior? Had he never budged, had he found Clara in the evenings to share a few stimulating and yet consoling words with her, would they right now be discussing a book on the state of America's soul? Would they be mulling over which soup the war widow down the way might appreciate receiving? A couple of squeezes would be forthcoming. He would rub talc into the folds of her body. He'd do whatever would give her comfort; whatever activity both could enjoy. This might have been the life of Henry Fyre Gould: a self contributing to its own sphere.

When his actual self is a prison, walled by its yearning to reach *beyond*. To contribute to something *else and beyond*, as bad as any of the salon-goers —

— even in intractable Rajottama, a moment might come for him to say to the villagers *We know one another as well as potted ham knows its tin. Why should I waste my talents any longer? You are already self-sufficient. Now you shall carry forth all the lessons we have learned together.* But would he recognize the arrival of this catapulting moment?

The new year's routine makes him wonder whether he has achieved enough. Eventually its activity gulps in men who when the sun plummets must cease talking and help sweep the dirtyard and fetch tree-hanging cloths. But festivities gestate in the hives of women to explode everywhere else. According to the New Year, Henry is just another useless man, already an outsider. *I'm doing fine*, he tells himself again, *all this is temporary, much more remains to be done.*

The rule is, and no one's exempt, Henry and Nani must present sweets to their neighbors. 'That's the custom, you must,' Johnny snorts, stuffing his mouth with a steaming rase kavili Nani has made. These last days, not immune to village tradition, she too had worked with brown palm sugar, finally completing her labors on the eve of the new year.

The next morning finds Henry limping from the house with Nani a step or two behind him. On her head she carries the basket of goods, its sweetness unable to cover a dank liverlike scent, the canal wafting its nightsoil their way.

Yet the canal swarms: men are striding royal upon rocks laid bare

346

by the governmental dam having been lowered. Close to their wives and daughters, they roost. And make their way to tiny islands amid the slow-flowing water.

'It's clear,' he cannot keep himself from commenting to Nani, 'just how much the villagers enjoy the lowered dam.'

'Before the gov-ern-ment built the dam, all this was vil-lage, Sir,' answers Nani. Saucy girl! she stares off into that place she always stares off to, nowhere he has known. How is Henry supposed to respond to her when she shows this sauciness?

'I'll wager Johnny told you that,' he manages.

They continue on, Henry's cane tapping its lopsided rhythm. Once he sees her mouthing *wa-ger:* this must be a word the monk never taught.

Henry stretches to gather for his botanical scrapbook a leaf here, a branch there. Like a child he surrenders his findings to Nani to carry atop the sweets.

'It was my fam-i-ly,' she says. Why does she sometimes emerge so suddenly?

'What?'

'I know about the dam not from Je-han-gir but from my fam-i-ly. Maps,' she says, as though that explains anything. 'Maps be-fore the dam.'

He nods, not understanding the insistence. 'Fine, maps.' Why should women be so moody? how can he meet her? Or what had he done to her to occasion this outburst?

The day's brightness could perversely depress him; he has reasons to be cheerful, but the monsoon has permanently suspended itself. Again the villagers have been fearing drought. Will he be blamed? Under the striping of trees, they walk. Below the model garden they start to hear the spirited boasting of the new Welsummer chickens, courtesy of the American Catalogue.

Unfortunately, the barnyard fowl have proven to be so aggressive (the first day alone seven were mauled dead from their penmates' beaks) that to avoid future bloodbaths, every morning (after each bird is released from an individual cage) even the females have to be corded in place atop the eggs. And the roosters sit like mutinied rulers: bound to iron thrones cobbled together from discarded coffee-sorting machine parts. Still, none of the birds stop trying to peck holes into the ground: Henry hasn't figured out yet how he is going to force them to mate without everyone dying in the process.

He may have to make an early killing and order a more docile breed. How could he have known from the catalogue that these Welsummers would be prone more to the laws of aggression than to the rituals of love?

At the temple the Buddha sits with his eerie head still noosed in those orange diapers. The morning chant has just begun with its nasal melody:

> I take refuge in the Buddha, the Dhamma, the Sangha

Henry does not notice his own sweat until Nani offers him a blue handkerchief monogrammed with Madame's three initials. He also notes the girl's wearing Madame's pearl drop earrings, those he gave her as a gift.

'Those earrings make your skin more cinnamon. No, more chestnut,' trying to compliment her, 'or hazelnut, you know? A real color. Not like me. White. Sick-looking. You can see my veins. White!' He pretends to spit at his bare arm in disgust. He would do anything to get a real smile from her: and this last jest is the first thing to work all month. He's rewarded with a mona lisa.

'But you are not white,' she corrects, 'you are pink, Sir.' A tiny but worthwhile reward.

After the temple the two pass below the market with its vagrant dogs sniffing boarded-up stalls just before the bridge. Above, they see Manu climbing toward town with a group of men Henry has never seen. When one of his friends drops a canister so that papers go tumbling, Manu continues walking uphill, letting the man gather them, but Nani has already run to snatch one flyaway for herself. In Sinhala, the small poster shows a rice farmer carrying a tiny cartoonish nation of people, all borne on his muscular arm, also proclaiming the date and time for an event.

She quickly slips the paper into the waist of her lungi. As they are about to cross the bridge, at the turnstile Nani gazes ahead and hesitates. A monk from another village is crossing the bridge toward them, like a cotillion dancer holding aloft an end of his orange robe. Henry urges her on.

'I pre-fer not, Sir.'

'Don't start,' says Henry, detecting the people's superstition — that a monk, encountered when one begins a journey, brings bad luck.

'You wait or . . . I meet you la-ter.' She runs, a banshee out of hell down the road. Back toward the house with her lungi tight around her sleek hips.

The elderly monk crosses the bridge, nodding at Henry before continuing up the hill, anesthetized to the tumult he'd caused. Henry shouts at the dodging back of the girl, *come back or else!* He cuts himself off, though there aren't any witnesses from the village. Still Henry suppresses the unsuitable. No imprecations can unseat the ancient mind that gets hold of her: a thing that breathes her like some terrible afflatus. *Naeve gilunaa, banchung,* he tells himself, a new saying he has learned from Johnny. When the ship is sinking, make merry. There must be good techniques for unseating superstition. Good techniques, he is coming to think, are everything. He doesn't know them yet. Not with her, at any rate. She is gone.

VI

ANIMALS

Yet while I was speaking to them thus, they did not know me, and they would enquire of one another, asking: 'Who is he that speaks to us? Is it a man or god?'

— The Buddha, *Maha Parinibbana Sutta*

76

THE HIRED MAN has bad spit technique.

He turns the jellied pig too slowly. Either the man's lassitude or calculated indifference has made the pork skin crackle and burn into a black-edged landscape. Burnt can sometimes taste better but this man goes too far. 'What's your name anyway?' demands Henry. 'Where'd you learn to cook?'

Since the official new year had ended yesterday, Henry decided not to change out of the special ceremonial tunic Nani had sewed for him. He is trying to keep his mood correspondingly festive and spontaneous: he has thrown away his ashplant cane (though he still limps and the dogbite has changed from indigo to what she calls a healing green-yellow). He has gone wrong, he thinks, with so much planning. One should plan less, and use good technique nonetheless. Yet he cannot keep up with his new spontaneity program: his impromptu yard party fails to be at all impromptu.

It came about this way: after all the new year pots had boiled over, he'd wanted to host something real friendly, American style. Like an outdoor barbecue. Something where he could just be himself for once. Free and plain with the Rajottamans. He'd invite *them* into his sanctum sanctorum, as it were.

Nani had not protested. No, she'd only made a little moue and acquiesced. 'Yes, sir.' She had apparently decided on perfect agreeability as a formula for survival, and why should Henry be against this?

A few minutes after Henry's demand about his culinary background, the assistant chef answers Henry in badly truncated Sinhala: 'I am pig-turner.' Henry hadn't noticed this bad Sinhala while hiring the man in the market. Partly because it had happened so fast: the man had appeared out of nowhere, practically right in front of him, a light-skinned man bearing the face of a weary shark, running a makeshift market stall with a sign affirming JELLIED PORK FOR SALE CHEAP NUTRIFYING PERFECK FOR CEREMONY: ARRANGE IN ADVANCE.

'I am perfeck pig-turner,' repeats the man. For all his difficult speech, the pig-turner had initially proven responsible, bringing — remarkably on time, on the stroke of 11:30 A.M. — the prepared animal from god knows where. Now it is noon and the man shows a new stubbornness. 'Why care who I am? I sell pig. I bring it. I cook for you.'

Johnny is in the house overseeing Nani; Joseph the gardener is sweeping the drive. As usual, no one's there when real help is needed. 'Step aside, please,' Henry tells the perfect pig-turner, who needs no convincing to abandon his post for the bench. 'I'll take care of it.'

Henry limps to hunch down by a fire he'd built too high. He tries to burrow sense up into that man's tired face. 'Could you go see if there's any coal slip? You know, to lower the flame?'

The former pig-turner rolls off toward the general direction of the house. With lanyard and rocks, Henry tries to reel and pike the iron spit into a set position, but nothing holds. He is forced to sit there with clothes grubby and the flesh smoke surging into his mouth and eyes, the pig's sad face spinning uncontrollably before him. He yanks it still. As soon as he'd seen the man's sign, the first day of the new year, he'd thought pork might be a nice delicacy for the people, signifying bounty, much as it had each December, the pig almost swallowing its apple on a platter in the Harvard dining hall. By obtaining something unusual, Henry thought he would make a gesture toward acknowledging this arbitrary new year, its midnight determined by a mercenary astrologist.

Without proper help, he is forced to hold and turn the pork, trying to keep from salivating. Burnt flesh. The smell of childhood: pork on the open breeze. Once the preparations are through they *will* be happy — Johnny and Nani have been kept in the dark about the main dish, partly so they too could be inspired by their employer's largesse and its reach.

His own face begins to bead with sweat from the heat; but this is a worthwhile heat; there should be good attendance —

— and up the drive here comes the first Pilima, Lester dressed in work clothes, face pointed in disgust — after him stumps Chollie, caning it. Henry had asked Lester Pilima to spread the word about the party, figuring Lester to be good as any telegraph service. Being a taxman, Lester must know the ins and outs of people's habits. To-day, behind him, the others would come —

'Pig?' yells Lester, from ten paces away, and then again, closer, so Henry's eardrums vibrate. The man so burlish. 'Pig? YOO-HOO! You're making *pig?*'

Henry continues to turn and then hold the spit. No riposte's possible. If the Pilima would use such sub-conversation, Henry would respond in kind.

'Fyre! I hope that's cooking for your drummer's dog?' asks Lester. From the house, Johnny bursts out carrying a tray loaded high with some kind of blended rice. Sighting the visitors, he sets the rice down on the porch and vanishes back.

'Pig?' Lester's still saying. He chortles, circles Chollie, strokes his toupee, taps the ground thoughtfully with a stick. 'Pig?' He checks with Chollie, who gazes at the ground as if to forbear shaming Henry. 'For the party, Fyre?'

Henry smiles up at Lester. 'I told you invite whomever you wanted.'

'PIG? Fyre!'

'Some prohibition against it?' Henry's eyes flitter, it could be taken as insolence, but the sun has escaped the trees' guardianship and flares down from behind Lester's head. 'Didn't the Buddha himself die from pork prepared by —'

'— a low-bred man,' Lester says, glancing behind him quickly at Chollie. 'That is correct. You insult us, Fyre.'

'This is true,' says Chollie, eyes still downcast.

'But you people!' No comedy enters Henry's voice; it comes out as a whine. He wipes his hands, rises to his feet, lets the contested pig spin or stay as it will. 'You'll make the tinned ham at the General Store sell out — we constantly have to reorder it — but you won't eat pig?'

Lester starts in talking about thieves, the drummer and son, at the store, pilfering ham. He says they keep a storehouse of it where the monster child is kept.

'No one else in the village eats it,' Chollie declaims.

But Chollie lies, Henry tells himself, the drummer and Manu especially wouldn't be stealing ham. 'The monk doesn't eat it?'

'No one,' says Lester. 'I forbade it.'

'*You* forbade it?' A village should not have too many heads.

'As mudaliyar.'

'Why didn't you come speak to me first?'

Chollie waves his cane. 'Lester is campaigning for office, Gould. He will be appointed to some high government position soon. This is why he leads us on the pilgrimage.'

'Great,' muttering.

'Trying to find a way to change it all from within,' continues Chollie, with a younger sibling's pride. 'Leadership in the village, Gould!'

All of Henry's attention focuses on not falling into a fit — but a vise is cranking his temples, tighter and tighter. 'So, Fyre,' Lester continues, as though in a chain of pleasantries. 'I actually asked *no* one to come here today,' he declares. 'This will make things easier for you.'

A long staircase beckons Henry down. The important thing is to refocus and there won't be any fits. He retrains his eyes on Lester.

'Fyre! your participation' — Lester coughs — 'in the new year can retain a good taste.' A tarpaulin of smoke hangs over the fire where everything but the pig's glimmering eye has turned black. The porcine snout is stuck in a call, its jaw-hinge opening and shutting in the heat as though it too wants to announce a last-minute campaign. And then the whole charred thing turns to blaze.

'Water!' yells Henry. The yard could catch on fire. The mango tree. The house. Everything. And these two clowns would just stand there berating him — even as Nani comes running in her best whites, calling 'Sir! Sir! Sir!' and heaving a bucketful atop the fire —

— until all that is left is a drenched pig.

Drenched pig? The visitors finally leave, the pig-turner accompanying them, all of them cryptic with warning and amused condolence. Johnny responds to Henry's request to 'just get rid of it' by borrowing gloves from Joseph and using for a hearse a wheelbarrow with a sorrowing creak which he pushes down to the canal. Inside the wheelbarrow, the black pig is covered now by a fine bright mucus, *some post-mortem desire for light*, Henry wants to write, but does not.

Instead from the bench he watches the death by water: the boy flings the pig with a good arm into the canal. Only for a minute does the fat beast float. When it finally sinks under, not a moment too soon, it gives up a tricky little larcenous burp, the last firecracker of the new year.

77

'WHAT DO THEY THINK I'm running here, an animal hospital?' he says to her. Because later that afternoon a lost cow barged up their drive. A bloated mother, speckled brown and white, it headed straight to the maid, where she knelt soaping lard ash from the grass.

'I like it,' Nani told him immediately.

Guessing where this was going, he told her just as immediately that it was a silly idea. So much else demanded her attention. Look at what she had not yet done. Her language lessons with the monk, for one thing. Hadn't she spent only two days learning English? had she ever started studying on her own? She didn't need a cow. The house and the garden and everything else needed more tending.

'I like it,' she repeated, a regular nanny-goat.

He saw she might not give in. She wouldn't just shoo the thing away. Her determination could sound almost vicious. 'I like it.'

The rest of the day, the speckled cow proved the nonexistence of Buddhism in the animal kingdom. It was so passionate about Nani that while she hung laundry, it pretended to be a cat and rubbed against the line. While she cooked, it slept like a sphinx, head bent slightly. She garlanded it with a palm braid, and Henry spied her stroking the brown and white bovine, speaking to it with a lover's confidence. In the evening, she even glided her cheek over its back.

This last gesture made him accept the new affectation. Can't beat them, then join them. Why should man not fully domesticate any kind of animal? Obviously the thing made her happy.

The next day, he joins her in petting the thing, only to have her say, 'She is in pain, Sir.'

'Then shouldn't we take her to a doctor?'

'No doc-tor can help.' That almost metallic determination.

'What kind of pain would that be, Nani?'

'No name.'

'We don't know whom she belongs to?'

'Us,' Nani smiles sincerely. 'Ours now?'

'Of course.' Only a slight pang in him. She cares greatly for this cow.

So it is that the cow grazes during Henry's morning on his bench. For now Henry does not want to read Wooves, not Wooves or the Ceylonese historians or even the perverse notators of amatory matters. He wants only to study his Sinhalese and suttas, to consider the monk and the village, the upcoming pilgrimage, and how to make plans watertight. The cow, Henry writes

> is an emblem of patience. Existence matters as much as achievement. If the mind were less foolish, the next patch of greener grass would never be enough to spur us on.

Plans for the Day:

1)
2)
3)
4)

78

OVER THE NEXT DAYS, planning starts to work again. Effects fold back in like tired birds to *his* impulses, investigations, motivations. Still, the first hint he gets that there might be intruders has nothing and everything to do with his wish for melons.

When he and Nani go to the market, several days running, they tie up the cow at home, so long as he can slip the pregnant mother mango-tree grass and make Nani smile. At the market there has always been chatter, the usual jungle telegraph, something he used to pay more attention to while now he tries to focus on fruit.

Because fruit-marketing unites him with her. It makes her unreasonably happy. Especially when they discourse on the consequence of certain choices — rambutan over banana, melon over starfruit — and stay undistracted by what he might overhear.

At one stand they linger over the last of the melons, two golden, cheap, shipped-from-South-Africa melons, according to the seller. Henry cringes at the implied colonial subsidies, but couldn't he go for a bit of sweet crunch, something to cool his hot tongue?

Then he hears them, ruminating about the weather — Looks like rain again? — in that English public school way of assuming all surrounding ears might be instructed by their superior accents.

'Worse than Brixton, this.'

'Storm clouds but no serious intention.'

'What's the diff?'

She wants to go on discussing the melons' respective ripenesses but he cannot. There are around him soldiers, in khakis and also blue uniforms, more like schoolboys on leave, ruler-straight boys with hair chopped abruptly at the rear as if a shearsman had gone mad with the desire to control anarchy. Confounding apparitions. Once, riding the Kandy–Colombo train, he had seen a similar flock of tall, well-brought-up boys. Young, spruce and eager in the king's employ, loud and very white, all qualities that put him to shame or at least make him feel his own promise thinning. Young and full of themselves and their repartee.

Seeing them in the marketplace — *his* marketplace — a burble rises inside him and his scalp tightens a few centimeters. He has to choke back what is after all the daft impulse to collar one of these young cheekies, pull him close, let him know who runs this village. The old heave and sough in his blood terrifies him, that being what he'd come here to inveigh against. Territorialism and its raw urges.

'Looks like we're in for a drizzle, doesn't it?'

Henry stops short, dazzled by the ruddy goodness of a captain perhaps half his own age, all clear brow and sincerity — every bit the type a nation chooses as father, leader, hero. Yet also resembling, strangely, a firm-jawed boar. 'You're not the famous foreigner, are you?'

This is funny but Henry can't budge. Nani's back can be seen far off in the market already.

'Chris the name. You're not eyeing those melons, are you?'

Did the soldier mean Nani? When Henry says nothing the boy goes on. 'Could feed at least four of us, you see —' He embarks on a long to-do about the mess-hall officer having taken the train down to Colombo to meet a shipment. Rants out long lists of things Henry has no need to learn: hours and programs and confused ration orders, meals and getting used to what they call porridge here.

With the force of a train collision, Henry gets it. This is a man with designs on not just his melon but Rajottama, being someone who has moved here in force.

Chris's face might as well be covered in marble, it has clearly been that admired. He hides behind such a mask readily, the apparent freckled vulnerability just another shield decoration. Chris? He has summoned squads of ruddy public-school variants of himself into Rajottama, 'for a good while, but moved in only these last few days.'

And over this new year period, he has blatantly made himself known. While Henry has been limping about eating sweets, roasting pork, overseeing watery funerals, having rapprochements with cows, planning —

— the British have come. And they are situated, far as Henry can tell, on the site of what Johnny has mistakenly called a *defunct* encampment. There are to be *other* foreigners at large in Rajottama.

Once Henry finds Nani, he lets her lead him home through the marketplace, where the happy buzz is high. The women think Chris interesting, that is all. Another new year augury. Their mothers had known of the *previous* commander on the encampment, the one who habitated at the camp long before but this Chris, a young version, he is so kind and solicitous besides. And handsome in that foreign way. Definitely a blessed boy. It almost makes them like the English.

As Henry passes the stand, Roshan leans over to whisper, 'Sir, everyone loves uniforms. The reason everyone's so friendly. If you wore a uniform and had all your strength back again, I promise, they'd love it too. Shall I have a uniform like theirs made up for you?'

On the way home, Henry decides. He will have to invite the leader over for a cuppa. He knows that much about the British. Calibrated hospitality. And no roast-pork-on-a-spit mistakes! He imagines himself leaning forward, broad American knees, the heavy drapes drawn, ginger tea served, playing up the fact of his wearing the native dress. He would borrow Johnny's spectacles and stare the captain up and down, all on home turf.

There's no doubt about it; with the British here, Henry stands the risk of having his fire stolen. He'd been planning to make the upcoming pilgrimage a volley against superstition and here the novelty of the Brits arrives.

These villagers would love any bauble, Henry thinks. Manu's poster had shown a rice farmer with a nation on his arm. Is it that the people want to settle onto an arm newer than Henry's? Had the Brits come purposely to undermine Henry? He will avoid them. He will not write back to any of the government agents. He makes a fist only to find it trembling. He'd prefer to be someone else right now. Some*where* else.

'The British have come,' he repeats dully to Nani, who shines back at him.

In the days following the new year's bad discovery he cannot help hearing the soldiers' pride, a medley of caterwauls, whoops and hollers echoing from the large olive tents above the temple. This is worse than firecrackers or Pali chanting before the gods. Rather than spy, he imagines the young soldiers quipping, stretching and calling one another decent sorts and fine fellows as they put water on for tea.

Instead (without willing it fully) he conjures a picture of himself sitting with those boys, blanketed by camaraderie, shuffling moisture-resistant wax cards printed in imperial blues and oranges. Trust could be a transplant. Maybe he is not being trusting enough, after all; maybe the jungle has finally got to him. He should relax a bit.

On Sunday night, a giant white sheet stretches up over the encampment. From below on the canal road, hiking toward it, Henry watches the film the British are projecting as it ripples upon the sheet. A colossal bluish-white actor with bushy eyebrows hangs from a tall building and makes the villagers gloat *anay!*, astonished in the dark.

When the tea invitation goes out, Chris Stout, a strong name, 'people from Bath,' won't hear of meeting anywhere but at the camp. 'We're the ones got to be hospitable,' he says. 'Please, dive in, be our guests. It's rationed stuff but all right enough. We're in Ceylon, aren't we?'

Home advantage. Henry knows this folly but lets the boy assert the awkward rights of youth. Every time they talk, invisible crows peck at his scalp. During the tea itself — noontime, standard-issue olive tent, metal cot proclaiming its competence, incessant talk of the vagaries of climate — the boy does prove himself clever.

'Been here a full monsoon?' he asks, flexing an arm, each sinew

361

with its own corresponding valley. And later: 'Talked much with the people?'

The session is a hunting game inside a miniature labyrinthine topiary. What is real about Chris Stout? He rivals the Sinhalese in his reserve, his friendliness and indirection. Boyish innocence in full artificial flower, faux as Henry's attempt to outplay English courtesy. Henry finally understands the phrase *foreign devil*.

Later, afternoon, at home the day of the devilish tea, the rains start up again, making the runnel near the house hard and fast, raindrops chased by the wind slanting down. Henry pretends to read in the library. Pretends to gather his thoughts in a room made cozy by the kerosene lamp's topaz light and by Johnny, lying on the chaise, scanning the Colombo paper, oblivious.

Without any notice (he'd given the boy only a brief summary of the interview with Chris) Henry intrudes on the quiet: 'Guy had my number from the start,' complaining, 'you know? That Chris practically cudgeled me with courtesy.'

Johnny lays down the paper and picks up the new little statuette he's been carving out of bark, a tiny thing. He twirls it into a blur. 'Henree, remember what we're after. You've got to learn not to let such officials get to you. Especially when they're English.'

Henry sits up straighter. 'You knew about this?'

'No,' the boy says immediately. Then takes a deeper breath. 'I wish I *had* known. This complicates things for us.' He waits. 'You're not thinking I've let you down?'

'I don't expect you to be God — you can't know *everything* that happens on this island,' Henry laughs. 'But the English soldier wouldn't have bothered you?'

'I'm from an island — he's from an island. Island people are different. We have thicker skins.'

As they both know, this approaches being a lie, insofar as Jehan is one of the world's most sensitive people. He can sense, for example, that Henree feels far too defeated in this moment. Not a favorable sign, not in this moment. Right when the boy in his telegrams has pressured Headquarters to publicly support Henree. Right when Jehan had practically put his own identity as spy into doubt because of the risks he *personally* had taken. All were risks for Henree, yes, for Henree's projects — but also for the new and reconstituted Jehangir. Perhaps for the future of an *American* Jehangir.

And could it have been the fault of all his accomplishments that Jehan was being punished? Subtly. With and because of and despite Chilkins, Jehan had rendered services unto Henree. And still was glad to stay unthanked. Yes, he had requested the checks for Henree's projects — had, also, secretly finagled Samankumar's complimentary article in the international *Tribune* — had even wrangled forth the supportive letter to Henree from Government Agent Colwether.

But had Whobody pushed *too far?* Was Headquarters now keeping Jonathan Nellie Whobody in the dark about new developments? About, for instance, the arrival of a British training platoon and encampment right in his own homestead, here in Rajottama?

Thus Jehan cannot just stand by and witness his American optimist-of-the-century flagging. That won't do. He moves to sit on their ridiculously overstuffed footstool. Closer to his employer so he can pat that swollen hand. 'Please. Don't let those uniforms get to you. We're taking abuse from every corner. First, the weather —'

Here Henree shakes the boy's hand free. He storms up. Ready to stamp off toward his room but halting on the threshold to stammer: 'Please! Not you!' his voice screeching like a regular madman's. 'Don't start in about weather. Ever since the English have come, that's all we hear. The big-deal obsession. Rain rain rain. Clouds. So what if there's rain? Water from the sky. Big deal! Rain!'

79

DURING THREE DAYS of storms without cease, housebound without regret, Henry draws up strategies for dismissing Rajottama's new military friends. He is Noah planning an ark in reverse. Send away the animals. Stay seated himself. He has the chance to work into a fine pitch the need for a question, not having yet found the right one. During his Sinhala lesson, held at Wooves' house — for once the monk did not mind the rain as much as his American pupil did — Henry has been able to maintain an inner calm, perfect equipoise.

They were moving from discussing the tricky idea of merit again, of *pin* and its economy, when, without wind, by some small magic the clouds parted or moved on to some unlucky dale beyond Rajottama. An effulgent sun burned through, glistening the muddy paths, floodlighting the library. A ghostly hope trickled back into Henry's mood. He may not have been betrayed, he reasoned. Trust was crucial. The right question would be resolved by a simple concrete answer.

As fraud inspector for the U.S. military and, briefly, New York State, Henry had known what effect you could get if you just nailed down the right question. His job had entailed the good fortune of tracing various interesting characters. One case had involved a charismatic man with resolute features, someone who'd advertised Harris tweed jackets falsely and then claimed, once cornered, that he had started a small village known to himself, family members and neighbors *as* Harris, right there in his good old American backyard, where he'd raised sheep not from the westernmost island of Europe but from his invented hamlet of Harris, Virginia.

In his single investigation Henry had asked the charlatan simply, 'On what basis is a Harris tweed identified?' at which the man stopped for a second and then broke down in tears, mumbling something about herringbone, ready to pay the punitive fine and sign a confession, if only to be rid of Torquemada Henry and his inquisition.

Another case, similarly dispatched, had involved a man who called himself Sabbatai Zion, who in an abandoned farmhouse had started a new religion in which the followers would achieve immortality if they helped put on puppet shows that glorified passion and its play. Henry had asked something along the lines of: 'Ever consider what might happen if one of your followers started his own religion?' This too had crumbled the whole edifice, shockingly, and soon the farmhouse became an abbatoir, with Zion acting as its humble butcher.

But one of Henry's favorite cases had been that of the female remedies husband-and-wife team, who hawked their snake-oil product at state fairs by having the wife pretend to be an onlooker in the audience, one who fell ill to female distress, only to be revived, at which point she would swear to dedicate her life to helping share with others a panacea that rivaled Mrs. Pinkham's. This couple had stumped Henry until he decided the perfect thing to ask would be, 'Can you show me your marketing routine from A to Z?'

In all cases, the question, aimed at the guilty conscience of the perpetrator, tended to elicit a siege of repentance. Once the perpetrators saw the irreversibility of his logic, they tended to want to sign, confess and bid Henry adieu. 'No more questions!' many of them had shouted after Henry.

Still, he has not been able to conceive of the dead-square question for Pandit. And there must be one.

As he walks the monk back to the temple, post-lesson, in the stifling day, Henry's hands find each other behind his back. He is trying to proceed in a sober, exemplary way. 'My only surprise,' he tells the monk, 'my question is how you could let this Chris's battalion use the temple grounds for their encampment.'

What Henry thinks is *and that you did so without telling me. And that you thought it a big favor when you let me start our Day of Altars upon your temple grounds. Where's your love of restoring Buddhism? of scaring away the baneful influence of foreigners?*

'It's not quite the temple grounds, is it, Colonel? They are just above the grounds! Doing no one any harm.'

The monk points out that it doesn't matter whether anyone knows what the soldiers are doing. After all, they're British and isn't this a British colony? The captains have their obligations to put soldiers where they please. Not every system is scrutable. If the soldiers are here or in Colombo, it doesn't really matter. 'In what country has liberation been an unequivocal success?' sniffs the monk.

'That's if the country's spirit has been broken.'

Henry had barely asked his question — it was the wrong one and the monk is acting temporarily insane. 'Saddhu, since they arrived, I always see the one called Chris everywhere.'

The explanation is worse than the situation. 'He's fine enough, Colonel. Does he interfere in the life of the village?' And the monk's crazy eyes deepen in meaning; his well-fed mouth is saying all sorts of wrong things.

If he could, Henry would bring back the early days in October or November. During them, sitting with the monk above the palm roof seemed as much a fulfillment of destiny as Henry Fyre Gould could have craved. He does not want to prove the monk guilty so much as he wants to harness the past into this moment. The future used to be theirs, certain as egrets clustering at dusk upon the mango tree. Why does his monk seem such a shape shifter, so far away?

The monk mentions to Henry that his progress is such that, for the next period, the two need meet for language lessons only on a weekly basis. 'Consider it an improvement, this movement to the weekly. That is, what's your word? A weekly *experiment*.'

The monk's sandals hit the temple's white plastered stairs. His ankles like inexorable poles plod up toward Rosalin-akka, waiting with her broom. As the monk enters his private chancel, she hurries after him.

Under the weight of a stultifying midmorning, for a few moments Henry watches the dust settle upon the stairs. The monk, for the first time, has forgotten to bow farewell to his student, who has been, according to repeated allegations, one of the most special in the monk's history.

80

TELEGRAPHIC DISPATCH FROM KANDY OFFICE TO 'CHILKINS' AND BLIND-COPIED AT SENDER'S REQUEST TO 'HEADQUAR-TERS' BY JONATHAN NELLIE AT 14:10, 1 MAY 1937:

HOPE IT IS A PEACEFUL SILENCE THAT HAS GREETED MY COMMUNIQUES FOR PAST TWO WEEKS. HAVE BEEN CARRYING OUT ALL ASSIGNED TASKS AND LOOK FORWARD TO FURTHER CONGRESS ON HOW BEST TO CONTINUE. MIGHT I PUT IN THE NOT UNREASONABLE REQUEST TO BE KEPT INFORMED WELL IN ADVANCE OF ANY UNUSUAL MILITARY MOVEMENTS EVEN IF SAID MOVEMENTS ARE ALLEGED TO BE ONLY FOR TRAIN-ING PURPOSES SHOULD SUCH UNUSUAL MILITARY MOVE-MENT OCCUR IN AND AROUND THE ASSIGNED REGION OF MY OWN DEPLOYMENT I.E. THOUGH THE NAME IS CERTAINLY WELL-KNOWN TO YOU RAJOTTAMA? REGARDS WHOBODY.

81

LAUNDRY LAUNDRY endless stains. She is thwocking the clothes on the rock hearing the song inside her. Laundry laundry. Far down the river, other women are doubtless hearing her beat it wrong, probably with nothing better to do than spy on their *coastal girl*. She has heard the duststorm of epithets in her widening wake and is sick of them all. No one has bothered to be her friend and after all is this village any better than the world of names she'd lived in at her sister's house?

Jehan had gotten so preoccupied he wouldn't teach her English even if she wanted him to. And Manu had awarded her a young boy's attentions until he got so busy he disappeared. She is condemned to fight for order in the Big House — the endless dirty laundry, for example. But she has her song, her Buddha and Vishnu, and she hopes for something greater coming along. Sometimes she waits on the log by the drive just to stare at the road. So what if the women sometimes gossip about her and how she sits and waits? or how she launders using the wrong rock and technique? It doesn't matter. The song is inside her, not them. They can't touch it. Anyway none of them do their laundry after four, and here she is, late in the day, beating out her song. Mischief has long been her savior.

As a child, she'd ambush her father in the dark, right as he came from his workshed, ready for dinner. She'd spirit herself like a little banshee onto his back so he would laugh. *Naughty gem*, he'd call her, smelling of sawdust.

Laundry laundry —

'— endless stains,' picks up a foreigner's voice. A man in a shirt like a brown bandage wrapped around his torso sits one rock above her. A boy really, with a face like Honree's, if lacking his dips and dents. The famous other foreigner — the one she hadn't looked at in the market! This boy could be made of pink boiled fruit except for the brown specks parading across his nose. In their blue, his eyes are strong and unrelenting, not like Honree's eyes, which are the color of water. Where this boy in his shirt is one pink piece. As if he could single-handedly guard for or against someone.

'Does it hurt you?' she asks back, tugging at her blouse without having meant to. He speaks good enough Sinhala that maybe she had misjudged him in that first meeting. Maybe in fact he is some kind of Burgher, someone who qualifies as a cockroach but who knows the language.

'The shirt?' He immediately understands. '*Should* it hurt me? Is it stained?' joking with her, speaking directly to her mischief. 'I'm Chris. You should know I'm also a flirt,' and because she doesn't know that English word she says back Manang kianne danae naeae, which is generally a good way to change the subject in most village conversations. Which he might know means *as for myself, I do not know.*

'You do know,' he goes on. 'Most likely everything. That's clear enough. What's your name?'

And this she doesn't want to tell. 'Guess.'

'Esmeralda? Genevieve? Susanna?'

She shakes her head. Like most of these people, possibly without knowing it, he says such embarrassing things. These people enter the world so foolishly and probably exit among similar shames.

'Then I'll call you Esmeralda,' snickering.

'Please don't. That's a disgusting name. If you have to call me something, call me Mala, which means *flow-er.*'

'Wouldn't I know that already, Mala?' Not one to hide his pride. Like Honree. He stands to survey the canal. 'See over there, the red?' She can't miss it; it covers the entire bank across. Croton never has a season, it blooms year round, insufferable red weed in any garden. 'That kind of flower, Mala?'

'That's silly. Please don't insult me. Croton is not really a flower.'

'But you are,' sitting down again, closer. 'Anyone would think you were a flower.'

'That's not true.'

'Prove it —' He skips stones across the water as though she could say anything she wants and he would take no offense.

'You are a stranger here. You have no idea what my place is here in this village.'

'Can't I guess? If you're a flower, you're a shy one, Mala.' He probably knows she enjoys this diversion. In that blue of his eyes, no harm can be done. 'But could it be, Mala, you're a flower who wants to come out?'

'You haven't told me anything about yourself,' she points out helpfully. 'Perhaps you are —'

'I'm a vegetable,' says the boy, 'you know, a *ladyfinger?*' and he uses the English word, which always gets her thinking of fancy women rather than okra, and the word makes them both laugh.

After a while the egrets come, winging it, harpoons across the sky. 'Should I be doing your laundry for you then, Mala?'

'Now that is really impossible.' He is sitting a little too close to her. Are his eyes too hard? 'I think, Chris the Falirt, whatever you are, I have to go back to the Big House.' And gathers Honree's underclothes, her skirts and Jehangir's pants into one wet parcel to stuff it all into her basket. Problem is, she hasn't finished rinsing, so tiny soap bubbles ride the surface of things.

'I don't know much about laundry, Mala, but if those stains aren't endless' — managing to pronounce such a hard Sinhala word! — 'doesn't seem to me like you've got a good hold on that. Can a person help you?'

'I'm needed at the Big House.' She begins walking up the path she had made herself among the sedge, leaving the boy in his awkward uniform. Just like some of the soldiers she had known! He tries too hard to keep her by the canal.

'Is he bad to you?' he asks her once she gets to the road. 'At the Big House?'

'No. Your questions, are they bad for you? What is it you're wanting, Chris the Falirt?'

'Me? I want to help with the laundry now and then?' and his voice so chirrupy and mock-innocent she can't help laughing again, even as she leaves him to his own thoughts, whatever they might be.

On this day laundry has been a better task than it usually is. Something is stirring in the world. It might be good fortune. In her altar room tonight, she will ask the Buddha and his helpers what to make of all this.

82

IT'S BEFORE DAWN that Henry wakes from a dream of tumbling with Lady B. to find Nani leaning over him in bed.

'What happened?' He jerks up.

She almost laughs. 'I come to help with clothes for the pil-grim-age and you call to me. Do not worry, Sir, Master, it is fine,' sweeping out. Once she is in the corridor outside his room, does she let herself laugh or sneeze?

That day he sees her crouching like an animal by the door to Jehan's cottage. She is peering through a hedge hole out at the road. From the stairtop, he clears his throat. 'We'll be out most of the morning,' he tells her, 'and we'll probably have lunch with the dance sisters.'

Now she jumps. Her interlocutor behind the hedge — invisible but for his shock of light hair — moves off. Was that the young soldier?

Is it Henry's imagination or has the hedge there begun to go bald, to afford her a better view of her roadside friend? Or friends? He will have to talk to the gardener about replanting — something thicker would be good.

'What, Sir?'

'The pilgrimage. To the forest monks. We have a meeting to discuss it. You'll be coming too, of course.'

She almost smiles. 'I like that, Sir.'

When that British soldier Chris is leisuring, Henry notes that he takes pains to greet almost every villager. He doesn't exclude Nani from his charm.

Seems that whenever the weather holds and she's out on the front lawn pinning and hanging — Johnny's whites, Henry's new native clothes, her bright cloths — the soldier comes in civvies, better than clockwork in his casualness.

Full of sandy-haired ruddy health, his young bulk leans on the tree. He addresses her pet cow. He chuckles.

'Talk to him often?' Henry asks her after one occasion, having limped down from the house while the soldier is still loping down the driveway.

The girl smells of bleach and citrusy sweat and something else. 'I talk to him when he talks to me, Sir. He keeps com-pa-ny. Helps me un-der-stand the village more. You like that, no? Learn English? Any-way, his language is good,' she finishes and covers her mouth. Though her voice is flat, her step away has a lilt, a bitter grace.

83

ONCE THE RAINS let up a little, Manu follows the movements of Chris and the British encampment closely. The day Chris calls in at the Pilima compound, the boy follows behind, hiding behind the palms. The children who usually tag him he banishes with a sharp *Shikshik!* — the same hiss he'd use to dismiss an evil spirit.

Today he will not be found out. He watches from his roadside coppice as the Englishman passes in those embarrassingly short pants, the kind only small boys wear, and a brown shirt that makes his arms seem uncomfortable slats strapped to the sides of his body. People have gone crazy over this monstrosity, these clothes. Manu cannot say why. Only that Rajottamans love uniforms.

The soldier is holding, visibly, a bottle of some English liquor, the kind for which many in the village would prostitute their mothers. The kind that shouts: a bribe is coming!

The Englishman does not falter or ask directions. In this, he is different from Jehan's pink man. He checks a map once, and makes a considered way to the gate of Lester Pilima's compound. What gives him such confidence?

Manu stays well-obscured as Lester comes to the gate. Reassuringly, Lester nods at his visitor, as villagers do to indicate someone is unwelcome or lower caste. Manu has seen Henry get this treatment far more than what Jehan can ever understand.

No doubt, a hundred paces off, Lester had recognized the bribe for what it was. Perhaps the Pilima will let some scorn enter his eyes, enough to make the Englishman fatally falter. The viper of the Pilimas' history will rise from behind Lester and spit on the visitor.

'Take your liquor!' Lester will sputter. 'Who needs your gifts? One foreigner is bad enough for our village!'

And despite the Pilimas' bad manners toward him and his family, Manu will again respect the Pilimas' history. He knows it backward and forward. There was the 1818 Pilima appointed by the English to work with the other Sinhalese chiefs. The Pilima was supposed to ask his fellow Kandy chiefs to hand over their kingdom. But brave man, the Pilima, he'd instead jumped to the rebels' side. He'd held forth vainly but courageously against the inevitable surrender. Perhaps Lester was not a true Pilima; still, he could have the family's viper sting.

What happens is different.

Some roughness in his soul, Manu watches as the Pilimas lose their history. Because what happens is that Lester fiddles with his hairpiece and smiles like a real sahib-sayer. Finally he takes the liquor; rather curtly, it is true, but takes it nonetheless. And retreats with another twiddle of his hair and a bright suggestion — in English! — back to his compound, which has just lost the world.

Did that happen? Manu forgets to make himself invisible again. Instead he and the soldier eye each other like two rams on the road.

'You're the temple drummer, aren't you?' the soldier asks, friendly enough, but with untwitching blue eyes. This alone is an insufferable rudeness. Is Manu a book, not a man, to be read? No Sinhalese would hold another's eyes like that.

'Yes, I like the drums,' Manu says in his best English. 'That is true, yes —'

The soldier accepts this and moves on six paces. Evidently another thought comes to him. 'You and your father might want this, wouldn't you?'

From another of his many pockets he pulls out a small tan bottle, another amulet. Manu has grabbed and hidden the bottle in his pocket so quickly even the soldier seems surprised. Why be surprised?

'Don't drink it all. Give it to your father too,' says the soldier. 'Cheers!'

Cheers? Manu hangs back and lets the soldier move off, a man who'd just gotten a bad bargain. His father *would* appreciate the gift. More than that kasippu-drinker, Lester Pilima, recipient of bribes. Because clearly there was nothing the drummers would be able to give such a soldier.

This is poverty's last gift. If anyone had been thinking of bribes, Manu for his part stays innocent. The drummers cannot be bribed. Because drummers cannot return any favors.

VII

THE CROSSING

꧁ ꧁ ꧁

182. Q. What did the Buddha think of ceremonialism?
    A. He condemned the observance of ceremonies and other external practices. These increase our spiritual blindness and our clinging to lifeless forms.

183. Q. But don't Buddhists make reverence before the statue of the Buddha, his relics, and the monuments enshrining them?
    A. Yes, but not with an idolater's sentiment.

184. Q. What's the difference?
    A. Our pagan brother considers his images not just visible representations of his unseen God or gods but that the images contain in their substance a portion of the all-pervading divinity.

185. Q. What does the Buddhist think?
    A. He or she reverences the statue and other things you have mentioned only as souvenirs of the wisest and most benevolent man in this world-period (kalpa). All races and people preserve and treasure relics of men and women considered in any way great. The Buddha, to us, seems more revered and beloved than any other, by every human being who knows sorrow.

84

ON THEIR WAY HOME after the long pilgrimage, the pomegranate sun slips into the horizon, into what they call a tank, a reservoir so still and full.

Returning after all these lauds, tributes and night services, all that idolatry is over with. Really the best thing to remark upon at this moment, Henry finds, are the tree trunks, the way they measure the shore and that vast manmade expanse. How their torquings resemble Nani's body. Yes: it was undeniable that her body at the water pump *had* twisted toward him, that first dawn after the pilgrims' arrival. Twisted toward; then away. That could still count as toward.

After three days of travel — of effort, of a moment at the pump, of nothing — the people's pilgrimage is coming to an end, he hopes.

Though she pretends to sleep in their cart — he turns back from guiding the bullocks to check on her — her mouth is pursed, its beacon pink stripe marking the lower lip's peeled skin. Ha, it's as though she already has some of him on her. Pink, he'll say when she wakes. *Pink?*

You are pink, Sir, she had said once.

What is she? Of the four qualities which Suba says a good woman must possess, doesn't she lack at least one? *Fair — tall — reserved — clever.* Would she fill that picture for others? Do they find her fair? sepia-skinned? That *fair* might mean *beautiful* — he'd have to ask Suba — signifies how the people stay sadly colonial to their last heartbeat. Perhaps too she wouldn't be considered *reserved:* on this pilgrimage she'd tried mightily to betray that other life you can so easily sense within her, depths below. But her forward movement, the way she thrusts out into the world! If she succeeds in camouflage, he envies her such a capacity.

More important: what does she make of him, his hands, big feet, hairy legs? His red nose and its propensity to sweat after a spiced meal? To her is he so much white sausage?

The closest she had ever come to telling him who he was to her: *You are pink, Sir* — that was it, the extent of him in her spoken life. Pink.

His tongue smolders with what could be said.

Silence, though — there's just her pursed mouth pretending to sleep and the rut of wheels on pocked roads. After the dam the caravan heads off the main road, without anyone consulting him, into yet another ancient village. Weren't they homeward bound? Henry wants his own bed! Do these people delight in hardship? The Ceylonese, they laugh while crammed together on such uncomfortable carts. What is unknown about leadership or consensus or plenary sessions here boggles the mind.

Entering a village they are greeted by smeared urchins who gather like lint, running ahead by Lester's cart, gasping out their help. 'Eden, Eden, Eden,' they whoop, pointing in every cardinal direction.

Once the pilgrims pull outside a house, the children fall wracked. A tall man with a nimbus of bright white hair emerges, and claps together the hands of Lester and Appuhamy.

'What selfishness' — tarred with fatigue Henry speaks to Nani's opened eyes — 'we detoured so Lester can meet a friend?'

'The man is an herb doctor,' Nani says in a low voice. 'Like Appuhamy.'

All this for a sorcerer named Aiden? But yes — the Rajottamans dismount their carts and wind through the dark town in a slow drove, yoked as tourists, coming onto an oversize field.

Here coir rope circles an area made seductive and aglow from hundreds of votives. Under a white tent's slow billows, an elaborate structure of wood, woven straw and flowers presides — a structure hardly unique, signifying nothing.

Sensing magic, Henry screws up his face.

In the tent, a string leads from a pregnant girl to the central altar. Amid dusky, wet-earth clouds of myrrh, a litter of small children make as if they own the girl, plumping pillows and fanning madly.

It starts to look doubtful that this evening will hold any redemption for Henry. Redemption he needs more than these sneering men and children do. Some eye from the sky could bother to take him in once in a while; hasn't it been eons since anyone has asked *his* advice? Men are all the while bringing coconuts filled with billowing smoke and rotating them before the painted deities.

'These are planets,' the sorcerer Aiden explains in a custardy English for the foreigner. 'The expecting girl is my niece.'

She leans back, sheer bloat stunning her, soaking up the men's attention. Henry's interest is held more by two trios of older men with smashed faces.

'Beira caste,' Suba whispers. 'Please! Mister Fyre, sit here!'

Here, there, what does it matter? So much scuffling. So many birds in a cage. One of the trios shudders and cues the others' singing; which means six elderly men cup their ears and emit some flesh-scraping melody:

> How sad so few men recall
> Those creatures who recall
> All our past acts!

At this, the drums start their pounding, cuing the sorcerer, who steps out, newly clothed, his face that of a depraved vaudevillian. Sure, there's some kind of stunning luminosity in Aiden. He has bound a sarong and thick red sash around such a boyish waist. It's not envy but a wind that chills Henry's bones. Aiden's torso is bare but for a blazing silver escutcheon — the silver armbands zigzagged around the arms, the earrings jiggling. With aplomb, Aiden hops rhythmically, flexes his feet. He knows his audience, he can make the children grab one another in fear, in glee —

All too horrible. From the makeshift stage comes a pretentious fanfare. It would be hard to subdue any of this but Henry's pen tries:

> What command Aiden possesses: a sorcerer chanting deep in
> some dream of his own, eyes fixed upon him. He licks his lips
> & his head vibrates.

Meanwhile, the three singers start calling out agreement with Aiden's public declamations. Do their thin faces mouth his own name? *Gould, Gould, Gould* —

No. It is just *O, O, O* that he hears.

Captivity and sudden death. He laughs, embarrassed, and scans for Nani, finds her seated a coquettish distance away, near the drummer's son. Her mouth and its pink stripe, how she bites her lip. In flirtation or pain? He'd have to talk to her about propriety before the villagers. That stare of hers, so coy toward the performer. If the field had not been so crowded, Henry would push — informally — through the dispensable others, squeeze in close by. But first he'd have to invent a task for her.

The sorcerer has started to dance in earnest. Like a woman, a man, a woman all over again. He becomes a mad syntax of wile and curve with a pot on his hip. Woman flywheeling a wand and then in labor pains, woman dimpling at the drumroll. Under the white canopy he undoes Henry with this dancing, these drums, incense and old men, crooners, pulling their earlobes.

Henry jams a kerchief to his nose. What god does Aiden possess to intrigue them all so absolutely? Henry's pen slips but he masters it:

> Does Nani envy motherhood? All the man's motion is for the
> pregnant girl's easy childbirth. This is the kind of collective
> spirit we must reproduce at the dance school. WHERE IS THE
> BUDDHISM IN THIS?

Aiden imitating a rooster's backward walk. Aiden at solemn moments, his prominent torso hovering above feet that start to whorl until he sinews for comedy like a real Hindoo. Such opaque intersections. All while the niece uninterruptedly chews her betel with rice and the people stay agog. Finally a bell signals intermission to the sorcerer's act.

Suba's chin juts into Henry's shoulder. 'How lucky the girl is!' hooting. Suba explains that now the child will receive blessings from Sikuraa, the same goddess as the planet Venus, a helper of women. 'These lines between the gods and us must be drawn lest we forget.'

'Lest we forget what?' asks Henry. 'Never mind.'

Though the ceremony continues inside, Henry sleepwalks like a gigantic slave into the night and its cool exotic. Under the sarong his sex stretches on his thigh soft as a loving finger. Impulsive, yes, to stand on his cart, a different kind of throne; but not so impulsive as what takes place under that canopy with that sorcerer's splay-footed dance. Henry Fyre Gould has undertaken so many journeys.

The very tips of his hands buzz. Power the magnet, power the snake. He will address those who have followed him out. In English he begins, his own voice a relief, beating back the night but drawing in the indistinct smudges of their faces. 'What happens when you vest too much in an object? What happens when the object gets shattered?'

Abraham in Ur had also been scared to smash his father's idols. But only with such daring could anyone be drawn back toward a tradition's truth. Henry's excitement lassos everything. He knows how to pull: to wrap them up and haul them back toward wisdom. This being what he can offer, a mere warm-up. And how their moonlit gazes stay in his thrall! 'No need to be sheep!'

For a second this hamlet turns into home: home, the swirl of lavender and gray, back when he was lecturing at the base of Central Park, at his most triumphant. Dazzling lights at the corner of his vision. It is true that old man Suba keeps calling up to him, a botheration and constant nausea, saying 'I am sorry, Mister Fyre.'

When Henry finally peers down, Suba explains that none of these people speak English. Henry would do better to have Suba translate for him.

'Never mind!' Henry didn't mean to have shouted. He just hates how at *his* moments, everyone tries to pounce. 'Tell them they can understand intention — or let them take in *ether!*' sounding like Madame, again without having planned it so.

But he *does* have a mission; and sometimes with these people, to outline a body you practically had to use shotguns. So Henry outlines: speaking of the mistake of myopia, the boon of Buddhism, the paganism of literal devotions. Among his audience the dance school sisters have come, there to watch Henry at his broadest coordinates. The tips of their saris cover their mouths — out of bashfulness or wistfulness or pride, he does not care, let them understand themselves. There's no codebook for such things. When the ceremony inside has an intermission, more renegades emerge to hear Henry. And this only fires him more.

Among their devil-may-care souls — he sees the majority of his listeners are not from his village — a little boy toward the front remains his most attentive audience, with a face unusually expressive. To the end the boy keeps up a terrific call-and-response.

Soon, though, a rushing jeer sends blood to Henry's ears, long before his final cadence has been reached. Why should he stop? A stream at first, perfectly ignorable; but the sound grows ceaseless, a roar enough to shake the hills, storm the region.

He does note when Nani, eyes unquiet, comes to lead the little boy at the front, taking him by the hand back to his mother. Such love and understanding she can show. There's surely something she's trying to save him from — he might not wholly know what — but she shouldn't worry. No one should.

Because if Henry stops to think of shame (even while stepping off his cart) everything might as well dribble away; he'd start losing himself to strangers. And who can afford that? Certainly, of all people, not Nani; not Nani most of all.

On the far-off dawn hills, women with heads flung back are crying out, shaking rattles high in the air. Alongside, masked naked men brandish and parry daggers, spearing staves that vomit trails of sparks. Dancing pigs in little capped outfits follow behind. All of it is a terrible rash against the sky.

Henry chuckles, incredulous, and the women fade.

'I'll drive for you, Fyre, yes?' offers Suba. He clutches the American's arm.

'Thank you.' This Henry will accept. His lungs ache with a desire to shout back at anyone but there is nothing to be said. His own palms stretched out before him are fascinating, angel-white, ten-fingered, mountainous, never before so tremulous.

As they begin the drive, he can't keep his mind and heart detached from frustration. If Buddhism is correct, his frustration and clinging would make him enter some fiery rebirth spiral a hundred million times over. But it is *grasping* that is bad, not *aspiring*. And in none of the suttas do they ever discuss the idea of the scapegoat. And wouldn't it be hard for anyone to practice Buddhism when the world keeps deriding you all the time, when you're reduced to thanking people for nothing more than a tempered scorn? His speech wasn't that bad. If the people spoke English better, they would've understood.

85

START ALWAYS with the coconut. Ax it into halves with one swoop.

Then perch yourself on the platform just above the ground. One leg here, another there. Make sure the little metal prong between is clean. Then you roll the coconut on it this way and that. Like a sister or auntie has shown you to do. Don't think of your coconut as a head because that is disgusting. Think only of the milk that will come once you press the coconut that petals out from around the prong.

While you core, it helps to sing a song from your childhood. No matter how fast you go, it always takes a while. But unless you grind enough, there won't be milk and not enough milk means you'll have a bad curry.

Once you're done with the nuts, chop onions into little tongues on a board you've wet down so you don't cry. When you get to the chilies, they are lovely. Long, green and waxy but angry inside. Even your fingertips smart as you chop — no matter how much water you use. Whatever you do, don't rub your eyes. You'll go blind. And you've got to peel the garlic, cut it into teeth and tusks. Then with the pestle, you grind the black and red peppers with the cumin and whatever else is on hand to make your curry. By the time you get to grating inguru, you've got to check the rice. Make sure the fire is steady but low under your oiled iron pan.

Tonight because it is a special night after the pilgrimage we have cashews that Jehan brought from the city market, many of them nestled together. After almost a week on the road, eating even a single cashew in a house with roof and walls tastes delicious. It's almost a reason to be reborn. Always it is good to put cashews in with the coconut's first milk. They soak up the flavor. It is when these cashews are at the stirring stage that he walks by, Honree, doing what he usually does, which means looking for something he has misplaced.

'Seen my book?' he asks. It is easy to let him understand in many little ways but really only in one big way when there is cooking going on and thus no freedom to talk. And Honree knows but doesn't like to admit he knows: how easy it is to talk without words.

There had been that first day in our journeys when we became one village on the path, so many other villages flowing into us and each hanging its flags on different trees. And all Honree did was squawk around like one of his bad chickens. Trying to keep up with everyone all at once, his mouth working the whole time.

In a crowd, such talking is not possible. You have to be mindful mindful mindful about everything. Who and why. And what. Someone never taught him this. And no one had ever taught him how to walk barefoot, he the only one with shoes clodhopping over all the vines and paths. Meanwhile, he kept asking everyone for a map.

Then there was that first night. We had finally arrived thirsty and tired at the jungle hall, a hall without walls where howler monkeys shrieked their happiness at having guests. We women were supposed to stay up all night. To chop and grind, to cook curry for the forest monks. But first we had to eat dinner. For the first time, during that dinner, Rutaeva became a village for me: all the men and women, together on mats. And I among them.

I among them but then Honree had to sink himself across like a sorcerer studying me. Each time he wrote something down, I knew he was trying to get me to look at him. From me he'd get no look. Let him go find a doll from one of those traveling shows, if he wanted, a doll to jerk from strings! But next to me was Manu courting my laughter out. The boy doing nothing, just balancing a plate atop his head and making faces. Still I laughed. Such a young boy never knows when to stop!

Because of him I was angry. I wanted to hear the story of why that boy had gone astray from me. Do you do anything else other than try to win girls all the time? I whispered to that boy.

He took what I said wrongly as an invitation. After a pause too long and full of meaning he said, No, all I ever do is try to win *one* girl.

Just to shun that pause, I had to laugh and make Honree stare again. But about all these looks I wasn't about to complain exactly. Because that night who wasn't looking? Even the high-and-mightys. Even some of those Rutaeva men who wish to act as if Nani Bandu is the low girl! Even the Pilima men and their friends.

In me a happy life was starting again. People were looking. Everyone knows when such a happy life begins again.

Across the way Suba was forcing Honree to talk about the stale pork that killed the Buddha. Even though Honree's rumpled pink mouth was saying Yes, yes, of course, the pork, his eyes cried something else (as did Suba's). They all wanted something, yes yes of course, and that something was from me was how it appeared.

Late that night most people curled into sleep under their cloths like hard little cashews but a circle of us on the porch listened to Suba reading aloud about the Buddha in his early days, Buddha a prince untempted by those palace dancing women. I among the listeners too until I saw Honree tottering around in the candles' bad light. For once his face was more than pale ash — it almost had color.

Peculiar how I wanted to rise and tease Honree. But more than that I wished to sink and hide, stay in the low brush behind. So that's what I did. Mischief should be called a protector god. Because of mischief, hiding was not such a bad moment. Actually it turned out to be a very nice moment. With Suba's calm voice and Honree looking for me, Little Gem warmed by the dark had come back into me.

The most important thing is never forget and let onions burn. If you're prone to forgetting, if you don't slice perfectly, you must fry on a low fire. Anyway a low fire's always better — so long as water jumps on the oil's surface and the onions melt into yellow and sometimes black sugar, then the curry will be fine. Your patience is better than cumin, there to help everything else. On the pilgrimage, when the sun rose that first day, I wasn't hungry so I let the others eat and went off to bathe alone at the camp's single well and tap. Just after dawn in my lungi with my hair down and shoulders showing like we're used to — but he is such a stranger!

He came running as though to tell me something important. Really I knew he had nothing to say. Like a dark blot on the hilltop he stopped — stared — and then became some bird flying down at me. All I could think was: This crazy wants to eat me.

So I said before leaving him: Use this water for your bath.

And left my bucket. But when I passed he did nothing human, only stared — so were the moons of my breasts rising? did he see the tops lighter like his room's mirror had once shown?

I tugged the cloth up higher but certain eyes you cannot escape. Of course the cloth was wet on me. If you're an elegant lady, only your cousin-brothers will see you like this. But here we don't bother about shoulders. We have shoulders all the time. Shoulders and wet cloth. Had I known the words, that's what I would've said. But I couldn't tell him. What would I have said? that it was rude to watch unless asked? And hadn't I been spying on him, just a little, while he slept? Maybe he was punishing me.

'Medusa hair,' he whispered just before I left. What sense did that make? His breath surrounded my shoulders like creepers. Who had trained this man to have his too-hot breath?

When you cook curry, dogs always come sniffing. Here they're mad with skinniness. That's why dogs learn certain houses. They know I'm the kind that gives rice. Because of Honree's accident, he doesn't like if I feed the dogs or really anyone but him so if he's around I hiss those curs away. He has no idea how much I do to help him. So many times on this pilgrimage, I hid things or helped him, which usually means the same thing.

Hiding and helping. Like when all the monks came forward on the jungle path toward our hall, Honree was standing in their way. I told him, Get to the side! which meant to hide himself more. And he did what I said, he stood behind Lester Pilima. Because I had been watching and was the first to see the monks coming from far through the green, bits and jots of orange starting to stick together, butterflies of orange becoming exquisite men on the path with their robes and parasols. They emerged into the sun. All twelve of them looking pure and unafraid of the jungle, the one where we'd heard leopards howl their love sounds.

While Suba and Lester Pilima washed each monk's feet with the care you'd give little newborns, my heart beat out a strange rhythm. Finally, monks — and each stepping into the hall. Each having meditated for years, that's how it looked. That morning the women, I among them, had braided all the areliya garlands and placed everywhere small candles.

When we sat before the shiny-headed monks to chant precepts and do some bavana, I sneaked a look at Honree whose eyes were tightly shut. He was rocking back and forth and calling out too many times, Buddham saranam gacchami. Still there was something fine in the way he moved. For a second, I considered his mouth, full like a child's, not like a butterfly's wings, what a child's mouth might mean on a hip and its curve. Then I missed the second chant.

But the monks, they couldn't match us. During the dharma talk the senior monk was talking about false consciousness, papanca this and papanca that. But you could tell all the monks with their fans up and fans down were tired or didn't care what they were doing. Even though they would eat our food later. During the dharma talk, I noticed they mostly burped or yawned or just fanned.

The women and I among them stood in line afterward to talk to the few of the monks and when we didn't all get a chance at darshan, Kumari said these monks were disappointing. To the forest monks, we were just another village who'd come to devote ourselves and grab merit for a better rebirth. These were not monks like the old days. Even if I hadn't met any of the old-time monks, I still agreed. Everyone was chiming in.

'Used to be different.'

'Show no love for the commoner.'

'Now some monks are wicked, you can tell —'

'They accept such a large offering from us.'

'Meditators! on their cushions!'

'And only speak a memorized dharma talk —'

'From one of the sermon books!'

'He didn't even know which village we all were from. Or who our monk was.'

'No, one laughed when he heard it was our Pandit Thero. Can

you believe the impudence, saying our monk is a good one for trouble?'

This was another point where I'd tried to help Honree. But he'd just shoved in and asked the young monk what was meant by our Pandit being a good one for trouble? The monk had laughed and covered his mouth. Said he didn't gossip. Then he added that our monk Pandit Thero was a known man to some of the monks from their monastery days. I could tell Honree wanted to pry into this man with his oily face but that would have been bad so I gestured to save him and said something like Mahattea, shouldn't we pack?

But when he wants to be, Honree is very good at ignoring me and that was a time when he was good. Instead of listening to me, he asked the monk: What is it about Pandit Thero?

And the young monk hemmed and hobnosed and said only that they had heard Pandit had a very good post now, did he not, even if it *was* just a little out of the way there in Rajottama, no?

This was when Pushpa had said Rajottama wasn't so out of the way because our village guards the Sacred Tree and isn't too far from the Great City! The young monk was wrong!

But the monk just answered Honree and Pushpa and all the women and me among them waiting to talk: 'Yes, yes, good wishes upon you too.'

That's all he said and then like a jellyfish closing he rushed back to his monks. Back with them just to float back to their hermitage on their path with their clean feet and even more gorgeous golden sandals.

The problem with curry is you have to change your flame constantly, depending on your sauce and its circumstances. With a thick sauce, you dampen the flame. With a thin sauce, you must find more banana refuse to coddle the fire until the smoke licks up. If you're making cashew chicken curry with the bad birds Jehan will bring later from the coops, you need to worry once the cashews start to dance around in the coconut cream. Too soon the little ones can grow fat with the oil floating to the top. I am not ignorant of the difference between a good curry and a rushed one. Among the sisters — even if Eka never let me cook once she married — they used to call me the best cook. At that time Little Gem was good enough for them.

The evening after the bad dharma talk we left the forest monks to travel toward a huge pomegranate of a sun. I had never seen the sun look so bloody. We turned into a village where a sorcerer named

Aiden was ceremonializing. The point was to invite Sikuraa planet to help birth Aiden's niece's child. But in the middle of the ceremony (when Aiden was dancing with his nice silver breastplate and head-piece tinkling) Honree got upset and left the canopy.

So silly, this pink man, he'd gone outside to stand on our cart. Why must he get so fired up in this language which helps no one? He himself doesn't know the answer.

He started in talking about truth, that much I understood, and about his most favorite thing: *super-stitching, super-stitching.* But while he was speaking, there was a small nephew of the great Aiden's who stood in front. He had talent, that boy, imitating this book of a man with all sorts of movements. He was swelling and then smacking his bare chest. Pointing angrily at the throng of us. Smearing the kohl bindi-dot between his eyes.

Generally mocking this foreigner of mine.

It was at the back of the group that the cackle began. Nobody was listening, dawn was stabbing us, most were cold and stiff after such a long rainbow of a night. As people do — as I would maybe do if I didn't know Honree — everyone was looking for excuses to laugh and move. I heard them.

'*Anay,* isn't this cockroach a rare one?' they roared, throwing coins at the stage to unsettle Honree. But I knew him, and knew he would just keep yammering on. He acted like a big statue, didn't give in at all. But the cackle, it became a regular babble and then my pink man, he couldn't make himself heard.

Even if he didn't know better, *I* knew. So I took that little mocker of a boy by the hand and led him away from making fun.

Because never should you treat a guest like that, even if a guest is going on and on. Never is it nice. More than forgetting full-moon day, such treatment, treating a guest like that — this gets noticed as a much bigger sin.

86

Her faculty of surprise is virtually infinite. At least, those surprises she bothers to show him. Like her gift for decoration. Henry had no idea she could be such an aesthete. He decides that were he to try to graph her he could never succeed. She would be horizonless.

The first night after their return from the pilgrimage, she set a table moody and noble enough to make a king envious. On a fine cloth — one with an embroidered crimson stork flying over yellow marsh reeds — she has placed:

> a polished bronze tureen of pumpkin curry
>> pinwheels of okra pooled in turmeric-golden coconut oil
>> tiny green chilies striping jeweled onion slices
>> a bronze spoon, carved into an elephant's trunk

pointing to hunks of chicken from the first and last of the noisy Welsummers.

Now stripped of nationality and stewed with cashews, these chickens are Henry's pride. They can't peck each other to death anymore. Of course, the girl — so thoughtful! — has prepared enough of the fine imported samba rice, tiny eyes of grain, to feed a conquering battalion.

Had Madame given up her lama to come keep Henry company in Ceylon, *she* would be the one wearing the Indian necklace of colored cut-glass beads which Henry had won in a salon card game. At the time he thought he'd gift Madame with the necklace in a moment of tearful reconciliation. Instead, tonight, struck by the picturesque table, before the guests arrive, he gives the necklace to Nani.

'You and I, we survived the pilgrimage,' he tells her. He breathes on her, trying to clasp the thing at her nape. 'We helped each other, didn't we?'

She assents or doesn't. Who could say? Her performance for the moment is to linger and shrug. And move away at the behest of an eternal errand.

Better than remembering is to look at her now, aglow in the new necklace: he loves how its prisms catch and reflect the votives' rays. Tonight in the candlelight all the dinner guests' eyes sparkle, tremendously. Their faces revive him, they ravish him. Were it not for outlandish Ceylonese taboos, Henry would hug them all with a seaman's embrace.

He had carefully arranged seating arrangements like an elaboration of his heart and vision. Home again, at a celebratory dinner, he is back in control. For the first time in the boat of a house, his Nani will take her place at the table on Henry's propitious right side. Just beyond will be Johnny, followed by the drummer's son Manu, now stretching out those insolent legs, and Regi anchoring the prow, scrawny shoulders cloaked in ceremonial white.

The last seat stands empty.

On the other side of Nani presides Pushpa Pilima, hair oiled neatly; her Samitha next to her, talking with his hands to Lester, who adjusts his toupee, surveying the guests with a captor's benevolence.

And finally, at the end, near the drummer, beloved but remote, the two dance school sisters have roosted, Kumari and Sonali. Their saris may be threadbare but the women are a crowning glory for Henry. The sisters can so often wipe out everything else. Straightforward and splendid, true supporters, they are a just configuration. Culture, humanity, substance. Almost as good as his boy.

'Johnny has been phenomenal ballast for us,' Henry is telling Pushpa. 'He manned the house during our pilgrimage.'

He watches Johnny slide around the table and slap Manu on his knee. *Moves like me now*, Henry cannot help thinking. *A kind of son.*

And now, safety-valved into a good mood, Henry stands for a toast of *teleje*.

'I'm almost too grateful seeing all of you. Come sit. You, Lester, whose family name and past devotions brought us interviews with hermit monks at our Mecca. We can never forget the experience.'

The others' hands tremble raising the unwieldy goblets. In a rush of grandiosity, Henry's undeterred. His mood is dawning and he must finish.

'Samitha, you who watched so well over our possessions while traveling. You, Pushpa, who always gives good advice. Of course, we're always grateful to Nani, for her help,' glancing away quickly to his right.

He can't help touching her smooth hand. Lilac, silk, talc. Even her hand rounds out toward him. Johnny breaks the momentary spell with a complicated set of coughs.

Once the boy's finished, Henry nods. 'And Manu. Your roadside ceremonies with your father' — he nods at the drummer — 'gave the people faith to carry on and . . .'

Henry notices the empty chair.

'We forgot to invite the monk,' Henry reprimands Johnny.

A quick consult follows. Johnny is stricken. The sisters set down their goblets. Should Johnny be sent to bring the monk?

'Beg pardon? The monk will have eaten already,' Johnny states. 'Monks are not supposed to eat after twelve noon. Anyway, while you've been gone, the Brits have been feeding him. That's what I think, at least.'

Even worse. 'Would you mind, Johnny? — we've never had him for a meal. He'll be especially flattered that it's you coming to bring him.'

'Righto.' The boy marches out into the gathering dark, the egrets in their night tree cooing at his approach. From the table it's all too easy to hear how the boy stumbles on the stone stairs set into the wet hill, how he stumbles and falls but collects himself, cursing in hoarse accents.

It's easy to hear the worry in Henry's assurance to the gathered: 'My trusted aide's fine, surely —'

'Shall we eat before these flies ruin the food Nani has made so well?' asks Pushpa, stroking the hair off her face.

Henry insists that Nani serve all of them immediately. They should begin eating together in democratic American style. 'Come,' he cries, 'no time to waste.'

Among the guests, however, there prevails a most stringent courtesy.

Thus the foreigner is the first to begin eating, rice falling in an uncivil rain from his fingers. After a conspicuous pause the high-farmer caste, Lester, Pushpa, Samitha, begin to mix rice with curries.

Here is when Regi, without meaning to, cues his son and the dance sisters. Finally, seated next to the foreigner, Nani, a girl from somewhere along the coast, eats at the same moment as the man of her house.

Henry stays impervious to this fastidious choreography. He chastises Nani for turning slightly away from the table's circle of flickering faces. And dares again to touch her eating hand. He would pull her back into that happy circumference but she won't budge. When he asks why not — and really, why not? — she says in unhushed Sinhalese that tonight's customs are peculiar already; to alter too much too quickly would not be right.

By the time the foreigner's aide stalks into the dining room, only Regi — pleased at the charm exhibited by himself and his son, the general warmth rendering him an equal dinner companion among these Madames and Sirs — only he continues to feast on his third helping of rice.

This dinner rewards him, Regi thinks. Three helpings is not so much. Not even four. Maybe five. During this ambitious trip, the pilgrims have recognized his true worth, his indispensability in their petitions to the gods. Even the famous sorcerer Aiden had practically bowed at his feet!

Regi is nothing less than a servitor of ancient tradition, divinity's own channel. And his own paddy's rice had never, but never, tasted like this. So dainty, possessing the pearled ivory color of temple carvings. He smacks his lips loud with satisfaction.

'Where's our monk?' Henry demands of Johnny.

'He's making his way here. He sent me on,' Johnny explains, shiftily, popping a salted tamarind into his mouth.

'What, does Pandit have a problem with eating this late?'

Johnny grimaces. 'What do you think? Your monk was pleased enough to come. If you want to know, he says he's actually quite hungry. He even complained that community donations toward his lunch today had been a bit sparse. "During the pilgrimage we didn't see much food at all." Turns out the British failed to feed him.'

'Oh!' Henry quavers, guilty. It is so hard to keep everyone happy. And yet for the village of the future to succeed, there must be a modicum of happiness among everyone.

'When he comes, check his round cheeks,' Johnny's saying. 'Your teacher's no forest monk, Henree.'

A frown crosses the Pilima contingent across the table and Johnny silences himself. He carries on with the meal service, however, nodding to Nani as she serves him rice, cupping his hands immediately over his plate to signal *enough*.

'True our monk's no forest monk. Because he's a village monk, that's why,' Lester intones after a sufficient pause, with all the sanctimony such a bear could manage.

'We are glad to hear you express it so plainly,' Pandit says from the shadows. 'Why should we grumble when we are happy to be here among you?'

No one knows how long the round monk has been standing in a corner of the room left dark by the waning votives. His buttery voice doesn't hide the gloom of one who's remained back from the jollity of an extended trip. Before the pilgrimage, Pandit had begged off, saying that these particular forest monks were 'known' to him, making his knowledge sound unpalatable. He'd said his time would be better served reading scripture than studying how monks get served their rice.

'Come sit, saddhu,' Henry directs, rising from the table. He would give anything to find happy footing tonight. 'Holy man. Please. We've missed you so much. Some of the forest monks said they knew you, I think.'

Henry pulls the chair next to the drummer, who pays no mind. Regi is set on serving himself more of the chicken curry.

'Regi,' Pushpa hisses from her end.

The drummer stares at her. '*Rasay*,' he says without ceasing to eat, '*hari rasay*. Really delicious. The girl's cooked well, Sir Henry.'

'Please, Pandit, sit,' Henry invites the monk.

Even in the lick of dim taperlight, the monk looks ill at the idea of sitting next to the drummer. And the drummer's chewing grows more exaggerated. He gulps down his food with violence and stretches over the table to ladle himself the last of the ladyfinger pinwheels. His scrawny shoulders and right hand reinvolve themselves in the scooping and proper mixing of his dinner.

'We will sit here' — Pandit indicates a bench against the wall.

In what Henry sees as Lester's customary show of aggressive respect, the Pilima stands abruptly, with Pushpa and Samitha following his lead. One half of the table has abandoned their seats.

Why doesn't everyone calm down? Henry wonders.

'I won't have it!' he declares. A mock boisterous tone takes him over. He's aping his idea of a good host. Annoyed that the words emerge as if a human heart is missing. 'After coming so far! They've treated you poorly while we were away, right? We must return you to proper spirits. Please. Pandit. Saddhu. We have Welsummer chicken from the new coops!'

Inspired by his role — gracious, seigneurial — Henry forgets himself. He seizes his teacher's shoulders and pushes him to sit down.

All awkwardness, the monk must sit next to Regi.

Pushpa cries out as though she chokes on her tongue. The dance school sisters, still seated, nudge each other. Forced next to the lowly drummer, the monk glances away from the man licking his fingers and grunting. With the same hand, the drummer reaches for the elephant ladle.

'Manu! at least tell your father to stop eating!' Pushpa whispers.

Manu leans back in his chair, relaxed, his long legs stretched before him. The boy shrugs and smiles. He makes a swilling sound to ask *how can I restrain my own father?*

Henry takes the serving spoon from Regi's plate and demands that Nani should bring more of the ladyfingers. Is there no extra? Hurriedly, Henry ladles rice into a sprawling heap upon the monk's plate, some grains spilling onto the holy man's lap. 'Take this,' he insists. 'Nani, serve him.' And like the host he has learned to be in this country, a good man and a righteous host, Henry stands over the monk to compel him to eat. 'Pandit, eat, please.'

Fascinated, the dance school sisters lean toward each other; Lester can't control his rolling shoulders; Pushpa leaves the room.

'Pandit, please, eat —' Henry invokes what he knows is the formidable power *over* the guest in this country; because why should it be wrong for the monk to rub elbows with his own temple's servitor?

As though any doubt remains, Henry commands: 'Eat, Pandit, holy man. Saddhu.'

Manu offers up his low tuneless hum as the monk and the drummer both mix their rice with gravy. The men pinch their rice — at this, Regi sniggers toward his son. With their right hands, both monk and drummer raise and chew and swallow, raise and chew and swallow.

Will no one move? 'You can eat!' Henry tells the others. 'Aren't you hungry? This isn't a performance! What were we discussing? Please continue!'

But Pandit finishes his meal long before the drummer and jumps up, snaring his robe on the chair. 'Thank you, Colonel Fyre. For your salutations. Your company. Your kind thoughts.' A fresh wind blows into the room.

'Will you not have tea?' Henry coaxes.

'Who drinks tea at this hour?' Pushpa shrieks. She's lost control, there at the threshold, folding and refolding her napkin. O would they not all contain themselves? Just for a moment, just for his benefit? But no, they *would* cast glances, every one of them, here and there, Henry can see that much; Manu at Jehan and then all around the table, everyone.

'Stop looking around!' Henry shouts at no one in particular, softening, 'please?' But after his voice comes a rude hiccough and hiss from what has been underneath the dinner-table conversation — the dying fire in the next room.

Johnny seemingly cannot help his mouth's ironic twist. 'At least something's eating.'

Triggered by his words, which they probably don't understand, the dance school sisters give in to hilarity. And these are his loyal ones, *his* women, Kumari and Sonali but now convulsed in laughter, forced to use the ends of their saris to wipe their eyes; mute and contorted by a trembling vise, the sisters wave their hands as though they've become weak paws.

Thank God that it is Lester who wants them to shut up, that it is Lester who stamps his foot. 'It's just fire!' says the Pilima. 'Stop it! This can't go on' — but even during this outburst Regi goes on eating and the monk still hovers holding his robe and all the while the women are unable to stop their heave-haw-ho laughing.

'Stop it!' cries Lester, coming to loom over the sisters, the women upsetting glasses on the tablecloth and toppling over, hunched as epileptics. 'Madness!' shouts Lester Pilima at them, 'madness' — and cannot help it, it seems, he must rage into the other room. Where, apparently, in his attempt to dampen the fire, his toupee falls off, straight into the hearth. For all the assembled hear a louder crackle and spit and then the Pilima reemerges, bald and utterly furious, saying not a jot as he stomps out, followed by the scent of scorched hair.

Immediately, the dance school ladies also excuse themselves with wordless apology, napkins pressed to lips.

Here the monk redrapes himself, clearing his throat. 'Thank you, Colonel Fyre. We must prepare for a dharma talk tomorrow. Also our lesson. You'll forgive us, we hope.' And he backs out the door past Pushpa.

One by one the remaining guests offer the customary bow to Henry and leave in a terrible silence, interrupted only by the fire eating the last of Lester Pilima's famous toupee.

'What?' Henry turns to Johnny, to Nani. And louder: 'What is it? What?'

After that, it is just the egrets who talk back, birds hooting into the Rajottama night, informing anyone who listens of their annoying satisfaction.

VIII

THE ELEPHANT'S LOOK

Whoever is overcome by this wretched and sticky craving,
his sorrows grow like grass after the rains.

— *The Dhammapada*

87

Before the pilgrimage, the monk had assigned Henry the Buddha's words on desire. A few days after the dinner, Henry reclines alone in Johnny's cottage, reading. Rereading. Trying to nail in the idea of desirelessness. Sometimes evenings here are too subdued. As much as he wants to, he might not succeed in the way he once thought possible in Ceylon. He must accept that possibility. Acceptance — Henry has long tried to tattoo the idea into his brain.

When his father was dying Henry could not give him a reason to live. All the reasons seemed selfish: all smacked of desire. Of fear of change. Of fear of being left a true orphan in the world, stripped of the one certainty of his existence.

'Whatever's best, Father,' he had said, a week into the final illness. He'd hated the words even as he said them, but did not know what else to convey to his father, the fallen rector with his face paler than whey. The sudden inefficiency of the body revealed — so much dross to carry around a prophetically small self. Did an ant have an equivalently weighty soul? 'Whatever's best.'

What the son said was a way of offering a gift. Henry had already been working hard to denude himself of the usual mortal passions and clinging. *Whatever's best.*

'Are you some kind of Cathar zealot? Don't you think I've been a good parent to you?' his father had wheezed back. It was a conservative voice, Henry had noted, trying only to observe, aiming for pure Buddhist detachment.

'Of course,' Henry had answered after only a moment of hesitation. 'Taught me what you could.' As though it were the night sky, he stared at the wrinkles in the waistline of the stocky, wry nurse he'd hired. There was no way to make wisdom flourish. He was making up rules for himself as he went along. *Show no emotion* had become one of these rules. Allow the dying to resolve their own attachments.

'So' — and his father had waited for his rasping cough to stop — 'no elixir you know of?' the old man managed to say.

'Acceptance? maybe equanimity?' And Henry cut himself off because he couldn't say more without choking. He started up again. 'That's the puzzle, I think, for us both, the benevolence of the world, yes, but also equanimity —'

The man's face had turned bitter, two chevrons flushed high on the cheeks. 'Then you'll get to eat your equanimity even if you don't have me,' the old man had said quite clearly before rolling away from Henry and the nurse. He uttered his final words: 'Equanimity! A son of mine? Good night.'

Three hours later the eminent rector from Westchester County had stopped breathing. The nurse said he went without a struggle. 'This sort makes you wonder why anyone ever bothered to invent the idea of the spirit,' she said. She was a charter member of the Skeptical Inquirers Society and this gave her a righteous faith. 'He listened to his body. He put up no fight.'

No fight. That may be the ticket. Through the open door, the scent of wet earth gusts in. In the yard above, Nani must be hanging up laundry, chattering to her speckled cow as though to a foolish, beloved child.

'All alone?' the monk asks out of nowhere.

The book clatters from Henry's hands onto the red-polished floor, along with tiny pressed leaves from the seasonless seasons he's passed in Ceylon, seasons of rain and no rain, seasons lacking winter, summer or fall. The monk and Henry bump heads. A peculiar harmony: they laugh together.

'Come, come,' the monk says, handing Henry the book, the crumbling leaves.

All's well, thinks Henry. His monk's returned and Henry wants to have returned to his monk. Teacher and student mount the stairs to the main house's front room. They resume their usual seats as though the celebratory dinner had given offense to no one, had poisoned nothing.

> Like water on a lotus leaf or a mustard seed on the point of a
> needle, he who does not cling to sensual pleasures — him do I
> call a holy man.

They lay aside the scriptures only to discuss the cultural plan. The monk has new views. And the monk has not forgotten Henry. For this reason, he is suggesting something radical, sure to appeal *because* it is so radical: to move the orphanage children off the plantation, which, before the colonizers, used to be — did Henry know? — the Pilimas' land.

Instead let the children be housed in vacant houses across the canal, in Monkeyheadside, upon the dance family's compound. There are enough empty rooms in that yellow house. More can be built, lean-tos, it takes nothing.

'But we've already renovated,' Henry begins. 'Lester Pilima himself oversaw it.'

The plan will proceed better, explains the monk. The school, the dance conservatory. Better that Henry's efforts not be a piece here, a piece there. When international observers come, they will be impressed by the consolidation.

How thoughtful. His ingenious Pandit. Always aware of Henry's goals. The monk explains that the dance family's compound can easily be made ready. Apparently he had spoken with the school sisters and, fortunately, the women had shown a lively interest.

Why hasn't Henry thought of this himself? To enlist the old dance hall as an actual, physical bridge linking the orphanage, the school and the culture conservatory. Why should a canal separate the three entities?

He envies the monk's clarity. The simplicity of his life, the grace of his orange robe draped with such care around a Buddha's full body. Once the monk leaves, Henry caresses the scriptures, overwhelmed with pride.

> He from whom lust and hatred, self-glory and hypocrisy have fallen off like a mustard seed from the point of a needle — him do I call a holy man.

88

RECHARGED, HENRY SETS the move across the canal in motion, delegating the details to Johnny. He memorizes a sutta a day:

> The craving of one given to heedless living grows like a creeper. Like the monkey seeking fruits in the forest, he leaps from life to life (tasting the fruit of his karma).

But two weeks pass without the monk appearing for language lessons. Each day Henry enters an X in his Village Book. A day without the monk is like a day without . . . The rain stops and starts. On the fifteenth day of May, the monsoon having entered a holding pattern of morning rains, scrawny Rosalin-akka appears.

In her staccato Sinhalese she relays that Pandit is temporarily indisposed.

Before she makes her skittering departure, on impulse Henry asks her: 'You like your job?' He is importuning the monk's right-hand server only because absence from Pandit has made him bold or desperate.

'An honor, Sir.'

'Why's that?'

Her eyes averted. 'It doesn't matter my family, Sir. I go every day to the *uda malua*. Maybe you cannot understand. I go to the top platform closest to the tree where no one else goes. I find good merit this way. I serve the Buddha and our holy lord. I can be reborn a high woman next life.' Her humility stirs him. 'I become a monk myself maybe.'

Rosalin-akka the former prostitute with her unshielded body that has known so many men and lives. Johnny had told him how, in her working days, young men would strip coins of the valuable surface metals and give her a fake wage. Or they'd leave the coin on the window tied to a thread so the next one could pull it and use it. Then after too many rages, stalking her offenders in the streets, Rosalin returned to the fold by becoming a temple server. Henry wants to offer something but has nothing to give. She instead presents him with a small gift from the monk, something to deposit straight into his perturbed, restless heart. Pandit has sent along a pamphlet with a note on its cover:

A Joke: All of the enclosed comes from monks spending too many years of self-restraint in meditation! Do not take it too seriously, Colonel.

In the disturbing pamphlet are pictures of short-torsoed men thrusting hot pokers into the orifices of women standing on their heads. Anuses squeaking open, yellow starbursts over them. Maze-like knotty bodies with infinite possibilities. Three-armed children, mischievous tongues. Untold tortured flight.

Henry's concerned. 'Did Pandit tell you anything else?' He doesn't mean to harangue the woman, he just wants an answer his pride can bear.

Eyes like cinders, she shakes her head, leaves on deft feet. And the echo of her sentences rings in his head: *Mang . . . mame . . . mang . . . .* I. I. I. *Mame mame mang.* This is her message: I and me. She loves what she does. Believes as well that she can do no better. He thinks maybe he should learn from her, a thing or two, learn from her readiness to deal with what life dishes out.

89

BEFORE DAWN one morning Nani raps on the glass door. 'Please, Sir, please come help.'

Sweet words. *Come help.* He jumps into the better tunic and pants she had sewn for him.

Early-morning mosquitoes and their arguing clouds just outside his room mean no one had lit the citronella sconces last night. Sad how no one remembers his foreign body with its foreign needs. The bugs buzz thick around his head and neck and some kind of distant thunder booms. Another thunderstorm? but usually they come later in the morning. *Come help.*

In the hall he finds her. 'What is it?'

She puts a finger to her lips to make him follow without protest.

Which he does. This is the kind of thing that is understood between them. It will soon become something he turns over again and again in order to find its navel.

The patio has become a bloody mess and at the center, Nani's speckled cow is felled, lowing in anger. Henry laughs. A small calf head tries to poke out of the mother's sex. 'Some kind of reveille.'

'What you did with the rain?' pleads his maid. 'Please now with the cow?'

Henry is not good at these things. He could argue with her. Or he could just address the situation: the birth of a calf. 'I am clumsy,' he remonstrates but she doesn't understand. He mimes himself slipping, stumbling. 'We send for a vet? a doctor?'

'Sir, what you did with Roshan, Sir?'

Help will be the only answer she will accept. *Come help*, she'd said. Kneels, he does, rolls up his sleeves. And helps. Amid gushes he begins to yank and heave in good faith, all a continuation of the dream he'd been having in which Nani had offered up a lily floret from between her legs and the air had turned rose plush. A raving spastic maniac, the cow with her bellows shakes the patio's white lattice.

'Sir needs help?' asks Nani.

Speaking is a formality. He hauls and pulls; finds a gap and steers around some awkward angles. By some crookery and internal groping he lugs the head out. And is ready to continue with the rest, panting, his hand deep inside the cow's innards. But another purple head pops out —

— a two-headed calf! —

— both little nappy heads blinded by placenta.

'Miracle, Nani, look —'

But she is crying, ridiculously — why would she cry at this? — her face beginning to close in.

'Nani? now I need your help —'

Nani kneels beside him, hand a tentative mirror of his, slithering into the cow from her side. Blood-spattered they finger the slippery bifurcated mass inch by inch all the way out. The mother's legs are sculling some invisible waters and strike Henry's thighs.

'Hold tight,' muttering, practically expecting a grenade at this point, 'we've got you.'

Nani suggests they raise her. A standing birth might be easier: this will be a small feat to manage. But it is as she says; on her four legs, the mother widens. Here they begin pulling out the one leg, knobbed and piebald, another right after, the last two hardest, wrenching until the speckled calf wobbles and falls flat on the ground with its two exhausted heads. And Nani with her own neck strained holds the mother up, keeps that bloated pornography of a thing from falling and crushing the newborn.

What is romantic in any of this? The calf's out; the mother barely stands. But without planning, blood everywhere, he grabs her. Nani by the waist, Nani finally by the waist, what a waist to grab —

— even as she holds up the cow. This is funny, that he grabs her in the middle of all this blood and she grabs the cow, is he laughing now? All without thinking. He laughs into kissing the part at her hairtop and smells rich coconut.

The moment surprises everyone; the cow moans, shows her teeth, pulls away.

It is ineffectual for Nani, still crying, to turn her head away, just a bad imitation of something; still her turn creates a sliver of space between her and Henry.

The cow is licking its little beastlet. The newborn with its two heads wobbles up, begins its nosing and pushing there at the tips of her engorged teats.

A lawless moment, out of season. Henry releases his maid and for the first time she says 'Thank you' but he doesn't know for what exactly. Whether it was stranger to kiss Nani or see a calf with two heads suckling at its mother's udders, Henry can't say.

Unable to know life amid all this blood, he affects a joviality he doesn't feel: 'Back to sleep?' That's all he asks. 'See you!' and follows up on his words, heads straight back to bed.

Nothing further has been sorted out when he wakes at noon, varnished with afterbirth. And having dreamt of naughty fingers. Only to find her leaning against his wall, wiping his shoes with meditative pleasure. She could have been there for hours, just watching him.

Now *he* thanks her. For — he invents — for everything. For cooking so well after the pilgrimage. And again for removing what he'd realized much later had been a mocker during his pilgrimage speech.

'That was terrible! those kinds of things can set a speaker off entirely,' he explains nonsensically. When she starts her laugh, he persists: 'You lose your point.' He doesn't need any more mockery. Not now. Somewhere he has the possibility to become another person: the one who understands everything. Even the source of her laughter.

90

Diwa, pronounced *diva*; tongue; taste; island; sky; firmament, region of the stars; Swarga, the paradise of the gods; a verbal root, which among many other significations, means to play, to sport, to romp, to gambol, to be glad, to rejoice, to be mad or frantic with joy, to be inflated with pride and passion; to wish, to desire, to love; from this root are formed all the words which are used to express that class of beings usually denominated in our language, gods, deities, divinities, etc., i.e., beings wholly given up to every species of pleasure and the indulgences of every corrupt passion; the Swarga or residence of these beings, which for want of more appropriate terms is called paradise, heaven, etc., signifies a place where every sensual passion is gratified without interruption or restraint, see also *devi*.

he writes.

91

HE IS SICK with waiting for everything to happen in his model village. Or for his mood to stabilize. Instead he spends full mornings in bed. He gets her, without too much prompting, to sit with her needlepoint nearby and talk openly and clearly of her childhood, one familiar to him even as he cannot cite its details. Here he discovers more than what he thought were her gifts. For one thing, Nani is a storyteller.

What is the difference between stories and antiques, between stories and jokes? Not much in her case. She is an admirable survivor of some ancient humor, that's what he thinks. A survivor with more than half a tongue left.

And is it possible that in these last few days she might look on him with more gratitude? It is; she does. Could she have something like love for him? at least affection?

The cow had mattered in a way he still doesn't quite understand. She had thought he'd had powers when he worked the rains, she says, and when he'd helped Roshan's child, then as well, but it was the cow that let her know for sure. He doesn't need to ask what she now knows. Because he would sacrifice his heart to go on listening to the euphoria of her voice. He lies abed, half-listening to the rain of her Sinhalese.

92

BUT SHE DISTRIBUTES her stories in bits. She won't reveal herself too quickly to him. She says he already knows about her father's death and he did know it — as a fact — though it is a dreamlike bit of lore, as if he'd been told the story in his sleep. While the last week of May fades into June he often asks about her cow and its doubled calf, a cheap ruse to get her to linger. And when she's gone, he notices the plants.

They have begun to grow outside Henry's window in strange distorted shapes. He hasn't succumbed to Wooves' illness. It's nothing like that.

At first he leaves the french door to the front room open to allow everything time to circulate. But first the day's storm and then that infernal heat lifts off the canal so he decides instead to close himself in with the mildew and rot. And slams the door so hard the glass cracks into a giant web. He sits staring out the half-cracked door onto the garden and the ancient mango tree.

On January 4, 1887, without relevance to anything else he had written before, Wooves evidently had taken a melancholic turn:

Pruning is the most important operation in a grape vine because it has a direct relationship with yield. In grapes, flowers are produced on the current season's growth. Therefore, the aim in pruning is to get enough new growth without impairing the vigour of the vine.

Had the civil servant been imagining a trellis? Either he had built one or not, either it remained standing somewhere or had been destroyed.

How long has Henry been sitting in the room considering Wooves before she enters and exits with her eternal laundry? The thing of which he is sure is his feet's baffling half-weight, like liquid sacs incapable of movement. And the laborers have begun to redecorate his head's inside. Their sledgehammers fall upon his temples in steady counterpoint.

93

IT IS THE LOCAL FEVER that has laid siege to Henry, the herb doctor Appuhamy had told Johnny. With his employer ill, the boy becomes an unstrung horse. This morning he enters a bit watery at the edges. He dismisses Nani, kneels at Henry's bedside.

'You've got such rings about your eyes, Henree. Haven't been eating margosa leaves, have you? Slept at all?'

Words don't will away pain. What answer would satisfy Johnny?

Every bone in his body feels broken; he plods through an opaque syrup; the heat alone sizzles his organs with a vile energy which could either purify or kill. Prickly eruptions under the skin make his sweat cling to every surface.

'If hell's heat, I know hell,' Henry mutters to Johnny. Is the boy still in the room? He is. All that remains to do is reread Pandit's pamphlet about the dire Avici. 'This Avici hell,' he tells the shadowy boy, 'it makes other hells more tolerable.'

Johnny leaves him to it.

- This Avici is the fitting punishment for one who enters the order of monks from bad motives, covetousness, or deceit; out of greed or gluttony; desirous of gain, fame, or reputation; or otherwise unsuitable, unqualified, unfit, unworthy, unseemly.

- This monk shall incur a twofold punishment, which will prove ruinous to all his good qualities; in this very life he shall be scorned, derided, reproached, ridiculed and mocked; he shall be shunned, expelled, ejected, removed, and banished.

- And in his next life, like foam which is tossed about, up and down and across, he shall cook for many hundreds of thousands of kotis of years in its hundred-league miasma, its ardent, blistering inferno.

- And when he has been released thence, his entire body will become emaciated, rough, and black; his head swollen, bloated and full of holes; hungry and thirsty, disagreeable and dreadful to see, his ears all torn, his eyes constantly blinking, his whole body one putrid mass of sores and dense with maggots, his bowels afire and blazing like a mass of fire fanned by a breeze, helpless and unprotected, weeping, crying, wailing, and lamenting, consumed by unsatisfied longings.

- He that once was a religious wanderer shall then, now a large demonic beast, a Preta, rove the earth bewailing his fate.

'Nani!' Henry cries out, throwing down the monk's pamphlet.

Her feet whisk like cloth over stone but his head is slow in turning toward her. Moving too fast hurts and he sees her through a dull cloak. Light, speed, distance — these were not made for him. His sickness has reduced him to a throb. And the gestures of his weak ineffectual paws.

She offers him something.

'Dirty water?'

'Coconut,' she says. 'To cool you.'

He quietly accepts the gift. Childhood summers were better than this heat. Speech costs more effort than its worth. But that pounding. He has to know what that pounding is. Henry applies himself to the glass, a strange cold assertion.

'The monk has come today,' she continues. 'With a helper.'

'Oh?' What matters is the drink, its gurgle down the throat to cool the interior. His organs free themselves of their moorings, unchained from the parabolic tyranny of brain and heart, vaulting democratic at last in a coconut milk bath.

Think of something positive, he instructs himself.

The Nani of his first meeting. A numinous goddess at the threshold. Or as she was, rising from the patio fire within the vastness of the house, its corridors all in flight away from the stove. Her wide uptilted gaze with its reproach. The one that compelled him closer and then bowed away. Memory keeps her on a rotating semicircular battery, turning for and against, endlessly showing between skirt and sari top that tight swath of back, a kaleidoscope in sepia.

Nani of the recent pilgrimage, a bivalve medusa by the waterpump. Early morning with the others at tea, her cloth stopped short of those gleaming bare arms, her heft of hair undone to her waist. She shivered when he ran downhill. As though Colonel Henry Fyre Gould, late of America, and Nani Bandu, a woman who rubs the insides of his work-grimed clothes, who dusts his most-loved books, were unacquainted guests. Her girderwork of shoulders with their perfume and stubbornness. Nothing of her on that pilgrimage would acknowledge him. No timid announcements of love. Only the shiver. And her speech: *Use this water for your bath.* Was such harshness necessary?

You're entertaining an obsession, he kept telling himself, unable to sleep, thoughts distending his head. Enough to make him lie outside on the patio where prolific stars blurred the sky into long streaky cuts. He wanted to peek again into the cooking area to see her among other women and their caldrons, the piles of husked coconut shells and eviscerated greens.

Should he add more of himself to the world? or subtract? What was there in the world that wasn't Henry? For once he wanted to see her choose him. Smile in recognition of him. 'Nani, Nani, Nani?' he said to find the name within himself. What was it that always made her glance away from him? No flourish and curlicue had brought her closer. Only perhaps —

— the cow? She may have deduced the dark is better and is drawing the blinds against the stalking croton.

'What?' he manages.

He's received a letter from the government agent. From Colwether. He tries to focus his eyes upon the dancing world.

My dear Colonel Fyre Gould:

Thank you so much for your gift of four healthy, happy and clucking Welsummer hens. A wild bunch, but the rooster has helped all of us abide by a regular schedule.

'I can't read,' he complains, 'this is ludicrous.' He gives her the job he used to give his wife — could she read aloud for him? And then realizes her English is not yet up to the task, so squints at it:

And, thanks to you, our holidays will be much fuller this year. We are all so impressed by your perseverance in raising chickens in this climate, given the local diseases.

They say there is no story on this earth that doesn't in some way mention an egg or a bird. So it is with your story here, apparently.

Be that as it may, we thought we might ask your thoughts on coop construction in other parts of the island.

Please advise us as to when you might be able to pay a visit to our seat in Kegalle. The recent troubles, with village unrest mere copycat imitations of India, no doubt, soon to die down, prevent us nonetheless from traveling ourselves.

Also, here follows a belated congratulations on the continued excellence of your write-ups in the International Herald Tribune, The New York Daily Post, and The Times of London.

Innovative and respectable traditions continue in your work, here on our isolated island. No Anglican or Catholic missionary has ever achieved quite so much as you have in your time. You really have gone head over heels in love with Buddhism, and this must stand in your favor among the people.

Every life has its little fancies, I suppose, from poultry to what you call, in your interviews, parinibbana(sic).

With every wish for success, I remain,
Yours truly,
Mr H.A.J. Colwether
Government Agent for the Uva Province
In the Honorable Employ of His Majesty the King

'What's this other thing?' he demands. 'Why are you wearing that loose dress?' It is gray and mantles her completely like an inverted Dutch hat.

'A house dress,' she says. 'Many women wear this. Better. Cooler.' He shrugs. 'Not better. Worse.'

'And the monk sent a note. He asks you to come to the temple to-mor-row. If you are able.'

A current of pain flashes straight into his temples. This government agent nattering on about fancies and poultry. Even the monk. Demanding his every vital fiber. They don't understand that he cannot *pay* visits when this whole country imposes its massive debt *upon* him. Spiriting its viruses and plagues and misbegotten ideas upon his broad American back. Sinking through the floor and back to his New York salon would be heaven.

But Buddhism (his mind catches on it) — isn't it still waiting for Henry Fyre Gould? As is the village. As are the people. They need him.

'No mail from anyone else?' He craves just a word from Madame; why wouldn't she write him? 'Think you might bring some brandy?' he asks.

Could brandy provoke what old German homeopaths called the healing crisis? Through an aching mantle, he nonetheless sees Nani's lips purse.

'That's ri-di-cu-lous,' he thinks she says.

'Then talk to me. I need distraction.'

'What to tell?'

'Sit here. Take this. Only my hand, right? Tell me a secret from your life.'

'There is nothing. Your hands are so cold.'

'About your mother?'

'I already told you. After I was born an-other sister came and both died. I never knew her.'

'Your father then.'

She consents with some reluctance and then changes her mind. Puts down that hand that feels like a swollen birth-knot and rises to straighten the dusty kidney-shaped mirror that hangs in Henry's room.

When she first came to the house, never having been in one with wooden roofs and glass windows, she had seen her face for the first time in that mirror. One day her father had said her face would be beautiful. When she arrived in this house, her father's words had returned in a clownish echo. *Would be.* Wouldn't she do anything to remember his voice?

'I remember now,' her pink man is saying. Jarring her. 'Your father. You say we discussed him before — so begin with — why you never married?' He takes her hand again, the cold offering like love. The things he call workmen in his head must have subsided.

She shakes her arm free of him.

'You do not understand what is the life here.'

'What what.'

'A woman in Ceylon. On a small island, everyone can know everything.'

'Sit and tell me. Then I'll know, right?' He won't give up.

He plays with her hand as an infant would and she has the urge to bundle him in her arms. All that pink mass close to her chest, hers alone. She would kiss his forehead, make his suffering go away, let him rest against her heart. 'You are sick. Better sleep.'

'For you,' he says, blue eyes amiable, 'I can always, always stay awake.'

Always? but he falls asleep before she even gets to the idea of soul.

94

WHY SHE TOLD no one is clear to no other soul but her own.

She should've known what to do. Hadn't she seen grim-faced girls in consultation with the washerwoman? She knew certain things. She knew the Dobie woman was the one to wash the first day's clothes. The one to make young girls surrender any bangles they had the misfortune to be wearing that first day.

Hadn't she roamed through the village enough to see young girls locked in that terrible roadside hut for seven days? Surely she'd peeked. Surely she knew that one day she too would need to consult the Dobie.

Instead when she finally saw red on her underclothes she chose to say nothing to anyone.

During the day she watched in fascination as between her legs the red widened into a blot and then a blossom.

I'm not dying, she sang to herself. Happy that even her skin felt heat and damp with more sensitivity.

Would her dark cloth be marked? Even then she would not appeal to the Dobie's ministrations. Why could she not wash it herself? Almost all her life she had been using the riverstone. How unimaginable it would be to have to confide to those crooked teeth and the rapid smile of the Dobie.

No one was awake in her sister Eka's house so Nani stole a rag from the kitchen and headed to where the river ran widest. Seated upon the pelican-shaped stone, Nani studied the foamy tumble over the rocks where the channel narrowed. Across the way lay a clearing and beyond, a forest pricked the low sky. A warbler lived there who called out her name — *who Nani Nani Nani?* She didn't want too much good fortune rained on herself alone so she'd tried to train the bird to call out the names of her sisters as well. But across the river the bird questioned, *why Nani Nani Nani?*

The river tightened precipitously at that bend. Stories told of boys who disobeyed their fathers, attempting to escape the village for the coastal capital. They tended to perish in their flimsy boats. The exceptions ensured others would die following their lead. At the moment when those doomed hearts reached their most exultant peak — breathing the crowded air of cities, stroking unimaginable pleasures — a slim brown hand not of man or woman stretched up from the riverbed to pull those young fools into their watery destiny.

It may appear gentle but the river recognizes the wicked, one song cautioned.

Nani hummed a single note to the rhythm of water spilling over rocks. She rose to see behind her on the stone the faintest vermilion butterfly-mark. Humming all the while, she squatted to paint more broadly, with a remaining thread of dampness, the wings of the blood-drawing.

So involved in her work was she that she didn't hear the other voice which picked up the river's accompaniment. When she noticed, she couldn't see who owned the young and ironic parrotlike singing voice. She knew its words:

> See the charms of women sporting by the river,
> Confusing people who see them,
> Such women in glory surpassing
> The goddesses sporting inside the river.

The song fell ugly and hard on her ears. The youthful voice started up for a second round. Something gave her the courage to shout: 'Who's there?'

A tease, the voice broke into a donkey's bray. After which it paused with some solemnity. Though still across the river, when it recommenced, the singing came from closer, turning gentle and pleading. Anger corkscrewed her up to her feet so she could glare across the way. All tricks! She walked up and down the uneven riverbank trying to find the jester.

> The face like a full moon,
> Forehead covered with golden bead.
> When young men see such beauties,
> Our hearts burn with eternal fire.

She shouted, 'Would you please be quiet please!'

> O lovely gemlike ones! Leave that tempting gait.
> Remove the jewels from your body.
> Come with your scented cloths to rub our feet,
> Let your hands know a future better than your dreams.

She would turn into an old maid weaving hair with her toes if she tried to find the glib voice singing its many loves. Then she saw the boy in the clearing. Stockstill, with only his mouth moving. A slim tall young man, was it? Awkwardly angled, his cheeks mere hollow triangles. Spectacles. A boy's newly hoarse voice. His intonation like a radio song.

> Girl! As we are of one age,
> Come, let us go to the fields.

She could not believe such impertinence and determined to be as rude as the boy and hold his shielded gaze. Centuries gave her strength because he wouldn't know all the legends she did. She knew them all. She knew about the crone who appeared as the young maiden at the riverside, withstanding the rudeness of boys whose mothers' milk still foamed about their mouths.

The story sprang into her half-memory and steadied her all the more.

Who knows, she tells Honree, letting herself stroke his arm. He lets out the faintest snore, which makes her continue in the Sinhalese of old storytelling grandmothers — maybe one day other young girls will find themselves feeling stronger than I did in the spot. My feet fought with each other. One foot wanted flight and the other wanted to stay there forever.

Sheltered underneath a pillow, Honree laughs. Has he been awake and listening? 'You have a good sense of revenge,' he says nonsensically, fighting for air. He comes up speaking his bad Sinhalese. She doesn't know what if anything he has understood.

There is a part of the story she did not dare tell even his half-sleeping soul. Nothing about how once the hollow-cheeked young man had finished his song, he stared at her with his blind glaze. Nothing about how he wiped his mouth with the back of his hand as though a good curry's stains remained. Nor does she admit what she noticed: the lips he wiped were so unusually generous, a crimson butterfly would envy such a mouth.

There'd been no fleeing a horizon mantled in such sadness, the one she found when she came home.

'Where've you been?' her sister Deka had asked.

'Out.' Her hands could do little more than flop about, dead fish.

Deka must've seen blood on one of her hands. She always had a martyr's specially honed instincts and must've guessed which kingdom her charge had entered. Before anyone could say anything, she had Nani turned around and brought outside.

She called out to the other sisters, to the twins scraping coconut meat into splinters. 'You! Suji! Hatara! Get the Dobie!'

Everyone knew Suji hated the washerwoman and her ilk. A leer crossed her face and she imitated the woman's thin tight features.

'Hurry!' called Deka, not letting go of Nani's shoulders. Deka came alive at moments like these, when her martyrdom had a chance to spirit itself into action and show its necessity. She overdid her usefulness now, wiping Nani's face with spit and tucking the girl's naughty hair behind her ears. The way Deka spoke, Nani could have believed Deka was endowing her with the key to all realms, the condensed, urgent information only encountered in dreams.

'The roadside, Gem. A hut, you understand. Seven days. See only the Dobie. Don't see men, no one except your family and the Dobie. Otherwise, you get a lifelong curse.'

Nani felt important suddenly but said nothing — she stopped only to grab a book she'd left under their pawpaw tree. And she allowed herself to be led by Deka. One foot still wanted flight but she managed to follow. A shock of tears overcame Deka as she handed her charge to the thin-featured Dobie, who flashed crooked teeth and said nothing.

When the Dobie began with her cracked and leathery hands tickling all over Nani's body, Nani could not stop laughing.

'What's the matter, you're hiding some jewelry from me? Know how girls suffer if they hide anything from me?' the Dobie asked, poking her nose into Nani's neck, making Nani laugh more. 'It'll do you no good,' she warned. 'You hide heirlooms from me now, your time won't pass easy.'

Nani reduced herself to commands to her legs and bare slats of feet. The Dobie practically pushed her along the road and into a hut behind some trees. Only after the Dobie had padlocked the door from the outside did Nani release her breath.

Flowers covered the swept sand floor. Not just white areliya buds but blossomed coconut and paddy seeds. A fancy tin cup and an earthen jug big enough to hold several weeks of drinking water on the side. And a musk of welcome you wouldn't expect in a dungeon.

She drank like she'd never seen water, like she'd never see it again. With damp wood matches strewn by an oil-pot stump, she lit the stinking wick. The oil-pot's light dwindled slightly the din of the outside animals, monkeys, leopards, distant elephants. Through cracks in the woven cadjan that made up the walls, she saw night had wrapped quickly around the hut.

Scared, she opened the single book she had thought to bring with her:

> The prince beheld his father in a dream, wearing dirty clothes, with disheveled hair, falling from the top of a knoll into a pit filled with bones and dung. At that time he beheld the seas dried up, the moon crashing on the earth, the whole world enveloped in darkness. He saw too the king's elephant's tusk breaking into thousands of pieces.

She couldn't read for long. Instead she fingered the floor's blossomed coconut flowers and paddy seeds and lay down on that pillow with its burnt stick beneath. Nearby was a pot of rice and a stone mortar and pestle positioned as though to crush or guard her from being crushed herself like dried chilies, ginger and pods of cardamom.

In her dream, she approached the mortar as a tiny girl, seeing the map on her father's cabinet being mashed inside. The Dobie, an even tinier woman in blood-stained clothes, tried to climb up and over the map. *Help me, daughter,* she cried. *I cannot climb fast enough.*

Was the Dobie trying to get in the door? Nani rose, enervated. 'Yes?'

No answer. She tried to remember the signs the Dobie had said she would give when entering to remove the soiled clothes, to bring more rice. Raps? A nightbird's hoot? Nani stopped breathing and heard nothing until the low song filled her ears.

Outside her shack, she realized, stood the riverside boy with the hollow triangles for cheeks. 'I won't offend you by entering, girl,' he said. 'Let me help sing away your seven lonely days.'

Now she was glad for him. When he told her his odd name, she leaned against the door of the shack.

Every night, alone, she awaited his footfall. She begged him to tell her stories and he did, turning gentle when speaking of the priest.

'If it hadn't have been for the priest, you see, girl, I would never have found you,' he said, explaining how the priest had told his aide to help maneuver the girl, the unfettered girl who'd been seen playing with a group of riverside boys, real brutes.

Odd news impressed her visitor. Not that she had been the leader of a gang of boys, but that she already knew how to read two languages.

This boy grew sweeter than the fruit he brought her, fruit he pushed through a hole the pair bored through the hut's walls. One day he brought her something she'd never tasted, ripe rambutan, the insides a shockingly fleshy red star, the juice dripping off her fingers. She loved his offerings but more than them, she loved his stories. She kept him awake until just before dawn, speaking of his plans and family, his mother's yard, the cruel friends he'd known. How much he loved the radio, always the radio.

He never tired of telling her how certain he was that he would never become a clerk. He was her first friend.

Twice over seven nights in that dark hut surrounded by night animals, the boy told young Nani how, if he could, he would stroke her thick hair. But this was the only impropriety he allowed himself after that first impudence, his riverbank song. One late afternoon, finished with her reading, she began to dance. She stopped once she realized he'd come, braving daylight to bring her an especially fine mango. But he waited politely, glancing away while her sweat cooled and her breathing returned from its ragged rhythm.

He never imposed himself. Not on that day or any other did he suggest entering the hut.

'I love you too much to touch you,' he whispered one day. 'And you're too Sinhalese for us to know each other. But after you get out, maybe just once you'll let me see you dance? maybe you'll dance for me?'

'I'll do it now,' she said, 'and for us.'

She was as impelled by the insistence of his voice as by the shame it hid. What did he mean, she was too much a Sinhalese? Was he a Tamil?

'So many Indian Tamil women chose Sinhalese kings as husbands,' she'd told him. 'We're not that separate, are we?'

And without choosing, that day she danced the demon dance. The whole time she did it, her arms flung out, hips drunk and knowing, she knew his eye was pressed to the hole to see her. When, exhausted and panting hard, she had her turn to steal a look through the hole, she saw the new moonlight lying like money on his face and his finger whipping to his lips as though to shush her. But never would she give him away. He was her friend, her alone and secret friend.

And his presence, she knew, she trusted, wouldn't curse her. Because the whole time he courted her — she realized that was what he was doing only later, once it was too late — he stayed outside the hut. Not once did he dare cross the threshold over which no man should ever come.

On their last day, he admitted he'd been the one to spot her leading the small boys' riverside games. He'd been the one to ask the Christian priest if he could receive the task of setting this outrageous girl straight.

'The priest told me I could come tame you, pardon the expression. But then you made me sing to you instead. I couldn't help it. Blame your beauty for my impudence. Once I really saw you, all I wanted to do was sing to you, never bring you in line.'

95

WHEN LITTLE GEM emerged from the hut a woman, she had none of the sick face that lingers on those who have been isolated. She needed no dusting off. When people asked how her time in the hut went, she dismissed their questions with a brisk *Fine*. She made herself glad and hearty to get on with living, until her sadness sneaked up on her.

The hollow-cheeked friend was nowhere to be found. Not at the river, not on the main road. Had the priest called him back, had he retired in shame from their time together? She didn't know where to find him. Instead of leaving her with fine memories of a time spent quickly, he left her with superstitions ignored, a promise unfulfilled, a fruitless guarantee of a friend which made her belly ache with loneliness.

Late at night on the riverstone she sang to him.

Her sisters grew certain she had finally gone batty. This littlest one fully deserved what they all had to share, they said, the family's ill, ill fortune.

In keeping with their ideas, Little Gem was the first to be married and the first to lose her marriage.

Soon after her time in the hut, an old man with jowls — but a coffee plantation to his name — had come by whistling for the tallest daughter. The youngest one.

This wasn't fair. The sisters blamed sorcery. They said The Groom — as they called him — had worn his shirt inside out for a month, under a sorcerer's instructions. This was how he got Little Gem and her stubbornness to marry him out of turn.

At dawn on Gem's wedding morning, Indian rains washed down from the north and doused multitudes of tiny coconut-oil lamps. Earthen pots spilled arecanut flowers into tiny heaps onto the planks of the poruwa, the small wooden stage that had swelled overnight. Rivulets scattered all the previous night's forethought: young coconut leaves, five-petaled flowers, fine paddy and betel leaves laid to lead the eye toward where the blessed couple would stand.

No one tells the same story.

Those standing near the sisters say that at the wedding's end — after the last local girls had finished braving the rains with their clenched-jaw songs, after Nani's hands had been joined with the groom's and water poured over — the two of them had stood tall together.

In this new custom of wedding ceremony, registration and ready-made ritual which had come in the missionaries' pouches, a local woman had agreed to preside. She'd tied their thumbs with thread and waited while The Groom pushed milk rice into Gem's passive mouth. The sisters smarted.

'She's usually so hungry, isn't she?' whispered Suji. 'What happened?'

Had the sisters' father been alive, it would have happened properly. He would've made a round of calls, spoken with a merchant, flashed his enigmatic smile everywhere and enough that other parents would press other grooms on the elder sisters. That Little Gem should be the first to marry — !

'Maybe it bodes well for us,' Hatara told Suji.

By the time The Groom and Little Gem circulated to hand out betel leaves and white scarves to the gathered elders, the rains had abated. The betrothed barely gazed at each other. 'You can tell they will be good together,' Deka piped up. She had pinned her hair to flow down her back in hopeful waves. Her thin lids fluttered, making her eyes look surprised. She stood ready for more surprise from the few men close to her age at the wedding.

Eka scowled at Deka. 'How can *you* tell?'

The priest beckoned a boy from the village, young Gemunu, to come bow with floorscraping ceremony and slice his machete down through a giant husky brown coconut. The local presiding woman hurried toward the two halves, hiked up her skirts and balled up her body to better study the broken shell. Her brow furrowed.

Those standing next to the sisters muttered, 'Lucky girl, finding a man like that.'

Such luck can be dangerous. The local presiding woman rose and shrugged, holding her tongue about the oracle's predictions.

As the newlyweds walked toward the waiting bullock cart bedecked with garlands, the sisters sang only one thing, faltering like rain's last drops: 'We wish you well, Little Gem.'

That was all they needed to say. Because they'd taken pains to ensure that all signs aligned. Their hands clasped in supplication and their eyes seethed with a semblance of good intention. Their mouths quirked at the strain of having had to smile so long. Nani knew all this was a struggle for them.

Still, she wants Honree to think kindly of them.

'They did their best given their fear,' she says, still pacing the room. She doesn't watch the pink man's mass on the bed.

Her sisters had done what they could. They knew about the noose of historyless, unmarried family. They knew family could prevent any outsider's entrance. In such a stranglehold, they could suffocate into being chief guardians of others' histories, doomed to tell the same stories in undying repetition.

'You're a lucky girl!' the groom's ancient father kept saying to her. 'Very lucky!' repeated as the newlyweds had to pass over the strewn flowers and through the new pelt of rain.

'I am sure.'

Nani demurred. Though her arm linked in her husband's, her eyes were unable to see anyone other than the creature now holding her as though she had always belonged to him. Tasting metal, she could not see the cart, the hand that pulled her up, the faces streaming past in attitudes of blessing.

They all seem so happy, it occurred to her. It's my wedding day. Why are they so happy?

Even her fingertips were numb.

If they are happy, she thought, what am I?

I am lucky. I am luck itself.

96

HONREE IN BED demands the next installment. 'Author! author!' This lifelike pink humidity of him. Sick and she can take care of him, man and infant, slave to his bed and with a gift for seducing her into this tide of speech. For a moment she will give up the power she has discovered in silence.

She starts in the middle. She talks to the Honree who is bedridden but usually stamps about not listening well to anyone. She talks to the mildewing walls, the big windows, the garden alive with fireflies. Talks to understand this life herself, incanting it as though she herself were the village's eye, as though she could see herself from a great distance:

No one's story is the same. Sweet young Gemunu from the village had been hired to stand guard in a hut not far from where girls bathed openly in the river. A discreet distance away from the new couple's bungalow. Of course, no one bathed on the wedding day because there would be a boy in a hut, a boy alone, even if he was to guard the newlyweds against blood-stalking beasts.

Now Gemunu swore that he had slept three full days prior to the wedding in order to sit dead alert on that most auspicious of nights. Elders had informed him that whatever happened on that night would weigh on the couple's future life. At any cost, Gemunu would need to prevent gratuitous omens.

Only later did new stories emerge, hints circulating that empty arrack bottles had been found buried near Gemunu's hut. Others owing favors to Gemunu's father protested that the bottles had been drained during the wedding, at a moment when Gemunu could not have been there. But to most, the arrack became evidence that Gemunu (everyone forgave him, he was after all *young* Gemunu) couldn't have stayed awake the whole night. A boy alone in the jungle's slither might be drawn to indulge more than usual. This wasn't uncommon in older men, why should it be any different for a young boy? Some recalled that his grandfather had died of the stuff.

All the more reason to forgive the grandson. You couldn't control men. And the boy could hardly be called a bounder. If nothing had happened, who would've cared whether the poor low-caste boy had taken in a little sleep?

Gemunu for his part vowed that the matrimonial bungalow's curtained window glowed with candlelight until late. Sadly for his character, it sounded as though the boy lied when he said that from his distance he could hear the newlyweds whispering.

After they trimmed their tapers, he swore, he kept guard until morning's first birds.

No one said return would be easy. But no one had said much of anything. The wedding and the death were as one in Nani's mind.

Nani considered that had she been a man returning, she would've been a celebrated hero. *You've survived your wedding night,* they'd say. *Not to mention all the other onslaughts. You're a boon to the family.*

Instead her sisters hid their faces from her when she entered the house. They withered her with avoidance for days.

'Won't you talk?' she finally asked Deka outside the back door where a few chickens squabbled.

'It's bad luck,' said Deka through her fingers. 'You'd wish your fate on me?'

Nani realized time would never again exist in words she had known before. *Day, week, month.* No words belonged to this new time. This moment would mark forever: the earth of Deka's fingers and her gleaming forehead, the way her hair tangled over a bright yellow blouse. The heat pressing down on the two of them.

'I will always remember this,' she said to Deka.

'It's horrible,' Deka said through her fingers. 'Shouldn't make me talk with you.'

Deka went on to explain. *Nani* should stay in the dusty workshed, not in the house and bed with the sisters. All Nani could hear was that *Gem* had disappeared.

Her eldest sister now called her by her birthname. Nani.

The sisters thought that what had happened on the wedding night was this: their sister's charmer had flung off a wedding's illusions. Little Gem may have possessed womanhood's standard allure. But others in similarly miserable circumstances would have proven much sweeter. A better match. Once The Groom truly saw his bride, they surmised, he realized he'd married a stubborn, petulant, dreaming girl. Perhaps no virago, but no angel either.

He came to his senses.

In short, the very morning of Nani's return, Eka, Suji and Hatara decided (with Deka abstaining) that Nani's groom had finally understood the terrible responsibility he had taken upon himself. And then he had died on the spot.

Three mornings after Nani's return, Suji and Hatara changed their minds. The twins figured that their unpredictable sister had been upset at her groom for wishing to abscond. She had finally realized the benefit of the wedded life others had prepared her to lead. And then their little sister had promised to cast dishonor upon him as a man. Once The Groom saw his desperate situation, he had committed suicide.

Whatever the truth, after the funeral, the worst of it was that The Groom had left none of his papers in order. And his father failed to recognize any of Nani's claims to her husband's holdings. She was a widow but as bad off as before.

Every day the father arrived to pester Eka about details of her little sister. Was the girl a black magician? Had she been born under the wrong planet? Nani became expert at hiding whenever this vile man came by.

At night she gazed into the jungle's stubble, curious whether the stars spelled redemption. In a breathy voice she sang the riverside boy's song:

> Girl! As we are of one age,
> Come, let us go to the fields.

Close upon Nani's return, Eka managed to find herself an older husband. Though from outside their village, he was of the same caste as their family. If half-blind and possessing a tendency to drink, he nevertheless succeeded at ingratiating himself with a surly half-smile into a foreman position at The Groom's father's coconut plantation. Eka's husband laid drink aside long enough to build a house in the Bandu compound. For his pains, Eka soon birthed him a set of sons whose demands upon her allowed her to have a tendency toward illness. She hired a wet-nurse. A servant. A houseboy. A cook. And all the while she lorded it over the other sisters, who found their own solutions.

Curdled, Deka still combed her hopes and put them to bed with her at night. The twins had each other.

But in the scheme set by Eka, Nani was lower than even the houseboy who slept on an outside mat no matter the weather's vagaries. In turn, Nani's only salvation was the books she scavenged. When those failed, she had the silky freefall of sleep.

When later Nani reflected on why she had stayed on for years under the reign of Eka, she thought it had something to do with the story of the loyal donkey who covered for the rebellious guard-dog. The donkey who brayed at the thief, to be rewarded only by further beatings from her drunken master for waking him.

Her wedding night had shocked Nani into a world not of her invention. Now she accepted what was given and kept herself from complaining if all proved less than her desire. Wasn't desire the root of evil? Her gods helped, her Buddha helped, why should she complain?

She understood the story of the dog and the donkey. The dog with all his complaints had gained no more freedom than the donkey.

As people do in insufferable circumstances, she became loyal to her principle. Her principle being generosity, she was more loyal to it than to any other person. She gave to them all indiscriminately. To Eka and her boorish husband and boys and servants. To shamed

Deka and the twins. She became more loyal to her principle of giving than to the memory of her departed father. She offered hours of sweeping the yard, of grinding spices, of stirring pots. If she had an extra piece of skirt cloth, she offered it to a sister who needed a house rag. When she wasn't hungry, she gave the extra rice for her dinner to the houseboy.

She kept only one book and one change of clothes. Because she would give. Then give and give and give some more, becoming the perfected principle of giving.

Until one day when her shoulders felt to be breaking and her heart (she knew it) had turned soggier than her own wedding platform that ill-fated day and she had just about enough of fists and gibes and begging for meals and the houseboy's sneer.

And in so doing, finally she gave herself something life-size. She did what had been waiting in her those long uncounted years. Such confidence as she'd been born with is a drumbeat that might go into muffled hiding but never leaves a body. She'd given enough.

She rolled up her mat, memorized her father's map and used a last hidden coin to embark upon the train, the one that would never bring her back.

97

SHE IS RIGHT. Honree had either been listening to this halting version of her life or had retreated into his pink-man trance. She admires the sheer crepe of the sheet she had bargained for and then bought for him. It suits him. How the crepe flows down his poke-out shoulders, down over his squiggly, funny-alphabet hairs. How it pleats over the groin, coming to that doubled furrow between the legs.

Now her finger traces his throat to where a yielding flag of skin collects, crinkled at the base. If she could, she would run away from everything with him. He would be a different man if he could be lured away from all his plans.

Far away, he might behave more as he does when he's bedbound. Better and softer. The way he was after they brought out the calf.

He is always racing two minutes behind his ideas. This is why she can never look at him while she speaks. She has to stare out the gauzy curtains and speak beyond the careful garden plots of the Big House. But since he's asleep she can play with him.

It's no difficult job to pull the sheet down in order to better examine that chest's coarse red and black hair, what she knows so well, hair the colors of a toy soldier, what he so proudly displays as he bathes. It's clear he's proud of this hair. How funny. She skims her palm to where his shoulder anchors his hand down and inventories the sharpness of his ribs' outward hull.

Near her childhood home, an old beached ship had rotted its innards, giving her and her gang of boys the chance to play in its briny, moss-lacquered shell. Now she plays with this pale curvaceous hulk, sapped by the day, almost feminine.

Too many directions, Honree, she instructs the sleeping man. *You should slow down.*

She has never been so close to any man. What she feels for him may be the stuff of love songs. On impulse, she draws close to his neck, finds the smell that pulls her closer, caught between the milk of almonds and that afternoon's pol curry. Underneath everything, always a baby's scent. A few weeks into his stay here she had taken pity on him — then he had a muttony scent, how could any of his plans work? — and, without the water, had taught him how to use the basin and the well out back. How to pour cold water down one's spine. She had taught him to use the stick after meals on his teeth and tongue, and it has worked, his breath is finally sweet.

Before, even from a distance, his stink had pulled her toward him, a tidal wave of pity for such a man, a slave slurried by his odd activities and ideas and lazinesses. Not to bathe! He had such funny ideas!

Now in his sweetness she practically owns him.

Are you mine? she asks that pallid man.

Only his breath ever answers and she wants to eat him for dinner. She wants to eat him up into herself so he has no history before her. She will be the first, the only, the memorable, the one to make him slow down. There is something sturdy to him, more than that boy Manu who pretended to welcome her into Rajottama and then made her so lonely. Has Manu shown his true self? Too busy and neglectful with his posters and events, his big secret — too rude, too absent.

On the bed she lies, staring away from Honree. Instinctively, she pushes her rear into where his warmth slumbers in those foolish pajama bottoms. She pulls his heavy slack arm around her for once, tries to breathe in rhythm with him and drifts off to sleep.

When she wakes with a jolt, his hand is traveling under her loose dress, leaving a line of goosebumps. His hand acts like a familiar visitor, guessing a roundness and a hollow before it arrives. A cold hand talking. Saying her womb holds the strings to the goosebumped kites the hand stitches together on her skin's surface. Saying he's not awake, or he is, but won't volunteer any sign he's out of his dreams.

Later we can say we were dreaming, she tells herself. *We fool-ish two* she mutters in her borrowed language.

Outside people call for them. The shades are drawn and the door bolted. *He must be sleeping,* she hears that singing boy explain outside.

She remembers the boy's hand, how it had offered her fleshy red rambutan fruit through the hole in the door. And the boy's refusal to know her as the girl in the hut, the one he'd wronged by disappearing. And how after the first meeting in this house she knew it was impossible to love someone who could forget, or pretend to forget, as much as her singer had.

Where Honree would not be one to disappear. He would keep her laughing with his hats and stormy ways.

For a sliver of a moment, his eyes open into hers. What color are they? His maker had been struck with indecision, making them green or gold-flecked blue, the color of the sea shattered into a thousand seconds. Up close his face is so distorted, all nose and cheek flesh, she almost giggles but instead closes her eyes.

We're not ashamed, she thinks, *but we should stay alone. And silent.*

He grabs her wrist, his leg pulls her close, she arches away. He slams his hand into the small of her back, she turns toward him. All the while they act out flight and union, sea and fish, they are alone and their eyes squeeze shut. Their hands stroke and slap as though there will be no repercussions, as though they free themselves of time, exactly the way shamelessness descends on immortals.

And his voice in Sinhala, breaking the spell: 'I can't believe you desire me.'

Morning finds her without that hulking frame in the bed. She is ignorant of his whereabouts, of what he thinks of her ingress. But she feels criminal delight. Not at him, at the fact of herself. What she has been able to get away with in this one short life!

IX

BLUE VEINS

❧ ❧ ❧

Thus are the Buddhas incomprehensible, and incomprehensible is the nature of the Buddhas, and incomprehensible is the reward of those who have faith in the incomprehensible.

— *The Mahavamsa*

98

'THOSE SOLDIERS were not bad people,' she tells Henry a week later. Ever since they'd begun to split a bed, her pink man understands Sinhalese much better.

He is interested, rolls strands of her hair between swollen fingers, a merchant appraising silk thread.

'Anyway, some had come from villages like ours,' she says. Some hadn't known why exactly they had joined but still clipped their hair and put on that funny uniform with its visored cap and useless braid. She'd understood their desire to surrender to something larger than the lives they had known.

What she knew less was how they'd decided not only to serve the rulers but to take on their vices. It was clear the bottle helped pass nights away from families, gods and normal terms of address. She almost understood. She only wished that during the brief time she stayed near the camp she could have had some similar escape. All she had was her single book.

'What was the book?' he murmurs, only half-listening.

They'd called her Little Sister and made her a tent. They'd invited her to partake of their sugar-mud coffee and fires but not the late-night games with bottles. They'd seemed decent at first. She'd lain awake in the empty tent that felt like a bullock's inside skin and read past the words of the book, a compendium of herbs she'd received from the herb doctor last new year's at home.

The book was in the underground language she'd thought only she and the late doctor shared. It reminded her of home. She'd stared past the words and wondered: What next?

Henry loves this story of her stay among the soldiers. This had been part of her journey toward what she calls the Big House. Toward Rutaeva. Toward *him*.

'Did they look at you?' he asks, running a finger up her side. 'Did they enter your tent at night?'

'It wasn't for long,' she says, her face shuttering closed. 'Only for a week after my wedding.'

'Then what?' he says. His teeth shuck her of the lace sari top, this bodice she wears. The marvel of her navel and her waist's swale meet his tracing lips. 'You will think of me later,' he says, 'any time you remember those shoulders, I mean soldiers.'

'You must take off your shirt if you touch me. That's the new rule. Your hat too.'

His sweaty self complies. On the chair, ceremonious, he places his funny hat and the tunic she'd sewn. Then they may be stripped of the world in this room, vacant but for them. Everything unspoken can fall away.

Soon he will be privileged with *her* eyes, *her* mouth, *her* ears. He'll know what it was to grow in her family, to eat that rice, to escape on a noisy train and come to a house where her hands had dusted and cleaned before they knew for what.

It's not wrong for her to hope that this tall mysterious foreigner could gain some understanding. She sees the flicker at the back of his watery eyes. A flicker with the quality of a verdict. He does know something. What it is she can't say. She has noticed the dark islands of his eyes, how they become black seas whenever she crosses his vision.

'Then what happened?' this foreigner asks her. His hands insist on roaming her thighs. 'What happened with the soldiers?'

Is he what she dreamed of as a child?

'Then I returned home. Then I died for a while.'

He is already in her and does not hear the last part. All the kites on her skin shrivel. 'They treat you well?' she thinks he asks. He digs out her insides. Trying to poke out some truth. 'You love them like me, love them this way?'

On the other side of the door, in the library, the boy stands.

He is stealing a book to read in his cottage. It is Henree's confidential Village Book that he wishes to read. To cover his theft he grasps his shoes and an old almanac to his chest. And tries to hold his breath.

With his shiny shoes he cannot keep himself from pressing his ear to their door late at night. His exhalation is hot and short and not right for a spy but he knows about stifling it. Only the moon falls into the front room with its perennial dust and opened books.

430

The boy's finger flies to his mouth. More than anything in life he hates being sentenced to the realm of the ignorant. He will not hiccough at the surprise of their coupling. He tells himself there is no magic to this. No surprise. He'd heard her telling stories to the stork; he was not an unspeculative sort; hadn't he seen this coming?

Behind the door the sheets are rustling. Though not from his own experience, he knows exactly how the two appear in their link and fastening. Their bodies entwine; there might be some show of Henry's physical prowess, some touching to soothe all nerves — it is maudlin. Which does he want to be? He can almost see the pink shipwrecked beast, feel the girl's thick hair stretched into wings over the pale body.

Could the two inside love each other? Jehangir could love some-one like her.

Someone like her. Finally the stories touch his memory, slam through his core, make him know her.

That is *his* girl in there, the girl from the river and the hut: Miss Rambutan Fruit, the backwoods dancer. Nani? A stiff agitation seizes him. He has heard enough. The boy will not wait until dawn.

And all this while he'd thought she loved Manu. He'd had har-rowing knife-point sights of her, how she'd walked with Manu from the market. Her kneeling by the hedge to talk through its lozenge-shaped hole if Manu walked past on the road — her soul submit-ting, some delicious laziness overtaking her. She'd both splashed her smile about and vanished more when Manu came to talk with oth-ers. Jehan had not begrudged her this love for Manu, whatever kind it was, pungent-familial or friendly or threatening-romantic, there not being that much difference. Something between *them* — that he could have forgiven. But here the girl of the hut, of his own youth, entangles herself with a foreigner.

With a bird of a man, a fish, a spiteful terrible something sleeping in the mirror.

One of the almanacs thuds to the floor. Jehan's hands have lost vo-lition. He turns to flee but cannot help it when one of his shiny shoes also crashes to the ground. He is fused to the spot. For a decisive moment the sheets do not rustle. And then it must be the man who emits huge rattling wheezes. Like some fallen leviathan or at least a satisfied pink man.

And the boy believes she must have heard his spying. But a girl of her background will not shame him. She knows the importance of normalcy, and he banks on this, slouching off to his cottage with its sparse furniture and immaculately red-polished floor.

To distract himself he reads from the new revision, a smaller Buddhist catechism:

Q. What are the duties to be performed by man or woman towards friends and others?
A. i. To give presents
   ii. To speak kindly
   iii. To do suitable acts for them
   iv. Not to dispute with them

99

THE NEXT MORNING she hears what she thinks at first is a strange rain with a sagging rhythm and a spread hand. Then she realizes it is the boy, battering a southern drumbeat on the teapot. The boy in the kitchen tapping. She has slept too long and grabs the cloth to wrap it around her waist. From the bed Henry raises a slack arm, astonishingly like a cadaver's. 'I'll do that for you?' he asks before rolling to his other side. She cannot have this chattering Jehan boy knowing too much about her. There has been that dangerous look in his eyes for many days. She hooks her sari top and ties her hair in a knot heading out the door.

Because she is aware of the other man's smell on her she tries to hurry by but Jehangir is leaning on the kitchen counter, a strange panic lighting him up, not letting her pass.

'You came for tea?' she asks with a peacock's cry, hard to control, 'With ginger?'

Her hair falls loose behind her and he snorts, 'You came from bed.'

She will keep things small, so starts gathering lonely cups left around the kitchen. A gnawed bone fallen on the ground. A scarlet spoon.

'That's mine,' he says. 'Leave it there. Is there some kind of festivity going on?'

She makes her way, brushing by him, and — she'd expected no

less — he follows her outside in his noisy, gloomy way. Through the lattice he watches her quickness scrubbing a pot. 'Is it difficult for you?' he asks finally.

'Anay — how do you mean?'

His mouth hangs askew, wounded, cracked. Just like that he should not be trying to enter some breach in her usual reserve. He should not be allowed out or in. He does not look safe anymore with his ember eyes.

'We know about each other,' the boy finally says, bottled up. She sees the words stay difficult in his gorge. Yes, he must have fallen under some bad cloud not to have remembered this before. He takes off his spectacles, the eyes swarming black holes, shadowed underneath. How could she have enjoyed him so much once? What bad demons had crossed him since? A sympathy snares her and she can almost see him in the region of what he used to be — a boy on the verge of fulfilling himself. Through the lattice he almost redeems something resembling that boy from the hut.

'You didn't take me to heart at all?' her singer asks, the last part falling. She doesn't understand what he means.

But clearly she'd been wrong to think he'd remembered. Their almost indecipherable murmurs, the river feeling they'd brought each other, their hands like heavy tongues into the Dobie's hut, the welcome intrusion, his polite-bishop's request to see her face, her dance, it had been better than fruit, trumpets, dawn, choice.

Then, there had been a tender sky over them. But she'd been wrong to think that in this house he'd made a silent pact with her. She'd thought the house had become their blank room, words swept to the corners, that they were never supposed to talk of the past. Now that he remembers, he is heavy with motion, he wants to make her recognize something, he is a rock forcing itself against water. His copper lips, she had thought them handsome, now jabbering this bad talk. He blasts and rips everything. But can't he see the nonsense of saying anything *now?*

It is her lover's mistake. As though before his sleep Honree had lacked the courtesy to close the door behind him.

She realizes the possibilities: the boy could have stood on the rolling hill below their room the whole night and swooned to her cries. Or worse. He could've been right outside the door creaking and making the wood saw and heave. She had wanted to think it a covey of river rats.

But Jehan is no rat. Not someone you can so easily wish away.

His lips are the only insistent reminder of the riverside boy who'd cheered her during seven solitary days. When his eyes had been calm and he had lulled her with stories. Now he's all trembles. Saying something about whether she wants a baby.

'What?' And then, realizing she wants only quick accord from him, she outstares him with what she hopes is something of her sister Eka's sharpness. 'Don't worry about me. We have our history. It is just history —'

— the red flesh of the fruit he had brought her during otherwise soul-crushing days, she remembers. Across the boy's face, his version of memory; a hand wanting to fly out to her.

But at least he has a foreigner's sense of politeness. He can be distracted by small courtesies. She gives him his tea in the courtyard. Milk, no sugar, no ginger. Wishing he would leave.

'You know how old he is?' asks Jehan in a hushed tone.

She'd been wrong. 'No,' she says, 'and I don't want to know.'

'He must be in his late forties. At least.'

'Yes.'

'And there are rumors about him and a Russian lady.'

'Thank you.' Her sobriety serves her. 'Now I'm going to the canal to do the wash.'

After this, whenever she sees Jehan with his combed, oily hair and his finger flying to his butterfly lips, she can no longer ignore that awful insinuating desire of his. The desire to mark himself on the new terrain she and the other man create, just upstairs from the boy.

He doesn't want to make any choices himself. She thinks he's afraid. Or lazy. Wants just to be inside them, or beneath, on the continents they shift with their grappling, to rise on the sparks and floaters they let off into the broad night.

100

ADORATION, AFFECTION, ARDOR. Attachment, care, commitment. Consecration, dedication, devotion. Sheer fondness, friendship and inclination. Liking developing into passion tempered by regard, respect, tenderness. Imbued with warmth.

There are at least fifteen words Henry can think of to denote love in English. Ceylonese has only the one. *Adare*. And *adare*, Pandit had hinted, is itself a loanword from the Portuguese. How can he get the monk or anyone to yield up the language's amatory wealth? Henry is swimming in her and not even the English can yield the word fresh enough to put in his Village Book, which he's misplaced.

Had he conquered her? Was he asking the right questions? He wanted to think it was not the worst part of him that wanted to pull her down and into him, but the beast inside felt old and oily, his own hands like stained leather on her clean body, even as he sank into her shimmer, the sex and light and perfume that unvexed him, that he wanted to drink in. He went hoarse trying to tell her how for the first time he could know the presence of love or freedom or abandonment all over. Away from her he found himself remembering the small bit of conjuring he had learned.

There is a point where the Buddha's meditation guidelines speak of how to put an image before another's eyes. One banishes darkness and says *May this eventuality appear before my father's eyes*, for example. This is just a wish, not witchcraft. Henry believes it will harm no one if in the meditation sessions (which Pandit had encouraged him to begin privately), he practices the smallest bit of compassion voodoo.

May Nani see a lifetime well-spent in loving me.

Sure, he hopes he attains proper merit through his Buddhist intentions and practice. And yet it would hurt no one if he pelted his wish upon the universe. *May I stand central in Nani's eyes.* He cannot believe how she gives herself up to him so readily each night, her laugh in his ear, slowing his hand until he behaves more calmly, less bewitched.

So all the ways he seeks to please her are careful ways. He leaves a pollen-flocked purple wildflower in her wardrobe. When she asks who brought it, as though it were a noble inheritance, he won't say. He sets on her spice ledge a hummingbird-shaped bottle of English rosewater, for which he had traded a pen in the open, taboo, *other* market. In the dark he feeds her an apricot, so she will be enamored, thinking perhaps she had never tasted one, and he is right; she says the skin is like his, she makes him suck the engraved pit and riddles him *now what is that like?* He is eager for any portent about their future, writing her name in elaborate blue-inked Sinhala on an ancient ola leaf he had purloined from the temple, and then leaving the leaf on his desk for her to find.

In the day around the boy she refuses to look at Henry.

Negligible old man, he tells himself when he needs to move his mind away from her. It would help if he had his Village Book. But he feels like an amputee; the book is lost; he can notate nothing about her. Nothing — because there is just one book for one village. One woman for one book. There will be no others.

101

'WHAT IS IT NOW, I'm searching,' he tells Johnny. Now that his strength returns these June mornings he treasures his solitude. Just before the rains, a later moment will always compete with an earlier, time so precious. Meanwhile the boy has begun a bad habit of dawdling. He sways in the library's early dawn like a tree with nothing better to do. A stranger and navigator, caged, hair falling over his eyes in an uncustomary fin.

'I want to ask something, Henree.'

'Tell me the topic of next Saturday's meeting and I'll let you do anything.' This is not a world of leisure that they live in, no matter how early the hour. Because business doesn't die when one doesn't do it. And Henry — no one would say he's not getting back to the business of things, this business of hope.

His aide, who might be having a bad day, thrusts forward not the longed-for Village Book, but the leather one in which appointments are kept. Henry scans the minutes of past and projected topics and meetings but what is there to set his soul aflame?

Proper Construction of a Poultry House — 50 attendees

Bee-Keeping for Pleasure and a Village's Profit — 44 attendees

Utilization of Manioc Leaves for Livestock: A Metaphor of Self-Sufficiency — 30 attendees

'Nice records,' says Henry, voice headlong as a child's. 'So where do we start?'

'You covered manioc last time, weeks ago. Got a minute?' There is melodramatic color to the boy's movements. He pulls without meaning on the drape cord, releases it, holds the sill as though it were a bridge railing. His fingers finally stretch for help up to his neck and he leans over Henry.

'Can it wait?'

'When would you *not* be busy, Henree?'

The day's ambivalent gray light enters through the theater of the mango leaves, playing up this one, scorning another, renewing nothing. Had she slept in? Such leisure would not be undeserved. First they always have to pass through the grating of their strangeness. Then she stays up all hours tending to him and his appetites.

'Suppose I told you, Henree, your character is a cold one.'

Henry is not unhappy to enter *this* topic with the boy, discussing how culture gives us our ideas about what character means, how coldness can be variously interpreted, and the impossibility of naming anything with certainty in this one life.

Exasperated, the boy tries again. 'You know, Henree, given the attention which has been drawn recently to our little project . . .' The boy's words tumble: there is the stream of funds (recently tripled) from Chilkins, maybe the government agent himself —

'Your doing, my boy.'

Yes, he says, and goes on — there are Henry's dreams of sharing the culture through the dance and the drums with the orphans, a winter-through-summer pleasure for every boy and girl, no matter their caste —

'You're always my eloquent Aaron, Johnny . . .'

There is holding on to all that Henry has built up.

Henry stretches himself out on the settee but some meteor falls inside. No glances had been trailing him, Henry had thought. Recent deeds feel dingy in the probing. 'What?'

Finally Johnny gets to it. 'Scandals don't fall lightly in Rajottama.' He speaks as though stones pile up in his throat — the boy cannot speak well. 'Anywhere. You can't go on pretending to be naive. Public attention isn't good for any of us.'

He regards his boy. Somewhere there must be a compromise between this boy's Hebraic face and all future delicacies of cusp and guzzling flesh.

'Henree —'

The boy sits near his boss, who happens to be noticing as if for the first time the godawful silver ripplings in the living room's tepid dark. Not a fit, no. The clouds turn the interior a mawkish milk-pail gray. What is the boy saying?

He tells Henry certain things go together as well as — as well as a ball of hair atop a bowl of soup. He says it is time for Henry to quit with her.

'A bowl of soup?' Henry knows what he means. 'There are many *hers.*'

Inescapable poverty, Johnny is saying, you don't understand, certain actions stand to jeopardize all those orphan boys having food enough to eat. 'Your idealism, Henree. Wasn't I with you in all that?'

'Aren't you still?' Henry asks, a little alarmed.

The boy rattles on about all the children from the beggars' village; the beggars' cook who prepares one hundred and fifty kilos of rice a day just from Henry's checks; the model garden almost good to go. Or what Henry speaks about in the lectures. About registering marriages. 'I did so much for you, for that —' It would be difficult to calm this boy, so nettled, kneeling before him, the voice thick: 'There are actions that would squander it all for a temporary . . .'

Outside the gardener is chewing and spitting betel, evidently enjoying his gargle. Birds crash through the trees; someone on the canal faintly reprimands a bull; two men pass by singing a drunken marching song.

The boy can't say it, he slams his hand into the settee right by his employer's leg, raising dust, coughing. 'Dammit, Henree — !' Jehan hides his hand under a pillow. 'What you're doing will jeopardize our projects.' In a flash, if asked, Jehan would be on glossy American streets with the man, saluting American girls, hearing American voices and pianos and owls. He would enter rooms with American doorknobs and candelabra and rum and manners — but Henree is embracing some other Henree, sitting like a chess piece that can suddenly go in any direction. Henree has to be shaken to be reminded who he is. And also must be reminded what he had portrayed himself to be, long ago on the Colombo dock.

Jehan is on the point of grunting out to the man the whole truth. Everything that Jehangir Nelligodam and Jonathan Nellie had done so far to help Henree. *I have turned myself inside out for you,* he would say. He would give his unassailable account. All the efforts that have left Jehan unzipped, unbuttoned, cloven, treading curiously around himself. And then Henree would not dare play cavalier with Jehan's life and everyone else's. He would not waste a boy's good faith just like that. Or would he?

'Why don't you stop kneeling? Can't you come sit here? We'll talk in a straight way, calmly,' says Henree.

'Because you don't know how to listen,' says the boy, 'how to see,' awfulness spiraling inside. He wants to retch up judgment against the man.

'John, you may be my aide and trusted . . . but if you do not . . .'

Was the boy asking him to sacrifice her? The blue of nights when her tracing fingers and choices reprieve all of life's motors. That underwater smile she offers. Her rear's warmth pressed into him. Her front and belly asking him to enter any cleft he can find. Deep fingers tunneling into the blue and her dastardly confidence. Her *Honree* so much better than that earlier mockery of *Sir*; Johnny would surely feel it the same if it could be explained. A caught moment like a portrait on a bathhouse wall; a landscape forlorn and unspoiled; her fine pink-stripped lips so much better when they don't taunt from far away. Now he can shush the teasing with a kiss. This is not classic folly. It's different.

'Henree, you don't need me to tell you this,' each word sharp. 'You always say we're a team. Or maybe I heard wrong, but the first thing you said —'

'Coming up the mountain, sure. But Johnny — how to say this? I'm not so sure you're speaking. Forgive me. From the kind of self-interest. Which approaches enlightenment.'

Johnny's face coarsens. 'Oh stop it.' Ready to explode or cry. 'Please don't.'

'What?'

'Not now. Please. I can't take it anymore. Don't unload your Buddhist Buddhism on me *now*. I was hoping for something better from you.'

This is no ten-second battle, it's a war. Once again Henry should have stayed more hidden so as not to be ambushed. At this point all his findings about her are tentative. He would miss the nights more than anything he's ever known. They've discovered ways to locate each other.

Outside there is a cool gray light and what the boy is saying, it could all just dissolve, couldn't it, leave him with her? The boy is at the bookshelf, stroking up some dust. 'I remember when you used to be honest, Henree.'

Henry tries to keep an angel's calm. But now the boy has gone too far — things are starting to go a bit blotchy. 'Isn't it possible you're speaking out of envy, Jonathan?'

All angry eyes, no lids. The boy storms to the door, gray light lances upon him. 'It never occurred to you my name is Jehangir? JE-HAN-GIR.'

Jehan*gir?* Henry goes on speaking. He must. Even though no one's any longer in the room with him. 'Don't get mad. Please. Take it down the hatch. Certain projects cannot be *ours*. Certain things are speculative. We share in the labors but know different things. We must leave certain projects to *others*.'

As he half-guessed, the boy is right outside. But spitting. 'Others.' Each time the boy says the word he spits. 'Others. I *am* your others. You haven't figured it out yet.' He spits again. 'There are no others before me.' Waits. 'You really think your talk means anything to anyone else? You know how much I've taken you and your ideas on? How stupidly? Way beyond what anyone might have asked me to.'

'I'm not denying it,' says Henry feebly.

'My stories have kept you well-covered. You have any clue how many times I've had to explain you to people?'

Henry raises himself. Shaggy, weighted. Maybe it's true, the whole village is going downhill. Maybe he has gone too far. '*Who* asked you to help me?'

'Doesn't matter.'

'What are you always hinting at? Where are you going?'

The shout comes from below, on the way down to the cottage. Each word bitten off. 'O master,' a namby-pamby tone. 'O sahib Henree. I'm off to get enlightened!'

Now Johnny really can't hear. Henry apologizes anyway from where he leans against the door frame. 'Please. Have you ever really been alone?' lips pressing the wood. 'Is it a crime? can't someone save *me* for a change?'

Hearing only weeping — his own — humiliating and juvenile in the book-muffled room, he sinks to the floor. And whispers, 'All else, don't you get it, I have to predict or contrive. It's me who has to make it happen. Too much gravity. But. This. She. Just came.'

And as though the room has waited for him to finish, it begins to unravel, tiny silver triangles everywhere, preparing him for a fit.

On the other side of the second door, rather than go comfort her chipped shell of a man, she backs away slowly. She wants him to recover himself. Without her. He is hers once he's strong and inhabiting passion again. Bedbound is one thing but wailing dampens all kinds of fire.

She steps away with mindfulness. Even if she has given up on personal silences, this house rewards her for attending its quiet. Now she uses it. The quiet has become her own version of slave. It bends to her will.

X

FOR LANKA WAS
KNOWN . . .

. . . to the Conqueror as a place where his doctrine should
thereafter shine in glory, and he knew that from Lanka,
filled with demons, the demons must first be driven forth.

— *The Mahavamsa*

102

THE WORST PART about it is her cries. Long sunderings of the night, her calls begin at the top of Jehan's ears and cut in. Her cries are a dagger become a million tiny blades, piercing his veins to end embedded as tiny pricks of remorse. An aggravation beyond language, one which makes him wish to cheat his own distressing pulses. Even the sight of his own veins makes him quake. As though he has become a boy once again with the priest's nubby hands steepling before him.

It might be Henree's one-too-many errors which fling the boy uncomfortably far from what he'd hoped might be the windfalls of his temporary assignment. But it is her ruckus which wrests Jehan from bed. The moon's slave, he paces the garden's fug. Just outside their door, the mango tree is sick with perfume. Inside the redolent room, forever pounding the bed, the couple's panting is worse than that of mangy dogs whose raw pustular tongues hang lopsided before the monsoon.

One night he's certain he'll throw himself into the canal and spiral floating on his back, then turn over onto his stomach, drifting heedless of the sharp teeth of the government-built dam just before the bridge. He'll explode from heat. He shouldn't let them do this to him.

No, the worst part is their coy daytime smirks. And the girl's preoccupation. Always dreaming. As though he doesn't know. If they didn't smirk so much, he wouldn't be angry. Words can't express Henree's hypocrisy. Does he think his ideas about marriage don't apply to a local girl?

Once, this girl loved Jehan. The boy is sure. One night in her seclusion hut he heard her. So softly whispered the jungle wind behind him could have spoken instead, but she repeated herself. She loved her riverside singer. Her Jehan. Once he finally remembered why she had been so familiar to him (that first sight of her on Henree's threshold) she does him the disfavor of forgetting, purposely.

One day in the kitchen, she says something sharp and unnecessary: *It could just as well have been the wind speaking to me.* And then never says anything more than that, only choosing nighttime to ricochet her cries into his bones. You can tell him to stop, Jehan often thinks. Tell him to stop. He likes to repeat the first phrase he learned from his radio. And he could use a radio here: *Today on the Choice of America, the tongue of today and tomorrow, a winning combination!*

After three more months (HQ having long ago requested a reasonable extension with a proportional augmentation of stipend) Jehan could just up and leave Henree. And Rajottama. The arguments. The model this-and-that.

He has Oxford waiting for him. Perhaps an enchantingly neurasthenic earl's daughter on a boat on the Thames whispering cold annoyance with her pedigree. Later she'll marry him and secure his citizenship. They will joke about building grand engineering marvels of bridges and channels all the way from Ceylon to England. Their children will have light but impermeable skin and scamper about a manor in which the help need not be trained and will memorize nursery rhymes he never knew: *Pussycat, pussycat, o where have you been?*

I've been to London to visit the Queen. He will spend years in books. Accrue degrees and respect from his fellows. Perhaps he might end up Oxford's first Ceylonese don and lecture on literature or jurisprudence. On whatever the curriculum needs most. Awards will spill out of his full pockets, which he will occasionally unburden with some philanthropic gesture of a public work. An anonymous scholarship for young stragglers who in childhood days were stung by being called coconuts, white on the inside. The Nelligodam Centre for Social Welfare. Or: The Nelligodam Centre for Young Jockeys.

It is true that Jehan has crossed over to Henree's side. He hadn't meant to. Yet the man's positive belief can seize the boy and reassure him. Something in Henree's forwardness has made Jehan half-believe in the idea of states united. That there should be a country that claims all others in its continent as American.

Yes, he is sympathetic to Henree. It is natural. Hasn't he for too long been telegraphing off into darkness? He writes — they never answer. Clearly the British mistrust Jehan if they nonetheless mistrust Henree more. And they expect Jehan to stand straight as an apostle carrying out his functions? When they never inconvenience themselves? When they never tell him about the troops arriving? Is he supposed to say grace for this? They persist in thinking Henree an American spy when Jehan knows the worse truth. Henree can often be just an original American fumbler — Henree, who thinks the British are more behind him than ever. Henree, so easily duped. Henree, who doesn't realize how dangerous it is to invite the enemy into your house.

Meanwhile, the colonials must think all clocks have stopped in Jehan's life. Or that his is a dispensable life. That he has boundless time to work for them.

They are having their afternoon tea. They are pursuing their promotions. Going to London to frighten the mouse under the throne. Or taking the air along the coastal strip of park near Colombo's Galle Face Hotel. Every so often they pretend to help by sending checks to Henree. Keeping their true motives obscured. It has been a giddy descent. Despite the checks. Despite the gift of Chilkins' nervousness. Why do they never answer him? He has begun to slack off from sending telegrams every week — let alone every other day.

Jehan is entertaining these thoughts the next morning, watching Henree sidle among the crowd in that beaming blind magisterial way. Yes, Jehan has led Henree to a contest but now goes on strike, privately. For once Jehan will not run around smoothing life out for his employer.

A sorcerer from a few villages over has summoned Rutaeva's local wizard, Appuhamy, to a kind of duel. There is to be a contest of whose magic is superior. At Isaac's Marsh, not far from Regi's, sand surrounded by torpid palms and sesame plants, the people are gathering to watch two competing sorcerers perform the usual tricks against each other. Coconuts which no one can lift. Sand stuck to the feet of the dancing sisters. Much chanting into limes at the base of the trees.

Jehan lets the Yankee sidle down and up in the crowd, bobbing greetings. *Today I won't bother to tell Henree to take off that terrible hat.* In radio dramas from Jehan's childhood, foreigners always made a big to-do of raising their hats. Today Jehan lets the American stay unconscious of everything. How when a person of a certain caste sits on a stool, others of a lower caste rise and leave. Finally Henree crouches awkwardly, a prisoner to the warlocks and their competition. Jehan's heart hardens into ice.

But he stays sitting. Today he will do nothing. Even as a monkey in a gold cap escapes from Appuhamy, only to pass over Regi and Chollie. Even as the monkey rushes to perch on Henree's shoulder where the beast, named Diwa, performs a demoralizing imitation of Henree's smile.

Jehan likewise does nothing as, nearby, Chollie and Regi snarl about the monkey; about Chollie's cane that the monkey had stolen; about the paddy. Instead, Jehan continues to follow the game of ground carom played by young boys nearby. At that age he would have lacked guts enough to join them.

Being two things at once, the lapdog of both emperor and empire, has lost all charm for Jehan. It is not the lost novelty. It is the eternity. Three months from today could stretch like forever. Yet it would be imprudent to quit Henry now. The structure of these ghostly movements — the British coming without Jehan's knowledge right into the heart of Rajottama — makes Jehan think the American purifier a better bet.

Henree has not gone totally bad. He just has to be brought back in line. He must not be permitted to keep fornicating away their shared dreams. Surely he will come back to his own.

Jehan once loved the idea of a square deal with the British. He spies for them; they send him to their homeland. The ungloved truth of it is that he hates their condescension. Probationary prisoner Jonathan Nellie and the crown colony had undertaken a gentlemen's agreement. A free exchange of information, now rescinded. Perhaps they restored the camp merely to justify the amount of Ceylon's security build-up. Or to ready their boys for an armed struggle off the isle. Somewhere that wouldn't concern Jehan. They had left him in the dark. He did not know how long these Rajottaman Brits were to stay, or who was supposed to get them out.

So while Henree may have slipped, one could hope he'd find his way *beyond* the girl in the house. It wasn't impossible. The straight route would return. Shipshape. Everything could move forward again. And while Jehan may not always love the terms of Henree's proposals, is there not something special about the man's immediacy? Even a Janus head knows when it has seen something good. In that constant sprint toward righteousness, isn't there something that involves Jehan far more than he likes to admit? Hadn't he started to think like the American?

The development the boy had never expected — he (still and still) admires Henree. Far more than the dry bureaucrats at Headquarters. Admiration had tugged him in worse than any jungle vine.

Still, a middle ground exists. And to refresh HQ's memory of its promises, it wouldn't hurt Jonathan Nellie to send in a report on Henree more frequently. Perhaps tomorrow. A few harmless notes, then:

1) This contest could provide a convincing bit of primary local color.
2) Tell them of H's programmes and lectures.
3) Of H's uneasiness with the British encampment.
4) Of H's correspondence with those who stand outside the inner British loop.

If he could, Jehan would be no one's spy and just live fully within his skin. He'd be Dakshan, the impish boy leading the game of carom, rowdy and free to aim at spontaneous targets. A boy comfortable with himself. Better yet, Jehan would be Manu. Anyone reporting to himself alone. But had Jehan's particular destiny marked him out, always being the good son to anyone but himself?

The tree-lined squares of Oxford have never seemed so far away from Jehan than they do in the moment of Henree's bleary and complicated smile upon his aide at the contest's close. 'Johnny, walking home?'

'Righto,' answers the boy, finding himself again ready to save Henree's face. He jumps up, brushes dirt off his trousers. 'Quite the row, wasn't it?'

'Quite,' Henree borrowing and then hiding behind the boy's plummy accents, 'almost worth our while.'

'You did well in going.'

'Your suggestion, Johnny.'

'Please.'

'You've always been my godsend.' Henree swallows, clearly rolling up for a big one. 'Don't deny it. No one could lead as well as you. Every day I thank my great good fortune for the gift of you.' He is orating to the fields, his scarless, swollen hands holding a bunch of invisible grapes. 'I am lucky! You've taught me to love this country. And I even loved this contest because of you. I couldn't stop thinking how much you mean to me. To everything I've done here. I could have ended up so differently without you. That's why I could view the thing in good humor.'

Jehan does what he can to smile back at his Henree. His employer. There is a stickiness to the American. He is increasingly something not so easily wished away.

On the walk home, the boy repeats a mantra to himself: *Remember, Jehan, this man is your ticket out. Not in. Remember — out.*

103

JULY STARTS like an offensive and then turns a savior. All the while Henry's unable to get his childhood Robert Frost out of his mind. He composes a folksy little ditty which he hums without cease in the front room:

Child's Lament

Never to walk, never to sigh,
Never to know the reason why
You gave me life and took it away.
Only You would know,
Have their gods earned such play?

While he hums, Nani lies in Henry's bedroom, her blood retreated from the surface of her skin. In the middle of the night, they'd found the odd creature, webbed in crimson, a pulpy sac nestled against her leg. This little tadpole in the last candlelight, frog legs no bigger than Nani's ring finger, an umbilicus still slinking into the very heart of his woman.

This would have been their child and Nani screamed with knowledge.

The creature's mouth was open too in some sympathetic last gasp. But it was Nani's scream and not the creature's that made blood and the umbilicus splotch out of her womb, blood pearled with a rare white tissue. Immediately after, she knelt on the bed in her sarong, her hand to her crotch, embarrassed at the dark purpled outpour which ruined his bed. Henry loved this small propriety. He saved the membranous umbilicus in a handkerchief but didn't know how to dispose of it.

Toward morning she lies there, the center of the rambutan fruit, an exhausted woman against the marbled scarlet star shape. And despite all the kitchen cloths Henry has brought her, the correct cloth, the nappy cloth, the pans of warm water and the crumpled rags and drinking water and special herbs she tells him to take from her tiny bag, his voice a semiquaver, despite his new ability to tend to this self-reliant woman, she still bleeds, waking up faint only to fall into a delirious sleep again in which she calls out Johnny's name, the monk's name, the names of others, even that of the drummer's son, Manu.

Manu?

She never calls Henry.

'Come on,' he goads her. 'Say it. Henry. *Honree.* Come on.' But her lips stay tight in delirium.

And the household, it has stopped. Henry wants no one to know why. The rains have stopped but there will be no breakfast, lunch or marketing. That is his wish as well.

The jungle becomes an ignored relative, repossessing the house with its slithering dampness. In this regard, Ceylon is quick. Piles of dead leaves and vines immediately conquer the sills and thresholds. The spiders regain Nani's carefully cleaned kitchen. Dust collects in such big and hairy corner clots that Henry keeps thinking small animals wait to pounce on him.

While the spiders purl and the dust collects, she bleeds. Henry thinks she's bled for twelve hours continuously, but it might have been thirty-six.

He has not slept, nor has he seen the boy; it could be any day. He should probably call for someone but whom would he want to tell? The herb doctor Appuhamy? the Western doctor from the capital, some five, six hours away?

It is not because he nurses her that she's so hard to quit. More that she makes him proud even in sickness. But he manages it, leaves her for the first time, expecting no reproach from anyone or anything. Over philology books in the front room what awaits him is the reliable serenity after loss. There must be a German word for such serenity. After all, despite everything, the two of them have produced a child with their love, a tiny sprite of their flesh.

> Never to walk at noon, or wrinkle
> Toward the Sphinx's last moon,

he writes on a scrap. He envies the child who's known her womb in a way he cannot, a child who has known nothing *but* her womb.

'Told you,' Johnny says, slashing with his old energy into the front room. Maybe the boy has overcome his pique. Or at least is managing to hide it. Hard to tell with this double-blaster.

'Told me what?'

'They're selling it at the market for pulp,' the boy says so triumphantly that at first Henry thinks They, whoever They are, are selling his little routed baby. Henry is lost imagining villagers bargaining over the pip — tiny grubs of tissue afloat in a merchant's giant colored vat. He asks the boy what he means.

'Your favorite project, Henree, your catechism, how can you smile?'

'I don't believe you. They memorized it, Jehang —'

'You just call me Johnny. No. You're wrong. They're selling it.'

'What — children!'

'Your project depends on these *children.*'

Henry waves his hand in a great feign of laxity and pedagogical delight. 'Then let them leech themselves.' But how quickly beatitude can vanish. He paces. 'Let them enjoy the facade of their own religion. How can anyone stop a suicide?' He sits down, he rises, he hits his desk. 'If it's done, it's done.' Which makes Johnny issue a conclusive sigh. He stares pointedly at Henry's locked bedroom as though a succubus lies behind.

Since Henry doesn't prod him, Johnny is the one to break the silence, demanding, 'What *is* it exactly you're doing right now, man?'

'Talking with you.'

'Where are your projects? Are you staying or going? I can't run everything alone. They need you at the school. *And* in the garden. And in the store. Not in bed.'

But Henry's tranquility has returned, a shred of it. He explains that if all the children care about is a furtherance of worldly acquisitions, selling their own catechism, for god's sake, he can do nothing. For now what will help him know the truth is solitude. Just solitude and meditation.

From inside his bedroom Nani calls out Henry's name, piping in the request for a glass of water: *Honree!*

'A new type of solitude and meditation, Henree?'

And Johnny bolts. In his hasty departure, he forgets his spectacles, the flimsy wire contraptions sitting like a cock-eyed joke upon the table. Fuming, he returns to whisk them away. As though Henry had no right to be alone in their company.

Once Nani recovers from their mistake, a week after the tadpole, they begin a honeymoon. Everything else reels away. She becomes a very young girl. Henry sees it happening. Her deep eyes are rimmed with coastal blue, her wrists slim, her shoulders broad. In every way she is correct, a law that cannot be disobeyed. Something rebounding all the more strongly after loss. He has never been more alive and revisits the moment of the miscarriage over and over.

First she suffered the pains, said she'd dreamed of a white elephant carrying a lotus in its white trunk, like the dream of Queen Mahamaya, the Buddha's mother, her name meaning Great Illusion —

— then Henry was holding her hand as the old blood, all her body's preparation for future love, surged out, suturing them tighter together.

He became her maid, draining her bedpans of blood, letting his bed turn into a red quatrefoil and then a dyed sheet with its delayed account of their coupling. All this was admittedly complicity.

The sheets bore witness to their kind of marriage ceremony, a divorce in reverse. The lies. The bed and bedpan. The bloody water which he poured into their plot of lavender out back. The umbilicus he buried at the base of the mango tree. All were rites.

The shape of the village, of Madame and his faraway life and the half-brother to the event, little Daniel, everything melted into a distant and slumbering beast. Once he decided to remain near the girl, he felt as close to her as if they were both dying. But he had never so fully endured the burdening privilege of awareness. He delighted in this godlike vision she bequeathed him, near to blood and guts and death.

Small moments shoot up between them. Fresh habits while she regains her strength. He rubs her feet until she cries, *Touching our feet is taboo, don't you care?* in her fine English, letting him know how much she had degraded herself so early on by stroking his feet. And she loves it, she cannot get enough of his swollen hands around her feet. He nuzzles and sucks the babylike balls of her toes as though they were tiny berries, delicious round promises of their life together.

Stop, she whispers, laughing in pleasure, tickled.

Egypt, 30 B.C. — Cleopatra dissolves pearls in vinegar and credits the potion with her seduction of Julius Caesar and Mark Antony. Many Egyptians find asp venom much less successful as an aphrodisiac,

he reads to her. She ambushes him in the dark, crowing at him as though he is bounty successfully hunted. She lets him take her onto his broad stork's back, spinning her around the room.

He learns now of her mischief, how she had been examining him while he slept. In this way, was it, she had entered his dreams, making them tumble out from her.

'Were you always this way?' he asks. 'Such a devil? How come I didn't know?'

'Sometimes I am one of the many kinds of shy,' she says. 'Before I was not me with you.'

'Myself,' he corrects her.

'Yourself was one of the many kinds of shy?' she teases him back, having chosen to speak in her own way. 'That I myself cannot believe.'

Rome, A.D. 68 — A man's potency is boosted if his genitals are massaged with asses' milk, presumably applied by an attractive milkmaid.

Sometimes he gropes her to get past all taboos. The ones he knew instinctively as a child, the *shallyouhelpmewithmygirdlewhatanideasillyboy* early mornings, seeing one of the maids refracted in her dusty mirror, stays and slips, the flesh both retreating from black straps and spilling over, the snap of the hooks.

At such moments, he touches Nani indiscriminately, aching for a sliver of flesh, brown, a woman's, toying with all taboos, and she always seems to know when he absents himself, she takes his hand and puts it away, she holds it to his mouth, she brings him back to her breath and specificity.

She has become the small sphere to which he can give, all blaze on the gunwale.

He sometimes whispers to her and realizes he is thinking of his childhood Matthew, the boy he would hide in his steepled hands. There is nothing beyond her, she understands all, they both have been waiting for this ease between them.

Mundane joys make up July. Finally, after the rains, the wind thrashing the trees, she keeps endowing him with the bravery to venture out again.

He teaches her his limited understanding of finances and book-keeping. Though there is little enough to do — the monk and Lester Pilima having taken over so much of the General Store and government accounting — with the books she is fast and more than competent, catching line errors he has made.

'From now on, because of you,' he tells her, 'all books will be clear,' meaning the sum of his existence. He whispers to her every-thing. The problems with the village. His unease about the British squad. And how Johnny's nonchalance about the squadron is also troubling.

But that matters less than her listening: increasingly the big life outside is lived by Henry like a puppet show. It is only for her. So she can hear its story in the hour of the raucous egrets. He never talks of what he left behind in America. Instead he describes running around in the day's humidity, meeting with this faction and that fandangled caste.

For a few nights he avoids her in bed in order to remember his adulthood, their separation. But then he finds himself jealous of every surface she brushes against or sits upon. The kitchen countertop and her meditation pillow before her pagan idols. Her Buddha and Vishnu and her carefully sewn white areliya garlands. He cannot stop the craving to drown in her, to let their skin seal to-gether.

'Do I heal or hurt you?' he cannot stop asking her.

'*Eeka naemae,*' she tells him. 'Neither. You are not a god! That I show you my care' — her lips tracing his swollen red fingers — 'isn't that just enough? *Aethi?*'

Everything begins to please him again. The idea of mildew. Old needles, weeds, procreation. Caste fights. Jock itch. Sweet tea. Sex. God. He begins again to compose flattering letters urging Madame to come. She can reinvigorate his vision. She would, at the least, charm these weird villagers. Let Madame bring on her pyrotechnics; her dancing roses; the stuffed monkeys.

Dear Elena, Ceylon has begun to crack without you, one letter opens. *Dear Elena, Your trusted friend now calls upon your talents* is how the one he finally sends starts.

July 18? —

Sent off 2 more letters to Elena.

Orphans successfully moved across the canal to the dance conservatory's family compound. Men took cots across the swinging bridge only yesterday. Children happy & even more ready than usual to learn their culture.

Our monk possesses such forethought.

School now held in a large dance hall, annex to Kumari's house. All have united their efforts. Now the orphanage so nicely renovated on this Elephant side of canal stands empty. Must find appropriate use for what has become a vacated mansion on Pilima land.

Now, too, the prickly yellow jakfruit has become full & sweet, no longer a vegetable.

They call it by a new name. Hanging from the tree, its scent, recalling green apple & vetiver & lavender, something from childhood, was strong enough to let Nani know the massive thing was ripe — & ready to pick.

The innards surprise. Pulpy yellow sacs, delicious when delivered by another's hands.

People promise that by August the fruit will become unbearably sweet.

104

'IF THE MAN is going to insist on *not* helping us, you see, he's never lifted a finger, he doesn't even know how to get rid of the British camp,' Lester is saying through the door to his wife, who is knitting in the front room, a habit she'd picked up during meetings of the Colombo Ladies' Charitable Society. She'd made it clear to Lester that if he had to smoke his cigar, a special gift from the young lieutenant, he would have to stay outside on the front porch and talk to her through the door as she wasn't abiding with all the bad habits he had picked up in her absence. She hadn't come all the way up to Rajottama just to smell someone's cigar smoke.

Lester had put forth a strong invitation that she be back home for July and August — ostensibly because he wanted to be a man with his wife, as he'd said, to live as others did. He had a deeper reason. He would barely admit to himself that Manik's presence alone — maybe a carefully prepared visit — would get the foreigner to leave. Because the man was a bad one. While *she* was an unquestionable good.

Once she had arrived, his hope was that if Manik could hear the litany of his woes — how the American kept meddling with the monk, with Chollie, the tappers, the drummers' land and Lester's campaign — she might get riled up enough to do something. That had been his thinking. Instead, after he wound up and finished, she lets out a sigh. Her yarn has gone rolling on the floor and stops on the threshold of the door between them.

'Can I come in now?' he asks.

'Not if you're still smoking.'

To Lester's perpetual chagrin and lust, her voice never loses that Pilima confidence, that buff of a woman content with herself or her pedigree. He finds that, for him, pedigree and woman are barely distinguishable. And it is in her shiniest voice that she proceeds to tell him that most of his village concerns are below the level of the daisies, they are at the cowdung floor. Such are the new free and cultivated expressions she has picked up in Colombo among the suffragists. He is not too tired to tell Manik how living with her aunt has made her into a rougher woman.

While he speaks, he is trying to bend back one of the brass roosters he had recently installed by the front door. One had been tilted forward so it pecks rather than preens. This is probably the work of the new serving boy, the last of many — another boy getting more fractious as the days go by. Lester studies the rooster's angle and considers firing the boy. His wife asks him does he really want to hear what she thinks?

'That's what I'm here trying to find out,' says Lester between puffs.

She tells him it is high time for him to stop worrying so much about the foreigner. He should devote himself to something higher.

'Like to you?'

'To the campaign,' she says. 'To take one example.'

Lester explains to her, using rhetorical skills paralleling those taught in monasteries, that for a man to win any support, he must first rid a village of its cancers. The cockroach is a cancer. If the cockroach stayed, people wouldn't believe in Lester. But listening to his dried-up concerns, his wife laughs. She doesn't accept such logic as soon as she should. She wonders aloud whether it is the people who want the cockroach to leave or would it be just Lester?

This distresses him. That she would chop him away from something he holds in high sentimental regard. The villagers. *His* villagers. He lists Chollie, Pandit, and surely others until she interrupts, saying it wouldn't hurt Lester to read a few Buddhist suttas a day.

From inside the house, her voice is victory. He can't stand how she polices him and then trounces him so snootily. He's forced to lean in and exhale a cloud at her. To remind her she'd married a devout man. A man whose devotion she would never fully comprehend.

She sighs. 'Yes, the forest monks said you would reach nirvana sooner than most people. Still you could look at a verse once in a while. Even just glance at the foreigner's catechism.'

Here is his coup. He tells her about the boys he'd hired to sell the catechism. That the catechism would soon be long gone. He knows in saying this that she had very much admired the pamphlet, despite her native distrust of the cockroach. Lester then informs his wife he is a busy man. And reminds her he hadn't asked her to return to Rajottama just to get him to make apologies all day long. He doesn't care if she is scornful, smiling inside. He is through, thank you, with apologies and excuses. Because, and she could tell him if he understood it wrongly, had the historical Pilimas become great by using excuses? For him, Lester, he would not allow himself the *leisure* of any more excuses.

105

THE WIND HAS STIRRED Henry into a better optimism than any before. Clouds in clear profile whip all over the canal, the light stenciling between trees. The world is gray and white and (often enough to inspire hope) a shocking king's blue.

Having found the greater goodness of life all over, he is about to make a routine stop at the dance school when he hears the male voice inside the hall. Laughing with Kumari in a pseudo-Sinhalese. The American stops outside the arched door and listens.

'*You* make it seem easy,' the man says. 'Had no idea it was so complicated.'

'Already you know more than he does,' Kumari encourages him, her voice possessing what Henry finds to be an unmercifully girlish lilt.

Inside the golden hall like a refuge for the afflicted is the British soldier in civvies. 'Chris the name. Glad to meet you,' his ruddiness says, pretending to forget the two have encountered each other, and over tea at that. He perspires so winsomely, so boyishly. 'Kumari here,' he laughs, 'she's just putting me through my paces.'

The woman stands back as if Henry had surprised her and a lover in bed. Though her heavy drum is slung from a strap around her neck, she balloons with some irrepressible joy.

Henry looks up at the boy: from his unlined face, Chris must be only in his late twenties. But how rugged his stature. He's the kind future generations are proud to claim in a cracked daguerreotype: *My great-grandfather in the Foreign Legion, I inherit my broad bones from him.* No wonder Kumari doesn't know where to sit.

Instead she frets like a nervous filly. Her fingers tap the drum's tautness. She's hospitable, she's thrilled, her voice skits about the higher registers — all in all she acts as though she's never met such a *nice* foreigner as Chris.

'Check in later,' Henry says, hoping he doesn't sound as rude as he feels. No one cares about him; caring must be an inconvenience for people. He delivers an official report: 'You're doing well, that's clear, no need to do much of anything here.'

As he walks, each time his feet flap the ground he hears *MUCH much MUCH much*. He hopes it's only a headache coming on.

106

SHE SAW HERSELF living with the pink foreigner in a house across the platen seas. A house lacking only Jehan and the garden. Across the seas was almost unimaginable. A land with no clouds. A land stocked high with tins and bright cracker packages forever grabbed and ripped open by loud pink large-boned men.

Try as she might, she couldn't picture Honree in a family. No mother, no father, not even neighbors. Not even childhood's skinned knees.

Then she envisioned life at the drummer's compound as Manu's wife.

She'd have to care for what would be her father-in-law: Regi's hands would grow too obstinate to play drums at the temple; Manu would never be there. She saw herself cooking rice in the back with Ruwini, her mother-in-law, trying to avoid the sight of Ruwini's marked stomach. She would be waiting for Manu to return to their private hut. Waiting and cooking in a simpler life, hiding the heat of her desire for his smooth drummer's back.

Manu was a boy, she reminded herself for the umpteenth time. Like Henry's, his groin rushed to his face when he talked to her. But this rush was a sign from a world far from the one in which Honree's groin lived.

She had checked. The boy's little packet of goods would nestle closer, more one with his body than Honree's almost detachable tubular sack — little child's walnuts, a cluster of fruit. Pendulous, lacking a pulse. What sort of children would issue from a bag hanging so far from the body, so bloodless? She couldn't begin to guess.

With Honree, at the beginning, she had expected their sortie to be more than just thrust and heave. Still there were times when she felt his hands yearned to contain all languages. Times when he seemed to understand within her skin how it had been growing into the woman lying beneath him. That was her wish probably and not the truth speaking.

A truth was that the presence of the foreigner bearing down every night made it hard. Hard for her to imagine Manu as being any different from Honree. The truth was also that her problem was color. The present caged her. She could not bring the boy's brown before her eyes. Brown as opposed to the everpresent pink.

One dawn Honree went to Durbbhiksha so she took advantage of the rains having stopped to do a huge cleaning. As she was hanging the laundry later that morning, *he* appeared. Manu the drummer boy. Fresh at her patio and she tittered. He didn't understand anything of any plan. He was foolish and young. And knew so little. For example, that she had dreamed of him many times, in many colors. Once in a dream he had entered her. Another time she had entered him.

But in life, he was ignorant and far too sudden. That morning, he came up behind her and her line. His hands crept around her waist faster than any spider's hook. His lips warm and pressed against her neck. She spun and laughed — he still caught her — but she covered her mouth, tittering. She had this problem of laughter and this wasn't the first time.

'Stop!' he implored, though he was the one who had grabbed her.

When she could finally speak, she managed to explain to him with words she'd never used in any dream: 'You can't,' she told the boy. 'Oyaate baeae.'

She didn't think he understood why. She had no room for him, for his velvet eyes and disorder. He was part of nothing, she could not explain him to herself, and still there was something that needed to happen. Her laughter wouldn't stop. She felt she had been instructed in this. By whom or what she couldn't say. She had never laughed so hard.

'I'm funny to you' — he was already whippersnapping away — 'everything I've done and I'm funny.'

Just as quickly as he had made his advance he was spooling out a long ribbon of things about his *organizing* about his *trying to impress her* about it all being *for nothing unless she realized what she was throwing away*. He was adolescent and impressive and lovely in his moodiness. This was what struck her. His self-importance. It made his easy charm more complex. She could love a boy who thought of himself in such deep relief, with such difficulty and grace. He had cared for her, it was clear. But then this time he left for good.

After that he never came round again. The few times she saw him in the marketplace, she tried to wish him hello. He eluded her as swiftly as he had first sought her out. Not friendship, and not courtship, only the pull between them stayed. And in his heart, she knew, he couldn't deny that pull.

Sometimes while whacking cobwebs out of the ceilings or hanging laundry, she thought it must have been her titter. She'd learned no one likes to be a laughingstock. It was true she hadn't pushed his hands away so much as she'd laughed them away.

She would do it differently if he tried again. Wouldn't Manu try? She wouldn't laugh this time. She would turn and take his humorous tragedy upon herself. His aches and braggadocio and quiet smile — she'd suggest they flee Rutaeva, just the two of them together, on the train in a whole new plan.

But he never would approach her again. Or would he?

107

'C'MON, FRIENDS, should it be that hard to find?' asks Henry, thumbing his beard, which Nani had cut for him that morning. A little too short? But she must have done it in the fashion of the country. 'Tell him,' Henry urges Johnny. 'It shouldn't be too hard.'

The meeting among the drummer and his son, Henry, and Johnny, all gathered in Wooves' library, hasn't been going smoothly. No one knows who should be addressed.

'You tell him, Henree,' Johnny insists. 'Your language is good enough by now, isn't it?'

Manu has been ignoring Henry's insistence to sit. He is too proud to sit in any chair offered him in Henry's house.

'We find the documentation,' Henry snaps his fingers. 'Then no dispute, right?'

'Henry —' says Manu.

This Manu calls a white man by his first name like some internal needling voice. How different he is from his father who stammers *SirHenry* as though taught the name in the crib. Johnny's struck dumb too, evidently able only to rock back and forth behind Manu. As though Johnny owns him. Or wants to.

Henry knows Johnny and Manu are friends. They spend hours by the canal as though able to share secrets. Often their third wheel is the radical Nandana who has taken up residence in an unknown habitation somewhere 'by the tracks.' These days with Manu spending more time in Rajottama again — having returned after a period of 'traveling' — it seems that every time Henry needs Johnny, he has to drag the boy up from his post with the drummer's son or the radical, a creature who breathes politics. Everywhere in the village Nandana pastes his handsome posters with their curling red and gold borders. Most have scenes of farmers holding nations on muscular forearms, the same as on Manu's poster. Or they show joyous rice farmers and women in Kandyan dress, turbans and saris dancing around a beatific paddy, which — if life were truly depicted — would show tired peasants shuffling in at four in the morning to harvest rice. Nandana is devoted to the idea of a nation of Sinhalese, Tamils, Muslims together. At least this is what the elderly Anglophile, Subasinghe, has hinted. 'You'd do better to get rid of him, am I correct?' he'd said, sticking this riff into a discourse on the Buddha's extrasensory perception.

This makes no sense — why would Henry get rid of some boy who has always been kind to him? Anyway, *get rid of?* From what universe does such a phrase come? And why should whittling occupy three intelligent boys so much?

'My father's a holy man. A temple server,' Manu is telling Henry. 'Still the monk wrote in a clause. To steal his land.'

Henry has Johnny translate *clause*. If Johnny has a clever sense of humor, he doesn't show it today.

'A clause like that, Henry,' and Manu explains, the next day the monk can get his father off their ancestral land. Worse, the monk had sanctioned the tappers to build on Regi's compound, right over Manu's monster brother's room.

Henry reassembles his face into credulity. Confidence like this boy has could make anyone a believer. But this blithering goes too far. Nani steps into the room and seeing who's there, a deer in an invisible forest, she just as speedily steps out.

'It's truth,' Manu continues after a pause. His face falls only a bit and he explains more: the monk had kicked out all of Henry's students and made them move to the dance school. Then the monk had asked the washermen to transform the old orphanage into his own additional private home.

'I'm sorry, Manu, you're a wonderful boy, really, but our cultural plan, it has so many details,' confiding in sweet accents so the boy takes no offense. 'You'd have a great head for understanding it too. Some other time I'll explain it all to you.'

The boy has a commensurate graciousness, his eyes faint pools. He tells Henry there is an expression among the Sinhalese — blindness can kill.

'Ho yes,' haws the father. 'Hee ho, yes.'

Manu carries on: did Henry know the monk wants to live like a lord on Pilima land? did Henry know the monk comes from not such a high caste? But should the monk fulfill his sneaky wishes over others' bodies? Was there a magna carta for that?

Henry's monk? a satrap?

Manu's likable enough but he doesn't know Pandit's dignity. Meanwhile, Henry tasting his index finger, salt and Nani, understands: the boy knows Pandit as a boss, not as one upholding the Buddha's doctrine. This youth with his folk face fails to recognize how some men transcend. That some, like Pandit, know the Middle Way. This comprises Henry's renewed faith in his monk. Without faith he would be lost. A man like Pandit would never connive to dispossess the drummer.

No, it must be that this boy has the same problem as all his people. A problem of esteem — he can't recognize his own worth. This is the son of a man who panders to the gods, who beats his small hands raw upon his daily drums. Pandit, for whom they play, is an avatar of loyalty. He'd be loyal to a *dog* who'd served him as many years as the drummers.

The problem is, Henry decides, Manu's taken on the message of the colonizers. Of the Dutch, the Portuguese, the British. The boy fails to recognize virtue in Pandit, a servitor of Buddhism. So instead he comes running to a foreigner.

Henry tries to explain some of this to Manu, who grows more stubborn and (Henry does not solicit the thought) almost sultry in his stubbornness. Johnny watches the entire exchange with his pro-

464

prietary mien. Henry wants to turn on him too. Everyone's annoying today. Nani won't bring tea. And Johnny is acting as though Manu's some kind of toy poodle trained to rear back on upholstered legs.

Be calm, Henry. He leans forward, all patient American knees and forearms.

'See here,' pointedly. 'If it weren't for the monk, I wouldn't know enough Sinhalese to talk it occasionally with you.'

'All right,' Manu muses in English. 'Let us speak how *you* choose.' He spits out *you* as though it should rankle.

'We'll find that book for you.'

Manu makes for the door. 'Until next time then.'

His father jumps up. 'Blessings upon you,' and Regi gives his Sir Henry a bow.

'What was all that about?' Henry asks his aide.

Johnny doesn't wait. He rushes out, to what, to reseat everyone, to uncle and mother the father and son.

All right, so it wasn't the most successful meeting. But advancement can be found anywhere. This land is still free. At the very least, Henry counts his blessings: he is not blind; he knows the boys are friends. Sure he can see it. There's some private love between Manu and Johnny. As interesting and unsettling as a cursory tightrope act.

'You two are David and Jonathan!' Henry tries to joke as Johnny reenters.

The boy grimaces. 'So?' The tone too bright.

'You tell me. This an A-1 problem? The monk, Regi's land —'

'A-1? to be honest, I don't know.'

Henry had only heard the boy when drunk admit he didn't know. This admission could be taken as a whimper, a bad sign, but Henry's not going to think like that.

Most importantly, he doesn't want Johnny to get pulled too far away from their shared history in the library. The history with its cloister's light. The boy shouldn't drift away from that. From all the times Johnny's pulled open the curtains or shelved a book.

'All this is a half-problem,' sniffs Henry, 'for half-people.'

'These half-people are your ingredients.' The boy is only temporarily lost to him. Henry has not ruined anything. And he will not plead. Above him the creaky, never-used chandelier rocks back and forth. All is reparable.

108

THE NEXT DAY at the temple the monk tries to mark the sounds Henry cannot pronounce differently: *seed; bone; truth; uncertainty; satiation; sufficiency; testicle.* Henry listens closely.

The tongue retroflex, the monk says. '*T* is different from *th*.'

Tintinnabulation. Henry leans over the old language books.

'Is it true you're having some sort of discussion with Regi about his contract?'

The monk's eyes lift. 'That's what his boy says?'

Henry assents.

Pandit explains, beaming, that these people don't understand that in the temple books this famous clause of theirs has been there for generations. 'Do we sin by mentioning the clause?' Evidently, if the drummer fulfills his functions in a manner the temple's leadership deems respectable, *proper*, his land remains in his family. Of course, everything would be passed to the *first* son — primogeniture being one of the oldest laws.

'So why's the family protesting?'

'The man is a raving illiterate, Colonel. And that boy of his loves trouble.'

Henry mops his face with his father-in-law's silty handkerchief. He cracks his knuckles. Listening, he tries to piece together the monk's statements. To wit:

> The document with the contract is unobtainable.
>
> Anyway, Manu would be unable to read the first sentence of even his own death warrant.
>
> Many families invent false titles regarding what the temple owes them.
>
> They do this because they want something for nothing and forget what is, after all, their job: serving the temple.

The monk leans into Henry's face and tells him to stop taking notes, just to think — wasn't Henry hired by the Yankee government to come help the people of Ceylon, and if he failed at his job, wouldn't someone else replace him?

Henry tries to correct the monk's impression.

'We must've been mistaken. Didn't you say your Madame was part of the government?' At this the American recoils, explaining he came here of his own initiative, that Madame was never part of any government, not that he knew of.

'No government behind you? Still, Colonel, if you were this drummer, you wouldn't renege on a generational contract, would you? Of course not. You Yankees like to say your word is your bond. You'd never do such a thing.'

Behind the monk's back Manu passes by the open door, carrying his drum. He raises a quiet hand to Henry in a semblance of gratitude.

'Pardon?' Henry stammers, guilty.

'You'd never do such a thing, Colonel.' The monk has an unhealthy enthusiasm.

'I'd never do such a thing.'

'But as you were saying,' continuing, 'to get the retroflex, your tongue must be back. Like so. *Aethi.*'

'*Aeti. Aeti.* I can't do it. *Aeti.*'

109

PANDIT HAD BEEN GAINING a foothold: on what exactly he could not say. In countless ways, the Yankee was ceding to him. Pandit himself felt like the great dam at the origin of the canal, far above Rajottama, able to collect water not just from two rivers but from the sky.

He would gather everything in; and once it was in, what would he do? There could never be enough somehow; he was righting something far greater than the wrongs visited on him in life, the times he'd been overlooked or unfairly surpassed; he was righting something greater than anyone could guess. Even having been posted to Rutaeva.

Slippage! A good position, this Sacred Tree Temple; yet Rutaeva was so far removed from Kandy town's Temple of the Tooth, the great Maligawa, where attending monks allowed devotees to see the gold room and casings which (deep inside, on velvet beds) held the Buddha's tooth, the unimaginable shining tooth.

Yes, Pandit had done well; had especially struck tender alliances that needed caring: with the Yankee; perhaps even with the English Chris (they nodded as they passed each other these days). As the Yankee would say, he just needed to map out some possibilities.

With such thoughts buzzing about, he thought it might be sensible to telegraph his old mentor, Sucharita, who had retired from the monastery in order to pursue an anonymous life as a farmer in the south.

If Pandit didn't wholly understand his teacher's decision, he accepted it nonetheless as being a part of some greater plan, much as the grains of wood in his table belonged to a forest long since dispersed. There *must* be a design to such a huge renunciation.

And Pandit's approach would be simple, direct — *his* mentor, unlike so many, disapproved of hedging. The former student would inquire whether Sucharita knew of any opportunities for serving *even if only once a week* at the Temple of the Tooth — what an honor it would be to work in the company of such esteemed monks! Could there be a way to confederate — whatever that could mean — or progress? He wanted the kindly old man to take an interest in his once promising pupil, as a sconce does in its candle. To take an interest in Pandit, whom he had warned so repeatedly: the old teacher rapping it into him, how one must love the world even as one gives up all attachments to it, reminding him that over-cleverness in a monk could become a liability.

Pandit's words:

> HONORABLE SUCHARITA AS WE CONTINUE IN RAJOTTAMA
> MAY WE ALSO FIND SOME WAY TO SERVE THE GREAT KANDY
> MALIGAWA YOUR ADVICE NEEDED ON HOW BEST TO SERVE
> PANDIT.

In the telegram, forty words cost the same as thirty, but Pandit had nothing else to add.

And as he was dictating this to the swing-shift clerk — who had decided karma and commerce were one, apparently, in terms of reincarnation possibilities, and had decided to *donate* the cost of the telegram to the monk — Pandit idly eyed the last telegram, with its proper name still affixed: Jonathan Nellie (according to this swing-shift clerk, happy to be of service and inform a monk of anything), a boy who on a weekly basis — and at the start even more frequently — sent to Colombo's colonial administration a report on Henry Fyre Gould, an American foreigner in Rajottama.

In other words, what Pandit had hazily suspected: Jehangir was a spy. Why shouldn't Pandit have known it earlier? Of course, to a monk, the clerk wished he could tell more 'especially to such an esteemed monk, one who leads such a holy village! Your tree! A wonderful place, Rajottama!'

What was it about that boy Jehangir? In him the monk could trace the lineaments of his own childhood. All the orphaned boys who threw themselves on the indifferent graces of cities. Or all the boys who retired to some plot of land where rice would always be inferior, weevils would beset them, and there'd always be a kind of tattoo on their heart saying *lost or bad father — plus no money.*

So while Pandit had transcended such a fate via strict monastic discipline, its four-in-the-morning risings with your feet still cold, and no food served after three, while he'd lifted himself over striving, Jehan was still jailed. You could practically hear the clink of the chains, see that though he'd pretended to escape being a clerk by attaching himself to the foreigner — like a little self-fattening leech! — he remained a clerk. Because Jehan was a spy, which meant, after all, a glorified clerk, one beholden to some screened but still unforgiving master.

Discovering the telegraph business had been a serendipity for Pandit, the most reassuring kind. Life had confirmed what dislike had merely guessed.

110

THE AFTERNOON has mellowed into a perfect day — low wind, clouds stretched across the sky, a promise of rain, Henry's climate-magic having worked. Or not. At Regi's, a smoky wisp from the kitchen fire undulates above a gathering of people, most with their hands crossed.

What is Henry's monk doing chanting over a plot on Regi's land, just off from the subterranean monster baby room? *Beneath this earth beats a heart*, Henry writes on a scrap from his pocket. He needs to delay. To take in what is happening.

Chollie the midget presses forward in front, tiny and powerful, men arrayed behind. And the sky turning threatening. The Yala should be over, but for once no one seems to care a jot about weather or Henry's role in it.

And Henry can't make his tongue work. Aiming to joke, 'Your heads won't melt,' Henry tells the crowd. 'When it rains, I mean.'

No one answers, they are praying too loudly in their sacred tongue. *Buddham saranam gacchami.* 'Know how big this thing's supposed to be, Johnny?'

'Shh, we'll find out later, Henree.'

The dwarf greets Henry as *Fyro*. 'We consulted Appuhamy!' he exclaims, exaggerating an apology. 'The sorcerer! you know this is the most auspicious day for months! we couldn't wait!' Chollie also informs Henry that the monk had agreed to title the tappers' half of Regi's land. 'For our new temple! The venerable Pandit said he could build his library! Actually in the orphanage you rebuilt!'

Henry questions the need to build at all on Regi's land.

Chollie's eyes slit into knives. 'Time for sharing! This was the site where in eighteen-hundred-you-know the Pilimas stood against the British. For us an important site! Just luck for that drummer that he's gobbled up such history! All these years and it's time for him to share!'

The first man bends low, trowels into earth shot through with dead jungle roots and blind insects, forking his clump of soil up high.

Chollie is saying something but Henry cannot hear. The dirt spray shoots out like a fountain, effectively filling Henry's nostrils, gaping mouth and eyes. He is at a loss.

Afterward, Henry hikes up Regi's hill: above them, apart from them. Regi is still nowhere to be found. The American sits under a palm tree watching them clean up after their 'ceremony.' What he will call a betrayal. He has nothing to report to his temporary Village Book, a stray card in his pocket. He tries doodling a house with strong structural support against winds and monsoons but gives up. He tries sketching Nani's form. Nothing works. He tries writing one of his drivel poems to cheer himself:

Beneath this earth there beats a heart
Which once held mirth, which now is dark.
When rulers fall, they fall too hard
For us to know where was the heart.

But I have seen where is the heart
And have conceived that sight was warped.
But who could guess this one great fear —
My tongue will cleave before all ears?

His drivel is designed to distract from the events in which he'd just unwillingly participated.

'Only an expansion, Colonel!' the monk had explained midway through the ceremony. 'We were going to offer the toddy-tappers your lovely orphanage. But of course we need that land for the temple holdings. For our library, isn't it? —' as though Henry didn't know what was happening. As though Henry in his adult life had never encountered greed. As though they lived in a mythical time before greed had been unleashed on the world. 'For the books you and I study together, Colonel. We'll shift to the orphanage site and oversee the books from there.'

How many books and how many rooms does a monk need to live in? It's a riddle Henry doesn't speak, a riddle which cancels its own humor before arriving at the punchline.

But the worst was the dwarf's invitation at the ceremony's close. 'Come tomorrow, Fyro!' Chollie said. 'We're celebrating! Finally the monk is giving our caste its own temple!'

An ear that knows, desire which binds
That truth of kings, the beggar's Art.
Why will men bury the world below
The search for wealth — diseasèd hearts?

Henry's done with his drivel, the betrayal ceremony's over, and he leaps up to follow his monk through the crowd, his tongue returned. 'So what is it?' Henry badgers Pandit. 'Dislike? Is it dislike? Did the drummer do anything to you?'

The monk responds with a quote. ' "Good is the acquisition of wisdom. And good is the avoidance of evil." Number three hundred and thirty-three.'

'But —' and Henry tries to quote back perfectly:

> He who is free from craving and attachment, perfect in un-
> covering the true meaning of the Teaching, and knows the
> arrangement of the sacred texts in correct sequence — he,
> indeed, is the bearer of his final body . . .

'Is truly called the profoundly wise one, the great man,' Pandit overlaps. 'Don't think your teacher forgets.'

'Right, so, please. Tell me what it is? you find the drummer e-e-evil?'

The monk mouths the word *evil* helpfully.

'If you must know, Colonel —' Here his teacher brings him to the side of the celebrating throng of toddy-tappers. He whispers, 'Your Regi's been embezzling ivory from the Buddha's image house. Those people will never admit such things. They close ranks. This new generation rebels! Older people used to think it an honor just to empty the temple's waste. And this, stealing the finest inlaid ivory in the entire Kandyan kingdom! You can understand why we might prefer someone who could just pay rent. Like Chollie.'

Henry flails. He praises Regi's devotion to the temple, hints at the bad merit the monk might accrue, sings a few lines of nonsense. 'This might be bad for you,' he threatens Pandit, 'you might wish to reconsider.'

'Pardon us, Colonel — what you don't understand about Theravada Buddhism could, dare we say, fill another *two* libraries! Built on anyone's land.'

Henry sneezes. His body is too sensitive all of a sudden, practically iridescent. 'You're not supposed to insult your students.'

'You still don't understand karma, Colonel.' The monk launches into a small dharma talk. About how karma isn't necessarily individual. Saying it's not like some Western luggage with your name on it that you drag from life to life. Karma can also be lateral. That karma affects all of us. A bad person is a bad person, he says, and we must shield ourselves from bad people. 'Your problem is you believe in the constancy of soul and we don't. *Anicca*, remember, the no-soul.'

'Regi dedicates himself —'

'Colonel. There are only a few who dedicate themselves to a painful rebirth in order to help others. Your Regi is no bodhisattva. He's a bad influence. He has the kind of karma which infects the very air around him. Trust us.'

Trust you? Henry tries to understand the leaps between the monk's sentences but instead he envisions Regi's eyes: blue-specked and pleading earnestly above those rolled-in shoulders. Henry understands why the monk's favorite concept might be the no-soul. Evil gets distributed wherever you want it, Henry thinks, with the no-soul.

Anicca.

Other monks might be better, he stops to write. The monk waits a few paces ahead, appearing amused as Henry writes,

> but I've discovered one straight from the pages of
> Machiavelli. Over all his rebirths, he has no continuous soul.

Henry realizes everything that has happened. Manu was right. Months ago, the monk had decided to transform the renovated orphanage into his own living quarters. Henry had slid, easy as a bead on a rosary. He'd helped the monk move the orphans across the canal. He'd even assisted Pandit in bequeathing drummer's land to the toddy-tappers. He'd been blind to everything.

> Disillusionment a bitter fruit

Pandit knows more about divide and conquer than any at the British encampment. And still insultingly insists on pelting Henry with his rational voice: 'Colonel! Don't take it hard, as you say. We must keep our minds on the task ahead. We won't talk about this matter again. Not during our language lessons. Not on our walks.'

My monk — Henry writes to keep his calm. On the other side of the card he sees, blurred, the faint purple traces of Madame's handwriting. This had been her send-off card to him, the card James had handed him, and now over the last of her message he writes *my monk my monk my monk. My monk*

> has (almost) disappeared.
> Beneath this earth there beats a heart.

111

LESTER HAS A THORN in his foot the Sunday in July that he assembles five men to discuss the problem of the foreigner, his aide, and their continued stay in Rutaeva.

Six to discuss two. The numbers feel safe.

The five take their time settling down on the Pilima benches, on the Pilima porch, in the Pilima compound. Chollie, Suba, Lester. Lester's brother Samitha. The monk, who sits slightly apart from the other men but who would expect anything less or more?

For his part Lester is trying to use the elaborate wooden tweezers he'd borrowed from Chollie at the pink man's store to extract the thorn. The tweezers keep splintering. Bad product *would* come from a bad project. He has more pain in his foot than when he began. 'Don't mind me,' says Lester, involved with his foot. 'I'm suffering but let's start.'

His wife, Manik, is still up from the capital. Dressed in white she rolls to sit in her elegance at the end of the men. Each shank is attached to its own lubricated cog; fat and gristle slacken her movements, each forward motion accompanied by a sink-down-and-around. She is the kind of woman who gives men comfort so long as they can pretend she's interested in them.

Her habits are expensive and Lester thinks that if after today she's not interested in working with him in driving out the American, it's better for her not to stay too long in Rutaeva. She would drive her husband crazy. Let her do ladies' work in education and the like in Colombo. After her sojourns in Colombo, for the first week, she will sometimes have a young girl's smile. But then she starts to find something — his cigar smoke, his trivia — there is always something. Now he thinks he'd found the way to make her pay attention to the problem of the foreigner. The drought and then the flood had ruined much of the Pilimas' coconut plantations farther down the mountain.

Following her advice, later today he *will* mention to the men his need for support in the new campaign. No flags of surrender here. He had hinted about the petition many months ago, before the pilgrimage, just to see whether there might be interest in his representing the village.

From those who have queried him, even those who are known flatterers, it is clear he is wanted. Lester would like to present a petition to the civil administration. There is no reason Lester Pilima shouldn't be elected the local county's sub-deputy government agent. There has been no one in the position for years. But he has to make his way toward this carefully. Otherwise his men will feel used.

'Be careful.' Chollie brandishes his cane for emphasis. 'You break the thorn off wrong and your foot can swell. Turn black. Worse than having a wife who stops cooking for you.'

'Fine.' Lester waves this off. 'What are we going to do?'

No one knows the exact reason for the meeting. Something about the foreigner and his boy was all Lester had told them. They are mostly honored by the sovereignty of drinking Pilima glasses of Pilima coconut juice from the Pilima plantation coconuts. And by Manik, last of the Pilimas, who checks on them now and again without saying anything. There they sit, tended to but silent, for five whole Pilima minutes. Six minutes. Seven.

Lester watches the hands move on the fancy gilded pocketwatch *Made in the U.S.A.* he got on barter from the pink man's store.

'This boy of his — probably a spy!' Chollie ventures finally. 'Been seen more than once at the telegraph office in Kandy!'

'Good,' says Lester. 'Now we're getting somewhere.'

'This is like the dams and roads and jobs we were supposed to be given by the English. Instead we had our temples ruined,' continues Chollie, a student hungry for more praise, rummaging through history and veering off the point.

Lester tries for patience but this whole council thing has never suited his nature. He calls the serving boy to bring on the Pilima kasippu.

'Sorry, saddhu,' he apologizes to Pandit. 'A little alcohol will help this meeting go faster.'

'No need to apologize' — this is the first thing the monk has said and the laymen startle — 'we're here for important business.'

The monk is an ally. Unlike another whom Lester had to include, an older man who has always irritated him, Suba the self-righteous Buddhist.

Where the Yankee doesn't know certain things, Lester does. A certain kind of older man can get sniffy if excluded. A certain kind could hear about the meeting anyway and go talking up the wrong trees.

'What I think is,' Suba says now into the silence, 'the boy was hired by some plantation, am I wrong? He's a Tamil —'

'Or something,' Chollie snarls. 'Doesn't belong anywhere clearly.'

'Whatever he is,' Suba goes on, 'the boy was the one to hire their gardener.'

'A Tamil for sure,' Chollie says. 'Lentil-eater, that gardener.'

'A hill-country tea type if I ever saw one,' Suba finishes.

Chollie, Lester and his brother Samitha slug down their kasippu. It is particularly hot and burning today. 'Good man!' Chollie burps.

At this, barely covering her disgust, Manik rises and retreats inside the house. The men can hear her conferring with Pushpa. Spaces between the Pilima shadows are long.

'You listening?' asks Suba.

'Yes, yes.' Lester's surprised at how useful Suba's proving to be, a kind of touchstone.

'I think,' and Suba's voice slips to a high pitch, 'the boy is probably an agent for a plantation in tea country. An envoy looking for a way to chuck us off our land. He's filing reports on all of us. He's the one controlling the foreigner, not the other way around.'

Later when Lester wants to remember when Rajottama started to change beyond question, he will remember this meeting. How Chollie used words, at certain junctions, like judicious pellets. At the time, this reassured Lester. There would be soon an equilibrium they would like more. There were measures at hand. 'On what evidence?' Chollie was saying, prosecuting.

'The telegrams the boy sends every other day in Kandy town.'

And Lester will remember, too, how Pandit refolded his robes, and spoke Lester's own thoughts. 'Telegram or not, why else would the foreigner have an assistant who is a Muslim or Tamil —'

Chollie interrupted. 'Or close to a Tamil.'

Out on the road, the serving boy was chasing away a crown of crows feeding on a ruptured rat. When the crows circled the boy, he ran but only Chollie laughed. Lester repeated the news, to understand it better himself. 'You're saying Fyre is being controlled by the boy. Not the other way around.'

Samitha's hands began to move until Lester translated. 'My brother's saying he saw the foreigner's aide talking to the British commander.'

'Chris,' intoned Chollie.

'It's clearly a conspiracy, am I wrong?' said Suba. 'That boy —'

'Definitely a canker,' the monk cut in, 'a true colonial. He defines one of the evils that make Rajottama Rutaeva. We become Slippage because of him.'

Lester will always remember the night the boy had appeared at the night training.

A ghost on the periphery. True, he *had* seemed possessed by the god of cemeteries. The very next day Lester had seen the boy in town, but had avoided being spotted by the boy's destitute gaze. Yes. He could remember it as though he had seen it himself. The boy *had* headed in the direction of the telegraph office.

'All signs add up, am I wrong?' Suba was asking.

'He's clearly the one to be gotten rid of,' announced Lester.

'You all are terribly, terribly wise,' the monk would second. Inside the women were whispering loudly, unintelligibly. 'Gentlemen, it's been a wonderful meeting.'

'Are we not discussing how all this is to be done?' Suba whined. 'Methodology — by the way,' addressing Lester, 'you have been kind, freeing us from paying taxes to the British.'

This was an act which Lester, as self-appointed taxman, had been able to accomplish easily. A very minor redirection of funds from the foreigner's store toward the colonial center. And all for what he believed to be the benefit of the village.

Only Chollie and the monk knew about this necessary diversion: both men had helped Lester. And there was no wrong in this. What Rutaevan had ever asked to be taxed? Similarly, which Rutaevan had ever *requested* the foreigner and his store? It had been only appropriate to rechannel the funds of something unwanted (the store) to something equally unwanted (the colonial taxes).

No one hurt — and who had *not* benefited? Lester had been a liberator unto the villagers. No taxes, and no harm done to anybody.

It was, rightfully, Chollie who got the last word. 'We'll find out more about the foreigner and his friends' — a meaningful wave of his cane around at the assembled — 'gather more information.' He held Lester's gaze a second. 'No use risking anything needlessly. But the day we see danger,' the cane trembling, '*any* danger to *any* of us — our way of life here — that is the day we pull back their ropes. Understood?'

112

AT THE END OF JULY Henry decides he will publish a compendium of Johnny's folk tales. He particularly likes the one he'd heard at the beginning, about a mountain she-demon who stalks men —

Bauddhilima, the reborn soul of every pregnant woman who ever died in birth. Every village has its Bauddhilima, even if she some-times goes by the name Villaraeni. She can become bigger than a house. Only virgins — or wet-nurses with their blouses stained by milk — can stem the wrath of the she-demon.

'But men,' Johnny had warned him in a tone of mock dudgeon, back when they were still getting along so perfectly, 'she stalks men to cut off their organs. There *are* a few ways men can fend her off. You hear Bauddhilima cry in labor and that's exactly when you have to shoot with a rifle. It's terrible' — the story drew him on — 'wherever you shoot, if you do it correctly, in the morning, same site, you find seven spotted lizards. That's what happened in my village.'

'How do you know so much about such a fairy tale?' Henry had teased — the story amused him as much as, admittedly, it froze the crease of his testicles.

As a child, instructed by his mother, Johnny had every night thrown urine into the night to keep Bauddhilima away. As he ma-tured, he grew braver. Because you can also ensnare Bauddhilima: you pour coconut oil on a palm leaf and keep it outside your door. Johnny had bravely done this and true to legend, during the night, she had come in her easiest apparition: a radiantly nude pregnant woman who rubbed the oil into her belly.

'She hurt my eyes,' the boy had rushed to say, 'it was my first time and probably my last.'

With such vagueness, was the boy testing Henry's own super-stitions? 'Dreams are like that,' Henry'd said. 'You'll see other women.'

'Of course, a dream,' his aide had agreed readily.

The swale and swerve of Nani make Henry understand how the she-demon might have appeared to the young boy. Such a vision would be too tempting to question. Nani and the point of her berry nipples, their surface like crimped rosettes. Her sleep breath and how she never finds safe mooring, her feet either tired or agitated but doomed to their task of climbing an endless and tantalizing se-ries — trellises, hog's backs, mountains.

The whirring arrives slowly on a Saturday some days after the be-ginning of what people are calling a drought. But there's never a monsoon in July so how can they call it a drought? These people.

Henry turns to Nani and asks, *Hear that?* She slides her hand over his ribs toward his compressed heart and murmurs, *No, go to sleep.*

Anyone would call Friday a renaissance. A week's work completed in a day. He'd single-handedly supervised his crackerjack team of wage laborers. Who'd complain? Things are on the up and up, he waited to tell her that night. He loves her more than ever; and his men are good, consistent workers, proud of their new money and status in Rajottama. He'd wanted to impress her and told her all the workers' children would have clean shirts and butter from now on.

'Silly,' she'd said. 'Clean shirts are good but who needed butter before?' Had she not been swift in leaving to go bathe outside, he would have pounced on her challenge.

On Friday morning, Henry had found a compelling straw-and-wire-scrap Buddha seated at the head of the intended cucumber row, the thing serene enough to stare anyone down, auguring riches beyond riches of communal belief in Henry and his project. A belief shooting to the moon far beyond any Maryland nitrogen-fixed earth. He would not tell her what the Buddha had spelled out to him; but he'd stamped his foot, too happy at his good fortune, knowing that one day he might understand what the Buddha really meant. It wasn't exactly a dead black crow, was it?

Now he listens to the rhythmic flapping, a song sweet as the lapping of oars in water. Friday afternoon his workers had stayed on to sow and ensure the garden's completion by evening. Henry'd picked his way home early over a pleasurable field, spotted with yellow wildflowers and cracked cow pies.

And had then fallen still, dumbfounded.

Feral dogs by the trees had snapped at some new winged insects. Wondrous creatures. Someone's will was apparent in this fierce diversity; if not a creator's will, then surely some organizing cosmic force. Little marvelous bugs, colorful as children's tinny whir-toys.

Nani's hand now travels to his lips. He clasps the long grace of her fingers into a kiss. So what if her digits are a bit thick around the joints? Even poets had lovers with a bit of dross clinging to them. It could be from the work he has her do. He *must* be in love, he thinks, to find her hand to be such a touching document to their shared labors.

He congratulates himself. One day she would rest in a house he would build her by the sea, one with a true bathtub under a tree. He could see her leaning over him, scrubbing his back with lemon and salt and soap. Her hair long and maternal. The two of them would twist and twine in a hammock without peering eyes and knocks during long afternoons of productive leisure and what he would schedule in as a necessary rejuvenation of the body.

For now, his vision is meat enough to nourish the two into fits of inspiration — yes, he wants to write, *the meat of inspiration* — and there's no question about whether work remains to be done, or whether she's qualified.

Like one of the mangy feral dogs, he chews lightly at her finger, making himself laugh. She turns over, her legs restless in half-sleep, the delicate ball of her foot climbing her calf.

Before she fell asleep, he'd wanted her to mark the day's success. Not every Friday flowed so smoothly, after all. And so what if he was also fatigued; he was required by the law of spine and groin to stroke her back until she turned toward him, her body more willing than her face. Hard to be sure. Once he enters her, he almost loses himself in her dissolving against him, a thick wash she hides during working hours.

But close to the height of things, why did she have to spoil it all by crying out, venomous words, *Honree, you speak my language one day?*

The devil of bad timing. She shouldn't have spoken at that moment. Now he tries to regain his mood. He should get up, sleep or catalogue, this last always the most appealing choice.

Another choice: he would enjoy one day hearing Nani in labor. Could a man in one lifetime try to hear all the sounds the world had to offer?

After his Argentinian gambling ring had netted enough to cover steamer fare, Madame's friend, the Bolshevik chicken farmer, finally landed in Uganda and later told Henry of the clucking dialects among central Africa's pygmies.

Henry cannot imagine how many sounds there must be in the world. The wind's rustle in Antarctic ice floes. The echoes of copper pennies falling inside a diamond mine. The sound of his beloved's voice when she believes herself alone.

What would she say, *when will you learn my language?* He's trying, wouldn't everyone just quit and see that?

The hum outside has increased, odd and compelling.

He doesn't dream it. But he's kind, he won't wake Nani again because he needs her to be awake later to check whether the orphan-age leaf-porridge program has been instituted — a particular pride of his.

Yes, he was the one who'd taught the boys to sow the leaves out back. Even Chilkins had been impressed by this line item. Via Johnny, the agent had earmarked funds for the restitution of this in-digenous staple. All is linking, the joy of it, there will be no misfor-tune.

As silently as a loud man knows how, Henry rises and pulls on the loose pants that still hold the shape of yesterday's kneel-in-the-muck gardening. If only he could grow accustomed to tying that damned knot in the front or side or wherever they hang the thing, he too would wear the cloth sarong. Yes, he'd tie his with the low-caste's knot. But that native game has become too cumbersome — and out-side the egrets are humming. He knows nothing; he hurries across the room's sacred nighttime threshold into true night where no stars shine. Where the moon hides behind a low cloud shifting north to-ward the tank. Before having made any decision, his head vibrating, Henry's bare feet hop him over the gate.

The gardener stands still as always, out on the road beyond the gate and gawking with an existentialist's curiosity at the canal.

'Hello, my continental philosopher,' Henry greets him.

Unsurprised, the gardener touches his turban and points to the sky, lips parting with a hearty delight. Henry points back, glad this night rests warm enough on his bare chest.

Stones on the road wake his feet: he turns up toward his fields and the first model garden. His crackerjack team has sown gourd. Only a month ago, the plants began snaking a slow dance up his cane trel-lises.

To get over the long hump made by the new subsidiary irrigation, each of his steps must be high. Each recalls the shovelfuls with which the villagers had dug the channel, a plan agreed to by the monk and the Pilimas — some of the time these people had their priorities straight.

Henry had appreciated the laborers' good humor. Brick by brick the villagers had built, some cursing under their breath. In their po-sition, Henry would probably curse too. So he'd wanted to show how much he was one of them. To the man whose curse he'd heard in full, he'd sent back a waggish little riposte. 'So you want me to be stricken with cholera?' he'd asked and then pantomimed the disease:

Henry staggered and clutched his gut until the workers cheered like excited children.

This was before he hired the all-new and permanent crackerjack team of laborers, capable of setting everything right. Anyone who chaffed him now would see their myopia later. In the next season, all will understand Henry's wisdom.

He coughs.

An insect has flown pell-mell into his mouth. He gurgles and spits. The same one — another? — lodges in his eyes. He arrives. But what had arrived first: a droning cloud hovering over his fields. A rain blacker than night. A mass fixed on breathing upon his fields.

He pauses midstep, ready to run back and wake Johnny. But the boy hails him, seated on the fencepost. How can the boy sit there — ironic, starched, white-shirted and statuesque, hands folded into a patient mudra — when fields are being destroyed?

'You didn't wake me?' Henry shouts at the preternatural boy, a boy made stiller by the cloud raging around him.

'What to do?' Johnny's shoulders shake without mirth. 'It's already done.' The boy's calm fells Henry. 'Anything we save now would be infected. Might as well return to sleep. Nothing can be saved now.'

Already racing, he is. Something must be saved. Through the cloud of bugs, he chokes on their soft bodies, spits them up, rushing. But the boy's right: every single corner's gone.

At dawn, only the most persistent bugs remain. And this is when the British regiment marches up. How easy life could be if you were one of these soldiers: calibrated, perfect, handsome in daily training.

The ruddy boy orders his underlings at ease on the road. All the better to view Henry's disgrace. He saunters up to Henry to speak an irrelevance: 'So sorry,' is what Chris says.

'You're a god now? Is it within your powers to give back my f-f-field?' And Henry tries to correct this bitterness. 'Thank you. Forgive me. Nothing to be done now.'

'Right, then.' The soldier leans back under his royal blue cap. 'Good luck, then' — a chin chucked at Henry, a wave. Back on the road he orders the boys to continue their march: cadenced steps simple for the untroubled of heart.

Why would one person's field be chosen for destruction when no one else's is touched? A few minutes later, Henry calls out so only Johnny can hear him, 'They'll get you too, Chris!' Giggling, 'Later if not now! Trust me, pink man!'

The day starts from behind Elephant Mountain and flattens into Henry's face, a light far too bright and dead and gray. He blinks. Villagers are massing in the field, looking as happy about disaster as about ceremony.

One woman positions herself near Henry and doesn't once cease her dolorous chant. Her drone melds with the whine of the last flies. As though she were a stray Henry hisses her off but tricks like this don't work; she won't abandon her post so easily. A veritable barnacle, she is, one that allows more villagers to approach. As though their red-barked colonel has been newly stripped and revealed in this shirtless and stupid state. Each villager touches Henry's leg or hand. Does being disaster's object make one holy?

'Tell them to go away,' Henry begs his aide.

'Can't, Henree. They think their touching takes away a bit of your misfortune.'

Henry stares at the cruel waking dream. Why did this hovering mass choose his Eden and not another's? The malevolent joy of the black insects is the most infuriating. Every now and then he leaves the fence and dithers about swatting random bugs. This is what he is doing when Lester booms up from the road, 'Best thing for it, right?' Such geniality's more irritating than any devastation.

Irritation is too small a word. By noon, Henry begins to admit the field is gone along with hours of labor.

It is not just the heavy snake gourds that are lost. Pumpkins are lacerated, radishes pecked, yams demolished, spinach stilettoed to lacework. Every single vegetable is corrupted. All injury, mischief, ravage. Forget his subscriber service and the model anything. Forget the Red Cross lady's praise of his industry. Months of labor! All right, so he hasn't been monitoring the garden. He has been busy. Some would say lax. But is this universe so unforgiving?

What could Henry have done that would be so bad as to merit this? Some do fall among thorns, his father had preached, and the thorns grow up and choke them.

Against Johnny's orders, a few villagewomen are stealing as souvenirs vegetables festering with the black bugs. 'Explain how they'll rot their own gardens, Johnny,' feeling his pose of apathy already devoid of charm.

483

'They don't have gardens, Henree. They just want to remember you and the day.'

'I'm not dead yet,' doing a little skeleton dance on the fence. 'Look, friends. I'm not dead.'

Once the mood of celebration has lifted, the people of Rajottama finally seem to understand he doesn't want talk. Or chant. Or touch.

But what does register on Henry is this: their sincere faces, bucktoothed smiles, a watchfulness. Around him has formed a half-circle of silence and respect.

And seeing this, he is rushed with love. '*This* is what I've cultivated!' he tells himself, trying to cheer up. The sower soweth the word. His crackerjack team stands only a few feet away. From their quiet gossip he understands their belief: Mister Henry has made no mistake.

They are loyal. Even the temple prostitute stops by, carrying her scrawny broom. Whether to dispel Henry's bad fortune from herself or to express sympathy (Henry would be the last to know) Rosalin-akka strews at Mister Henry's feet fine white areliya and Job's tears. When she backs away, the drummer pushes Manu forward. Apparently Regi wants his son to commiserate in his English. 'We're sorry, Henry,' says Manu. 'This should not happen to you.'

Henry laughs again. He squeezes an insect against his forearm and watches the blood jet out in a tiny hopeful glyph. Should it be taken as an omen?

'Thank you,' to the drummers, 'that means' — what can anything mean to Henry right now? — 'so much.'

Nani arrives and urges upon him a flask containing a calming but bitter tea doctored with god knows what. Johnny calls it balm of Gilead. Still Henry cannot leave the scene of the disaster. He feels he's a linchpin. Should he leave prematurely, the world as he has known it will swallow itself into its navel right at the snake gourd field.

By half past twelve, the deputy government agent shows up. One of his unscheduled inspections? But *today?* The donkey-drawn rickshaw and the white suit are such incongruities that Henry laughs. The man has no clue.

'Bad day for a visit,' shouting to Chilkins. 'Should turn around right there.'

On more formal occasions Chilkins has been both clumsy and munificent. Thanks to Johnny he has signed, sealed and passed to Henry checks for prodigious sums. Today, with a solicitude honed after years of civil service, the expert hides his smile.

'One feels you to be in civvies today, H'nry,' the deputy says, smiling at the despairing man and his bare chest. 'At least it's not raining, right? Count the blessings.'

Fortunately or not, the weedy Brit takes the gentleman's route: not to shame Henry *too* explicitly. He seems to want to treat the entire debacle like a missed putt. The two men are to have a decent conversation.

Yet Chilkins doesn't give up an expert's grip. With graceful brio, he starts. Says he recognizes the ambition of being worthy of better fates than mass infestation by snake gourd maggots.

'But you know, H'nry, it's difficult,' harrumphing, brandishing his walking stick at the ruined field as though saying *It's difficult to obscure my authority*. 'Snake gourd? *Trichosanthes anguia?*' Waves his arm. '*Trichosanthes* draw the worst beetles. Quite a concerted effort there.'

'I sent my plans to you, didn't I? there at the Federal Building —'

'One never came across them. This gourd's an exhaustive feeder. Did you supply the creepers with five tons of cattle manure per acre? Should tell you, gourd beetles feed on young leaves. Had this — all — been inspected early on, one might've noted telltale cross-shaped markings. This type of infestation can be controlled. Yes, I told a chap from Canada the same thing, and not long ago either. But no harm done. You're kept busy, aren't you? Your house, your servants. Your other little pet projects —'

Henry can't not interrupt. 'Why this particular plot over any other?'

'Monocrop in one area for too long,' laughs Chilkins. 'First thing any farmer knows. Worsened by the heavy rains and then the drought.'

Henry disbelieves him.

Chilkins lifts a perished baby gourd from the ground. He shakes off the dirt. 'Shouldn't take it too hard. No matter what, you'd have had problems later.' The man hands over the surprisingly light thing but Henry refuses it.

'Hollow!' Chilkins thumbs an imprint into the flesh. 'Second-generation gourd fly had already set in.'

'But w-w-we took precautions. We even consulted some colleague of yours.'

'It's this area, H'nry. False hopes. The plan was rotten from the start. One should know a hawk from a handsaw. Should monitor better. This consultant of yours, was he in the government's pay or yours?' His leap from paper shuffler to expert horticulturist having been accomplished, Chilkins gentles his tone.

'Your consultants outside the government don't risk anything by being optimistic. These fellows wish anything on the peasants just to have an extended lab for their own hypotheses. Development types. Problems come if one roots something here that has no business growing this side of up-country. You wanted your homespun Ceylonese confection mixed with your Yank ideas. And your hired chaps agreed. That's what they were paid for. Take it from one who knows. Administered this area since 1930. Seven years, H'nry. Give one credit for knowing a few things.'

As the foreigners speak, Pandit advances, holding his parasol as though ready to swat barbarians. Why should the deputy agent and monk greet each other with such warmth? *I know a lot about nothing.* Henry eyes his monk who has chosen to stand by silently, hands united into an icon of sympathy.

Henry will not be deterred. He must finesse Chilkins, squeeze the man for every last bit of information. No future decisions should be made without information.

'How could the garden have been rotten from the start?'

'Flies. Maybe a month ago these creatures laid eggs in the ripening fruits. The things hatched and fed on the tender flesh. That's how it's moldered in patches. As though that weren't enough —'

It hurts Jehan to watch Henree practically cover his ears. Poor Henree would deafen himself if he could. And Chilkins, playing at deputyness, he won't stop. He speaks with the same scolding and bored pose he would use while disputing cricket scores.

Jehan thinks he knows. This spectacle is orchestrated as pure revenge. Pure revenge for the port scene in which Jehan had finagled British support for Henree's projects. And that had just been a youthful stunt. But a bad stunt now, a stinking stunt — it is all Jehan's fault that this man shames Henree.

And Chilkins is on a roll. 'Full-grown maggots emerge from the fruits only to fall on the gourd, you see. They pupate. Give rise to the second generation of flies. Better than Malthus. You went too far in your ambitions. You could not have escaped *some* kind of scourge. Especially' — sniffing about with distaste, from his glance it might as well be corpses putrefying around them — 'given your insistence on using *homespun* pesticides. Say you'd stuck with tried-and-true English Surrey brand, as one usually recommends — an import your villagers have always used — you might've had a fighting chance.'

'That's — all too expensive, I don't know, Chilkins —' Henree attempts.

If Jehan could, he would cut Chilkins' throat to stop all this grandstanding. But words fail to come.

'H'nry, p'raps take this entire affair as a message. Quit while you're ahead. Stop fussing with native fertilizer and gardening. These people are happy enough eating rice and their curried grass. Ask yourself why bother? Leave them be. Forget your model this and that. Stick with your school and your little culture projects which may one day tour. Think of perhaps even a hospital. Such projects, they're good for the island. No one would think you were meddling —'

'Excuse me —' interrupts Jehan.

'You're saying quit while I'm ahead,' says Henree. Too earnestly!

'Excuse —' Jehan tries again.

'Yes. Something like that.' Chilkins sniffs like the rabbit he is. 'Could use some water, actually.'

'Is this about the government needing land for rubber?'

'Of course not. Really, your little cultural things are quite nice. My colleagues were anticipating your troupe. Dance, is it?'

'I can't believe this is happening to me.'

'H'nry, don't indulge in self-pity. It's unattractive in any guest, and especially in one enterprising like you. You tried too much. This affair could have ended much worse,' surveying around. The man might as well be a sundial clocking time and shadow. 'Field could have been more decimated than after a chena. You Yankees can never recognize your luck. As you say, get out while one's ahead. You should call yourself lucky.'

'Right,' says Jehan's boss, showing Chilkins his empty palms.

113

TELEGRAPHIC DISPATCH FROM 'CHILKINS' TO HEADQUAR-
TERS, AT 13:04, 28 JUNE 1937:

WHOBODY CEYLONESE SUBJECT CONTINUES TO NEED
SURVEILLANCE. MAY BE SHARING SECRETS WITH YANKEE IN
VULNERABLE EPOCH. REQUEST PLACED TO STOP ALL MON-
IES. CONTINUED SUPERVISION BY THE UNDERSIGNED SEEMS
ADVISABLE FOR TIME BEING. REGARDS CHILKINS.

114

IN TOWN THIS MONTH, Manik Pilima shops for vegetables in the throng of stalls near the bridge and titillates the market.

Usually a servant shops for the last real Pilima but these days Manik could be a villagewoman herself. She sniffs the greenness of fruit. Her petticoat's as proudly white as the lowest washerwoman's. And her skirt is tied with ruffles and knots identical to those in Kumari's own sari.

Kumari has just finished reweighing an amber bottle of coconut oil with care. A few days ago she was cheated. But she almost drops the bottle when she realizes a Pilima stands behind her. The real Pilima. A woman she last saw years ago, a woman she always hears so much about. The one who is scented with cities.

So what if others think this Manik Pilima woman puts on airs? Pilima manners are her due. Not everyone descends from so illustrious a family.

And Kumari believes her own clan holds as grand a past as the best Pilima. Not every family receives an honorary name from a king. Not every family is linked to the local herb doctor. And the gods do not choose every family to dance and drum for them.

*   *   *

The two have never spoken so Kumari takes her time deciding what she'll say to the Pilima. Neither too uppity nor too humble.

'You must find it hard to return, Pilima nona,' begins Kumari. She holds the image of her ancient king and the gods at the center of her heart like a set of precious keys. At first she flushes. Is Manik pretending she doesn't recognize Kumari at first?

No, the Pilima rescues herself. She compliments Kumari on her sari, which is, after all, a special one.

After this initial bumpiness, the women slowly cozy up to each other, slipping away from the oil-seller's interest, standing apart from the market. After all, a bond exists. Years ago Kumari came to Manik's mother's funeral. There she performed a terror of a dance containing all the rage a bereaved daughter could desire.

Since each woman bears such a strong sense of her own superiority, the two quickly find a shared dialect. They begin with the oddness of rain this past monsoon and move on to how the village of Rajottama is esteemed in the capital, about which Manik generously exaggerates.

Then they scrape upon the work of the foreigner in their midst.

'He's become a nuisance,' Manik asserts. 'The coconuts are ruined. And he can't even read our politeness. No one's going to *tell* him to leave, he should just understand it.'

'Certainly not, we're a hospitable people,' murmurs Kumari. 'We've done him so many favors.'

'But who knew about his aide? Each time I see him I can't believe it. That boy might stay on and on.'

'He's the worst,' agrees Kumari, before her sister joins the women.

Kumari only hushes her vendetta against Jehan because of her sister, Soni having entertained a small devotion to the boy. For some reason his careful speech, slicked hair and slipping spectacles translated as class to Soni. Kumari, for her part, had never been fooled by him — even if she remains a covert fan of the pink man. But she won't admit that to Manik, and she'll also spare her sister from any shame before the Pilima.

Instead Kumari jokes about the foreigner's beloved Buddhist catechism pamphlets. The boys now sell them to the pulp trader at the market. Little does the author know, or does he? He gives such books away for free when the paper they are printed on is more valuable than the type and illustrations.

'He expects everyone to memorize what we already know here . . !' Kumari thumps her heart hard enough to produce a cough. 'He gives the children chits to use at the General Store. When the children complain those bitty pieces of paper fly away, he gives them money instead. Such a man! He thinks they come to school for his education?'

'What can such a man know?' Manik's voice is surprisingly soft in assent.

Kumari is embarrassed, suddenly remembering Manik's sister-in-law is the schoolteacher. She rushes in: 'It's good others take care of the store accounts. Otherwise, where would we be?' She studies Manik, trying to find a new place where the two women can meet in some common feeling.

So far, Kumari believes she's managed to quake superstition under the bovine exterior of Manik Pilima. But Kumari's tongue is boiled by desire: she wants to be recognized as *someone who knows things* by this untoward audience of a high-caste Pilima.

Manik Pilima must remember the snake gourd failure, Kumari continues. Everyone's talking about it. This strange pink stork is a man blind to bad omens. One who persists beyond the point where a reasonable man would understand a divine message.

Whether they consider the pink man, his aide, or even that strange servant girl he has, servitors of such foolishness should not be allowed to infect the bounty of Rajottama. An area long graced — and here Kumari allows her tongue to release the flattery which she'd managed to restrain — by the noble, superior history of a family such as the Pilimas.

As she sings the Pilimas' praise, Kumari's oil drips outside the badly corked bottle, and two drops stain Manik's purple skirt. Unthinkable. Manik notices the stains after Kumari does. And yet Manik, such grace in the woman, saves the lower-caste from shame. She waves away the drops, even argues for them as part of the design.

'You're right. We've survived well enough without him,' Manik agrees slowly — she returns a favor to Kumari by using the ambiguous *we*. 'We'll certainly continue to prosper without him.'

115

Then the venerable Ananda said to the Blessed One: 'How, Lord, should we conduct ourselves toward women?'
   'Do not see them, Ananda.'
   'But, Lord, if we do see them?'
   'Do not speak, Ananda.'
   'But, Lord, if they should speak to us?'
   'Then, Ananda, you should establish mindfulness.'

Too long has passed without Madame responding to his letters and Henry realizes he must step up the call if he sincerely wants her to make the junket to Ceylon. She really could help bolster everything. She would inspire the people. And would inspire him.

When he finds the heap of discarded planks from the old coffee plantation, he reckons it to be a sign, despite the fingers of paint curling and splintering off the boards.

If she'll insist on silence — it's already July, eleven months here with no answer from her — perhaps he'll build a meditation tower in her honor. With her name on it. Then she cannot refuse to answer, she cannot refuse to come.

And dammit, he'll build right on that snake gourd burial ground. 'A tower with a three hundred-sixty-degree vista,' as he explains to the drummer's son. Even Madame's charlatan lama could live in the tower. To himself he says: *Be average. Tell yourself you love to fail. This way nothing can surprise you.*

'Too bad for them,' he tells Manu. It's July's last day and they are investigating their own boot hill, the snake gourd cemetery. Henry is speaking of the wage laborers who'd refused to work on that land. A vengeful deity had leveled it, their leader had explained. He was sorry but the crackerjack laborers couldn't return to such a bone field.

It was because of this labor strike that Henry had been forced to announce the plan for the meditation tower at the last meeting. After the sparsely attended event, everyone had lingered in gossip and

I'll work for you was all Manu had said, simply, sullenness conspiring with effort. And despite the boy's limp hands, Henry had accepted.

Since the boy's demeanor fit Henry's own mood, Henry didn't need to know *why* the boy had volunteered. It was enough that he had come forward.

What Henry doesn't know is that the boy was urged to volunteer by his father.

'It's true,' Regi had whispered to his boy during the boring lecture. 'Drummers like us shouldn't get vain about height. True that if you get too high up like the toddy-tappers you see what happens.'

'So why are you telling me to do this, appachi?' Manu had whispered back. 'If it's not the way of drummers?'

His father smelled of betel and illness. He'd been a good father, not one to be disobeyed. There are only two things Manu has kept from his father. His love for the pink man's maid. And what he had organized, furtively, against the British. Because, talk about vain efforts, he had done the last thing just to impress the first. And nothing had worked.

Other than those two times, his whole life Manu has listened well to his father. Who says now: 'We need the land and we need the foreigner with us. Puta, I'm telling you, this would be the quick way, maybe the only way. If you don't do it for yourself, do it for your old aching father. Or your future children.'

Henry had seen the two heads staring at him during the meeting. Regi's support had warmed him enough that he made a mental note to inquire later how they were proceeding with their land, their temple duties, their child, and any other small talk he could summon to keep at least one faction behind him.

So when Manu appeared after the meeting, Henry heard the boy's offer as originating in good if morose faith. Despite his hands hanging by his side like they'd lost all will. Without thinking twice, Henry took the boy on. Manu would be his sole worker on the project.

A project to finally lure back to his side both Madame and charm.

Henry begins the habit of spending calm mornings in the site of his previous failure, seated on a rock that hugs his body just right. As his tower's plans change, he writes longer and longer letters to Madame.

One version of Henry's plan shows the meditation tower resembling the famous tower in Paris. Another is similar to a prison's pan-opticon, a precarious translucent nest perched atop an upward beak. It resembles something of his childhood's comics, the visions of the twenty-first century. The boy for his part appears to ignore the daily slips of paper and plans he receives from the foreigner. He agrees only to make the tower higher than the temple.

In only a few days the boy's own crazy-quilt construction emerges, with all of a honeycomb's puffs and curves. It rises over the field like a drowsy god's dream. In the long room at the top, Madame will be able to meditate. Meanwhile, Henry writes in his temporary book:

> The boy works with the force of a demon escaped from hellfire.
>
> What the Hindoos call karma yoga = the way Manu throws himself into work with such abandon.
>
> A true meditation.

The Tower of Manu doesn't astound only Henry. Everyone is amazed.

The boy's there powered by some internal axle that says he can trust ladders and nails at the break of day and maybe not much else. He hangs tarpaulins past the evening hour when colors glare and mothers stop calling children in. He and the tower soar toward each other like true lovers. Sleeping and waking the tower must rise before him. Lonely would not be the word you would apply to his labors as the tower has become his company. Johnny will come sometimes, just to scrape around with a spade or hand up tools. He will dirty his shoes and hands and leave them unwashed for much longer than the duration of his actual help.

And Henry has seen, too, that Manu's friends from other villages drop by occasionally to plead with the boy to come join some activity or another. This event, that meeting.

But Manu stays alone. There are depths to this boy that Henry could never have guessed during his full-time drumming days near the Sacred Tree. The drummer's son is a good one for muzzling himself. Even when his strange friends come, at least while Henry's there, the boy remains high on the scaffolding. One hand waves down, the other keeps its grasp on the hammer Henry has given him.

Here at the edge of the village the air is mild and taciturn, a world away from the life of the canal. But the boy is as possessed by the project as would be someone hacking through jungles. In this determination there is beauty enough to break Henry's heart.

Manu will never come home with Henry for lunch but he does accept Nani's food if Henry brings it to him in the field.

On Thursday of the second week, Henry watches the boy tuck into rice and his second, now his third curry with an appetite so prodigious and enthusiastic that Henry wonders whether he had ever known such potency, at any age, seventeen or beyond.

He sees that the boy, in pride at his own work, has carved his name in English into his hammer's handle. Regi and Manu is how Henry had known them. The *drummers*. He'd never thought to inquire into their family's name. In the Land Rights Bill the drummer was just referred to as Temple Servitor Regi, grandson of yet another Reginald. But is Bandu not Nani's last name? Or is Bandu the Ceylonese version of Brown or Smith?

'Manu *Bandu?*' exclaims Henry. 'Ban*du?* you have the same last name as my domestic!'

It takes Manu a moment to understand. Then he shrugs, as though Henry has slighted him. 'That must be it then,' slurring the Sinhala. '*Eeka tamay.* She wants to move forward.'

'Forward?'

'Higher, better. Upward. Never mind' — the boy swallows — 'who'd expect you to understand?'

'I know about moving forward. You're talking of caste?'

But the boy, like so many of them, has a birthright ability to stay orbitless, soundless when it suits him.

116

As she and henry make love that windy afternoon (the click of the gardener's shears not far from the open windows, rain starting in) there is a surrender the like of which Henry's never known. Not in meditation, and never in success.

And this surrender comes about not so much because of the progress of the tower or the discovery of new allies in Manu and a potentially recommitted Johnny. It isn't because the monk has suddenly demonstrated his moral worth — he hasn't — or because the townspeople are rallying — they're not. It isn't because Henry's nonetheless optimistic about Durbbhiksha, the next village over.

It is perhaps because he is finally slowed down enough to be with her — at the fulcrum where he can't say where she begins and he ends. He hasn't sacrificed his personal history or autonomy. Those too sit there, along with his folded clothes, to be worn or doffed. But something (greater than himself) has just chosen to doff them. *So this is what the Buddhists mean*, his thought is thought. They are making their slow way through afternoon love. *This is the self stripping itself of Self.*

He sees her luster, sees the cascade of hair spreading on the pillow and thinks she's there to be known; he can hold this gaze until she clasps it unblinking and also unafraid; such firmness; an ability to hold her own against any waffling in him that could be impressive or obfuscating or remote. She has lived a long sort of troubled life herself; has some corner mischief but still always that resolve that rests in her blue-rimmed eyes.

Today those eyes are not so spooky, no, they recognize him. They practically choose him. I will stand upon my watch and set me upon my tower. No language is perfect enough for this exact fact to be communicated. It is just known in this best and most simple type of silence.

XI

DISAPPEARING KARMA

When the Guide of the World, having accomplished the salvation of the whole world and reached the utmost stage of blissful rest, was lying on the bed of his *nibbana*, in the midst of the great assembly of the gods, he the great Sage, the greatest of those who have speech, spoke to Sakka who stood near him: 'A man is come to Lanka from the country of Lala with seven hundred followers. In Lanka, O Lord of gods, will my religion be established, therefore carefully protect him and his followers and Lanka.'

— *The Mahavamsa*

117

WHEN A PERSON goes so deeply into an event, it cannot be rooted out in twenty conversations. Not in thirty. What happened that night happened quickly. How could creation take so long and destruction be practically instantaneous?

At the knock Henry had risen, tying a cloth inexpertly around his waist. 'Who is it?' he'd called.

'Jehan, please, come, it's important,' this last finished even as Henry, having dropped the heavy silver key not once but twice, bent down, fumbled and reinserted it in the keyhole.

He opened his bedroom's garden door to the electric darkness and Johnny whose face was traced with water as though with dew. Still half-asleep, Henry stroked his aide's soft face. 'You're sweating,' he teased the words out. 'Your shirt's stained. Don't tell me you've been working on the tower at this hour?'

'Come immediately. *You* put on a shirt.'

Henry let himself be led by his gasping aide to the garden's stone bench, through the wet weeds among the trees. Near the nayingala flower stood, enduringly, his gardener Joseph, gnawing and spitting some kind of seed out, a whole spray of them. At their approach the gardener vanished without a step into the stripings of moonlight, his arms skinny out from an undershirt.

The boy's face toward his employer was an absence of tints, the words coming out with bad lapses. Johnny hadn't been able to sleep. He knew he shouldn't have kept himself awake by walking at night but he'd had little choice. On impulse he'd gone to the canal, to the market, finally to the old snake gourd field. There he'd contemplated the tilt of Manu's tower, and even his own minor handiwork of the day, when he heard someone calling to him. A voice from a throttled mouth. He saw no one on the scaffolding but the voice came from within.

He circled the structure dividing up possibilities. What he finally saw at the back shocked him down to his knees — Manu had fallen.

The boy lay contorted next to the scaffolding, completely caught, face twisted, hammer still in his hand. He could have been pulverized into the ground but Johnny had found him. His friend had probably worked past sunset. Had probably grown dizzy from hunger or nerves and fallen.

At least that's what Johnny thought at first. But who knows? Something else might have happened. It was hard to make out Manu's whispers. Johnny stooped closer. He tried to avoid seeing the unnatural turns in his friend's neck. His ribs and ankles. Tried to avoid hearing the whistle in his breath. Manu couldn't remember much exactly. Had lain there for hours. Until he heard Johnny's tread he had been going through the suttas and the precepts.

'What I mean is he stayed religious to the end,' Johnny said, an odd animal whimper in his voice, 'I mean he stayed calm.'

Johnny had lain beside him in the tall grasses. Had asked again, *Sure you don't want me to get anyone?* But the boy had insisted.

'Time,' the boy kept saying, and something else. First Manu made Johnny promise that his father would be cared for. And that Johnny would help Regi reclaim his land. Because otherwise Regi would have little reason to live. And that if Manu's nationalizing group came, Johnny would tell them to go on with their activities. Against the British, Manu had said, 'you —'

— and Johnny couldn't promise *of course* or anything else because those were the last understandable words out of the low-caste's royal mouth. He wouldn't describe what happened as the boy's life fled him.

Against the British? What Henry wanted to know immediately, gut thorned, was where the boy could be found. 'He died just like —' and Johnny glanced away. The gardener had been skipping stones out toward the canal with great method. What they heard was mainly the thirst of water swallowing stone after stone. 'What are we going to do?' Johnny asked.

What can contradict death? Henry took the boy's arm and pressed it to his chest in a flabby, awkward embrace. 'What is ever to be done?' he asked gently.

In answer they walked toward the canal, Johnny apart from Henry, enough to impress an obscure guilt upon the American. At one point Henry heard himself telling the boy that it was not he, Henry, who had brought this about, and anyway who had ever poured water without spilling a drop? Even to his own ears he sounded like a pouting child and he fell silent.

Deep in the thick weeds they found Manu, brow smooth and eyes a glassy velvet, a figgy scent starting to rise. Nearby, the market bull-ock nosed along, ropes dragging. Jehan asked what the American was starting to do, pulling at Manu's wrists. Whispering: where was Henree planning on taking the boy?

'To the ditch at the back there, in the field.'

This is Henree's solution. He will not bury Manu properly. He will forbid a funeral and not tell Regi, at least not immediately. All of this muttered back makes little sense. 'You're not seeing the bigger picture,' he tells Jehan, hands describing arrowshafts. Just where Jehan had lain beside his friend. Henree is saying some-thing about understanding grief. Of course there could be a moment of silence or a proper ritual later, a spiritual repose, but nothing stands to be gained by gossiping about the incident. He knows about people overheating with this type of thing, he should be listened to on this one, everything is so close to arriving, this should be kept quiet.

And the boy will not help drag Manu. Instead stands a vertical stilt.

Henry raises his voice at such obstinacy. 'This could damn every-thing.' He studies the sky where no stars clash. Because his own face feels frozen into some tragic mask, he can't really move his mouth. He tries to tell the boy something, about how not to risk overattachment to something. To someone.

'Buddha buddha buddha?' Johnny combs his fingers through the dead boy's hair. 'Now?' Henry wants to run away from the boy's curses but Johnny has already started. About a cover-up, Henree, cover-up — would that be part of a new plan? A potter's field? The model village? A meditation on the deterioration of the flesh?

But in response Henree is quiet and horrible, saying is it not possible the British had come to get Manu for his nationalizing activities?

A final absurdity and Jehan sinks to his knees. This is not a moth, it's a boy, he almost retches at Henree. Everyone will know. Every-one. Henree will be implicated no matter what. As will Jehan. You can't go around bashing justice when it suits you.

But Henry cannot understand why his aide has started to care so much what others think. The boy meanwhile is having difficulties breathing. He stammers, hands kneading the air. He stumbles up, backs away. But also tells his employer he has other channels him-self, he can pursue it on his own.

Logic, conclusion, logic, conclusion — there is a desert to cross and it is taking all Henry's strength to keep from looking at the boy. 'I need to trust you on this,' he tells Johnny, 'now more than ever. If you want, we'll tell the father, we'll tell Regi.'

You know I'm dying to think you're someone different — a reflection breaking off inside Jehan, a bent ray, a chilled blade. He is fingering his sleeve-hooks, he is youth and anger and everything in between, his eyes hurt when he looks at the man — *but what you're saying, it's starting finally to disgust me.*

The ligatures are melting. Beyond the field they hear someone setting off down the canal in a boat, an aged man singing a song, oars sifting through.

'Whose side are you on?' asks Henry. 'You might as well be working for *them*.'

The boy sticks his chin out at Henry. 'So what if I were?'

There is a silence between them which lasts longer than it takes for a child to be conceived. Everything is landing in the weeds of this field. In the snake gourd field and the boy who won't be dragged.

Henry manages to shimmy, kick and roll Manu into the ditch. The dead boy lands mouth open, splayed, a careless arm akimbo as in Ceylonese dance, right up the side of the hole.

'So maybe I'm not with you but still on your *side*,' Johnny has just said as though to himself. This distinction between Johnny's employment and faction confuses Henry. *Had* his boy been working for another side? You could never know for sure what went on behind that face. At one moment it would look as though it came from dining with the rich among chandeliers and carpeted boxes while the next moment it would be lost and unknown, unholy, an urchin's, the face of a cat, bird, horse. Now it hates him, that is all Henry knows, the hinge on one's own tomb, full reproach and nothing else.

The market bullock butts over to them with interest. Henry, in trying to remember what is important, considers the risk of the bullock sniffing something appealing and falling into the ditch alongside Manu. It takes great effort to push and shove the overtame beast away. The fake hunter-beggar has trained it to be unafraid of humans and their rules. For the bull this is just another calm August night.

And the land, that is what Johnny wants to know, as if all this speech were necessary. Because, he says, maybe nothing can be done about the loss of a life, but there had been the promise Johnny had made.

As a child in morning song, Henry would imagine himself alone with God on a speck of land in the middle of an ocean filled with broken but still floating eggs. Let everyone else sing *Excelsis,* he would sing *eggshell seas.* He thus offered up his own private and uncommon love song to God. Once he wondered whether the daydream was more mundane, having to do with his first real memory of his mother, cracking eggs before his eyes, swirled landscapes in a glass bowl.

During morning song only Henry and God communed amid the seas. Now he feels himself far from God and farther from mother, who could not have imagined how alone he is. Here with a vengeful basilisk, an aide, pawing dirt onto a dead boy. This aide in a sea already too crowded with gods.

'They should call this Totinsel,' Henry is saying — land, no land, the greater good matters, not this damn island mentality. He is wiping his brow with the back of his hand and gestures behind. Maybe the dawn will catch up with them.

'Will you be good enough later to see about getting laborers over here, to continue the tower?'

'I don't understand, Henree,' Johnny shovels the last of the dirt onto the face and coughs. 'To continue *what* again?' He sizes up his employer. 'Or that's the point, isn't it. It doesn't matter what. *Continuing* is the thing for you, isn't it? Having a goal so *you* go on hiding.'

As they cross down to the canal a small parade of turbaned children on the opposite bank, replete with kazoos and large feathered masks, marches solemnly forward in an elliptical moment of their own devising. A man costumed as a large green parrot leads his charges, ignoring Henry and braving on, tooting a mock funereal threnody across the water and into the early dawn.

118

ONE OF THE LONGEST NIGHTS any of them have ever known. They've retired to the kitchen lit by the oil lamp with its ghoulish spluttering. His Nani presides quickly and quietly. Over her lover; over his aide. She offers the two men various liquids and cloths where what might be Manu's dried blood is scrawled upon Johnny's clothes and skin. How much does she understand?

What he decides at the tiny table where they had eaten their first meal — what Johnny wants is excessive. That Colwether should be the one to interfere? The head government agent? That Colwether should forcibly return acres of land to Regi?

Henry's insides quake. Genuine, passionate, hopeless. It was less than a month ago that Deputy Chilkins picked up the hollow snake gourd and sealed a kind of doom by saying *trichosanthes anguia*.

'Please!' he tells the boy. 'Not Chilkins or anyone like him.'

'You have to give that up,' says Johnny, the voice wheedling Henry like his own conscience. 'I'm not saying Chilkins, who is a sort of fake really. It should be Colwether, he'll make sure justice is served.'

'You know him?' This is just to stall.

The boy doesn't, Chilkins is the one they know —

And, inside, Henry dies a little. He stiffens his neck, his heart: there is nothing more for anyone to say. The boy rises to pace, in a fine rage, saying something about this time it not being about *Henree's* pride, the man can't be selfish, this time Johnny must be listened to, he had promised Manu. And then starts over.

Henry will let his aide cool down. Already this evening the boy has cried, stomped off, returned, complained of illness. Vituperated. He needs to incline back toward himself. Come back to his crop. Then Henry can listen.

But there is also a deadness skulking in from his fingertips. A fruitful land unto barrenness. From the edge of some shadowy, still crater he perceives the night as a ghastly event. The place where the earth sucks itself in even more. All Henry wants is to make a success of something and then the crater and its suck happen. As though it's come to scatter hopes abroad.

Yes, of course all this is a terrible thing. He is not at the edge of a crater, he *is* the crater, blood inroading in from fingers and taste-buds. This is the kind of thing that makes you retreat to some still-born place until that same hide-and-retreat has you erupting in a greater action than ever before: you have little choice.

Mostly you must fight off that unutterable deadness you'd found waiting for you.

No. This is the kind of thing where you want it to have been exactly the day before. That's it, for Manu the day before could have been intervention. Turn back the clock, the day and all the rice harvested in it. All the mosquitoes killed, satin embroidered, cloth dyed, dances learned, hair woven, goiters scratched, words exchanged, shadows fallen.

It would be the day before or the day before *that* when the boy in all his angelic beauty had saluted you and you'd felt that burn of respect travel up your throat and into the insufficient words you were able to muster, whatever they were — *Hello, Manu!* or *You're keeping our project healthy, you're helping to save us!*

Or just: *Good luck my friend!*

Hammer-tonguing it if you say good luck. Because how can bad luck exist in the world? Why would some be born into a streamlined unquestioned existence, others into famine? Some with a mother and others without? Why would some enter into the kind of privilege where everything is said to happen for the good? Where golden elites get to ponder whether or not they create (rather than fall victim to) their destiny?

How could anyone create anything here? No. What happened to Manu was simply bad luck. Extend it over a few lifetimes and Henry'd call it plain old karma.

Whatever Manu's karma, it was essential to grasp that the word *projects* did not describe Henry's plan. No, each is no mere project. Each is a dream. And dreams depend on another, dreams *stack*, each a turtle upon a turtle upon a turtle all the way burrowed back down to the fiery guts of earth and first creation.

The details might seem petty, Henry remonstrates to no one. He recites them as comfort to himself. The newest strain of chickens is due to arrive. Is that just so many puddles of champagne? Yes, and the second garden in Durbbhiksha is about to grow into what the original model was meant to be. A dribble of funds created next month's event, when truly international observers are supposed to come see the first Ceylonese dance gala, here in Rajottama. Turmeric-yellow costumes, swept unassuming roads, the local announcements. And the dance company due to tour the island. He would tell Nani about it all. Each a turtle upon a turtle upon another. Each important.

With none of these able to function alone. Out lost in the garden somewhere he is sure his Village Book has lain rotting for months. Wooves' plans and his own accounts have grown sundried and faint, suckled moldering into the viperish groundroots like everything else, a book without qualities.

'Where did my book go anyway?' he demands.

Johnny ignores this and issues yet another skinless proclamation: That if Henree Fyre Gould continues to think this selfishly, he will always be stained. From the boy's compressed tone it is clear he is a hothead too close to the affair. Someone who wants immediate action. Follow-through.

Everything will be marked. No one can wash this one out for you.

'And,' murmurs Henry, ' — beg pardon — if no one sees the stain?'

119

WHEN REGI STOMPS up the drive the next day and the day after — why wouldn't he, he is searching for his son — the impression that this strange storm-tossed voice makes is so frightening that Henry hides. Animals, trees, houses. All would shudder away from such a sergeant.

Nani tells a lie for Henry, explaining how the foreigner's gone and left in the middle of the night. *Eyaa enawa aeti*, maybe he'll be back sooner or later.

Were Johnny there he would be hacking up his guts. Seems that if giving Regi his own tongue would alleviate Johnny's guilt, the boy would do it, skipping tongueless and liberated on the hills. The boy doesn't understand that there are times of surplus and times of loss and the most important thing during times of loss is to conserve. Stay tight. Lucky that Johnny's gone when Regi comes. Some light falls on the old tub.

Some. But the dogday sun turns its rancor on Rajottama. When he does get the chance, Johnny talks. He has untelescoped himself enough to blab and now won't stop. Talk talk talk. Haranguing Henry. Enough to drive anyone mad.

'I *promised* him,' the boy keeps saying, 'so what in bloody creation are we doing for Regi?'

He gnaws his fingers, shudders, breathes his deadwood voodoo onto Henry. And Henry isn't ready to do anything. He maintains meditative composure. Tells the boy he'd prefer to sit tight for a while. And this rationale the boy fails to understand. His mouth turns that humbling gray, the mettlesome gray that is everywhere, the one screaming that life is disapproval.

By the third day the harangue's gone on too long. It has become a siege and rushing of the fortress. So Henry turns back on Johnny with surprise speed: '*Who* promised him,' he says, referring to Manu without wanting to mention the boy's name. '*You* promised. *Don't rush, Henree*, you always say, *don't say always or never*. I wouldn't have promised him anything.'

This hushes the boy into a sham boredom, a dense humid void he stays in for the next few days, little Ceylonese sleepwalker. His whole being is an argument for structure, bent and collapsed into itself. At such times he is no one's ward, not even his own. He is walked, he is absented, he flits among mango trees examining the rotted fruit. As if he could hope to conceal himself and his slender figure far from the world.

After this he appears at the dinner table wan and refusing to eat. When, at one such dinner, Henry has finished his curries and dessert — he chews ultra-methodically so as to keep Nani nearby, taking his time swallowing the last of the sweet apple bananas, like an expert trombonist — Johnny takes hold of his employer's shoulders. An inescapable touch, something in other times guileless but not today. It is pure recrimination, all clawed vulgate, even this boy's unsteady hand.

He is saying, 'I may still be with you —' the boy's tone tight enough to signify each word's cost. His face seraph and corpse and something scarily beyond: '*Why* still with you, I can't even explain anymore — but forget me being *of* you. Make your own decisions. Forget my standing *behind* you.'

Henry coughs in surprise; the boy only finishes after Nani leaves the room.

And Henree's tone is mild but he cannot hide his own tremble: 'Did you, though? *Did* you ever stand behind me one hundred percent?' And from the boy's guilty look, he almost realizes, bitterness rinsing his insides, this boy is not A or B or C, not anything within any known alphabet, this boy may have been semi-living with his Henree always a semi-truth.

So chaos still reigns the next morning when Regi storms into the library. Johnny is whittling a giant amorphous damascened stick, some drossy petrified rage, and doesn't glance up from his work. In a different way, the drummer's face is sharpened, lacking the slightest gleam of divinity, another firebrand maddened into another request.

Regi wants an official investigation into his son's disappearance. Or at least for Henry to file a missing person report. And Johnny will not translate what is, after all, Henry's polite enough response to the drummer, a response interlarded with courtesy, qualifications, understanding, dismissal.

Using his own English-clotted tongue, Henry has to explain that he cannot quite trouble the government agent at the moment, could Regi aim for a bit of patience in the matter? And that perhaps Regi might like a few extra chits to use at the General Store?

'Let's keep it between us,' adds Henry.

'Between us?' Regi laughs.

Henry alone has to hold the drummer's glare. *You're falling farther than you know, Sir Henry*, the drummer's anger says, *you're practically gone.*

And Henry's Sinhalese does not translate to the man. Or else Regi plain chooses to misunderstand.

In the next week, Regi cannot be tied down long enough to keep his boy's disappearance quiet. Stray people and animals are subjected to the story. All their shared moments, Henry's gifts and Regi's candles and that private altar visit, all this gets relegated to the past. Regi and his blabbering — this is the colorful folk life Henry would rather escape. Henry wishes he could just temporarily manacle the man's mouth and wrists.

Apparently the drummer must go wild with his story. He kindles it in buyers at the marketplace, among women penitents at the temple, amid tattling idlers on the road. He sets rumor to run so tall and high in the grasses, no one can dream of stopping him.

'Manu was killed,' says the father to anyone he meets, 'and the foreigner's not letting me make an investigation!' He leads them on, preempts skepticism: 'Even if the boy's just disappeared, the foreigner's not letting me know why.'

Why hasn't Henry thought of it before? An attack of insomnia grants Henry a temporary solution. He will *appear* to satisfy Regi's desire for an investigation: he'll mount his own personal inquiry. In this way two birds will be killed — he'll also get to tap the hindered pulse of the village. Johnny'll consent to help him of course.

Everyone will come around.

And as he predicted, Johnny is as enthusiastic for this task as for anything since Manu's death. Not a surging — but enough of a faithfulness to a trust, enough to make the boy say *Who knows,* sounding as though he too wanted to convince himself the death had been an accident. That Manu had fallen like an earthward spirit from Henry's tower and then just transubstantiated. As though the boy's death had not been hidden by Henry himself.

'Who knows,' says Johnny, convincing himself. 'Everything's possible. Someone might've had it in for him. We don't know what league we're playing in.'

All Henry hears again is *we,* a tutelary genius of a word. *We.* A stark union. Maybe Johnny's come over to his side again.

As they make their rounds, some villagers swear to Johnny that on the night Manu disappeared they'd witnessed a cricket game between boys of high and low caste, between boys from high up the mountain — who came from homes of plenty, of linen-filled cupboards — and others, boys of nothing, boys from homes sunk into the valley. They claim Manu (of nothing) had fought with an upper caste (of plenty), and had nearly killed him.

'Go ahead, guess,' they guffawed, 'that underdog Manu ran, scared of his own skin. He knew someone would revenge all over him.'

The plains in Henry's brain are vast, thunder dry and booming, ricocheting. No one's signals are clear.

Others sneer that the drummer and son had quarreled over temple duties. Of course the drummer must be lying. He's trying to distract everyone from the fact that he'd always held his son hostage to his job. A few villagers hint they think the monk and drummer are keeping the boy locked in the temple's dungeon.

But the motley informers who tell Johnny that Manu had tried to join the night gamers upset Henry the most. *Night* gamers?

Reputedly, while Manu and the night gamers had the same goal, the night gamers did not accept Manu and his insurrectionist, all-caste boys from other villages. 'Manu and his types were too low caste.' *Insurrectionist* boys? Some say when Manu disputed any exclusion, they saw him killed and thrown into the canal, his body waterlogged bigger than a bull's. Others had seen him and Nandana running away.

'What night gamers?' Henry asks his sulky aide. 'The afternoon cricket players?'

Johnny says Henry could go ask, since he knows well enough where Manu is.

'Which games?'

Henree can talk to Pushpa, says the boy — Pushpa with her fancy Chinese methods, because who knows, Henree, maybe Pushpa was behind those games.

'I, my friend, behind *night* games?' Pushpa asks, elegant eyes crossing. 'Chinese methods? Who said? No, you've never understood how things work in our villages. There are always fashions —' she elongates the English word. 'They die! Compared to what we know, you've been here maybe half a second.'

Her short fingers snap, bayonet-quick. 'You've never listened to me. You just came here. You came and, beg pardon, *squatted* in that terrible house on land that belongs to us. To the Pilimas. You never offered any rent. We would have refused, that is true — but you never offered. Listen to me. If these games of yours existed, they were for our young. Probably a way for them to avoid that nationalist nonsense! The other towns have it and we don't. I didn't want to teach you but I tried anyway. We have no problems with the British. We in Rajottama are very lucky, correct?'

She smiles, pulling her shawl tight around her shoulders on a warm enough night. 'Excuse me for speaking as a barren woman, my friend. Even a childless woman knows this — no infant ever realizes just how young it is.'

Henry has seen Rajottama's boys walking the road singing in a safe pack. Night gamers and insurrectionists?

The boys have been good, even deferential. They've behaved like little adults. Their only impishness has been that shadow-cloud of orphans. Or the ones who stop him repeatedly on the road to ask *What time is it?* so as to make him fumble for his elaborate pocket-watch, Madame's gift.

Night games? Of course, in his planning, he had decried a lack of organized, self-improving entertainment for the Rajottaman children. But he'd never denigrated what he saw as their native respect for him.

Night games would not be respect. Night games would be will-ful connivance. If they had been truly respectful, just one of them should've told Henry or Johnny. If night games existed, they served a single function, he thinks: repudiation of Colonel Henry Fyre Gould.

'Tell me, boys and girls were playing military games at night?' Henry asks once the baby on the woman's hip stops squalling.

'Maybe not at night but at dusk, toward evening, after the devil's wife disappears,' the beggarwoman hoots back. The devil's wife is sunset but Henry can see this woman bears sympathy for the general phenomenon of *anything* setting, whether it is the sun or herself or the devil's wife.

He is stunned into watching her extreme eyes and the red-haloed smile. She hands the baby to an older girl inside her hut and resumes weaving long black human hair, using her square toes as a loom. She has already made the fleecy arm of one dark sweater and it hangs, an amputee, off her ankles. 'If they had a good judge around here,' she says, 'the boys never would've needed to fight. But anyway, Regi's boy, he was a bit wild-tempered, don't you know?'

Henry catches a fifth of her meaning, enough to believe she speaks the salty truth of the village. *Wild-tempered*. As he gets up to leave she explains something with great pride: the sweater she is weaving and sewing is a gift for her grandchild, 'the lightest-skinned of them all.' And also how sorry she is to see such a spirited boy as Manu gone. Henry should accept her condolences. But of course the world continues; the best are always taken first; nothing lasts; life is suffering and illusion. We must always cultivate detachment; we must also cultivate, apparently, the brittle clichés that follow so swiftly on all deaths.

Over tea, Kumari, the more dramatic of the dance sisters, lowers her voice. 'Regi's son set the lead by avoiding his father's profession, no? By not playing the drums with great enthusiasm, no? Manu may have driven someone somewhere mad. If you'd wanted to control him, beg pardon, should've done it earlier.'

'Boys from up valley descended on Regi's son 'cause he was from down valley,' her nephew Dakshan declaims through a lock of hair. 'Up-valley boys hate down-valley boys. Like foreigners and Sinha-lese. Same same.'

Appuhamy the sorcerer tells Henry that everyone agrees. 'All know it was a caste incident.' Boys from farther up had referred to the drummer boy's low-caste ancestry. 'You cannot understand such things.'

'None of the Elephantside high-caste witnesses did a thing,' says a pruned, polished man whose hands stay locked behind his back. 'Instead those high people let the boy be massacred in cold blood before their eyes.'

And people are sure the boy was killed.

'For all we know,' Henry says to conclude each interview. Robbed of speech, he begins to talk at buckshot level. 'For all we know, Manu could return tomorrow.'

Then he begins to believe his own words.

As he stands on the old snake gourd field, he lets himself imagine the boy coming back. It would be a nostalgic, precipitous gesture, the boy's desire to finish his own work.

The boy's velvet eyes would gaze at his tower, still listing in homage to its maker. Henry's wage laborers had been right about the cursed field. Now the tower has become an oversize cenotaph. By some absurd law of anti-probability, *once* cursed can quickly become *twice* cursed. Just as money attracts money, ill luck brings on its cousins, who stay and stay and stay.

120

WHY DID NANI never tell Honree what she knew of the night games?

Manu once chose to confide in her. He said he saw her like the canal, always moving, never the same. Never graspable but constant. Drummer's son, how much he had courted her. Manu's seduction tactics relied on surprise and the endless resource of a boy's bragging.

Nani might be pounding laundry at the canal and the boy would startle her into dropping a cloth so it floated downstream. Only he could dive in quickly enough to save the cloth and bother to tuck an extra new petticoat into her basket as a gift hidden for later enjoyment. A petticoat perfect enough to make her wonder how he had measured her so carefully. Or as she carried vegetables from the market, he'd trace her shoulder, make her jump so gourds tumbled from her basket down the road like fallen kings' heads. Her exasperation was matched only by his readiness to restore all that was hers. It became a routine between them.

Everything moved in its way toward tempting music. She couldn't help but laugh at his exaggerated courtesy. She called him *cousin.*

The boy evidently liked her coastal freedoms, the way she waved her hand to dismiss all questions. She braced herself against the wind. Did she like working for the foreigner? To him, he said, she was strength itself. Obviously, he thought, *she* had chosen the house, had selected her duties. When he spoke this way, she was sparked.

He began to broach the subject of his own ideas, of the two of them, beyond these brief moments. But he appeared to guess that behind her wide brow, she might be laughing at him as just a boy. He was too well raised to ask her age but once ventured that she must be only a few years older than him.

'You know you're charming,' she had dared back and told him.

He must have sensed his velvety eyes had driven women crazy. She was not blind to the dark that glides on a river's bottom. So was the problem for her that he'd always be a temple server?

She wasn't that ambitious, was she? Because she'd always liked his pride. He wasn't in the least ashamed of his father, of his lineage descending from the first Brahmins to bring over the Sacred Tree's sapling, he'd said, struttingly.

So what, we two have a similar ancestry, she would tell herself, mostly believing it, but never aloud, so as not to embarrass. Calling him *cousin* was one thing, saying *kin* would be another.

She told Manu that his father reminded her of someone in childhood, of the doctor who'd taught her to read. He called this an invitation and she laughed, said it wasn't, said it was only passing a moment together.

The day he seemed to know she would never encourage him — though he must've known, even a little, that she loved him, however much she could — he'd slipped up from behind whispering. Before that day, they'd lived what he said had been a life's romance for him.

To win her, he revealed, an elderly friend had told the boy he needed to develop a secret. Something to reveal a wealth of future intimacy. He had begun his activities in other towns for long enough for her to note that time stretched between his visits. The friend had been right. She had found herself missing him.

When finally he told her, during the rainy season, she had gotten angry.

'You stayed away just to tempt me?' she scolded. 'Foolish boy! I wasted time thinking of you!'

'Why call it a waste?' And he spun on her, trying to kiss the back of her neck, as though he'd always wanted to steal up on her in this way. 'You just admitted it. You loved me. You love me right now.'

'As a brother. A cousin.'

'It doesn't matter,' he said. 'Nothing works with you. Let me just kiss you' — and before she could answer his lips were clamped on her cheekbone, determined to suck out the resistance that kept her from him.

Once he let go, she was vain enough to insist on hearing the entire story.

So what if he'd invented a secret in order to win her. Piqued, she tried to disguise his appeal and the effect of his flattery.

'Sharing a secret is much harder than other kinds of honesty,' the boy had essayed, borrowing one of his elderly friend's formulations.

Impressed, she'd sworn to keep the boy's faith. And then she'd listened. Inspired by the contest of winning her admiration, Manu had been traveling to other towns to learn from organizers how to train youth for a rebellion against the British. She remembers hearing the words *organizer, training, something better than the night games because it would include all the castes.* She had to admit that he intrigued her almost as much as his courtship's innocence pleased her. But she showed this intrigue too late, after she had laughed at him, after having not taken him seriously.

No one would ever know that on nights Honree split her — even after the day when she'd sent the boy out of her life with her laugh, her terrible laugh — she kept Manu at her mind's periphery. He was her secret, a wildflower.

At his disappearance from his father's house, she wondered whether the boy's last thoughts in Rutaeva were that she might have betrayed him to Honree. He might've believed she had told his secret. The thought chewed her heart's nib.

Soon there might be little left inside her chest. She knows how the best never return. It is always in the dead of night that you learn about rotting things. She has collected enough collisions, crumbled soil in her hands, listened for when life begins to turn full and golden again. Now one more had left her and she will have to find some new way of making amends with what another rips out of her.

121

TORN UP INSIDE, not torn, he prefers mostly to pretend to nap, scratched by the new jute-and-chicken-feather pillowbed, and it is from this lair, two weeks after Manu has gone his way, that Henry hears: the encampment soldiers have organized a cricket game for Saturday and another Sunday-night showing of an outdoor cinema film.

Johnny twiddles his thumbs, leaning against the door, reporting. He's back to his metallic competent self. 'Not coming, Henree?'

'I'll think about it,' Henry says, fancying himself Nero. But as the boy leaves, Henry raises himself from the pillow to ask: 'If you hate me so much, why stay linked with me?'

'I don't.' And that could cut deeper than hate.

I don't hate you or *I don't stay linked to you?* 'Then why not?'

'You still have half a chance to do right. Otherwise, maybe there would be something like —' The boy doesn't finish. 'Anything else?'

'How *is* cricket played anyway?'

Henry doesn't come but walks by it, descending from the upper road as though he always preferred this winding leaf-cluttered path, its paisley of dappled light, even if it stretches inconveniently far above the canal. In the English cleared plateau, he sees Chris and the other damnably athletic soldiers. In their center, like a field of spuds, some ten young Ceylonese boys hunch trying to understand directions. And along the rim, women with children squirming up their hips watch this vain endeavor, overjoyed.

The night before, lost in bad dreams, Henry had scratched his face enough that now a slight gust stings the cuts along his jaw. He ducks to shield himself from both the wind and being seen on the field road. His head he keeps flush level with their playing ground, concealed behind a half-falling palm tree with a diseased trunk and long leaves pecked with holes like those of the snake gourd flies. This is not my fault, he thinks, these holes. I wasn't the one that diseased this tree. The new refrain: *This is not my doing.*

'Mallet it full on!' chipper Chris is shouting, two bright balls of red high in his cheeks. He'd seem to sacrifice his own mother if these boys would just play the game right, he is that much the picture of patriotic glee and health. For the occasion he's donned a smart little tweed golfer's cap, and now stops running about demonstrating in the center of those spudlike listeners only to stop with hands on his hips. 'Thread those balls through.'

The boys act as if they're trying to memorize Chris's face even as they take their positions at the baseline, one little prophet after another ready to hit.

'Come, no bad sports, no thinking —'

A tall boy Henry's seen before punts hard, and must have punted well, because the onlookers cheer with more enthusiasm than Henry's seen even during his small cultural pageant at the dance school. *Is this after all what they want to teach their children? How to propel a puck through space?* He watches the people's faces and can imagine them in some odd switch, pink and white with astonishment, cheek by jowl, their fortunes allied intimately to their respective teams. The children run around in random patterns and then stop, exhausted, so much flung-about cigarette ash.

'A brute of a ball!' calls Chris. 'Good consistency, though. A regular beaut. New batsman! Bounce ball!'

As far as Henry can see, it is all just winning by opportunism. A give-me, takeover kind of game. But is there any other kind of game? In the final analysis, all games rotated around this idea: my will is greater than yours. Or some might substitute *ability* for *will*, which Henry didn't really believe in, all men having been created equal, each able to produce his own Valhalla if he trusted in it enough and had compassion for the other valhallas around him.

'I would think you need to find the outside edge! The wicket has to play the ball too! It needs some encouragement! Keep it plumb as anything!'

One small boy stands crying by the side, runtish, fists gouging out his eyes, drawing Henry's attention the most. Could be Daniel, mop-headed Daniel who truth be told lacked talent with games, Daniel who played until the first defeat, or whatever he called defeat, who'd then quickly change the activity, invent his own games.

'Can't give up, son,' Henry had counseled him constantly, punching the kid's gut with a football, 'think of Job and his trials,' sounding to his own ears too much like his own father with all the godawful platitudes that meant nothing. Now Henry wants to go console the little crying pariah on the side, the game's runt, bring the tadlet's spirits back up to par, but instead, out-caste himself, he hangs back, hidden, but not well enough.

He is sighted. No one can hide here. It's a covenant among the trees on this island. 'Should come up, really,' Chris calls out, ringing tones across the field, good tones for mother England, better for commanding. 'Today they're giving everything out there. Going into the double figures. Particularly severe. Best innings I've seen in play. Still want seven runs to win. They're dawdling up the pitch. Sun's in the fielder's eyes. It's great fun.'

A bit dizzy. 'Maybe next time.'

'Next Saturday, then,' chirps Chris. And returns his attention to the next boy, coaching: 'Remember — give 'em a bit of long handle! Ah, you're a stylish left-hander. Your grasp this way. For gentleman's form hold higher. Lower is peasant's form. Ah, last two wickets disappointing, men.' And, as Henry had guessed, Chris is not above jingoisim. 'Do it for England!' he erupts, whether for Henry's benefit or to express an inner soul, no passerby could guess. Chris equals the very picture of saintly, beastly self-satisfaction. 'At the neck! Keep your eye on it. And follow through —'

Henry had hoped the sortie would raise his own mood. That in spying on another nation's pastimes, he would be regranted his own mission's relevance. Along the roadside, the wind has picked up, sharing the scent of young ginger plants and nettling the hedges and trees. Something in this orchestration does cheer him, the banal grandeur of a sunny day. Heading back, he will drop in at the temple, though climbing the temple stairs, it is hard to hold the cheer. The game must have left him distempered.

In the monk's study, Pandit has been reading yesterday's papers on the smashing game played between England and the West Indies. 'A regular blinder, Colonel!' he exclaims. This sport must be worse than maggots, it is that airborne and contagious. 'You've seen this, Colonel? The English lost their best player to the navy. Called up. Things getting a bit messy. Which way are the Yanks heading?'

'In cricket?'

'No, no — this fuss over occupation. Or you want to talk cricket?'

Of course the two will have tea together, the monk insists, even if it is a bit early. Rosalin-akka and her tremor are sent for. Of course Pandit's heard about Manu but not the night games.

'A terrible nuisance for us as well!' says the monk. Henry knows Pandit is marking time in the conversation. Still, Henry might be able to push toward the upper galleries. 'Really we understand, Colonel, the boy might've left on his own. That family loves attention! Were you not the one who told us so?'

The monk claims it to be a common enough case, the father seeking an excuse to stir up some noise about his son, a rotter really, one who couldn't get along with anyone — had Henry ever stopped to consider that perhaps the *father* was the one to drive the son out?

'Manu was doing well with all his projects.' Even to Henry's hearing, his response makes no sense. It is just a tally in the accounting of Manu's character, some insertion into the divine record. He has to keep his own story straight.

For the first time in their acquaintance the monk looks to be fighting off some bad demon. He bunches his brows, inclining his head so the skeleton hints from one cheek. Opens his mouth, thinks better of it, closes it; calls again to Rosalin-akka to hurry with the tea.

'What we need to tell you, Colonel — ah, would you look at those boys! At it again!'

Henry joins him at the window.

'Senseless amusements! Colonel, this makes me wonder sometimes.'

Two boys, each energetically heaving rocks into the canal at the spot where the bank lies flush, there where unattractive yellow suds skim over the water's brackish tapestries. A competition is on; who can skew in the larger stone, farther, with a more full-hearted kerthunk.

Henry cannot stop himself from starting in about Manu. The boy's father is owed the land, is he not? And at this sally, the monk does not seem to know what to do with himself, whether to race or stay still. Of course, Henry had hoped the boy's disappearance might have brought about some change of heart for everybody. That Henry's raising what could be called the boy's specter would force the monk's hand toward the good.

They sit to their tea with a silence between them, ended only when the corners of the monk's mouth rise as though a better man could peek out from behind the curtain. 'You know,' says the monk, absorbed in the ritual of pouring cream into his cup, pinkie raised like a flag, 'there's something else. Your boy Jehangir has been seen telegraphing the British.'

'Normal enough.' Henry would say anything just to tamp a strange seething inside.

'Normal for a spy, you mean. May I speak directly? I've researched the matter. He bought passage to England for himself so long as he kept tabs on you for a year or longer. You consider that normal, Colonel?'

Henry cannot decide what exactly he came here for. 'Drizzling again, is it?' is all he says. The monk had just told him Johnny was a spy. But the monk is never to be believed again. He tries to fit the monkey jigsaw of it together. Pandit calling Johnny a spy could mean Johnny is as loyal as they come. But these are unpleasant times and bad words to hear.

The two men drink their tea in this breed of silence, while the fingers of new rain start to drum the temple's roof.

Once done with his cup, the last he'll ever share with the monk, Henry rises and slams in his chair. He *will* say something — has nothing to say — can only note that warped square of light coming off the monk's forehead. The chin that begins a royal double when the monk looks down. Which he does now.

'So soon, Colonel?' The curtain back up, performance on.

'Have things to attend to,' looking for his hat; yet he'd come without one, hadn't he, there was nothing to do but be gone. The paradox of dissolution is how it sharpens resolve. Henry will have to pursue the land matter for Regi on his own.

But the monk asks who had told the colonel about the night games. Had it been Pushpa, no, it wouldn't have been her, he figured it must have been the colonel's aide, Mister All-Aboard, Jehangir with his Muslim name, who had *tutored* Manu. 'We thought you were a fraud inspector before this, Colonel —'

'I liked Manu.' Henry feels his responses qualify him to be the ripe old age of three. In the time it takes the monk to redrape his robes, Henry wipes his brow like his own father and exits into the breeze where the rain has just stopped; walking the path toward the stairs —

— not having bid any kind of proper goodbye, wanting only to do what was just and also to orient the fearful butterflies in his gut. Forward, go forward, pursue this justice thing. No one's hand raises to him, he bows to no one a farewell.

His search on behalf of Manu will be a good cause, the one he believed in all along, the vision behind their projects. It will really be for Johnny. And he'll do this without telling the monk a thing.

The monk who's come to talk to him from behind: 'You know, Colonel, if it's any consolation, turns out it was the son, not the father, who'd been stealing ivory from our temple's Buddha statues? Such thievery and in a sacred house!'

'You told us that before.'

'We tolerated it mainly because the father is such a scapegrace. Both father and son have been so difficult to, how would you say, accommodate.'

'That's great,' Henry, lackluster, turning to descend the stairs.

'You say the apple tree doesn't fall far. Of course we find it a pity the boy had to disappear. But he was up to no good. He always disappeared for days on end, Colonel. He'll probably return.'

'Goodbye, saddhu,' says Henry. Monotone, doesn't the monk get it? 'Is it that you're jealous of the family?'

'Listen, Colonel,' and the monk's greasy voice thins in the wind. 'Manu probably went to the city to look for work. You don't know about this. They always end up somewhere on the edges of things, his kind, they scrabble.'

122

WHEN THE BUDDHA was dying, his most loving disciple, Ananda, sick from attachment, spoke to him:

> For truly, Lord, when I saw the Blessed One's illness it was as though my own body became weak as a creeper, everything around became dim to me, and my senses failed me. Yet, Lord, I still found some little comfort in the thought that the Blessed One would not come to his final passing away until he had given some last instructions respecting the community of monks.

There have been no last instructions. It is night and feels like it will be shrinking night forever. Henry is pacing the canal road when a cow bellows just behind him. Is that Nani's speckled cow with its woven necklaces? He idly pinches the thing's hide and it moves on. Around Henry fireflies twinkle in no design, peaceable and unaware of any cow or the cranky piano music pounding amid the palm trees.

The British have their film playing on a sheet above and beyond him. A man, playing a tramp, has just presented a dead rose to a woman with ironed hair.

'*Anay,*' the villagewomen cry, 'how lovely.' Amid the glow of fireflies, Henry's villagewomen are enchanted into love.

They wanted parlor games! Henry says to himself, changing his mind on the path so he turns back home. Home where he can retrench.

But first he shouts once at the screen, the screen on which a man curtsies and then bows to the woman: 'You want them, I can give you parlor games!' shouts Henry. 'I'll give you stuffed apes and flying roses and parlor games! I'll give you parlor games until you beg for cricket!'

Over the next few days, Henry begins to realize that the British have more reason to be interested than he might have suspected. He knows that it's Chris especially, ruddy chipper Chris, who has an interest in spying on Henry.

Even his temporary village book never remains where he leaves it.

'You moved this?' he asks Nani about the flimsy book. Before he left for his half-hour walk that morning, he's sure he'd left it on the chaise longue.

'*Aey, mang keranne oonae unaade?*' she asks. Shouldn't I have?

'No, and if you want to learn English, you should speak it more often. I'm sure I didn't leave this on the desk.'

Later, the night's too windy for sleep and they lie in bed together listening to leaves and twigs pelt the walls. Distracted, she strokes his hair, grown long and nestled in tiny curls at his skull's base.

'Like a snake,' she murmurs. 'Or many snakes.'

'What?' he bolts upright. Something muddy and turbid flows through him.

'Like snakes, your hair's like snakes.'

'Who taught you that word?' he asks.

'Snake?' She laughs and lies back down with him. 'Come here and tell me a story, snake.'

He turns to her. In the bands of moonlight her face is possessed. The pink stripe across her lower lip becomes a demon's warning. 'Just t-t-tell me who taught you that.'

'You did, silly,' she says in Sinhalese. 'Like this —' She makes her hand into a serpent's wiggle along his ribs. 'Now come here and sleep a bit.'

123

JEHAN IS at the telegraph office wondering what at this point Headquarters might need to know. Today the clerk is a new one and has reddish eyebrows that fly toward the room's corners as aging people's often do, all body hairs those of a blind cat who orients by sonar. Perfect hairs for a telegraph clerk. The man probably has more of a clue than Jehan does about the real destination of his messages to HQ.

So many words flying out to some unknown worldly address c/o Chilkins. Words about Henree.

These many months Jehan has possessed just a code number and a sense that Chilkins — that gadabout — forwards his messages to the appropriate sources whenever and wherever he pleases. Somewhere Henree must be a famous man.

But really, why do the British care whether Jehan monitors his charge or not? Why do they augment his stipend for him to stay on a few more months? Just a few more months. Jehan could have written pure fiction about his charge and despite any taxing on their patience and imaginations would they have cared? Jehan can feel the shape and contour of their interest in the Yankee like a wicket that opens to let in a bit of light, if rarely.

And the Yankee believed that because he got letters from Colwether and nice reports from the Red Cross that what everyone had been doing in the model village mattered. This last month Jehan kept wanting to puncture the Yankee and his big balloon of rhetoric. But puncturing helped no one.

Meanwhile no one from HQ had kept their captive Jonathan Nellie informed. He has begun to obsess over it, the British encampment having moved in. That for months, since before the famous pilgrimage, Chris has been there with his boys. Chris! Annoying Chris! As inscrutable as the soldier probably would call a subcontinental native!

Even Chilkins has started to hang pretty low on the invisible ladder that must exist. Jehan figures he himself must then be for HQ like the runtiest of fleas smashed under the lowest rung of the ladder abandoned in a forgotten project somewhere in the out-station.

This is why Jehan had, in a recent communiqué, made the suggestion that Chilkins get himself invited for tea with Chris. At this putative tea party, Jehan thought he might figure out some of the details of his own situation, more than he would understand directly from Chilkins, pitiful weedy creature all too hungry for free goods.

But during the tea all that had happened was disaster and debacle. Cups had spilled on Jehan's best shirt and he'd had to undergo awkward quizzing about Manu which had, as Chris put it, stirred up the whole village. And about this Jehan would not say a word.

One night when Jehan was talking late with Manu they'd listened, the two of them, to the grinding of water from the government dam. A phantom, orphan boat had appeared out of nowhere, floating downstream, and they had laughed at this escapee. Eventually Manu had fallen asleep. By moonlight Jehan had tried to discern his friend's features. The drummer's son had an unimpeachable integrity that anyone along any canal would crave. No one could be like him. But then no one could touch his heart. That night Jehan could not imagine a single way to embrace his friend as a brother might.

Anyone, no matter who he was, would take Jehan's sincerity wrongly. Just an embrace would be thought wrong. And yet maybe that was the surprise truth in life: there is one person who understands your sincerity, one who reflects it back to you in the right way.

In the camphor air of the telegraph office, Jehan can't breathe. 'Hold on a minute,' he tells the clerk's eyebrows, which in response raise and lower meaningfully over tortoise-shell glasses.

But outside offers no relief. The air itself struggles through the heat. Either there had been no wind or it had died, but still toward the Temple of the Tooth, barefoot monks sit unburned by the sun, cool as orange lotus leaves in the neat formations of their faith. Which are the true believers and which enter only to be housed and sheltered?

Manu would never have wanted to be a monk, while eons ago, Jehan *had* wanted this destiny, improbably, and this (he felt) left him many notches less than Manu. Jehan had practically spied on his own mother's womb.

From behind the tangle of swords that is his mind these days, Jehan spies out over to Queen's Hotel with its columns and uniformed guard. And there is Henree, standing there speculating, troopless, sniffing suspiciously about himself. He is not wearing his silly net hat; his hair's off-brown pigeonishness makes him bare and young. The Yankee could be any anonymous traveler thunked down in the town center, naked as all travelers are.

Hard to tell whether Henree wants to be invited in or pushed out. Had he just emerged from the hotel with its serenity and afternoon teas, its battalions of white-uniformed waiters and their *ayubowans* and *bohom istutys* and constant rewatering of the potted palms? For the first time Jehan gets it — Henree has never been sure about his own destination.

The boss has spotted his Johnny, who dutifully waves a hand across the square but does not go meet him. Instead, signaling a telegram, Jehan backs into the office with its camphor air. He begins his dictation to the clerk:

SUBJECT APPEARS

— he pauses and considers his own future —

TO BE AWARE THAT ALL HIS EFFORTS AGAINST HRMTK AND OTHERS ARE SHORT-LIVED AND INEFFECTUAL. THIS CORRESPONDENT'S SINCERE BELIEF IS THAT THE SUBJECT'S TENURE ON THE CROWN COLONY ISLAND OF CEYLON WILL BE LIMITED AND AS SUCH THERE SEEMS TO BE LITTLE REASON TO CONTINUE TO DEPLOY THE USE OF OBSCURED PERSPECTIVES IN FOLLOWING SUBJECT'S MOVEMENTS. REGARDS WHOBODY.

This he writes out of loyalty to Henree. Or is it loyalty after all?

Jehan hates Henree for being a man without a clear destination. They have undergone a lovers' spat and a war. Henree has either done the wrong thing or the only thing, Jehan cannot decide. But there is still always the possibility of escaping everything.

Perhaps immediately he and Henree should head back to New York. There he and Henree could start a different life, one with patios, hammocks, train rides. Without Nani. Jehan could be the journalist, Henry the householder. They'd drink coffee and listen to American frogs while a stateside joy descended in their hearts. Together, fresh, Jehan being the one to steer this time, something better might be created, there in New York.

This thinking is all proof of how much the Yankee has infected him. Jehangir laughs aloud and the clerk's eyebrows draw together sternly: 'Are you against something here?' he asks.

'No,' says Jehangir. 'Actually,' he laughs again, 'I seem to be against very little.' He throws his arms wide. 'Even you could probably have me. Get it?' He leans in close. 'I'm what you'd call pretty free for the taking.'

'Free for the taking, aha.' At this the clerk rubs his nose as if from a violent itch. More antenna-like hairs protrude from this nose and at the rubbing they all go haywire. But there is work to be returned to, the eyebrows signal as much. 'That's the end of it, then?'

'No,' says Jehan. 'Sorry. Not quite yet. There's a little more I have to add and then a kind of sign-off. It's worth it, though. You're almost there. Don't give up faith yet.'

'Aha,' says the clerk. 'That'll be one rupee to your account, sir. If you don't mind my asking, why must you Ceylonese speak in riddles all the time?'

124

WHEN SHE RETURNS at two from marketing, Henry asks with whom she has spoken.

'I do not usually speak with many people, Master,' she says. Her spookiness has returned and right when he needs her the most. She places her basket of gourds down and cringes like a dog beaten one too many times.

'But Nani, look at me.' He presses his fat thumbs hard against her cheekbones and goes on speaking, even though she keeps her eyes closed. 'No one?'

'I spoke to the herb seller. And I saw the herb doctor. You do not know that Kumari and Sonali speak to me not often. Today they both said hello.'

'That was it?'

'There was too some demon-stra-tion the soldiers did in the market. Some kind of knife that cuts *pol* quicker.'

'Coconut. Look at me.'

'Co-co-nut.'

He lets her go. Sucks his finger before asking, 'Chris talked to you?'

'Who is Chrees?'

Now he knows. He leaves her in her kitchen with the gourds but this goes beyond doubt. She shouldn't be so naive as to feign innocence. Showing a bit of knowledge would help her case more. Before, he is sure, she has used the name of Chris.

She knows the name! and is hardly one to forget! He had seen her confiding in the man. She'd nudged in close to the Brit. As though the Brit were a lost family relative come to divide spoils.

Squeezing his fists tighter than pigeon hearts, Henry wills himself to keep control.

That evening he leans on the kitchen countertop and calls to her. She comes from stirring rice over the fire, her face illegible.

'If there is anything you need to tell me, you'd tell me, right?'

She nods, and laughs in an odd terrified screech which ceases at his grimace. At his blunt fingers tracing her chin and coming to rest in the penetrable pulsing hollow under her jawbone.

'You can tell me.'

Behind him, Johnny stumbles into the room, cursing softly.

Henry stops. 'That's all right,' he tells Nani. 'You go. Go now.'

Johnny listens tight and close to what Henry tells him. The boy's solemnity has returned, as though he's struck some kind of bargain with Manu's departed soul. He takes off his spectacles to hear better. What needs to be done is not simple. There are procedures.

The boy's presence must seem natural. He should have a cloak and friendship should be as good a cloak as any. After a short period spent circling the target, the target itself could be stolen.

The last ripple of light makes Johnny's cottage into a cave's open mouth. Henry has followed Johnny down to explain what needs to be done. He sits across from the boy, close, but not too close to threaten. His eyes are moist, he can feel them, he hopes this gives every word greater import. 'Consider how the Trojans took over,' Henry says. 'Knowledge is fundamental. Can a man survive without knowledge?'

Johnny looks to the walls of his cottage as though the gold eel-like script from through the windows could explain all.

'We're against an enemy now, Johnny,' Henry says. Something makes him use this ragged vulnerability, right when he hadn't intended it. 'A conspiracy. They're using any means. *We are going to use any means.* You understand me?'

'Could I not?'

Somewhere off the canal road, a rice farmer squawks to his cattle. It could be any one of the local paddymen. Henry can see it: the mud, the faceless farmer balanced on the little board attached behind, fanning up a sprayed V of dirt, the cattle's recalcitrance as they turn the bends. A never-ending web. The sound bounces off the canal with full-hearted perversion. Henry is only temporarily distracted.

The truth is, if Johnny's being sarcastic with his *could I not*, this doesn't sit well with him. He would like to wipe any insolence off the boy's face. To give Johnny a gentle slap, refasten his head. Recently a lot of water has passed under the bridges.

But only one tactic truly overcomes sarcasm: a heightening of sincerity. He takes Johnny's hands in his, the dry in the wet; he is almost sick of being polite to everyone and wants to cut to the chase, bawl out his urges. Instead, he imitates the boy in coughing. And then proceeds: 'These people' — and now the dry throat helps — 'get it, Johnny? These people are anti-Henry all the way.'

Above him he feels the two selves. The pitch-perfect sincere one and the speaker, both cavorting in a spectral gavotte claiming all speech to be false. He is guilty only of trying to read the boy's face but rises with what he hopes is a monumentality fitting to the new mission: a subset and variation on the old mission. Dusting himself off, Henry lumbers heavily to the door, simultaneous in acting and feeling.

Feeling and acting. It is not bad to leave Johnny with a monumental image. That's what some people need, a stoic front and rear. Let the boy take the idea and run with it. Let the boy be on fire just as he would be for an old general who needs a bit of excitement from young hearts.

Henry sustains his act all the way up the stairs. He allows himself to shout down to Johnny only once, to say through the banana leaf fringes, 'You *are* leaving soon, aren't you?'

125

A CHANGED CONSTELLATION. At the camp Jehan begins his program slowly. He moves about like a numb man who knows manners and not much else. Now he has come to Chris not for himself —

— but to save Henree, who may be some last thing to be saved before Jehan jumps ship himself. Always there's the chance to cut loose from everything. Only the means remain to be discovered.

To Chris, then, he offers help with Sunday's film night. How gladly would Jehan hide from this vestigial longing, to save his boss from such obsessions. But he is obedient to Henree's urge and also mired in making sure Chris knows that he, Johnny, will pose no threat.

'Thanks,' Chris refuses, 'we have a detail tagged out for that unit.' A polite enough rejection.

He would like to tell the officer they share a common boss in the crown colony — but cannot. Jehan, being part of the cloak-and-dagger services, had as a condition of employ promised never to divulge even to a British lieutenant what headquarters truly employ him. He cannot introduce himself as Jonathan Nellie, royalty's spy extraordinaire, a colonial success, something to wash the oneupmanship off Chris's face. Jehan would like to. But he is obedient to his two patrons: the English (his past) and Henree (his future?).

If Jehan's mother hadn't given birth to nothing and then to him, maybe he would feel less significant but he cannot shake the sense that meaning attaches to every single thing he thinks and dreams. He has a destiny to follow through and so must kill himself with this temporary obedience to everyone. Above all, he must stay undercover. He does this so well that Chris continues to spurn every one of the boy's offers to help.

For the first time Jehan studies cricket rules with the fervor he used to bring to his childhood catechism. The same ravaging urgency runs through him. Saturday finds him returning home mud-covered and shins bruised from a mistaken run.

'You ask anything?' Henree says, his body a shattered column against the doorjamb.

'It would be too early' — they have fatigued the boy, draining him into this simple act of scraping mud off his shoes — 'he's not dumb. He knows I work with you, Henree.'

'He's friendly?' A swollen red hand clutching upward.

'Enough for your purpose.'

'Don't play games. I'm done spectating on others' spectating. You can understand that, no?'

'Enough, Henree, I said . . .'

Just to win one thing would be cause for a celebration. *Some*thing.

'He's friendly enough, I said.'

126

FOR MOST TASKS Henree used to propose, the boy's enthusiasm would rise, a body arcing to meld with its twin, a will soldered to his. Urgent command was transformation itself. Jehan wished everything to make sense in the village's grand scheme.

But the capacity to reason at any complicated level, he's losing it. These days all Jehan sees is a single color before him. Something rising, a crimson recalling Manu, a hue that greets him as he awakes and when he throws his body down to sleep. Red Manu. Black Manu. Red again. There are days when he forgets who employs him and he becomes just a set of arbitrary hands in the arbitrary world of work.

All he sees is that there are right reasons and wrong reasons to help Henree.

Wrong reasons include Henree penetrating Nani, his body stuck within hers, a dead man enclosed in a tight space. What Jehan cannot help but imagine: the steam and gyrating muck of it all. And Henree's jealousy of Chris the spy arises from this same muck.

Even though the couple has fallen into some implacable silence, Jehan still imagines their cries making the white curtains billow out. Just the idea of their perfidy is enough to render the boy an insomniac's insomniac.

But right reasons remain (despite Manu, despite Nani) and they include the vision that made Jehan first believe Henree to be his ticket.

If Jehan stays on board Henree might still be a compass out, still offer a ticket. Only when Jehan is dispirited beyond words does he wonder, a ticket to *what?* After this apprenticeship to frustration would he still want New York evenings? Even the quadrangles of Oxford? He may have satiated himself on ambition by now, at least for a while.

Yet while Henree has made him undergo a trial by fire, unreason of reasons, a manic fiddler, Jehan still believes in something of Henree. He believes in the way the American has learned how to say Rajottama, and pronounce it perfectly, suspended for a second in the middle of the two Ts like no other pink tongue could manage. Rajottama. The way he never calls it the unproud name, Rutaeva, the word for Slippage.

No, he says it perfectly. Rajottama.

And Jehan also believes in the way the man wants to see himself: a lone pioneer whose stubborn perseverance will win out, will help ease others' lives, will impose a greater meaning on an environment that resists it. That's what Jehan still works for: *that* Henree. The strangest part for Jehan: despite everything, this is a man who dedicated himself to helping a people not his own. Didn't that mean he was good? A man who without pay or honor has shown some eminent and exponential desire: *to be generous.* Even if this desire is a hunger that feeds upon itself more than any fat cat gnawing fish. Even if Henree's hunger to be generous has killed the boy who was the best thing Jehan has ever known.

If Jehan could have anything, what he'd really like is to return to see his mother, back in her village. He'd like to be there in a serene time to help fix her doors and chairs and string laundry lines, stand at the foot of the range and embrace her. To see that face fill up with hope again before he decides whether to continue with the British or give Henree up for broke or run away. *Run run run away* shrieks his blood. He is hardly unaware of the fact that HQ in Colombo has been depositing a tidy stipend to an account under Jehan's name. The reminder comes monthly.

He could just so easily leave Henree, forget the States and England, instead withdraw his sum and press it into his mother's hands and become anonymous again. Be his mother's god and give her reprieve from her widowed skin.

But Jehan Nelligodam, slated to be a clerk, cannot yet truly give up Henree, much as he'd like to. He knows this.

He writes in the margins of Henree's old Village Book,

> This is still a man who can care, a man who knows how to care
> so far from home.

127

NANI INSPIRES DISGUST in Henry. Not disgust, repulsion. She now repels him almost as much as she incites desire and Henry blames her.

He blames her for the British spies upon him, for Manu, for the maggots feeding on gourds in his first field. When Henry is in Johnny's cottage, just the way she parts the overhanging palm leaves on the path outside repels Henry. He can read guilt in her uptilted eyes, even while they blink and flap with that damnably feigned innocence. Once Johnny gives him final proof of her engagement with Chris, he will remind her of the importance of truth in the village of the future.

No deceit should be allowed between intimates. She will remember the habit of honesty and how to reinhabit the body he has known, though these days she behaves as though his avoidance has punched her concave.

He writes an addendum to the catechism:

> Q. What are the duties of the wife to her husband?
> A. To show affection to him; order her household aright; be
>   hospitable to guests; be chaste and honest; be thrifty;
>   show skill and diligence in all things.

Yet so often when he reads the texts the words garble into filigreed seaweed. Lost chains without purpose which fail to make sense anymore. What did the Buddha mean:

Weeds are the bane of fields, desire the bane of mankind. Therefore what is offered to those free of desire yields abundant fruit.

He turns to his own writings, to the editions of his Buddhist catechism — the overripe fruit of his labor with the monk.

> Q. Through what Western religious brotherhoods did the Buddha Dharma mingle itself with Western thought?
> A. Through the sects of the Therapeutae in Egypt and the Essenes of Palestine.

He can't remember why it matters that little schoolchildren memorize this exact fact in the village of the future. *Why this fact and not another?* His broken pencil scratches her rough-hewn silhouette into the top of the desk used by the mad Englishman Wooves.

> Rome, A.D. 50 — Pliny the Elder wrote that ginger pounded into a paste and spread on stomach, scrotum, and anus has aphrodisiacal powers.

He wanders the house like a hungry ghost only to find himself entering her private perfumed altar, the one she thinks he has not known about, the one from whose door he used to spy on her — touching her lavender and spreading tiny petals. She is laundering at the canal and will not return. He is safe lighting the candle before her pagan idols, the first sign of her betrayals.

O white plaster Buddha, he intones, seated on her cushion, *O foolish statue of pagans, O brown-faced cuckold face of Vishnu.*

She has not spoken to him for days. He stares at his pocketwatch with its traced mandala as though it, too, might provide answers. And fingers the stale white areliya garland from yesterday, the careful petals placed in lotus form, all the while envying her safe harbor here. Trying to make his own ritual, he breaks his pencil and dusts graphite onto her altar.

Nani whistles at a dog before circling the house. She pads through the patio carrying her basket of wet underclothes to hang on the line stretching from the kitchen to the old wing. When something scuffs inside her altar, she thinks the dog has come to sniff her rice offerings to the Buddha.

This is when Henry bolts from her secret cushion but not quickly enough. She pulls him out with a force which lists him onto the patio and into the old dog's hostile path. After she has slammed the awkward altar door after herself, the dog continues to bark at Henry.

From inside the sanctum, her voice sounds a muffled echo. 'You have no right!' she yells.

The dog will not stop barking. *Whore*, Henry thinks in nonsensical response. *His fingerprints are upon you*, he tells her.

He has yet to hear the day's report on Chris from Johnny. 'What took you so long?' he asks, not waiting to hear her answer. He steadies himself before pacing into the house.

She calls after him, reverberating into the patio. 'Laundry! I was doing laundry! Only laundry!'

128

THAT EVENING Johnny comes upstairs with spectacles off and presents Henry with the piece of paper, a handwritten scrap. The words sound operatic in Henry's mind and call out a litany of sins upon the Englishman's head.

> does not seem to notice our encampment here. Has been carrying on usual activities which so far appear limited to excessive interest in a native maid, resuscitation of a sad little garden, a poorly attended dance school and much talk of

'Think he means me?' Henry asks his aide needlessly.

Johnny beams and shudders with what Henry thinks is pride at his success. The boy did well in procuring such a revealing document. According to Johnny, the young officer had left his tent to bring Johnny a picture of his own wife back in the green and pleasant land. While he was gone, Johnny had prised the scrap out from under a bedpost.

'That wife bit must've been some kind of ruse,' says Henry.

'Really, I found it there!' Johnny says, a rush of anxiety fluttering his hands.

'Of course you did. What I mean is, it doesn't take a detective to know that such a man wouldn't be married. You never saw a picture of his wife, right?'

'No, I, he never showed me one.'

'Exactly. He probably left to confer with other officers about you or me. You did well and you've only been there a few days. Interesting. You wouldn't expect him to have such fine handwriting. It almost reminds me of yours. Lacking your perfection, of course.'

To be mentioned in the first scrap they have found is a proof of both methodology and sanity. Henry feels perverse about his great satisfaction. And Johnny says many things. He says he knows that Chris keeps locked away a giant blue portfolio containing hundreds of such pages. Pages upon pages of the soldier's views on Rajottama, scraps amounting to a journal. So far Johnny has been unable to get his hands upon it. He will bring it to Henry bit by bit.

'The man has it out,' Johnny explains hastily, 'whenever I arrive. But he keeps a key around his neck, you see, and locks the portfolio away into a box, a steel box, after I enter. Perhaps I can read the pages and report back to you?'

'You are up to the challenge, I know.'

'Thank you, Henree. For you, I am still up to it.'

'That sounds ominous.'

'I've never *not* been up to it.'

129

FOR TWO NIGHTS, she doesn't enter his bed at all. The third night he's in the front room, restless, inhaling kerosene and memorizing the Buddha's last sermon. When light from behind the house flattens through the curtains' crack, he rises, hazily, to go find her.

In the patio she's stirring the fire and rattling pans as if noise could hide her absence.

'Come,' he says, taking her by her broad shoulders. Oddly pliant, a music box ballerina, she turns under his hands as he leads her to her private altar.

'Don't stare at me that way,' he says. He opens the door. 'Look here.'

He lifts her brown-faced Vishnu and smashes it on the ground. Strange that the head severs from the neck but the body stays whole. He squats with the pieces and laughs up at her.

'Can you glue him back? Or will he heal overnight? I watched him all night and he didn't do any special tricks for me. Can you make him glue himself? Maybe you're propitiating him out there? In the jungle where you come from? Where you have a new lover?'

She will not answer. She turns and runs through the house and hides herself somewhere on the compound.

'I'm not searching for you!' he shouts. 'Superstitious — come out. Ollie ollie oxen free!'

But she doesn't play the game right. When he checks the kitchen for the tenth time, her usual citadel, the laughing god still ogles up at him, his eyes an untarnished troublesome blue and the head still whole. He kicks the godhead so it skitters like a puck on cropped grass.

'You're not to go there!' he tells her with some hope that she hears, — wherever she is — hidden somewhere in the empty house. 'That altar's forbidden and this is the last time I'll tell you.'

130

At times one easily finds hope to be a non sequitur, a nadir, a whey-faced myrmidon,

but hope rests mainly on Johnny's progress in the encampment. The boy's smart to spy on the British when they think they are the only spies. Henry sees signs of espionage everywhere.

These are days when suspiciously humanlike imprints cut into the fresh morning mud outside his bedroom door. Rubber bullets lie scattered on the road just outside the gate. Birds alight on the branches in a drugged daze.

While waiting for the scraps of reports and espionage, Henry tries not to count his tribulations. The monk. The locusts. The child he and Nani lost. If Johnny can find out what's being written about him, if Johnny can reveal in what manner the British spy has gained access to Nani, Henry will be able to dig in his heels again. To start over. With the village and with her.

For now he lives to catch the boy as he saunters past the gate and the gardener. Each moment the boy's accent grows truer to what must be his childhood's radio cadences. With Johnny gone to the encampment, Henry inspects the front yard near the blood-seeded nayingala flower which summer's approach has withered.

Stupid flower, he thinks. He knows about its poisonous yam-root, popular in Ceylonese stories of suicidal love. *Monsoons and droughts have passed over me too but if anything I've grown stronger, not shriveled.*

He has let his beard grow, has traveled leagues from his birth-place, from his father's corridors and succession. He has traveled so far, he has used his pluck and talents, has tried to know when to hold and when to fold, he'd kept boundlessness at bay by strict inner con-trols. There has been risk and work, neither one excluding the other. Only to arrive at this stone bench under the ancient mango tree, awaiting his boy's news of the Britishman spying upon Henry. Of the colonizer courting his woman.

All he accomplishes during these few days is the barring of Nani's altar, using giant beams that Joseph helps him with. The rest of the time, he sits on the garden bench. While he cannot see the encamp-ment, sometimes he can hear the whoops boisterous and defiant during cricket games — or the piano tinkling.

He has suspended all lectures and appearances. When Kumari comes one afternoon to remind him of the international audience arriving next week — she has done much with the new repertory — he encourages her.

'Great,' he says, magisterial at his bench. 'Maybe I'll come see you,' he lies. He pokes the cramp in his leg with a stick and lies again, promising an increased travel and costume allotment to be forwarded by Johnny.

Kumari remains among the last of the regulars who dare disturb him. A few garden laborers visit that evening to pick up their weekly salary from Henry's hands, not Johnny's. They make merry about the random quantities of chits and cash which he hands them from his bench. Some model things are continuing in a model enough way, Henry notes, but refuses to write his observations.

When Chollie the dwarf comes among them, with his invoices and reports of money spent at the General Store, Henry demurs. 'I'll check next week. For now, do whatever you think best.'

'We must have a strategy,' he repeats when he sees Johnny. This is his new mantra.

After Henry's own heart, the boy would rather discuss strategy than Buddhism and the village. They consider the best ways to gain Chris's absolute confidence. Henry grills the boy on the man's qualities. Does he hold back in speech? Does he commit errors in consistency? Does he ever allude to his past?

This is a game which they can both outfox.

The two never meet in the mad Englishman Wooves' house anymore, preferring their old-time bench. Or even better, the mournful breeze inside Johnny's cottage. The wired windows and ill-fitting door barely contain the jungle. And Henry comes to lie on the straw mat Johnny leaves out for him.

'They want me to enlist,' Johnny tells him that night. Henry knows he means the British. 'They say I'm as fit as any Crown subject. They want me to live at the camp.'

The boy hesitates — it's clear he doesn't want to join Chris's regiment — but he gets the answer from Henry's face. 'You're right,' he says immediately, as though mesmerized. 'It'd be the only way for us. My cloak will be the key to knowledge.'

Henry lurches to his feet. For the first time, he takes the boy up against his chest; folds him in; his hands on the harsh shoulderwings. After all, things are patched up with his boy. 'From the beginning, you've been a gift,' he tells Johnny. 'Loyal to the end. I'm sorry about everything.' He would pitch all the innings. 'You're really the son I never had.'

At this all volition seems to spill from the boy's body. His spectacles slip lopsided on his nose, he falls into his boss, cut from the strings. Strange unpredictable boy. Peristaltic heaves shake Henry's broad frame.

Henry strokes that oily hair. He is flummoxed. Having intended a murmur, he states too loudly to the room what his own father used to say: 'No one's any better or any worse than you. You have every fighting chance in the world.'

On a scrap of paper:

> Eggs in a boat's dark hold, clustered together. At a wind,
> they crack against each other and solder into one egg huge
> enough to splinter the ship.

The boy packs his tent with an efficiency Henry has grown to love. He is direct, clean and compact. Everything his awkward body would suggest he's not. His mode an overcompensation for the spectacles, the hair, the herky-jerky movements. As he packs, the boy offers Henry one of his last few chairs and watches from the corners of his eyes.

'Sure you want me to do this?' asks the boy, almost ready. 'To *enlist?*'

'Why not? Isn't that what we agreed?'

'So long as you're sure.'

'Why make everything sound so final?' But Henry does wonder, in a brief silence, *Do I push the boy too hard?*

'As long as it fits your goals. Because you and I might not know enough to be so cavalier —'

'What did I tell you when we first met? Never disparage yourself, my dear boy.' He waves a hand. For old times' sake he musters up grandness, feeling himself to be imitating Madame. 'Never.'

'I don't exactly have a degree from Oxford,' the last two syllables fugitive.

'You always' — Henry searches — 'know more than you think.'

Each night, Nani has turned away from him, lying on the sliver of bed farthest from Henry, her majestic body screwed up like a little girl's. Even when she consents to be touched, every single muscle from ankle to neck strains away, telling him she is not his, confirming the Chris hypothesis.

Now he is alone in the house. Mornings, he summons enough enthusiasm to sit planning various enlightened reforms, penal systems, currencies. Afternoons, Henry oversees the gardener. He would like Joseph to clear a path from the great house to the boundary hedge, a clear plane allowing for a full vista of the canal.

While possessing an amiable countenance, Joseph is slow and requires Henry's continual supervision. Tired of making himself understood, Henry often retreats to the straw mat in Johnny's empty cottage. He prefers the floor, *this* floor, to the mad Englishman's chaise longue. Often he falls into the most satisfying half-sleeps he knows these days, sleeps in which arguments are mended, locks are picked, notebooks retrieved.

Only on his last day in the cottage does an argument among the birds rouse him.

'Don't smile, Sir Henry,' the drummer greets him, towering over the drowsy foreigner. Something about vegetables, Henry understands the drummer as saying. He sits up.

Johnny has not come back yet. He has failed to keep Henry abreast of much, whether regarding the village or the camp. Henry will have to ask the boy to come back to the cottage, back to him. Better to keep resources close during this time, the tether tight. Because too many odd people approach him — like this villageman in a ranting mood.

In the menace who stands before him, all spitting wrath and ire, Henry can barely recognize the shy Regi who once lit incense for him before his family idols. If Henry understands, the man prattles on about the family's sacred history.

' — keepers of the oldest historical tree in the world!' the drummer finishes.

Henry's embarrassed to be shirtless, the black and red tendrils of his chest revealed, a recent rash so apparent. 'Wait just a moment,' he tells Regi, before running up the stone stairs and into their bedroom.

Where is she? How can she expect him to distinguish between the clean and the worn in these unkempt piles of laundry? The last two nights, she entered after he was asleep and rose before him, exercising unpredictable ways. Doesn't he deserve a dependable woman? One who calls him by adoring names, as she did in the beginning?

Once he returns, it proves even harder to concentrate on the words emanating from Regi's gaping hole of a mouth. His voice resounds deeper than any Henry has heard in this village. It's as though the drummer has learned to speak for two men from between bone points and the carved-out sac of his heart. Henry fingers his catechism. He wants escape from having to stand there, a dimestore Indian forced to face a smoker, a child before such calumny.

Q. What is Karma?
A. A causation operating on the moral, as well as on the physical and other planes. Buddhists say there is no miracle in human affairs: what a man sows that he must and will reap.

'Don't read. Don't smile,' the drummer continues. 'I'm talking to you.'

Henry understands well enough what the drummer says. For generations his family has been linked with the tree. Henry knows that. Two thousand years ago the Buddha attained enlightenment under the same bo-tree, up in India. Henry has heard this too.

With representatives from eight castes, Regi's family (then Brahmins, just as all the castes claimed about themselves) followed a sapling from this great tree. Those long-ago Regis swore to help uphold the Maha Bodhi tradition over centuries. With calluses on Regi's hands, he has kept up his part of the bargain. With the blood of his second son, his temple and monk have failed him.

'Maybe you too have failed me,' he adds.

But the drummer has another point in mind. Something not at all about his family but about Nani. With his lineage he could arrange a marriage for Nani with a boy if not from their region at least from Anuradhapura.

Henry rises to stare down upon the man, to discern the code of these drooping lips. He is beset with the strange idea of stripping himself naked before the man, slapping his pale thighs and saying: *What can I give you?*

But he does not; and yet there's no tea ritual which could break or raise their urgency, no women to bring in saucers or to peer in from behind curtains. Henry's impulse subsides. Here in Johnny's bare room, softness has fled. The drummer and his son: the father now claims vengeance. And Henry had once, he remembers, foolishly promised something, just to shut the man up. He had promised to help find the boy.

Still, would the man not get to his point? Johnny has claimed that this many-shreds-from-a-coconut way of speaking is the village way.

But then had Henry profited any from all his Johnny's sayings? He would be rendered to bones and fat before he finds out a thing. Henry sits again, leaning forward, earnest forearms pressed to broad American knees. His forearms say *I'm making every effort to understand you but don't make things too difficult.* His knees say he's at home anywhere, even in a room with little furniture and a last cloying scent of talc.

'Listen,' wishing he had a parachute. 'I agree, my g-g-good man. But since the day is short, and work is long —'

Regi's head wobbles. His smile glints but the eyes stay riveted. 'Your Nani has left, Sir Henry. She told my Ruwini you did not treat her well. That she was crying in the mornings and you must make amends. She's staying somewhere nearby.'

Henry restrains his flighty hands from shaking the man's smaller hands clasped in quietude in his lap. 'You make some mistake, perhaps.'

'All we need,' the drummer says, 'is a small question here, a look there. Then we know and can live our lives. You don't know how easily snakes take over anthills. The demon Mohini can come disguised as one of our monks. An innocent boy gets killed —'

'He disappeared. I think you're mistaken.'

'This isn't like our Manu. We have reason to believe he was taken and need to know why. Just an investigation. No problem.'

Henry's stomach clenches at this man nattering on in that strange chest-cavity voice. The drummer's calloused hands sometimes punch the air, sometimes trace as though along the lineaments of precious gods.

'You have always cared, Sir Henry. You cared that the people believe you. Some say you cared too much.'

131

HE WOULDN'T BELIEVE IT but she had begged a ride on a cart rolling to Kandy town, to see the monks in the square. He would have called it crazy, but seeing the monks, she will know what to do. She had jumped onto a bullock cart loaded with sticks that used to mean death to her but now she was no longer afraid of sticks. Not because of him, it was her Vishnu who'd given her a last gift, his head off but freeing her of rules. No longer should there be the fear that goes with rules. And Vishnu had done his work well. Even as she passed a monk she didn't blink or jump off and turn back; she saw how things were now, nothing bad would happen to her again.

He had called this road their road because together they had walked it so many times. He would pick up a stick or red leaf and hand it to her. Had he never had a mother? A sister who stroked his hair at night? That he called this *their* road just because he and she had walked on it? He kept calling her too deeply. He thought he knew her name. Had he ever known her? How could she hold a future with him when he was so ready to break things? He had never known her.

There was a time when he'd called her in from outside where she was tending the garden and she came. He sat at his great desk. Nani, he'd said. Please, sit here. And she did, she did what he said, in his lap she sat, that was how they were spending those days, sitting, she on him, just because they thought they had the same idea at the same time.

'Did they ever tell you a kiss could matter to the world?' That was what he'd asked and she'd given the answer he wanted, slowly, pretending not to at first, ducking away so he had to strain like a bird at worms. And he had loved the game. Please give yourself to me, that's what she'd made him beg.

But that was the day when he finally did what he asked of everyone else. He gave himself too. Because the afternoon passed and even when night things were to be done in the house, she made him stay in their great chair.

'There are so many ways to begin a kiss,' he said afterward, when nothing needed to be said, 'and to continue it, and to make it never end. Nani, did you know that before?' he asked, but really he was telling how much he wanted it always to be that moment. Our moment, he called it. Did he ever give her room to answer? And she did not answer him then. And maybe there were good reasons to answer him and probably better reasons not to.

132

August 1937
The chicks have pecked out of the eggs & their heads float
for only a second, giant ungainly things, before their beaks
descend with final little bubbles. The undertow throws their
bodies against rocks outcropping from the shore. Soon only a
reddening of water marks the site. The shells remain golden
on the inside as their shards float into the shore. The people
run away from what they have seen. Still, the dead chicks
drained of blood continue to wash ashore. A sea of broken
beaks, matted yellow fuzz, eyes wide with the future.

'We're lucky. Usually we almost have to wear wellies to bed.' The
chief British agent Colwether has all the time in the world to savor
his own humor. 'Can you imagine? Wellies to bed. That would *really*
keep our women away.'

Henry doesn't appreciate innuendo. He is uncomfortable playing
staring games with this forceps-head. And to do this on Colwether's
own ground, in the stale heat of an oak-paneled office in a Dutch
building near Colombo's central port, where fans whirligig sound-
lessly overhead like some constantly self-congratulating innovation.

The Union Jack once flew over two fifths of the globe's surface.
Here is Henry from one of those two-fifths, the afternoon of Regi's
visit, sitting in a low chair stuffed with cushions which make him
shift like he has diaper rash.

But he shouldn't be judging any man on the basis of nationality.
He had in New York met the lovely English. The generous, intelligent, modest English, and Englishwomen too, like Lady B., an arts
lover down to her last pore. He had encountered the sophisticated,
witty and deep English, those who'd given him perhaps his best
ideas about the world and literature and formed his ideas of the true,
the important, the introspective. It is only his Ceylonese luck that
had kept him from this particular Englishness.

Or is he blinded by some anti-white prejudice that attacked him
once he set foot in Colombo? Maybe his colleague here, who for the
last half-hour has been trading little jokes and comments about the

weather with mainly himself, would appreciate it if he got business done right away and then for the remaining time they'd be free to talk romantic notions, spoonerisms and puns.

'Telling it straight' — he breaks agent Colwether from his thoughts — 'I'd like to request an investigation.'

'What are you implying, Gould?'

'Nothing. A low-caste man's getting robbed by our monk. I'm just indicating the need for a proper investigation, isn't that c-c-clear —'

As though to help Henry's stammer, Colwether's jaw opens, closes and opens again like a mocking jackhammer, mouth slowing into the rhythm of a pebble skipping down a mountain. Once silent, Henry cannot keep himself from jittering his knees back and forth impatiently.

'Gould, your Rajottama is not exactly your, let's say, Colombo. Not to mention London. Or let's say Vienna. Have you been to Austria? Lovely country. Shame about the Austrians.'

'I'm sorry, don't follow.'

'Your Rajottama is not a port. Not Jaffna or Galle. Your pet is hill country. Not even tea country.' Colwether gestures down at the sheaf of papers across his desk. 'It's not exactly our most pressing concern.' He is monitoring the clock on the wall, Queen Victoria etched on its face. Right now, both hands join just beyond her right nostril.

Henry must be diplomatic with this snake. Too forceful and Henry stands to lose. 'I'm just indicating the need. There should be a proper investigation into land policies.'

'Slowly! You've just arrived. Proper? With these people?'

'These people what?' The old stuttering takes him over. He's as bad as that poor temple prostitute with her endless tics. He imprisons his hands between both jumpy knees and continues to maintain, as much as possible, a straight gaze.

'These people, Gould! Often they throw dead bodies into caves and leave the site for twelve years. You follow me? When their brethren die, they'll leave the bodies until the stars say it is time to bury. You see? Letting the stars determine their timing? Don't start thinking logic applies here. Please.'

Even the agent's hushing is an exquisite sarcasm. His eyes rotate up to the fan each time he invokes the heathens. A different island's superstitions power his confidential tone.

'You probably don't know the extent, Gould. Their own priests don't even come to their funerals or marriages.' His gaze lurks like a surveillance guard's. 'I'd heard about you from others in the service. You had the reputation of being clean. But now you must listen.'

Colwether's exhausted finger pushes back from his fluted forceps temples some imagined stray hair as though elegant and gray-streaked like the rest of his perfect head.

Here is a life, Henry believes, *lived kicking and screaming under terrifying restraint.*

'Gould. This is what I know. As much as these people might grumble about authority, they fall apart without it. We're both men of the government, in a certain sense, aren't we? —' an eyebrow arched at Henry to see whether he acknowledges the flattery. 'We can talk, as you Yanks say, *straight*. We reward a man for the job he does. Nothing else. All those traditional enmities, those silly distinctions they insist upon, caste and blood and the like, we are nothing if not open-minded and' — he draws the word out — 'magnanimous. Magnanimous. We teach them tolerance of their own ways.'

The agent's hand now sweeps a broader panorama, one containing potential objections. Henry glances at the opposing wall where a faintly whitened circle shows the Victoria clock may have once hung. Why would it have been removed and hung directly across? Had it been taken for repairs? Henry's mind whirs nonsensically.

'You know, Colwether. I'm not requesting anything fancy.'

'No Scotland Yard?' And here the agent's cackle grows leisurely because it lacks mirth and possesses time in which further decisions can be made. Henry must wait and become aware of how such mirthless mirth fills the room in which these two servants of the people sit.

'No —' slowly, as if to a child or ape, Henry taking on the other man's mannerisms '— nothing fancy, you see.'

'Ah, but Gould, that's the crux, isn't it?'

Colwether's hands clasp in a falling house of delight, immediately disbanded. His long fingers point down a horizon of nonconvergent lines. 'The crux of Western philosophy. Unseat it, you have yourself a field to mine. I read Greek at Christ Church. You see — it's a tautology, my good man. You cannot have the brain knowing itself.'

'I'm sorry, I don't follow your point.'

If Henry could just finesse this gentlemen's game of tennis which Colwether was playing with him — Colwether has barely broken a sweat and Henry is panting.

'You mean well. You've heard of some misdoing. You feel powered by some manifest destiny' — a hand up to halt objections — 'all understandable, even if you weren't American. But one branch of our government cannot investigate another. There's your tautology. The brain can't know itself. The land policy we administer is the land policy we administer.'

Outside his office the steady shuffle of papers and the creak of footsteps on a lacquered floor never cease. 'You know, Gould, on islands not too far from here virgins get sacrificed quite often. There's an Africanus group even on Ceylon's northwest coast which shares blood with the rest of the population. Still they have to be muzzled at times or else it's said they eat human flesh. You don't know certain things. You can't afford *not* to listen to me.'

Afford. What can a person *afford?* Henry rises, feeling as though he has shat in his pants. 'Thank you,' he says, the courtesy out of his mouth before he has willed it.

'Enjoy the weather while you can,' Colwether says to the trumped back leaving his office.

What can a person afford and still be himself? Can he afford total defeat? What is there to hold on to? On the train ride back to Kandy from Colombo — one which ordinarily can make Henry cry great inner tears of joy, the thrill hits him so — he is a window zombie. Beyond the palm trees, great canyons and prehistoric mountain ranges open up into a great abyss. He cannot bear to let down one more person. Thinking to right himself, he orders black tea from a supercilious Sinhalese with a haughty British accent, who nonetheless like everyone manages to spill some of the scalding pot into his lap. You can't escape tea.

At least the man has the good sense not to laugh at his mistake.

Henry chooses to walk from town, returning past the Muslim homes on the main road. Back to his minor hill and its minor house with its flying buttresses. He can barely afford the walk. At the canal he stops and catches his breath before striding left toward his waiting library with his minor books. An undeniable ache spirals up his ribs for her. Maybe she has turned contrite, come back, cooked for him, turned down his sheets, anointed her neck and shoulders with sandalwood oil.

Maybe she has unsheathed herself of her clothes and lies there with her knifelike body at the center of his stained bed, full of risk and pleasure and everything that's not minor. She was the only one and she had also taken him away from himself. When he was young they had forced him to kiss the wooden crucifix, and then had given him a child's treat, a buttery cookie, and he'd felt it melting away in his mouth; he would never have it again, this would always be its first and last moment. He realizes he hasn't eaten in days.

The afternoon is clear. A dry wind rises off the canal as though cleanliness could be restored. It pushes him home, home where a new racket awaits.

Before his housegate hangs a death banner strung with coir — for Regi's son? The white flags lap the wind like angry little tongues. For a second Henry thinks he might be witnessing one of the rites attending his own funeral and burial.

A bear of a man ambles toward Henry, the long shadow hitting him first. Could this be the same man who shepherded volunteers toward a beggarmaid's altar? Underneath the flags, the man addresses Henry in the native tongue. Missing a fourth of what is said to him, Henry understands the tone. The impressive shoulder roll follows most of the sentences, but Henry is still forced to understand the Sinhalese.

'You know we never needed your help,' Lester begins slowly. 'We've always been just fine. We here in the high country in sight of the Great City' — he points in the direction of the great distant mountain of Kandy — 'have held onto the heritage we needed. We've never lacked.'

'I am not doing anything,' says Henry. 'Anyway I can't afford this.' He has the sense that as they speak, their words are being transcribed for some later justification.

'You are getting us in trouble with your Indian Christian coastal boy sent to live among them. Why else would you send him but to give us away?'

'To give you away?'

'Don't play innocent. Your work here is a monkey's sword-work. You don't do your best. You know sometimes karma cannot mete out the best punishment. A man may commit fifty murders, but he can only be hanged once. You should change your epitaph anyway. Doing your best? You forget simple things.'

'Like what?'

'Like we will always know more and better than you.'

Lester goes on about tradition, fairness and authority.

Henry stands there: once again a dimestore hunk of wood taking in every last word.

Upstairs, the heavier drapes closed, no one can tell whether it is morning or dusk. Only the crows outside try to remind them of night's approach.

They are in Henry's front room at cross-angles. Rather, Henry sits inside, the birds outside indifferent to all angles. The drummer pacing like this will better protest the cosmos. He'd followed Henry in, having hidden on the compound away from the Pilima.

Regi slaps his thighs, hunches over, howls. 'How can you tell this story? There will be no investigation?' Ground stamped, head shaken as though to wring justice from the skies. 'There *must* be an investigation,' whispered, hoarse with hatred. 'About my son! The land!'

A soul of apathy, the foreigner barely stirs.

'You don't care about any of us!' the drummer shrieks, changes to a squeal as if he were being tortured. 'You never cared nothing!'

Henry lifts his hand with consummate effort and lets it fall. 'Want me to sign something?' he asks. 'That's what I can afford. I'll sign anything. If you want.'

The drummer moans his disbelief, heading out the door.

Henry didn't know how she managed it. How she gathered her belongings. How she undid the beam blocking entrance to her altar — had the gardener Joseph helped? — how she must've bowed and whispered before her Buddha before stowing the god and the broken Vishnu in her valise. All she had left him was the dried lavender hung above the altar, the very last of the altars dismantled in Rajottama.

Fear drove her away, he told himself. *My fear.* Surprised that he found himself sitting before the emptied altar with his face wet.

Who is crying for Nani? he asked, wishing for a voodoo bridge between their hearts. A channel of light. If only his grip on her memory could lasso her back right here and now.

In the kitchen, just before the drummer came to pay another visit, Henry had been mooning and fingering the dried red chilies which she used to cook in his food. But he forgot to wash his hands afterward. When he wiped his eyes, the spice's sting made him scream in misery. He lay in the patio's center and imagined peeking up her tight colored skirts.

If only she could have moved with him through the gray corridors of cities. She would've seen his worth among others of his ilk. His irreplaceability. How he was different and better. His belly feels like nothing so much as a socked-out lamppost. He can't quiet his ache, this tumult that spins him, gives birth to pain.

Far off a train's insolent whistle sounds. She might be on that one. Where would she go? Back to the pagan forest gods? Back to her village by the sea, with her sisters there to mistreat her? To Johnny? But then he was still at the British camp. Would Johnny know the name of her village? The day before she disappeared she had cowered from him and shrunk into a hint of the old woman she would become. She'd shown teeth long and hard enough to surprise him.

The false promise of her strong wide shoulders and brows. The body that surprised him every second he touched it. He'd seen her eyes as uptilted, ready to find him amusing. They could have lived anywhere.

But he'd misread, had been a fool. Why should she matter to him as no other woman had? Life was just beginning inside him. She was wrong to leave. She shouldn't have done this. He could have been good to her.

133

WHILE HENRY is lying there, the whistle sounds again but it is a fake if loud train whistle issued from a great distance, at the train station, true, but by a man in a smart yellow cap who guards Rutaeva's platform. Behind the guard waits a sad-eyed elephant rigged up in white and gold after the annual Kandy perahera.

Useless signs hang off the beast's back advertising lodgings during the parade that had already passed unwitnessed by Honree. The station guard is a Sinhalese who blows his whistle and clips his heels together like a soldier or idiot, making his beast shift weight in protest but the guard doesn't care. He smiles all the way down the platform at her.

She sits on the station bench with her belongings and gifts rolled up into the same hatbox she had when she first came. Since that first day, the station has shrunk into something less than her memory. It is hot and August and next to the bench there lies a skinny beggarwoman with two leprous stumps for legs. She keeps stretching her palm frond cone up like an elaborate hand waving toward Nani.

Sometimes the beggar's palm rubs Nani's ankle as if the ankle itself were money. *Anay, give me something. Anay, rich lady spare something.* What Nani has in her hatbox are the broken heads of her protectors and her single volume. No coins. Only the lavender bookmark and the embroidery hoop but not much else and all in her hatbox.

And still she has become a rich lady to someone and for this gift of a compliment she smiles down at the woman with her beggar cone.

A man selling fried balls of dough comes down the platform. He speaks through his nose calling *Vadevadevadevade* and is selling to Nani and the beggar and the guard but finds no takers. There are no last parade-goers crowding the platform and for this too Nani is glad. Beyond the tracks is a brick wall that crumbles as though it had been dynamited imperfectly and beyond that is a mutated palm tree that reminds her of the two-headed calf someone must have taken from her.

The last day she had seen her calf, Appuhamy had been telling her to banish the pink man. But a pity how the doctor must have worked some of his magic on Honree. He had made Honree run savage.

Sorcerers could do this and it had been her fault — she should not have sat so close on that same log with Appuhamy and then cooked food for Honree, but at first the doctor had been so polite. Then he had touched her arm to make sure he got his sorcerer magic deep into her marrow. There was no way she wouldn't have rubbed some of that disti into her pink man. The last man remaining for her. Strangely, one she had trusted.

Now that she thought about it, it seemed very few people hadn't been working on Honree. In the village they all wanted to do something different to him. Bring him closer or tear her apart. The day after the doctor came, even Manu's father visited to try to get her to stay with them in his compound. When she refused, Regi was so angry he said he would spread rumors that she was with child.

But maybe she was.

Maybe the sorcerer had brushed something else into her. A demon child. She rubbed her belly and the beggar at her feet said more ingratiatingly *Anay rich lady good food for me? Many blessings.*

The air sticks in her throat. Again the man down the platform blows his idiot's whistle. She doesn't know where the next train is going or where she will find the money to pay for it or even where she wants to go. She just knows that after a year and a day or more of hiding in the Big House, it is time to get onto something that will take her where there wouldn't be pink men going savage. That's the last thing she needs. She has no use for wildness. She doesn't know how to unhex that particular spell.

Inside her is a calm spacious temple and she has been through something she thought would be correct but she has to give it all up now and return, make that temple better. Somewhere the Buddha waits for her. Somewhere he will take her in. She will get on a train and let the train tell her where the Buddha wants her to go. Not to her sisters but to a better place. She will trust that by now the god of trains and her Buddha know her and won't take her to her sisters.

All would be better if she had closed things up with Honree but he might have pulled her down into his madness and no train could have been found then. She has no luxury to spare. Everything is pinned on this next train, which will know what is best. The train will be her new protector.

134

WHEN THE DRUMMER returns to the house the next day, it is to find the foreigner sprawled in the patio like a blind man. The drummer wants to wait for nothing, least of all the righting of hearts. He has a tale to recount which goes something like this:

> There is a story we tell of the donkey and the dog. Both were owned by a master who was particularly stingy and cruel, a master unusual both in the degree of his boorishness and his tendency to overvalue possessions. The master's one joy in life came when he dragged his two animals out of their shed. There he would beat the beasts until a livid script of welts rose upon their flesh.
>
> Do not think that in his own mind the master beat for arbitrary reasons.

He beat out inescapable facts. That his younger and more irresponsible brother had more success than he. That crops spoiled easily. That there was no one of suitable rank with whom he could drink. That all the local village's bootleg kasippu tasted of death.

Even kasippu couldn't cure him since life in its bounty of surprises visited grievous headaches upon him. He beat his animals even for their inability to cure him of his painful head.

How could I have ever bought and fed such dumb beasts, he would cry, the stick raising itself yet again.

You, female donkey, you're a weakling unfit to carry any burden. Where is that foal you were to bear me so long ago?

Dog, you are no better. A worthless whelp good for nothing. Bad at herding cattle, worse at protecting my belongings. You increase my property only by the dung you deposit over the stall and yard. I have to hire someone even to take care of your terrible messes! Both of you — such ingrates!

Over the years, the two animals worked hard for the master. They bore such treatment in silence, and learned not to watch the other when insults and beatings rained down. Seeing another's blood and welts made one's own pulse too difficult.

One night a thief in the neighborhood happened to see that the lights in the master's house were out. In order to get a good approach from the master's yard, he had to sneak by the animals' stall.

The donkey in her stall heard the noise and knew the footsteps to be those of someone stepping into the yard for the first time. Of one who felt even greater guilt for his presence than she did. Though the dog on his rope noticed the sound as well, he gave no sound.

What's the matter with you? scolded the donkey. You dog, you're the one on guard!

What do you think? snorted the dog. We have a master who mistreats us so terribly. Why should I care if a thief comes to take all his beloved property? Wouldn't we stand a chance of improving our lot? We might even escape.

Oh, you don't know, said the donkey. You are young. A new master could be much worse. Better the pain we know than the one we don't.

A worse master? I don't think so, said the dog, pretending to return to sleep. He was not long after adolescence and found himself enjoying this pose of careless arrogance.

Don't you think we'll suffer much more if we don't do the

jobs we were bought for? continued the donkey. Irrepressibly, she wished to get a rise out of the dog. For example, she lectured the dog, the primary trait which the master hired me for was my great loyalty.

What are you talking about? You're wrong! said the dog, getting excited despite himself. How can anyone see loyalty right off? Anyway, I'm the one whose value to the master is my intelligent loyalty. Your value is probably more in stupid perseverance.

Hear what you're saying. If that's so, you're falling asleep on the job, said the clever donkey. If you're not being persevering, you're not fulfilling the dictates of your job, and someone else must attempt to.

So saying, the donkey commenced to bray. She let her bray come so forcefully that she shocked not only the dog but her own self. Raucous, she succeeded in scaring off the thief. While the thief had already gained entrance to the house in which the master lay sleeping, he nonetheless ran off with his empty hands and greedy stomach.

However, the donkey's clamor also roused the master from his drunken stupor. Her new bray so excited her that she did not stop to hear whether the thief had left or not. The master descended into the donkey's stall. There he beat her with a club rather than a stick. For days after, the loyal donkey was covered with festering sores and flies. So weak had she become, she could barely rise from her strawless stall.

On the day she recovered, the dog sidled over to her stall.

See what I told you, said the dog. Guilty of an ancient habit, he covered sorrow with cruelty. You see what happens, he continued, when you're so foolishly obedient. To survive, you have to be crafty. Like me. Am I wounded?

And despite her crippled knees, her festering sores, and the leering dog's face, the donkey still thought she had been right in taking over her companion's job.

From this story we have the expression *like the donkey who did the dog's work* to speak about one who bumbles.

135

WHEN REGI finishes the story, he gives travel advice to Henry who still lies dazed on the floor. 'If I were in your place,' says the drummer, 'I'd go off with other beasts of my own kind. Why stay when you can't do any more damage? All I want to know' — but here his hands betray him by shaking, as though it takes great control to keep from wringing the foreigner's neck — 'why a ditch? Why kick my son into a *ditch?*' he cries.

' — Johnny who told you?' Henry attempts to say, 'Was it Johnny?' but cannot make the name more than *honey*.

As the drummer leaves, he wails into the empty house. 'Why not find your own resting place? For my honor, for Manu's name, Sir Henry, spare us. Spare us the effort?'

136

HENRY DOES MANAGE to find his way back to Slippage.

He had spent time high up in the tea country, a week if not longer, up among the planters. The last of the Raj raised on their barstools with their whiskey sours and racing card results. The way they tolerated and teased one another for little foibles and scandals, pretty young boys on the tracks, public reportage in the *Tribune*, new jowls and the horses they had sired carefully. Raising them to be sixteen hands. Decca Star a foal and GoForBroke. Their gins hot down the hatch. He had listened to them singing their ironic songs in the billiards room with its red-leathered interior and mohair seats and the sad moosehead. They were busy flaring their nostrils and veins, putting on a brave show for most of the night and day as the last bits of empire started to topple around them. He had been stoical listening to their gibes about him as a Yankee. His broad accents and foolish belief. He had played that for them too. Praising the industry of the

Nuwara Eliyans he saw rising early. Each tending a plot of land, no matter how small. He had even tried to lead them in songs none of them knew.

And then been stoic and a little drunk himself as they had called him Colonel and quoted aloud from his own catechism that they had long ago gotten hold of, what they now used for quizzing games. They asked him was it after all true about how Buddhism is the only religion never to kill anyone?

In the green light of the banker's lamps, there was Clive the Tamil planter and Tommy the dapper manager of the Hill Club with his young wife and prospects and Pink Cheeks who oversaw the golf course and had a small bit of property nearby. The colonel had tithed his money to Pink Cheeks. And then the colonel let himself be attached to a small English girl abandoned by a captain. He let her gray slender body remind him of someone else's in the middle of some rakish midnight caper on a gray soft bed in a room whose wallpaper he couldn't make out. The last night there, he had met forceps-head Colwether hunched over his drinks on his way off the island, waiting for some buzzercraft to take him off. And Pink Cheeks had whispered that there had been a spot of fraud controversy around the government agent, and no doubt it could have come from what the colonel's own investigation had turned up. As if confirming what Henry had done, Colwether's face hung slack as a batwing's, ashamed, disintegrating. When Henry dreamed whiskey dreams later that night, he took it as another riddle. It was Johnny he had seen, tall in the corridors, the boy's skin beautiful and translucent, a beacon and signal home.

As he rattles on a rented trapset downcountry from the tea land, Henry hears the voice of his trusted aide explaining the villages.

Don't call it Slippage, call it Rajottama. It means universal king, I believe.

It was a mistake to run away from everything for a week without his Johnny. He will have to inquire regarding developments in the terrible cantonment. Perhaps the tea country and its lost royals solved nothing. But Henry knew enough to know he had been due for reprieve from the mess of Slippage.

His driver took the wrong route back to Slippage, a long circle up from Kandy town, and they ride to his house's main gate amid the vapidity of dusk — after the sun has delved into the lowering sky but before the crows and white birds come to celebrate night. A smell of smoke and turpentine and tiny drunken men still carnivaling in his skull, Henry pays the driver far too much and this makes the man take a while to understand that he and his trap are to slip away quietly, please.

Over the hill's base are still strung tiny stained death flags, bright pieces in the moonlight. Only Joseph the Tamil gardener is there, above, seated on a stump by the house, turbaned and chewing betel. A low wind has started up, far away there comes some shouting, and Joseph doesn't stop cleaning his mamotty blade as he watches Henry climb.

A new clasp holds the gate. The gardener smiles as Henry fumbles it. When the clasp fails to come easily, Joseph descends to lift it for the foreigner and they walk to the house side by side. Across the front door a large nailed battering ram blocks access, as though Nani had decided to lock Henry out, as though a flying column has fallen. The gardener shrugs. He leads Henry to the small cubicle by the outdoor fire, where the gardener himself has slept for his brief spells. A straw mat on the floor his bed, another straw mat his roof: his heaven and earth accounted for.

Sleep, the gardener seems to say. *You cannot enter your house but you can stay here with me.*

Shaking off his stupor, Henry rushes by the man's hospitality. He hurries to the patio and the kitchen. Upon all the doors to the house giant battering rams are nailed.

Come! Henry indicates to the gardener. Help me!

Patient, the man provides a handrest for Henry to step upon, so that he can try to unhinge the upper Dutch windows. He is able to lever himself up. Straining, he breaks through the top of the window. Catapults into the kitchen, lands on his knees. Grunts. And then manages to stagger toward the front room.

Dusty in here, he can hear his aide say. *Henree, open the curtains.* But there is no aide, rather only the putrid stench of old meat.

'Nani?' calls Henry.

And knows she is gone for good. Only a faint echo, a stench and an echo, greet him from the house's bowels. In the front room he knocks into the settee.

'Johnny?' he calls out, a sharp pain in his gut, liver the seat of anger. 'Johnny?' before his eyes have fully adjusted.

He draws the ponderous drapes. Across the windows more diagonal battering beams bisect the pale moonlight entering past the mango leaves. All his own papers still piled over on the desk. Diagrams for what? Sweet redolence and no gaslamp anywhere, only a long strange wrapped bundle waiting for him on the settee.

His hands slap the bookshelves until he grabs the lamp and lights it with piss-damp matches he ferrets out from deep in his coat pocket.

What catches the orange light best is a pair of spit-polished shoes. Once the shroud is pulled down there are the shoes and they are barely on. From them rise legs become angles never meant to be married. Poor sluggish and helpless legs. O my boy. The knees are known in his palm like a private god while the lamp falls and the glass crashes with the kerosened wick still sputtering.

It is not impossible to see how stained the shirt is. Such a bad white, tea-brown and worse. The light is going out but not before the head is there with its triangular hollows and the spectacles so badly crooked, which must be their last joke. And how stained the shirt. The mouth hangs open unseemly, the bluish eyes shine with a conscience illiterate. All this under a neck sliced crossways and then placed neat as a splint for a hybrid plant right back atop the body.

Now this could not be Nani's work. She is long gone and had no shred of any of this in her. It is the others wherever they are. And whoever. Even if they're not watching right now, he feels them.

Jokers who placed the star-tipping boy with a white banner tied across his chest in the bow of a child or gift. And they steeplejacked his hands over his chest in a mock greeting. *Ayubowan.* All to make the boy ready to lead and be led like human nature on that first day in the middle of things, at the port when he had offered that gift of his life.

And you had taken him on for the ride. He made promises to you. *And you to him.*

The last of the matches is enough to light another lantern to read the rough note they pinned to the boy's shirtfront:

> Remains of a spy found in our camp this morning. Returned in state found. Probable local retaliation for subject's nationalizing activities, trespasses against state and region, unlawful

agitation, espionage, actual cause unknown. Local authorities to be informed.

Yrsr,
Chistopher Watkins
Colonel of Regiment Q74
Rajottama Village

Is this the handwriting of one for whom English is not a native language? Is this fraud or truth? And the original morocco-bound Village Book lies open on the table.

A life worth nothing — should it be worth going on living? You disappear like this, Johnny, make it nothing. Why so heavy when scooped up in these arms, life worth what when heaviness is a boy in these arms. A boy who couldn't live in paper or glass. A face like plum wine and one of the spit-polished shoes clattering off. A boy hewn down, fallen against the sputtering lamp. A head in danger of doing the same, clattering off. If things are going to stay together the boy will have to be strapped.

Cord can be found in the kitchen. The door opens out easily enough and the inner courtyard's walls are smooth cool plaster like unfolded skin. By the kitchen the gardener sits in his cubicle expectorating betel but her mortar is what gives off the astringent scent of old chilies.

The cord curls on the lower shelf where it should be. Is there anyone ever in the next room? She lived so correctly. If you sneeze in that moment it means she thinks of you. Retrace the steps and wrap the rope carefully over the head and under the spit-polished shoes and around the chest too skinny to carry anger. What is more solid than red brick? The curve of his back if aimed shooting toward the stars. What is more solid than the boy? Sage as a law of nature and unangry, his two lives traversed now requiring a double cordage.

Only the shirt's stained. How could that throat be cut and then cleaned up to lie in wait? They must have done it to Johnny for him to be so everlasting clean. What look to be made of bamboo but are really a boy's fingers? Murmuring helps keep the head on. A child takes over the father's work when the boy has obviously lost all sense and led one too many lives, but now to carry the Village Book when the boy is heavy.

Is it all in your shoes? But we must keep the shoes on if we want to keep the head on.

*   *   *

On down the path. Through the swinging gate and down the canal road, it is hard to see and one can easily stumble. There was the milking of cows and ringing of bells as a child, the arctic fox rug before the fire, when now the whole bundle could collapse, still the gardener comes to close the gate after all volunteers.

And out on the canal road, someone curses the dark.

'What is it?'

The driver from Nuwara Eliya has lingered and turns his unsurprised beamy face. 'Damn wheel,' he mutters. 'Had it fixed before but it's running irregular.'

Turn to the driver, offer some help.

Perfect, Johnny, how you do it. 'If I help you?'

Let me lay you down, my boy, on this dirt they call a road. 'Listen —' to the driver '— if I help you, will you take me back?'

'I'm not taking the dead,' says the driver.

'He's not dead, he's suspended,' in English and the driver will accept this. But the wheel is difficult and the driver anyway had not expected much expertise.

'You know, I'm sure my old vehicle is up there, we can use your bulls and take it,' said in half-English. Still the man understands with the grace of those who know how to find rice from nowhere.

The driver considers. 'But what about my cart?' he says finally.

'You can keep my cart.' Generous. But the weight of Johnny would make anyone gasp. — *Are your shoes staying on, my boy?*

The driver lets out a whistle of appreciation at the spacious thing, this bullock wagon. In the few minutes it takes to be linked to the driver's bull, the dogs across the canal do not cease their wailing.

'You can take me back to N'Eliya,' said once they orient down the driveway toward the canal road. The boy would slump against the legs of anyone who held him. — *Stand straight, my boy, none of this is proper.*

'I don't go that way.' The driver is callous in his glance over his shoulder. 'But get in if you want.'

'Where are you going then?'

'Taking the Dambulla road to near Sigiriya. Having made a few stops on the way.'

Sigiriya? 'I'll go with you.'

The driver eyes the corded-up bundle. 'You must be having more money?'

Next to the pocket she sewed is the last of what Pink Cheeks left. A tithing. 'I do.' Ready for anything.

'Get in now,' says the driver. 'I'll stop near a market. You pay for us, I'll give you to come with me.'

Agree to anything. The boy stays clasped and there is no harm in proceeding without a plan. Because the boy still has an employer who can shield him.

The silhouettes of two ample women with their bags packed come rushing down the canal road, waving. Kumari and Sonali, the dance school sisters, the first grabbing the second's bag. 'You're leaving? We'll go with you, Mister.' Kumari is trying to hike herself up into the cart. Once there, she holds a hand out to her sister.

'I'm sorry.' This would flabbergast anyone. 'Where to?' The only concern is to stay still so as not to disturb Johnny.

'To a country where they give to eat and to wear,' Sonali says, meaning the sisters are ready to travel in search of husbands.

'No,' says Kumari, sitting next to him. 'We heard what happened and we want to go with you. The villagers. Your aide. Terrible things, Mister. Really, we must go with you, won't be any trouble. We can start a new village and dance school somewhere else.' Kumari peers through what seems like a great fog.

'Are you not happy here, Kumari?' mildly asked.

'Want these women or not?' says the driver. 'We don't have all night.'

'It has been ugly, Mister. You are a good man. Here are starting troubles. And we would like to be maids. See things. Help start some new place. Some place where there is no trouble history?'

Palms turned up.

'See?' Sonali accuses her sister. 'I told you he wouldn't want to. And who'd cook for Appuhamy if we left?'

'There will be no more Appuhamy and anyway he'd eat roots and be better off for it,' Kumari retorts, not pressing. She descends the cart with the grace of a deposed queen. 'We thought the world of you.'

'Finished with those ladies?' the driver barks.

'Sorry for you not to come.'

'Where are you going, though?'

'Sigiriya,' checking with the driver, 'the lion mountain.'

'And then?'

A weak gesture, again the hand waving. 'And then on. Thank you and good luck.'

Without waiting, the driver snorts and gets his bullocks to begin plodding.

Behind, Sonali is shouting something hard to make out.

'You should know your servant girl is safe with her relatives now.'

'Her relatives?'

'You didn't know? With Regi and Ruwini. They've taken her in as a niece. Maybe she is with child? What Appuhamy said. And they let no one see her.'

'Don't listen,' says Kumari, 'my sister can't help lying all the time.'

'Tell her I will always see her' — stopping when Kumari nudges Sonali — 'tell her she'll always be with me.'

But leaving them behind, up ahead he finds the flaming. He'd not seen this smoke when he'd arrived by the longer road. A chanting from the temple where the eyeless Buddha had lost its head-wrapping, staring blindly out, a pure white plaster loner, and above the Lord Buddha a sky lit the wrong way, conjuring wrong things. Premature dawn with the British camp bleeding soldiers, too many running out toward the canal, faces confused or sealed, hands on rifles, and inside the camp shrieking atrocious, girls' voices, something struck, clouted, splintering and cracking, dry wood and falling, a burnt-hair stench, petrol and turpentine, the blood in his ears throbbing, a vast calm opening up inside. His General Store ahead kindling a great hotter light, boys in muddied uniform crushing onto the rope bridge, swaying toward Monkeyheadside, the paddy there alight, overwhelmingly beautiful, smoke in the moonlight a live wall ascending, billowing to curl within itself. A colossal stinking wall.

Keep going, he tells the driver even as men run by covered with mud, disguised by mud, villagers hanging onto his bullock cart. Mud and contemptuous night have made them one, out from the camp, running along the canal, into it and calling from the surface, British, Ceylonese, Tamil, Sinhalese. Mud and fire and a young boy with a tender-bird face — young Upali asleep? — carried by his mother, running by. The bullock doesn't want to move forward so they stay stuck silent, benumbed where the market used to be, fruit-sellers and buyers, so many burned, by him runs a woman with her face bubbled, gas noxious, flames carried in the wind, little bits of fire scudding flying the palmtops. Running downhill then, men and boys holding giant torches like firespitting alligators, men disguised as giant parrot heads, huge patrons with bodies grisly naked into the dark and then the light.

What he is leaving behind — the mourning sounds of nothing. He had not done this. This is not his doing. He will not meet the eyes. These are the people of his village. He covers his face because he has good reason. A boy running by hands him a smaller parrot mask and a mask is not a bad thing, a mask can be used to hide from the smoke. To cover his boy Johnny, as well, Johnny who needs some special tending.

Alone with the boy, Johnny whose head will no longer stay upright on his body, he too a hollowness of a man in the cart finally pulling up the great hill. No one has made proper goodbyes but Rajottama is already departing behind them. And the cart's jolts are neither one nor many, only a godforsaken single shock, not his doing, driving the boy together with his carrier, joist and hitch and bone.

137

THE GARDENER JOSEPH was not so old a man that he could not see what happened before his own eyes. Nor was he that young that he did not know what it meant. When the tiny man with the long beard came, the gardener Joseph opened the gate for him. Joseph had no grudges. They called the dwarf Chollie and Chollie had never been polite to Joseph, but neither had he been rude. Joseph opened the gate. What else could he do?

With Chollie were three of his men. There's trouble in the village, one of them told Joseph. We found out your Jehan is a British spy. He must be called before a court of the people.

Not understanding fully, Joseph agreed. This was another of their plans. And Chollie, the short one with the beard, was the one who at his General Store sold Joseph betel to chew. Joseph bore no grudges. He choked a bit on his betel and coughed. None of them cared whether he coughed.

He let them into the house but the one they wanted was not there.

It did not take long for the big men who always traveled with the short man to return. They came lugging heavy beams and Joseph opened the gate for them. This is when they began to nail the beams to the house. Joseph did not help but followed them around to see how they did what they needed to do. The gardener thought this was another of the pink foreigner's plans. It was just like barring off the domestic's altar.

It was also interesting to see how the taller one strained to lift the shorter one onto his shoulders so the short one could pound the nails through the beams. The big one made faces as the short one pounded and Joseph guffawed without making a sound.

When Chollie stared, Joseph returned to his stump. He also admired their metal nails, shinier than those he was used to. When they were not looking, he took one for his room. And then another. When the two men were done, the gardener opened the gate for them and closed it after.

But they noticed this and decided to put a new lock on the gate. He watched how they did this from his stump where he ate his betel. He was the gatekeeper and would need to know how to work this lock. Once they left, he tested it.

It was a good strong thing, with two flaps coming down on each side of the gate. He was glad they had put it on in front of his eyes because it was a strange lock. But since he was a little boy living with his mother and brothers his fingers had always been quick. Which is why, after all, he went to the coffee plantation in the first place. You have to be quick to know which berries to pick and which to leave. And how to avoid where they spray the most poison. You don't go near the spray and then you could be lucky. He had not been lucky. Once for a whole season he had to pick in the most poisonous areas. That was when he had gotten sick. Now he was better in this big house.

Far away in the village the gardener could hear what sounded like a great big celebration. There were whoops and calls and firecrackers.

It was only when he saw some more of Chollie's men running by on the canal with blood on their faces that he questioned the celebration. He did not know whether it was blood or mud or paint but he assumed it was blood because only herb doctors wear paint.

He must have fallen asleep because when he awoke he was hungry and the noisy birds had come to the big mango tree. The sky was dark and he wanted to go out to the road and look at the canal. But before he could, voices kept coming. He knew one of the voices was the monk who used to come almost every day. The monk was not polite to Joseph but Joseph the gardener bore few grudges. When the monk came up the hill toward the gate, Joseph descended so he could open the gate for the monk, the dwarf Chollie, and a big man they call Lester Pilima. They always call him as though his two names are one name: Lesterpilima. With no one else do they always say the last name. Joseph knew his last name must be important. Or maybe there were many with his first name so they always had to say the last name.

Lesterpilima was polite to Joseph and Joseph the gardener always hurried to open the gate for him.

Behind the monk, Lesterpilima and the short man came some of Chollie's big men carrying an object smaller than the beams they used to nail shut the house but bigger than what they usually carried, which were their buckets of toddy. Joseph admired those men who carried toddy because they knew how to balance on ropes stretched high between the palm trees. If Joseph could carry a bucket and walk on a rope carrying a bucket of syrup, he would rather do that than be a gardener. It would be nice to be near the birds and sky with your warm syrup right there in a bucket. That would be interesting. On some days gate-opening was more interesting than others.

Today it was more interesting.

He opened the gate for the men and they walked by. The big object the other men carried dripped onto the path. When the monk saw that the other men had nailed beams over the house he got angry. The way he got angry was to shout and then remember himself. The monk walked over to where Joseph watched them and sat himself down on the stone bench. You should not have done that, the monk kept saying to the short one they call Chollie. Lesterpilima came over while the other two men were taking the beam off the front door. Lesterpilima was telling the monk it would only be a matter of minutes. The monk was nervous and kept glancing over his shoulder at the canal as though some monster would rise and bite him.

Joseph wanted to tell him the safest hour is after the birds come home. He didn't know why he kept silent. His habit around all these men was silence. Once the beam was down, they brought their object into the house. Joseph followed them like he had learned to do.

If the gardener wished to be see-through, no one ever saw him. Or if they did, later they might wonder whether it was true or not.

Did you see Joseph in the house? one might ask another. The truth was the gardener didn't know whether anyone ever talked about him. Or if they knew his name.

He was just interested to see what they did with the bundle. They laid it down in the front room that he had once helped the domestic clean. They had puffed the dust out of the drapes and curtains. That had been interesting one day, to see how she did it. But that is more women's work and not for every day. Is the girl here? the monk asked. No one answered the monk so he went into the patio. Outside he called the domestic's name. He returned with a face that did not say whether he was glad the domestic was gone.

Now for the first time they pulled the sheet off the object and revealed that tall boy Jehan. Almost every time Jehan had passed through the gate, he had said something to the gardener, unless he was with people. Then he had just nodded to Joseph. But Joseph always hurried to open the gate for him. The boy was good. Now he was dead.

They laid him down and then Lesterpilima asked the monk if they should write a note. That was when Chollie looked at the gardener and said *he* can tell him.

By mistake Joseph had stopped being invisible.

Tears fell down his cheeks but he did not mean them. Are you ridiculous? Lesterpilima asked the short man. He can't talk. That was when the gardener started to like Lesterpilima less. He would hold a grudge. He would be slower opening the gate.

Of course Joseph could talk. Once he had come to this town looking for work, he chose not to. He figured it would make things simpler for him. Most people were Buddhist and a few were Christian. Joseph was not only not Christian but Hindu and a Tamil like maybe the tall boy and he knew being these things could make life difficult. If he said nothing and let his nephew talk and only gave them a card with the name the plantation owner had written, then things would be easy. He had been right. No one had wanted to hear from him.

Once he got the job opening the gate at this big house, life had been easy enough. There was no doubt that this was an easier life than plantation life. It was good not to talk and better to send money to his wife.

The monk was already writing a letter. The short man arranged the tall boy's hands and put the monk's letter there. That should get rid of both of them, the short man said to Lesterpilima. They all paused and then for the first time the men let themselves laugh, the monk, Lesterpilima and Chollie. Joseph let himself laugh too, but it had been so long since he laughed that what came out sounded like the strange cry of an animal caught in a trap. He was as startled as they were. As they were leaving, before Chollie had his men renail the beam to the front door, the monk addressed Joseph.

You can stay here, the monk said. Where else would the gardener go? Anyway, Joseph did not like the monk. The monk began to laugh again. Joseph stood seeing the man's eyes close because of laughing so hard. This time he did not open the gate for any of them.

He let them close it, with the new difficult lock and all, by themselves.

138

FAR BEFORE DAWN and they have arrived in a place that never sleeps. Behind curtains into a back room in which Gould hears the first hint of that mocking voice through the curl of bluish smoke with its deep odor, burnt apricots or taffy.

What are you afraid of, Henree?

Are you mocking me, my boy? Here when I am keeping you together.

Do not be so afraid, Henree. Isn't your plan to know all layers?

All layers, of course. But what about those tea-country British? If I had not left, you'd be in better shape now.

Hazim the driver's friend places before himself a bronze tray on which sits a small oil lamp. He lights the lamp and never stops talking but his hands fly. His eyes glue to his knitting. The yarn between the two needles is amber, darkening under his superior deftness.

With the stuff become a gum, Hazim quickly thrusts it into a ceramic cup with a hole at the center and presses a silver-chased bamboo tube deep down. With a smile at the driver he quickly inhales the melted stuff until it bubbles and evaporates from within the cup. Blue smoke burns an apricot taffy stink and Gould can scarcely be aware of anything else. But Hazim lies against the cushions against the wall and with his eyes closed explains how to smoke.

At Gould's inhale, the tiny volcano at the bamboo's end does not disappear as neatly as it did for Hazim. While it had been predicted, the scorch still shocks. Though Gould's throat suppurates, miraculously it does not close into a cough.

He tries to stand up. *Aren't there other places for us to go to, my boy?*

But Hazim indicates the driver must take his share. And that the tall cockerel of a man should be made to sit down.

You don't mind if I lie down, my boy? Let me prop you against this wall. I will discuss current affairs with these two pleasant gentlemen.

What is it that so holds their interest? They talk commerce, trade, governmental regulations, plans and communities.

'Strange,' says Gould. 'You know I wasn't affected by your pipe.'

'Check your clock,' Hazim tells him, indicating the pocketwatch on a chain.

Hours have passed without Gould's head having moved from the same position.

'But I only smoked one pipe. You all have smoked four or five and you're still all right.'

'That's opium too,' says Hazim, handing him the crazy-making pipe.

The pipe is a handsome thing with its hollows. They're like his boy's cheeks combined with her shape. Or is this a new pipe whose indents catch the assembled group's lowlight reflections upside down? Seeing her in the indents fills him with peace. This must be a different pipe. Who is he to think he has nothing to offer? At that moment, sleep is the best thing he can give to the world.

Sunset or dawn the next day, the driver sets him down on the road before accepting payment and retreating.

So many places we've traveled, my boy. You were there with me in the barroom, weren't you? Those warm debaucheries before you lured me back to our house.

At their return to Sigiriya, the lion mountain, Gould is sure it's nightfall again.

Once before, the two had traveled to Sigiriya.

At the beginning of their life together, under a gibbous moon, they had slept outside what Johnny had assured him was the rim of the ancient palace grounds. Or rather, Gould remembered, Johnny could sleep, his hand flung loose like some character unafraid of crucifixion, his intelligent brow unperturbed and freed from his desire to help Gould. Gould had crouched forward to feel the night teem with sound and pale toward morning. A thin enfilade of sun had stolen the remains of his wake.

At dawn Johnny fed and watered the bullock; Gould started a fire for tea.

Waiting he watched daylight spill forth and reveal where they had slept. Legend claimed the careful water gardens flowed in endless trickle from underground for the first time after four hundred years. These ruins were cast on a small scale, tiny bricks leaning into one another rounded by centuries' weight and the eyes of those who would brave jungles to visit a forsaken site.

Here at Sigiriya, generations of royal sons had killed fathers until the last son managed to resheathe his sword after cutting his own throat.

Gould considered it good they had come.

He downed his tea without tasting the mug's tin or the thick sugar lolling at its bottom. Eager to get on he saw Johnny rolling a small cigarette, a habit indulged only when on the road. The cart stood tied in the shade. Without speaking the men left their belongings covered and tied, the cart near an old arecanut tree, to approach the park's casual symmetry.

The long walk cleared their memory of roads and houses and words, stripping them down to a necessary singularity of purpose. Minerals bled down the rock *mourning the centuries & the difficulty of being perpetual witness to kingly pleasures and violence or its later form,* Gould wrote of the two men's attempt to scale the huge face.

Up the stone stairs they started and Gould's breath started to heave and saw. Only now and then Johnny allowed himself to glance behind at Gould.

'This is just the beginning,' called Johnny, spitting.

Once he made Gould wince by calling him *old man.*

'What to do?' Gould had asked.

'Keep climbing,' said his guide through a new wad of masticated leaf, tobacco and lime.

Gould could not keep from panting.

'Cling,' Johnny instructed.

They pressed their bodies into that obscene heft. With blind feet up the escarpment, they found ancient indents left from some vanished scaffolding intruded upon the rock's integrity.

This was fearsome and made Gould call out once *Good god!* No matter the view he would not peek down at those brilliant ruined gardens.

And then they were inside the dull coolness of the cave with its bare-breasted undisturbed women dancing on walls. Johnny stood back, pleased at Gould's wonderment. Mannishly he folded his arms over his chest, as though he himself had just finished applying the last bit of ocher resin to the rock.

'They say King Kasyapa hired an artist trained in India to paint these.'

Still catching his breath Gould stood near one that had been defaced in the upper corner. What strange loveliness. The neck disappeared into chalky emptiness.

'When the painter had finished his work, the king blinded him,' Johnny said, perhaps thinking he recited the tale to himself.

'Was the king so displeased?'

'Our Asian kings liked to make sure no one else would possess anything like their commissions. This was the custom of the time, blinding the artist. To ensure originality.'

Gould had not invited the image before his eyes of a row of painters' glaring eyes strung up on a cord around a grinning king's neck.

He passed his handkerchief over his brow. He could use the water they had left behind.

'Why not say barbaric?' Johnny was still smiling at him.

But Gould could not sustain his end. He had to sit, and did, directly below the two ladies who had addressed him first. Of all the women in the cave, those alone or in pairs, these two interested him most.

While all the others were caught up in some private greed or supplication, envy or desire or worldliness, these two sang out a friendship. The tall one in front, with her bare round forward breasts and spacious eyes reflecting light, leaned naively into a future she appeared sure to decipher. She held a purple manel flower before her as though it were the key to all worldly pleasures.

Gould decided the one in the rear was the guardian, her eyes too intelligent and worldly to be otherwise. Her chest was covered and a shadow hand raised in a mudra like forgiveness. Another transparent hand upheld a platter of flowers as though to support the front woman, but her shoulders sloped. Burdened with greater intelligence, indulgent of the front one's blithe freedom, she was necessary, allowing her complement to step forward bare-breasted carrying only a flower into a larger world.

Cautious, she herself needed to be more graceful in her knowledge and smaller bones, hiding away her sensual being as a secret that would have time to emerge later. The more he studied them, the more he thought the two women were actually the same woman at different times in her life.

Just the thought of Nani prickled his pores with a guilty electricity.

> Because of eye and material objects, brethren, arises visual consciousness; the meeting of the three is sensory impingement; because of sensory impingement arises feeling; because of feeling, craving; because of craving, grasping.

The growing heat and stillness of the cave lay heavy upon him until Johnny scuffled outside.

'Touch this,' said the boy. 'Slippery, no? the famous Mirror Wall that women pilgrims wrote upon. An archaeologist deciphered their writing but went mad later, thinking he read words that no one else saw. Henree, from here you must climb to the top by yourself. Everyone should do it once in a lifetime. I have seen it hundreds of times and want to stay back. Believe me.'

Gould did not and wondered what would keep the boy from climbing with him.

As they began up the last stretch of narrow stone stairs, Johnny held tightly to the banister. Gould realized his boy was afraid of heights and spoke only to distract himself.

'They also say that the painter was in love with King Kasyapa's daughter.'

'Then what happened?' panted Gould.

'How could the great king be bothered with giving his daughter away to one more artisan when his palace had more than fifteen thousand slaves? The ones who built these very stairs.'

They had arrived at the lion's paw. A bulky stone conceit with its paws clenched. This was a beast that lived for the taste of another's blood.

'You see,' said Johnny, 'you enter through the belly. Some say the palace itself was the head of the lion. Though how could such a giant's structure be built back then? Our people are very literal. Keep your weight close to the rock and you will not have any problems. Don't worry about the hanging wasps' nests, it's not their season. If you have to glance down, do so only at the top.'

Many times Gould could have fallen.

Once, hands wet from effort, he is sure he will spiral to death below. His knees buckle. He imagines Johnny scooping his remains, stowing his skull. Pay attention to the task at hand, Henry, he rebukes himself, and has to keep repeating it as a mantra all the way to the top.

From Kasyapa's palace he tries to understand cause.

The story Johnny had told was of a king, attacked by his brother's army, whose royal elephant turned back at a marsh. Because of the beast's skittishness, the hand-picked soldiers, thinking their king had surrendered, scattered into the jungle. Without them, the king was sure he would lose. He withdrew his sword and pulled it along his own throat, resheathing it just before he fell from his howdah.

That was grace. What would make someone live with such grace and hubris?

Before his brother had come to kill him, the king had ruled from this plateau where only hawks and falcons sliced the sky, reflected in long pond gardens before the jungle. He had awakened each morning ignoring military strategy — how foolish it had been to build atop a mountain in isolation — with his only friend the mist skirting the distant ridges.

He had certainly walked naked on this plateau where now the grass is winning, insatiable mockery of prior desires. He had certainly rambled these terraces, made for his bare-breasted courtesans and children. And while he'd believed the Buddha enlightened, he himself had half-attained the Buddha's height on this natural Babel.

What lay beyond the horizon would have been less relevant.

No doubt, the king would have been partial to these stone stairs which created an illusion of immortality, stairs on a rock engraved by salty winds. He would have enjoyed light's falling, ethereal strips across a plain, and how smoke arose from woodlands where insurgents hid. How the sun cast shade only in his palace's barest niche. In the afternoons, he would have marked the cloud gods astride, giant looming shadows across the plains.

*   *   *

Was it in the Bible, Gould wonders, that a day in God's life could be compared to the utter erosion of a single mountain if a bird were to come once every thousand years to remove a single speck?

Thinking of this, he leaves the body of Johnny who has finally come to the top to see the panorama with him. Ignoring wasps and a scorpion's nervous rattle, he places the dead boy on a slab of what must have been some kind of smoothed stone throne for Kasyapa. The boy sits with hands in his lap, thumbs incongruously raised. If rigor mortis had not set in, Gould would have been able to push the thumbs back down. As it was he has to leave the boy, head cocked but the shroud arranged to disguise the faultline across the neck where skin slips so loose and papery. He leaves his boy with the heart staining a once-immaculate white shirt, thumbs raised ready to twiddle.

Gould descends in a glow of accomplishment and is not even perturbed when from below, looking up at the throne, he sees the first leopard steal up on Johnny.

He remembers Johnny's triumphing voice on their first trip: 'King Kasyapa was not a true Buddhist,' Johnny had said, shaping the word *true* with irony.

The pride of leopards must have hidden when Gould came up. Once he began the descent, the beautiful bright animals must have scented meat ready for the taking, must have understood Johnny as having been delivered up to them. It makes sense that they savage him in a frenzy of hunger satisfied. From a distance, their golden dance unrolls slow and luxuriant. It is no longer Johnny whom he has delivered. It is Gould's part in nature's cycle that he has fulfilled.

Feeling munificent, Gould forgives the king — parricide, suicide and false Buddhist. After all, the king had bequeathed him the right site for the boy to wait out eternity.

316

POSTSCRIPT: PARTITION OF THE RELICS

A victor am I over all, all have I known, yet unattached am I to all that is conquered and known. Abandoning all, I am freed through the destruction of craving. Having thus directly comprehended all by myself, whom shall I call my teacher?

He did not know what brought him there. But it made more sense than anything else that he had done for a long time. Easy enough to take the late train past the burst valley of Lizard Pass with Bible Rock looming through the night. Easy enough to leave his flapping hat and wallet at the train station in a coffin-size and scuffed wooden locker whose identifying number had been almost entirely scratched off. *Keep the key*, he told the astonished guard, a man with a skinny mustache filled in by oil pencil, *won't be coming back for a while*. And for once he did not have to stand a patient figurehead hearing all objections to his plan, he could just take the morning train down the coast with dawn a thin cold landside rime until the waters on his right also glimmered through palms and the train continued until it became night and he wandered into the town, quiet with an ember line glowing in the distance.

He walked into it as though he had been here before.

Around but not with him was a phalanx of bare-chested men with elaborate red and black paint and ash streakings upon them. Not with the men but alongside strode a few women whose hair had turned into livid snakes, matted dark and long, *outdoing Kali*, Gould thought, but stayed his hand from reaching into the pocket where once he had stowed his cumbrous Village Book. *You don't need to write a thing, Gould*, he admonished himself.

With his last coins he bought a length of red cloth from a nearby seller who almost stripped in order to show Gould how to tie the thing around his waist. Thank you, Gould did not say before unhanding the last of his money and folding himself back into the crowd with no fight.

One small toothless man in a white sarong whose scanty silver hair thickened into a knot at the nape attached himself wordlessly to Gould. This man pointed Gould to a massive mustard stone block of a building which had a placard missing a nail and saying A REST-HOUSE FOR PILGRIMS. And next to it a small pink soldier tangoed with another soldier on the lid of a can marked SHRIVER'S DOES IT BEST.

Past the best and worst of families strewn on mats in cubicles with doors opened against the viscous heat the two men walked. Past heaps of bodies stirring against one another and bare cubicles where single men engaged in bathing rituals or just sat stilled.

Once a door opened and one of the tall Kali-women came out hitching up her skirt. The white under her pupils fixed the two men in an odd brilliance before she passed them toward the end of the halls beyond which shacks clustered in the stench of excrement.

A bearded man with a stomach preceding him lumbered through this same open door.

'Ah,' said Gould's silver-haired friend, pointing to the man before backing away.

Gould understood the bearded man as the proprietor. 'Does Mister have any — ?' he began in Sinhalese.

'I speak English. We're full,' said the man. 'Season's started. Come back next week.'

Gould found himself neither pleased nor displeased by this answer. He checked behind him but his silver-haired companion had slipped away. This left him without effect.

'Of course,' Gould murmured. He nodded to the proprietor. '*Salaam.*'

The man smiled back. 'Better luck in a few days.'

Gas lantern light puffed the chins and sockets of fruitsellers calling out their trays of offerings. Gould walked by them without hearing their calls to come feel, come see, but he enjoyed the voices calling him further into the dream wrought by the perfumed jasmine necklaces hung over their stalls, the familiar areliya garlands, the baskets of woven palm.

It was neither too much nor too little.

He began walking across a bridge toward the first temple he could see but then people on the shores underneath were bathing and he turned back on the bridge to walk heedlessly down rocks set into the hill. He tore off a small section of red cloth meaning to use it as a towel later. The rest he wrapped around his broad hips so he could disrobe underneath and fold dirty khakis and grayed socks atop his boots on a muddy stone on which there was nothing and then set the morocco-bound Village Book above all else.

He went into the water then with only the cloth between him and it and watched children splashing each other revealing some ritualized war in their blood but he had no urge to write as the thought came and went. No more and no less than what was needed.

It was cold but this cold was fruitful, Gould thought, feeling its shiver penetrate his bones and move up his spine like an icy flame. He stood a stork in the water feeling the heat above and the cold below unclot into the same temperature. Around him women and men bathed in devotions of their own devising. One woman crossed her round arms over her chest to tug her ears. Her eyes rolled upward as she kneeled to the water, bouncing and finally submerging herself. She was perfect and around her others improvised variations but it was enough to see her alone rise sputtering and cleansed and repeat the tug, kneel, bounce, submersion.

Always it was to the water that they came and as more pilgrims entered fewer left so soon Gould standing there stock-still knew heat growing around him as bodies pressed close and bowed, kneeled and sank under. He felt he had fainted *but I'm still standing* and he was glad he had left the book on the first side of the water because now it was time to leave that soup and climb over small oily rocks to the other side where he ambled out stopping only to squeeze out a corner of the ragged cloth wrapped tight as wet snakeskin across his bones.

At the top he paused near the white temple he had seen from a distance. Now its bell clanged and clouds of resinous smoke emerged from its mouth but with the crowd pressing in close around its front, he would not enter yet.

I will go on, he said aloud, the words a destination in themselves, lost in the rising clamor of nose-flute and drums around him.

As he mounted to the path leading beyond the white gate, a small man appeared at his elbow, hobbling in a waistcoat with bulging pockets, huge unlaced boots and oversize trousers chafing the ground. It was his silver-haired friend, who smiled at him without teeth and handed him a morocco book. Keep it, said Gould. The man's smile gaped larger and he pulled a length of white cloth out of one of the waistcoat's pockets and proffered it. Gould hesitated, realizing it was his friend's own sarong, but the man insisted.

The cobblestones made his feet tender. The rest of him delighted in walking with bare chest into the night whose heat had lessened since the bathing with other bodies. He tore off two small pieces of the white cloth and wrapped the soles of his feet in the cloth. The whole while his friend stood over him watching with some great patience. He then gave Gould the red towel cloth and Gould wrapped it around his wrist.

Past the gate they stood and prophets raised large consecrated coconuts to their heads for an infinite suspension of a moment and then smashed the nut down so it would break into halves. The milk gushed out and the halves were studied and approved or received with disappointment in their faces, which then indicated to others the urgency of hurrying to the great temple.

For a moment Gould thought he saw Johnny among the jerking men but except for the slicked hair the man was another. And so Gould was not ready for the great temple. It would await him as it had waited forever. For now enough to see men and women and striped fruit and flower trays being brought into those incandescent first halls.

He shook his head at his friend who seemed to understand and then beckoned Gould to come with him on a different path away from the noisy crowds and gossamer lights and incense. They passed quiet huts and tents with dull fires still burning, surrounded by trees thick with vines and the palpitation of insects. Only once did Gould have to stop to tighten his foot bandages but then through the jungle he continued over thorns and creepers and stones and finally past a sulfurous hot pool. They came to a small clearing where Gould's silver-haired friend (whose eyes reflected moonlight) made a glance significant with pride, by which token Gould knew an empty cadjan hut with a swept sand floor was the man's dwelling.

Gould found he was tired enough that the straw mat laid upon the ground was the world's finest feather bed plumped with pillows. He laid his reeling head upon the thing and his friend offered him a mealy drink from a flask. He made some kind of bow on the threshold and pushed the cross-barred door closed to let Gould enter the dreams which had also been awaiting him like a team of wild horses.

He was dragged by them as though tied on the ground behind and woke several times in a confused heat with his head disconnected from his body. Spinning off with a strange fever he had not known before, his mind went wild upon nothing. If only there could be some cooling hands offering some cooling drink . . . Once when he thought he heard his friend pacing about outside he called out and heard nothing but the hiss of sulfured water and the answering spasm of night insects. He recognized then that some beast had stalked his fevered body, having known the prey to be fattish meat easily torn from bones. Flesh that could deliver itself easily to hunger. He could feel the heat working on disintegrating his flesh from the outside and searing in toward those broad bones quickly losing their nationality. To his wondering finger the fat of his arm had become a hot goo ready to dissolve.

I will go on, he heard his rough voice whisper from the straw mat into his body. But he was scared to leave the hut to which he had come and in one clear instant saw ordinary health must have deserted him for him to have been led so easily to such a mad jungle hut.

At dawn insects ceased and when the light increased he wrapped his dry cloth around him and pushed open the door weighted on the outside by a heavy stone. In that bright lucidity of early morning the jungle clearing showed itself with the goodness of paradise and Gould thought he had been foolish to have so believed those terrifying dreams though his own flesh burned unbearably.

Hanging from a tree was a huge parcel covered in white cloth. When Gould undid the cloth he found a flawlessly dressed-out deer. For only a second he considered whether the gift had been offered by his father, who had often taken him hunting upstate when he was a bitty boy and who had once left an entire deer for him to dress out alone. When the boy, frustrated, had given up, his father had returned and showed him for once without preaching how carefully one had to use the knife. How to remove the bilious sacs and carve close to the bone in certain difficult angled spaces.

Behind his shack a forking of fumes rose. A reddish hot pool gave off its sulfurous smudge and closer a small fire smoked in a ring of stones. A flare of hunger rose from his stomach but better not to eat yet because the burn within still flamed his skin and swallowed most any other sensation.

In the crook of the tree lay some twine and a curved knife still bloody from preparing the deer. Gould had to stare at these two offerings awhile until it became clear what medicine was intended. No sin would ever ripen from this.

He sat on the stone that had weighted the door. It was working in the sulfured air that made it necessary to sing a song composed of nonsense syllables and melodic lines familiar and surprising and keeping his hands at their labor. He began with his feet, strapping cool strips of meat onto their sweltering tops. Slowly he tied pieces to his calves, his thighs, over his groin even, and finally to where it was most needed. He pressed the cool venison to his chest from which all fires emanated and wrapped the meat around his neck without choking himself, and when he had succeeded, sat completely covered in strips of raw deer. Almost completely satisfied and cooled for the first time since arriving in this flaming town.

But it was his thirst that kept him from full enjoyment and he studied the last piece of venison laid across the rock in the shape of a shoehorn or an island. It lay there wet enough for him to bring it to his lips and suck on the meat until the capillaries disgorged themselves into his mouth so that when he was done he laid the deer down bloodless and dry, finally satisfied as his head ceased to reel.

Perhaps he sat there the entire day.

Only the flies came to witness.

He had no desire to move except to follow the tree's shade around the rock. He managed to suck the blood from strips he had tied onto his wrists, feet and calves, and his mouth hung open in satisfied rictus.

But he had moved enough. Only once, perhaps it was afternoon, did he think of her, possessed by a ridiculous picture of her searching among a heap of empty coconut shells. She threw some aside, saved others. Now what would that be about? She was saying something, drawing the blinds, knowing he would prefer the dark. But then he could dismiss the thought easily and return to sitting. The thought of her was no less and no more than what was needed. Forget her. She was no more there than the deer or the stone or the hut or the sand.

Toward evening, a herd of elephants thundered in heavy and slow from the horizon. The ground shook and there was no fear or movement in him. He was sure they were elephants long before he saw them come. It was neither hard nor easy to follow them to the hot sulfur bath near his camp. These were beasts who could eat a hard fruit whole and excrete it intact with the contents disappeared. They had destinies to conduct.

A baby elephant glanced first at the others and then plodded into the hot pool. There in the purpled light a smell of drastic burnt elephant leather came up and the call scraped the inside of his ears while the baby's eyes rolled upward until through the fumes they turned smoky. The stink of charred meat strengthened only when the rest of the herd plodded in swifter and swifter. He knew what he was seeing. A herd of elephants in a screech of trumpets choosing to end right before him. He did not move but could see their clouded eyes and hear the last of their cries even after they stopped making them. The pool was filled with them and their sad gray flapping skin floating unstitched at the top of the bubbling pool. And no one but him had contained the sight. This was neither good nor bad.

When night came with its own kind of heat he himself rose and made his way with the meat covered only by his red sarong. Just before the large path on which the people approached the giant white dome he came across a group of men hidden by the last trees, men with long hair whose cheeks were pierced by scarlet arrows and from whose bare backs hung metal hooks, thrust through their scanty flesh. They paced before a double row of incarnadine coals. He sat quietly at the outskirts and watched them chant before a smudged altar on which sat a figure *blacker than death*, but he had no urge to write. Then in turn they were walking over the coals as though those sizzled red eyes formed a soft carpet. Their heads held straight. No hesitation about them. This was neither bad nor good nor too little nor too much.

The only bothersomeness was the voice beginning in Gould's head and he wanted to forget it, thinking it no more than her — the deer stone hut herd the circle of men — but he could not banish it so easily and it was saying things which sometimes Gould could not keep himself from saying aloud in his hoarse voice parched of all liquids but deer's blood. The voice was reasonable at first, speaking of thorns with some insistence. Thorns that were thrust away because they could not be taken with hands, said the voice, and yet the man that shall touch them must be fenced with iron and spear staffs and all should be utterly burned with fire in the same place. He almost understood.

But why should he be the one inflicted with this voice, hadn't he made enough of an effort to escape?

The voice cared neither to answer nor to ignore but had proceeded on to instructions. Take away with you the innocent blood. Take it from your father's house. That the blood should return forever upon the head of yours. Do not fence any further, nor there commence any force, nor go forth thence any whither.

He sat there trying to contain the voice and eventually the men had left and after the coals died it multiplied itself not even doing him the courtesy of speaking singly but all a loud rabble telling him that young lions were roaring upon him and yelling and threatening to lay waste to his land entire and that his cities be burned without inhabitant single.

He felt betrayed. He had put forth his trust and had been betrayed. He sat in shock at his betrayal.

How long had passed he could not say.

Now the voice had quieted into a single constant friendly strain, again more reasonable and familiar saying if a man put away his wife and she go from him into the arms of another shall he return unto her again? Shall that land be greatly polluted? But you have played the harlot with many lovers yet you may return again to me, you may lift up your eyes.

He glanced about him and still it was night and he thought to leave the voice in the jungle and continue on toward the great white dome of the temple where day and night passed unobserved.

Not to enter yet. Rather to choose the spot which when the sun returns might be blessed with shade. Having seen neither too little nor too much, he found his way by the lights and came to sit just below the arch of the great temple.

The reasoning voice had stayed friendly enough that he could speak it aloud without any fear of reprisal and like a reverse drinking it soothed his dried throat to speak the words aloud.

A few times people returning from the temple offered him fruit from their trays and he ate what they offered with a quietness borne of the reasoning voice which allowed him to taste every moment of fruit. He knew the meat strapped to him did not smell pleasant and that people who offered him fruit also held their noses and reached across a distance to him but he did not mind. He was only grateful to the generosity of their reach.

What need for shame? the voice asked and further asked Gould to speak it aloud. Had shame not only devoured the labor of our fathers from our youth but our own labor?

We lie down in shame and our confusion covers us, he said obediently.

He decided there was no need to return to the elephants or the clearing or the hut. The voice had returned to being his ally and approved the decision because it was a plan and not a plan. What harm was there in sleeping against the great arch? He was free to sit and do nothing but give voice to the reason emerging within.

After some days his coolness would return to him. All this was promised and so it came to pass. And the meat had begun to rankle upon him so his skin crawled with the idea of maggots feasting on his flesh but it was fitting tribute to the voice to keep the meat upon him as the meat and voice had brought him back into health's flickering world. He was shiny waxen fat with meat and underneath his flesh was shriveling until finally he removed the meat and with the voice hung in abeyance he offered the tied strips to a fine-eyed priest to burn.

The priest returned with ashes and coconut milk to pour over the seated man's rancid flesh, a gift to restore him to breathing a less rotted air. How appropriate of you, he said to the priest, whose eyes were two fireflies but did not understand so he continued on to tell the man in his ash and eyes and long bundled hair a story the voice had roused him to tell. He spoke of how children gather wood and fathers kindle fire and the women knead dough and all are making cakes to the queen of heaven and all are pouring out drink offerings unto gods and how he knew to accept this, he did not anger at the children for their practices.

The priest stood there listening with eyes focused on a point beyond but bespeaking what Gould understood as an especial gift for understanding so Gould decided to repent of his own queen, his prince. Once I sawed off a limb, he began to the priest. I sawed off and I ungathered her wood. I ungathered her and unkindled her fire and unkneaded her bread and poured the drink back into the bottle. In that alone lay the shame of my desire that I had not let her be without me. I tell you that I had set my face to enter with the strength of my whole kingdom and take upright ones with me, thus had I desired to do, and for aid had taken the daughter of women and corrupted her. But never did I know whether she stood by my side for me. I had turned my face unto the isles and wished to take many but a prince for his own behalf had caused the reproach offered by me to cease, had caused the reproach to turn upon him and himself alone.

And then I have come here, he said, knowing he would not be able to finish, I walked hard as I could and turned toward this fort of your own land. Can you not tell me how to go on? And into the bowl the priest had handed him he let clatter the first of many coins from those who gave silence and those who took pity and those who showed love.

AUTHOR'S NOTE

The Far Field is no history of Ceylon but a novel, a fiction refracted from and departing from the country's history, a book with aims more literary than documentary: the characters and events of the years 1936–37, as well as much of the Ceylonese topography, are conflated or invented. This book, as none could, does not encompass modern Ceylon/Sri Lanka in all its permutations. For instance, a great population of monks, whether in Sri Lankan villages, cities, or the country's diaspora, could be called wise and compassionate.

Within this novel's scope, then, if one searches for contemporary correlates, it is primarily caste discrimination that bears addressing, as it runs as a poisonous, subliminal discourse in Sri Lanka. This is especially apparent in the ongoing 'ethnic' strife, which (shortly after independence in 1948) was exacerbated by a ruinous separatist language policy in the schools, thereby segregating generations of Tamils, Sinhalese, and Muslims and encouraging murderous nationalisms on all sides. It is quixotic but perhaps necessary to hazard the guess that the current war — laden with its symbols, tanks, suicide bombers, Baby Tigers who at age ten wear cyanide capsules around their necks, and thousands of refugees, many living in inhuman camps — could be resolved not with military power but with a devolution of power into some form of regional autonomy, potentially in the form of federal states, which would nevertheless safeguard the good humor of the cities' majority nationalists.

For additional material, the reader might consult Michael Ondaatje's *Running in the Family*; Gananath Obeyesekere's *Medusa's Hair*; *Ravaya*'s publication *Sri Lanka: 50 Years of Independence*; Leonard Woolf's *Village in the Jungle*; anything by Richard Gombrich; and anything published by Kandy's Buddhist Publication Society, Delhi's Asian Educational Services, or Adyar's Theosophical Society.

What remains beyond all this, historical or fictional, should be considered encouragingly vast territory for others to explore.

— June 2000

ACKNOWLEDGMENTS

To those who helped endlessly — Nandana Weerarathne, a genius of justice, and Karuna Abeysekera, the great teacher. To Gananath Obeyesekere, who helped light a way, and Darini Rajasingham, who helped lighten it. To the Fulbright Commission of Washington and USEF/IIE of Colombo; to the former Cummington Community, to Macdowell Colony, and to Fundacíon Valparaíso, all generous granters of time to write. To the Sri Kanta, Pereis, Rajapakse/Amararathne, and Potuhera families. To the Bibile travelers and war zone election monitors. To all who helped who cannot be named.

To David Rothenberg and Marta Ulvaeus of *Terra Nova* (MIT Press) and to David Lynn and Marilyn Hacker of the *Kenyon Review*, all of whom published ur-excerpts. To Michael Ravitch, an entire literary community from the start. To Sharon Guskin for her dreams. To those with lessons about how to savor: Carolina Garcia, Suzanne Kingsbury, Josefa Heifetz, Keren Stronach and Josh Greenbaum, Madeline Goff, Sue Johnson, Becca Bahr, Adrienne Weiss, Ed Sarkis, Lynn DiOreo, Rina Carvajal, Rina Harari, CPS mentors, Marilyn Chandler, Tom Strychaz, Sheila Ballantyne, Myra Paci, Nick Bakos, Jim Shapiro, Mary Caplan, Katya Tripp, Stuart Karlan, Amit Rai, Ifeona Fulani, Chris Buhner, Simon Liebesny, Amy Russell, Yaels Melamede and Teplow, Ira Sachs, Lisa Sitkin, Martina and Tomas Rheinhart, Lee and Linda Ward of Fayetteville, and Marlene Haerbaut. To the late Suzanne Levine, Rose and Joe Ziglin, Michael DeSimone, Sally Belfrage, Emanuel Meidav. To Peter Matthiessen for being at times a beacon and at times an anchor.

To the great strength of humanist and agent Bill Clegg, to Heather and Corey, and to Kathy at the Robbins office. To the vast-minded godsend, persevering editor Eric Chinski. To the Houghton producers of both Boston and New York. To Lenora Todaro for her perspicacity. And to my family, Josh, Tamar, Wil, Mae, and Tsvi for their humor, belief, and example. To Victor, Emmy and Danny, Liza Lerner, Diana Naparst, Margrons, Teichers, those of Haifa, St. Louis, Scotland, France, New York, and Berkeley, for their radiance. To Stan Stroh for the richness of his inner life and faith.